Shadows of Betrayal

Dragons of Vacari

T.A. McEvoy

DRAGONS OF VACARI

T McEvoy

Copyright Registration Number: TXu 2-478-639
Library of Congress Control Number: 2025905013

Book Cover by: NovelStormDesigns.etsy.com
Map by: Rob Donovan (Snikt5 on Fiverr.com)

First Edition: 2025
Printed in the United States of America

978-1-964250-14-4

Imprint: T McEvoy

DRAGONS OF VACARI

A Word Before You Begin

Welcome to The Dragons of Vacari series!

This saga is a tapestry of interconnected stories, where each book weaves its own unique arcs and resolutions into a larger, overarching adventure. As you journey through these pages, you'll uncover ancient secrets, forge powerful alliances, and witness epic battles that will shape the fate of Vacari. Some mysteries will unfold within a single book, while others will span the entire series, revealing their secrets piece by piece.

If you love high-stakes adventure, legendary dragons, and a richly crafted world, you're in the right place. This series is filled with thrilling dragon battles, deep friendships, and the enduring struggle between light and darkness.

Planned as a nine-book journey, The Dragons of Vacari is an epic undertaking that will unfold over time, with each installment crafted with care and dedication. In the meantime, stay connected and explore exclusive content on my YouTube channel, where I share behind-the-scenes insights into the world of Vacari:

https://www.youtube.com/@theresamcevoy612

Your patience and support mean the world to me as I bring each chapter of this story to life. Thank you for joining me on this adventure — I hope you enjoy the twists, turns, and surprises that await!

You'll come across the term Crystalbow in this book. This is not a typo — it refers to a specialized weapon tied to one of the characters you'll meet. The unique spelling is deliberate, used to reflect the weapon's significance and rarity within the world of Vacari.

I have always loved dragons.

In the world of Vacari, they are far more than beasts or background legends. Here, dragons are living, thinking, feeling beings — with their own choices to make, burdens to carry, and destinies to shape.

My dragons are characters in their own right, with voices, emotions, and personalities as complex as any hero or villain. Some are fierce protectors, others clever schemers, and a few... well, a few might just surprise you along the way.

I understand this approach may not resonate with every reader. But for me, it is part of what makes Vacari truly alive. Dragons are not merely part of the world — they are the world, woven into its very breath and heartbeat.

Thank you for stepping into their story. I hope you enjoy meeting the dragons of Vacari as much as I've loved bringing them to life.

— T.A. McEvoy

Dragons of Vacari

World Map

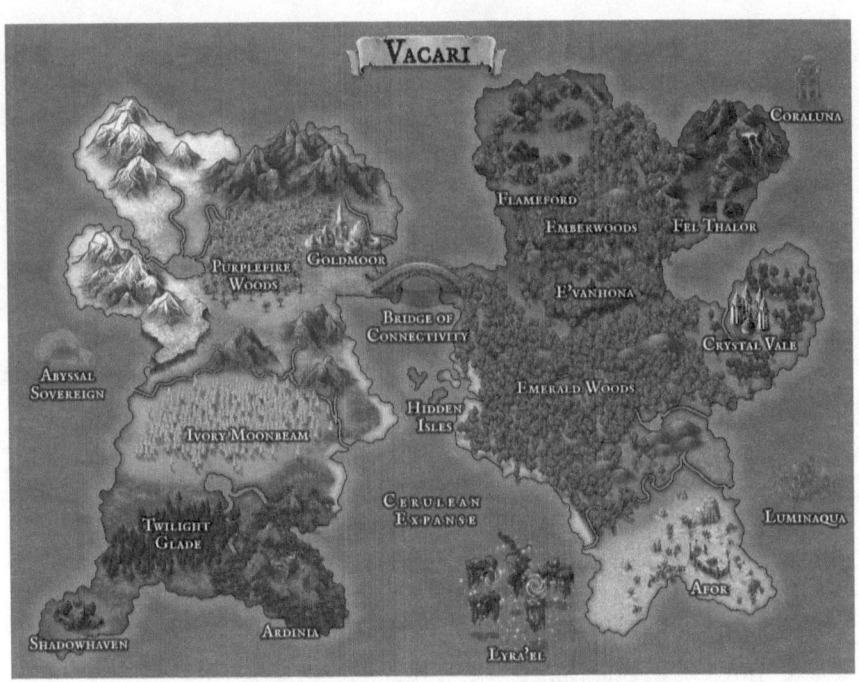

DRAGONS OF ACARI

List of Characters

- **Keisha** (Eladrin) – Courageous adventurer with elemental magic, skilled in archery, driven by justice, bonded with Kimras, the Gold Dragon.

- **Lord Karrenen** (Eladrin) – Master of magic with unmatched arcane command.

- **Thalorian** (Moon Elf) – Skilled warrior and rider of Verdantia, deeply connected to nature.

- **Kaelorn** (Luminara) – Trusted leader by the fae, dedicated to the harmony of Emerald Woods.

- **Qellaun Deadcrusher** (Druchii) – Fearsome warrior, formerly in service to Phoenix and Vuarus.

- **Lyra Deadcrusher** (Druchii) – Cunning sorceress with a mysterious past, once allied with Phoenix and Vuarus.

- **Ong Swifthammer** (Human) – Loyal warrior, married to

Keisha, bonded with Amara, the Amethyst Dragon, and an accepted member of Eladrin society.

- **King Manard** (Human) – Respected King of Crystal Vale.

- **Gailen** (Human) – Brave prince of Crystal Vale, bonded with Aurelia, the Crystal Dragon.

- **King Alex** (Human) – Noble King of Goldmoor.

- **Queen Jeanne** (Human) – Queen of Goldmoor, ruling alongside King Alex.

- **Valeon** (Human) – Hesitant yet earnest young man seeking his place in Vacari.

Noble Dragons

- **Kimras** (Gold Dragon) – Regal leader, known for wisdom and benevolence.

- **Aurelia** (Crystal Dragon) – Mysterious and ethereal, possessing vast ancient knowledge.

- **Verdantia** (Emerald Dragon) – Deeply connected to nature and the vitality of the world.

- **Amara** (Amethyst Dragon) – Spiritually insightful, with an aura of power.

Dark Dragons

- **Zylron** (Red Dragon) – Treacherous and fierce, mirroring fire's unpredictable nature.

- **Glaciera** (White Dragon) – Ruthless and cold-hearted, embodying winter's harshness.

- **Xalzorath** (Black Dragon) – Cunning and ruthless, his dark heart as cold as the night.

- **Nocturna** (Obsidian Dragon) – Cold and unbreakable, her dark power mirroring volcanic stone.

Divine and Significant Beings

- **Aeliana** – Guardian of the Mystic Realm of Ardinia.

- Lysander-God of the Sea

- **Mysterious Person** – Powerful figure within the dark divine realm, motives remain hidden.

Others

- **Pumpkin** (Panther) – Mischievous young panther with a mysterious connection to Keisha.

- **Casper** (Cougar) – Queen Jeanne's companion and protector.

DRAGONS OF VACARI

Various Locations

Main Realm

Vacari

Vacari is an enchanting realm where nature's vibrant tapestry weaves together diverse landscapes, fostering a peaceful coexistence among elves, humans, dragons, and merfolk. Majestic cities like Goldmoor and Crystal Vale thrive in prosperity, their gleaming spires and flourishing trade routes nestled amidst lush forests, shimmering lakes, and serene oceans. Ancient magic flows through the very soil, influencing both the land and its people, while the skies above remain guarded by the vigilant wings of dragons. Vacari's rich cultural heritage reflects the harmonious balance between its peoples, sustained by an intricate connection to the natural and mystical forces that shape the land.

Main City inside Vacari

Goldmoor

Goldmoor, the shining jewel of Vacari, radiates a harmonious fusion of elven grace and human ingenuity. Majestic spires, adorned with intricate gold and silver filigree, reach toward the heavens, their gleaming surfaces catching and reflecting the sunlight like beacons of prosperity. The bustling streets form a living tapestry of elven elegance and human vitality, where vibrant marketplaces brim with goods from every corner of the realm. Artisan stalls display exquisitely crafted wares—delicate elven jewelry, sturdy human armor, and magical artifacts—while the aromas of exotic foods fill the air. At the heart of the city stands the grand castle, its walls a testament to the unity between elves and humans, built with precision and artistry that mirrors the strengths of both races. The city hums with life, laughter, and camaraderie, celebrating the enduring bond that has forged not only a shared kingdom but a shared destiny.

Notable City inside Vacari

Crystal Vale

Crystal Vale, a mesmerizing gem nestled in the heart of Vacari, stands as a testament to the perfect fusion of elven grace and human ingenuity. Its crystalline structures shimmer like diamonds, refracting sunlight into breathtaking cascades of light that dance across the city. Elven and human artisans work in harmony, crafting architectural wonders—delicate bridges that span glistening waterfalls and elegant towers that soar toward the heavens, their surfaces glinting with ethereal brilliance. The city's pulse resonates with the unity of its people, and nowhere is this more poignantly symbolized than in the union of Ong Swifthammer and Keisha. Their marriage, a celebration of love and alliance, echoes eternally through the crystal spires, binding the city's legacy to their story.

Celestial Realm

Lyra'el

Lyra'el, the celestial realm, is a magnificent and ethereal domain where dragons and celestial beings converge in harmony. Floating high above the mortal world, this radiant realm is bathed in the soft glow of starlight and cosmic energies. The skies shimmer with hues of gold and silver, and vast, crystalline mountains rise from the celestial plains, their peaks touching the heavens. Here, dragons of divine origin soar alongside majestic celestial beings, their forms radiant with the essence of the stars.

In Lyra'el, the boundaries between time and space seem to blur, creating a timeless sanctuary where both beings of incredible power come together in unity. The realm pulses with an ancient magic, one that governs both the heavens and the mortal world below, and its inhabitants are entrusted with the balance of cosmic forces. It is a place of unparalleled beauty and serenity, where the celestial and draconic realms intertwine, their destinies forever linked by the will of the stars.

Dark Cities inside Vacari

Fel Thalor

Fel Thalor, once the forsaken city of the Druchii, now stirs with life once more, yet remains a haunting monument to its dark past. Its once-majestic spires, though still scarred by time, rise defiantly against a brooding sky, casting long shadows over the streets where whispers of ancient power still linger. The air is thick with the weight of forgotten rituals, as if the city itself remembers the blood sacrifices and dark magic that once permeated its core. At the heart of Fel Thalor, the sacrificial altar—a grim relic of the Druchii's ruthless practices—has stirred from its long dormancy, as though waiting for its masters to reclaim their sinister legacy. Though no longer abandoned, the city remains shrouded in an unsettling stillness, a place where the line between past and present blurs, and the presence of its dark history can be felt in every stone.

Old Flameford

Old Flameford, once the formidable stronghold of the warlock Phoenix Shadowwalker, was a city cloaked in darkness. Its ominous atmosphere, enhanced by the oppressive hues of black and red that covered every building, created an ever-present sense of dread. At its heart stood the Dark Tower, a foreboding structure that pierced the very heavens, once the source of Phoenix's malevolent power. This was the seat of his dark rule, where nefarious plans were forged and dark magic flowed freely—until the alliance rose against him, driving him into exile.

However, Old Flameford has since undergone a dramatic transformation. While the tower still looms over the city like a grim reminder of its past, the landscape has become even more treacherous. Evil dragon lairs now scatter the land, their dark inhabitants adding to the already sinister aura of the city. These draconic overlords have made their homes among the crumbling ruins, solidifying Old Flameford as a place of darkness where evil continues to fester, waiting for the moment to rise once again.

Shadowhaven

Shadowhaven lies on the edge of Twilight Glade, adjacent to the foreboding Cerulean Expanse. This dark and shadowy city is a place where the light barely penetrates, and an air of mystery and danger lingers over every corner. Once a thriving figure in Goldmoor, Maldrak now rules over Shadowhaven, having been exiled by King Alex for his treacherous actions. Under his iron grip, the city has become a haven for those who seek to escape the law, as well as those drawn to its darker energies.

The architecture of Shadowhaven is as oppressive as its atmosphere—blackened stone towers and gloomy streets blend into the ever-present twilight, illuminated only by the faint, eerie glow from hidden sources. Maldrak's influence casts a long shadow over the city, where whispers of rebellion and secrets seem to thrive in the gloom. Its residents, a mix of outcasts and dark-hearted souls, have adapted to this realm of constant dusk, living under the ever-watchful gaze of their exiled ruler.

Though menacing and dangerous, Shadowhaven also holds a certain allure for those seeking power or refuge from the light. It is a place where alliances are forged in the shadows, and where Maldrak's dark ambitions may one day extend far beyond the city's borders.

Forests inside Vacari

Purplefire Woods

Purplefire Woods, awash in a mesmerizing kaleidoscope of purples, stands as an enchanting testament to nature's vibrant palette. Every shade, from deep amethyst to soft lavender, blends harmoniously with the gentle rustle of leaves, creating a forest alive with color and serenity. This breathtaking realm, beloved by Keisha for its beauty and tranquility, became the perfect setting for her union with Ong in a magical wedding ceremony that will forever be etched in the hearts of those who attended. The regal shades of purple that drape the trees and blanket the ground serve as both a backdrop and witness to this sacred event. Beyond its beauty, Purplefire Woods is a vital passage, guiding travelers through its enchanted paths toward the majestic city of Goldmoor, making it a place of both natural wonder and symbolic importance.

Emeraldwoods

Emeraldwoods, a lush, verdant realm bathed in the soothing embrace of emerald green, serves as a breathtaking passage to Crystal Vale. The vibrant hues of the forest, coupled with its serene ambiance, create an enchanting landscape where nature feels alive and welcoming. This sacred forest witnessed the engagement ceremony of Ong and Keisha, marking the union of their souls in a celebration of love and harmony. Beneath the emerald canopy, they pledged their bond, setting the stage for the joyous festivities that awaited them in Crystal Vale. The forest stands as a symbol of new beginnings, a tranquil sanctuary where love and life intertwine before travelers continue their journey to the majestic city.

Emberwooods

Emberwoods, a captivating forest bathed in fiery hues of red and orange, stands near the volatile volcanic region, lending it an otherworldly glow. Despite the inherent dangers lurking within, the forest retains a haunting, untamed beauty that entices both awe and caution. Traveling through Emberwoods is a perilous journey, as it leads to the formidable Druchii stronghold of Fel Thalor. Now, a new layer of mystery and challenge awaits all who venture there. Copper dragons and pixies have woven their magic to create an intricate, twisting maze at the very gates of Fel Thalor, a cunning trap meant to confuse and thwart the evil Druchii. This enchanted maze, alive with illusions and deceptions, tests the wit and endurance of any who dare to enter, making the path to Fel Thalor even more treacherous than before.

Ivory Moonbeams

Ivory Moonbeam, the mystical home of the Sylvan Elves, is a realm bathed in hues of white and ivory, its landscape reflecting the pure, radiant beauty of its name. The trees, with bark that gleams like polished pearl, rise tall and graceful, their leaves and flowers shimmering with a soft, ethereal glow beneath the moon's gentle light. The entire forest comes alive at night, as the moonlight casts an otherworldly brilliance upon the landscape, enhancing its serene and enchanting atmosphere.

The Sylvan Elves, known for their deep connection to nature, dwell harmoniously within these enchanted depths, their lives intertwined with the magic of the forest. The pristine color palette, dominated by shades of ivory and white, reflects the purity and tranquility that permeates Ivory Moonbeam, making it a sanctuary of peace and wonder. Those who wander through its glistening paths feel the quiet magic of the place, as though they've stepped into a world untouched by time, where nature and mysticism reign supreme.

Twilight Glade

Twilight Glade lies in the delicate balance between the ethereal beauty of Ivory Moonbeam and the mysterious darkness of Shadowhaven. The color palette of this enchanted forest reflects its name, with soft hues of purple, blue, and gray blending seamlessly into the landscape. The interplay of light and shadow creates an ever-changing tapestry of colors, as the sunlight filters gently through the thick canopy by day, casting dappled shades across the forest floor. By night, moonbeams weave through the trees, their silvery glow dancing upon the ground, adding an air of quiet magic to the glade.

The forest itself seems alive with the subtle transitions of light, as if caught between two realms—one of purity and one of shadow. Twilight Glade serves as a mystical bridge, embodying both serenity and mystery, a place where travelers can experience the magic of both worlds. The shifting hues create a dreamlike atmosphere, inviting those who wander through to lose themselves in the tranquil beauty and the soft whispers of the wind

Sub-Areas inside of Vacari

Shimmering Coast

The Shimmering Coast stretches along the borders of the Cerulean Expanse, where the ocean's azure waves gently meet the land. This radiant coastline serves as a peaceful convergence point, where merfolk from Coraluna emerge from the depths to bask in the sun's warmth and converse with visitors from the surface world. The coast is named for the way the waters shimmer and sparkle as sunlight dances across them, creating a breathtaking spectacle of light and color.

More than just a place of beauty, the Shimmering Coast acts as a vital meeting point between the realms of land and sea, fostering friendships and alliances among different civilizations. Here, merfolk and surface dwellers exchange knowledge, form bonds, and strengthen ties between their worlds. The coast has become a symbol of harmony, a place where the boundaries between ocean and land blur, and the people of both realms come together in peace.

Hidden Sub-Realm inside Vacari

E'vahona

E'vahona, the hidden jewel of the Eladrin, was a sacred gift from Kadona, the benevolent goddess of light. Shielded by divine magic, it remains untouched and unseen by the evil Dominion, a sanctuary of peace and purity. Crystal pathways wind gracefully through the city, leading to homes seamlessly crafted from a delicate fusion of crystal and wood, blending the natural with the ethereal. Within the enchanting boundaries of E'vahona, the Eladrin share their lives with magnificent companions—majestic wolves and mythical creatures like Pumpkin the panther—who roam freely, adding to the city's mystical charm. The air carries the gentle, harmonious melody of nature, resonating with an otherworldly beauty that reflects the close bond between the Eladrin and their divine patron. E'vahona is not just a city; it is a living testament to the light and protection of Kadona, and a place where magic and nature dance in perfect harmony.

The Sacred Grove

Nestled within the heart of E'vahona, a breathtaking garden flourishes under the divine caress of Kadona, the goddess of light. Crystal-clear waterfalls cascade gently from moss-covered cliffs, their soothing symphony echoing throughout the lush, vibrant landscape. The air is perfumed with the delicate fragrance of exotic blossoms, their brilliant hues creating a mesmerizing tapestry of color and life. Elaborate pathways, adorned with luminescent flora, weave gracefully through the garden, guiding visitors on a journey through this enchanted paradise where ethereal creatures roam freely. Butterflies, shimmering in the soft glow of the flora, dance in a harmonious choreography, while the gentle hum of mystical energies pulses in perfect resonance with the natural world. In this sacred space, the beauty of nature and the divine touch of Kadona converge, creating a serene haven of peace and wonder.

Sub-Realm inside Vacari

The Hidden Isles

Tucked behind a mystical barrier, The Hidden Isles emerge as a sanctuary of breathtaking beauty. This ethereal realm, a collection of isles adorned with vibrant flora and encircled by cascading waterfalls, welcomes only those who can pass through its enchanted protections. At the heart of these mystical isles stands a majestic golden castle, a symbol of the noble dragons' grandeur and the sacred meeting place for allies from various races. The crystal-clear waters below reflect the brilliance of the azure sky, while the air hums with the harmonious melodies of unseen creatures that dwell among the isles. This hidden paradise, untouched by time or conflict, is a place where nature, magic, and dragonkind exist in perfect harmony, offering refuge and counsel to those deemed worthy.

Ardinia

Ardinia, a haven of enchantment shielded by a magical barrier, unfolds as a breathtaking realm where nature's beauty reigns supreme. Towering trees, their branches adorned with blossoms in every imaginable hue, stretch toward the heavens, creating a lush canopy that murmurs the ancient secrets of the forest. Crystal-clear streams weave gracefully through the ver-dant landscape, reflecting the vibrant colors of the surrounding flora and adding to the tranquility of the realm. In this mystical sanctuary, nymphs, fairies, and the elusive white unicorns roam freely, their presence adding an ethereal grace to the serene atmosphere. Occasionally, the skies above Ardinia are graced by the majestic flight of Pegasus, a rare and awe-inspiring sight reserved for those fortunate enough to glimpse the magic that thrives in this protected paradise.

Cerulean Expanse

Beyond the shores of Vacari lies the Cerulean Expanse, a vast and seemingly endless ocean teeming with life and untold mysteries. The azure depths of this boundless sea conceal countless wonders, from vibrant coral reefs brimming with marine life to the forgotten shipwrecks of ancient vessels long lost to time. The ocean's surface glistens under the sun's rays, reflect-ing a shimmering, almost magical light that stretches to the horizon.

Beneath the waves, the merfolk dwell in majestic underwater kingdoms, their cities crafted from coral and pearl—a breathtaking testament to the beauty and grandeur of the ocean realm. These hidden cities are sanctu-aries of peace and wonder, where the ocean's currents carry stories of the deep and where nature and magic intertwine. The Cerulean Expanse holds many secrets, its waters whispering of adventures yet to be uncovered, making it a place where both beauty and danger coexist in the vastness of the sea.,

Underwater Kingdom inside Vacari

Coraluna:

Coraluna, a mesmerizing underwater kingdom, unfolds as a realm of vibrant beauty beneath the azure waves. Vast coral reefs, adorned with a kaleidoscope of colorful corals and teeming with exotic fish, create a breathtaking tapestry that stretches across the ocean floor. Lush underwater plants sway gracefully with the gentle currents, their movements in perfect harmony with the ebb and flow of the sea. The merfolk, diligent and wise, tend to the well-being of their aquatic home, ensuring that Coraluna remains a thriving and serene sanctuary. King Oceanous, a majestic and benevolent ruler, watches over the kingdom with compassionate eyes, guiding his people and maintaining the delicate balance of the underwater world. In Coraluna, the harmony between nature and its inhabitants creates a tranquil and magical realm, hidden beneath the waves yet brimming with life.

Luminaqua

Nestled in the heart of the ocean's embrace, Luminaqua stands as a stunning testament to the ingenuity and harmony of the Aquanar Elves. This underwater haven is a marvel of elven and aquatic architecture, where the boundaries between nature and artifice blur, creating a breathtaking spectacle. The city's structures are masterfully crafted from luminescent coral, casting a gentle, ethereal glow that bathes Luminaqua in perpetual light. Towers and buildings, adorned with pearlescent shells, shimmer like jewels beneath the caress of the ocean's currents, their surfaces reflecting the serene beauty of the underwater world. The city's layout flows seamlessly, mirroring the graceful movement of the tides, with elegant bridges and pathways connecting its various districts in fluid harmony.

Luminaqua is not merely a city; it is a living, breathing masterpiece, pulsing with the ocean's rhythm and the spirit of its elven inhabitants. The Aquanar Elves live in perfect balance with the sea, their culture deeply intertwined with the ebb and flow of the tides. Life in Luminaqua is a dance of elegance and resilience, as this sanctuary, hidden in the ocean's depths, has withstood the test of time. A glittering jewel in the vast underwater world, Luminaqua remains a beacon of beauty, unity, and strength, a place where magic and nature are forever intertwined.

Underwater Realm inside Coraluna

Abyssal Sovereign:

Nestled within the ocean's depths, Abyssal Sovereign is a magnificent underwater realm governed by the divine watch of Lysander, the God of the Sea. This ethereal kingdom is a breathtaking display of aquatic wonders, where vibrant corals sway gently with the currents and schools of iridescent fish dance in perfect harmony. The tranquil kingdom is adorned with stunning structures, masterfully crafted from seashells and precious gems, their surfaces reflecting the divine touch of Lysander. His protective aura envelops Abyssal Sovereign, ensuring that no darkness or malevolence can breach its serene depths.

The merfolk inhabitants, guided by their benevolent ruler, maintain the flourishing marine life, tending to the ocean's vibrant ecosystem with care and devotion. Under Lysander's divine leadership, Abyssal Sovereign has become a haven of peace and beauty, where the sea's mysteries and magic coexist in perfect balance. It is a realm untouched by conflict, its calm waters a reflection of the god's power and wisdom, a sanctuary beneath the waves where tranquility reigns supreme.

Neighbor Realms

Afor

The Neighboring Realm of Afor has undergone a dramatic transformation over time. Once a vast, treacherous swampland where Phoenix and the Druchii were exiled, Afor's landscape was forever altered when Vuarus, the god of the abyss, was released from his imprisonment. His chaotic power scorched the land, transforming the swamp into an unforgiving desert, a barren region of shifting sands and desolation.

Since the defeat of both Phoenix and Vuarus, Afor has begun to rebuild. Amidst the harsh desert, new cities have emerged, built by resilient inhabitants who have adapted to the unforgiving climate. Yet, due to the realm's dark history, the Noble dragons (Bronze) maintain a vigilant watch over the region, patrolling the skies and ensuring that no lingering threats arise from its troubled past. Though Afor still bears the scars of its dark legacy, life continues to flourish as its people and their noble dragon protectors carve out a new future in this once-forsaken land.

Etharyon

A secluded realm of ethereal beauty, Etharyon is home to the Moon Elves. Known for its harmony with nature, the realm features Silvaraen, a serene valley city glowing with bioluminescent lights, and Aerindral, the Sapphire City, a cultural and diplomatic hub with canals and sapphire-inspired architecture. Etharyon embodies clarity, wisdom, and resilience.

DRAGONS OF ACARI

Dedication

Tom Vick

To my wonderful boyfriend, Tom—thank you for reading every draft of this book. Since we met, my life has improved in more ways than I can express. Your constant encouragement, always having my back, and reminding me that I can achieve anything means the world to me. A special thanks for handling all the marketers and promoters—though they seem too scared to contact you after they're told to! Guess you've got them figured out, huh?

DRAGONS OF VACARI

Also, by T.A. McEvoy

The Elves of Vacari Series:

The Wicked Published 11-01-2023

Shadows Unveiled- Published 12-05-2023.

Vacari's Resurgence: Healing Bonds 04-12-2024

Dragons of Vacari Series:

Rise of the Ancients 12-02-2024

Shadows of Betrayal 04-21-2025

Celestial Convergence (coming soon)

Explore more about each book and series at: https://www.tamcevoy.com/

Contents

Prologue
Shadows of the Abyss

The air in the Abyss cavern pulsed with energy, pressing against the lungs, whispering uneasily to the soul. Even in the absence of its master, the walls thrummed with the echoes of Vuarus's power. A lone servant of the fallen god traced their fingers along the jagged obsidian, memories unfurling like shadows in the dim light, memories of servitude, of wrath endured, of expectations once as unbreakable as the chains that had bound a god.

Once, this place had been the heart of fervent rituals and trembling prayers. Blood and fire had been offered in desperate devotion, for to disobey was to summon wrath beyond mortal comprehension. Here, the god of the Abyss had been both prisoner and master, his influence stretching far beyond his shackles.

A voice shattered the silence low, steady. The figure's jaw tightened, shoulders stiff with suppressed turmoil.

"Do you remember me, Vuarus? Or was I just another vessel cast aside?"

The void swallowed the words, yet the cavern trembled in response. A deep tremor rolled through the Abyss as if the darkness exhaled a slow, ominous breath. The chamber pulsed with an eerie, unnatural light, a sickly green hue slithering across the walls, distorting shadows as though the god's essence still fought to claim dominion.

And there, bound in celestial chains, Vuarus loomed his crimson eyes seething with divine fury.

The figure's breath caught. Muscles coiled with tension, an instinctive shudder rippling through them. They forced themselves still.

"You seek my favor?"

The voice was not merely heard. It was felt, reverberating through bone and soul.

The figure knelt, the weight of the Abyss pressing them closer to the stone. "I seek purpose, my lord. In your shadow, I will find it."

"Purpose."

Vuarus's laughter rolled like distant thunder, vast and mocking. The figure flinched as the sound scraped against their resolve like jagged steel. Every rumble sent tremors through their body, chipping away at certainty.

"You serve because I demand it, not because you wish it. In serving me, you will learn only the truth of your insignificance."

The chains groaned as the god leaned forward. His breath, thick with the acrid scent of brimstone, scorched the air between them. Each word is carved into the figure's resolve.

"But perhaps you will prove... useful."

The memory fractured, dissipating like smoke into the abyss, leaving behind only the bitter taste of anger, a fury reignited by the thought of Vuarus's demise.

The noble dragons had taken him.

United with the elves and the people of Vacari, they had struck him down, severing the one constant in their existence. That loss simmered beneath the surface, unspoken yet undeniable, fueling a resentment that had yet to find its reckoning. A wound that could never heal.

The figure's hand trembled as they pulled it from the rock.

Vuarus was gone. His divine presence was extinguished, torn from the world.

Yet his absence had left a void not only in the Abyss but within the figure's very soul. A hollowness that festered with anger, an ache they refused to name. As if something essential had been wrenched away.

"It's all in motion now," they murmured, stepping away from the wall. Their eyes glinted, caught between defiance and fear. "You set me on this path, Vuarus. Every step feels like a descent into chaos, yet I cannot turn back. Whether it leads to salvation or destruction, I will walk it to the end because I have nothing else to cling to."

Their footsteps echoed into the vast emptiness, swallowed by the ever-hungry dark.

But the Abyss was never truly silent.

The shadows stirred, whispering of treachery, despair, vengeance.

The figure stiffened as a chill slithered down their spine.

"Failure."

"Betrayal."

"Loss."

The words struck like needles of doubt, threading through the cracks in their resolve, daring them to falter.

Yet still, they walked on.

Chapter 1

Call of Home

The twilight of Etharyon bathed the land in a silvery glow, casting long shadows over the rolling hills and distant spires that pierced the horizon. Mist curled around Gailen's boots as he stood at the edge of the overlook, gazing at the vast expanse of the Shimmering Plains. Below, the silvery grass swayed like waves in a quiet sea, and the faint shimmer of winding rivers wove ribbons of starlight across the landscape.

His gaze was distant, his thoughts as restless as the mist swirling around him. The cool air carried the scent of damp earth and distant pines, grounding him even as his mind drifted. A deep, familiar ache settled in his chest, nostalgia entwined with uncertainty, pulling him between the past and the path ahead. This land had shaped, tested, and strengthened him in ways he had never imagined. Etharyon had become a part of him, its lessons etched into his very being.

Yet, as much as he had grown here, something stirred deep within him. A longing. A pull toward the home he had left behind.

His fingers tightened around the hilt of his sword, the familiar weight steadying him. Memories of his father's voice, stories told beneath starlit skies, noble dragons soaring above Vacari, each one a tether pulling him back. It was time.

A shift in the mist drew his attention.

Kaelorn stood nearby, his luminous glade-fire eyes catching the faint light—striking, otherworldly, reminiscent of the fae. He had traveled alongside Gailen for years, bound by shared battles and unspoken trust. Yet tonight, something felt different. There was a weight in Gailen's stillness, an unspoken tension, as though unseen thoughts pressed upon him like the mist clinging to the plains.

"You're quieter than usual," Kaelorn observed, calm but edged with curiosity. He stepped closer, movements fluid as the drifting fog. "What's on your mind?"

Gailen did not respond immediately. His hand lingered on his sword hilt, fingers tightening before he exhaled, the sound carrying quiet resolve.

"I've made a decision," he said at last.

Kaelorn tilted his head, his brow furrowing slightly. "A decision about what?"

Gailen turned to face him, his expression resolute. "I need to return home."

Kaelorn blinked, the words hanging between them. "Home?" he repeated, confusion flickering in his tone. "I thought Etharyon was your home."

A faint smile touched Gailen's lips, though it carried a hint of sadness. "It is not. My home is Vacari, across the border." He paused, letting the revelation settle in the air. "That is where I come from. That is where I need to return."

Kaelorn studied him in silence, surprise mingling with contemplation and a hint of concern. He knew the dangers of returning home after so long, the weight of unresolved pasts and lingering ghosts. Yet, he also recognized the determination in Gailen's stance, the resolve that left no room for doubt.

Behind them, the others had taken notice. Thalorian and Valeon remained quiet, their gazes fixed on Gailen, curiosity evident in their expressions.

Thalorian was the first to speak. "Vacari," he mused, his silver brows drawing together in quiet contemplation as he folded his arms across his chest. "I have heard whispers about the Eladrin and Sylvan Elves who live there. Their history, their power... fascinating, if the stories are true." He stepped closer, the faint light catching in his silver hair as he regarded Gailen. "If you are going home, I want to come with you. It might be an opportunity to learn more about them—and to establish ties between them and the Moon Elves."

Gailen shrugged slightly, a faint smile tugging at his lips. "All I know are the rumors, Thalorian. I have never met an Eladrin or Sylvan Elf myself. For all I know, they might be nothing more than myth."

Thalorian's expression did not waver, determination glinting in his jade fire eyes. "Even myths have roots in something real. If there is a chance, I would rather see it myself."

Gailen nodded. "Then you are welcome to come along. We will find out if there is any truth to the tales."

Kaelorn rested a hand on his hip, a knowing smirk curving his lips as he cast Gailen a sideways glance. "If you are heading back to Vacari, I am coming too. Someone must keep you out of trouble."

Gailen raised a brow. "Out of trouble? I did not realize that was a full-time job."

"With you? It always is," Kaelorn shot back with a grin. Then his expression softened, and his gaze drifted toward the horizon. "Besides, this might be a chance to rebuild something that was lost long ago. Etharyon and Vacari once had strong ties before things fell apart."

Gailen frowned. "Fell apart, how?"

Kaelorn hesitated, his brow furrowing as if sifting through fragments of a past not entirely his own. He exhaled slowly, the weight of untold stories pressing against his thoughts. When he finally spoke, his voice was quieter.

"There was a man. Manard, his name was. He came here long ago, and an alliance was in the making. But then he died, or so they thought. His fiancée found another, and they had a son. But the boy... he grew up here, trained as one of us."

Gailen stiffened. His breath caught, an invisible weight pressing against his chest. His pulse quickened, a dull ache forming at the back of his mind as memories stirred hazy, incomplete. A chill ran through him, though whether from the cool air or the sudden realization, he could not tell.

The name struck a chord deep within him, resonating with something buried, something forgotten yet familiar. Fragments surfaced half-forgotten stories, distant echoes of his father's voice, moments dismissed as a childhood fantasy. His fingers curled into fists, tension rippling through his shoulders.

Manard. The name rang in his mind like a distant bell. His expression remained neutral, but the revelation hit like a hammer inside.

That name... my father. But why didn't he tell me?

Kaelorn glanced at him, unaware of the storm beneath Gailen's calm surface. "Maybe this trip will mend those old ties," he said. "And who knows, perhaps there is more history between our lands than we realize."

Gailen exhaled slowly, Kaelorn's words pressing against the unspoken memories he carried. Doubt and longing tangled within him, whispering of untaken roads and truths yet uncovered. His past called to him like an old song, familiar yet distant.

Would returning home bring answers? Or only more questions?

He had no certainty, only the weight of history left behind. Still, he nodded, keeping his voice steady. "Maybe."

Valeon, who had been leaning against a nearby tree, finally spoke. "Well," he drawled, smirking, "if Thalorian and Kaelorn are going, then so am I. I am not about to miss out on an adventure."

Gailen turned toward him, amusement flickering through his earlier turmoil. "Adventure, huh? More like trouble if you are involved."

He glanced at Thalorian. "And for the record, he's the one who gets into trouble, not me." Laughter rippled through the group.

Valeon raised his hands in mock surrender. "I cannot help it if trouble follows me. It is not my fault I am irresistible to chaos."

Kaelorn rolled his eyes, shaking his head, though he could not suppress his grin. Thalorian chuckled softly, his usual reserved demeanor cracking just slightly. For a moment, the weight of uncertainty lifted, replaced by camaraderie. And for now, the road ahead felt a little less daunting.

Gailen turned to Thalorian, and his brow raised thoughtfully. "Do we need to head to the Moon Elves? Let them know about your decision to leave?"

Thalorian gave a short nod, his expression calm but resolute. "We should. They would worry otherwise, especially if I disappeared. It would not reflect well on us."

Kaelorn leaned against his staff, arms crossed. "Then it is only fair I do the same. I will need to inform the King about my departure. He will want to know why I am leaving."

Valeon chuckled, a smirk widening across his face as he spread his arms theatrically. "And that, my friends, is what makes me special. No obligations, formalities, just me, the road, and my undeniable charm."

Thalorian gave him a flat look. "If by 'special,' you mean utterly incorrigible, then yes."

Kaelorn shook his head with a quiet laugh while Gailen shot Valeon with a knowing grin. "And yet, somehow, you're still here with us."

Valeon crossed his arms, feigning pride. "Of course. Someone has to keep things interesting."

The faint hum of flowing water and rustling leaves welcomed Gailen and his companions as they stepped into Silvaraen. After days of traversing rugged terrain and uncertain paths, the city's tranquil beauty felt almost surreal, a stark contrast to the weariness of their journey. Here, the air was crisp, filled with the soft chime of wind bells, a delicate reminder that they had entered a realm untouched by the burdens they carried.

The city unfolded before them like a dream. Silver towers rose gracefully against the cliffs, their gleaming spires stretching toward the sky. A cool breeze carried the scent of blooming nightshade, mingling with the murmuring of a distant waterfall. Lanterns lined the pathways, casting a soft, ethereal glow over gardens of shimmering plants while the faint chime of wind bells wove a gentle melody.

Silvaraen's tranquility stood in stark contrast to the weight of their mission and the uncertainties that lay ahead a timeless sanctuary, untouched by the struggles of the outside world.

Thalorian led them through the main thoroughfare, his steps measured as though he was already beginning to miss this place. The sight of the silver towers bathed in moonlight stirred memories of childhood lessons beneath the great tree, of nights, spent tracing constellations with his elders, of whispered laughter carried on the wind.

Each step forward felt like leaving a piece of himself behind.

This was home, the place that had shaped him, a sanctuary where duty had often felt lighter. No matter how far he traveled, returning to Silvaraen felt like stepping into something eternal.

"It doesn't matter how often I leave and return," he murmured, more to himself than the others. "Silvaraen always feels timeless."

They reached the central forum, where a few Moon Elves had gathered near the great silver tree. Their gazes turned toward Thalorian as he stepped forward, expressions a mixture of curiosity and quiet reverence.

A moment of silence stretched between them before he finally spoke.

"I've made a decision," he began, his voice steady yet respectful. "I will be traveling to Vacari with Gailen and his companions. There is an opportunity to learn about the Eladrin and Sylvan Elves and forge a bond that will benefit both our people."

A regal Moon Elf with hair as white as starlight stepped forward. Her silver eyes held quiet wisdom, her voice calm as she regarded him.

"The Eladrin are said to be elusive, their magic powerful but hidden. Even their city remains a mystery to most." She inclined her head slightly, her gaze filled with both pride and caution. "Be careful, Thalorian, and if you find them, bring back stories and an alliance we can be proud of."

Another elf, younger and more curious, glanced at Gailen. "You've never seen an Eladrin?"

Gailen shook his head, and the elf smiled faintly. "They exist, though finding them will test your resolve. Their city is veiled in mystery, a place whispered in twilight tales. Only those with unwavering will and the patience to follow the echoes of the unseen will uncover its secrets."

Gailen nodded thoughtfully. "Then persistence will be our guide."

The weight of the journey ahead settled within him, yet beneath it stirred a quiet determination. They would find what they sought no matter the obstacles, and doubt would not take root.

The elder's expression softened, her gaze lingering on Thalorian with pride and sadness. "Go, then. May the moonlight guide your path, Thalorian. You carry the hopes of Silvaraen with you. Bring back what you find and remember your home will always be here, waiting."

The sun dipped below the horizon as the group entered Aerindral, casting the city in a warm glow that danced across its sapphire-toned stone. The streets shimmered as though carved from liquid light, and the canals winding through the city reflected the hues of the sky, creating a mesmerizing interplay of blues and silvers. Lanterns, shaped like crystalline flowers, flickered to life, their soft light casting an ethereal glow over the bustling streets.

Kaelorn led the way, his pace steady and purposeful. His fingers curled into fists briefly before he forced them to relax, the weight of old regrets pressing at the back of his mind. The city's beauty was unchanged, yet it felt different now. It was a place both welcoming and distant, a reminder of all he had left behind and all he had yet to prove. His jaw tightened slightly, memories surfacing like ghosts in the dusk.

Every step carried the weight of duty, the echoes of past failures whispering at his heels. But he pushed forward, resolute.

This journey was more than diplomacy. It bore the weight of history, of choices that could alter the future of their people. He had seen alliances rise and fall, trust forged and broken. And with every step toward the Royal Hall, he wondered if this time would be any different.

"Aerindral's beauty never fades, no matter how many times you visit," he said, glancing back at the others. "But do not let it fool you. The King values results over admiration."

They passed through the Azure Market, where vendors called out in melodic tones, offering wares ranging from shimmering fabrics to rare gemstones that captured the city's light within their depths. The air was rich with the scent of sweet herbs and freshly baked bread, mingling with the faint metallic tang of the canals.

Gailen inhaled deeply, letting the warmth of the market's aromas chase away some of his lingering tension. Beside him, Valeon let out a contented sigh.

"Now, this is the kind of welcome I appreciate," he murmured, eyeing a vendor stacking golden loaves onto a cart.

The Royal Hall stood at the city's heart, its domed roof gleaming like polished silver. Guards flanked the grand entrance, their armor reflecting the sapphire glow that permeated every corner of Aerindral. They nodded as Kaelorn approached, stepping aside to allow the group entry.

Inside, the hall was no less breathtaking. Soaring ceilings bore intricate carvings of waves and stars, while the floor beneath them was a mosaic of blue and silver tiles, each catching the light and casting it in shifting patterns. At the far end of the chamber sat the King of Etharyon, his robes, a deep navy trimmed with silver, a crown of elegant simplicity resting on his brow.

Kaelorn stepped forward and bowed low.

"Your Majesty," he began, his tone respectful but firm. "I have come to inform you of my plans. I will be traveling to Vacari alongside my companions, seeking to reestablish the alliance and trade that once flourished between our worlds."

The King leaned forward slightly, his fingers lightly tapping the armrest of his throne. His expression remained unreadable as he studied Kaelorn, searching for unspoken truths. Silence stretched between them, heavy with the weight of past decisions.

Finally, he exhaled, his grip on the armrest tightening momentarily before he spoke.

"Your intentions are noble, Kaelorn, and your efforts commendable. But the road you travel will not be without peril." His voice was measured, carrying both caution and hope. "The history between our worlds is... complex, and alliances are not easily mended."

Kaelorn met the King's gaze with unwavering resolve. "I understand, Your Majesty. But this is a step worth taking. If we can rebuild the trust between our people, there is much we can achieve together."

A faint smile touched the King's lips, though his eyes remained serious. "You carry the hope of Etharyon with you, Kaelorn. Be careful and remember your actions will speak louder than any words. If you succeed, the bonds we once shared can be restored."

Kaelorn inclined his head. "Thank you, Your Majesty. I will not fail."

The King rose, his gaze sweeping over the gathered group.

"To all of you who embark on this journey, may the light of Aerindral guide your steps, and may you return with the stories and strength that will bind us once more."

As they stepped from the Royal Hall, the city's glow seemed brighter, reflecting the King's cautious optimism. Kaelorn walked ahead, his expression thoughtful.

"Well," he said finally, glancing back at the group. "That could have gone worse."

Gailen smirked. "Careful, Kaelorn. You are almost starting to sound optimistic."

A cool breeze met them as they stepped into the streets. The scent of the canals and the hum of Aerindral's night filled the air. The city had begun to quiet, its sapphire glow softening as lanterns flickered to full brightness, casting long, dancing shadows across the cobbled streets.

Gailen turned to the others, his voice steady but firm.

"We have had a long day, and the journey will not be easy. Rest tonight, and let your horses recover as well. We leave at dawn."

Thalorian inclined his head, his usual composed demeanor unshaken. "A wise choice. We will need our strength for what lies ahead."

Kaelorn gave a slight nod, his gaze lingering briefly on the glowing spires of Aerindral. "Dawn, it is, then."

Valeon stretched, his grin lazy, his tone laced with mischief. He shot Kaelorn a sidelong glance, nudging him playfully with his elbow. "Try not to look too serious, Kaelorn. You might scare off all the fun before we even begin."

Thalorian rolled his eyes, muttering something about Valeon's unmatched talent for theatrics, while Kaelorn merely shook his head with an amused sigh. Even Gailen could not suppress a faint smile—their familiar and effortless banter eased the weight of the day's events.

"You mean I get to sleep in a real bed tonight?" Valeon added, stretching his arms above his head. "You do not have to tell me twice."

Gailen smirked but said nothing more. A quiet warmth settled in his chest as he glanced at his companions, their camaraderie, a steady presence amid the uncertainty. He had seen too much loss to take moments like this for granted. The road ahead remained uncertain, the weight of their choices yet to unfold, but one truth remained: whatever awaited them in Vacari, they would face it together.

The city lights shimmered around them as they dispersed, casting long, wavering reflections across the sapphire stones. The night stretched overhead, vast and silent, as Aerindral stood as a watchful sentinel—a city steeped in history, bearing silent witness to the beginning of a journey that would test them all.

Chapter 2

Return to the Land Beyond

The first light of dawn crept over Aerindral, casting a soft golden glow against the city's sapphire-hued stone. Gailen took a steadying breath, letting the morning's tranquility settle over him. The sight before him was a quiet testament to how far they had come and the uncertainty ahead.

For a fleeting moment, he allowed himself to exist in the stillness.

As the sun's light touched the canals, their surfaces shimmered like liquid crystals, reflecting the shifting hues of the sky. The bioluminescent vines that clung to Aerindral's walls slowly dimmed, yielding to the morning's embrace, while the distant hum of a waking city stirred softly in the air. The cool dawn breeze carried the faint scent of mist and earth, punctuated by the occasional chirping of early birds and the gentle lap of water against the canal walls.

The streets were quiet, save for the rustle of wind through the vines and the occasional soft splash of water from the canals.

Gailen adjusted the straps on his pack, and his gaze fixed on the city gates ahead. Thalorian and Kaelorn stood nearby, both already prepared for departure. The Moon Elf was, as always, composed and unreadable, while Kaelorn's fae features betrayed a flicker of impatience.

Thalorian turned toward Gailen, his voice calm but pointed. "One of us should fetch Valeon. Unless you wish to see if he decides to grace us with his presence."

Kaelorn chuckled softly. "He did say he had no responsibilities. Perhaps he took that as permission to sleep in."

Gailen exhaled through his nose, shaking his head. It was expected yet still exasperating. He should have known.

Valeon possessed an almost supernatural talent for ignoring the morning sun, as though waking early was a personal affront. This routine had played out enough times that Gailen no longer needed to wonder how it would end with him dragging Valeon from whatever tangled mess of blankets he had cocooned himself in.

Yet beneath his exasperation lurked something more complex.

Something was infuriating about Valeon's ability to remain so... unbothered. He shirked responsibility at every turn, defying structure, duty, and expectation, and yet Gailen could not deny the peculiar comfort of having someone like him in their ranks.

An anchor of a different kind. A reminder that not everything had to be weighted with gravity.

But that did not mean he would let Valeon sleep through their departure.

"I'll get him," Gailen muttered, his tone tinged with reluctant amusement.

As he strode back toward the inn, his mind wandered briefly to Valeon's uncanny ability to defy expectations. No matter how often he evaded duty, he remained a constant, a presence that disarmed even the most irritated of companions. Gailen had never decided whether he envied or resented that effortless charm, but he did know it always fell to him to ensure they kept moving forward.

Finding Valeon was as easy as expected. Sprawled across his bed, one arm flung dramatically over his face, and he looked as though he had spent the night fending off some great catastrophe rather than simply sleeping.

Gailen rapped his knuckles against the doorframe. "Valeon. Get up. Unless you want us to leave you behind."

A low groan escaped from beneath the blankets. Valeon rolled over, squinting up at Gailen as if betrayed by the very concept of morning. His dark hair jutted out at odd angles, and his sheets clung to him in a chaotic tangle, a fitting reflection of someone who had fought valiantly against waking up and lost.

Gailen crossed his arms. "It is time to go. The rest of us are ready. You do not get to hold us up just because you have decided responsibility does not apply to you."

Valeon sat up, ruffling his hair with a lazy flourish, a smirk tugging at his lips despite the heavy sleep in his eyes. He stretched his arms overhead with a contented sigh before flopping dramatically back onto the bed as though debating whether getting up was even worth the effort.

He finally relented, stretching exaggeratedly before flashing Gailen a mischievous grin. "Fine, fine. But for the record, I ensured my beauty sleep did not go to waste."

Gailen rolled his eyes, turning back toward the door. "Just don't make me regret not leaving you behind."

Valeon looked annoyingly well-rested despite his late start when he joined them at the gates.

Gailen shot him a sidelong glance, shaking his head in disbelief. "Unfair how you always look like you've had a full night's rest."

Valeon merely grinned, stretching with exaggerated satisfaction. "It's a gift."

Thalorian raised an eyebrow but said nothing, his posture composed as ever. Kaelorn shook his head with a faint grin, the corners of his mouth twitching as if suppressing something more amused.

Gailen tightened the strap of his pack. His gaze flickered toward the path beyond the gates, stretching toward lands he had not seen in far too long. "It is time," he said, his voice quiet but confident. "Let us head home."

The group had been riding for hours, the sapphire glow of Aerindral long behind them. The steady rhythm of hoofbeats filled the air, blending with the rustling of leaves and the distant calls of unseen birds. The journey had been uneventful, but the weight of what lay ahead settled over them like a quiet haze. Though little was spoken, there was an unspoken understanding among them. Each was lost in thought, preparing for the challenges awaiting them in Vacari.

Gailen glanced over his shoulder, watching as the last traces of the city faded into the dense trees of Etharyon. A quiet sigh escaped him.

Aerindral had been a sanctuary, a place of safety and respite, yet it was not home.

The sight of it vanishing into the distance left a strange, hollow feeling in his chest. Perhaps it was relief or something closer to longing. Either way, the call of Vacari settled more firmly on his shoulders with every passing mile.

The narrow trail wound through towering trees, their branches forming a shifting canopy of light and shadow. The air was cooler and rich with the scent of damp earth and moss, and the stillness of the forest stretched around them like an unspoken omen.

At the front of the group, Thalorian rode with practiced ease, his posture straight, his gaze scanning the path ahead. His fingers instinctively brushed against his sword's hilt, a subtle but constant reminder to remain prepared. A slight furrow marked his brow, his ears attuned to the faintest shifts in the forest's sounds.

After a long stretch of silence, he finally spoke. "We will need to stay vigilant. The path to Vacari is not obvious. It is easy to miss if you are not looking for it."

A dramatic groan came from the rear of the group.

Valeon slumped in his saddle as if the mere thought of a concealed path drained him of all energy. "Hidden paths, of course," he muttered, throwing a hand in the air. "Why would it ever be easy? No one ever says, 'Oh look, a clear, well-marked road to our destination.' No, it is always hidden, difficult, or cursed."

Kaelorn smirked, glancing at him sidelong. "Would you rather go back and sleep in Aerindral while we handle it?"

Valeon shot him a mock glare. "If the universe truly wanted us to succeed, it wouldn't make everything so inconvenient."

Kaelorn rolled his eyes while Thalorian let out a barely audible sigh, choosing to focus on the trail rather than Valeon's theatrics.

Gailen smirked, already used to the routine. "You act as though this is unexpected."

Valeon straightened slightly in his saddle, feigning deep contemplation. "Unexpected? No. Unacceptable? Absolutely."

Thalorian's expression remained composed, though a faint glimmer of amusement flickered in his gaze. "Complaining will not make the path any easier to find. Keep your eyes sharp. We will need everyone to ensure we do not miss it."

Valeon sighed in defeat. "Sharp eyes, sharp mind," he muttered. Then, after a beat, he added, "Fine, but if we get lost, I reserve the right to say, 'I told you so.'"

Gailen glanced back at him, a smirk tugging at his lips. "I'll hold you to that."

The group pressed on, the sound of hooves muffled by the soft forest floor. The trees loomed taller, their shadows deepening as they ventured farther from the roads well-traveled. The path ahead remained elusive, but Gailen could not shake the quiet hum of anticipation.

They were getting closer. Closer to the hidden road that would lead them home.

The group rode in companionable silence, the steady rhythm of their horses blending with the rustling of leaves and the occasional trill of unseen birds. Sunlight filtered through the dense canopy, casting shifting patterns across the forest floor.

It was Thalorian who finally broke the quiet.

"Gailen," he began, his tone thoughtful. "What types of forests does Vacari have? I have heard the land there is... diverse."

Gailen glanced at him, a faint smile tugging at his lips. "Vacari has four main forests, each named for the unique hues that define them." He paused, his voice steady but touched with nostalgia.

"There is the Purple Fire Woods, where the trees glow faintly violet at sunset. Ivory Moonbeam, where the trees shimmer white under the moon's light. Then there's Emberwoods, known for its vibrant orange and red canopy."

His expression softened. "And, of course, Emeraldwoods. That one surrounds and protects Crystal Vale."

Thalorian listened intently, his gaze distant as he processed the descriptions. After a moment, a glint of wonder shone in his jade fire eyes. "Unique names for unique places," he mused. "I cannot wait to see them for myself."

Kaelorn chuckled softly, warmth threading through his voice. His eyes crinkled at the corners as he glanced at Gailen, a quiet admiration in his expression, whether for the man himself or the land he called home.

"Sounds like they are as remarkable as you, Gailen," he said. "Living in a land with so much... vividness must be special."

Gailen's smile widened slightly, his thoughts drifting to Emeraldwoods.

He could almost see how sunlight danced through its emerald leaves, and the scent of damp earth and wildflowers filled the air after the rain. The memory wrapped around him like a familiar embrace, grounding him in something longed for yet always present.

"They are special," he murmured. "Emeraldwoods especially. It is not just a forest; it feels alive like it watches over Crystal Vale."

A wave of nostalgia washed over him, tinged with the quiet ache of longing. He could almost hear the whisper of leaves carrying stories of old and feel the peace that settled in the heart of the towering green canopy.

Thalorian nodded again, his curiosity now tempered by something more profound, a newfound respect. "A land worth protecting."

Hoofbeats filled the quiet forest trail as the group pressed onward, the dense trees closing around them. With each passing hour, the air grew heavier with the scent of damp earth and moss, and the occasional droplet of moisture dripped from the moss-laden branches overhead. Shafts of golden sunlight pierced through the canopy, casting shifting patterns on the ground as the wind rustled through the leaves in a hushed, whispering sigh.

Despite the uneven terrain, Valeon rode slightly ahead of Gailen, his usual smirk firmly in place.

Gailen's lips curved into a knowing smile. "Come on," he urged, motioning them forward. "We're close."

The others exchanged curious glances but followed without hesitation. The distant sound of water grew clearer, blending with the gentle murmur of the wind through the trees. Then, as the last of the underbrush parted, they emerged onto a vast, open expanse.

Shimmering Beach stretched before them, its pale, sparkling sands glowing faintly under the afternoon sun. A wave of emotion surged through Gailen: relief, anticipation, and a quiet reverence for the land he had left behind.

Vacari called him home, and he answered. Untouched. Radiant.

The sight of it stirred something profound within him, a silent promise that this journey was more than a return. It was a homecoming.

The grains of sand, fine as powdered quartz, shifted softly beneath their boots with each step. In the distance, waves lapped at the shore, their rhythmic hush blending with the whisper of the ocean breeze. The air carried a briny tang, mingling with the faint scent of sun-warmed drift-wood and salt-kissed stone. Beyond, the water stretched clear and endlessly, mirroring the vibrant hues of the sky.

A grand stone bridge arched gracefully over the water, its elegant design a testament to timeless craftsmanship. It was more than a connection between two lands. It was a bridge between the past and the present.

Valeon released a low whistle, shading his eyes as he took in the sight. "Well, that is something. But more importantly..." He wandered toward a flat rock near the beach's edge and dropped onto it with exaggerated relief. "Time for a rest."

Gailen chuckled, shaking his head as he crossed his arms. "Good timing, Valeon, considering we have officially arrived."

Valeon froze mid-stretch, blinking up at him. "Wait. This is Vacari?"

Gailen's grin widened. "It is. Welcome to Vacari."

Valeon groaned, flopping back onto the rock and throwing an arm over his eyes as if suddenly burdened by the weight of the journey.

Kaelorn smirked, nudging him lightly with his boot. "If exhaustion were an art, you'd be its greatest masterpiece."

Valeon exhaled a dramatic sigh, his chest rising and falling with mock weariness. "Finally. I thought we would never make it."

Thalorian stepped forward, his gaze lingering on the bridge and the shimmering waters. Though he had never set foot here before, there was something familiar about this place.

It was as if the land whispered to him, a distant echo of a history beyond his grasp.

The gentle curve of the bridge and the endless horizon stirred a longing he could not name, a quiet certainty that this place held more than beauty. It held meaning.

A flicker of reverence, nostalgia for a place he had never known, softened his jade fire eyes.

"It's beautiful," he murmured. "The stories didn't do it justice."

A land worth protecting.

Gailen nodded, his voice quieter now but no less confident. "It always has been, especially to the people of Vacari."

Kaelorn exhaled slowly, his gaze sweeping across the shoreline. There was something in the air, a hum beneath the surface of reality, a quiet magic woven into the land itself. It was not just beauty. It was a presence, something living, something waiting.

"Vacari doesn't feel like just a land," he said at last. "It feels... alive as if it remembers. You are right, Gailen it is worth protecting."

Gailen said nothing, but as he stared across the endless stretch of water and sand, a quiet resolve settled deep within him.

Chapter 3
Unmasking the Heir

The morning sun glinted off the shimmering waters, its soft light casting playful reflections across the sand. Gailen exhaled slowly, letting the warmth seep into his skin. For a fleeting moment, the world felt untouched by duty or danger.

Yet beneath the serenity, anticipation coiled in his chest. This was Vacari, his homeland. But after so long away, would it still feel like home?

The faint scent of salt lingered in the air, mingling with the sun's warmth to create a moment of quiet beauty. The rhythmic crash of the waves blended with the golden light, wrapping them in a soothing tranquility.

The group was packed and ready to move except for Valeon, who perched on a rock near the water's edge, cupping his hands around his mouth as he called out over the waves.

"Mermaids! Come out, come out, wherever you are!" His tone was sing-song, his grin wide and unapologetic. He could almost picture their shimmering tails flicking playfully just out of sight, feeding his mischievous thrill at poking at the impossible.

Thalorian cast a glance at Kaelorn, who rolled his eyes in exasperation. Gailen rubbed his temples as if warding off an impending headache.

Kaelorn smirked faintly, caught between admiration for Valeon's unwavering confidence and the sheer absurdity of his antics. He had done his fair share of reckless things in his youth, and though he would never admit it, he found Valeon's antics more amusing than irritating.

It took a special kind of boldness to call out to creatures that may or may not exist with absolute certainty.

Did Valeon genuinely believe in the impossible, or were his antics merely a distraction to keep reality from pressing in too close? Or perhaps, in his way, Valeon refused to let the world be ordinary.

Leaning forward, hands theatrically cupped around his mouth, his eyes glinted with mischief. "Your prince charming awaits."

Just as he prepared to call out again, the water rippled. A sleek, silver-blue dolphin leaped gracefully from the waves, twisting in midair before landing with a loud splash. A burst of seawater crashed across the shore, drenching Valeon in an unexpected cascade.

He sputtered, blinking away the water as the others erupted into laughter.

Kaelorn arched a brow, torn between amusement and the temptation to shove him off the rock entirely.

Thalorian sighed, arms crossed, his gaze flickering between Valeon and Gailen. His expression was a careful mask of patience, though the slight furrow in his brow betrayed his growing exasperation. "If we let him continue, we'll still be here by nightfall."

Gailen pinched the bridge of his nose before striding toward their wayward Wildcard. "Valeon, get up."

Valeon turned, feigning a look of wounded pride. "What? I am making diplomatic overtures. Isn't that what we are here for?"

Thalorian's jade fire eyes narrowed. "If the merfolk wanted to meet you, they would have done so by now. Let us go."

Valeon shrugged lazily, turning back toward the water as a gentle breeze stirred its surface. "Patience, my friends. Charm takes time." His lopsided grin caught the sunlight, defiant as ever.

Gailen did not indulge him. He stepped closer, grabbing Valeon's arm and hauling him to his feet. "Enough. We are leaving. Crystal Vale will not wait for you to play ambassador to imaginary mermaids."

"Imaginary?" Valeon echoed, smirking. "You wound me, Gailen."

"Keep it up, and I'll wound you properly," Gailen muttered, though his tone carried more exasperation than malice. A faint smirk tugged at the corner of his mouth, betraying his reluctant fondness for their resident troublemaker.

Thalorian chuckled as he turned toward his horse. "A shame. The merfolk might have been our best chance at losing him."

Valeon shot him with a mock glare, brushing sand from his cloak as he followed. "I see how it is. You would all miss me the moment I was gone."

"Unlikely," Thalorian replied smoothly, without missing a beat.

The beach faded into the horizon behind them as the group rode onward, the scent of salt giving way to the crisp, earthy aroma of the towering Emeraldwoods. For Gailen, the sight of the verdant canopy stirred something profound within him, a vivid echo of home.

He remembered racing through these woods as a child, his laughter carried by the wind as he chased after his father's lessons on tracking and survival. The scent of pine and damp earth pulled forth memories of quiet evenings by the fire, stories told beneath star-lit skies, tales of noble dragons and the guardians of Vacari.

Each twist in the path felt like turning a page in his past, a reminder of where he had come from and how much had changed since he last rode this way.

Once, he had left these woods as a boy, brimming with dreams of adventure. Now, he returned as a man, burdened by loss, responsibility, and the understanding that the world was far less forgiving than he had once believed. He thought of the day he had left.

The somber farewell with his father, the quiet sorrow in his eyes as they parted. The weight of expectation had settled on Gailen's shoulders that day, though he had not fully understood it then. His mother had been gone long before, her absence a void that had shaped him as much as his father's lessons.

The lessons learned beneath this canopy now felt distant, overshadowed by the burdens he had carried ever since.

And yet, as he returned, the forest seemed unchanged, as if waiting for him to find his place among its whispers once more.

The soft crunch of leaves beneath their horses' hooves was the only sound in the hush of the trees, save for the occasional distant call of a bird. The air was cool and damp, rich with the scent of pine and moss, offering a welcome reprieve from the sun's warmth.

Gailen rode at the front, and his expression caught between uncertainty and quiet resolve.

He glanced at his companions—Thalorian's unwavering composure, Kaelorn's sharp awareness, and Valeon's ever-present smirk.

They had trusted him this far. But before they reached Crystal Vale, they needed to know something. He could not delay much longer.

So lost in thought, Gailen did not notice when Thalorian pulled his horse to a stop beneath an archway of intertwining vines.

Gailen's horse bumped lightly into Thalorian's, jolting him from his reverie.

Thalorian turned in his saddle, one jade fire eyebrow raised. "Distracted, are we? Or are you as impressed by this as I am?"

Gailen blinked, following his gaze. Before them lay a small, circular grove bathed in a soft, ethereal light.

The space was no more than fifty feet across, its boundaries defined by perfectly arranged trees that formed a natural wall, enclosing the clearing in quiet serenity. The grass glowed faintly, as though imbued with magic, while delicate flowers bloomed in every shade of green imaginable, their petals shifting subtly as if responding to an unseen breeze.

A faint, sweet fragrance filled the air, carrying hints of fresh rain and wild herbs. Somewhere in the distance, the gentle trickle of water blended harmoniously with the rustling leaves.

The trees formed a perfect ring, their leaves shimmering faintly as if touched by something beyond the ordinary.

Gailen's voice was quiet, almost reverent. "This is new." His gaze swept the grove, lingering on its untouched beauty. "It wasn't here when I left Vacari years ago."

Thalorian tilted his head, curiosity flickering in his eyes. "Interesting. The forest seems to have grown while you were away."

Kaelorn and Valeon rode up beside them, each taking in the grove with varying degrees of interest.

Valeon arched a brow, his lips curving into a smirk as he tilted his head slightly, deciding whether the scene before him was impressive or merely another curiosity to jest about.

Kaelorn, however, was attuned to something more profound. His fey heritage made him sensitive to such things, and he recognized the magic immediately old, yet vibrant, woven into the very essence of the grove.

It was not wild or chaotic but intentional. The forest had shaped this place with purpose. His gaze flickered toward the trees, where faint motes of light shimmered and danced before vanishing into the foliage, hinting at the presence of hidden fae.

Valeon whistled low. "Nice spot for a picnic. Should we expect mermaids here, too?"

Kaelorn cast him a wry glance, his smirk sharp. "Careful what you wish for. You already got the attention of one sea creature today."

Thalorian exhaled through his nose, shaking his head. "If a mermaid does appear, I hope she drags you straight into the lake."

Gailen shook his head, his expression sharpening as he decided. "We should rest the horses before we go any further," he said, gesturing toward the grove. "Let's take a moment here."

The group nodded, leading their horses through the archway. As the grove's peaceful ambiance settled around them, Gailen took a deep breath. The time had come.

As they stepped into the grove, the air shifted. Sunlight filtered through the canopy, casting golden rays across intricate statues scattered throughout the clearing.

Each one depicted a dragon, its form crafted entirely from leaves and flowers, the artistry so lifelike that they seemed on the verge of waking. The statues' poses felt intentional, as though they were guardians of the grove, silent sentinels watching over secrets woven into the forest's ancient magic.

Gailen wondered if these figures were remnants of a forgotten age, echoes of stories lost in time, waiting for the right soul to uncover them.

Thalorian dismounted first, his jade fire eyes widening as he examined one of the statues. "Remarkable," he murmured, reverence threading through his voice. "They look as if they could breathe at any moment."

Kaelorn ran a hand along his horse's flank, the warmth of its coat grounding him as he studied another statue nearby. The intricate details of the dragon's face were too precise, too natural, as though the stone had been coaxed into shape rather than carved.

His horse shifted uneasily, ears flicking forward, sensing the same subtle energy humming through the air. Kaelorn's voice was quieter when he spoke. "This is no ordinary craftsmanship. It feels as though the forest itself shaped these... as if it holds a consciousness of its own."

Valeon, predictably, let out a low whistle. "Impressive, I will give it that. But if one of them moves, I am out of here." His hand twitched toward his sword, half-expecting the statues to stir.

Gailen dismounted last, his movements slower, more deliberate. As his companions explored the grove, he cleared his throat, drawing their attention. "I have something to tell you before we reach Crystal Vale."

Valeon opened his mouth, a smirk already forming, but Kaelorn quickly shook his head. One glance at Gailen's serious expression, and Valeon held up his hands in surrender.

"All right, all right. Serious time."

Gailen exhaled, steadying himself. His pulse thrummed in his ears, the air around them growing still. The weight of anticipation settled over the group.

Thalorian's gaze sharpened. Kaelorn folded his arms. Even Valeon, ever the joker, tilted his head, watching intently.

For the first time in a long while, the grove was silent, as if waiting for the words he was about to speak. The weight of his past pressed against him, as did the hope that his companions would understand. This was the moment.

The bridge between the uncertain boy burdened by duty and the man who had forged his path—a path shaped by trials, choices, and the truths he could no longer avoid. He only hoped they would accept the truth as he had come to accept it himself.

"Years ago, I left Crystal Vale for a reason." His voice was steady, though the past still lingered at the edges of his words. "I needed to prove myself—not to others, but to myself. Growing up in the shadow of my father's expectations and my mother's legacy was... daunting. Every decision, every step, felt predetermined. There was little room for me to define my path. Leaving Crystal Vale was not an act of rebellion. It was a desperate need to discover who I was without the weight of a crown looming over me. I had to stand somewhere where no one knew my name. I had to learn who I was when no one expected me to be anything."

Thalorian nodded slowly, his expression thoughtful. "A noble goal. But why not go to another city here in Vacari?"

Gailen's lips curved slightly. "That might have worked... if I were not Prince Gailen. The son of the King of Crystal Vale."

Silence fell over the clearing. His words settled between them, shifting the air like an invisible tide.

Thalorian's expression remained composed, though a slight furrow formed between his brows. Kaelorn tilted his head as if reevaluating everything he knew about Gailen.

Valeon, on the other hand,... stared. His mouth was slightly open. Finally, he broke the tension.

"Wait a minute." He squinted at Gailen, pointing an accusatory finger.

"You mean to tell me... you could have gotten me that armor I wanted years ago? Instead of making me work for it?" His mock indignation was only half-masked by the playful grin tugging at his lips. "You're holding out on me, Your Highness."

Laughter shattered the lingering weight in the air, easing the moment enough to let it breathe.

Gailen shook his head. "I don't think that's how it works."

Kaelorn placed a hand on Gailen's shoulder. His voice was calm, steady. "There is no need to apologize. You had something to prove to yourself. That is something worth respecting."

Gailen's smile softened. His gaze flickered between his companions—Thalorian, Kaelorn, and Valeon. For the first time in years, he felt lighter. Freer.

"Thank you."

As Valeon's quip faded into chuckles, Kaelorn tilted his head, his expression contemplative.

"How did your parents take your decision to leave?" he asked. "Few would expect the heir of Crystal Vale to walk away."

Gailen's smile dimmed slightly, replaced by a more somber expression. "My mother passed years ago," he said quietly, his voice tinged with lingering sorrow.

He could still picture her gentle smile as she read to him beneath the trees in Emeraldwoods, her laughter like the soft chime of bells. The memory was a painful reminder of what the Druchii had stolen from him, leaving a wound that had never truly healed.

"A Druchii assassin took her life in Emeraldwoods. I was young, but I remember the loss vividly."

Silence settled over the grove. Thalorian's expression darkened, his jaw tightening as he absorbed Gailen's words.

Kaelorn nodded slowly, his gaze steady. "And your father?"

Gailen straightened, his tone more measured. "King Manard understood. He knew I needed to prove myself, even if it meant leaving Crystal Vale for a time."

Kaelorn frowned, the name sparking immediate recognition. His shoulders tensed slightly, a flicker of unease crossing his face.

"Manard," he murmured, thoughts racing back to their earlier conversation. "I mentioned him before. He was the one who once sought an alliance with Etharyon long before your time. I knew the name sounded familiar." His thoughts churned, recalling fragmented stories—whispers of alliances and betrayals tied to that name. The pieces did not fit neatly, but the unease lingered as if the past had left a shadow he could not yet grasp.

There was more to this than coincidence.

Gailen exhaled, absorbing Kaelorn's words. "That would have been long before he married my mother. But it is something I intend to ask him when I see him." A new weight settled over him as realization took hold. "If it's true, it means a stepbrother exists somewhere in Etharyon."

Kaelorn's gaze darkened slightly, his mind already working through the implications. A long-lost heir. A broken alliance.

History had a way of repeating itself, and something told him that Vacari's past was far from done shaping its future. He lifted a brow slightly but said nothing, simply nodding in acknowledgment.

The weight of Gailen's words lingered in the air for a moment before he shifted his stance.

"We've rested long enough," he said, his voice steady again. "It's time to head to Crystal Vale."

The group mounted their horses and made their way out of the grove, the towering trees of Emeraldwoods guiding their path toward the Vale. A sudden gust of wind stirred the leaves, sending a cascade of petals swirling through the air, their motion eerily deliberate.

In the distance, an unseen bird made a low, mournful call, its cry fading into the forest's hush. Gailen suppressed a shiver, the sensation of being watched lingering as they rode onward.

The soft rustling of leaves accompanied them as if the forest murmured secrets in hushed tones. Gailen cast one last glance at the clearing, where the solemn dragon statues stood, unmoving.

And yet, he could not shake the feeling that their journey had just begun. That the land was watching. Waiting.

For what was to come next.

Chapter 4
Return to Crystal Vale

High above Crystal Vale, a pair of glimmering shapes emerged against the backdrop of the towering peaks. One, a shimmering silver-blue, the other, a brilliant translucent emerald, soared through the sky, their wings cutting through the air with fluid grace. Sunlight refracted off their gleaming scales, casting a cascade of prismatic hues over the valley below like fragments of a dream. They moved in perfect tandem, majestic and otherworldly, silent sentinels watching over the city they called home.

Gailen inhaled sharply, his gaze locked onto the spectacle above. "I never thought I'd see them again," he murmured, awe and nostalgia threading his voice.

Valeon blew a low whistle, shielding his eyes from the dazzling display. "You never mentioned they put on a show. If this is their idea of a welcome, I feel honored."

Kaelorn's sharp gaze followed the dragons' path, his fae senses tingling from the raw energy radiating off them. "They are not merely showing off," he said. "Their magic is woven into the very fabric of this place. This is more than a spectacle. It is a sign of protection and power."

As the group approached Crystal Vale, Gailen's heart quickened. The familiar silhouette of the city rose before him, framed by the towering peaks of the surrounding mountains. Yet, as they neared the main gate, he reined in his horse, his eyes narrowing at the change.

The air thrummed with energy, a quiet hum of magic lingering in the space around the newly adorned entrance. Sunlight caught on the crystal formations, sending rippling bands of color dancing across the stone as though the city had been reborn.

The gate had always been grand, a steadfast symbol of the city's history, but now it gleamed with renewed life, infused with the vitality of the crystal dragons. Large emerald and crystalline structures adorned the archway, refracting sunlight into brilliant patterns that shimmered across the walls.

His companions exchanged glances, each reacting in their way to the mesmerizing sight.

Valeon gave another low whistle, shaking his head slightly, still glancing toward the sky where the dragons had disappeared beyond the peaks. "Even I have to admit, this is impressive."

Kaelorn's sharp gaze lingered. His fae senses were attuned to the ancient magic woven into the crystals and their resonance thrumming in his bones.

Thalorian inclined his head slightly, his disciplined composure giving way to a flicker of quiet admiration.

Intricate carvings of dragons, unparalleled in craftsmanship, wove through the crystalline structures, casting a kaleidoscope of light onto the ground.

Gailen felt a surge of pride and nostalgia, reminded of the strength and artistry that symbolized his homeland. Kaelorn's gaze remained on the carvings, absorbing the power imbued in every delicate detail. Thalorian traced his fingers lightly over the etched dragons, his touch careful, as though honoring the artisans who had shaped them. Even Valeon, ever irreverent, seemed momentarily subdued, his smirk giving way to contemplation.

Gailen dismounted, stepping closer. His fingers brushed the smooth surface of one of the crystals, his brow furrowing. "This wasn't here before," he murmured.

A voice broke through his thoughts. "It's something, isn't it?"

He turned to see a middle-aged woman pausing nearby, her arms laden with baskets. She smiled warmly, nodding toward the gate. "The crystal dragons did that. They restored the gate after it was destroyed a few years back."

"Destroyed?" Gailen asked, unease flickering in his chest.

The woman's expression darkened slightly. "Yes. During the attack by Phoenix Shadowwalker and his abyssal dominion. The gate was shattered, parts of the city burned, homes lost, and lives upended. It was a dark time, but the crystal dragons helped us rebuild stronger than before. They wanted to leave a reminder of their protection." Her smile returned as she gestured toward the gleaming crystals. "Aren't they beautiful?"

Gailen nodded slowly, his gaze lingering on the gate. "They are."

The woman studied him for a moment, tilting her head. "You seem familiar. Have we met before?"

Gailen's lips curved into a faint smile as he adjusted the reins of his horse. "Perhaps. It has been a while since I was last here."

Recognition lit her eyes, but she said nothing more, simply nodding before continuing.

Thalorian and the others dismounted behind him, gazes drawn to the gate. Kaelorn stepped up beside Gailen, his senses attuned to the subtle energy radiating from the crystals. The presence of the dragons still lingered, their essence woven into the very magic that pulsed through the structure.

A quiet emotion stirred within him, something deep and unspoken as if the resilience etched into the gate resonated with struggles he had never put into words. He let the feeling settle, not fully understanding it but knowing it carried weight.

Like a distant melody, a faint vibration thrummed through the air, resonating in Kaelorn's core. He paused, absorbing the moment. The hum of magic called to something ancient within him.

"Impressive work," he said softly. "It speaks of more than just restoration. It hums with purpose, woven with the will of those who rebuilt it. It is a declaration of resilience, of strength reborn."

"Of what?" Valeon asked, his tone light as he leaned against his horse. "Fancy gates mean fancy people?"

"Of resilience," Kaelorn replied evenly, his voice steady, gaze intense, as though weighing the weight of the word itself.

Gailen said nothing, his hand still resting on the crystal. A flood of memories washed over him: childhood days spent racing through these gates, the distant echo of his mother's laughter, and the heavy gaze of his father as he chose to leave.

The weight of the past pressed against him, mingling with the uncertainty of what awaited inside.

Taking a deep breath, he turned back to his companions. The gate stood as both a reminder of past struggles and a testament to the strength of those who had rebuilt.

"Let us go. It is time."

The group moved deeper into the bustling streets of Crystal Vale, the lively hum of the city enveloping them. Market stalls lined the roads, and vibrant displays of goods were drawing the attention of passersby.

Predictably, Valeon could not resist.

He plucked a ripe piece of fruit from a vendor's stand, tossing it into the air before catching it with a grin. "I'll take this one," he said, biting into it. Then, glancing at Gailen, he added with a wink, "You can pay for it, can't you? Prince of the Vale and all that?"

Gailen sighed, shaking his head as the others chuckled.

The vendor, initially startled, laughed as recognition dawned. "It's fine, Your Highness," he said warmly. "It's on the house."

Valeon tipped an imaginary hat, earning an amused shake of the head from the vendor. "You've got a way of making even a simple transaction entertaining," the man said with a chuckle. "But don't push your luck, lad."

Gailen exhaled through his nose, shaking his head with exasperation and amusement. Valeon had an uncanny ability to walk the line between trouble and charm. Somehow, he always landed on his feet.

Kaelorn gave him a nudge. "One day, Valeon, your charm will get you into trouble."

"Not today," Valeon replied, his grin undimmed.

As they continued toward the castle, Gailen's attention was drawn to a quiet grove off the main road. Sunlight filtered through the trees, casting a soft glow over a magnificent dragon statue. Its crystalline form refracted the light, sending a rainbow of colors dancing across the surrounding foliage.

A nearby citizen noticed Gailen's gaze and approached with a warm smile, her eyes bright with pride. "Beautiful, isn't it?" she said. "After the crystal dragons helped us rebuild and protected Crystal Vale during the dark days, the people wanted to honor them. That statue represents Aurelia, the ancient crystal dragon."

Gailen's chest tightened at the mention of Aurelia, a familiar ache settling deep within him. The name carried the weight of history, whispered bedtime stories, and childhood wonder now layered with the grief of time lost. His mother's voice echoed in his memory, filled with reverence whenever she spoke of the excellent crystal dragon, her words painting Aurelia as both protector and legend.

That same reverence pulsed within him now, an unspoken promise to honor the past and safeguard the future. His fingers curled slightly at his sides as a memory surfaced of his mother's soft and awed voice as she recounted the dragon's unwavering presence.

He recalled the story she had told him as a child, of Aurelia's radiant form soaring over the Vale, her mere presence as a beacon of hope and strength during the kingdom's darkest days. That tale had shaped his understanding of leadership, teaching him that true strength was not just about power. It was about offering hope when all seemed lost.

Standing before the statue now, he felt a renewed sense of purpose.

The craftsmanship was exquisite, perfectly capturing Aurelia's grace and power. Her crystalline wings were etched with ancient runes that shimmered faintly in the light, their inscriptions a silent hymn to the past. Her eyes, carved from a deep emerald, seemed almost alive, watching over the Vale with eternal vigilance, a guardian who had never left. The delicate curve of her wings seemed poised to take flight, while the glimmering light within her crystalline form symbolized the hope she had brought to the city in its darkest hours.

Thalorian stepped into the grove, his movements quiet as he approached the statue. He hesitated momentarily, his gaze tracing the dragon's form before inhaling deeply as if grounding himself in its presence. His usual composed expression softened a flicker of something unspoken passing across his features: respect, perhaps, or reverence.

Then, with careful steps, he moved closer, his posture shifting into one of silent acknowledgment. He ran a gloved hand along the sculpture's base, tracing the intricate carvings with contemplative stillness as though absorbing the reverence in the stone. Turning back to Gailen, he spoke softly.

"It seems the crystal dragons are deeply respected here."

Gailen nodded, his expression thoughtful. "They always have been."

"They've earned it," Thalorian said quietly. "I'm glad they were here to help my home when it needed them most."

For a moment, the group fell silent, the weight of the grove's significance settling over them. Then, Gailen turned back toward the road. "Let us keep moving. We are almost there."

As they made their way through the city, Kaelorn's sharp eyes caught sight of a towering tree nestled in a quiet corner of a plaza. Its branches stretched high, their leaves a vibrant mix of emerald and gold, and perched among them were birds unlike any he had seen before. Their plumage shimmered in the sunlight, shifting colors as they moved a kaleidoscope of iridescent greens, blues, and silvers.

Kaelorn slowed, his gaze locking onto the creatures, curiosity flickering across his face. "What are those?" he murmured, stepping closer, his movements careful, deliberate.

The others paused, following his gaze. Gailen studied the birds, his brow furrowing slightly. "I'm not sure," he admitted. "I don't remember seeing them before."

Thalorian joined them, his jade fire eyes scanning the creatures with quiet intrigue. "Remarkable," he mused. "Their colors almost seem alive."

Kaelorn remained transfixed, a deep sense of familiarity stirring within him. The birds' presence resonated with something ancient in his fae blood, an echo of forgotten knowledge hovering beyond his grasp. His fingers twitched slightly, an unconscious response to the pull he felt toward them as if they carried a message only he was meant to understand.

"I wonder if they're native to Vacari or something... new," he murmured. The words felt hollow compared to the instinctual certainty creeping into his bones. Recognition fluttered at the edge of his thoughts, not a memory but a sensation as a song half-remembered. These birds were more than creatures of beauty. There was something deeper, something unseen.

The air around them shifted, the moment stretching into something delicate and weighty. The soft trill of the birds wove into the rustling of golden leaves, creating a melody that hummed through the space with quiet reverence. One of the birds tilted its head, iridescent feathers shifting, before releasing a melodic call that was clear, resonant, and almost otherworldly.

Valeon, for once, was silent. Thalorian's typically composed demeanor softened as he studied the birds, his usual measured distance momentarily forgotten.

Gailen exhaled, a quiet smile forming as nostalgia flickered in his eyes. He could almost hear the distant echoes of childhood laughter, the careless joy of racing through these streets, stealing sweet pastries from the market stalls. He remembered the indulgent chuckle of a vendor who pretended not to notice those days had felt endless when his worries were small, and the world stretched vast with possibility. Now, they were echoes of another life he had long since left behind.

He drew in a steadying breath. "My father will know. We are at the palace."

With a final glance at the tree, Kaelorn fell back into step with the group. The birds remained perched, their shimmering forms a lingering mystery, as though silently observing their progress.

Ahead, the palace's towering spires pierced the sky, gleaming in the afternoon light. Their grandeur was unchanged, yet to Gailen, they felt different, weighted with expectation, with the past he had left behind and the answers that awaited within.

His gaze lingered on the highest spire, anticipation and unease tightening in his chest.

The years had changed him. He had fought battles, made difficult choices, and carved his path. Yet, stepping onto this familiar ground, he wondered if his father would see him as a leader or as the boy who once ran through these halls without a care. Would he be welcomed as the man he had become, or would the shadow of his past still define him? The thought weighed heavily, a reminder that home was not always as one left it.

He had dreamed of this moment for years, yet standing here now, the weight of expectation settled heavily upon him. Would his father recognize the changes in him? Would he measure up to the man the kingdom needed him to be?

The grand doors to the throne room swung open, revealing a long hall bathed in golden light streaming through stained-glass windows. The scent of polished wood and aged parchment lingered in the air, mingling with the faintest trace of incense. Their footsteps echoed softly against the marble floor, each step carrying the weight of the moment as they advanced toward the throne.

Gailen's breath caught for a moment, and memories of racing through this hall as a boy, the laughter of childhood now distant, echoed in his mind. The polished floor reflected the intricate murals on the walls, each depicting scenes of Crystal Vale's rich history. At the far end, atop a dais, sat King Manard, his regal presence commanding the room even in stillness.

Thalorian leaned toward Valeon as they stepped inside, his voice low but firm. "Try to be on your best behavior."

Valeon smirked. "I'm always on my best behavior."

Thalorian gave him a pointed look but said nothing more as Gailen moved forward, his boots echoing in the quiet chamber.

His father watched him intently, rising slowly from his throne as Gailen approached. Stopping a few paces away, Gailen inclined his head and began to bow, his movements precise and respectful.

But before he could complete the gesture, King Manard descended the dais swiftly, purposefully. He stopped before Gailen, his expression softening, and without a word, he enveloped his son in a firm embrace. A small tear escaped his eye as he murmured, "Welcome home, my son. I was unsure if you would ever return."

Gailen stiffened briefly, caught off guard by the rare display of emotion. For a heartbeat, he felt like a child again, lost in the warmth of his father's embrace. The scent of aged parchment and steel clung to the king's cloak, a familiar comfort from his youth.

He exhaled a breath he had not realized he was holding and slowly returned the embrace. For a fleeting moment, memories of his childhood rushed back when his father's arms had felt like the safest place in the world.

The unexpected emotion tightened his chest, reminding him how much he had longed for this connection, even if he had not admitted it to himself.

"It's good to be home, Father," he said quietly, the weight of the years apart reflected in his tone.

The room was silent, the moment heavy with unspoken truths. King Manard exhaled slowly, his grip tightening briefly on Gailen's shoulders as if reassuring himself that his son was indeed there. Gailen, in turn, swallowed hard, his fingers flexing at his sides as he absorbed the weight of his father's presence, the years apart settling between them like an invisible barrier yet to be crossed.

The weight of their separation hung thick in the air, the quiet stretching between them not as a void but as a bridge slowly being rebuilt. Thalorian and Kaelorn exchanged glances, their respect for the reunion evident in their reserved expressions. Valeon, for once, held his tongue, his usual smirk replaced by a thoughtful look.

King Manard stepped back slightly, his hands settling firmly on Gailen's shoulders. Gailen took a steadying breath, his chest rising and falling as he fought to suppress the flicker of uncertainty stirring within him. The weight of his father's gaze was grounding and daunting, a reminder of the expectations that had once defined him.

The king's gaze swept over his son, a mixture of pride and contemplation flickering in his eyes. "You've changed," he said, his voice filled with quiet pride. "There is much to discuss, but it is enough to see you standing here for now."

Gailen nodded, a faint smile touching his lips. "There's much I need to tell you as well."

King Manard's gaze shifted briefly to the companions standing respectfully behind Gailen. "And I imagine your companions are part of those stories."

"They are," Gailen said. "They have stood by me through everything."

The King nodded, his expression warm. "Then they are welcome here."

He turned to an attendant. "Prepare suites for Prince Gailen's companions. They are honored guests."

The attendant bowed deeply. "At once, Your Majesty."

Manard then turned back to Gailen, a faint smile softening his regal demeanor. "Your room is still as you left it, though you can change it as you see fit."

Gailen inclined his head. "Thank you, Father." He turned to his companions, gesturing toward the doors. "Make yourselves at home. You have earned it."

As they began to leave, Valeon stretched exaggeratedly, a grin spreading across his face. Thalorian shot him a sidelong glance, his expression unreadable, before shaking his head slightly in quiet amusement.

"Finally, a luxurious bed. I could get used to this."

Kaelorn rolled his eyes and reached out, giving Valeon a light bop on the back of the head. Valeon yelped in exaggerated offense, rubbing the spot with a dramatic flourish. "Unbelievable! First, I am denied the royal treatment, and now I suffer abuse? Truly, my suffering knows no bounds."

Kaelorn smirked. "Mind your manners, Valeon."

The others chuckled as Valeon rubbed his head, muttering something about a lack of appreciation for his humor.

Gailen shook his head with a quiet smile, watching their easy camaraderie. Moments like these reminded him how much had changed, not just within himself but also in the bonds he had forged. These were not just his companions; they were his family now.

He laughed, the sound light and genuine, watching his companions disappear through the doors.

Once they had gone, King Manard placed a hand on Gailen's shoulder. "Rest for now, my son," he said quietly. "We will speak later. There is much to discuss."

Gailen inclined his head. "Of course, Father."

But anticipation and trepidation stirred within him as his father turned back toward the throne. The conversation ahead felt heavy with unspoken questions and years of distance, and he braced himself for what was to come.

His gaze drifted across the throne room, lingering on the ornate pillars lining the chamber, each etched with the history of his ancestors. He remembered tracing those carvings as a child, imagining the great rulers who had come before him. The weight of being home settled over him, both comforting and heavy.

The familiar scent of aged stone and polished wood surrounded him, stirring memories of childhood evenings spent listening to his mother's stories in the grand hall. He recalled one in particular, the tale of Aurelia, the ancient crystal dragon who had once soared over Crystal Vale, her wings shimmering with every color of the spectrum. His mother's voice had carried such warmth as she described how Aurelia had shielded the city from darkness, a guardian woven into the heart of its history.

Standing within these halls, he could almost hear the hushed wonder in her tone, the way she had assured him that Aurelia still watched over them, even if unseen. He could almost hear the distant echo of laughter from years past, a stark contrast to the quiet solemnity that now filled the space.

This was home. But it was not the same, and neither was he.

With a steady breath, he left the room, his thoughts swirling with the days ahead.

Chapter 5
Echoes of Command

The skies above Flameford grew heavy with an unnatural gloom, heralding the arrival of a force from the void, a presence ancient and insidious, its unseen tendrils weaving through the volcanic air like whispers of forgotten nightmares. High above the jagged, molten landscape, a single black dragon sliced through the air with deliberate grace. Xalzorath, the Ancient Black, was a shadow made of flesh, his massive frame towering like a fortress of darkness, his serrated wings cutting through the air with lethal precision. The wind howled in protest as he moved, swirling ash and embers in chaotic spirals around him as if the very elements recoiled from his presence.

As he descended, the air around him seemed to grow heavier, a suffocating pressure coiling through the volcanic currents like an invisible storm. The molten rivers below flickered erratically in response to his presence as though wary of the abyssal force that had entered their domain. Even the dragons that called Flameford home instinctively tensed, their gazes tracking him with wary reverence, an acknowledgment of the power he carried within his void-like form. The jagged edges of his scales seemed forged from charcoal, shimmering faintly with an aura that devoured light and left an impression of a fathomless void. The rhythmic beat of his wings sent tremors through the volcanic air, stirring ash and embers into faint eddies that shimmered briefly before fading into the heat.

Within Flameford's grand cavern, Zylron stood motionless, his imposing crimson form bathed in the molten hues of the fiery pools. The Ancient Red's crimson eyes narrowed as he sensed the shift in the air, his claws flexing against the basalt floor. Beside him, Glaciera stirred, her posture regal and unyielding, like a sentinel carved from frost. A flicker of tension coiled within her, buried beneath the icy veneer she had perfected over the ages. Xalzorath's presence always brought a shift in balance, a reminder of old grudges and unspoken rivalries that ran deeper than time itself. Though her expression remained impassive, a quiet calculation ran through her mind—his return was no mere coincidence, and she intended to uncover the actual reason behind it. The Ancient White's presence was no less commanding, her alabaster scales laced with gray striations that spoke of age and experience. Her piercing gaze held a quiet authority, a glacial stillness that clashed with the molten fury surrounding her, like frost meeting flame in an eternal battle of opposing forces.

The air around her carried an unnatural chill, the temperature plummeting in her immediate presence. The basalt beneath her claws cracked subtly under the strain of opposing elements. Her icy gaze flicked toward the entrance, where the black dragon's approach grew imminent.

"He's here," she said, her voice a low, frosty tone that sent chills even through the volcanic heat of the cavern. Her gaze momentarily lingered on the cavern's entrance, an unreadable flicker crossing her icy features, something between wariness and anticipation. The weight of history and unspoken tension coiled around her words, as though Xalzorath's arrival was not just expected but deeply personal.

Zylron's lips curled into a faint, humorless smile. "Xalzorath never lingers on the edges. He is a dragon of presence."

Moments later, Xalzorath appeared at the cavern's threshold, his vast frame filling the space with an oppressive weight. He strode forward, each step deliberate, echoing in the ancient chamber. The black dragon's spiraling horns twisted like the gnarled roots of a dead tree, and his piercing gaze, darker than the most bottomless abyss, swept over Zylron and Glaciera with cold calculation. The air grew heavier with every step he took, the faint hum of power radiating from him like an unspoken threat. Zylron's claws flexed subtly against the basalt, his tail flicking once in unconscious response. At the same time, Glaciera's icy breath misted before her, the temperature around her dropping ever so slightly, a silent reaction to the weight of the Ancient Black's approach.

"Zylron," Xalzorath greeted, his voice deep and resonant, carrying the menace of distant thunder. "It has been... many lifetimes."

Zylron dipped his massive head slightly, his crimson eyes never leaving Xalzorath's. "Xalzorath. Flameford welcomes you. Your absence has left a shadow here that even time could not erase."

Xalzorath's lips curled into a faint smile, his teeth glinting like razors in the dim light. "And yet, Flameford still stands. I see you have kept it... warm."

"We endure," Zylron replied smoothly. "In anticipation of your return, a section of Flameford has been reserved for the black dragons. You will find it spacious and untouched, a canvas for your brood to reshape as you see fit."

Xalzorath tilted his head slightly, his abyssal eyes darkening with a calculating intensity. "A gift... or a constraint?" His voice carried a pointed edge, each word laced with doubt. "You extend this courtesy, Zylron, but tell me, does it come with chains hidden beneath the surface?"

Zylron's wings shifted slightly, embers glowing faintly from his maw. A deliberate display of controlled power, a reminder that while he extended hospitality, he remained a force to be reckoned with. "A gift, Xalzorath. You and your kind are Flameford's guests, and it is only right that you feel at home." Despite his steady tone, Zylron's mind churned with calculations. He knew the Ancient Black's arrival was both a boon and a risk—an ally who could shift the balance of power, yet one who might unravel their fragile unity.

Xalzorath's gaze lingered on Zylron for a long moment, his silence heavy with unspoken tension. Zylron met his stare without flinching, though a flicker of fire pulsed briefly in his throat, betraying a quiet wariness. He understood the weight of that silence. Xalzorath was not simply assessing him but measuring the depths of his resolve.

Then, his voice returned, quieter but edged like a blade. "We are here for more than Flameford's courtesy, Zylron. You know this." His tail flicked once, scattering loose fragments of basalt with a crack, his movements smooth and deliberate, as though he carried the weight of inevitability with every gesture. Unease rippled through the gathered dragons. Wings shifted, tails flicked. Some lowered their heads in reluctant acknowledgment of his power, while others tensed, claws scraping against the basalt floor.

"I joined this alliance for two reasons. The first is simple: revenge." Xalzorath's tone bristled with restrained fury. "Drakthor, my predecessor, was slain by the Noble Dragons. Their treachery runs deeper than the darkest caverns. That debt remains unpaid."

Zylron inclined his head slightly, his expression unreadable. "Drakthor was a formidable dragon. His death echoes through us all."

"The Noble Dragons believe themselves untouchable," Xalzorath hissed. "I will ensure they learn the error of that belief."

Finally, Zylron spoke, his voice steady yet edged with steel. "We all have our reasons, Xalzorath. Let Flameford be the forge that shapes them into a weapon strong enough to shatter our enemies."

"And the second reason?" Glaciera's icy voice cut through the heavy air, drawing Xalzorath's abyssal gaze.

The cavern fell silent momentarily, and a strange shadow flickered across Xalzorath's expression—an unsettling hesitation as if the weight of unspoken truths coiled within him. His abyssal gaze darkened, his thoughts spiraling toward a past he refused to acknowledge. A force beyond his control, beyond even his vast understanding, loomed at the fringes of his mind, pressing against him like a phantom whisper he could not silence. An uneasy shift, like the ghost of a memory clawing at the edges of his mind, a weight pressing behind his abyssal gaze. Unspoken tension lingered as if he wrestled with a truth too vast or terrible to voice. "The second reason... is one I cannot ignore. There is a presence, a command, from one who walks in shadows darker than ours. Their will cannot be denied. Already, their influence weaves through the fabric of our world, pulling strings none of us can see. Flameford bears traces of their hand, a force that shapes our path, whether we recognize it or not."

Glaciera stiffened slightly, the faintest glimmer of frost spreading instinctively across the basalt floor beneath her talons, her mind racing with the echoes of old warnings. She had heard whispers of a force moving unseen in the world, a power even the most ancient dragons dared not name. Was this the same presence she had feared for so long, the one that had haunted the edges of forgotten lore? The thought sent a chill more profound than any frost she could conjure, but she forced her expression to remain impassive. A reflexive reaction to the looming presence. Behind her icy gaze, a swirl of conflicting thoughts flickered fear, defiance, and a grudging recognition of the power at play. It went against her very nature to concede to another, yet the weight of this force was undeniable and unrelenting. Her talons dug into the basalt as though anchoring herself against the chilling weight of the revelation. "You speak of them."

Xalzorath's lips curled into a thin smile. "I see I need not explain further."

Zylron's fiery eyes burned hotter, a growl reverberating in his chest. The molten pools flickered in response, casting restless shadows across the cavern walls. Glaciera's breath came slower, the frost at her feet thickening, while Xalzorath watched, his gaze unreadable, absorbing the tension like a void. "Their power is undeniable, but their motives remain... obscured. You trust this figure to lead us to victory?"

Xalzorath chuckled, though it was a sound devoid of mirth, a quiet acknowledgment that trust had never been part of his nature, and Zylron, of all beings, knew that well. "Trust? No, Zylron. But their authority is absolute, their knowledge boundless."

Zylron's claws flexed against the basalt floor, his mind turning over the implications of following such an unknowable force. Doubt gnawed at the edges of his resolve. Was this the path to power or a descent into something far more dangerous? He had spent centuries carving his place in Flameford, ensuring its strength, but now, the weight of an unseen hand shaping their fate unsettled him. To align with such a force was an opportunity and a risk, one he was not sure he was willing to pay the price for. Glaciera's icy breath hung faintly in the air, betraying a tension she could not entirely suppress, though her expression remained composed. "They have orchestrated events far beyond what even we can comprehend. To ignore their summons would be to invite destruction. Even the blackest shadows tremble in their presence."

Glaciera's gaze narrowed, and something unreadable flickered through her icy eyes. "And still, no one knows who they truly are."

"Does it matter?" Xalzorath replied, his tone cold and unyielding. He held Glaciera's gaze for a fraction longer than necessary, his tail flicking once, deliberate and measured as if punctuating his certainty or masking something more profound. "They demand obedience, and we will give it for now."

Zylron's wings tensed slightly, his mind churning with unease. Submission had never come naturally to him, and the thought of yielding to an unseen force set his instincts on edge. He had fought for dominance his entire life and clawed his way to power with fire and fury. And yet, here he stood, weighing the cost of defiance against the certainty of annihilation. Was it indeed submission or merely survival? His claws flexed against the basalt, his inner turmoil hidden behind the heat of his glare. He had built Flameford through force, ruled it through fear, and shaped it into a fortress no one could challenge. Yet now, the game had changed. Power did not reside in fire alone but in the whispers of the unseen force that had summoned them here.

Glaciera's icy gaze flicked downward for a fleeting moment, the faintest crack in her composure betraying the storm of thoughts racing behind her calm exterior. Trust is irrelevant. Their presence gnaws at the edges of my being, relentless and insidious. It seeps into my thoughts, twisting them into shadows of doubt, a force so absolute it leaves no room for rebellion. But fear alone is not enough to control dragons. They must offer more, something we cannot refuse. Compliance is not a choice but a necessity, and I cannot fathom the depths of their power or the cost of defiance. What matters is what they promise a reckoning.

The air around Flameford grew heavier once again as if bowing to a second formidable presence. From the horizon, the silhouette of an immense dragon emerged, her wings slicing through the sky with an elegance that belied her fearsome reputation. Nocturna, the legendary Obsidian Dragon, soared over the jagged peaks, her obsidian scales gleaming like liquid night, absorbing and warping the light from the lava streams below. Her piercing silver eyes, streaked with violet, swept over the volcanic city as she descended toward the cavern entrance.

A murmur passed through the watching dragons, their postures shifting, some in wary reverence, others with subtle unease. Even the heat around the lava pools wavered, reacting to her presence as if the elements themselves recognized her power.

Zylron's wings flexed instinctively, a subtle sign of preparation, while Glaciera's frosty talons dug into the basalt floor, betraying the tension beneath her calm exterior. Even Xalzorath tilted his head slightly, his abyssal gaze darkening, the faintest flicker of something unreadable passing through his expression as he weighed the significance of her arrival. The

cavern grew silent, each dragon acknowledging Nocturna's commanding presence in their way.

Inside, Zylron stood with Glaciera, both sensing her arrival before
she even touched the ground. The Red Ancient shifted his stance
slightly, his crimson gaze fixed on the entrance. Glaciera remained still,
her frosty demeanor masking her thoughts.

Nocturna landed with a force that sent tremors through the basalt
beneath her talons. She moved with the calculated grace of a predator,
and her head held high as her gaze swept the cavern before settling on
Zylron.

"You," she said, her voice smooth yet edged with suspicion. "You are
the red dragon following the orders of this... mysterious figure?"

Zylron met her gaze without flinching, his wings slightly unfurling in a gesture of authority. As a red dragon, he was accustomed
to instilling fear in all who opposed him, his presence alone enough
to command deference. Yet here, among those he was meant to ally
with, he navigated a precarious balance, asserting dominance while
conceding to an authority beyond his understanding.

"I am. Zylron, Ancient of Flameford. Welcome, Nocturna. You and
your kin are expected. A section of Flameford has been prepared for
the Obsidian Dragons. You are free to make it your own."

Nocturna studied him for a moment, her silver eyes narrowing.
"Expected. By whose decree?"

Zylron's tail flicked, embers sparking from his maw. "The same figure who summoned you here. Their will unites us." His voice remained
steady, but a flicker of doubt lingered in his crimson eyes, hinting at a
quiet wariness of the authority he had outwardly accepted.

Nocturna let out a low, rumbling chuckle, menace wrapped in amusement. It echoed through the cavern, reverberating off the basalt walls like
distant thunder, sending faint vibrations through the stone. "This mysterious figure. I do not bow easily, Zylron. Nor do my kin. And yet, I am

here." Her gaze shifted briefly to Glaciera. "When will they reveal their intentions?"

Zylron's voice was steady as a molten rock. "Soon. The figure will call us together to explain their expectations. Until then, Flameford is yours to prepare."

Nocturna tilted her head, the light catching on the jagged edges of her scales. "Do you know who they are? Or are you as much in the dark as the rest of us?"

Before Zylron could reply, Glaciera stepped forward, her voice cold and measured. "No one knows who they truly are. Only that their power is absolute enough to command even the greatest of dark dragons."

Nocturna's eyes locked on Glaciera, the faintest glimmer of intrigue flickering through her expression. "Absolute, you say? Then we shall see if their will holds when their identity is revealed."

Glaciera's icy gaze did not waver, though a subtle shift in her stance, the faintest tensing of her wings, hinted at the quiet strength behind her resolve. To yield was against her nature, an affront to everything she had built herself upon. Yet the weight of this force pressed upon her, demanding more than mere defiance. It required calculation, patience, and the will to navigate a path she did not yet trust. "The question is not if their will holds, Nocturna. It is whether we are prepared to follow it."

A tense silence followed, broken only by the distant sound of molten rock shifting in the pools below. Its heat was thick in the air, carrying the acrid scent of scorched earth and sulfur. Nocturna finally inclined her head, her expression unreadable.

"Very well. I will find a place for my kin. When the time comes, we will be ready."

Without another word, she turned and strode toward the deeper tunnels of Flameford, her presence leaving a faint chill in her wake, a stark contrast to the searing waves of heat that radiated from the molten rivers. The temperature warred, an eerie testament to her power. Frost clashed against the oppressive heat, sending crackling tendrils of steam into the air, a ghostly mist that curled and dissipated as the elements fought for dominance.

Zylron watched her go, his gaze sharp.

"She will be a formidable ally or a dangerous enemy," Glaciera remarked, her voice low.

Zylron's eyes flicked toward her, a faint smirk curling his lips, one of knowing amusement but with an edge of calculation lurking beneath. "Then let us hope this mysterious figure's will remains... absolute."

The Tower of Shadowwalker loomed in the heart of Flameford, its dark spires stretching toward the ashen sky, a testament to the control and ambition that pulsed through the volcanic city. Its shadowed peaks seemed to watch over Flameford, embodying its raw power and precarious unity. Forged from fire and shadow, the tower pulsed with sinister energy, a silent reminder of the authority it once wielded under the Shadowwalkers, masters of deception and unseen influence. Under the mysterious figure who claimed it, that authority had shifted. No longer shrouded in deception, as the Shadowwalkers' rule had been, it was enforced through an unrelenting grip of power. Where the former rulers manipulated from the shadows, this new force commanded outright, binding the dark dragons with an authority that left no room for subtlety or dissent. The air around the tower rippled faintly, a distortion in reality as if the structure were a living entity breathing in the darkness that fueled it.

Deep inside, in a chamber dimly lit by molten streams weaving through the floor, the mysterious figure stood cloaked in layers of shadow. Their presence filled the room, an aura of command impossible to ignore. A faint hum of energy radiated outward, seeping into the stone itself, making the walls pulse subtly—like the slow, measured heartbeat of something ancient.

The air shifted as Qellaun entered, his movements careful but confident. The faint rustling of his armor accompanied his steps, blending with the flickering hiss of molten streams that cast restless shadows along the chamber walls. A brief hesitation flickered in his silver eyes as he stepped fully into the chamber, as if instinct warned him against drawing too close. The oppressive energy clinging to this place was unlike anything he had encountered before, a force that weighed on the mind as much as it did the body. He bowed slightly, his gaze respectfully lowered.

"They have arrived," Qellaun announced, his voice steady but laced with deference. "The Black and Obsidian dragons are here. They are... preparing their habitats as you instructed."

Standing unreadably still, the figure inclined its head ever so slightly. "As expected."

Nearby, Lyra worked at a long stone table, the surface strewn with ancient scrolls, inkpots, and strange tools of arcane origin. Her deliberate movements and unwavering focus hinted at more profound knowledge, as though her work was key to the unfolding events. Each precise stroke of her quill seemed to weave a fragment of the intricate plans shaping the future of Flameford. Her delicate hands moved swiftly, tracing symbols and transcribing sigils with precise care—ancient glyphs imbued with binding enchantments and forgotten prophecies, their meanings lost to most but crucial to the figure's designs. The glow from her work illuminated her face, etched with quiet focus. A single droplet of ink splattered against the parchment, and there was a slight flaw in her usually meticulous script. It was a minor mistake, yet her fingers tightened around the quill, betraying the pressure she placed upon herself.

The mysterious figure turned toward her, their voice cutting through the silence. "Continue with the scrolls. They will be needed soon."

Lyra paused only briefly, enough to nod before resuming her work, though her grip on the quill tightened for a fraction of a second. A flicker of hesitation crossed her features, an unspoken thought she quickly buried beneath her steady strokes, her quill scratching against the parchment with renewed focus. Her face held a subtle shadow of something more ambitious tempered by control. Her eyes glimmered with the dangerous allure of darkness and the promise of power within her grasp should she remain on this path.

The figure's attention shifted back to Qellaun. Their shadowy form emanated an almost imperceptible hum of power, a resonance that prickled against the skin, sending an involuntary shiver through the air. The very stones of the chamber seemed to absorb it, a faint tremor rippling beneath the surface as if their presence altered the foundation of the space itself. Qellaun fought the instinct to step back, his muscles tensing against the invisible force pressing upon him.

"Inform them I will meet with the dark dragons... later."   Qellaun bowed again, his head dipping lower this time. "As you command."

The figure turned away, gazing out a narrow window overlooking Flameford's blazing expanse. Molten rivers snaked through the land like veins of fire. A reflection of the chaos they sought to harness. Their grip tightened slightly at their side, the weight of their unseen influence pressing against the world's edges. Soon, the pieces would move, and Flameford's fate, the fate of all, would be sealed in shadow and flame. The lava rivers reflected faintly in their shadowed outline, casting an aura that seemed to shift and change with the light. For a fleeting moment, their eyes narrowed as if glimpsing something beyond the horizon, hidden within the flickering light of the molten depths. A sign? A warning? They could not yet say.

Behind them, Lyra's quill continued its steady rhythm, the only sound in the chamber as Qellaun departed.

Outside, Flameford churned and roared, the gathering darkness brimming with the promise of chaos. Whispers of rebellion stirred among the restless. Shadows crept where none should be. And the slow but sure crackling of fissures formed in the fragile alliances that held the city together. The wind carried a distant, eerie howl, though whether it was the call of a dragon or something else lurking in the abyss remained uncertain. The darkness deepened, its tendrils reaching further into Flameford, setting the stage for the unknown ahead.

Chapter 6
Council of Shadows

The heart of Flameford pulsed with restless energy, its fiery veins stirring with the anticipation of looming conflict. Rival factions vied for dominance over the dark dragon tribes, their ambitions smoldering like embers waiting to ignite. As the seat of power for the dark dragon tribes, the volcanic city stood as a bastion of molten fury and ancient dominion, its cavernous depth sheltering long-buried secrets. That tension reached its crescendo in the dark cavern beneath the city.

At the center of the obsidian dais stood a figure cloaked in shifting magical shadows, tendrils of darkness writhing like living extensions of their will. The gloom around them deepened, amplifying their presence with an otherworldly menace. The shadows coiled and stretched, drawn to their power, a testament to the authority they wielded. A spectral glow pulsed from the runes etched into their robes, each sigil binding the darkness to them. The eerie light highlighted their unnerving stillness, an unspoken display of the ancient magic anchoring their dominion.

Their presence weighed upon the chamber. Some dragons shifted uneasily, talons scraping against the stone, while others instinctively lowered their heads, a silent concession to the power radiating from the figure. Around them, the leaders of the dark dragon tribes stood assembled, their massive forms exuding strength—yet even their combined might seemed to wither beneath the figure's shadow.

Zylron and Glaciera stood closest to the dais, the tension between them and their shadowed leader palpable. Zylron's tail flicked once—a brief but telling display of agitation. His wings shifted in a restrained motion, simmering frustration barely contained beneath his deep, resonant voice. Glaciera's claws pressed faint imprints into the frost-laced stone, her stance poised, betraying a tension she refused to voice. Her gaze remained locked forward, cold and unwavering, but the faint twitch of her tail belied the unease she would not admit. The Red Ancient's crimson eyes burned with restrained defiance, while the Ancient White's icy composure masked the sting of past wounds, the bitter reminder of their last battle with Kimras and Amara.

The figure's voice sliced through the silence—resonant, razor-edged.

"Zylron. Glaciera." Cold menace dripped from each syllable. "Before we move forward, let us not forget the cost of your recent... failures."

A chill crept through the chamber, unnatural against the bubbling streams of molten rock. The contrast between fire and frost heightened the tension as if the very elements recoiled from the power that hung in the air. The gathered dragons remained silent, their gazes fixed on the two Ancients.

Zylron's claws flexed the faint scrape against stone, a whisper of defiance in the oppressive stillness. The sound reverberated, mingling with molten rock's slow, rhythmic drip, each sizzling drop adding to the charged silence. The other dragons exchanged wary glances, their unease a quiet current through the chamber. Doubt and defiance warred within Zylron, but his expression remained carefully measured. He would not show the turmoil that burned beneath his skin.

Glaciera's tail flicked, frost thickening beneath her talons.

The figure continued, voice taut with contempt. "Kimras and Amara still breathe." Their shadowed form darkened, the runes on their robes flaring. "Their leadership is the linchpin of the Noble Dragons' unity. As long as they stand, they inspire hope and fortify their defenses: Kimras, the strongest of the Metallics. Amara is the unparalleled force among the Gems. Without them, their alliances would crumble."

The figure's tone sharpened, each word edged with scorn. "Their survival preserves the unity of the Noble Dragons and emboldens their resistance. Every moment they live is a threat to our plans. And why?" A pause—weighted, deliberate. "Because of your incompetence."

Glaciera bristled. Her icy gaze narrowed, irritation flaring beneath her composed exterior. A sharp chill radiated from her form, frost creeping farther across the floor. A slow exhale escaped her, visible in the air like ghostly mist. The bitter memory of their failure gnawed at her pride. "We were outmaneuvered," she said, voice clipped. "They had the forest's magic shielding them—and Ong's dragonlance."

"Spare me your excuses," the figure snapped. Their shadow pulsed, the dais trembling beneath them. "You were humiliated. A mere mortal weapon crippled you. Worse, you allowed Keisha—an Eladrin—to tip the scales against you."

Zylron stepped forward, molten eyes locking onto the figure's shrouded form. His voice rumbled, restrained fury simmering beneath each word. "Keisha's magic was no small interference. Her bond with Kimras is unlike anything we have faced. Together, they disrupt even our strongest attacks. You sent us against them without the proper support."

The shadows deepened. The runes on the dais flared, reacting as though stirred by the figure's ire. Their voice turned to ice. "Do you think I summoned you here to question my decisions, Zylron? No. I summoned you to correct your failures. You live because I still see value in you. Do not make me question that."

Silence thickened the air. The molten streams crackled, their rhythmic bubbling an undercurrent to the rising unease. The acrid scent of sulfur clung to the chamber, the oppressive heat pressing against scales and skin alike. Tension coiled like a beast preparing to strike.

Glaciera's frosty aura deepened. The floor beneath her shimmered with a thickening layer of ice. Nearby dragons shuddered, their breath misting in the sudden chill. Some took cautious steps back, talons scraping against the ice-laced stone, while others tensed, their gazes flickering between her and the shadowed figure, uncertain of which force to fear more.

Her voice was like frost-laced steel. "We live—and we will not fail again."

The figure's gaze flicked to Glaciera. Their voice, softer now, held no less menace. "See that you do not. Your failure was not merely a blow to your pride. It was a blow to us all. The Noble Dragons see their survival as a victory. A weakness in our forces." Their shadow stretched, swallowing both Zylron and Glaciera in darkness. "That perception must be shattered."

A final command, sharp as a blade.

"Kimras and Amara must fall. The Noble Dragons cannot lead if their leaders are dead."

Zylron's tail lashed, embers scattering across the cavern floor. "It will be done. They will not escape us again."

Glaciera lifted her chin, her voice cold and resolute. "Their reign ends here."

The figure straightened, its shadowed form exuding a quiet menace, a chilling presence that seemed to leech the warmth from the air. The torches flickered uneasily, their flames guttering as if recoiling from the oppressive force radiating from the dais. Acrid smoke curled through the chamber, mingling with the faint crackle of flames sputtering in defiance.

Around them, a ripple of instinctual unease spread through the gathered dragons, the subtle shift of wings, the scrape of talons against stone, the flick of a few restrained tails. Yet beneath the stillness, an unspoken resolve lingered—a calculated determination to dismantle the Noble Dragons' unity and secure dominion over Vacari, no matter the cost. The runes on the dais pulsed faintly, their glow in rhythm with the figure's thoughts, a silent promise of the reckoning to come.

"Good." Their voice was a blade, honed and unforgiving. "Remember this moment, both of you. Let it fuel your resolve. There will be no second chances."

The chamber's tension ebbed slightly as the figure turned their attention to the others. Yet the sting of failure still hung in the air, a sharp reminder of the cost of underestimating their enemies.

The oppressive weight in the cavern thickened as the figure's gaze swept over the towering forms that stood beyond Zylron and Glaciera. Xalzorath, the Ancient Black, loomed apart, his massive frame merging seamlessly with the surrounding darkness. His abyssal eyes gleamed, unblinking, a silent storm of restrained power churning beneath his stillness. Though his composure remained intact, a flicker of tension rippled through him, betrayed by the faint twitch of his wings. The weight of the figure's commands gnawed at his pride, yet he did not speak, his gaze locked and unyielding.

Beside him, Nocturna, the legendary Obsidian Dragon, was a stark contrast. Her silver-streaked violet eyes studied the figure with quiet curiosity. A slow, deliberate coil of her tail signaled deep contemplation, while the faintest tilt of her head suggested she was weighing every word with calculated interest. Though her posture remained composed, her mind raced through the possibilities, each order a thread in a complex web of advantage and risk. Striking too soon might expose weaknesses in their forces, but waiting too long could allow Aurelia and Verdantia to fortify their defenses. Every move had consequences, and Nocturna intended to ensure theirs led to dominance, not defeat.

The two ancients' sheer presence was formidable, yet even their power paled beneath the weight of the figure standing before them.

The figure's voice, calm yet commanding, filled the cavern.

"Xalzorath. Nocturna. Your assignment is not one of destruction—yet."

Xalzorath's wings twitched slightly, but he remained silent. Nocturna's tail flicked, her focus sharpening.

"You will fly to Crystal Vale and Emerald Woods. Observe. Watch. Bring me a report of what transpires in those lands. Most importantly, I want information on Aurelia and Verdantia—the Ancient Crystal and Emerald Dragons. Their movements, their alliances, their vulnerabilities. Learn everything you can."

A ripple of tension passed through the cavern, a subtle shift that spoke of Xalzorath's dissatisfaction. The figure's shadow deepened, their tone hardening.

"You are not to destroy the forests or the cities—yet. Your purpose is to observe, nothing more." A pause, deliberate. Then, with cold calculation, "However, you may let yourselves be seen."

A hush fell over the chamber.

"A distant shadow over Crystal Vale or Emerald Woods will remind their inhabitants of what lingers beyond their borders—a harbinger of dread, a whisper of the inevitable. Let the farmers pause, their hands tightening on their tools as an unnatural darkness sweeps the land. Let the children playing at the tree line freeze mid-laughter, their instincts whispering danger. Let the bravest warriors glance skyward, a cold shiver crawling down their spines as a silent omen passes overhead."

Nocturna inclined her head slightly, her tone smooth but edged with curiosity. "And if they seek to engage us? If Aurelia or Verdantia appear?"

"Then you retreat," the figure commanded, their voice firm and unyielding. "I do not need a show of force from you, Nocturna. I need information. Do not mistake observation for permission to act."

Xalzorath's wings twitched once, his jaw tightening as if restraining the words that burned to be spoken. His mind seethed with unspoken defiance, the indignity of inaction grating against his very nature. He was a predator, a conqueror—not some passive observer sent to hover like a carrion bird over the battlefield. His deep, rumbling voice finally broke the silence.

"You send us to skulk in the skies like fledglings—to observe when we could crush."

The figure turned sharply. A sudden, suffocating power erupted from their shadowed form, consuming the cavern instantly. The air thickened, clawing at the dragons' lungs with an oppressive weight, forcing them to gasp as tremors rippled through the stone beneath their talons. Even the molten streams seemed to dim, their glow flickering as the heat surrendered to an unnatural chill.

A biting frost slithered over their scales, numbing limbs, creeping into wings, and seeping into bone. Breath turned faintly visible, starkly contrasting to the once-searing air, now void of warmth. The cold licked at their spines, an eerie perversion of the volcanic chamber's molten embrace. The weight in the air pressed down like an invisible force, undeniable and unrelenting.

Xalzorath's wings drooped slightly, his frame locking beneath the crushing presence, while Nocturna's tail froze mid-flick, her breath catching as if the very essence of the room conspired to smother her defiance. Around them, the gathered dragons shrank back, their towering forms betraying flickers of unease as the power bore down upon them all.

The figure's piercing gaze locked onto Xalzorath then flicked briefly to Nocturna. Both dragons froze, their immense strength momentarily dwarfed by the sheer weight of the force before them.

"You will obey," the figure intoned, their voice low but resonating with an otherworldly force that pressed upon their souls. "And you will remember your place. This is not a request. It is a command."

The oppressive power lingered a moment longer before finally easing, retreating like a receding tide, leaving only a cavern thick with heavy silence.

The dragons shifted uneasily, their massive forms betraying subtle signs of discomfort. A few exchanged wary glances. Others bowed slightly as if their instincts compelled them to acknowledge the figure's unassailable dominance.

Xalzorath inclined his head begrudgingly, his voice subdued but laced with reluctant fire. His jaw clenched as his nature warred against submission, but he forced himself to comply.

"As you will."

Nocturna nodded, her tone smooth yet measured. "It will be done."

The figure straightened, their shadow retracting slightly as they approached the exit. A faint shudder rippled through the gathered dragons, some inhaling sharply as if releasing a breath they had not realized they were holding. Without another word, the figure ascended toward the upper levels of the Tower of Shadowwalker, their form vanishing into the darkness.

In their wake, the air seemed to hum faintly, as if the chamber bore witness to their plans' weight. The flickering torchlight cast restless shadows upon the cavern walls as though the darkness pulsed in anticipation, eager to heed the figure's unspoken will.

Behind them, the leaders of the dark dragons exchanged glances. Unease glimmered in their eyes, a mix of skepticism and silent calculation. Some appeared burdened by the weight of their orders, doubt shadowing their expressions. Others remained still, minds racing, measuring the risks and weighing the advantages. The storm had yet to break, but its whispers had begun—a thread of wariness weaving through the ranks, unspoken yet undeniable.

Silence lingered as the figure's shadow faded, broken only by the distant crackle of molten rivers far below.

Xalzorath turned sharply toward Zylron, his abyssal eyes narrowing. The Ancient Black's wings flexed slightly, and his voice was a low growl of frustration.

"Who is this... being?" His words carried weight, thick with suspicion. The others exchanged uneasy glances, though none dared echo his bold question. "I have never bent to another's will. Not once. And yet—" His voice faltered. His claws scraped against the stone, a restless motion as though trying to grasp the weight of what had just occurred.

Nocturna's silver-streaked violet eyes glimmered faintly as she studied him. Her tail curled subtly around her talons, a flicker of tension betraying her composed exterior.

"The same power that held us in place." She paused, her voice smooth but taut. "You have felt it before, haven't you?"

Zylron's crimson gaze met Xalzorath's—unflinching yet resigned. "Yes." His tone carried the weight of certainty. "Both Glaciera and I have stood beneath that power." A pause. "It is... unlike anything we have known. It commands not through strength alone but through something deeper. Something unnatural." He exhaled sharply, his tail flicking with unease. "Even Phoenix and Vuarus, the only ones who ever commanded our kind, wielded power in ways we could understand. This... this is different."

Glaciera's voice, cool as frost, cut through the stillness. "We know as much as you do." Her shoulders stiffened slightly, tension rippling through her poised frame, resisting an unseen weight. "Their power is undeniable, but their identity remains a mystery. We have asked, but there are no answers. Only commands."

Xalzorath snorted, his wings twitching in irritation. "I do not like it. I do not like being at the whim of one whose face is hidden, whose strength comes from shadows. It is unnatural."

Nocturna's gaze flicked toward him, then back to Zylron and Glaciera. "And yet, here we are—all bound by the same force. Whatever this being is, their power cannot be ignored."

Zylron nodded, his tone heavy with reluctant agreement. "That is why we follow. Not out of loyalty. Not out of trust. But because we must." His voice darkened. "Whatever this being is... their power is absolute."

Glaciera's cold gaze swept across the gathering. "And until we know more, we move as commanded." A pause. Then, lower sharper. "For now."

A tense silence settled between them, an unspoken understanding passing in the stillness. One by one, they turned, each departing toward their place within Flameford.

Xalzorath and Nocturna lingered a moment longer. Their gazes locked, a silent exchange passing between them—one of measured thought, of quiet calculation.

Xalzorath's frustration simmered beneath his composed exterior, his mind racing through the implications of their submission. Nocturna, ever calculating, studied him with quiet scrutiny, her expression betraying nothing—yet hinting at the same unease that coiled in his chest.

For all their power, they had been reduced to mere instruments of an unknown will. A reality neither could ignore.

The thought burned.

They were conquerors, not pawns. Yet they had been forced into submission, shackled by a force neither chosen nor understood.

Xalzorath's wings twitched with restrained tension. Nocturna's tail curled slightly, unreadable yet calculating.

The Ancient Black's gaze flicked toward her, his voice low, grim. "Let us do what is required and watch closely. If answers are to be found, they will not be handed to us."

Nocturna inclined her head slightly, her voice smooth and resolute. "Agreed. For now, we fly to observe—but we remain vigilant."

With a final glance at the cavern, the two dragons spread their wings and departed, their massive forms vanishing into the tunnels leading to their domains.

Behind them, Flameford churned.

The ancient city stirred, restless beneath the weight of the gathering storm.

Chapter 7
Bonds in the Vale

The warm glow of late afternoon streamed through the towering stained-glass windows of the royal hall in Crystal Vale. Sunlight, bathed in vibrant greens and golds, filtered through the intricate glass-work, casting shifting patterns across the polished marble floor—reflections of the bittersweet emotions stirring within Gailen. Pride swelled in his chest for his homeland's resilience, yet a lingering unease settled in his bones, a reminder of the burdens awaiting him after his long absence.

The stained-glass windows depicted tales of triumph and unity, testaments to the kingdom's endurance. Beyond them, Crystal Vale gleamed with life—cobbled streets bustling with vibrant marketplaces, the Mage's Tower standing watch over the city, and lush gardens mirroring the hall's tranquil elegance. The intricate mosaics painted the chamber in shifting hues of green and gold, a reflection of the land's enduring prosperity.

At the far end of the hall, King Manard stood framed by an arched window overlooking the city. Though regal and commanding, his presence carried an unmistakable warmth. Beyond the glass, Crystal Vale stretched into the horizon—marketplaces alive with chatter, rolling emerald hills embracing the kingdom like a protective shield.

Gailen entered his footsteps, a measured echo against the marble. His posture was upright, yet a subtle hesitation in his stride hinted at the mix of reverence and unease that came with stepping into the royal hall once more. He had barely reacquainted himself with home before being summoned. The emerald-green tunic he wore caught the light, blending with the rich tones of the chamber.

"You wished to see me, Father?" Gailen's voice was polite, though curiosity edged his tone.

King Manard turned, a small smile playing on his lips. "Indeed, my son. I have news that requires your attention."

Gailen arched a brow, already sensing the faint undertone of mischief in his father's voice. "And what news would that be?"

The king stepped forward, folding his arms behind his back. "I have taken the liberty of arranging a dinner tonight. A celebration, if you will. Allies and friends of Crystal Vale have been invited to join us."

Gailen blinked, his mind racing. A formal gathering meant scrutiny, expectations, and the inevitable weight of diplomacy. He had barely settled into the rhythm of home, and now he was to be placed at the center of an event laden with unspoken implications.

"A dinner? Tonight?"

"Yes," King Manard confirmed with an unbothered air. "A welcome home feast in your honor."

Gailen tilted his head, brow furrowing. "I don't recall you mentioning this to me."

His father's penchant for surprises had not changed. Yet now, Gailen understood the true purpose of this feast. This was not just a homecoming—it was an introduction. A moment for him to meet the allies who had shaped the kingdom's fate in his absence and to take his place among them.

Manard's smile deepened, a chuckle escaping him. His eyes gleamed with fatherly amusement, a blend of pride and mischief. Gailen felt a familiar exasperation bubbling up. His father's surprises were rarely straightforward, and this one undoubtedly carried more weight than a mere feast. It was his way—lessons woven into unexpected turns, always ensuring his son remained on his toes.

"Father's privilege," the king said with a teasing smile. "You'll meet the allies who have stood with us—and see why their friendship matters."

Gailen sighed, his hands resting on his hips. The weight of duty settled over him like an old cloak—familiar yet constraining. He had spent years carving his path beyond the kingdom's borders, and now the expectations of royalty crept back in, unyielding as ever. He had not attended a formal royal dinner in years, and the thought of enduring one again made his shoulders tense. Since leaving Vacari, he had seldom faced such obligations. Yet now, they loomed once more, unavoidable.

"I see. So, I have no choice in the matter?"

"None whatsoever," the king replied with a chuckle. "Consider it a royal obligation."

Gailen shook his head, a wry smile tugging at his lips. "Very well, Father. Since I have no other option, I shall do as you wish."

Manard clapped a firm hand on his son's shoulder, the warmth in his touch softening the weight of duty in his words. "Good. Though tedious at times, you may find these meetings invaluable. Our allies have stood with us through trials, both seen and unseen. Tonight, you will begin to understand their importance."

As Gailen turned to leave, his father's voice stopped him.

"Oh, and one more thing, Gailen."

He paused in the doorway. "Yes, Father?"

"Extend an invitation to your companions," the king said. "They have stood by your side through much, and their presence at the table will honor their efforts. It is time others see the strength of those you trust."

Gailen hesitated, then nodded. "Very well. I will let them know."

The king smiled approvingly. "Good. The bonds of camaraderie and trust are as vital as those of diplomacy. Do not underestimate their worth."

A flicker of curiosity sparked in Gailen's eyes. "At least tell me who will be in attendance." He wondered whether the evening would bring unexpected allies—or those whose presence might complicate the reunion.

Manard grinned, a knowing gleam in his gaze. "Patience, my son. The answers await tonight."

Gailen studied his father, sensing the unspoken weight behind his words. This was more than a celebration. It was a turning point—a moment when he would have to prove himself among those who had guided the kingdom in his absence.

As the king turned back to the window, his expression grew contemplative, his gaze fixed on the sprawling city. Beyond the walls of Crystal Vale, challenges loomed on the horizon. Tonight's feast was only the first step in fortifying the kingdom's future.

Gailen lingered momentarily and bowed slightly before stepping into the hall beyond, readying himself for the night ahead.

The cool breeze of the courtyard was a welcome reprieve from the formality of the royal hall, yet Gailen's mind lingered on his father's cryptic words. He had endured enough formal dinners in his youth to know they were never merely about food and pleasantries. Beneath the surface, there was always something more—a negotiation, a lesson, or an expectation. Tonight, would be no exception. More likely, it was an opportunity to assess those who had aided Crystal Vale in his absence and measure their loyalties and intentions.

He found his companions in the small garden courtyard adjacent to the castle's east wing, a tranquil space draped in flowering vines and shaded by towering oaks. The soft rustle of leaves and the faint scent of jasmine wove through the air, mingling with the easy camaraderie of those who had fought by his side.

Thalorian, ever composed, sat on a stone bench, sharpening his sword with practiced ease, his jade fire eyes flicking up as Gailen approached. Kaelorn leaned against an ancient oak, his vine-like arm markings catching the dappled sunlight. Valeon sprawled on the grass, idly tossing a coin into the air, catching it with effortless flair.

"Gailen," Thalorian greeted, straightening slightly. "You look as though you have news."

Gailen stopped at the center of the clearing, hands resting on his hips. "That I do," he admitted, his tone carrying a mix of duty and mild exasperation. "My father has scheduled a dinner for tonight."

Kaelorn raised an eyebrow, pushing off the tree. "A dinner?"

"Yes." Gailen exhaled. "It is for allies and friends—those who have recently stood with Crystal Vale. My father wants me to attend to... reacquaint myself with them. And he has extended the invitation to you as well."

Thalorian nodded, setting his sword aside. "I will gladly attend. It sounds like an opportunity to understand those who have aligned themselves with the kingdom."

Kaelorn arched an eyebrow, amusement glinting in his glade fire eyes as he shifted, one hand resting on his belt. A chuckle escaped him, a gesture of effortless charm. "I have survived banquets where every word and gesture could lead to scandal or worse. This should be child's play." The corners of his mouth twitched upward in a faint smirk. "Aerindral's feasts trained me well for these things. At least here, I will not have to navigate a dozen political traps between courses."

Before Gailen could reply, Valeon sat up abruptly, blue-gray eyes gleaming with mischief. "Food? People? A chance to stir up some fun? Count me in."

His grin was disarming, but Gailen caught the briefest flicker beneath it—something keen and calculating. Valeon, for all his levity, was always watching, constantly weighing more than he let on. Perhaps he was hoping someone at the dinner would finally confirm the existence of Merfolk, or maybe he was measuring the alliances present, anticipating the undercurrents of power at play. Or maybe, just perhaps, he was ensuring he played his part with charm and subtlety. Beneath the jesting, Gailen knew one truth—Valeon, ever the wanderer, was still searching for a place where he truly belonged.

The group exchanged looks, exasperation mingling with amusement. Then, as if on cue, laughter broke the tension, filling the courtyard with a shared warmth.

"I should have expected as much from you, Valeon," Gailen said, shaking his head with a smirk. "At least I can count on you to keep things... interesting."

"Always." Valeon flashed his most disarming smile.

With their decision made, the group dispersed to prepare for the evening. Thalorian returned to his sword, though a faint smile lingered on his lips. Kaelorn strode toward the castle with a quiet, thoughtful air. Valeon lingered a moment, spinning his coin one last time before tucking it away and following, whistling a carefree tune.

Gailen watched them go, a flicker of gratitude settling within him. He had walked many paths alone and faced trials where trust had been a luxury he could not afford. Yet here, at this moment, he was not alone. These were not just allies but steadfast companions bound by shared struggles and an unspoken understanding.

He would face the evening with them by his side, whatever the evening held.

Kaelorn walked through the quiet grove near the palace gardens, his steps slowing as he reached the heart of the secluded sanctuary. The serenity of the place washed over him, easing the tension in his shoulders. Ancient trees stretched their gnarled roots like silent sentinels, their branches interwoven in a canopy of dappled gold and emerald light. He drew in a slow breath, quiet gratitude settling in his chest for this brief moment of peace amid the turmoil of recent days.

Perched among the twisting branches, a flock of birds with shimmering plumage moved in fluid grace, their feathers glowing faintly as they shifted between hues of silver and gold. As they fluttered from branch to branch, the soft rustle of their wings filled the air with an almost melodic rhythm, lending the grove an ethereal, otherworldly stillness.

Kaelorn's glade-fire eyes lingered on the creatures, a quiet longing stirring in his chest. He envied their existence—unfettered, free of expectations, without the constant need to prove their place. They did not have to explain themselves or shape themselves into what others would accept. They simply were. He wondered, not for the first time, what it would be like to live without hesitation, without the weight of always guarding parts of himself.

The birds moved with effortless grace, their luminescent glow reminiscent of his magic—both a gift and a burden. Like them, he carried something rare, not easily understood by those who did not share it. Yet where they soared unbound, he remained caught between two worlds, never truly belonging to either.

He exhaled and moved to a nearby stone bench, leaning forward slightly as he studied the ethereal creatures.

"Beautiful, aren't they?"

Kaelorn glanced up as King Manard approached, his expression warm as his gaze followed Kaelorn's to the luminous birds. Without hesitation, the king stepped closer and sat beside him, his presence unassuming yet commanding.

"They are," Kaelorn replied. "I have never seen anything like them. What are they?"

"They're Etherwings," Manard said. "Messenger birds, but unlike any others. They can carry messages across realms—even to those hidden from mortal eyes. Their magic makes them invaluable."

Kaelorn tilted his head, intrigued. "I imagine they were useful in times of war."

Manard's expression darkened slightly, shadows of memory crossing his face. His shoulders tensed, his fingers curling slightly as if grasping something unseen. "Indeed. During the first occupation of Goldmoor, when Phoenix Shadowwalker led his forces with dark magic, they became a lifeline. His armies swept through the region without mercy, but the Etherwings carried messages to allies hidden deep within the forests—even to those beyond this realm."

Kaelorn studied him. "But something changed, didn't it?"

The king sighed, his gaze softening as he watched the birds. "Yes. During the second attack, Phoenix returned—with Vuarus at his side. That war nearly plunged the entire realm into darkness. The forests were ravaged in the onslaught, and with them, we thought the etherwings were lost forever."

Kaelorn leaned forward slightly, his voice quiet with awe. "But they returned."

Manard nodded, a faint smile touching his lips. "They did. The fairies and nymphs worked for years to restore the forests after the war. And when the trees regrew, so did the Etherwings. Their return was seen as a promise—that renewal is always possible, even after great destruction."

Kaelorn leaned back, absorbing the tale. His gaze traced the graceful arc of the birds' flight, his fingers unconsciously brushing over the vine-like markings on his arms. The weight of the king's words settled deep in his chest, stirring something profound within him—a recognition of resilience, of survival against forces greater than oneself.

The Etherwings had endured devastation and returned, their presence a quiet testament to perseverance. And in their renewal, Kaelorn saw his own. He, too, had walked through fire and emerged scarred but unbroken. He had carried the weight of his heritage, both treasured and burdened by the magic in his blood. The sight of the birds—so radiant, so un-bound—was a quiet affirmation that he was not alone in this struggle.

"Thank you, Your Majesty. That's... remarkable." His voice was soft and reverent. The story resonated deeply, and a quiet understanding took root within him.

Manard's gaze shifted to Kaelorn, his expression thoughtful. "And what of you, Kaelorn? You are no ordinary companion to my son. That much is clear."

Kaelorn hesitated the weight of past judgment pressing down on him. Then he exhaled and smiled faintly. He had spent years enduring the whispers, the wary glances, the unspoken doubts about his mixed heritage. The world had not always been kind to those who straddled two realms, belonging fully to neither. Despite the king's kindness, caution still lingered in his chest.

"No, I am not," he admitted. "I am Luminara—a mix of human and fae. It is rare, I know."

Manard nodded, his sharp gaze lingering on the markings along Kaelorn's forearms. "I thought as much. Fae magic runs through your veins."

Kaelorn followed his gaze, watching the intricate vine-like patterns etched into his skin faintly shimmered in the grove's light. "Yes. It is not something I share freely, but you deserve to know."

Manard nodded in understanding, his expression kind. "You have nothing to fear in Vacari, Kaelorn. The allies of this realm will see you for who you are, not just your heritage." His voice was steady, firm. "It is a gift, and I imagine it has made your path extraordinary and difficult."

Kaelorn rose from the bench, a small smile tugging at his lips. The king's words lingered in his mind, a rare reassurance that here, in this kingdom, he might not have to hide who he was. The acceptance Manard offered was unfamiliar yet strangely comforting.

"Another time, we can speak more about my heritage," he said. "For now, I should prepare for the dinner."

The king smiled warmly. "Of course. But know this, Kaelorn—I will hear your story when you are ready to share it."

Kaelorn inclined his head respectfully, then turned toward the palace. The cool night air brushed against his skin, carrying with it the distant hum of the Etherwings as they glided through the trees. Their soft glow lingered in his periphery, a quiet echo of the magic that had touched his life.

He walked purposefully, yet his thoughts remained on the king's words, their weight settling over him like an unseen mantle.

Tonight, there will not be just another dinner.

It would be a test. A moment of reckoning.

He would face it as he always had—with quiet resilience, with unshaken resolve.

As the Etherwings vanished into the canopy, their luminescent glow fading into the twilight, Kaelorn pressed forward.

Whatever the evening held, he would meet it head-on.

Chapter 8

Arrivals and Anticipation

As Keisha and Ong approached the shimmering gates of E'vahona, the faint hum of protective magic filled the air, a constant reminder of the divine barrier shielding the city from the outside world. Forged from ancient Eladrin magic, the barrier was both a defense and a declaration, a testament to E'vahona's sacred seclusion. Within its embrace, knowledge flourished, untouched by corruption, its secrets safeguarded from those who might seek to exploit them.

The city was revered as a bastion of wisdom, yet it remained shrouded in mystery. Its luminous gates guarded arcane relics and long-forgotten truths known only to a chosen few. Among its most coveted treasures were the Celestial Orb, said to grant glimpses into other realms, and the Echoing Codex, a tome that recorded whispered truths across from the ages. Their existence inspired both awe and speculation, further cloaking E'vahona in myth.

Before the gates, Lord Karrenen stood in regal stillness, his violet robes embroidered with golden filigree that traced intricate runic patterns. The ambient glow of the crystal pathways reflected off the fine threads, giving his attire a subdued brilliance. His silver hair was braided with jeweled clasps that marked his rank, a silent testament to his authority and the gravity of the occasion.

Keisha quickened her steps slightly upon seeing him, offering a small smile and a respectful nod. "Father."

"Keisha." Lord Karrenen's baritone voice carried the weight of centuries, yet warmth softened its edges. His gaze flicked to Ong, his expression composed but cordial. "Ong."

"Lord Karrenen," Ong replied with a slight bow, his tone steeped in respect.

The Eladrin lord's sharp eyes swept over them, taking in their formal attire and the sleek form of Pumpkin, who padded silently at Keisha's heels. "I see you are prepared for the evening."

Keisha nodded, adjusting the folds of her gown. Tonight would be her first official dinner as Karrenen's daughter, a role she was still growing into. The thought sent a flutter of nerves through her, but she straightened her posture, determined to meet the evening confidently. This was more than a mere formality; it was a test, a moment to prove her place among the Eladrin to those who had long watched her from a distance.

The rich emerald fabric of her gown, adorned with subtle gold embroidery that shimmered like sunlight through leaves, reflected her careful preparation. She took a steady breath, pushing aside her uncertainty. "We are. And you?"

Lord Karrenen gave a slight nod of approval. "As ready as one can be for such occasions. Let us not keep the Crystal Vale delegation waiting."

Without another word, he raised a hand and the shimmering barrier before them parted, revealing a portal-like pathway bathed in golden light. As they stepped through, the air grew cooler, carrying the crisp scent of pine and earth.

When they emerged, they stood just outside the Emeraldwoods, where towering trees stretched skyward like emerald spires. The forest, Crystal

Vale's first line of protection, pulsed with ancient magic, a silent guardian woven into the land. The air was rich with the scent of moss and wildflowers, mingling with the crisp freshness of pine.

Keisha inhaled deeply, letting the familiar aroma settle her nerves. The scent stirred memories of childhood walks beneath the vast canopy, of whispered stories carried by the wind, of the quiet strength the forest had always provided. This land recognized her just as she recognized it.

Her connection to the forest was unlike any other. Magic bound her to it, a bond of both strength and vulnerability. When the woods thrived, she felt their joy, energy filling her with quiet harmony. But when they suffered, she suffered with them. Their pain echoed through her veins, stripping her of magic as indeed as fire devoured leaves. She had once nearly lost herself when the land had been wounded, her power fading like dying embers. Now, as she stood within the Emeraldwoods once more, she felt their contentment thrumming beneath her skin, a quiet assurance that, for now, all was as it should be.

Beside her, Ong inhaled deeply, the familiar scents sharpening his focus. The crisp pine carried echoes of quiet nights spent beneath the boughs, of battles fought in the shelter of these woods. The floral undertones evoked memories of past travels, times when peace had been fleeting, and every scent carried the weight of experience. This place had changed, yet it had not.

Keisha and Ong moved in quiet tandem, their steps in rhythm with the pulse of the land. Sunlight filtered through the dense canopy, casting shifting patterns of light and shadow on the forest floor. The hum of insects and the occasional birdsong wove a serene melody, blending with the rustling of leaves in the gentle breeze.

Keisha paused, letting her gaze drift over the verdant expanse. A faint smile touched her lips. "It's been a while since we've traveled this path."

Ong adjusted his sword belt, his sharp eyes sweeping the trees with a warrior's vigilance. A distant rustling in the underbrush caught his attention, subtle, deliberate. Nothing emerged, yet he remained alert, attuned to the presence of something unseen lingering beyond sight.

"Too long," he said, his voice low. "It is as beautiful as I remember."

Lord Karrenen stepped forward, his presence both commanding and at ease. "Come. The Crystal Vale is not far, and the evening awaits us."

As the group set off, the shimmering portal behind them collapsed into a cascade of golden embers, vanishing into the ether. The Emeraldwoods stretched before them, both a natural guardian and a spiritual threshold to Crystal Vale. Keisha felt the forest's subtle magic hum beneath her skin, reassuring her that all was as it should be. Yet, beneath the familiar harmony, a sense of anticipation lingered. She wondered what awaited them within the crystalline halls while Ong's vigilant gaze hinted at his readiness for any surprises the evening might hold.

Goldmoor gleamed beneath the morning sun, its gilded spires catching the light in dazzling arcs across the land. The scent of freshly baked bread drifted from bustling markets, mingling with the crisp morning air, while the distant clang of metalworkers shaping gold echoed through the grand avenues. Streets paved with gilded stone reflected the city's splendor, elegant banners fluttering gently in the breeze.

Queen Jeanne stood before an ornately carved mirror within the grand palace's heart, fastening the golden clasp of her flowing ivory cloak. Her refined features carried a quiet determination, and her gaze switched to her companion at her feet. Casper, the golden-furred cougar, sat watchfully beside her, his piercing amber eyes scanning the room as if sensing the importance of the occasion.

King Alex entered, adjusting the straps of his traveling gear. His broad shoulders and steady demeanor radiated authority, but his expression softened as he approached his wife. "Are you ready, Jeanne?"

She brushed a stray curl from her face and nodded. "As ready as I will ever be. It has been some time since we last visited Crystal Vale."

"And even longer since we crossed through Purplefire Woods," Alex remarked, his gaze drifting toward the horizon's golden glow. "The path should still be safe, but we'll keep our guard up."

Jeanne's lips curved slightly as she glanced down at Casper, his steady presence offering quiet reassurance. He had grown into a powerful companion, his unwavering loyalty a comfort in uncertain times. "With him by my side, I feel safe enough."

The cougar let out a soft, knowing growl, his tail flicking lazily.

Moments later, the royal couple and their escort exited the palace, passing through Goldmoor's gilded gates. Beyond the city's radiance, the vibrant hues of Purplefire Woods awaited—a breathtaking contrast where golden rooftops gave way to the forest's enchanting violet glow. The trees, named for their faintly luminescent bark, cast an otherworldly shimmer as the light of day waned. It was a realm of quiet majesty where nature and magic intertwined in serene harmony.

The journey through the woods was tranquil, the soft crunch of leaves underfoot blending with the distant calls of woodland creatures. Jeanne found comfort in Casper's presence, his graceful movements mirroring her calm yet unwavering resolve. His sharp eyes flicked between the shifting shadows, ever watchful, his senses attuned to the unseen movements within the trees. He was more than a protector; he was a companion who understood her in ways words could not convey.

As they walked, Jeanne's thoughts drifted to Keisha. She had raised Casper since he was a cub, and Jeanne hoped she would see how well he had grown under her care. More than that, she longed to reunite, to share in the bonds of friendship and trust that had not faded despite the passing of time.

Alex walked slightly ahead, his sharp gaze scanning the forest with the vigilance of a seasoned ruler. As the group emerged from Purplefire Woods, a grand stone bridge stretched before them, its arches adorned with carved vines and golden leaves. Below, a river sparkled in the afternoon light, its waters flowing toward the heart of the Emeraldwoods, where towering green canopies beckoned them onward.

Jeanne paused at the bridge's edge, taking in the breathtaking view. "It's beautiful," she murmured, a note of quiet awe in her voice.

Alex smiled, placing a hand on her shoulder. "It always is. The sooner we cross, the sooner we reach Crystal Vale."

With a final glance at the violet woods behind them, the royal couple stepped forward, Casper padding protectively at Jeanne's side.

As they entered the Emeraldwoods, the vibrant green canopy stretched high above, filtering sunlight into shifting patterns of gold and jade. The interplay of light and shadow gave the forest an ethereal charm, as though it, too, welcomed them home. Birds chirped in the distance, their songs weaving into the rustling of leaves, a tranquil melody that followed them along the path.

Excitement stirred in Jeanne's chest. After so much time away, she looked forward to reuniting with old allies to rekindle the trust that would fortify them against the growing darkness. The shadow of unrest loomed over the realm, whispers of an unknown force moving in the distance. Dark dragons stirred. Ancient powers awakened. The bonds they forged tonight would shape the battles to come.

Alex's stride was steady, his silence a quiet testament to the weight of diplomacy ahead. Jeanne knew he was already calculating the risks and promises that awaited them in Crystal Vale.

The journey continued, the Emeraldwoods unfolding before them, its lush beauty a prelude to the crystalline majesty of their destination.

Ahead, a small group gathered near the forest's edge, preparing to enter. Ong stood near the path, his hand resting lightly on the hilt of his sword, dark hair catching the dappled light filtering through the canopy. Beside him, Keisha adjusted the drape of her emerald gown, her fiery red hair a vivid contrast against the verdant surroundings. Lord Karrenen, resplendent in formal Eladrin attire, stood nearby, exuding quiet authority.

At Keisha's feet, Pumpkin lounged gracefully, her sleek black form a striking presence against the forest floor. Green eyes gleaming with serene awareness, the panther flicked her tail lazily, her muscles stretching languidly. Yet, for all her relaxed posture, her gaze remained fixed on the shifting shadows of the trees, ears twitching at the faintest rustle in the underbrush. She sensed something, perhaps nothing more than the unseen movements of the forest's inhabitants or something deeper, something lurking just beyond perception.

Keisha reached down, brushing her fingers against Pumpkin's fur in an unspoken exchange of trust. Their bond ran deeper than words, forged through years of silent understanding. The panther was more than a companion; she was an extension of Keisha's instincts, a guardian attuned to unseen things.

King Alex smiled as he took in the scene. "I see you have brought a unique companion," he remarked, his voice warm with curiosity.

Keisha turned, inclining politely, lips curling into a faint smile. "Pumpkin goes where we go. She insists."

Ong chuckled. "And trust me, Your Majesty, it's best not to argue with her."

Alex let out a good-natured laugh. "I do not doubt it. She looks as though she would win any argument."

Beside him, Queen Jeanne knelt slightly, extending her hand toward Pumpkin. The panther sniffed it cautiously before allowing the queen a brief, measured pat on her sleek head. Nearby, Casper observed the interaction with quiet curiosity, his golden eyes sharp yet unreadable.

Ong stepped forward, his expression shifting from lighthearted to severe. "King Alex, if you and the queen do not mind, I suggest we travel together through the forest. Vacari has been increasingly threatened—dark dragons and other forces have been spotted near the borders. Safety in numbers would be wise."

Alex glanced at Jeanne, who gave a slight nod, her gaze carrying both warmth and understanding. Traveling with trusted allies was a welcome comfort, especially in uncertain times.

"A prudent suggestion," Alex agreed. "We'll gladly join you."

Lord Karrenen, standing a short distance away, gave a nod of approval. "A united front is always stronger."

With that, the group formed a steady formation. Ong and Karrenen took the lead, their strides confident and sure. King Alex and Queen Jeanne walked side by side in the center, their presence calm yet commanding. Keisha moved alongside Ong, her fingers grazing Pumpkin's coat as the panther padded silently beside her. Casper remained close to Jeanne, his vigilant gaze sweeping their surroundings, a silent sentinel attuned to every movement within the trees.

The journey through the Emeraldwoods was uneventful at first. The forest was alive with the quiet symphony of rustling leaves and distant birdsong. Sunlight filtered through the towering canopy, casting shifting patterns of gold and green across their path. Yet, beneath the tranquil beauty, a shared vigilance lingered.

At one point, a distant rustling in the underbrush drew a momentary pause, hands instinctively drifting toward weapons. Pumpkin's ears perked, her emerald gaze locked on a shadowed hollow between the trees. The group stilled, breath held, waiting for anything to emerge. But after a moment, the sound faded, leaving only the soft hum of the forest. A silent agreement passed between them, and they pressed on, their awareness sharpened despite the lingering calm.

As the trees began to thin, revealing the shimmering spires of Crystal Vale in the distance, an unspoken relief settled over the group.

To Keisha, the city represented a return to her roots and the weight of expectations she had yet to meet. The halls of Crystal Vale had once been unfamiliar to her, but she had carved a place within them, claiming a role she had once questioned. Yet even now, a part of her wondered whether she had proven herself enough.

Ong remained alert, ever the protector, knowing that unseen threats could linger even within the city's walls. For King Alex and Queen Jeanne, Crystal Vale was more than a familiar city. It was a diplomatic battleground where alliances could be forged or broken. Lord Karrenen, ever composed, seemed to anticipate already the intricacies of the discussions to come, his mind navigating the labyrinth of politics before they had even stepped inside.

Each carried its own purpose and burdens, yet a single undercurrent ran through them all: this was more than just a homecoming. It was a step toward something greater.

As they approached the city gates, their crystalline surfaces gleamed under the late afternoon sun, their soft glow a beacon against the encroaching dusk. The sight evoked a profound sense of reassurance, as if the gates promised sanctuary amid the rising uncertainty in Vacari.

The guards at the entrance straightened at the sight of the approaching party, their expressions shifting between recognition and respect.

Alex turned to Ong, offering a nod of gratitude. "Thank you for your escort, Ong. It is reassuring to know Crystal Vale has such capable protectors."

Ong inclined his head slightly. "It was my honor, Your Majesty."

With a silent command, the gates opened, their crystalline arches parting to admit the travelers.

As they stepped into Crystal Vale, the city welcomed them with its ethereal splendor. The air shimmered with magic, the polished stone streets reflecting the sky's hues, the elegant spires rising like frozen light against the evening sky. The quiet hum of enchantments wove through the city, a testament to its ancient heritage and enduring grace.

For all its beauty, the city was more than a sanctuary. It was a crossroads of fate.

And tonight, within its crystalline halls, the path ahead would unfold.

The banquet hall of Crystal Vale was a masterpiece of shimmering elegance. Its crystalline walls refracted the golden glow of the chandeliers into a mesmerizing array of colors. Light scattered in delicate prisms, casting shifting hues across the gleaming marble floor, while the soft murmur of conversation wove through the grand chamber.

For a fleeting moment, the hall's beauty lifted the weight of recent troubles, filling the gathering with a sense of renewal and wonder. Yet beneath the splendor, an unspoken awareness lingered- the dark dragons still stirred, and the unknown force commanding them remained a shadow on the horizon. Peace, as ever, was fragile.

Each detail of the banquet reflected both tradition and careful diplomacy. The long dining table, adorned with polished silverware and delicate elven goblets, had been meticulously arranged to honor the assembled guests. The sparkling walls, reflecting a unified brilliance, served as a reminder that unity was not just an ideal but a necessity.

As the group entered, their footsteps echoed softly against the polished floor. The hall hummed with anticipation, and the early arrivals engaged in quiet discussion. Meanwhile, the delicate strings of a harp filled the space, its melody weaving seamlessly into the atmosphere.

At the far end of the hall stood Aeliana, a vision of ethereal grace. Her silvery-green hair cascaded over her shoulders, flowing like liquid moonlight beneath the soft glow of the chandeliers. Her gown, woven from shimmering threads that seemed to hold the essence of the stars, shifted subtly with each movement as though touched by unseen magic. Smooth violet eyes reflected warmth and wisdom, speaking to her role as guardian of the fairies and nymphs of Ardinia.

Keisha's face lit up when she saw her, her steps quickening instinctively as relief and joy washed over her. Aeliana's presence was a familiar light in uncertain times.

"Aeliana!" Keisha called warmly, her emerald gown sweeping gracefully as she moved forward. Pumpkin padded silently behind her, emerald eyes gleaming as she followed.

Aeliana turned, her expression brightening as her gaze met Keisha's. "Keisha," she greeted, her melodic voice carrying across the hall.

The two embraced briefly, their bond evident in the familiarity of the gesture.

"It's been too long," Keisha said, stepping back but resting a hand lightly on Aeliana's arms. "I didn't know you would be here."

Aeliana smiled, her expression soft and fond. "I would not miss it. The bonds between Ardinia and Crystal Vale are more vital now than ever." There was a pause, then, with quiet warmth, she added, "And any chance to see old friends is a blessing."

Keisha nodded, the tension in her shoulders easing. "Agreed. How are things in Ardinia?"

Even as she asked, a flicker of unease stirred in her chest. Whatever darkness threatened Vacari would inevitably reach Ardinia. The struggles they had endured and the fragile peace they had fought for felt like they rested on a blade's edge.

Aeliana's gaze grew thoughtful, her voice softer now. "Peaceful, for now. But the darkness gathering in Vacari concerns us all, for its reach extends beyond borders. What threatens one of us threatens us all."

She hesitated, then continued, "The fairies and nymphs have begun reinforcing their wards around the sacred groves. We can only hope it will be enough."

Keisha's smile dimmed. Her fingers brushed against the fabric of her gown as unease settled more heavily in her chest. She knew, deep down, that hope alone would not be enough.

Exhaling slowly, she steadied herself. "It is good that you are taking precautions. Vacari has been through too much already."

Aeliana inclined her head slightly as if reading the unspoken weight behind Keisha's words.

The two women continued their quiet conversation, their connection rekindling as the others in the hall settled in. Around them, voices murmured, alliances solidified, and the uncertain future loomed beneath it all, waiting, watching.

The doors to the banquet hall remained open, a silent signal that the evening's gathering had yet to begin formally. Though the hall hummed with conversation, a subtle undercurrent of speculation wove through the murmurs. Where was King Manard? Had an urgent message delayed him, or was there a matter demanding his attention before the gathering?

Keisha exchanged a glance with Ong, sensing that whatever kept the king was no trivial delay. A quiet tension settled in her chest. Was this a sign of deeper troubles or the weight of duty keeping him from the hall?

At the palace entrance, King Manard stood with his hands clasped behind his back, his gaze lingering on the pathway leading from the guest suites. The soft glow of Crystal Vale's crystalline spires bathed the courtyard in ambient light, but even the serenity of the evening could not entirely mask his curiosity.

Then, at last, footsteps echoed along the stone pathway.

Gailen approached with his companions. Thalorian walked slightly ahead, his usual composure tinged with mild exasperation. Kaelorn strode beside him, his tall frame relaxed, while Valeon trailed behind, adjusting the cuff of his tunic with an easy grin. His unhurried demeanor stood in stark contrast to the measured strides of his companions, as though he carried none of the burdens that seemed to weigh on the others.

But Valeon was never as carefree as he appeared. Beneath the teasing and laughter, doubt lingered—an ever-present whisper that he did not truly belong. He masked it well, weaving mischief into his words, playing the rogue with practiced ease. But even as he jested, his sharp eyes missed nothing—the tension in Thalorian's stance, the flickers of thought in

Kaelorn's gaze. His role, however unspoken, was clear: to remind them all that amidst duty, there could still be levity.

"Ah, there you are!" Manard called out, stepping forward. "I was wondering if you'd gotten lost in my palace."

Thalorian dipped his head apologetically. "My apologies, Your Majesty. We had... a minor delay."

Manard raised an eyebrow, the corners of his mouth twitching with amusement. "Oh? And what caused this delay?"

Thalorian's composure cracked just enough for a faint smile. "Valeon. He could not decide what to wear tonight."

Valeon grinned, utterly unrepentant. "Well, Your Majesty, one must dress to impress at such an important event."

Manard let out a deep, hearty laugh. "Does Valeon always make you late, Gailen?"

Gailen, standing just behind Thalorian, shook his head with a rueful grin. "More often than I'd care to admit."

Laughter rippled through the group, breaking the last remnants of formality.

"Well, then," Manard said, gesturing toward the hall, "let's not keep our guests waiting any longer."

Together, they made their way toward the grand doors, their voices mingling with the soft ambiance of Crystal Vale's evening air as they prepared to join the banquet.

As the grand doors swung open, a radiant cascade of gold and crystal hues spilled into the corridor. Gailen and his companions stepped into the hall, drawing glances from the guests.

Thalorian walked with quiet confidence. Kaelorn's gladefire eyes flicked across the room, taking in every detail with measured curiosity. Valeon's grin remained firmly in place, but his ever-watchful gaze noted the subtle shifts in conversation as they entered.

And King Manard followed last, his regal bearing effortlessly commanding attention.

Kaelorn's gaze settled on Aeliana, and his composure wavered for the first time that evening.

She stood near Keisha, her shimmering gown catching the light like woven starlight, her presence radiating effortless grace. Something about her felt almost otherworldly—quiet confidence, a wisdom that seemed older than time.

For a moment, Kaelorn hesitated, drawn in by something unspoken. Her aura carried the mysticism of fairies and nymphs, the unseen magic of realms beyond mortal reach. He found himself wondering what had shaped her wisdom. What secrets did she carry beneath that serene expression?

Turning slightly, Kaelorn leaned toward Gailen and murmured, "So, nymphs and fairies are just rumors, are they?"

Gailen chuckled, his voice low but amused. "Well, I never met any, so how was I supposed to know they existed here in Vacari?"

Behind them, King Manard let out a booming laugh, the sound warm and infectious.

Gailen grinned despite himself, the laughter easing the last traces of tension in his shoulders.

Valeon's smirk widened. Thalorian sighed quietly but did not bother hiding his amusement.

Manard clapped his son on the shoulder. "Oh, my son, you will soon find that some of what you believe to be mere legend is far more real than you think. You will learn, in time, that truth often hides within whispers of myth."

Gailen shot his father a sidelong glance, intrigue flickering behind his eyes. What else had he dismissed as mere stories? What other unseen wonders lay hidden within Vacari?

"I suppose tonight's just the beginning, then?"

Manard smiled knowingly. "Indeed."

As they moved deeper into the hall, their footsteps blended with the murmurs of conversation, the soft strands of music weaving through the air.

Gailen's curiosity simmered just beneath the surface. The evening had only just begun—but already, he had the distinct feeling that the world he thought he knew was about to change.

Chapter 9

A Silent Threat

With quiet confidence, Thalorian approached Lord Karrenen, his silver hair catching the soft, refracted glow of the crystalline hall. The walls shimmered like captured starlight, intricate carvings reflecting hues of blue and white, while delicate crystal chandeliers cast a warm, ambient glow that danced across the polished floors. His sharp features bore an air of refinement, his pale skin faintly illuminated with a silvery sheen that hinted at his celestial heritage. The effect accentuated his jade fire eyes, lending him an almost otherworldly presence. Dressed in elegant yet practical attire that reflected his Etharyon lineage, he halted at a respectful distance before the Eladrin lord and inclined his head.

"Lord Karrenen," Thalorian began, his voice steady yet carrying a subtle warmth—an undercurrent of self-assurance and respect. His words bore the measured cadence of one well-versed in diplomacy. "I am Thalorian of Silvaraen, hailing from the Etharyon realm. It is an honor to make your acquaintance." He paused, his gaze keen yet tempered with courtesy. "If I may ask, are you one of the reclusive Eladrin I have read about in my travels?"

Lord Karrenen straightened slightly, his silver eyes meeting Thalorian's with quiet dignity. Though his expression remained composed, a flicker of something unspoken passed through his gaze—a guarded warmth, carefully restrained. "You are correct," he said, his tone measured yet kind. "I am Eladrin, though we are not as reclusive as we once were. The past circumstances have... compelled us to take a more open role in this world."

Thalorian inclined his head in understanding, his curiosity deepening. "Then the legends of the Eladrin's grace and wisdom must still hold."

Lord Karrenen allowed the faintest smile, touching his expression with quiet pride. With a subtle gesture, he indicated Keisha, who stood nearby in a flowing emerald gown. She was poised, yet the slight tilt of her head and the way her fingers brushed the fabric of her sleeve betrayed a quiet curiosity. Her green eyes flickered with interest, assessing Thalorian with an observant yet warm gaze.

"Allow me to introduce my daughter, Keisha," Karrenen said, his tone softening as his gaze lingered on her—a fleeting but telling sign of paternal care.

Keisha turned, her vibrant red hair catching the light in shifting shades of copper and flame. Her emerald eyes appraised Thalorian with quiet intrigue, their depths thoughtful. After a moment, she spoke, her voice poised yet touched with certainty. "By your features, you appear to be a moon elf. Am I correct?"

Thalorian's lips curved into a faint smile, his posture subtly straightening. "You are perceptive, Lady Keisha. Yes, I am a moon elf."

Keisha studied him a moment longer, her gaze lingering with quiet contemplation. She had always been fascinated by the nuances of elven cultures, and meeting a moon elf in person was an opportunity she would not take lightly. The moon elves' celestial connection made them unique, their magic entwined with the rhythms of the night sky. Rarely did they venture so far from their kin, and she wondered what had drawn Thalorian to these lands.

"I have heard of the moon elves, though meeting one in person is a rarity," she mused. "Your people are known for their quiet strength and celestial bond."

"True enough," Thalorian replied, his tone modest. "The night sky has guided us for centuries, yet there is always wisdom beyond the stars."

Keisha's smile softened, and Lord Karrenen inclined his head slightly, his expression both approving and contemplative as if weighing the significance of Thalorian's presence. A flicker of curiosity stirred in his gaze, a silent calculation that hinted at deeper considerations beneath his composed exterior. "It seems this evening is filled with rare and welcome introductions."

Thalorian bowed slightly, his demeanor composed. "Indeed, my lord. It is an honor to be in such company."

Their conversation continued, and a quiet accord formed between them. Respect and intrigue wove through their words, the evening unfolding with the promise of more profound revelations. Yet beneath the polished courtesies, an unspoken tension lingered—an awareness that unseen forces were shifting. Whispers of dark dragons, long thought extinct, stirred uneasily in the hearts of those who understood their true menace. Shadowed alliances, forged in secrecy, threatened the fragile peace they sought to uphold. The echoes of fate intertwined their destinies, the specter of conflict looming just beyond the veil of the present.

The hum of conversation faded as King Manard rose from his seat at the head of the grand banquet table. The crystalline hall shimmered with soft luminescence, its surfaces refracting light into intricate patterns that danced along the walls. A faint chime resonated through the air as the delicate crystal fixtures shifted slightly, their harmony blending with the hushed murmurs of the gathered nobility. A subtle undercurrent lingered in the hall, the crisp touch of the evening breeze filtering through the towering windows, carrying the scent of distant pines and the cool hush of twilight. All eyes turned to the king, his commanding presence effortlessly drawing the attention of nobles, warriors, and guardians alike.

"My friends, my allies," Manard began, his deep voice reverberating through the hall, "it is with great joy that I welcome you all here tonight. This gathering is a celebration and a moment to honor the bonds that have carried us through these trying times."

He paused, his gaze sweeping across the assembly with quiet pride before settling on the young man at his side. "Tonight, I wish to introduce someone who is not only my son but also a warrior in his own right. Gailen has returned to us from the Etharyon realm, where he has spent years proving himself and honing his craft. A skilled swordsman, he has also mastered the bow, his precision rivaling even the finest archers."

A ripple of interest passed through the hall as the assembled guests turned their attention toward Gailen. He stood with composed restraint, though his fingers curled slightly at his sides, a fleeting, telltale sign of the weight he felt under their scrutiny. Though his posture remained sure, a flicker of uncertainty crossed his gaze before he inclined his head in acknowledgment. Murmurs of approval spread through the gathering, the curiosity in their eyes evident.

Manard placed a steady hand on Gailen's shoulder, his tone gentler now. "This evening marks the beginning of what I hope will be many opportunities for you all to know my son. Tonight, we celebrate. There will be time for deeper bonds to form in the days to come."

Further down the table, Keisha caught Ong's gaze. With a subtle nod, she prompted him to rise. Straightening, his blue eyes steady and keen, Ong turned toward the king and Gailen.

"Your Majesty," Ong began, his voice rich with both strength and ease, "I speak for all of us when I say we look forward to knowing your son. He has much to offer." A knowing glint flickered in his gaze as he added, "Including Aurelia—the ancient crystal dragon who watches over Crystal Vale, her name carrying immense weight and wonder."

A hush fell over the room. The name sent a subtle yet undeniable ripple through the gathering. Some nobles exchanged brief, knowing glances, while others leaned slightly forward, their curiosity barely concealed. Aurelia, the ancient crystal dragon. Her legend was not merely a tale whispered in passing but a cornerstone of Crystal Vale's history. The mere mention of her name carried reverence, admiration, and an unspoken gravity that few dared to question.

Gailen's brows lifted slightly, intrigue flashing in his expression. Around him, murmured discussions threaded through the hall, speculation weaving its way into quiet conversations.

King Manard chuckled, his eyes glinting with amusement. "Indeed, Gailen, it seems you have already drawn the attention of more than just those in this hall."

Gailen turned to Ong, a faint smile tugging at the corner of his lips. "Then I suppose I have even more reason to make the most of this evening."

Soft laughter rippled through the gathering, easing the moment as the banquet regained its celebratory air. Yet, beneath the mirth, Gailen could not ignore the weight now tethered to his name. He had barely set foot back in Crystal Vale, and the expectations upon him already loomed heavier than before.

Ong, meanwhile, watched the exchange with quiet satisfaction, knowing that the mention of Aurelia was but the first ripple in a tide of deeper discussions yet to come.

The festive air of the banquet shattered as hurried footsteps echoed beyond the hall, accompanied by urgent voices. Conversations faltered in mid-sentence. Goblets were set down with barely concealed tension, and a few guests instinctively reached for weapons, their hands tightening over hilts. A ripple of unease spread through the gathering, the air thick with unspoken apprehension. Noble and warriors exchanged wary glances, their murmurs fading into a heavy silence.

King Manard rose swiftly, his regal composure giving way to the sharp focus of a leader sensing imminent danger.

"What's happening?" Gailen asked, stepping to his father's side, his tone edged with concern.

"We'll find out," Manard replied, already striding toward the doors, Gailen and the others following close behind.

The night air carried an unmistakable tension as they emerged onto the palace steps. The city's crystalline towers gleamed under the moonlight, casting long, silvered shadows across the courtyard. Yet all eyes were drawn skyward.

Circling above the distant edge of the Emeraldwoods and Crystal Vale, two vast shapes loomed in the darkness, their massive forms unmistakable.

An Obsidian Dragon, its scales gleaming like polished black glass, cut through the air in calculated arcs, its movements precise and predatory. The deep whoosh of its colossal wings sent gusts of wind rushing through the treetops, rustling leaves and carrying an eerie chill over the assembled onlookers. Beside it, a Black Dragon swept its abyssal wings in slow, deliberate strokes, each beat disturbing the air like an unspoken challenge. They did not attack. They circled—watching, waiting, testing.

The Obsidian Dragon's head swiveled with eerie precision, its molten eyes gleaming with dangerous intelligence as it scanned the land below. The Black Dragon let out a low, guttural growl, a deep vibration that thrummed through the air like a warning. Their synchronized flight was not an act of random aggression but a display of dominance, a silent proclamation that they were not afraid to cross these skies. Their shadows stretched over the treetops like creeping specters, a dark omen against the moonlit expanse.

Below, whispers of unease rippled through the gathered onlookers. Warriors tightened their grips on their weapons while others exchanged wary glances. Some murmured quiet prayers, barely audible pleas for the return of the Platinum and Celestial Dragons to stand against this encroaching darkness. Children clung to their parents' robes, their wide eyes caught between fear and awe.

But the night was not absent of its defenders.

Above the treetops, two luminous forms held their ground—Aurelia, the Crystal Dragon, and Verdantia, the Emerald Dragon. Their radiant scales shimmered with an ethereal glow, their presence a stark contrast to the darkness creeping through the skies.

Gailen's breath caught as Aurelia's voice rang out, clear and commanding, reverberating through the night. There was no hesitation, no uncertainty, unshakable authority.

"Dark dragons, leave this place. The Emeraldwoods and Crystal Vale are under the protection of the Noble Dragons. Your kind is not welcome here."

Kaelorn's sharp gaze tracked the circling dragons, his hand instinctively brushing the hilt of his blade. The tension in his chest settled into something steadier—a quiet readiness. If battle came, he would not hesitate. Yet, as he studied their movements, a realization struck him.

"They're not attacking," he murmured to Gailen, his voice low. "They're testing boundaries. Watching how far they can push before we respond."

The Obsidian and Black Dragons hovered high above, their burning eyes locked onto the noble guardians below. The night seemed to hold its breath, the weight of the moment coiling tighter.

Then, with one final, defiant glare, the dark dragons turned. Their wings beat against the air, sending spirals of wind cascading below as they ascended, disappearing into the vast expanse of the night.

For now, they had chosen to withdraw.

But no one watching believed they were truly gone.

King Manard drew a steady breath, exhaling slowly. Relief flickered across his face, yet the tension remained in the subtle curl of his fingers. His measured stance balanced composure with unease, his gaze lingering on the darkened skies as if expecting the threat to return at any moment.

"That could have been far worse," he murmured.

Descending the palace steps, he approached Aurelia as she landed effortlessly, her crystalline scales reflecting the soft glow of the city's lights.

"Aurelia," he said, inclining his head in gratitude. "You have our thanks. Your protection ensures the safety of our people."

Aurelia dipped her head in acknowledgment, her tone calm yet resolute. "It is my duty, King Manard. Emeraldwoods and Crystal Vale will not fall under their shadow."

Her silver-blue eyes shifted to Gailen, her gaze piercing yet kind. "Gailen, meet me in the glen tomorrow. There is much we must discuss."

Gailen straightened, nodding with quiet determination. "I will be there."

With a final nod, Aurelia spread her wings and ascended once more. The gathered onlookers watched as she and Verdantia returned to their posts, their luminous forms vanishing into the night's expanse.

Manard placed a firm hand on Gailen's shoulder. "Come. The evening may yet hold some peace. Let us return to the hall."

With a shared sense of unease and gratitude, the group re-entered the palace, though the memory of what they had witnessed clung to them like an unshakable shadow. Questions pressed at the edges of their minds. Was this merely a warning—or the first move in something far greater? The night had not brought battle but left an unspoken promise of storms yet to come.

As the banquet hall emptied and the weight of the evening's events settled over the guests, Gailen turned to his father, his expression thoughtful.

"With the dark dragons so close, do you think it's safe for everyone to return home tonight?"

King Manard regarded him for a long moment before nodding. "A valid concern. I will extend the offer for our guests to remain within the protection of Crystal Vale."

Turning to the gathered attendees, he raised his voice. "Friends, tonight has been eventful in ways none of us anticipated. You are all welcome to stay safe in the palace. Rooms will be prepared should you choose to remain."

Aeliana stepped forward, her serene presence drawing the attention of those around her. To those who had witnessed her magic before, she was a humbling sight. Her connection to the currents of magic was as effortless as breathing as if she existed between the physical and ethereal realms. Some regarded her with quiet reverence, while others, unfamiliar with her abilities, watched with fascination.

"Your generosity is appreciated, King Manard," she said, her voice melodic. "But I will travel on the currents of magic. They will carry me safely to where I must be."

With a gentle smile, she lifted her arms, and in a swirl of shimmering light, she vanished, leaving behind a faint hum of energy.

Keisha turned to Ong, her expression questioning. Ong met her gaze before glancing at Lord Karrenen, who regarded them with calm authority.

"I will return home," Karrenen said, his tone resolute. "You both stay here. Speak with the others in the morning. There is much to discuss."

Keisha's heart clenched at her father's decision, duty, and concern warring within her. She understood the weight of leadership and the sacrifices required, yet the thought of him facing danger alone gnawed at her resolve. Beside her, Ong exhaled quietly, his brow furrowing in silent worry. He said nothing, but the slight tightening of his fists betrayed his unease—a reflection of the same apprehension Keisha felt settling deep in her chest. Though his composure never wavered, she recognized the weight he carried—the quiet resolve of one accustomed to shouldering burdens alone. Memories of past moments flickered in her mind, reminders of his resilience and the dangers he often faced without sharing the weight of them.

Her gaze lingered on him as he turned away, and her resolve hardened within her. She would honor his trust and see their mission through.

With that, Lord Karrenen strode toward the exit and, like Aeliana, disappeared into the night. Keisha and Ong exchanged a knowing glance.

Nearby, King Alex and Queen Jeanne conferred quietly. Alex placed a hand on his wife's shoulder, his voice low but firm. "It's safer to remain here tonight."

Jeanne nodded in agreement, her hand briefly brushing Casper's head as the great cougar stood watchfully by her side. "Then we'll stay."

Manard motioned for an attendant. "Prepare a suite for the King and Queen of Goldmoor."

As they were escorted away, Ong approached King Manard and Gailen. "We'll discuss all of this in the morning," he said, his tone steady but determined.

Manard nodded, his expression grave.

As the guests dispersed toward their rooms, Valeon trailed behind, crossing his arms with a dramatic pout. His blue gray eyes narrowed in exaggerated offense.

"Honestly, how am I supposed to enjoy myself with such interruptions?" he grumbled, his voice laced with theatrical indignation. "How dare those dark dragons ruin my night!"

The outburst drew amused smiles. First from Kaelorn, then from Gailen, and finally from the others. The ripple of laughter broke the solemn mood, a brief reprieve from the weight of the evening.

Their footsteps echoed softly through the halls as they retired, but the questions lingered.

Was this merely a show of power? Or is it a precursor to something far worse?

Sleep would not come quickly, not with the weight of uncertainty pressing upon them.

Chapter 10
The Obsidian Shift

As the first light of dawn crept over Crystal Vale, its crystalline towers shimmered in pale gold and silver hues. King Alex and Queen Jeanne stood near the palace gates, the quiet weight of morning settled around them. Casper, the Queen's loyal cougar, prowled at her side, his keen eyes flickering between shifting shadows, attuned to every subtle movement. Each sound tensed his muscles—a silent guardian ever watchful. Even as Jeanne rested a steadying hand on his back, his instincts remained razor-sharp, sensing the lingering unease from the night before. The city's crystalline structures glistened like freshly fallen snow, their fleeting reflections dancing across the quiet streets. An uneasy stillness clung to the air as though even the winds hesitated, unwilling to disturb the fragile peace.

King Manard approached, his expression calm but resolute. "You've decided to return to Goldmoor this morning?"

Alex nodded, his voice firm. "We leave at once. It is best to reach home swiftly, given the unrest in Vacari."

Manard's gaze flicked to Casper, the fabulous feline's graceful yet powerful form at odds with the usual means of royal travel. "Under normal circumstances, I would suggest one of the younger Crystal or Emerald Dragons for a swift journey, but that may not be an option."

Jeanne offered a small smile, her fingers tracing slow circles through Casper's fur, a quiet motion that steadied them both. "I would never leave him behind. And I doubt he would take kindly to dragonback travel."

Manard chuckled softly before his expression turned serious. "Then I insist on providing a royal escort. My guards will ensure your safe passage through the Emeraldwoods and Purplefire. We cannot take risks after last night's events."

Alex hesitated before inclining his head. "Your generosity is appreciated, Manard. The path will be safer with your guards accompanying us."

Jeanne turned to Casper with a fond smile. "Looks like we'll have company, my friend."

Within moments, a small contingent of guards, clad in armor bearing the crystalline insignia of Crystal Vale, assembled at the gates. Their leader, a tall man with a vigilant demeanor, saluted sharply. "Your Majesties, we are ready to escort you."

Manard clasped Alex's hand firmly. "Safe travels, my friend. Send word when you arrive in Goldmoor."

"We will," Alex replied. "And thank you again."

The royal couple began their journey with the guards forming a protective perimeter. Emerald Dragons watched over the sacred woodland as the group moved steadily through the lush Emeraldwoods. Morning light filtered through the trees like rippling emeralds, the earthy scent of moss mingling with the sweet aroma of blooming wildflowers. Crossing the bridge into Purplefire Woods, they entered an enchanting twilight, where violet trees cast an ethereal glow upon the path. The presence of the Amethyst Dragons infused the air with a quiet magic, their unseen vigilance a source of reassurance. Though the guards remained alert, they carried themselves with measured confidence, trusting in the ancient protectors of the woods.

Jeanne exhaled softly, the glow of the trees easing the lingering unease from the previous night. Yet, a watchful presence seemed woven into the air, an awareness that stirred beneath the surface. The guards exchanged wary glances, fingers instinctively tightening around their weapons despite the tranquil beauty surrounding them.

Jeanne drew closer to Alex, her voice hushed. "These woods feel alive," she murmured, her gaze flicking toward the faint, pulsing glow within the bark.

Alex nodded, his brow furrowed, sensing the same uncanny awareness. Even Casper's usual calm gave way to a low growl, his ears twitching as he scanned the path ahead, every muscle taut with vigilance. A faint, sweet aroma clung to the air, tinged with the sharp, wild scent of magic, setting the guards further on edge. The violet glow bathed the surroundings in a dreamy twilight, lending the woods an otherworldly serenity that whispered secrets beyond mortal understanding.

At one point, the escort leader raised a hand, signaling the group to pause. A faint rustle echoed through the canopy, blending seamlessly with the natural harmony of the woods. Weapons were drawn, sharp eyes peering into the dense foliage. Yet, after a tense moment, the unease faded, swallowed by the tranquil melody of the forest.

As they neared Goldmoor, the city's golden spires came into view, their radiant glow a welcome sight. The towers, kissed by the sun, cast long beams of light over the cobblestone streets, which gleamed like polished gold. Banners, gilded in rich embroidery, fluttered like whispers of prosperity in the breeze. The warm scent of sun-baked stone mingled with the tang of metal from the bustling forges, starkly contrasting with the ethereal fragrance of Purplefire Woods. The distant hum of market chatter replaced the hushed whispers of enchanted trees, grounding them once more in the familiar reality of home.

By mid-afternoon, they passed through Goldmoor's grand gates. The contrast between the mystical twilight of Purplefire Woods and the city's golden brilliance was striking. As they stepped into the familiar warmth of their palace, a collective breath of relief passed through the travelers. Yet, the tension of their journey lingered, a quiet reminder that the shadows they left behind were not truly gone—only waiting.

Alex and Jeanne turned to thank their escort, gratitude clear in their expressions. Casper prowled ahead, ears flicking toward the slightest sound, his sharp gaze darting between shadows—a silent sentinel attuned to the unspoken tensions surrounding his queen.

"Manard's kindness is a reminder of why our alliances matter," Jeanne murmured, brushing Alex's arm.

"Indeed," Alex agreed, his gaze lingering on the distant horizon. "These are uncertain times, but with allies like him, we stand stronger."

The royal couple entered the golden halls of their palace, their journey complete—yet the weight of the night's events remained, a whisper of unfinished trials yet to come.

After ensuring Queen Jeanne and Casper were safely settled, King Alex made his way to the outskirts of Goldmoor, where the golden spires of the enclave stood like sentinels against the horizon. This sacred space, reserved for the Gold Dragons, radiated warmth and serenity, an unspoken promise of guidance and strength in the days ahead.

As Alex approached, the familiar silhouette of Kimras emerged from the golden mist, his massive form stepping forward like a legend woven back into reality. His immense frame shimmered, scales catching and refracting the morning light like liquid gold. Each step carried a regal weight, his wings tucked neatly against his sides, exuding an unspoken promise of power. Resting near the enclave's edge, the mighty Gold Dragon fixed his intelligent gold gaze on the approaching king.

"Alex," Kimras greeted, his deep, resonant voice carrying warmth and concern. "You come with purpose."

"I do," Alex replied, stepping closer. "Something happened last night in Crystal Vale."

Kimras inclined his great head, his expression sharpening. "Tell me."

Alex recounted the night's events—the dinner, the sudden commotion, and the confrontation between the Noble Dragons and the dark dragons circling Emeraldwoods and Crystal Vale. "Aurelia warned them to leave, and they did. But I must tell you, Kimras, they were no ordinary dark dragons. One was a Black Dragon, and the other... Aurelia said it was Obsidian."

A low growl rumbled in Kimras's throat, his amber eyes narrowing. "The Black Dragons do not surprise me. With Drakthor's death, I expected them to join the conflict. Vengeance is their nature. But the Obsidian Dragon... While they are gem dragons, their temperament often aligns with the dark ones. That part does not surprise me."

Alex nodded slowly. "Yet their involvement still raises questions."

Kimras shifted, his massive wings folding tighter against his body. "Indeed. The Obsidian Dragons have long remained on the fringes, content in their isolation. For them to openly align with the dark dragons suggests a greater force compelling them. The mysterious figure we have discussed before must be behind this. If they can command both Black and Obsidian Dragons, their influence is more dangerous than we feared."

A heavy silence settled between them. Alex frowned, the weight of Kimras's words pressing into him. "What kind of power could unite such disparate creatures?"

Kimras's gaze turned distant, his thoughts shadowed by the echoes of ancient wars, the ruins left smoldering in the wake of devastation, and the cries of those who had once believed themselves safe. He had seen darkness consume Vacari before, alliances forged in desperation, and kingdoms left in ruin. He had carried the weight of leadership through it all. As history threatened to repeat itself, he wondered if their choices today would be enough to prevent another age of destruction. "The threads are fraying," he thought grimly. "If we cannot hold them together, Vacari may never recover."

"Power that transcends brute strength," Kimras said at last. "Fear, persuasion, or control of such magnitude that even those who would resist feel compelled to obey. Whoever this figure is, they have moved beyond mere schemes. They are building a force capable of shaking Vacari to its core."

Alex's mind raced. Were the dark dragons acting under coercion, or had they truly allied with a greater force? If so, how many more would follow? "Could it be fear, or have they been promised something—greater power, perhaps, or dominion over lands they've long desired?"

Kimras's gold gaze sharpened. "Whatever their motivation, it stems from desperation or ambition. Both are dangerous when paired with such formidable allies."

The two fell into contemplative silence, weighed down by the enormity of the threat. Alex's thoughts churned with strategy—how to protect his people and forge alliances strong enough to counter this growing force. Kimras, meanwhile, pondered the ghosts of past conflicts, each memory a warning of how fragile peace could be. Together, they stood at the precipice of something vast, unspoken tension thickening in the quiet space between them.

After a moment, Kimras straightened, his voice decisive. "Amara and I will increase our patrols over Goldmoor and Purplefire Woods. If the dark dragons return, they will not go unnoticed."

Alex inclined his head, gratitude evident. "Your vigilance is invaluable, Kimras. Goldmoor is safer with you and Amara watching over us."

With a final nod, the king turned back toward the palace, his thoughts a storm of unease and determination. The weight of looming conflict pressed upon him, but his resolve burned like tempered steel beneath it. He would not allow Vacari to fall into darkness—not while he still had the strength to fight.

In the distance, dark clouds gathered over Flameford, their shadows creeping toward Goldmoor—a silent omen of the battles to come. The storm was rising, and with it, the fate of Vacari hung in the balance.

Chapter 11
A Call to Protect

The soft knock at the door broke the morning stillness in Ong and Keisha's suite. A delicate crystal chime echoed faintly from the hall, signaling the arrival of a royal attendant. Ong glanced toward Keisha, who sat near the window, her vibrant red hair gleaming in the sunlight as she brushed through its silky strands.

"Come in," Ong called, rising from where he sat, sharpening his blade.

The door opened, revealing a young attendant in the elegant livery of Crystal Vale. His posture was poised, though the urgency in his expression betrayed the calm facade.

"My lord, my lady," he began with a slight bow. "King Manard requests your presence in the throne room to discuss the events of last night."

Keisha set her brush aside, her green eyes meeting Ong's. A flicker of concern passed through her gaze, but Ong's steady resolve grounded her, offering unspoken reassurance amid the turmoil of recent events. Their silent understanding was a quiet anchor in uncertain times, a reminder that whatever awaited them, they would face it together.

"It seems our morning has already been decided," she remarked lightly, her tone edged with humor.

Ong nodded, turning to the attendant. "Tell His Majesty we will make our way there shortly."

The attendant inclined his head. "At once, my lord." With that, he stepped back and exited, leaving them to prepare.

Keisha rose gracefully, smoothing the flowing sleeves of her gown. "Given what happened, this isn't unexpected."

"No," Ong agreed, fastening his sword belt with practiced ease. "We should hear the king's thoughts—and offer our own."

Pumpkin stretched with lazy elegance by the hearth, her sleek black fur gleaming in the light. She flexed her claws against the stone floor, the faint scratching sound a quiet reminder of her presence. A low, rumbling purr escaped her as if sensing the shift in their plans. Keisha smiled, scratching behind the cat's ears before glancing back at Ong. "Shall we?"

"Let's not keep the king waiting," Ong replied, gesturing for her to lead the way.

With Pumpkin padding silently behind them, they exited their suite and made their way toward the palace, the weight of unspoken questions hanging between them.

The journey was brief, and they were swiftly escorted into the grand hall. The crystalline walls shimmered faintly in the morning light, alive with a quiet energy hinting at the coming discussion's gravity. A faint hum resonated through the chamber, carrying echoes of past deliberations that mingled with the crisp scent of polished stone and parchment. King Manard stood near the throne, speaking with an attendant, his expression thoughtful.

"Ah, Ong, Keisha," Manard greeted warmly, turning toward them. "Thank you for coming so promptly."

Ong's sharp eyes scanned the hall for familiar faces. Noting the absence of Prince Gailen and his companions, he stepped forward. "Your Majesty, with respect, this discussion may benefit from Prince Gailen's presence, along with his companions."

King Manard's lips curved into a knowing smile as if he had anticipated the suggestion. His gaze held a glint of amusement and wisdom, reflecting his understanding of those gathered before him. "You are not wrong. Thalorian and Kaelorn will join us immediately; they are disciplined men. As for Valeon, well..." He chuckled. "He enjoys his mornings a little too much."

Ong allowed himself a wry smile. "Then perhaps just the prince and his companions—if Valeon cannot be roused."

Manard's laughter filled the hall, and a rich, genuine sound rippled through the chamber. A few attendants exchanged amused glances while one guard allowed a faint smirk to break his otherwise stoic expression. "We'll see what the attendant can manage."

Still waiting nearby, the attendant bowed deeply before hurrying to deliver the summons. Meanwhile, Ong and Keisha exchanged knowing glances, silently bracing themselves for what promised to be an eventful conversation.

The soft knock on the door of Gailen's suite was met with a muffled groan. Thalorian, already awake and fully dressed, strode to the door and opened it, revealing the palace attendant. The young man's posture was as formal as ever, though his tone carried a quiet urgency.

"Prince Gailen," the attendant said, inclining his head respectfully. "King Manard requests your presence in the throne room, along with your companions."

Gailen sat up in bed, rubbing the sleep from his eyes. "Understood. Thank you."

The attendant bowed and departed, leaving Gailen to swing his legs over the side of the bed. He glanced at Thalorian, who stood ready, arms crossed in his usual composed stance.

"I assume Kaelorn is already up?" Gailen asked, stifling a yawn.

Thalorian nodded. "He is on his way to the throne room already. The challenge will be Valeon."

Gailen sighed, a smirk tugging at his lips. "Then we'd better make sure he doesn't miss this."

Minutes later, the two found themselves outside Valeon's door, standing in a corridor adorned with intricate crystal sconces that cast a calm, ambient glow. The crisp scent of morning dew drifted through the open windows, carried by a cool breeze that brushed against their skin, refreshing in the early light. After knocking repeatedly to no avail, Thalorian pushed the door open. Inside, Valeon lay sprawled across the bed, blankets tangled haphazardly around him.

"Valeon," Gailen called firmly, his voice full of exasperation and wry amusement. He tapped his foot loudly against the floor to emphasize his impatience. "Unless you've decided the king can wait on your beauty sleep, it's time to get up."

A muffled groan emerged beneath the blanket as Valeon pulled it tighter over his head. "It is too early. Whatever it is can wait."

"It's a summons from the king," Thalorian said, his tone clipped. "So no, it cannot wait."

When Valeon made no move to rise, Gailen and Thalorian exchanged a look of shared determination. Without hesitation, they stepped forward, each grabbing an arm. Valeon thrashed in protest, groaning dramatically as he tried to pull the covers back over his head, but Gailen and Thalorian were relentless, dragging him from the tangled mess of blankets.

"Fine, fine!" Valeon grumbled, stumbling as he tried to untangle himself. "I am awake. No need for the rough handling."

"You'll thank us later," Gailen said dryly, already heading for the door.

Still muttering under his breath, Valeon trailed behind them, his complaints barely audible. Gailen merely shot him a dry look while Thalorian, unimpressed, responded with a pointed glare and a deliberate tap of his foot against the polished floor. "If those dark dragons show up again, I'm blaming all of you."

The trio made their way toward the throne room, Valeon's quiet grumbling providing an ironic counterpoint to the steady resolve of his companions. Thalorian merely shook his head in silent exasperation while Gailen smirked, clearly entertained by Valeon's protests.

Upon entering the throne room, they found King Manard rising from his seat, his gaze sweeping over them with measured intensity. The crystalline walls pulsed faintly with arcane energy, a subtle vibration tingling in the air, heightening the moment's weight. The tall windows bathed the grand space in soft morning light, casting an ethereal glow over the gathering.

"Thank you all for coming," Manard greeted, his voice calm but edged with urgency. His gaze lingered briefly on Valeon, who slouched with casual indifference.

Thalorian sharply glared and murmured, "Be polite, Valeon."

Valeon straightened slightly, raising his hands in mock surrender, his faint smirk betraying amusement. "Of course, always the gentleman."

King Manard's lips twitched in the barest hint of a smile before his expression hardened. "Tell me about the dark dragons from last night. What did you observe?"

Ong stepped forward, his stance steady and composed, each word deliberate. He glanced at Keisha, a silent reassurance passing between them before he addressed the room. "Your Majesty," he began, his voice grave, "there is a figure uniting the dark dragons' shadowy force driven by vengeance against the noble dragons."

The room grew still, the air thick with tension. A subtle shift rippled through those gathered. Keisha's fingers tightened slightly at her sides, Manard's jaw set with quiet resolve, and even Valeon, for once, sat motionless, his usual smirk absent.

"Kimras and Amara dealt with Zylron and Glaciera months ago, but their defeat did not end the darkness. It is spreading. More dark dragons are answering this figure's call," Ong continued.

Keisha's voice was quiet but laced with sorrow. "This is no coincidence. The timing and coordination all point to someone orchestrating these movements with a singular purpose."

Manard's sharp gaze swept the room, meeting the eyes of each person present. Ong's words hung heavily in the crystalline hall, leaving even Valeon uncharacteristically silent. For a moment, the only sound was the faint hum of the crystalline walls, as if the city held its breath.

The silence was broken by Gailen, his piercing blue eyes narrowing in thought. "Why? What does this person have against the noble dragons?"

Keisha's gaze dropped momentarily, her voice faltering before she raised her head. "Because of what happened years ago. They believed my powers could anchor the darkness and amplify their control, and it cost me almost everything."

Gailen's brow furrowed as he turned toward his father in confusion. King Manard stepped forward, his tone measured but grave. "Phoenix Shadowwalker and Vuarus sought to sacrifice Keisha to the abyss. They believed her powers could tether the darkness and grant them dominion over it. Kimras and Amara stopped the ritual and saved her, but the cost of their actions still ripples through time."

Keisha's hands clenched at her sides, a cold weight settling in her chest, sorrow welling at the thought of the noble dragons being unjustly targeted. A whirlwind of memories surfaced—fear, pain, the suffocating grasp of darkness that had nearly claimed her. Her voice barely rose above a whisper, laced with guilt and uncertainty. "So, it's because of me."

"No," Ong said firmly, stepping closer and wrapping her in his arms. "It is not your fault. None of this is your doing."

Manard's voice was resolute as he shook his head. "Ong is right. The noble dragons acted to protect not just you but all of Vacari. The darkness they sought to unleash would have consumed us all."

Gailen nodded, his voice steady. "My father's right. This is not on you. You were their target, their victim, but never the cause."

Keisha leaned into Ong, her fiery red hair catching the light as she exhaled slowly. Whoever was behind this was blinded by their anger, unable to see the noble dragons for what they were—protectors. The weight of that truth pressed against her chest, heavy with sorrow. "I understand, but it doesn't change the fact that this figure's vengeance stems from that moment."

Manard's gaze swept over the group, determination etched into his features. His hands curled into tight fists at his sides, his stance firm with unyielding resolve. "Be that as it may, what matters now is how we confront this threat. We cannot allow their plans to retake root. The unity of the dark dragons must be broken before it strengthens further."

The weight of his words ignited a shared resolve in the room, a silent agreement among those gathered. Thalorian straightened, his expression grim yet determined, while Kaelorn exhaled slowly, his fingers flexing as if grasping an unseen weapon. Even Valeon, usually one to scoff, remained uncharacteristically quiet, his brow furrowed in thought. The revelation of what had nearly happened to Keisha left him momentarily stunned, his usual flippant demeanor replaced by a rare moment of solemnity.

Ong stepped forward again, turning to the king. "Your Majesty, it is time to prioritize dragon-back training. I know you have been cautious, but time is not a luxury we have anymore. We must establish riders who can protect Emeraldwoods and Crystal Vale and prepare them to safeguard all of Vacari."

Manard studied Ong momentarily, weighing the risks against the urgency in his advisor's eyes. His instincts had long urged caution, but hesitation could cost them dearly now. Finally, he nodded slowly. "You are right.

The time for caution has passed. I will convene the council to find suitable locations for training and ensure we gather the best candidates to become dragon-back riders. Vacari's future may well depend on their readiness."

The atmosphere in the throne room remained heavy, but the resolve in the eyes of those present burned brighter—a silent vow to stand united against the darkness looming on the horizon.

Gailen turned to his father, his blue eyes unwavering. A storm of emotions churned beneath the surface: the weight of responsibility, the fear of failure, and the silent pressure of living up to expectations. Doubt flickered in his mind, but he forced it aside, gripping onto the determination that had carried him this far. "I will become a dragon-back rider, Father."

His voice held steady, though a flicker of hesitation lingered in his eyes. Memories of the dark dragons' power and the burden of leadership pressed heavily on his mind, yet resolve flared within him. He clenched his fists subtly, reminding himself of what was at stake—not just for his kingdom but for all of Vacari.

King Manard studied his son carefully, his expression a mixture of pride and concern. "Are you certain, my son?"

Gailen met his father's gaze and smiled, his confidence unwavering. "Yes, Father. I am."

A hush settled over the room, the weight of Gailen's declaration sinking in. After a moment, Thalorian stepped forward, his silver hair catching the crystalline light. "I will join as well," he said, calm and resolute. "The dragons will need allies who understand strategy and precision."

Kaelorn shifted, opening his mouth to speak, but Ong met his gaze with a knowing look. "Kaelorn, your abilities would be better utilized in Emeraldwoods. The fairies and nymphs need someone they trust to coordinate their defenses and prepare for the worst."

Kaelorn hesitated, his gladefire eyes reflecting his inner deliberation. Finally, he nodded. "You are right. If Emeraldwoods is threatened, I will ensure they are ready."

From the edge of the group, Valeon finally broke his silence. "And what about me?" he asked, raising an eyebrow. "I don't think dragon-back riding is quite... suitable for someone of my reputation." His sheepish grin carried a hint of genuine hesitation.

Gailen couldn't suppress a chuckle. "In other words, you're afraid of riding a dragon."

Valeon smirked but did not deny it, though the thought of being so high above the ground, with nothing but a dragon's back beneath him, sent an involuntary shiver down his spine. "Call it self-preservation," he said, crossing his arms in mock defiance. While he respected the noble dragons, soaring through the skies on one's back was a challenge he was not ready to face. Thalorian sighed audibly, shaking his head, while Kaelorn chuckled under his breath. Even Manard's lips twitched slightly before he masked it with a composed nod.

Gailen clapped Valeon on the shoulder, his tone light. "That is fine. You can work with the royal guards and Kaelorn. There is plenty to be done that does not involve dragons. You could also train with the healers. They will need someone who understands strategy and compassion to coordinate their efforts."

Kaelorn rolled his eyes but could not hide his amusement, a faint smirk tugging at the corners of his mouth.

Ong stepped forward, drawing the group's focus. He took a measured breath, his gaze sweeping over those gathered, ensuring he had their full attention before speaking. "I will speak with Aurelia and Verdantia about the dragon-back training. With their guidance, we will ensure those who step forward are prepared for what lies ahead."

The group nodded in unison, a shared sense of purpose binding them together. Despite the daunting challenges they faced, determination shone in their eyes.

As the meeting concluded, the weight of their decisions lingered in the air, a reminder that the fight against the encroaching darkness was only beginning. Gailen exhaled slowly, feeling the enormity of what lay ahead. "This is just the beginning," he thought, steeling himself for future battles. The path ahead would test them all, but they had taken the first step for now.

Chapter 12

A gift from the Moon

O ng tightened the clasp of his sword belt, adjusting to its familiar weight as his thoughts churned over the discussion ahead. He could feel the gravity of the task ahead, the pressure of ensuring Vacari's survival pressing against his chest like an unrelenting force. His mind raced with the questions he would pose to the ancient dragons Aurelia and Verdantia. Known for their vast knowledge and unmatched foresight, Aurelia embodied the fiery passion of wisdom. At the same time, Verdantia was the serene voice of reason, each a cornerstone in guiding Vacari through its trials. Their wisdom was a beacon of hope against the rising threat, and he felt the weight of the kingdom's fate pressing heavily on his shoulders. Ever the steady presence by his side, Keisha adjusted her cloak, ready to accompany him. She briefly wondered what challenges lay ahead, knowing that every step they took now would shape the fate of Vacari.

As they moved through the polished crystal corridors, Thalorian approached, his silver hair gleaming under the morning light streaming through the high windows. His expression was composed, but an unusual gravity lingered in his demeanor.

"Ong," Thalorian said, his tone steady yet thoughtful, "may I have a moment of your time? You and Keisha, both."

Ong stopped, exchanging a glance with Keisha before nodding. "Of course. What is it?"

Thalorian gestured toward a nearby alcove where the Emberwings perched, their iridescent feathers shimmering in hues of gold and crimson. The faint hum of their magic filled the space, casting a warm, ethereal glow around them. The space, alive with the faint hum of the magical birds, was secluded and serene. They followed him, curiosity sparking between them.

Once inside, Thalorian turned, his jade fire eyes meeting Ong's. "I have both a request and an offer. The Moon Elves of Silvaraen are famed for crafting weapons of unmatched precision—tools born of magic and purpose. Among these are the crystal-emerald bows, designed to bridge strength and elegance in battle."

Keisha's green eyes widened slightly, wonder flickering within them as her gaze lingered on Thalorian. A memory surfaced—her father once spoke of the Moon Elves' bows, calling them whispers of the stars woven into form. She had always imagined them as distant myths, unattainable relics of an age before hers. And yet, here was Thalorian, offering to bring those weapons into their hands. She could not help but reflect on the stories she had heard as a child—tales of the Moon Elves' unmatched craftsmanship and ability to weave magic into every creation. The idea that these legendary weapons might now play a role in protecting Vacari filled her with awe, and a quiet determination stirred within her to see their potential realized. Her red hair caught the soft glow of the Emberwings' plumage, accentuating the awe across her features.

"The crystal-emerald bows are legendary and are perfect blends of strength and elegance. I never thought we would see them here."

Thalorian nodded, his expression serene but resolute. "It is true. And I believe they could serve Vacari well in this growing peril. I want to return to Silvaraen to retrieve these bows and bring them here as a gift from the Moon Elves. They can provide the edge you need."

Ong crossed his arms, his thoughtful gaze moving between Thalorian and Keisha, his fingers tapping lightly against his elbow as he considered the implications. The offer was generous—too generous. While the prospect of the bows was enticing, a nagging doubt lingered in his mind. What unspoken expectations might accompany such a gift? His jaw tightened slightly, the weight of leadership pressing down on him as he considered the risks of accepting aid without knowing the full cost.

"And you're certain this is something the Moon Elves are willing to give?"

Thalorian's lips curved into a faint smile. "Silvaraen thrives in unity. The Moon Elves have long understood that no kingdom stands alone when darkness rises. If Vacari falls, the balance shifts for us all. The threat against Vacari is a threat against us all. These bows are a gift and a statement of our commitment to this fight."

Keisha stepped closer, her voice filled with certainty and warmth. To her, the bows were more than just weapons; they were legendary artifacts of craftsmanship and power, known to be wielded by only the most skilled warriors. She had no doubts about their worth or the Moon Elves' sincerity in offering them. "Ong, these are not just weapons. They are symbols of alliance and trust. Vacari would do well to accept."

Ong inclined his head, his respect for Keisha's insight evident. He turned to Thalorian and extended his hand. "Vacari would be honored to accept this gift. Thank you, Thalorian, for bringing this to us."

Thalorian clasped Ong's hand briefly, his jade fire eyes steady. "I will leave at once to retrieve them. I will also bring back other Moon Elves skilled in battle and strategy to aid your defense."

Ong nodded, his voice steady. "Travel safely, and may the stars guide your path."

With that, Thalorian departed, his form disappearing into the gleaming corridors. Ong exhaled slowly, his fingers tightening at his sides. The Moon Elves' gift was an undeniable boon, but the implications of their involvement stirred uneasiness within him. Would this alliance bring salvation or merely shift the battlefield toward an unknown cost? Ong turned to Keisha, his brow furrowed in thought. The weight of the Moon Elves' offer pressed against his mind, the implications stretching far beyond weapons alone. Was this a sign of deeper alliances forming or a desperate measure in response to an unseen threat? He knew King Manard would welcome the aid, but he could not shake the lingering question of what price, if any, Vacari would be expected to pay in return.

"King Manard must hear of this at once. These bows and their bearers may shift the tide in our favor."

Keisha smiled faintly. "He'll be as honored as we are."

Together, they exited the alcove, their steps purposeful as they headed toward the throne room to share the news.

The palace halls hummed with quiet activity, the murmur of distant conversations blending with the rhythmic echo of footsteps and the rustle of fabric. Sunlight streamed through the crystalline windows, casting soft rainbows on the polished floors.

King Manard sat in the Royal Meeting Chamber, a grand hall adorned with intricate carvings of dragons locked in flight and constellations woven into celestial patterns. The walls bore ancient tales of battles fought in the skies, each etched with meticulous detail as if capturing the essence of history within the stone. Sunlight filtered through stained-glass windows, casting vibrant patterns on the polished marble floor. The warm glow carried a subtle warmth, while the faint scent of aged parchment and polished wood infused the chamber with an air of quiet dignity. His son Gailen and Kaelorn stood before him, and their conversation was casual yet purposeful.

"So, Kaelorn," King Manard said with a smile, "how do you find the city? I imagine it is vastly different from the forests of Etharyon."

Kaelorn chuckled lightly, his gladefire eyes reflecting the light. "It is indeed different, Your Majesty. But its beauty rivals even the most sacred glades of my homeland."

Their conversation was interrupted as the doors opened, and Ong entered, Keisha at his side. Manard rose slightly, greeting them with a nod. "Ong, Keisha. What brings you here?"

Ong stepped forward, his tone respectful but direct. "Your Majesty, I bring news from Thalorian. Before heading to Silvaraen, he informed us of a gift from the Moon Elves—crystal and emerald bows. He has gone to retrieve them and will return with additional support."

King Manard's brows lifted in interest, and he exchanged glances with Gailen and Kaelorn. "Crystal and emerald bows," he murmured. "That is no small gift."

Gailen turned to Kaelorn, curiosity alight in his piercing blue eyes. "Have you ever heard of such weapons?"

Kaelorn nodded slowly, his brow furrowing in contemplation as he ran a hand over his chin, considering the weight of the revelation. His fingers lightly tapped against his jaw, a silent rhythm of thought. The mention of the bows stirred memories of ancient tales whispered through Etharyon's sacred groves. He had always believed them to be myths, relics of a past that had faded into obscurity. Yet, if the Moon Elves had truly forged such weapons, their craftsmanship would be unparalleled, imbued with the magic of starlit forests and the wisdom of ages. The idea of wielding such a weapon filled him with reverence and intrigue. "They were rumored in Etharyon, whispered about in hushed tones. But none have ever been seen, at least not in my lifetime."

Gailen's lips quirked into a small smile as he turned to his father. "Well, Father, you were right. Sometimes rumors hold a fragment of the truth."

King Manard chuckled, his pride in his son evident. "You have chosen your companions well, Gailen. Thalorian's actions reflect wisdom and foresight that will serve us all."

He rose from his seat, his commanding presence filling the room. "We will wait for Thalorian's return to begin the training properly. His mission could mark a turning point in Vacari's fate. But in the meantime, we will announce the training program. Anyone who believes they have what it takes will be welcome to try. We will need more dragon riders than ever before if we are to stand against what is coming."

Kaelorn inclined his head, his thoughtful gaze fixed on the king. "A wise course of action, Your Majesty. The more prepared we are, the stronger we will stand."

Manard nodded in agreement, his gaze momentarily drifting to the grand map of Vacari etched into the wall. His eyes traced the borders, lingering on the mountain passes where battles had once been fought, the rivers that sustained the kingdom, and the distant frontiers that now faced an uncertain future. Every detail on the map told a story, a reminder of the fragile balance he was sworn to protect. As he studied it, he saw a kingdom and a diverse realm whose people stood united. Every region, from the shimmering coasts to the dense forests, played a part in the delicate harmony that held Vacari together. Their strength lay in warriors and the unity they forged across cultures and races—a force more potent than any blade. The weight of responsibility pressed heavier on his shoulders, knowing that this decision would shape the fate of many.

"Gailen, Kaelorn, Ong—spread the word. The future of Vacari may depend on the strength of those willing to rise to this challenge."

The group shared a solemn understanding, each feeling the weight of what lay ahead. Ong envisioned the dragons' wisdom as an anchor to guide their efforts, their ancient knowledge a beacon through the uncertainty ahead. He considered the lessons they imparted—not just strategies for battle but the importance of unity, patience, and foresight. This understanding steadied his resolve against the rising tide of darkness. Keisha thought of the alliances they were forging and how trust could become their most vital weapon, her heart brimming with cautious hope. King Manard reflected on the resilience his people would need, silently vowing to lead them through the trials ahead with strength and conviction. Together, they would ensure Vacari was ready to face the storm gathering on the horizon.

Silvaraen's soft silver-blue radiance and ethereal glow greeted Thalorian as he emerged from the magical currents, their swirling light leaving a lingering shimmer on his cloak. His muscles tensed briefly from the sudden shift between realms. The familiar strain of magical travel settled into his limbs before dissipating. He exhaled slowly, steadying himself as the energy faded, grounding his senses in the air of his homeland.

A gentle hum resonated in the atmosphere, the magic still tingling against his skin, carrying the faint scent of moonflower blossoms drifting through the city. Crystalline towers stretched high, catching the perpetual moonlit sky in a cascade of prismatic hues that seemed to pulse with life. The currents had carried him swiftly and smoothly, their energy a comforting presence, a tether to the heart of his people. The quiet thrum of magic in the air was as familiar as the steady rhythm of his own heart. He strode through the city's grand plaza, his steps purposefully as he approached the council chamber of the Moon Elf elders.

Inside, the chamber was bathed in a soft, silvery light that seemed to emanate from the walls themselves, casting an ethereal glow upon the smooth crystal floor. The radiance evoked a deep sense of nostalgia in Thalorian, a reminder of the nights he spent as a child marveling at the craftsmanship of his people. It filled him with pride and a solemn awareness of the responsibility resting on his shoulders. The air was thick with an ancient, almost tangible magic, humming faintly in the background. The elders, their expressions serene yet attentive, sat in a semicircle on elevated seats carved from shimmering moonstone. Their flowing silver hair and robes, adorned with intricate runes, lent them an air of ageless wisdom and unyielding authority.

Thalorian bowed respectfully. "Elders of Silvaraen, I bring news from Vacari, where darkness gathers and threatens the balance we all hold dear."

The elders exchanged glances but remained silent, waiting for him to continue.

"Crystal Vale faces a growing threat," Thalorian explained, his voice weighted with urgency. "The dark dragons are rallying under a mysterious figure cloaked in shadow, whose identity and motives remain unknown. Their influence spreads quickly, leaving destruction and fear in their wake. The people of Vacari are preparing to defend their realm, and I believe we can help them. I request permission to bring crystal and emerald bows crafted by our people to aid their dragon riders. And if any among us wish to stand beside them, they would welcome our strength."

The eldest among them, a tall figure with eyes like starlit pools, leaned forward slightly. "Your request is bold, Thalorian, but not without merit. If Vacari falls, it will not be long before the darkness turns its gaze toward Etharyon."

Another elder nodded. "The bows you speak of are our pride, crafted with precision and imbued with our magic. Each is enchanted with spells that guide its flight, ensuring unerring accuracy, and woven with protective charms that resist wear and corruption. The arrows loosed from these bows strike with an ethereal force capable of piercing even the most formidable dragon scales. These weapons carry the history of our people, their craftsmanship unmatched by any other realm. They are as much a symbol of unity as they are a tool of war. They must go with our blessing to aid in this fight."

The chamber grew quiet as the elders conferred, their gazes meeting in unspoken understanding. One elder tapped his fingers against the armrest of his moonstone chair while another absently traced the runes on her sleeve. A faint shift in their expressions—an arched brow, a subtle nod—hinted at the weight of their deliberation before the eldest finally spoke. "Your request is granted. The bows will be prepared and sent with you."

Thalorian inclined his head deeply. "Thank you, Elders."

Thalorian arrived at the storage hall the following day, its towering crystal walls faintly illuminated in the morning light. The air was cool, carrying the subtle fragrance of lavender, mingling with the crisp scent of polished crystal and aged parchment. The distant murmur of attendants moving about their tasks and the soft flicker of magical runes cast a hushed reverence over the hall, a calming presence amidst the tension of preparation. An ornately adorned wagon awaited at the chamber's center, its intricate carvings and silver inlays glinting with enchantments. Runes flickered softly along its sides as attendants moved carefully, ensuring everything was in place for the journey. The wagon was filled with beautifully crafted crystal and emerald bows, their polished surfaces gleaming with the faint glow of enchantments.

As Thalorian secured the wagon for travel, a rustling sound behind him drew his attention. Turning, his gaze fell upon a group of Moon Elves, all armed and dressed for a journey. Their expressions were resolute, their eyes alight with determination. Each carried a weapon or tool marked with personal craftsmanship, a sign of their readiness and deep connection to their cause. Their posture spoke of unyielding resolve, a silent promise that they would stand with Vacari no matter the cost.

"What is this?" Thalorian asked, his jade fire eyes widening in surprise.

A younger elf stepped forward, her silver hair braided tightly. "We heard your call, Thalorian. Vacari fights for survival, and we will not let them fight alone. Our place is with you."

Emotion swelled in Thalorian's chest, his throat tightening as he fought back the sting of unshed tears. The sight of his kin standing ready to fight alongside Vacari was almost overwhelming, a testament to the unity he had always hoped for. But he kept his tone composed, his voice steady despite the raw emotion. "Your choice honors our people and the bonds between realms. Thank you."

With their numbers greater than he had anticipated, Thalorian felt a pleasant shock ripple through him. He had expected a handful of warriors, but the sight of many willing to fight filled him with renewed hope. Smiling faintly, he led the group to the city's edge. A swell of pride and gratitude filled him—his people had answered the call without hesitation. Their willingness to stand beside Vacari was not just a gesture of alliance but a declaration that the fate of their realms was intertwined. He exhaled slowly, steeling himself for the journey ahead, knowing that this was only the beginning of the battle. Magic had carried him swiftly to Silvaraen, but the return journey would be made by traditional means. The wagon wheels creaked as they began their long trek back to Vacari, the silver glow of Silvaraen fading behind them.

Chapter 13
A Luminara's Path

K aelorn stood in the royal meeting chamber, his glade-fire eyes thoughtful as he spoke with King Manard. The king exhaled softly, his ice-blue eyes narrowing in consideration, the weight of experience evident in his gaze. "I'd like to meet the fairies and nymphs of Emeraldwoods," Kaelorn began, his tone both curious and resolute. "Their wisdom and connection to nature are legendary; I believe we could learn much from them."

Manard nodded, his expression contemplative. "They are cautious, yes, but for good reason. Their connection to the natural world makes them protective of it and themselves."

Kaelorn's brow furrowed slightly as he considered Manard's words, his fingers absently brushing the hilt of his blade. He let out a slow breath, his thoughts shifting between admiration and concern, weighing the lessons of the past against the uncertain future. The weight of history and duty pressed against his thoughts, stirring a quiet resolve. "I've always admired their ability to preserve balance," he said, his voice tinged with admiration and determination. "To walk in harmony with the world rather than seeking to bend it to their will is a strength I fear we have forgotten. Their way reminds me of what Etharyon once aspired to and what we must strive to protect."

"In Etharyon, we once shared a similar bond with nature, but over time, we allowed our ambition to overshadow our harmony with the world. We have lost much in understanding how to coexist with it."

The faint sound of footsteps echoed through the chamber, interrupting the moment. Ong, passing by, caught the tail end of their discussion and could not resist interjecting. A grin spread across his face as he turned to Keisha, who stood nearby. "Keisha," he called, his voice warm with amusement, "think you could arrange for our friend here to meet the fairies and nymphs?"

Keisha turned to Kaelorn, her green eyes reflecting both curiosity and amusement. A thoughtful smile played at her lips as she studied him, sensing the weight of his request and its sincerity. A breeze from the open windows carried the faint scent of blooming jasmine, reminding her of the nights spent under the emerald canopy, listening to whispered secrets of the forest. The familiarity of those memories filled her with quiet reassurance, a connection she hoped Kaelorn would come to understand. Memories of her time in Emeraldwoods flickered in her mind of moonlit glades where the fairies danced, the soothing hum of the nymphs' whispered songs, and the gentle rustling of leaves that carried secrets older than the kingdom itself. She had once been an outsider, earning their trust through patience and sincerity. It was a bond she cherished and hoped Kaelorn could forge as well.

"I believe that can be arranged," she replied with a smile. "Kaelorn, you will come with me to Emeraldwoods. They trust me, and I think they will trust you if I vouch for you."

Kaelorn inclined his head, a faint smile touching his lips. "I would be honored," he said, his tone steady but with a hint of eagerness betraying his calm exterior.

As they prepared to leave, Valeon strolled into the room, his casual gait and ever-present grin making his entrance as notable as his timing. "Where are you two off to?" he asked, glancing between Keisha and Kaelorn.

Kaelorn sighed, his patience visibly tested but intact. "To Emeraldwoods, to meet the fairies and nymphs," he replied, his tone clipped but polite.

"Sounds... enchanting," Valeon drawled, his grin mischievous. "Off to gaze at fairies and be charmed by their magic, are we? Perhaps you'll return speaking in riddles and poetry." Kaelorn's jaw tightened slightly, though he quickly masked his irritation, while Keisha's lips twitched in a faint smile, clearly accustomed to Valeon's antics. "But I think I will leave the forest frolicking to you two. Someone must ensure the palace does not run out of wine."

The grin on Valeon's face faltered for a moment, replaced by an almost imperceptible flicker of thoughtfulness, his gaze momentarily distant, as if recalling a time when he, too, had believed in something more significant. A shadow of an old memory passed through his eyes, perhaps a regret left unspoken or a past he preferred to bury as if something in Kaelorn's words had struck a chord, a fleeting memory, or an unspoken sadness. It passed as quickly as it came, leaving only his trademark playfulness behind.

Gailen, standing nearby, shook his head, his piercing blue eyes glinting with exasperation. "Father, you still claim I picked good companions?"

Manard chuckled, his eyes sparkling with amusement. "Even the best choices come with... colorful additions," he said, the warmth in his voice softening the humor of his words.

The room filled with light laughter as Valeon wandered off, his usual carefree stride intact. However, his fingers briefly tapped against his belt in a rare moment of quiet reflection before disappearing around the corner, searching for his next meal. As Keisha and Kaelorn began their journey to the edge of Emeraldwoods. Keisha glanced at Kaelorn as they walked, her voice quiet but thoughtful. "The fairies and nymphs value sincerity primarily. They will see through any pretense, so just be yourself."

Kaelorn nodded, rolling his shoulders slightly as if easing an unseen tension. A slow breath escaped him, and he clasped his hands behind his back, grounding himself in the weight of her advice. "I will keep that in mind," he replied, his voice firm yet humble. As they approached the forest, Kaelorn could not help but feel anticipation and reverence. The path ahead promised new connections and discoveries, but the camaraderie of those left behind ensured that even the simplest moments carried warmth.

Kaelorn and Keisha walked side by side as the crystalline towers of Crystal Vale receded, giving way to the emerald-hued path leading into the forest. Their footsteps made a soft crunch against the mossy ground, the earth beneath them pulsing faintly with the magic woven into the land. A quiet sense of anticipation settled between them. Kaelorn was eager to experience the magic of Emeraldwoods firsthand, while Keisha, nostalgic yet resolute, understood the importance of their visit. The air in Emeraldwoods was alive with energy—a harmonious blend of rustling leaves, the faint hum of magic resonating from the trees, and the delicate scent of blooming flowers.

As they approached the forest's entrance, Kaelorn gazed at the towering greenery. "This is the Emeraldwoods," he murmured, his glade-fire eyes bright with wonder. "It's as if the forest breathes."

Keisha nodded, her expression warm. "It does, in a way. The magic here is part of its life force, just as it is a part of me. My elemental magic is rooted in the forests; through it, I can feel the energy that flows through every tree and blade of grass."

They stepped beneath the vast canopy, dappled light filtering through the leaves in shifting patterns. Keisha led the way, her steps sure and purposeful. After a while, she turned to Kaelorn, her voice gentle yet firm. "We are going to the glade at the center of the woods. It is the best place to meet them."

Kaelorn nodded, his curiosity piqued. He had heard many stories of the Emeraldwoods, but standing here, feeling the magic hum through the air, was entirely different. A flicker of memory surfaced from his last visit to this enchanted place—the way the air had shimmered with unseen energy. The anticipation stirred within him, a quiet thrill at the thought of rediscovering its wonders. "I saw the glade not long ago, when Gailen had us stop to rest during our journey through Emerald Woods," he said quietly. "The dragon statues—woven from flowers and living shrubs—weren't there when Gailen left Vacari, or so he said. Lanterns hung from the trees, swaying gently in the breeze, casting a soft light over the clearing. Even in stillness, the dragons seemed alive, as though waiting to draw breath. The moment was peaceful... almost sacred. It's stayed with me since."

Keisha smiled, tilting her head slightly with a faint pride in her voice. "It is a tribute to the dragons. The fairies created it after the Emerald Dragons helped restore the Emeraldwoods. That glade symbolizes what we can accomplish when we work together."

Kaelorn's gaze lingered on the path ahead, his respect for the forest and its inhabitants deepening with each step.

When they reached the glade, it was as breathtaking as Kaelorn remembered. The dragon sculptures, woven from blooming flowers and intricately shaped shrubs, stood proudly among the natural splendor. Sunlight streamed through the trees, illuminating the vibrant colors and filling the space with a serene warmth.

Keisha gestured to a spot beneath a large tree near the center. "Let us sit here while we wait. They will come to us when they are ready."

Kaelorn followed her lead, lowering himself onto the soft, mossy ground. The incredible, velvety texture pressed against his palms, grounding him in the forest's embrace. A soft breeze stirred the leaves, carrying a faint, melodic whisper that almost sounded like laughter. He glanced around, his glade-fire eyes narrowing slightly. "Are they already here?"

Keisha smiled knowingly. "Perhaps. The fairies have a way of making their presence felt before they are seen."

As they sat in comfortable silence, the tranquil beauty of the glade enveloped them, a reminder of the magic and unity that had created it.

A sudden shift in the air drew their attention upward. The soft hum of magic intensified as Verdantia, the ancient Emerald Dragon, descended gracefully from the canopy above. Her shimmering green scales blended seamlessly with the vibrant hues of the forest, her presence both majestic and calming. A gentle breeze stirred the leaves as she landed, carrying the faint scent of moss and blooming flowers.

Verdantia's wings sliced through the air with effortless power, a rhythmic whoosh resonating through the glade as she glided lower. Each controlled movement carried the weight of her ancient grace, a harmony of strength and elegance that rippled through the clearing. Sunlight danced off her emerald scales, casting shifting mosaics of green and gold across the mossy ground as though the forest itself had come alive to greet her. As her talons touched the earth, a soft tremor rippled outward, and a faint glow seemed to emanate from her form, blending harmoniously with the glade's vibrant hues. She inclined her head toward Keisha, her emerald eyes glowing faintly.

"Keisha," Verdantia greeted, her voice resonant and warm. "You bring a guest."

Keisha rose, her warm and genuine smile, a glint of pride in her emerald eyes as she gestured toward Kaelorn. "Yes, Verdantia. This is Kaelorn. He is from Etharyon and wishes to meet the nymphs and fairies. He wants to work with them to protect Emeraldwoods from the dark dragons."

Verdantia's gaze shifted to Kaelorn, piercing and regal. A flicker of unease brushed his thoughts, but he met her gaze steadily, refusing to waver under her scrutiny. He knew this moment mattered, that his sincerity must be evident. He straightened unconsciously, his fingers curling slightly against his palm as if steadying himself under her watchful eyes. Bowing somewhat in respect, he spoke with quiet conviction. "It is an honor, Verdantia. Your guardianship of this place is extraordinary, and I would like to contribute to its protection."

Verdantia studied him for a moment longer before nodding, her approval clear. "Your intent is noble. I will ensure you have their ear."

She turned toward the dense foliage at the edge of the glade and spoke softly, her words carrying the weight of ancient authority. "It is safe. Come forth."

The air seemed to shimmer at her call, and the forest came alive. Fairies, their delicate wings glimmering with ethereal light, fluttered from the trees, their laughter like the soft chiming of bells. As they moved, petals swirled gently in their wake, and faint glowing trails lingered in the air, marking their playful paths. Nymphs emerged from the underbrush, graceful and serene as they stepped into the glade.

The fairies immediately flocked to Keisha, their tiny hands reaching out to touch her hair, which caught the light and glowed under their attention. As they laughed and fluttered about, a few began weaving small, colorful flowers into her vibrant red locks, their delicate fingers moving with practiced ease. Keisha smiled, accustomed to their affectionate gestures, and let them continue their playful handiwork. One fairy perched on her shoulder, its laughter like a melody as it played with a stray strand of her hair.

Keisha laughed softly, her eyes sparkling. "Kaelorn, let me introduce you."

Kaelorn watched the scene with quiet wonder. His glade-fire eyes reflected the magic of the moment, capturing the flickering lights of the fairies as they danced through the air. The beauty around him felt almost surreal, as if he had entered a world untouched by time. His breath caught slightly, his heart quickening as he absorbed the sheer harmony of the glade. Something deep within him stirred—a longing for the beauty around him and the sense of belonging it offered. With its unity and magic, this place felt like a bridge between the two halves of himself, offering him something he had never entirely known before.

His fingers brushed against the mossy ground, grounding him in the moment as though he feared it might slip away like a dream. The vibrant energy of the glade seeped into his very being, filling him with a profound sense of peace and purpose. Each delicate motion of the fairies and nymphs felt like a thread weaving into a more extraordinary tapestry—one he now realized he longed to be a part of. A quiet reverence settled over him, mingled with an unspoken vow to protect the harmony of this place. Bowing his head slightly to the fairies and nymphs, he spoke sincerely. "Thank you for allowing me to meet you. Your work here is a testament to the strength and beauty of Emeraldwoods."

Keisha smiled, sensing the beginning of something meaningful. The fairies and nymphs regarded Kaelorn with curiosity and warmth, their trust growing under Verdantia's watchful gaze.

As the fairies and nymphs continued to flutter and glide around the glade, one particularly bold fairy, her wings shimmering like liquid gold, flew directly to Kaelorn. She hovered before his face, her tiny, radiant eyes studying him intently.

"You're not human," she said, her voice chiming like a soft bell. "Nor are you fully fae. You belong to Luminara."

The statement lingered, heavy in the air. Kaelorn felt their scrutiny press upon him, a tangible force that quickened his pulse. Uncertain threatened to creep in for a fleeting second, but he steadied himself, focusing on the purpose that had brought him here. A flicker of uncertainty passed through him, echoing the times he had questioned where he truly belonged. Memories of standing at the threshold of two worlds, human and fae, surfaced in his mind, the sense of never fitting entirely into either. But as he steadied himself, drawing in a slow breath, he reminded himself why he was here. This was not a test of identity but of purpose. His pulse quickened slightly, a fleeting doubt whispering at the edges of his mind. But he clenched his fists, grounding himself in the weight of his purpose. He steadied himself with a slow, measured breath, pushing aside uncertainty and embracing the moment before him. The others turned their attention to him, and curiosity and intrigue were reflected in their expressions. Kaelorn straightened slightly, his glade-fire eyes meeting the fairy's unwavering gaze.

"I am," he acknowledged, his voice calm yet resonating with pride. "My heritage is of Luminara, a blending of human and fae blood."

The fairy tilted her head, her gaze trailing over him as if piecing together the story of his lineage. Kaelorn remained still, feeling the weight of her scrutiny. A twinge of anticipation stirred in his chest, but he met her gaze with quiet confidence, determined to prove his place in this world. Slowly, the nymphs and fairies gathered around him, their interest piqued. Their eyes lingered on his broad shoulders and muscular, agile build, which spoke of a protector's resolve. His deep chestnut hair, streaked faintly with silver, caught the light, further emphasizing his dual nature.

The soft shimmer of his skin became apparent as the sunlight danced across him, a mark of his fae blood. The vine-like markings tracing his forearms seemed to pulse faintly with life as if the forest recognized and welcomed him. The fairies and nymphs exchanged knowing glances, their gazes softening as they sensed the undeniable bond he shared with the woods, a connection both ancient and profound.

Kaelorn remained perfectly still, his respect for their curiosity evident in his calm demeanor. Yet beneath his composed exterior, a quiet exhilaration stirred. The air around him vibrated with an unspoken understanding, the weight of centuries-old magic brushing against his skin like a whisper of acknowledgment. Yet within him, he felt an intricate thread of connection forming, as though the forest was reaching out to embrace him. Each soft touch of the fairies and nymphs carried whispers of their trust, their ancient magic resonating with something profound in his core. For the first time, Kaelorn fully realized the depth of his bond with the Emeraldwoods, a humbling and empowering connection. He could feel their delicate hands brushing the leather of his armor, their fingers tracing the faintly glowing runes embossed in intricate leaf patterns. His curved blade sheathed at his side drew glances, its etched runes a silent testament to its purpose.

"You carry both worlds within you," another nymph said, her voice soft and melodic. "A bridge between realms."

Kaelorn inclined his head. "That is my role. To connect and protect both."

The fairies fluttered closer, their wings stirring the air in rhythmic bursts. They darted around him in playful yet deliberate patterns, their move-ments both graceful and inquisitive. A faint shimmer followed in their wake, trailing like golden dust as they studied him from every angle, their eyes gleaming with curiosity. Their presence felt like the hum of magic itself, a tangible force of nature acknowledging one of its own. The hum resonated within Kaelorn, a subtle warmth spreading through his chest and a tingling sensation along his arms as though the magic were weaving a connection between him and the forest. Despite their closeness, Kaelorn did not flinch or shift, his stillness a quiet testament to his acceptance of their scrutiny.

Keisha watched the scene unfold with a faint smile, recalling her first meeting with the fairies and nymphs. The scent of fresh blossoms and the soft hum of fairy wings had surrounded her then, much like now, a reminder of the trust she had once earned. The scent of fresh blossoms had filled the air that day, mingling with the soft hum of fairy wings and the distant melody of the nymphs' songs. Their laughter had been like wind chimes in a summer breeze, gentle yet full of life, as they wove delicate wreaths into her hair, a gesture of trust and renewal. She had been overwhelmed when she first stepped into the restored Emeraldwoods, tears slipping down her cheeks as she saw what they had done. The fairies had gathered around her then, weaving blossoms into her hair and whispering reassurances, their kindness easing the ache in her heart. That moment had forged an unbreakable bond between them. Even amidst the ruin, their laughter and trust had been a balm to her spirit, a symbol of hope and renewal. Seeing them accept Kaelorn, she felt a deep sense of pride and reassurance in the bond she had cultivated over the years. "It seems you've made an impression," she said lightly.

Kaelorn allowed a small smile to touch his lips, a quiet sense of belonging settling in his chest. He had walked the line between two worlds for so long, uncertain where he genuinely fit. But here, among the fairies and nymphs, he felt seen not as an outsider but as someone with a purpose, a bridge between realms. "It's a privilege to be among them."

The fairies and nymphs began to nod in quiet agreement, their curiosity giving way to a subtle acceptance. One fairy, her wings shimmering with a faint silver glow, reached out and lightly touched Kaelorn's hand, a silent acknowledgment of his presence. A nymph stepped forward, pressing a delicate vine into his palm, a symbol of trust woven from the very essence of the forest. Around them, the soft hum of magic deepened as if the Emeraldwoods recognized his purpose. The glade seemed to glow just a little brighter, casting soft, golden light that danced across the mossy floor and lengthened the shadows of the trees. The air felt warmer, humming with a gentle energy that seemed to embrace Kaelorn in a silent, magical welcome.

Keisha observed the fairies and nymphs as they hovered around Kaelorn, their curiosity gradually transforming into a quiet cama-raderie. Their once-inquisitive glances softened, their movements more fluid and welcoming as they acknowledged him as one of their own. She turned to him, a faint smile gracing her lips. "Kaelorn," she said gently, "I will leave you to get acquainted with them. But be forewarned, the Emerald Dragons watch over the fairies and nymphs. They will protect them fiercely if they sense any threat."

Kaelorn hesitated momentarily, a flicker of contemplation passing over his features. He met her gaze, his glade-fire eyes steady and sincere, the weight of his promise settled firmly within him. "You have my word, Keisha. I mean no harm. My only intent is to learn from them and to work alongside them to protect Emeraldwoods."

Satisfied, Keisha nodded, and a quiet reassurance settled over her. She had seen others earn the trust of the fairies and nymphs, but this felt different. Kaelorn was not just accepted; he was understood. As she turned to leave, she cast one final glance over her shoulder, her heart swelling with the hope that his presence here would mark the beginning of something greater. "Good. Then I will leave you here. They will guide you better than I ever could." With a final glance at the glade, she turned and walked back toward the forest's edge, her silhouette blending into the dappled green light as she returned to Crystal Vale.

Chapter 14
The Shadow's Grip

The dimly lit chamber of the Tower of Shadowwalker pulsed with ominous energy, the air thick with tension that thrummed with the enigmatic presence of the figure. Lyra sat hunched over a table, her delicate fingers tracing the intricate runes on an ancient scroll. A chill ran down her spine, unease coiling in her stomach like a tightening vice. Her pulse quickened, and an icy tension settled deep within her, gripping her with every passing second. A faint tremor ran through her hands. She forced herself to steady her breathing, but the tightening in her throat and the prickling sensation at the nape of her neck made it impossible to dispel the creeping dread curling around her like unseen tendrils.

The parchment was weathered and frayed at the edges, its surface marked with symbols that shimmered faintly in the dim light as if whispering secrets from a long-lost era. The faint, metallic scent of ancient ink lingered in the air—a testament to its age and significance. Her expression was one of intense concentration, though a flicker of unease danced in her eyes. The weight of the mysterious figure's demands pressed heavily upon her mind, each command a chain binding her tighter to their will.

She had seen what happened to those who failed. Whispers of their fates haunted the tower, their names lost to the shadows. The thought sent a shiver through her, but she dared not falter. One misstep, one moment of hesitation, and she could be next. The gnawing fear of consequences far worse than she could imagine clung to her like a specter.

"Lyra." The mysterious figure's sharp, commanding voice shattered the silence. "Continue deciphering the information hidden in those scrolls. I want every detail about the noble dragons laid bare."

Lyra's fingers hesitated—a barely perceptible pause—as doubts flickered in her mind. Was there no end to these tasks? No escape from the figure's relentless grip? With a quiet sigh, she nodded, schooling her features into careful neutrality. "As you command."

The figure's gaze shifted to Qellaun, who stood near the chamber's far end. His dark armor gleamed faintly in the flickering candlelight, the shifting shadows casting jagged lines across his face. "Qellaun, you will watch over the dark dragons while I attend to an errand."

Qellaun's jaw tightened, his fingers curling into fists at his sides. A cold prickle ran down his spine, the weight of responsibility pressing heavier upon his shoulders. The figure's orders had become increasingly unpredictable, and an unspoken dread coiled in his gut. Was he merely a pawn in a game he did not yet understand? His voice was cautious but edged with defiance, a subtle challenge in his stance as he met the figure's gaze head-on. "What errand requires you to leave now, of all times?"

Lyra glanced up from her work, curiosity momentarily eclipsing the weight of her task. "Yes. Where are you going?"

The mysterious figure turned toward them, their presence radiating an aura of unmistakable power. The air in the chamber thickened, pressing against Lyra's skin like an unseen force, while the candle flames flickered violently in response. A chill seeped into the stone walls, carrying a whisper of something ancient and unrelenting—as if the shadows themselves bowed to their will. "It is none of your concern," they replied, their voice cold and unyielding. "Do as I command, or I will find others who can."

The oppressive silence that followed was suffocating. Lyra and Qellaun bowed their heads, their protests swallowed by the figure's sheer authority. Their gaze lingered on them for a moment longer, ensuring compliance, before turning and striding toward the exit, their movements swift and purposeful. The heavy chamber doors groaned as they shut behind them, leaving behind an uneasy stillness in their wake.

The journey to Fel Thalor was shrouded in secrecy, driven by the figure's relentless pursuit of a power that was rightfully theirs. They had felt its presence calling to them, whispering in the darkest hours, promising strength that had been denied for too long. Soon, all would see this power belonged to them, and no one would dare challenge it. They believed this force could tip the scales of destiny in their favor, but it was fraught with peril and ancient warnings. Each step brought them closer to an ancient force, their whispers threading through their thoughts like an echo from forgotten ages. It promised strength, yet the weight of unseen dangers lurked beneath its allure. The figure's thoughts were singularly focused on a presence they had sensed over the past days, a power that called them from the shadowed ruins of the ancient city. They extended their will outward as they approached the towering remnants of Fel Thalor, its crumbling spires cloaked in an eerie mist. Their voice, a whisper across the void, echoed with chilling command.

"Come to me," they intoned, resonating through the ruins. "You have been hiding long enough. Fel Thalor awaits your obedience."

The figure stood still, their gaze fixed on the shadows that seemed to writhe with unseen life. A chilling breeze whispered through the ruins, carrying the faintest hint of something ancient and restless. The distant echo of a low, almost imperceptible growl sent a shiver through the air as if the ruins themselves held their breath in anticipation. The power they sought was tantalizingly close, and soon, it would be theirs to command.

Above the darkened skies of Fel Thalor, ominous clouds swirled in restless patterns. From the depths of the shadows, the summoned figure approached the ruins, his steps heavy with reluctance. Memories of past servitude weighed on him, a constant reminder that no amount of time had freed him from this tether. He could still hear his father's voice, the desperate pleas that had sealed their fate, offering their family's service in exchange for power he could never truly control. The echoes of that betrayal clung to him, a ghost of chains he had never been able to break. No matter how far he ran or how many years had passed, the weight of his father's desperate choice still dictated his path. Every command, every reluctant step forward, reminded him that his fate had been decided long before he had a say. And yet, deep within him, resentment burned a quiet, smoldering ember that refused to die, waiting for the moment he might finally reclaim his destiny. Each step felt like a betrayal of the freedom he thought he had won. The jagged edge of the city's remains loomed ahead, cutting into the mist like broken shards of memory. He paused just outside the shadowed gateway, his fists clenched and his breath uneven, as if steeling himself for the confrontation.

"Why now?" he muttered, his anger boiling beneath the surface. He knew the call could not be ignored, yet every fiber of his being screamed to turn back. With a resigned growl, he stepped into the ruins.

The mysterious person stood in the center of the decayed courtyard, their form draped in shadows that seemed to move with a life of their own. A chilling wind whispered through the ruins, carrying the faint scent of damp stone and decay as if the very air recoiled from their presence. Their presence was as commanding as it was oppressive.

The man approached, his defiance evident in his every movement. His jaw tightened, and his fists clenched at his sides, the tension in his body a silent refusal to submit. Every step forward carried the weight of his resentment, but he refused to falter. "What do you want?" he demanded, his voice echoing through the ruins. "Can you not just leave me alone? I left Flameford and all the darkness years ago, so leave me alone!"

The mysterious person tilted their head slightly, their expression unreadable beneath the shadowy veil. A slow, deliberate shift in their posture hinted at amusement, though their presence exuded an unsettling menace. When they finally spoke, their voice was deceptively smooth, laced with an undercurrent of quiet authority that made the air feel colder. "You are still under obligation to me," they said coldly. "And you will do as I command. I want reports from you regarding the noble dragons."

The man's eyes burned with fury as he shook his head. "No. I do not serve you. I will not do as you command."

For a moment, silence reigned, the tension between them crackling like a storm on the verge of breaking. Then, the mysterious person raised a hand, their fingers curling as tendrils of dark magic coiled and twisted through the air like living shadows. The energy crackled with an eerie hum, distorting the space around it as it surged forward. A blast of cold radiated outward, withering the moss beneath their feet and leaving a faint, acrid scent of burning air before slamming into the man with bone-rattling force. The blast hit the man like a hammer, slamming him to his knees. His breath caught in his throat, and the air ripped from his lungs as an icy force constricted around him.

"You forget yourself," the mysterious person hissed, their tone laced with venom. The words struck like a physical blow, the man's chest constricting as the air turned ice-cold. A searing pain coursed through his veins as if the magic were clawing at his very soul, leaving him gasping and trembling under its crushing weight. "You are mine, bound by the choices you made long ago. Do not test me again."

The man writhed on the ground, his strength waning under the oppressive weight of the magic. Fire lanced through his veins, each pulse of pain searing like molten iron. His breath came in ragged gasps, the sensation of drowning in darkness tightening around him like unseen chains. Every nerve screamed in protest, yet deep within, a spark of defiance still flickered, refusing to be extinguished. His defiance dimmed but did not disappear entirely, his gaze still holding a flicker of rebellion even as his body betrayed him. The pain threatened to consume him, but a memory surfaced of his mother's whispered words on the night his father sealed their fate. "You are more than the chains placed upon you." That truth, buried beneath years of servitude, burned within him now, refusing to be extinguished. Within him, a war raged, the crushing weight of submission against the burning fire of resistance. Every muscle screamed in surrender, yet his mind clung desperately to the fragments of his will, refusing to let go of the man he once was.

The mysterious person lowered their hand, the magic dissipating but leaving its mark. "You will deliver what I ask," they said, their voice like ice. "Or I will remind you of the price of failure."

With that, they turned and disappeared into the shadows, leaving the man alone in the desolate ruins. His breaths came in uneven gasps, his body aching from the lingering pain, but his spirit clung stubbornly to defiance. He pressed a trembling hand to the cold stone beneath him, grounding himself, unwilling to let the darkness consume him entirely. Though his resolve had been shaken, it had not broken, and he would not break.

As the shadowy form of the mysterious person vanished into the ruins, the man remained on his knees, his body trembling from the force of the magic and the weight of his despair. The silence that followed was deafening, broken only by his shallow, labored breaths.

He shook his head, his voice a whisper that barely escaped his lips. "I thought all the remnants of the past were gone, especially since Phoenix was killed," he murmured, bitterness lacing his tone. "My father's pledge to Maelgrim Shadowwalker should have ended with Phoenix's death."

Pushing himself to his feet, he cast one last glance at the crumbling spires of Fel Thalor. The ancient city felt like a cage, its jagged ruins encircling him like prison bars, closing in with every breath. The wind howled through the empty streets, its mournful wail echoing off the shattered stone. Beneath his boots, debris crunched with every reluctant step; each sound was a reminder that there was no true escape from this place or his past. Each jagged edge mirrored the shards of guilt and regret in his heart, a constant reminder of the choices that had chained him to this path. The memory of his father kneeling before Maelgrim Shadowwalker, pledging their family's servitude in exchange for power, haunted him. He had been just a boy, watching helplessly as if his fate was sealed with words he had no say in. Even now, the weight of that moment pressed against his soul, shackling him to a destiny he had never chosen. It coiled around him like an iron chain, each link forged from the choices of others, tightening with every reluctant step forward. No matter how much time had passed, the echoes of his father's decisions still dictated his path, a suffocating force that left no room for escape. Even the mist seemed to close in, a suffocating shroud that whispered of no escape. His heart grew heavier with each step he took away from the ruins. The path before him felt darker than ever, the chains of his past pulling tighter with every moment.

He knew the truth all too well. Just when he had begun to feel like he belonged in Crystal Vale among his friends and the new bonds he had just started to form, this shadow from his past resurfaced, tearing away any illusion of freedom. Once they discovered what he was going to do, what he had to do—they would never trust him again. Worse, they might even demand his death for the betrayal he could no longer avoid. But despite the crushing weight of that knowledge, he could not see a way out.

There was no turning back now. Not for him. His jaw tightened, and he clenched his fists as if bracing himself for the inevitable. A flicker of doubt surfaced. This was not a path he had chosen but one forced upon him by the decisions of others. The chains of his past had never been his to forge, yet they bound him all the same. A bitter ache settled in his chest at the realization, a silent war waging between resentment and resignation. He had never asked for this fate, never wanted the weight of choices made long before he could fight against them. And yet, the shackles held firm, tightening with each reluctant step forward. He crushed the thought beneath the weight of his resolve, forcing himself to accept what could not be undone. This path was his, and he would walk it to the end no matter the cost.

With a resolute expression, he turned his thoughts to those who trusted him, who would never know the burden he carried until it was too late. He would continue forward for their sake, even as the shadow of his past loomed more significant than ever. No matter the cost, he would see this through. And when the time came, he would face the consequences, even if it meant standing alone.

Chapter 15
Plans in the Dark

The Tower of Shadowwalker exuded an oppressive stillness. The air seemed to hold its breath as the mysterious figure strode through its shadowed halls. A faintly metallic tang lingered as if the stone had bled over centuries. A rhythmic creaking echoed distantly, like ancient beams groaning under unseen strain. Each step reverberated before being swallowed by the suffocating silence of the dark fortress, the sound dissipating as if absorbed by the very walls. Shadows shifted and coiled, their indistinct forms murmuring in hushed tones—a spectral chorus of forgotten voices, tendrils of darkness stretching and recoiling as if reaching for something unseen.

Qellaun and Lyra waited in the central chamber, their stiff postures betraying their unease. The silence pressed against them, thick and suffocating, until the measured click broke it of boots against stone, each step a deliberate intrusion that sent an eerie ripple through the still air. The figure's gaze swept over the two like the edge of a cold blade, piercing through any pretense with merciless precision.

"What have you to report?" The voice was sharp and unyielding, leaving no room for hesitation.

Qellaun inclined his head slightly, his tone carefully measured. "Xalzorath and Nocturna have returned from their surveillance around Crystal Vale. They await your presence in the Cavern of Ash."

The figure paused, their expression unreadable beneath the shadows of their hood. With a curt nod, they turned toward the shadowed corridors. "I will go to them."

Neither Qellaun nor Lyra dared to speak as the figure disappeared into the darkness. The tension in their wake clung to the chamber like a phantom, coiling in the stiff set of Qellaun's shoulders and the tight clasp of Lyra's hands. The air felt weighted, pressing against them like an unspoken command to remain silent.

The cavern was vast, and its jagged walls streaked with veins of shimmering obsidian that caught the dim, flickering light from volcanic fissures below. Heat pulsed through the chamber, carried by faint tremors beneath the earth. Xalzorath and Nocturna, the ancient Black and Obsidian Dragons, rested on the uneven stone floor, their immense forms barely contained by the cavern's space.

Xalzorath's dark scales absorbed the surrounding glow, their surface drinking in every flicker of light like a black hole consuming the remnants of a dying star. His abyssal eyes, devoid of reflection, fixed on the figure with unsettling intensity. Nocturna's iridescent obsidian scales gleamed, her angular features radiating lethal elegance. Her tail twitched, a subtle hint of restrained energy, while Xalzorath's claws flexed against the stone, a quiet display of latent power.

The mysterious figure entered without hesitation, though their grip tightened slightly at their sides. A slow exhale steadied their breath as they stepped forward, masking the flicker of tension that threatened to rise. Undaunted by the dragons' sheer presence, they moved with practiced resolve. The heat from the volcanic fissures prickled against their skin, but they showed no sign of discomfort, their movements fluid and deliberate. Their voice, calm and commanding, cut through the charged air. "You have something to report."

Xalzorath's growl rumbled low, reverberating through the cavern like distant thunder. "As commanded, we circled Crystal Vale and Emeraldwoods. The noble dragons are united. Aurelia and Verdantia stand vigilant."

Nocturna's voice was smooth yet sharp, laced with quiet satisfaction as if relishing the disruption she had caused. Her lips curled into a faint smirk, her tail flicking lazily against the stone, a silent reminder that she enjoyed playing with her prey before striking. "They warned us to leave, but not before they saw us. We made certain of that."

The figure remained silent, prompting Nocturna to continue. A sly smile curved her lips. "We interrupted something, possibly a dinner. The commotion we caused was... unexpected."

The mysterious figure's shadowy presence betrayed no reaction, yet a faint shift in their stance hinted at an unspoken thought, weighing the potential outcomes of their disruption—how deeply the noble dragons' unity had been shaken and what their next move might be. "Interesting," they said after a pause. "Even better to keep them unsettled."

Nocturna tilted her head slightly, her tail flicking again. "If unsettling them was your goal, we succeeded. They were far from pleased."

"Good," the figure replied, their tone cold and measured. "For now, their awareness will suffice. The time for direct action is not yet upon us."

Nocturna's eyes narrowed slightly, her tone shifting as curiosity gave way to a quiet challenge. "Surveillance alone will not bring the noble dragons to their knees. What is your plan?"

The figure stepped closer, their shadow stretching ominously across the cavern floor. "You doubt me, Nocturna?" Their voice, though calm, carried a chilling weight. "Patience. The time for action will come. For now, you will continue to obey."

Nocturna met the figure's gaze for a moment before lowering her head, though the tension in her body betrayed her frustration. Her claws flexed slightly against the stone, a silent display of the restrained defiance simmering beneath her submission. The air around her seemed to pulse with unspoken words, but she held them back, knowing the time to challenge would come. Xalzorath's low rumble of agreement echoed in the silence as the figure turned and disappeared back into the shadowed tunnels.

After leaving the Cavern of Ash, Xalzorath and Nocturna descended through Flameford's volcanic terrain, their wings stirring up heat waves as they maneuvered skillfully through the rugged landscape. The acrid scent of sulfur thickened with every beat of their wings, and the molten rivers below cast an eerie glow upon their scales. The oppressive heat did not trouble them, but the air shimmered with intensity, distorting the jagged rocks that lined their path. The thick air carried the acrid scent of sulfur, and the distant glow of molten lava painted the cavern walls in shades of red and orange. Their destination was a secondary cavern, where Zylron and Glaciera waited.

Zylron's crimson eyes narrowed as the pair approached. His claws scraped idle patterns into the stone. "What brings you here?" he rumbled, his voice heavy with suspicion.

Nocturna's tone was calm but firm. "We wish to ask again: what do you truly know of the mysterious person?"

Zylron growled low, his tail flicking in irritation. "Very little. Their power is immense, unlike anything we have encountered. It is as if they command the shadows themselves."

Glaciera, her white scales gleaming faintly in the dim light, spoke up, her voice cautious. "Have you felt anything else? Some other ancient power in Flameford?"

Nocturna's head tilted slightly, her sharp eyes narrowing. "Perhaps a faint presence," she admitted. "Why?"

Zylron's expression darkened, his brow furrowing as his jaw tightened, a flicker of unease passing through his crimson eyes. "After the battle with Kimras and Amara, something ancient stirred. We do not know what it is, but its presence lingers."

The silence that followed was thick with unspoken uncertainty, pressing against them like the weight of an impending storm. Glaciera's claws twitched involuntarily against the stone, a subtle betrayal of the unease coiling within her. The faint tremor of the volcanic terrain beneath them seemed almost alive, as though the land itself anticipated something monumental, something ancient stirring beneath the surface, waiting for the right moment to awaken and shift the balance of power. The dragons exchanged uneasy glances, their thoughts heavy with implications of an ancient power waiting to reawaken, a force that could tip the balance of the coming conflict.

The mysterious figure re-entered the central chamber of the Tower of Shadowwalker. Lyra looked up from her work, her fingers tracing faded runes etched into a weathered scroll. The tension in the air thickened as the figure approached her.

"What progress have you made?" they demanded, their voice sharp yet measured.

Lyra's gaze flickered over the scroll. She hesitated, her fingers pausing over the ancient runes before speaking. "Not much more has been revealed. However, these scrolls seem to carry a particular resentment toward Kimras."

The figure's shadowed face remained impassive, but their voice sharpened with sudden anger. "What did you expect? Kimras ruined Vuarus' plans. Of course, there would be resentment."

Lyra flinched at the harshness of the words, her eyes widening in shock. A flicker of doubt crept into her mind. Why had the figure reacted so strongly? Was there more to this connection than she understood? A strange sensation stirred within her, an inexplicable pull as if the figure's reaction resonated with something profound in her mind. Was there a connection between them and Vuarus that she had yet to uncover? She lowered her gaze to her work, her fingers trembling slightly as she resumed tracing the faded runes, the unease lingering in her thoughts.

Lyra tilted her head slightly but said nothing, returning to her work. The figure turned, shifting their attention to Qellaun, who stood at attention by the entrance.

"Qellaun," the figure said, their voice like a blade. "I have a task for you."

Qellaun stepped forward, his expression rigid. "Yes, my lord."

"Find out what was happening in Crystal Vale the night Nocturna and Xalzorath were there. Nocturna believes it was a dinner. I want confirmation."

Qellaun hesitated, a flicker of unease crossing his features. The task's weight bore down on him, not just the mission itself but also the fear of failure and the consequences that would follow. "As you command."

"And Qellaun," the figure added, their voice dropping to a dangerous whisper, "you are not to be seen. If you are discovered, you will face consequences."

Qellaun's bow was profound, though his discomfort was evident. "Understood."

As he departed, the figure turned back to the shadows. A slow, sinister smile spread across their lips, satisfaction gleaming in their hidden eyes as the final pieces of their plan fell into place. Soon, whispers of unrest would reach the noble dragons, forcing them to act, and when they did, the trap would spring, sealing their fate. Soon, the noble dragons would be drawn into a conflict they could not escape, and when the moment was right, the ancient force beneath Flameford would rise to seal their fate. Every move tightened the noose around their unsuspecting foes, and the power stirring beneath Flameford would soon be theirs to wield.

Chapter 16
The Moon Elves Arrival

The soft glow of moonlight bathed the landscape as Thalorian led the caravan of Moon Elves into Vacari. A quiet sense of duty weighed on him, mingling with cautious hope. He had spent years dreaming of this moment—the chance to offer his people a home, a sanctuary away from the shadows that had chased them. Yet, uncertainty lingered beneath his resolve, whispering doubts about the dangers ahead. Their movements were slow with fatigue, yet their eyes shone with anticipation, reflecting exhaustion and the quiet hope of a new beginning.

The Shimmering Beach lay ahead, its crystalline waters reflecting the starlit sky like a sea of silver and blue. A faint, salty breeze carried whispers of the ocean, mingling with the soft rustle of their footsteps. The Moon Elves, weary from their journey, gazed around with wide eyes, murmuring in awe at the beauty of this new realm.

"Vacari is... enchanting," one of the younger elves murmured, her voice trembling with wonder. "It feels as if the land itself breathes magic."

Thalorian's faint smile softened his jade-fire eyes, the moonlight catching in their depths as he scanned the horizon. "Vacari thrives on resilience. Its beauty reflects the strength of its people and the harmony of its magic."

As the group neared the resting grounds of the Shimmering Beach, a ripple of excitement moved through them. A noble bronze dragon soared overhead, its wings catching the celestial glow as it sliced effortlessly through the night sky. The dragon's shadow briefly blanketed the group, casting a fleeting chill over them despite the warm night air. Some elves instinctively tensed, a primal awareness stirring in their chests, while others remained enraptured, their awe tinged with reverence and unease. The moment passed as quickly as it arrived, leaving a lingering hush of wonder and caution.

"Look!" one of the elves exclaimed, pointing upward. "A noble dragon!"

The others craned their necks, their voices mixing admiration and disbelief. Thalorian paused, his gaze following the dragon's flight. A faint smile touched his lips, but his tone grew serious as he turned back to the group.

"Yes, that is a noble dragon," he said, calm but firm. "But remember, Vacari is not only home to such magnificence. Dark dragons roam these skies as well. Unlike their noble kin, these creatures are wreathed in shadow, their obsidian, crimson, and ivory scales absorbing the moonlight rather than reflecting it. Their piercing crimson eyes hold no warmth—only the hunger of an ancient malice that has long lurked in Vacari's depths."

The awe in their expressions dimmed, replaced by quiet determination. A silent understanding passed between them, their gazes meeting in shared resolve. One of the elder elves clenched his fist, murmuring under his breath, "We will not fail this land." Another adjusted the crystal bow at her back, her fingers tightening around its smooth surface, drawing strength from the weight of their purpose.

Thalorian continued, his voice steady. "That is why I brought you here. The crystal and emerald bows you crafted will aid Vacari's people in their fight. And your presence, your strength, will help preserve this land's magic."

The Moon Elves nodded, their resolve evident as they followed Thalorian into the Shimmering Beach. The water's edge glowed faintly with bioluminescent light. Their earlier exhaustion seemed to fade as they set up a temporary camp, their movements efficient and silent.

Thalorian stood at the edge of the camp, his gaze lingering on the bronze dragon as it disappeared into the distance. A flicker of hope stirred within him, but a gnawing unease swiftly shadowed it. The dragon's presence was a beacon of resilience and a harbinger of the battles yet to come. The forces rallying for Vacari's defense would be tested, and so would they. Even the noble dragons, with all their strength, could not halt the encroaching storm alone.

The gentle waves lapping against the shore provided a soothing backdrop as the Moon Elves worked. The cool sand was soft beneath their feet, and the salty tang of the ocean filled the air. Bioluminescent light shimmered like scattered stardust across the surface, casting an otherworldly glow on their faces.

Suddenly, one of the elves pointed toward the water, her voice filled with awe. "Look there!"

Two figures emerged from beneath the rippling waves, their forms sleek and radiant. With shimmering scales that caught the moonlight in hues of silver and sapphire, Merfolk swam closer. Their melodic laughter echoed softly as they observed the newcomers with curious eyes.

The Moon Elves hesitated, letting out quiet gasps as they took in the sight—this was the first time they had ever encountered merfolk. Unsure if their greetings would be welcomed, they offered respectful bows. "Greetings," one of them said, their voice laced with wonder.

The merfolk responded with fluid gestures, their movements graceful and welcoming, conveying an unspoken invitation to the newcomers. A playful silver-blue dolphin darted between them, its sleek body gliding effortlessly through the water like a blade of moonlight, leaving a faint trail of ripples in its wake. The scene was enchanting, a living testament to the magic that thrived in Vacari.

Thalorian stood slightly apart from the group, his lips curling into a faint, mischievous smile as he recalled Valeon's failed attempt to summon the merfolk upon their first arrival. This would be something to tease him about later. "I'll have to make a note to tell Valeon about this," he murmured. "He'd be insufferable knowing he missed out on seeing merfolk."

The Moon Elves watched the merfolk and dolphins for a while longer, their earlier weariness forgotten in the face of such beauty. The merfolk swam in gentle circles, their movements synchronized as though performing a silent dance for their enchanted audience.

After some time, Thalorian's voice broke through the reverie. "We must continue to Crystal Vale," he said gently but firmly. "There's still much to prepare."

The Moon Elves exchanged reluctant glances, their sighs quiet but heavy. The enchantment of the merfolk still lingered—the mesmerizing fluidity of their movements, the soft melody of their laughter, and the tangible hum of magic in the air—an unspoken bond formed in a fleeting moment. Yet, the weight of their journey and the responsibility ahead tempered their longing. Their purpose lay beyond the shore.

Gathering their belongings, they offered final waves to the merfolk, who responded with fluid bows before disappearing beneath the waves. The dolphins leaped playfully into the air one last time before following suit, leaving the shore quiet once more.

Thalorian and his companions set forth again; their spirits lifted, and their resolve strengthened. Yet, as they ventured inland, the air grew heavier, charged with the foreboding sense of a world bracing for war. The magic of the Shimmering Beach had been a fleeting reprieve, but it could not shield them from the darkness ahead—the looming threat of the dark dragons.

As Thalorian and the Moon Elves stepped into the Emeraldwoods, a collective sigh of admiration escaped them. The forest felt alive, its towering ancient oaks and silver-barked elms swaying gently as if acknowledging their arrival. Some of the Moon Elves reached out to brush their fingers against the rough bark, marveling at the energy thrumming beneath their touch. Others inhaled deeply, allowing the rich scent of earth and blooming orchids to fill their senses as if drawing the very essence of the land into their souls.

The foliage shimmered in hues of emerald and jade, dappling the mossy floor with shifting patterns of light and shadow. Shafts of sunlight pierced through the canopy, illuminating the forest in a golden-green glow. The air carried the crisp fragrance of wildflowers and damp moss, mingling with the soft rustle of leaves whispering secrets in the breeze. In the distance, the gentle murmur of a meandering stream added to the enchantment, its crystalline waters weaving a melody harmonizing with the pulse of the living forest.

"This is extraordinary," one of the Moon Elves murmured, their voice laced with awe. "It feels as though the forest itself breathes magic."

The group moved deeper into the woods, their steps light and reverent. Soon, they came upon an enclave at the heart of the forest, where small streams crisscrossed the land, mirrored surfaces reflecting the vibrant green canopy above. Sculptures of dragons, intricately crafted from blooming flowers and woven shrubs, adorned the space. These magnificent creations were the work of the fairies of the Emeraldwoods, who not only sculpted them but nurtured their growth, ensuring they flourished with vibrant beauty. Each dragon bore an ethereal grace, their forms so lifelike it seemed they might stir at any moment and take flight.

One of the elves halted, their gaze fixed on an enormous dragon sculpture, its head lifted as if gazing at the sky. The craftsmanship was exquisite—each scale and ridge was meticulously shaped to capture the dragon's majesty. Beyond its artistry, the sculpture carried a deep symbolic weight, a tribute to the noble dragons who once safeguarded this land. A wave of reverence washed over them mingled with an unspoken nostalgia. The sight stirred something profound within—an echo of ancient stories passed down through generations, tales of noble dragons who had stood as guardians and allies in times of peace and war.

"It seems the noble dragons are deeply respected here," the elf said softly.

Thalorian nodded, his expression contemplative. "The people of Vacari understand the balance the noble dragons bring through their wisdom and magic. Their reverence is well-earned."

They lingered for a moment longer, absorbing the tranquil beauty of the enclave, before continuing their journey toward Crystal Vale.

As they approached the gates of Crystal Vale, the Moon Elves halted, their eyes widening in awe. The city's entrance was a masterpiece of craftsmanship, its towering crystal gates shimmering in the sunlight like a beacon of purity and strength. Cascading waterfalls framed the town like a protective veil, tumbling down from the hills and mountains surrounding Crystal Vale. Their waters were more than mere beauty; they provided a vital source of life, feeding the lush gardens and energizing the city through enchanted channels. Beyond their practicality, the falls symbolize purity and renewal, and their ceaseless flow is a reminder of Crystal Vale's resilience against time and turmoil. Their flowing waters blended nature's grandeur with the artisans' brilliance. The thundering roar of the falls filled the air, creating a harmonious symphony.

"This..." one of the elves began, their voice faltering. "This is beyond anything I've ever seen."

Thalorian smiled faintly, his admiration evident despite having seen the city before. Crystal Vale's beauty was unlike any other, a perfect harmony between civilization and nature. Built around the land rather than over it, the city's design ensured that no tree was uprooted, no river redirected—every stone and crystal woven seamlessly into the untouched wilderness. "Crystal Vale is a testament to the resilience and artistry of its people."

The group moved forward, their initial awe giving way to quiet appreciation as they passed through the gates and into the city. The sound of the waterfalls accompanied them, a constant reminder of the natural beauty that blended seamlessly with the city's crystalline splendor.

The Moon Elves were unprepared for the reception that awaited them inside Crystal Vale. As they walked through the city's sparkling streets, the citizens stopped to greet them with warm smiles and kind gestures. Vendors offered samples of their wares, children peeked curiously from behind their parents, and passersby nodded respectfully.

One vendor, a cheerful woman with warm brown eyes and a weathered face, approached the group with a welcoming smile. Her hands, calloused from years of work, cradled a fruit basket as she extended it toward them. "Please, take these," she said, offering glistening crystal berries. "Welcome to Crystal Vale."

The Moon Elves accepted the snacks with polite bows, their surprise evident in their wide eyes and hesitant movements. Some exchanged glances, their fingers tightening around the delicate berries as if unsure whether to believe in such kindness. A few brought the fruit to their lips with tentative curiosity, their expressions softening as the crisp sweetness burst upon their tongues, the unexpected warmth of the welcome settling over them like a gentle embrace. The berries burst with an incredible, crisp sweetness upon their tongues, a delicate balance of honeyed nectar and a faint citrus tang that left a refreshing aftertaste. As they moved further into the city, one of the elves leaned close to Thalorian and whispered, "I did not expect such a welcome. Even in Etharyon, we are not always greeted kindly in some cities."

Thalorian's jade fire eyes glinted with appreciation. He admired how the Eladrin presence in Vacari had paved the way for greater acceptance of all elves, making their arrival here smoother than it might have been elsewhere. "Crystal Vale has always been a land of inclusion. They welcome even elves. But," he added thoughtfully, "the presence of the Eladrin in Vacari makes things easier for most elves. All except for one group."

The elf tilted their head, curious. "The Druchii?"

Thalorian nodded solemnly, his tone quiet but firm. A flicker of memory surfaced—old tales of betrayal and bloodshed, the weight of history pressing on his thoughts. He exhaled slowly, steadying himself before continuing. "Yes. The Druchii are an exception and with good reason. Their actions in ages past earned them a reputation that even the open-hearted citizens of Crystal Vale cannot forget."

The group fell silent, reflecting on his words as they continued through the city. They knew of the Druchii, the darkness they carried, and the weight of their past betrayals woven into stories whispered through generations. The memory of their treachery lingered a cautionary tale that reminded them of the shadows that could still linger even in a place as radiant as Crystal Vale.

Their path led them to another enclave adorned with statues of crystal dragons. The Moon Elves slowed their pace, their eyes widening with admiration and reverence. Some reached out tentatively, tracing the cool, smooth surface of the crystal with their fingertips as if hoping to feel the essence of the noble beings these statues represented. Others exchanged knowing glances, recalling tales of ancient alliances between their kind and the noble dragons. The sight reassured them, a silent promise that they were in a land that understood the balance between magic and guardianship.

The statues glowed faintly, their translucent surfaces catching the sunlight and refracting it into rainbows that danced across the enclave. These crystal dragons were not merely ornamental; they were the protectors of Crystal Vale, imbued with ancient enchantments that allowed them to sense disturbances in the land. Centuries ago, when Crystal Vale fell under attack, these guardians stirred from their slumber, their radiant forms coming to life to shield the city from destruction. Their magic, woven into the very essence of the land, had preserved the city through times of peril. Their watchful presence was a reminder of the city's guardians, standing ready to awaken and defend the realm should darkness rise again. After the Battle of Vacari, they played a crucial role in rebuilding the city, ensuring its resilience and prosperity. The Moon Elves paused to admire the craftsmanship, their earlier awe rekindled.

Thalorian turned to the group, his voice steady, though anticipation stirred within him. "You can wait here. This is as good a place as any for you to rest. I will go to the palace and speak with Prince Gailen and King Manard."

The Moon Elves nodded in agreement, their gazes still drawn to the intricate statues. Thalorian gave a faint smile before striding toward the palace, his steps purposeful as the city's crystalline splendor guided his way.

When Thalorian arrived at the palace, the guards greeted him with respectful nods and quickly ushered him into the grand hall. King Manard rose from his seat as Thalorian entered, his expression a mix of curiosity and anticipation. Beside him stood his son Gailen, his features calm and thoughtful, and Valeon, who leaned casually against a pillar, his eyes lighting up with interest at the sight of Thalorian. Memories of past battles and shared victories surfaced in his mind, fighting side by side in defense of Etharyon and cutting through enemy ranks with a rhythm only years of camaraderie could forge. He recalled Valeon's laughter echoing amidst the chaos, always finding humor even in the direst moments. Their camaraderie was built on trust and the thrill of combat. A knowing smirk played at his lips as if already formulating a quip or recalling some past jest between them. Their past camaraderie, forged in earlier skirmishes, was evident in his easy grin and gaze's faint sparkle of mischief.

"Thalorian," King Manard said, his voice warm. "It is good to see you returned safely. What news do you bring?"

Thalorian inclined his head. "The Moon Elves have arrived, Your Majesty. They come as allies and bearing gifts—emerald and crystal bows of exquisite craftsmanship. Their presence here signifies their commitment to Vacari's defense."

King Manard's brows rose in surprise and admiration. He paused, fingers resting lightly on the armrest of his throne, as he absorbed Thalorian's words. "The Moon Elves themselves? And they bring such gifts? This is unexpected. Their history of seclusion made such an offering unthinkable until now."

"I thought it best to bring you to them directly," Thalorian said faintly. "Their work deserves your thanks."

Gailen nodded approvingly. "It is no small thing to convince the Moon Elves to journey beyond their borders. This is a boon indeed."

Thalorian smirked slightly before glancing at Valeon. "You'll be disappointed to know you missed quite the sight. We encountered merfolk at the Shimmering Beach."

Valeon's eyes widened before his expression twisted into a dramatic pout, his shoulders slumping as he let out an exaggerated sigh. He crossed his arms, tapping his fingers against his sleeve as if physically restraining himself from launching into a tirade. "You're joking. Merfolk? And I wasn't there? That's just cruel, Thalorian."

Gailen chuckled, shaking his head. "We'll never hear the end of this."

King Manard laughed softly, and even the guards chuckled, some shaking their heads in quiet amusement. Thalorian's smirk grew. "I figured you'd take it hard."

Valeon let out a dramatic sigh before waving a hand. "Fine, fine. I suppose I will survive. But only because there are more pressing matters at hand."

Valeon straightened, his earlier nonchalance replaced with curiosity. "Well, let's not keep them waiting," he said, gesturing toward the door. "Lead the way, Thalorian."

Thalorian turned and led the King and his son through the city streets, attracting curious glances from passersby. As they neared the enclave, the sunlight refracting off the crystal bows created dazzling patterns, drawing the King's gaze even before they reached the Moon Elves.

When the group reached the enclave, the sight that greeted King Manard left him momentarily speechless. The Moon Elves stood in quiet clusters, their silver hair catching the light as they exchanged hushed words and knowing glances. Some rested their hands lightly on their bows, a silent gesture of reverence, while others observed the enclave with awe and quiet anticipation. The bows, crafted with breathtaking precision from emerald and crystal, were carefully laid out, their surfaces gleaming under the sunlight, casting dazzling patterns that shimmered across the ground.

King Manard approached the bows, his fingers lightly brushing one of them. The surface was calm and warm beneath his touch, an unusual contrast that sent a faint tingle through his fingertips. He could feel the magic humming within as if the bow were alive with purpose. The surface was calm and impossibly smooth, yet he could sense the delicate engravings etched into the crystal beneath his touch. The bow felt sturdy and refined, its weight balanced with precision, and it was a true masterpiece of craftsmanship. His expression was a mix of awe and gratitude. "Thalorian," he began, his voice almost reverent, "this craftsmanship... it is exquisite. I never expected so many Moon Elves to accompany you, let alone to offer such a gift."

Thalorian inclined his head slightly, his gaze steady, pride swelling. His people had come to the defense of Crystal Vale, standing alongside its citizens in a time of need. This was more than an alliance—a declaration that the Moon Elves would no longer remain in the shadows. "The Moon Elves understand the threat Vacari faces. I informed them of the dark dragons and their danger, and they chose to stand with us in this fight. They wished to aid in its defense. These bows are a symbol of their commitment."

The King looked at the Moon Elves and bowed his head deeply, his voice filled with sincerity. "You have my gratitude and the gratitude of all Vacari. Your generosity will not be forgotten."

The Moon Elves inclined their heads in unison, their quiet dignity speaking volumes. Thalorian observed them with a sense of pride and relief this alliance, fragile as it might have seemed at first, was now tangible. He knew the battles ahead would test them all, but in that moment, he felt a glimmer of hope solidify into certainty. The group began to move toward the palace, the weight of their shared purpose settling over them. Though the challenges ahead were daunting, their unity served as a beacon of hope. Yet, beneath that hope lurked the knowledge of the dark dragons' growing power and the uncertainty of alliances yet to be tested. Still, Thalorian dared to believe that this meeting was more than just a temporary pact. Perhaps it was the first step toward rekindling an alliance between their two kingdoms that could stand firm against the coming storm. He hoped that the mistakes of the past could finally be left behind, allowing their people to forge a future unburdened by old wounds.

Chapter 17
A Place to Begin

Golden light from the morning sun bathed Crystal Vale, glistening off its crystalline structures and casting an ethereal glow that made the city appear almost otherworldly. Reflections shimmered across the streets as the town awakened beneath the dawn's embrace. King Manard stood motionless atop the palace's tallest tower, holding a small scroll tied with an emerald-green ribbon. Beside him, an Etherwing perched, its iridescent feathers gleaming like liquid metal under the sunlight.

"You know where to go," the king murmured in his commanding and gentle voice. The Etherwing tilted its head, sharp eyes glinting with uncanny intelligence. With practiced hands, King Manard secured the scroll to its slender leg and leaned closer, whispering, "Fly swiftly to E'vahona."

The bird let out a quiet trill before spreading its luminous wings. With a mighty leap, it soared into the sky, a streak of light against the morning horizon. King Manard watched until it vanished, his expression serene. The Eladrin would answer as they always had—bound by honor and tradition. They were the foundation upon which alliances were built, unwavering in their word, steadfast as the stars. A faint smile touched his lips as he turned from the tower, anticipating their response.

"The Eladrin will answer," he murmured, his tone steady with quiet certainty. "They always do."

Miles away, Ong and Prince Gailen rode through the outskirts of Crystal Vale, the steady rhythm of their horses' hooves breaking the morning stillness. Their mission, simple in concept yet elusive in execution, was to find a secluded yet suitable location for training dragon riders.

"It needs to be hidden yet open enough for the dragons to take flight," Ong said, his brow furrowed. Their previous searches had led them to valleys too narrow, forests too dense, and rocky cliffs too treacherous. The dragons' weight, unpredictable landings and the need for secrecy made this task more difficult than he had anticipated. He exhaled sharply, scanning the landscape with renewed determination as the breeze ruffled his dark hair.

"Not to mention close enough to the city to avoid logistical nightmares," Gailen added, his piercing blue eyes sweeping over the rolling terrain.

Their path led them through a dense corridor of trees, sunlight breaking through the canopy in fractured beams. They paused as they emerged into a clearing, taking in the vast, open expanse. A small stream meandered through the center, its crystal waters glistening in the light. Above, the sky stretched endlessly, unobstructed and inviting.

"This could work," Ong said as he dismounted, his boots sinking slightly into the soft earth. He crouched by the stream, letting the cool water run through his fingers before inspecting it. "It's isolated enough, and the terrain seems manageable—solid enough for the dragons' weight, yet soft enough to absorb their landings."

Gailen dismounted with practiced ease, his gaze sharp with assessment. In his mind, he envisioned dragons soaring above and riders training below.

After a thoughtful moment, he nodded. "It is perfect. We will need to bring supplies and ensure the area is secure, but this will do."

Ong stood, brushing dust from his hands, his gaze lingering on the clearing with contemplative intensity. A quiet sense of responsibility settled over him. Crystal Vale had once been his home, where he had trained and lived until he married Keisha. Now, he had the chance to shape the next generation of dragon riders, ensuring the city remained strong and its defenders well-prepared. His jaw tightened slightly, the weight of their task settling deep within him. "I will send word to King Manard. Training can begin as soon as the riders are ready."

The two men exchanged a resolute nod before mounting their horses. As they turned toward Crystal Vale, an unspoken understanding passed between them—this place would shape the future of their people. It was a proving ground where legends would be forged. Behind them, the clearing remained still and untouched, waiting for the day it would awaken to the thunder of wings, the clash of steel, and the rise of warriors destined for greatness.

The Etherwing circled gracefully over E'vahona, its iridescent form glinting in the sunlight as it descended toward the grand terrace of Lord Karrenen's estate. The air here felt welcoming, infused with a quiet serenity that the Etherwing would undoubtedly love. This was where it could soar freely, its presence honored as part of the land's natural beauty. The estate, carved into the cliffside, gleamed with emerald accents, its terraces cascading toward a lush valley below.

Lord Karrenen, clad in flowing robes of deep emerald that mirrored the verdant hues of his homeland, approached the bird with quiet reverence. A sense of duty weighed upon him, a reminder of the countless times his ancestors had answered such calls—each one different, shaped by the needs of the time. Some had been calls to war, others to diplomacy, and others to safeguard the balance between magic and the mortal realm. He wondered, fleetingly, if this time would demand more than they could give.

The fabric billowed gently with each measured step, the embroidered patterns catching the light-like veins of living foliage. A flicker of anticipation crossed his face, his fingers tightening slightly at his sides. He had long expected this summons, yet the moment's gravity pressed heavily upon him. His people had always stood beside the dragons; now, their fate was again intertwined. The Etherwing extended its slender leg, the scroll tied with an emerald-green ribbon glinting in the sun.

With practiced hands, Karrenen untied the scroll and unrolled it, noting the emblem of Crystal Vale pressed into its seal. Each region in Vacari carried its distinct symbol, a mark of its sovereignty and legacy. His sharp eyes scanned its contents, and a faint smile curved his lips. "So, the noble dragons call for aid again," he murmured, his tone tinged with amusement and intrigue. His gaze drifted toward the horizon as he added, "And Keisha is already there. Of course she is," he mused. He had never expected that his daughter would always be involved in protecting Vacari, just as she always had been. How fitting. She and Ong remained in Crystal Vale after the dinner, staying behind when the dark dragons were spotted."

He turned to an attendant, handing them the scroll deliberately. His gaze lingered on it for a moment, considering the weight of the decision he had just made. No doubt the Eladrin would answer, but what consequences would their involvement bring? "Prepare a reply," he instructed, his voice steady and commanding. "Inform King Manard that we will send Eladrin, skilled in the bow, to assist in training. But remind him," Karrenen added with pride, "that he already has my daughter, Keisha, the finest archer in Vacari."

The attendant inclined their head, but Karrenen raised a hand, signaling he was not yet finished. "Also, inform him that we are sending mages. Magic on the ground and while riding a dragon are entirely different disciplines. Our mages will ensure the riders are prepared for both."

The attendant bowed and set off to draft the message. Once the response was prepared and tied to the Etherwing, Karrenen released the bird, its luminous wings catching the wind as it soared into the azure sky. He stood momentarily, watching it vanish, his thoughts lingering on a more profound concern. The dark dragons were a threat, but even more troubling was the unseen force pulling their strings. The question of who orchestrated their movements gnawed at him. With a steady breath, he turned to the gathered Eladrin behind him.

He called, his gaze sweeping over the assembled group with a quiet intensity. "You will travel to Crystal Vale. Your task is to train their people in using the bow and applying magic for battle grounded and airborne."

One of the archers, a tall figure with silver hair and eyes like molten steel, stepped forward, adjusting the bow strapped across their back with a measured, deliberate motion. "And the dragon saddles, my lord?"

"Bring them," Karrenen confirmed with a nod. "They are a gift to aid in the training."

The group bowed deeply before dispersing to prepare for their journey. Archers shouldered their intricately crafted bows, their quivers filled with arrows tipped in gleaming silver. Mages secured their spell books, charms, and enchanted artifacts, their movements deliberate and precise. A few attendants loaded the dragon saddles ornately carved and reinforced for comfort and durability—onto wagons. These saddles were not merely crafted; they bore the unique touch of the Eladrin elders, who infused them with their distinct magic, ensuring they adapted seamlessly to both rider and dragon, enhancing their bond in flight.

As the caravan began its journey, Karrenen stood on the terrace, his hands clasped behind his back, his fingers tightening slightly as if grasping an unseen weight. His jaw tensed, his gaze unwavering as he watched the departing figures. A slow breath escaped him, carrying the unspoken burden of responsibility that pressed heavily upon his shoulders. His thoughts lingered on the dark dragons, but the unseen force orchestrating their movements was the more significant concern, its influence woven into the shadows for too long. They had remained undetected for too long, weaving their influence from the shadows. But no secret remained hidden forever, and eventually, the mastermind behind this chaos would be revealed. He watched the line of wagons and riders vanish into the horizon, his unreadable expression betraying none of the thoughts weighing on him. "The balance must be preserved," he murmured, his gaze lingering on the fading caravan. The balance between dragons, magic, and the mortal realm had been threatened constantly at significant cost. This time, he hoped they would be enough. "May they succeed where others have faltered." Yet, his mind remained restless. Who was behind the dark dragons? Why were they targeting the noble ones? That answer could shift the course of the conflict or determine its end.

Chapter 18

Silent Threats

Golden light spilled over Crystal Vale as the sun crested the horizon, igniting the crystalline gates in a radiant shimmer. They reflected the vibrant green of the surrounding forests, creating an ethereal mirage. A caravan of Eladrin arrived, their presence unmistakable. Flowing garments of green and silver caught the breeze, intricate embroidery glinting beneath the sunlight. The colors, sacred to the Eladrin, symbolized harmony and resilience—green for their deep connection to nature and silver for the wisdom of their ancient lineage. The faint scent of ancient pine and jasmine lingered in their wake, stirring nostalgia in some, evoking memories of sacred groves and whispered songs beneath moonlit canopies. Their serene yet commanding aura turned heads as they passed, an almost ethereal whisper accompanying their measured steps. Atop their wagons, dragon saddles gleamed, each a masterpiece of unparalleled craftsmanship.

Prince Gailen stood poised and regal at the gates, awaiting their arrival. Beside him, Valeon leaned casually against a pillar, unusually quiet, his sharp gaze tracking the Eladrin's approach. Keisha was the first to step forward, her strides confident as she came to stand before Gailen.

"They've brought the dragon saddles," she said, pride and anticipation evident in her voice. "These are for the riders."

Before Gailen could respond, Thalorian stepped closer to the wagons, his moonlit jade eyes alight with curiosity. He stopped before one saddle, his fingers brushing the intricate designs etched into its surface. For a moment, his composed expression gave way to awe. "The craftsmansh ip... this is extraordinary," he murmured. "Each saddle is a work of art."

Prince Gailen nodded in agreement, his appreciation evident. "These will serve the riders well. Let us store them in the armory with the crystal and emerald bows until we can move to the training grounds."

The Eladrin bowed slightly, acknowledging the request with quiet grace. They turned and began their journey to the armory, carefully unloading the saddles and carrying them into the secure walls of the fortress.

Beyond the gates of Crystal Vale, in a secluded grove hidden by dense underbrush, a pair of sharp, calculating eyes watched the scene unfold. The faint rustle of leaves in the breeze masked his steady breaths, and the cool shade clung to his skin like a second layer, blending him into the darkness. Qellaun, the Druchii elf, stood motionless, his dark attire merging seamlessly with the shifting shadows. A faint breeze whispered through the underbrush, rustling the leaves like hushed voices conspiring in secrecy. His breath was slow and measured, barely disturbing the stillness, while his keen eyes flickered between the figures at the gate, assessing every detail with the precision of a predator lying in wait. His hand hovered near the hilt of his dagger, a silent gesture of readiness as his sharp ears tuned to every word exchanged at the gates.

His gaze lingered on Thalorian, noting the elf's silver hair and jade fire eyes. Yet, it was not just his features that held Qellaun's attention. There was an ease in Thalorian's stance, a certainty in how he observed the scene, which set him apart. Qellaun's frown deepened. Though the Druchii rarely concerned themselves with the affairs of other elven kin, something about this one unsettled him. A faint unease flickered in his silver eyes. "An elf," he murmured, "but not Eladrin... something else."

His attention shifted to Prince Gailen, whose commanding presence stood out even from a distance. Qellaun's lips pressed into a thin line as his gaze narrowed. "And who is this?" he wondered aloud, his tone laced with suspicion. "Another figure of importance in this wretched city."

Instinct urged patience. Any mistake would not go unnoticed—or forgiven. The mysterious figure who commanded his loyalty had little tolerance for failure. Though curiosity burned within him, Qellaun remained rooted to the spot, fingers tightening on the hilt of his dagger. Acting rashly would be unwise. For now, he would listen and observe, piecing together the shifting dynamics within Crystal Vale. The longer he watched, the more his mind wove potential schemes, silent calculations forming in the depths of his cunning gaze.

The enclave buzzed with quiet conversation, the usual formal divide between the Moon Elves and Eladrin dissolving as they exchanged ideas. They spoke of their homelands—the Moon Elves recalling the silver-lit glades of their forests, while the Eladrin shared memories of their emerald strongholds. Hope flickered in their words, a shared desire that their lands might be a guiding light for the unity of all realms. With them working together, unity would be easier to achieve. While there had never been hostility, years of separation had left their connection dulled, a rift formed after an attack in Etharyon during King Manard's visit for trade negotiations. The talks had died in the aftermath, leaving the relationship between their peoples strained. Now, their growing collaboration was all the more significant. Precision and discipline defined the Moon Elves, while the Eladrin's centuries-honed expertise with the longbow lent them an air of practiced grace. Both sides leaned closer, their discussions animated as they debated the best methods and locations for training.

The Moon Elves emphasized replicating the challenges of flight and movement, while the Eladrin advocated for open spaces, ideal for perfecting accuracy and range. Their contrasting perspectives gradually wove together, creating a shared vision.

Unnoticed at first, King Manard stood at the edge of the gathering, his arms crossed and expression contemplative. A faint furrow creased his brow as he observed the interplay keenly, his sharp gaze shifting from one speaker to the next, absorbing their points with quiet intensity. His sharp gaze shifted from one speaker to the next, absorbing their points before he finally stepped forward. His commanding presence brought the enclave to an immediate hush. Conversations faded, backs straightened, and a few instinctively shifted to stand at attention, their gazes locked onto the king with renewed focus.

"Pardon my interruption," he began, his tone thoughtful yet firm. "Why not train them in the same location as the dragon riders? It is secluded, open, and would provide the opportunity to combine bow training with learning to ride dragons."

The group exchanged glances, a wave of realization rippling through them. Nods of agreement followed, and an elder Eladrin, his silver hair shimmering under the sunlight, stepped forward. "That would be ideal, Your Majesty. Combining the two trainings would foster skill and unity among the riders."

A Moon Elf added, "It would also save time and resources. Training on the ground and adapting those techniques in the air could strengthen them quickly."

King Manard, ever the calm and composed leader, smiled, the consensus satisfying him. This was more than just a strategic decision; it was a step toward something more significant. Perhaps the realms would follow if the elves could unite for a shared purpose. The thought lingered, filling him with a cautious optimism. "Then it is settled. I will inform Prince Gailen and Ong to begin preparations."

He nodded once more before striding purposefully from the enclave, his determination evident in the sharp click of his boots against the stone streets. The unity between the elves only solidified his resolve as the plan took shape.

Within an hour, the preparations were complete, a testament to the efficiency and cooperation between the Eladrin and Moon Elves. Their seamless coordination ensured that every task was handled precisely, reinforcing their commitment to the training ahead. Wagons laden with dragon saddles, bows, and provisions assembled near the gates of Crystal Vale. A small contingent of soldiers and citizens had gathered, the buzz of anticipation filling the air as final checks were made. Soldiers inspected their weapons and adjusted their armor while attendants secured the dragon saddles and packed the provisions correctly. A group of Eladrin and Moon Elves exchanged final words, confirming their training schedules before departure.

A sudden ripple of surprise passed through the crowd as a sleek black panther padded into view. Pumpkin glided forward silently, her powerful muscles shifting fluidly beneath her obsidian fur. Pumpkin's emerald-green eyes glowed with an almost otherworldly intelligence, locking onto the gathered onlookers with a calm yet assessing gaze. Following closely behind Keisha and Ong, the panther's presence commanded immediate attention, her tail flicking once in mild amusement at the murmured reactions of the crowd. Sunlight played across her obsidian fur, accentuating the effortless grace in each measured step. Her emerald-green eyes glinted in the sunlight, and her every movement radiated quiet grace.

"What in the world is that?" someone murmured, their voice tinged with caution.

Ong chuckled, his tone warm, a knowing glint in his eyes as he crossed his arms casually. "This is Pumpkin, our companion. Do not worry. She will not harm anyone unless there is a threat."

Thalorian stepped forward, his curiosity evident. He stopped at a respectable distance, his jade fire eyes fixed on Pumpkin. Turning to Keisha, he gestured toward the panther. "May I?"

Keisha's lips curved into a faint smile. "Go ahead."

Thalorian extended his hand slowly, letting Pumpkin sniff at his fingers before she leaned into his palm. Pumpkin let out a contented purr as he stroked her sleek fur. "A magnificent creature," he murmured, admiration gleaming.

Gailen watched from a distance, his expression a mixture of hesitation and intrigue. Ong noticed and grinned. "Go on, Your Highness. She does not bite unless you are an enemy."

Encouraged, Gailen stepped closer, though uncertainty still lingered in his mind. He had never been this close to such a powerful creature, and a flicker of doubt nagged at him—was he truly accepted, or was Pumpkin merely tolerating him? Suppressing the lingering tension in his shoulders, he forced himself to move with steady intent, unwilling to show hesitation in front of the others. He could not help but wonder why Pumpkin seemed so at ease around him. Had she already decided he was no threat, or was there something more to her quiet acceptance? He had never been this close to a predator of such size, but Pumpkin's relaxed demeanor reassured him. Taking a steady breath, he extended his hand with cautious determination. With careful movements, he reached out and petted Pumpkin. She tilted her head slightly, her purr deepening as she basked in the attention. Keisha laughed, unable to hide her amusement.

"Alright," she said, her tone teasing. "She is enjoying this far too much. Let us get moving."

Pumpkin let out a low, playful growl, her tail swishing sharply as the attention stopped. She huffed dramatically, flopping onto the ground for a moment before bouncing back to her feet with a flick of her tail, her playful nature unmistakable. She gave Keisha a sidelong glare before padding along with a reluctant flick of her ears, her dignity intact but her displeasure clear.

The group chuckled at the panther's antics, shaking off their brief moment of levity. The warmth of the exchange eased some of their tension, momentarily shifting their focus from the daunting challenges ahead, learning to ride dragons while mastering magic and archery from their backs. For those who had never flown before, the task was intimidating. Yet, as they exchanged glances, the lingering smiles spoke of camaraderie and strengthened resolve. The journey ahead would test them, but for now, the shared laughter and Pumpkin's playful spirit reminded them that they were not alone.

Still, beneath the moment's warmth, unease lingered. The looming threat of the Dark Dragons weighed on their minds, and they could only hope their training would remain unnoticed. Their success would determine the fate of the land they loved, its safety resting in their hands. The dangers ahead had yet to reveal themselves fully. Smiles lingered as they glanced at one another, the camaraderie strengthening their resolve.

The group had just begun moving through the gates of Crystal Vale when a subtle movement caught Pumpkin's attention. Walking calmly at Keisha's side, the sleek panther suddenly froze. Her emerald eyes narrowed to dangerous slits, locking onto something unseen. A low, menacing growl rumbled from her throat, sending a ripple of unease through the group.

In the shadows beyond the gates, Qellaun had drawn his dagger, his crimson eyes locked on Prince Gailen. The title "Your Highness" had reached his ears, kindling a dark intent. Silently, he crept closer, his blade poised to strike.

Pumpkin's growl deepened, her muscles coiling like springs before she sprang forward. In one fluid motion, she planted herself between Gailen and the unseen threat, her teeth bared and tail lashing in warning.

The group halted abruptly, every gaze snapping toward the panther. Keisha's sharp eyes swept the shadows and found Qellaun, his dagger catching faint light.

Ong reacted instantly, pivoting to face the Druchii with measured precision. His hand rested on the hilt of his sword, and his voice rang out, calm but cutting. "Qellaun," he said, his tone sharp as steel, "you have one chance. Leave immediately and never return, or Pumpkin will happily tear your Druchii hide from your bones."

Qellaun hesitated, his silver eyes flickering between the growling panther and the formidable group before him. For a moment, his grip on the dagger tightened. Then, with a frustrated curse, he stepped back into the shadows. Failure weighed heavily on his shoulders as he retreated, frustration twisting in his chest. He feared both the shame of retreat and the consequences that awaited him for his failure. He had calculated every move, yet still, he had been exposed. The pity of retreat burned in his veins, but more than that, the consequences of failure loomed over him. What punishment awaited him for his incompetence? His mission had been clear, and he had failed. His grip tightened on his dagger as he disappeared into the shadows, mind racing with thoughts of how he might salvage what was left of his purpose. His silver eyes burned with unspoken defiance, but the cold tendrils of unease coiled around him. The thought of facing the mysterious person's wrath darkened his steps, a stark reminder that his failure here would not go unanswered.

Thalorian's jade fire eyes followed Qellaun's retreating figure, his hand brushing the hilt of his sword. "Should we?" he began, but Ong cut him off with a curt shake.

"Not now," Ong said quietly. "This isn't the time."

Pumpkin stood frozen in place, her emerald eyes fixed on Ong with a look that could only be described as offended disbelief. Her tail flicked sharply behind her, silently protesting that she had everything under control. She had been ready to chase the intruder off herself, and now Ong had taken away her moment of triumph. Her tail flicked sharply behind her, a silent statement that screamed, I was handling it. She stared at him for a long moment, her posture radiating annoyance.

Keisha smothered a smile, leaning slightly toward Ong. "I think you've made her mad," she whispered, her voice barely hiding her amusement.

Ong glanced at Pumpkin and sighed. "She'll get over it."

Pumpkin huffed, turning her back to Ong with exaggerated grace as though dismissing him entirely. Her tail swished dramatically as she returned to Keisha's side, her dignity fully intact but her mood unmistakable.

The group quickly regained its composure and continued through the gates, though wary glances and tense shoulders hinted at the lingering unease. Conversations remained hushed, their usual ease dampened by the unspoken warning left in Qellaun's wake.

As they reached the open fields of the training grounds, their focus shifted. The arrival of the crystal and emerald dragons loomed ahead, drawing their attention to the monumental task at hand. The brief but unsettling encounter with Qellaun faded into the background, overshadowed by preparations for what would come.

Once the group settled at the training grounds, Prince Gailen broke away and approached Pumpkin, who had returned to Keisha's side. The sleek panther turned her emerald eyes toward him as he knelt, his voice low and filled with sincerity. "Thank you, Pumpkin," he whispered, brushing his hand gently over her head.

Pumpkin responded with a soft chuff, her eyes closing briefly as she accepted his gratitude. Keisha's expression softened, and Ong gave a nod of approval. Even Thalorian's usually unreadable features reflected a glimmer of warmth. Her sleek, thick fur shifted like flowing silk warmed by the sun under Gailen's fingers. The quiet exchange rippled through the group, easing the lingering tension. Keisha's lips twitched into a knowing smile while Ong's approving nod remained steady. Thalorian, composed as ever, seemed momentarily touched by the panther's rare display of trust. With a flick of her tail, Pumpkin conveyed her message: You're welcome, but do not forget it.

From a distance, Thalorian watched with a faint smile tugging at his lips. He went to Keisha and Ong, jade fire eyes glinting with humor.

"The prince appreciates Pumpkin's protection," he said lightly, "but being stubborn, he decided to thank her instead of you."

Ong chuckled knowingly. "It is easier to thank Pumpkin than to express it to anyone else. But," he added with a mischievous grin, "you might not want to tease him too much. The Eladrin have a habit of adopting orphan wolves and panthers. It is tradition."

Thalorian laughed softly, shaking his head in mock exasperation. "Just what I need. I am already juggling enough between Prince Gailen, Kaelorn, and Valeon. The last thing I need is an animal companion demanding my attention."

Keisha joined their laughter, the tightness in her shoulders gradually unwinding as the lighthearted exchange washed over her. Seeing Gailen and Pumpkin connect filled her with quiet satisfaction. At first, her smile was hesitant, but as the warmth of camaraderie spread, she allowed herself to be drawn in. The tension echoes lingered for only a moment before giving way entirely to shared amusement, her laughter blending effortlessly with the others. A sense of relief settled over the group. Gailen was safe, and for now, that was enough.

The camaraderie lifted their spirits, anchoring them in unity as they prepared for the challenges ahead. Yet beneath their laughter, the weight of their mission pressed upon them. Training riders, forging alliances, and standing against the dark dragons each step brought them closer to an inevitable confrontation. The shadows of war loomed, and time was running short. Every lesson, every bond forged in these fields, could mean the difference between victory and devastation. Failure was not an option. The fate of their lands rested on their success, and the trials ahead would test their skills and the strength of the bonds they had begun to build.

Chapter 19

The Dragon's Choice

Morning light spilled over the training grounds, casting elongated shadows as the sun climbed higher. The air buzzed with focused energy, the rhythmic movements of archers and instructors shaping the day's lessons with precision. Its golden rays cast elongated shadows over the artfully arranged targets and the trampled grass beneath eager footsteps. The Eladrin and Moon Elves moved gracefully among the gathered individuals, offering calm, precise guidance. They adjusted postures, corrected grips, and demonstrated the art of the longbow with practiced ease. Thalorian and Kaelorn, steady and commanding presences, offered quiet encouragement, their words instilling confidence in even the most hesitant trainees.

The steady rhythm of arrows striking targets filled the air, punctuated by the twang of bowstrings and the dull thud of shafts sinking into the straw. The scent of freshly churned earth and sweat hung thick, mingling with the crisp tang of oiled wood and feathers. Instructors paced among the trainees, their steady voices offering corrections and encouragement while murmurs of determination rippled through the gathered warriors.

At the center of it all was Keisha. Her crimson hair caught the sunlight as she moved effortlessly between the archers. She nocked an arrow with fluid grace, her fingers gliding over the smooth shaft of the arrow. The bowstring pressed against her fingertips, taut with potential energy, as the tension coiled through her arm like a drawn breath waiting to be released. With a sharp twang of the bowstring, her arrow flew straight and true, embedding itself deep into the center of the target. The wooden frame shuddered from the impact, the fletching still quivering as the shaft stood firm against the force of her precision. Admiration rippled through the archers she was teaching as she turned to instruct, her calm voice carrying across the field like a steady breeze.

A short distance away, Ong and Prince Gailen observed the scene. Gailen's piercing blue eyes tracked Keisha's fluid motions, awe etched into his expression. He marveled at her seamless control, how each motion flowed into the next with the confidence of someone who had spent a lifetime mastering their craft. It was not just skill. Artistry, a perfect harmony of discipline and instinct, inspired and humbled him.

"She's incredible," he remarked, shaking his head in disbelief. "The precision, the ease… she makes it look effortless."

Ong laughed heartily, folding his arms across his chest, his expression filled with deep affection. "That is because she is one of the best, Your Highness. Keisha's skill with the longbow is unmatched, and her magic makes her even deadlier." He paused, pride gleaming in his dark blue eyes. "I wouldn't dream of comparing myself to her, not with a bow and certainly not with her gifts."

Gailen's lips twitched into a small smile. "You sound proud."

Ong nodded, his tone softening with a mixture of regret and love. Regret for the hardships she had endured, for the trials that had pushed her beyond reason. Yet love, deep and unwavering, for the strength she had forged from the ashes of her suffering. A memory surfaced of Keisha, broken and drained after her capture and torture at the hands of Phoenix and

Vuarus. They stripped her of her magic and skill, leaving her to claw back from nothing. But she had fought, relentless and unyielding, reclaiming her power piece by piece until she stood more potent than ever before. "Of course I am. Keisha's talent is rare, and her heart is even rarer. I am unsure what my life would be like if I had not met her. You would be wise to listen if she ever offers to teach you." He gestured toward her with a wry grin. "She's taught many a warrior humility on and off the battlefield."

Gailen chuckled but kept his gaze on Keisha, admiration deepening. "It's no wonder Vacari holds her in such high regard," he murmured.

Ong's eyes followed Keisha as she stopped to help a young archer adjust their stance. "She's earned it, bow by bow."

Then, a sudden hush fell over the training grounds as if the earth paused in awe. The distant sound of beating wings grew steadily louder, a deep, resonant hum vibrating through the air as shadows stretched across the field. The sheer majesty of the approaching dragons commanded every gaze, silencing even the most determined whispers.

Sunlight reflected off radiant green and shimmering crystal scales, heralding their arrival. Aurelia, the ancient Crystal Dragon, led the procession, her translucent body refracting light into dazzling rainbows. Beside her flew Verdantia, the Emerald Dragon, her deep green scales gleaming like polished jade. Smaller Crystal and Emerald dragons followed, their wings beating in perfect rhythm as they descended with graceful majesty.

Gasps of awe rippled through the trainees, even the elves standing transfixed by the sight of the ancient creatures. A deep, resonant hum filled the air as the dragons' wings stirred the sky, sending a breeze tinged with the scent of earth and ozone. The ground trembled beneath their weight, subtle vibrations rolling through the trainees' boots. Swirling air carried dust and leaves, mingling with the sharp musk of dragon hide, wrapping the moment in an almost sacred aura.

Aurelia stepped forward, her crystalline voice ringing clear and pure, cutting through the lingering hush like sunlight piercing a storm. The weight of her presence commanded attention, her words carrying the authority of ancient wisdom. "You stand at the precipice of something greater than yourselves," she declared, her gaze sweeping over the gathered trainees. "Dragonback training is not for the faint of heart. It demands discipline, strength, and above all, trust."

Verdantia moved beside her, her voice deep and steady as stone, carrying the weight of centuries. The resonance of her words sent a shiver through the trainees. Some straightened their posture in quiet reverence, while others swallowed hard, feeling the moment's gravity settle over them. "Approach each dragon with respect. The bond between rider and dragon is not one-sided. If a dragon does not sense a connection, they will not consent to carry you. Their choice is as vital as yours."

A quiet resolve settled over the group. Some trainees exchanged nervous glances while others squared their shoulders, determination hardening their features.

Keisha leaned toward Ong, a smile playing on her lips, remembering how adamantly he had once refused to become a dragonback rider. Ong shifted slightly, a knowing glint in his eyes as he folded his arms, his stance relaxed but attentive. Do you remember when you swore you'd never ride a dragon?" she teased, amusement softening her voice. "And now you're soaring like one of Amara's own."

Ong chuckled, shaking his head. "How could I forget? There were moments when I thought she had let me fall to teach me humility."

Keisha's soft laughter twinkled like music. "You know she would never do that. But teasing you? That she enjoyed from the very start."

"She still does," Ong replied with a smirk. His gaze drifted to the dragons, now watching the trainees with sharp, appraising eyes. "And I doubt she'll ever stop."

Their smiles faded into quiet respect as they turned back to the field. Trainees began approaching the dragons—some hesitant and awed, others resolute. Elaris, a young elf with trembling hands, took a steady breath as she stepped forward. All hoped for the exact moment: the meeting of eyes, the silent agreement, the bond that would change their lives forever. Her heart pounded as she met the gaze of a smaller Emerald dragon, its intelligent eyes studying her with quiet intensity.

The ancient dragons watched in silence, their wisdom stretching back through millennia. Their keen eyes flickered with unreadable insight, sensing the emotions coursing through the trainees—nervous excitement, quiet determination, and lingering fear. Some exchanged knowing glances, recognizing potential or foreseeing futures yet to unfold. Their gazes lingered on those with inner fire and quiet resilience, assessing courage, patience, and will.

A wing flick or a slow blink hinted at their silent evaluations, as though weighing each hopeful rider's heart, not just their skill. Their nostrils flared, scenting each trainee's unique blend of strengths and fears, unraveling hidden truths deep within. Some dragons tilted their heads slightly, their expressions unreadable, while others let out soft, rumbling hums—signals of consideration or quiet approval. They sought more than bravery; they sought a resonance, an unspoken harmony woven into the very essence of their being.

As the trainees moved toward the dragons, anticipation hung thick. Thalorian stepped forward, his jade fire eyes scanning the gathered noble dragons with the purposeful intent of choosing the right partner. His stride was measured, his expression calm, yet Verdantia, the ancient Emerald Dragon, tilted her head slightly and spoke, her deep, resonant voice slicing through the silence.

"You will not need to select a dragon, Thalorian."

Thalorian froze mid-step, his brow furrowing as if he were trying to decipher a cryptic message carved in stone. Confusion flickered in his jade fire eyes as he struggled to grasp Verdantia's words. Why would he not need to choose? Had something already been decided for him? Slowly, he turned to face the tremendous emerald dragon. "I... don't understand," he said cautiously.

From a short distance away, Prince Gailen, who had been watching with casual interest, straightened and glanced over, curiosity flickering across his face. "What's going on?" he muttered under his breath. Standing beside him, Ong broke into a broad smile, a spark of amusement dancing in his blue eyes. Without a word, he turned to Keisha, who was already grinning knowingly.

Ong's wink set them off, their shared laughter breaking the heavy atmosphere before Thalorian could question Verdantia further. His frown deepened, frustration creeping into his expression as he glanced between them, feeling as if he had missed an essential piece of the puzzle. "What's so funny?" he demanded, his voice edging impatiently.

When their laughter only grew, Thalorian stiffened, his eyes darting between them. He spun around sharply, his frown deepening as if he had just walked into an inside joke he desperately wanted to understand. "What are you laughing at?" he demanded again, exasperation lacing his tone.

Keisha regained some composure, though a smirk still tugged at her lips. "I believe what Verdantia means," she said, her tone light but teasing, "is that you won't need to choose a dragon because she has already chosen you."

Thalorian blinked rapidly, glancing between Verdantia and the others as if waiting for someone to tell him this was a joke. "What? Are you serious?" he asked, his voice hovering between disbelief and mild panic.

Verdantia's luminous emerald eyes bore into him, calm yet unyielding, carrying the weight of an unspoken challenge. A strange sensation crawled up Thalorian's spine, a mix of reverence and unease, as if an invisible force pressed against his soul, testing his resolve. There was an ancient knowing in her gaze, a silent test that sent a shiver down Thalorian's spine. It was as if she were peering straight into his soul, weighing his worth with a gaze that held both wisdom and challenge. Lowering her great head slightly, she spoke again. "I sense something within you, Thalorian. You are not like the others. You are destined to ride an ancient dragon. I will instruct you myself, and your training will be different."

Thalorian opened his mouth, closed it, opened it again, then hesitated mid-breath as if his brain had momentarily short-circuited before exhaling sharply. "Well," he muttered, rubbing the back of his neck. "That's... unexpected."

From the sidelines, Gailen's grin widened as he broke into laughter. "Good luck, Thalorian. You are going to need it."

Ong shot Keisha a look though his amusement remained. He chuckled knowingly, turning to Gailen with an almost mischievous look. "And so will you, Your Highness."

Gailen's amusement faltered, his brow creasing. "What do you mean?"

The answer came swiftly. Aurelia, the ancient Crystal Dragon, stepped forward, her iridescent gaze locking onto the prince. Her crystalline voice rang with calm authority. "I will train you, Prince Gailen," she declared. "You are to lead the dragon riders of Crystal Vale should the day come when it must be defended. Such a role demands more than mere skill. It requires unshakable trust. Only an ancient dragon can guide you to become the leader your people will need."

Gailen's mouth fell open slightly, his breath catching as a weak laugh escaped him. He ran a hand through his hair, uncertainty flickering across his face before he shook his head, trying to process the weight of Aurelia's words. The idea of leading dragon riders was thrilling in its own right, yet a shadow of doubt curled beneath that excitement.

Was he truly ready for such a responsibility? Could he live up to the expectations placed upon him? His heart pounded, torn between disbelief and the gravity of sudden leadership. The enormity of the moment settled over him like an unseen mantle pressing against his chest. Doubts crept in—was he truly prepared for this role? And yet, beneath the uncertainty, a thrill of possibility stirred, igniting something deep within him. His mind wavered between fear and the flickering excitement at the idea of leading something greater than himself.

"Me? Lead?" he echoed, his voice uncertain.

He and Thalorian exchanged bewildered glances, a silent camaraderie forming in their shared disbelief. Before either could find words, Kaelorn's melodic laughter rang out from behind them, warm and teasing, a familiar sound between old friends.

"Good thing I'll be working with the fae in Emerald Woods," Kaelorn quipped, his gladefire eyes alight with humor, his words laced with the ease of long-standing camaraderie.

The matching glares from Gailen and Thalorian came instantly. "Don't start," Thalorian said dryly.

"You're lucky we're otherwise occupied," Gailen added, his tone mock serious.

The tension broke as chuckles rippled through the group, offering a brief but necessary reprieve. Though the weight of their roles remained, the shared amusement strengthened their resolve, a reminder that they were not alone, even in the face of great responsibility. Verdantia let out a slow, rumbling exhale, a sound somewhere between amusement and approval, while Aurelia tilted her great crystalline head ever so slightly, observing the trainees with quiet contemplation. Around them, the other dragons shifted, some stretching their wings while a few let out deep, resonant huffs as if sharing in the humor of the moment. The subtle movement in the air seemed to ease the trainees, their shoulders loosening as the gravity of their training momentarily gave way to camaraderie. Verdantia and Aurelia watched with patient understanding, their immense forms casting long shadows over the field. Around them, the remaining crystal and emerald dragons stretched their wings, keen eyes observing the hopeful riders who began stepping forward with nervousness and determination.

For some, this would be the first step toward a bond that would reshape their destinies, forging them into warriors, leaders, and protectors. Learning to ride a dragon was challenging, demanding resilience, adaptability, and an unshakable bond between rider and beast. It would challenge their fears, demand sacrifices, and force them to confront their strength or weakness within themselves. The trials ahead would test their skills and their hearts, pushing them beyond their limits and into the unknown. For Thalorian and Gailen, however, their paths had already been chosen whether they were ready.

The field grew quiet again as the trainees moved among the gathered dragons, the air thick with hushed reverence and an electric charge of anticipation as if the ground held its breath. Each step was measured, and their movements were cautious and respectful, just as Verdantia had instructed. The dragons' intelligent eyes followed their every motion; their sheer presence was awe-inspiring and intimidating.

One by one, the hopefuls approached, their hands hesitating to touch a dragon's wing, scales, or leg. The connection was immediate. For some, a dragon would slightly lower its head or ruffle its wings in acknowledgment. The joy and relief of those chosen were unmistakable, their smiles radiant as the bond began to take root.

Not all were so fortunate. A young woman stepped toward a crystal dragon, her breath catching as she extended a trembling hand. The dragon's eyes flickered over her, unblinking, as if weighing something unseen. Its nostrils flared slightly, exhaling softly, shifting its great head before turning away. She had dreamed of this moment for as long as she could remember, visions of soaring through the sky, of forging an unbreakable bond. Doubts gnawed at the edges of her mind, whispering fears of inadequacy. Had she trained hard enough? Was she genuinely meant for this? The dragon regarded her momentarily before huffing softly, turning its head, and rejecting her without malice. She hesitated, disappointment flickering across her face, but after a steady breath, she moved on to another dragon, determination hardening her resolve.

The sting of rejection settled in her chest like a weight, a silent question echoing in her mind: Was she simply not worthy? She fought against the tightness in her throat, forcing herself to breathe and move forward. She had come too far to let one moment define her. Swallowing her disappointment, she straightened her shoulders and set her sights on another dragon, determination flickering in her eyes like a rekindled flame.

Across the field, this delicate process repeated. Some dragons stood tall and aloof, their appraising gazes unwavering. Others bowed their heads or extended their wings, gracefully accepting the riders who had earned their trust. Murmurs of awe rippled through the group, and a sense of unity began to take hold with each new bond.

The crystal dragons gleamed beneath the sun's rays, their translucent scales refracting light into dazzling patterns. They shifted slightly, adjusting their wings with quiet grace, their majestic and serene presence undeniable. The emerald dragons exuded quiet power, their green scales glinting as though infused with the life force of the forest itself. A few let out deep breaths, their chests rising and falling steadily as if attuned to the energy of their newly bonded riders. Together, they were a breathtaking display of nature's majesty and ancient wisdom, their presence infusing the air with a quiet reverence. A subtle shift in energy rippled through the field, a mixture of awe and deep-seated respect that seemed to bind the moment in timeless significance.

Ong stood at the edge of the field, arms crossed, his expression of quiet approval. A faint nod accompanied the slight narrowing of his eyes, a subtle flicker of satisfaction betraying his thoughts as he observed the newly bonded pairs. When the final trainee found their match, he stepped forward. His voice carried with ease over the grounds.

"Well done," he said, his tone firm yet encouraging. "Each of you has earned your dragon's trust, but let me be clear: this is only the beginning. A bond is one thing; learning to ride them is another entirely."

A ripple of anticipation swept through the group. Some trainees exchanged nervous grins while others shifted excitedly, their eagerness palpable.

Ong's mouth curved into a faint smile tinged with challenge. The trainees instinctively straightened, their expressions shifting from excitement to focused determination. He knew most of them would not enjoy the inevitable experience of falling off their dragons, but it was a lesson every rider had to learn. A few exchanged quick, nervous glances while others clenched their fists, steeling themselves for the trials ahead. "Tomorrow, we begin your first lesson learning to ride."

The weight of his words settled over them, a mixture of apprehension and determination flashing in their eyes. Some clenched their fists, steeling themselves for the trials ahead, while others exhaled slowly, centering their focus. A few cast fleeting glances at their newly bonded dragons as if seeking reassurance in the silent strength of their companions. Around them, the dragons rested comfortably beside their chosen riders, their silent understanding a testament to the bond they had just formed. For all the promise of the future, both dragon and rider knew the trials that awaited.

Chapter 20
Price of Failure

The journey back to Flameford felt interminable, though Qellaun deliberately took a longer route, avoiding direct paths. He moved with practiced stealth through shadowed glades and over rocky outcroppings, his thoughts consumed by the weight of failure. Each step felt heavier than the last. Memories of Pumpkin's piercing green eyes and Ong's stern warning replayed relentlessly in his mind, an unshakable loop of regret.

"I should have struck faster," he muttered, frustration tightening his jaw as his crimson eyes narrowed. Yet, even as he voiced it, the truth lingered bitterly. His hesitation had cost him dearly. What was done could not be undone.

On the horizon, the jagged peaks of Flameford rose faintly, their silhouettes wavering in the heat rising from scorched earth. But Qellaun lingered at the fringes of his journey as though delaying the inevitable might change his fate.

The mysterious person's voice sliced through his thoughts, sharp and unyielding, like the crack of a whip in the silence—cold and emotionless, devoid of any trace of humanity. It carried a cold finality that sent a chill through his veins. Do not fail me again.

His fists clenched involuntarily, his breath hitching as a shiver crawled up his spine, and his pace faltered. A cold weight pressed against his chest, his breath shallow as dread coiled tighter around him. The thought of returning empty-handed sent a shiver crawling up his spine, each step forward feeling like walking into his grave. He knew the punishment awaited those who failed the shadowy figure controlling Flameford.

Perhaps I should leave, he thought fleetingly. But the idea felt hollow. The mysterious person's reach extended farther than he could run. He would be found, and disobedience would bring an even harsher reckoning.

With a heavy sigh, he adjusted the hood of his cloak and trudged onward, the charred expanse of Flameford creeping ever closer with every reluctant step.

The jagged peaks loomed larger as Qellaun paused on the outskirts of the ash-streaked land. His feet felt rooted to the ground, his silver eyes scanning the familiar yet forbidding horizon. The Tower of Shadowwalker pierced the dusky sky, its dark silhouette sending a fresh chill through him.

He was not ready. The thought of facing the mysterious person sent ice through his veins. He knew anger awaited him, the kind that did not forgive failure. If he were lucky, he would still be breathing by the end of it—but luck had never been his ally.

His hand twitched toward the dagger at his belt, seeking reassurance. The worn leather grip, molded to his palm from years of use, carried the ghosts of past battles. Once a symbol of his prowess, it now felt like a useless relic, its edge dulled against forces far beyond steel. Yet, a hollow ache settled in his chest as his fingers brushed the hilt. What good had it done against the panther? The steel had been nothing more than an empty promise of control.

"Qellaun?"

The voice startled him, and he spun to see his sister, Lyra, approaching. Her dark hair shimmered faintly in the dim light, and her sharp gaze carried a mix of curiosity and concern.

"You've returned," she said, her tone probing. "What's wrong?"

He hesitated, his jaw tightening before he exhaled heavily. "I was following orders, spying on Crystal Vale," he began, his voice tight and low. "But I overheard someone address a young man as 'Your Majesty.' I thought..." He glanced at his dagger, bitterness clouding his expression. "I thought killing him would please the mysterious person."

Lyra's eyebrow arched slightly, her lips pressing into a thin line. "And?"

"I failed," he admitted, his shoulders sagging. "I did not see that cursed panther of Keisha's. It was on me before I could react. I barely escaped with my life." His gaze darted toward the tower, haunted by dread. "The person will be furious. I am as good as dead. A beating or worse, something drawn out, a lesson in pain to remind me of my failure. The mysterious person does not tolerate mistakes, and mercy is not a word in their vocabulary."

Lyra studied him in silence, her sharp eyes assessing. A flicker of fear passed through Qellaun's silver gaze, brief but unmistakable. She understood that fear and knew all too well what awaited him, but seeing it in her brother, who rarely let such emotions slip, made her jaw tighten slightly. Her fingers tapped lightly against her forearm, a subtle but telling sign of her deliberation. She crossed her arms, shifting her weight slightly, the flicker of tension in her jaw betraying an unspoken thought. Then, she gave a slight nod. "Reckless as ever," she said, clipped but kind. "Still, you are my brother. I will go with you."

Qellaun blinked, startled. "You would do that?"

Her gaze softened, a quiet sympathy flickering in her eyes, though her words remained matter of fact, steady, and unwavering. "You will need someone to keep you alive when the person lashes out. Let us go."

Together, they began the long walk toward the tower, their footsteps muffled by the ashen ground. The acrid scent of charred earth filled the air, burning Qellaun's throat and making his stomach churn. A distant gust of wind howled through the jagged peaks like a spectral warning, and he swallowed against the bitter taste of dread rising in his chest. Qellaun's shoulders tensed with each step while Lyra's fingers hovered near the hilt of her blade, her sharp gaze scanning the path ahead. The silence between them was heavy, thick with unspoken fears, yet neither dared to break it. Each step carried them closer to the storm awaiting them, the looming punishment a brutal, unforgiving reckoning that would serve as both retribution and warning. He had failed, and the mysterious person did not abide failure.

A heavy, oppressive stillness filled the Tower of Shadowwalker as Qellaun and Lyra entered. The air was thick with the scent of damp stone and lingering smoke, and the faint flicker of torches cast elongated shadows across the cold stone walls. At the chamber's far end stood the mysterious person, their silver hair barely visible beneath the hood of a dark cloak. They turned sharply, their piercing gaze locking onto Qellaun like a predator assessing prey.

"Well?" the mysterious person barked, their voice cold and biting. "Give me your report. Although," they added with a sneer, "judging by your expression, it seems you've failed... again."

Qellaun flinched, his breath catching in his throat, fingers twitching at his sides. His stomach knotted, a cold sweat breaking across his skin as dread curled in his chest like a vice. Every muscle in his body screamed for him to flee, yet he remained frozen, trapped in the crushing weight of his failure and the inescapable wrath that loomed before him. But he forced himself to step forward, his voice faltering as he began. "I... I overheard someone call a young man 'Prince.' I thought if I killed him, it would please you." His hand brushed the hilt of his dagger nervously. "But I did not see the panther. Keisha's panther. It attacked before I could strike."

The mysterious person's eyes narrowed, their fury crackling like a storm about to break. Qellaun's breath hitched, his shoulders tensing as if bracing for a physical blow. Beside him, Lyra's hand flexed at her side, her stance shifting subtly, a silent, instinctive preparation for what might come next. Her fingers twitched at her side, her jaw clenching slightly in silent wrath. "A panther?!" they shouted, their voice reverberating through the chamber. "You let a beast stop you? You are more pathetic than I imagined!"

Lyra stepped closer to her brother, her dark hair catching the flickering torchlight, but she remained silent, her face an unreadable mask. Yet, her fingers curled slightly at her sides, tension evident in the faint quiver of her breath.

The mysterious person advanced, their cloak billowing slightly as if caught in an unseen breeze, their voice dropping to a venomous hiss. "Perhaps I should let Zylron handle your punishment. He would relish tearing you apart, piece by piece."

At the mention of the red dragon, Qellaun shivered violently, the color draining from his face. The thought of Zylron's wrath turned his blood to ice, and he struggled to steady his breathing. "Please," he stammered, "I'll do better."

The mysterious person's cold gaze bore into him, and he swallowed hard, the silence more terrifying than their anger.

It was Lyra who broke the tension, her voice calm but deliberate. "While my brother may have failed," she said carefully, "he still uncovered valuable information. King Manard's son has returned to Crystal Vale. Surely, that is worth some consideration."

The mysterious person turned slowly, their glare pinning her in place. Lyra stiffened but held her ground, her fingers twitching slightly at her side as she met their gaze head-on. For a moment, silence hung in the air, sharp and brittle.

They spat, their tone venomous. "You dare suggest leniency?"

Before either sibling could respond, Lyra's eyes flashed with determination as she thrust her hand forward, summoning tendrils of her dark magic. The air around her shimmered with an eerie, violet glow, the tendrils writing like living shadows. A chill ran through Qellaun as he felt the raw, crackling energy in the air, its unnatural presence sending a tremor down his spine. The shadows twisted and coiled, forming a barrier of inky black mist that crackled with raw energy. Yet, even as it took shape, the mysterious person's power surged forward, and a wave of dark magic erupted from their outstretched hand, a roiling mass of inky black and violet streaks that crackled with malevolent energy. The air hummed with an eerie resonance as the force crashed forward, distorting the space around it with an unnatural pressure. It tore through Lyra's fragile defense like a blade through silk, shattering the barrier effortlessly. The force slammed into them, driving them to their knees, searing pain burning through their bodies. Qellaun gritted his teeth, his hands clawing at the stone floor, while Lyra gasped, struggling to hold herself together.

The mysterious person watched their agony with cold satisfaction. Qellaun risked a glance at Lyra, his vision blurred with pain, and saw her jaw tighten as she suppressed a cry. Their gazes met briefly, a silent exchange of shared torment before they both lowered their heads, enduring in silence. After a moment, the mysterious person dropped their hand, the dark magic dissipating like smoke.

"Thank your sister for her intervention," they hissed, their voice dripping with malice. "But heed my words, Qellaun, fail me again, and it will not be Zylron who deals with you. I will feed you both to a far more dangerous dragon."

Qellaun and Lyra remained on the ground, panting as the echoes of pain slowly faded, a lingering burn searing through their limbs. Their limbs trembled, aching from the lingering tendrils of dark magic, and the cold stone beneath them did little to ground their spiraling thoughts. Qellaun clenched his fists, his breath uneven, while Lyra pressed a hand to her side, swallowing back the raw sting of their failure. Without waiting for further commands, they scrambled to their feet, pale, and trembling.

The mysterious person stepped toward them, their voice cutting through the silence like a blade. "There is a hidden gate within Flameford. The Druchii will access it as part of my plans to bring about the noble dragons' fall and the fall of the light in Vacari."

Neither sibling dared to meet their gaze, merely offering a brief nod of acknowledgment. Qellaun's fingers twitched at his side, betraying the nervous energy he tried to suppress, while Lyra's throat bobbed in a silent swallow as she fought to maintain her composure. Without another word, they turned and hurried out of the chamber, the weight of the mysterious person's threat and the implications of their words pressing heavily upon them.

Left alone in the dim chamber, the mysterious person moved to a throne-like stone chair at the room's far end. Settling into its cold embrace, they ran a gloved hand along the armrest, tracing the deep, ancient carvings of serpentine forms entwined in battle. Their lips curled into a wicked smirk as if drawing power from the throne's silent history of conquest and betrayal. Their thoughts turned to the man who had resisted their commands.

He will obey, they thought darkly. And he will bring me the information I need on the Prince of Crystal Vale.

A low, sinister laugh echoed through the chamber, bouncing off the ancient stone walls. The frigid air seemed to chill further, thick with malice as if the very stones bore witness to countless betrayals. Outside the chamber, Qellaun and Lyra quickened their pace, their breath unsteady. Neither dared to speak, but the weight of that laughter clung to them, wrapping around their thoughts like a noose. Lyra clenched her fists, jaw set in quiet defiance, while Qellaun swallowed hard, his pulse pounding in his ears. The echo of their failure followed them down the winding corridor, a grim reminder that escape was never an option. The mysterious person leaned back, their mind alight with schemes as the pieces of their plan for Vacari fell into place.

Chapter 21
Chains of the Past

The Tower of Shadowwalker stood silent, its ancient stones exuding a faint chill while a distant water drip echoed in the shadows. The oppressive stillness weighed on Lyra and Qellaun, wrapping around them like a shroud, each sound magnifying their unease. The air carried the acrid scent of old magic and the metallic tang of damp stone, pressing close like a whispered warning. The air within was still charged with the tension from earlier. Lyra and Qellaun were summoned again to the main hall, their expressions guarded as they faced the mysterious figure.

"I have an errand to run," the figure announced curtly. Their hood was drawn low over their face, obscuring all but the faint outline of their jaw.

Lyra opened her mouth to question them, but pain stole her voice. But she caught herself, the sting of dark magic still fresh in her memory. Doubt clawed at her mind—was it worth provoking them again? The pain had been unbearable. A warning seared into her very bones. She swallowed hard, forcing herself to stay silent. She could still feel the searing pain that had shot through her veins, the echo of an incantation reverberating in her skull. The cold grip of unseen tendrils had wrapped around her lungs, squeezing until she thought she might never draw breath again. Even now, the ghost of its presence lingered beneath her skin, a cruel reminder of the power she dared not provoke. Her fingers twitched at her side, but she forced herself to stillness, inclining her head in a gesture of reluctant obedience.

Qellaun mirrored her action, though his jaw tightened, his eyes briefly flicking to Lyra as if silently warning her not to press further. "Understood," he muttered, his voice measured but taut with restraint.

The figure's gaze lingered on them, sharp and unyielding, as though daring them to speak out. Both tensed under the scrutiny, their muscles rigid with unspoken apprehension. When silence prevailed, they turned sharply, the hem of their cloak brushing the stone floor like a whisper of finality. With a faint shimmer in the air, they vanished into the shadows.

Lyra exhaled, her shoulders sagging as she glanced at Qellaun. "I hate this."

"So do I," Qellaun admitted. "But we do not have a choice. Not yet."

They returned to their tasks, the air between them heavy with unspoken unease.

Through a hidden gate deep within the Tower of Shadowwalker, the mysterious figure reemerged far from Flameford, stepping into the heart of Fel Thalor. The portal shimmered momentarily behind them before fading into the volcanic gloom.

Fel Thalor's dark spires loomed against the horizon, their outlines wavering in the heat haze, while a low, mournful wind carried a faint, hollow whistle through the scorched crevices. Like unseen embers dying, a distant, eerie crackle punctuated the heavy silence, adding an undercurrent of cold unease to the fiery landscape. Their silhouettes were etched against a blood-red sky, wisps of smoke curling around their peaks, shifting in the heated air like restless specters. The sky churned, thick with ash, and the occasional flare of molten embers illuminated the darkness, casting eerie, flickering shadows across the ground. The streets were eerily quiet,

save for the faint echo of distant footsteps and the ominous roar of lava
streams carving through the landscape. Heat radiated from the ground in
shimmering waves, making the air hostile.

The figure moved with purpose, their steps deliberate as they approached the city's center. There, in the heart of Fel Thalor, stood the
infamous altar. Carved from black obsidian and etched with runes that
pulsed faintly, it seemed alive with ancient magic. Below it, molten lava
churned and bubbled, its oppressive heat turning each breath into a test of
endurance.

The mysterious figure paused before the altar, a flicker of tension tightening their posture, a mix of anticipation and restrained frustration. Their
gloved hand trembled slightly before steadying as if battling impatience
or doubt, then traced the runes with deliberate precision. The smooth
obsidian was unnervingly warm, almost pulsing beneath their fingertips, as
if it were alive and aware of their presence. Each symbol thrummed faintly
beneath their touch as though recognizing them. It was here, amid the
oppressive heat and suffocating silence, that power was repeatedly claimed
through blood and fear.

Placing a hand flat against the obsidian surface, they whispered in a
language long forgotten by most. The words carried weight, twisting the
very air around them. A subtle vibration rippled through the altar, and the
runes began to glow brighter, their light reflecting eerily in the surrounding
darkness.

The air thickened, pressing in from all sides as the figure muttered an incantation under their breath. Each word pulled something from the depths
below, stirring the molten core beneath the altar. The faint hum of magic
grew louder, a promise of power waiting to be claimed—or unleashed.

Still, the runes flickered faintly, resisting as though sluggish from years
of neglect, their power dormant after being untouched for so long. The
figure's patience frayed, and their tone sharpened as they repeated the
incantation, willing the ancient forces to respond. A low rumble echoed

from the depths of the altar, and the ground beneath them trembled slightly. The runes pulsed erratically, flickering between light and darkness as if struggling to awaken. A gust of scorching air swirled around them, carrying the faint scent of sulfur and something far older, something waiting.

Far from Fel Thalor, the man sat, surrounded by cracked earth and the faint hiss of steam escaping from fissures. The air carried the sharp tang of sulfur, and the distant rumble of unseen forces beneath the ground hinted at the land's restless nature. His fists clenched in the shadow of a jagged cliff as he stared at the scorched ground, his jaw tightening with suppressed frustration. A muscle twitched beneath his eye, and his breath came in shallow, uneven bursts, the weight of inevitability pressing down on him like an iron shackle. The summons had come, a sharp, unrelenting pull in his chest that refused to be ignored. It was a sensation both searing and suffocating, as though unseen chains wrapped around his ribs, tightening with every breath. His pulse pounded in protest, each beat a drum of defiance. His muscles coiled, rigid with futile resistance, as if bracing for an unseen blow. It was not just a call; it was a demand, an unyielding force that gnawed at his will and threatened to shatter it entirely. Yet he remained rooted to the spot, defiance flickering in his eyes despite the growing pressure.

"What's the point?" he muttered, shaking his head. "Nothing good will come of this."

Closing his eyes, he willed himself to resist the invisible force. But the air around him thickened, heavy with the promise of consequences. Before he could react, the ground beneath him dissolved into nothingness.

The world twisted violently, dragging him through space. When he landed, it was with a jarring impact on the obsidian platform near Fel Thalor's altar. The heat clawed at his skin, and the air shimmered with the oppressive glow of lava. Staggering to his feet, he found himself face-to-face with the mysterious person, their hooded form radiating authority and menace.

"You dare defy me?" the person snarled, their voice a venomous rasp, like cracked stone grinding in the heat, dripping with contempt and raw menace. The person hissed, their voice slicing through the oppressive air.

The man straightened, his lips pressed into a thin line. "I didn't ask for your summons," he said, his tone edged with frustration. "I—"

His words were cut short by a blast of dark magic that struck him with bone-crushing force. Agony exploded through his ribs, a cold fire burning in his veins as the impact sent him sprawling. A sharp, metallic taste filled his mouth, and his vision blurred at the edges. The sheer force of the magic left a lingering tremor in his limbs as though his very bones recoiled from its dark touch. His muscles spasmed, a violent shudder wracking his frame before numbing cold settled into his veins, leaving him breathless and weak. A dull ache spread through his chest, each breath a raw reminder of the power that had coursed through him. His fingers twitched involuntarily, the ghost of the attack still seared into his nerves. He crumpled to his knees, a cry of pain escaping him as the energy seared through his body. The mysterious person watched impassively, their hand outstretched, wielding the spell cruelly.

"Let this be a reminder," they said, their tone devoid of mercy. The magic surged again, its hum reverberating through the chamber.

The man clawed at the ground, gasping as the spell finally ceased. He looked up, his breath ragged, to see the person towering over him like a shadow of judgment.

"Never ignore my orders again," they commanded, their voice icy and laced with a cruel finality. The man's chest burned with defiance, but a flicker of fear gnawed at his resolve, a silent battle between pride and the searing reminder of his powerlessness.

The man nodded weakly, his resistance momentarily broken. "I... understand," he rasped.

The mysterious person stepped back, their gaze as sharp as the blade of a dagger. "Good. There is hope for you yet."

Shakily, the man rose, the metallic scent of the lava stinging his nostrils and the distant crackling of stone under intense heat filling his ears. Pain still burning in his limbs, frustration simmered beneath his compliance. "What do you want from me?" he demanded, his voice raw.

The mysterious figure tilted their hooded head, menace lacing their cold authority. "King Manard's son, Gailen, has returned to Crystal Vale," they stated. "I want information."

The man's fists clenched. "I cannot betray a friend. Especially not a prince."

A cruel smile shadowed the figure's lips, their voice a rasping, cold murmur that seemed to scrape against the air, thick with menace. "The pledge binds you still—by blood and shadow. You are mine."

Darkness chilled the air, and shadows writhed along the walls. "You will fulfill the obligation or face the consequences."

The man's defiance cracked. "The Shadowwalkers are gone! The pact should have died with them!"

The figure's laughter was a blade of ice, sharp and hollow, echoing through the chamber and seeping into the stones like a cruel memory. "The pact is eternal. Your servitude... inevitable."

His voice broke, bitter and desperate, as his fists clenched at his sides. "If Gailen learns of this... my life is over."

The figure instantly seized him, dangling him over the molten abyss. "Obey," they hissed. "Or suffer."

His body trembled. Defeat slipped past his lips. "It will be as you order."

The figure released him, their control absolute. "Good. Now, what have you learned?"

"Gailen... will be a dragon rider."

The figure's response was a low murmur. "Interesting. Report anything unusual. Do not fail me again."

They dissolved into shadows, leaving the man with his torment.

The Fel Thalor altar pulsed with a sinister vibration, thrumming through the stone and sending eerie ripples as if the chamber conspired with the darkness. A mysterious, cold glow seeped from its runes, casting flickering shadows across the walls as if the chamber breathed with ancient, unseen power. Cold magic crept under his skin, a mocking reminder of his bondage.

His voice cracked with anguish. "Why, Father? Why condemn me to this fate?"

The altar's hum answered only with silence.

With a bitter glance back, he turned from the chamber, the heat of the lava clashing with the cold weight of his burden.

"If I had known Phoenix passed the obligation... I never would have set foot in Vacari."

The night swallowed his retreat, the darkness feeling both a cloak and a cage, heavy with the weight of his choices. The jagged spires of Fel Thalor faded behind him.

Ahead lay Crystal Vale. And with it, the unbearable cost of his loyalty.

Chapter 22
Soaring Into Battle

The dragon riders moved across the training field, their newly bonded dragons circling overhead. The occasional roar or beat of mighty wings punctuated the air, blending with the crisp commands of Ong and Keisha as they directed the trainees.

From a shaded vantage point near the field's edge, Prince Gailen stood beside Thalorian, both watching intently. Their expressions were unreadable, but the intensity in their gazes hinted at the weight they carried—anticipation laced with uncertainty, the knowledge that their training would push them beyond their limits. They knew their training separate, daunting, and led by ancient dragons—would begin soon.

"Seems manageable enough," Thalorian remarked dryly, though his jade fire eyes did not leave the riders.

Gailen smirked faintly. "We both know it won't be this... mild for us."

A few steps away, Ong leaned closer to Keisha, his arms folded across his chest. "They don't realize yet, do they?" he murmured, his tone amused.

Keisha didn't lower her bow as she nocked another arrow, her emerald eyes sparkling with humor. "Not a clue," she replied softly. "But they will learn soon enough. Aurelia and Verdantia do not take things lightly."

Valeon stood further back, arms crossed, his gaze locked on the target range. His blue gray eyes tracked Keisha's next shot—the effortless way she drew, aimed, and released. The arrow flew straight and true, landing dead center.

"She's... impressive," he said aloud, half to himself.

Kaelorn, standing beside him, smirked. "What is this? Compliments from Valeon?"

"Hey, I can appreciate talent when I see it," Valeon said with a grin. Then his gaze drifted to the nearby food table, and his smile widened. "Speaking of talent, mine lies elsewhere. Back in a minute."

Kaelorn burst into laughter as Valeon wandered off. "Always eating," he muttered, shaking his head.

Gailen turned at the sound of Kaelorn's laughter, raising an eyebrow. "What is it this time?"

"Valeon," Kaelorn said with a chuckle. "I swear, he's got an unending appetite."

The group exchanged amused glances before returning their focus to the training field, where the reality of their upcoming trials settled over them like a gathering storm. The lighthearted moment faded as they watched the dragons overhead, a reminder that their skills would soon be tested in ways they had yet to imagine. Above, dragons soared against the open sky, their presence a constant reminder of the immense responsibility awaiting them all.

Aurelia and Verdantia surveyed the training grounds, their ancient eyes focused on the bustling activity below. With a nod to Ong and Keisha, they motioned for the dragon riders to bring their dragons back to the ground.

Keisha stepped forward, her commanding presence silencing the hum of conversation among the trainees. Some straightened instinctively, their expressions shifting from casual to focused, while others exchanged glances, anticipation flickering in their eyes. "Bring them down," she called, her voice firm but encouraging.

The dragons descended gracefully, their riders guiding them with varying skill levels. Once the dragons had landed, their massive forms shifting restlessly on the field, Ong strode toward the area where weapons awaited, his eyes scanning the trainees.

Keisha was the first to act, separating the magic users into their groups. "Those of you who can channel magic, step forward," she instructed. "Your training will focus on incorporating magic into your flight. This will be your primary role in battle."

A smaller group moved to the side, their expressions a mix of pride and anticipation.

Ong motioned to a different group of riders. "The rest of you, come here," he called, gesturing to the dragon lances nearby. He nodded toward the weapons, their long shafts gleaming in the sunlight. "See if you can lift them."

The riders stepped forward, gripping the lances and testing their weight. Those who managed to lift the heavy weapons easily were assigned to the lance group, pride flickering in their eyes as they realized not everyone could wield such formidable armaments. Their new roles were clear.

Meanwhile, Thalorian and Kaelorn busied themselves to distribute the bows. The emerald bows went to riders of emerald dragons, and the crystal bows were paired with crystal dragons.

One of the riders glanced at Thalorian curiously. "Why match the bow to the dragon?"

Thalorian paused, his jade fire eyes glinting with a hint of amusement. "Because these bows are not ordinary weapons," he explained. "They resonate with the energy of your dragon, amplifying their power and aligning with their essence. The color reflects the connection you share."

The rider nodded, holding the bow with a newfound sense of reverence.

Once every trainee had been assigned their equipment, Aurelia and Verdantia stepped forward, their imposing forms radiating authority.

"Return to the sky," Aurelia commanded, her voice resonant and firm. "Practice with your new roles. Learn the weight of your weapon and the power of your bond."

Verdantia added, her tone grounding and steady, "Your dragon is your partner, your strength. Trust them as you wield your weapons and fulfill your duties."

The dragon riders, now fully equipped and grouped by their roles, mounted their dragons again, tightening their chests yet setting their jaws with determination. Wings unfurled, and the air was filled with the mighty rush of flight as they soared into the sky, ready to begin the next stage of their training.

From the ground, Valeon stood with arms crossed, watching the dragon riders practice high above. He winced as one rider slipped from her saddle, letting out a small yelp before her dragon swooped under to catch her.

"Yeah, I'm glad I'm not doing that," he muttered loud enough for the group to hear.

Gailen turned, a mischievous grin spreading across his face. "Probably better for the dragon too. I am not sure they could handle your constant eating breaks."

Laughter erupted around them, Valeon scowling in mock offense. "Very funny, Your Highness," he grumbled.

Kaelorn chuckled, clapping Valeon on the shoulder. "Speaking of breaks, enjoy them while you can. You are coming with me to Emerald Woods soon. We need to check for any signs of dark dragons causing problems for the fae."

Valeon groaned dramatically. "Why does my job require all this walking? Can't we send someone with shorter legs?"

Kaelorn rolled his eyes. "You'd probably still find a way to complain."

Gailen smirked. "Or bribe someone into carrying you."

Valeon gasped in mock outrage. "Now, that is an idea worth considering."

The group shook their heads in exasperation, Ong smirking as he turned to Gailen. "How did you find this one again?"

Gailen laughed, his piercing blue eyes twinkling. "We met in a tavern. Valeon got in over his head, and we stepped in to help. After that, he just sort of... tagged along. Eventually, he learned to hold his own."

Valeon puffed his chest out, feigning indignation. "Excuse me, but I'm the best of us all, and you know it!"

Another wave of laughter followed his comment, even Valeon joining in before the group dispersed back to their respective tasks.

Kaelorn grabbed Valeon's arm, steering him toward the edge of the training grounds. "Come on, let us head to Emerald Forest. You can complain about walking while we walk."

"Wonderful," Valeon muttered sarcastically, glancing back at the others. "If I never come back, blame Kaelorn."

The group watched them leave, shaking their heads fondly as the pair disappeared into the woods.

As the day wore on, the training intensified. The dragons soared higher, their movements sharper and more daring, testing the limits of their riders' abilities. A crystal dragon twisted mid-flight, a daring spiral that sent its rider clutching the reins tightly, fighting to maintain balance. Below, Ong and Keisha watched with sharp eyes, their expressions a mixture of pride and scrutiny.

"Push them harder," Aurelia's voice resonated, her tone unyielding.

Verdantia added, her emerald gaze scanning the sky. "They must be prepared for every possibility. The dark dragons will not hesitate to exploit weakness."

The riders adapted slowly but surely, though not without struggle. Some wobbled in their saddles, gripping the reins with white-knuckled determination, while others overshot their commands, causing their dragons to veer off course. Yet, with each pass, their grips steadied, their movements became more fluid, and their coordination with their dragons improved. Magic users sent sparks of energy into the air, coordinating their spells with their dragon's flight paths. Those wielding bows practiced taking shots from precarious angles while the lance-bearers learned to steady their weapons during rapid dives.

A particularly daring move saw an emerald dragon weaving through the air at breakneck speed, its rider clinging tightly, nervous yet focused while aiming at a moving target. The arrow flew true, striking the mark and earning a chorus of cheers from the ground below.

From their vantage point, Gailen and Thalorian exchanged glances, their respect for the riders' determination evident.

"They're improving," Gailen said, his tone approving.

"They'll need to," Thalorian replied grimly, his gaze lingering on the horizon. "This is only the beginning."

As the sun dipped lower in the sky, casting golden hues over the field, the dragons landed one by one, their riders sliding off with exhausted but triumphant smiles. Gailen watched silently, a deep sense of pride swelling in his chest. This was more than just training; it was preparation for the battles ahead and the survival of their people. He exhaled slowly, the weight of responsibility settling over him like the twilight creeping across the sky. The training had tested them, but it also forged stronger bonds between dragon and rider.

Chapter 23
The Defenders of Emerald Woods

The skies above Emerald Woods churned, thick with the scent of scorched leaves and the metallic tang of dark magic, layering the air with tension and dread. Black dragons loomed overhead, their shadows swallowing the sunlight and casting the forest into an ominous twilight. A chilly wind hissed through the trees, heavy with the crackle of dark magic and the panicked cries of creatures fleeing for cover. Xalzorath, the ancient leader of the black dragons, circled like a living storm, his charcoal scales glinting and his eyes burning with merciless intent.

Below, chaos reigned. Fae scattered under the oppressive wings of the invaders while young emerald dragons darted through the canopy, their shimmering scales defiant as they shielded the fleeing fae.

Kaelorn and Valeon arrived, Valeon's mind racing with unease: too many enemies, too few allies. His breath came faster, shallow with tension, and his fingers curled instinctively around the hilt of his blade, seeking reassurance in its familiar weight. But failure was not an option. The tension in the air was suffocating. Kaelorn's gladefire eyes burned with determination, memories of past failures gnawing at him. Valeon, fingers twitching near his blade, fought the tremor of doubt creeping up his spine.

A fairy, no larger than Kaelorn's hand, darted before him, panic in her voice. "Please, help us!"

Kaelorn's command was swift. "Valeon, take them to the grove. Use the dragon statues for cover."

Valeon's resolve hardened, his pulse quickening as he tightened his grip on the hilt of his blade, every muscle coiled with urgency. "On it. Quickly!" he called to the fairies, leading them through the trees to a towering dragon statue. The stone radiated an ageless power, and Valeon guided the fae into its hollow sanctuary. His fingers brushed the weathered carvings of dragons frozen in eternal vigilance as the fairies huddled inside, their luminescent wings flickering like stars in the darkness. Positioning himself at the entrance, his hand firm on his blade, he vowed, Today, I fight protector or not.

Meanwhile, Kaelorn stood firm, his muscles taut and limbs trembling from the strain of channeling magic, the raw power surging through his veins like wildfire, searing and exhausting in equal measures. His past failures were a heavy specter behind him. He raised his hands, vine-like markings glowing as tendrils of earth-bound magic wove a protective barrier around the scrambling fae. The air thickened with magic and the scent of fresh earth. "This will hold," he whispered, though his heart pounded with the weight of the battle.

Above, a young emerald dragon's roar split the air, accompanied by the hot rush of wind from its wings and the faint sear of its breath, carrying urgency and defiance. It turned, wings slicing through the air as it sped toward the training grounds, its cry an urgent summons for Verdantia.

Kaelorn gritted his teeth, channeling more power as the black dragons pressed their assault. The magic burned through his veins, a searing force both invigorating and draining, threatening to consume him if he lost focus. "Hold the line," he muttered, his voice carrying the weight of his vow: I will not fail this time.

The training grounds erupted with tension, the sharp crack of snapping branches and the rich scent of earth churning beneath pounding feet, heightening the sense of urgency. The young emerald dragon landed in a rush, its wings snapping closed as it dashed to Verdantia. The ancient dragon's emerald eyes narrowed, her voice calm but urgent: "Trouble in Emerald Woods."

Thalorian's pulse quickened, his chest tightening with anticipation and dreading the battle he had only heard of was now his to fight. His fingers curled into fists, knuckles white, as a cold sweat slicked his palms. The weight of expectation pressed down on him, but there was no turning back now. He had heard of the devastation from Keisha and Ong now, and the battle was upon them. Without hesitation, he vaulted onto Verdantia's back.

"Hold on," Verdantia warned, her wings unfurling with raw power. They surged skyward, cutting through the winds toward the chaos.

Keisha, Ong, and Gailen exchanged tense glances. "This is worse than we thought," Ong muttered.

"We move now," Keisha snapped, sprinting for the forest. The others followed her urgency, matching hers.

From above, Aurelia's crystalline form glimmered as she addressed the paused riders: "Continue your training. I will return." With a mighty beat of her wings, she soared after Verdantia.

The battle in Emerald Woods was chaos. Flashes of emerald and black clashed mid-air as dragons fought viciously for dominance. The fire scorched the earth, and the acrid sting of smoke filled every breath, choking the air with its suffocating presence. Screams, roars, and the crackle of burning wood collided in a brutal symphony, every second raw and unforgiving. The emerald dragons clashed with black, fae cries piercing through fire and smoke. Kaelorn stood amid the turmoil, his magic weaving a barrier alongside young emerald dragons. His gladefire eyes blazed with resolve.

"Xalzorath!" Verdantia's roar shook the ground, scattering leaves and sending ancient and resonant tremors through the earth. The battlefield stilled. Her emerald gaze locked on the towering black dragon. "This is not your domain. Leave."

Xalzorath's answering roar shook the earth, his tail felling a tree with a violent crack. Verdantia tensed, her wings flaring instinctively as a protective growl rumbled in her throat. Around them, the emerald dragons bristled, their scales flaring with reflected light as they prepared for the inevitable clash. "This forest will burn, Verdantia. Your protection is meaningless."

Thalorian dismounted beside Kaelorn, his legs trembling from the surge of magic coursing through him, each pulse searing his senses with effort. Silvery vines flared from his fingertips to join the barrier, fortifying it against the onslaught. We cannot fail. The balance is at stake.

The arrival of Keisha, Ong, and Gailen rippled through the battle. Black dragons hesitated mid-air, their snarls briefly muted as they registered the power shift before some pulled back warily. Others launched into a fresh, furious assault. The reinforcements brought new strength. Keisha's magic surged into the barrier, its pulse forcing back the black dragons. Some faltered mid-air; others retaliated with blazing fury.

Gailen's eyes swept the battlefield. "Where's Valeon?"

Kaelorn, strained but unyielding, gestured to the grove. "Guarding the fairies within the dragon statue."

Gailen's jaw tightened, a flicker of concern for Valeon flashing in his eyes. He knew Valeon would do his best, but he was not a fighter. The thought gnawed at him before resolve set in. "I'm going to him." He sprinted toward the grove, leaving the battle behind but carrying its weight.

Ong met Keisha's glance, the warm rush of wind from dragon wings brushing past them, carrying the earthy scent of the forest and the distant tang of smoke. His resolve sharpened. Without a word, he approached a young emerald dragon, which lowered its head knowingly. In a heartbeat, Ong mounted, and with a powerful launch, they soared to join Verdantia and the defenders against Xalzorath.

The sky became a battlefield; flashes of fire and bursts of magic tore through the air. Wings clashed with bone-jarring force. Roars shattered the sky. The air burned hot, filled with smoke and chaos as emerald and black forms twisted and struck with deadly precision. Ong, wielding his dragon lance, struck true his blow, piercing Xalzorath's side, drawing a furious bellow from the ancient black dragon. The beast lashed out instinctively, his claws slicing through the air in a blind attempt to strike back, but Verdantia's emerald power slammed into him before he could retaliate, halting his attack. The beast's eyes burned with malice, but Verdantia's emerald power slammed into him before he could retaliate, halting his attack.

A second wave of magic crackled through the air, Aurelia's crystalline energy. She hovered above, her voice resolute. "Leave, Xalzorath. You have no claim here."

Xalzorath snarled, his claws gouging the earth as frustration boiled beneath his scales. He surveyed the battlefield, his forces faltering under the combined might of the defenders. Pride warred with reason before he spat a final threat: "This isn't over." With a signal, he and his dark kin vanished into the sky.

The battle haze lifted, but exhaustion weighed heavily on the defenders. Aurelia, her authority tempered with concern, asked, "Is everyone safe?"

Verdantia nodded. "We are. Thank you."

Aurelia's wings spread wide, her crystalline scales shimmering as they caught the fractured light, casting prismatic reflections across the air. "I return to the training grounds. They will need guidance." With that, she soared away.

On the ground, Ong dismounted, his breath heavy but steady. Nearby, Keisha's eyes softened with relief as she spotted Gailen and Valeon approaching, the fae safe around them.

Kaelorn stepped forward, his gaze softening briefly as he caught Valeon's expression—a flicker of relief mixed with lingering doubt, his lips pressing into a thin line as if questioning his place in the fight. It was a silent acknowledgment of the battle fought within and without. His voice carried rare warmth. "Good job," he told Valeon.

Valeon, flustered but proud, felt his chest lighten as a fairy darted up, planting a quick kiss on his cheek. "Thank you," she chimed.

The group's laughter echoed through the clearing, the tension momentarily broken.

Verdantia's firm but expectant voice carried the faint rustle of her wings folding and a subtle tremor, adding a textured weight to her authority. She turned to Thalorian. "Rest while you can. Your training begins soon."

Thalorian met her gaze with a nod, his eyes alight with determination.

With the battle behind them, the scent of scorched earth lingered in the air, and the whisper of leaves, stirred by a faint breeze, carried the echoes of the fight. Ong exhaled slowly, his gaze sweeping over the battlefield. "Another victory," he murmured, though the weight in his chest reminded him of the battles still to come. Keisha glanced at him, reading his thoughts without words. "For now," she agreed softly. But the road ahead was still long. Ong, Keisha, and Gailen began the walk back to Crystal Vale. The forest, bruised but standing, dappled them in the afternoon light, a fleeting peace before the next storm.

Chapter 24

Verdantia's Choice

Thalorian stood in the glen, his breath shallow as he steadied himself, his pulse a relentless drumbeat in his ears. The crisp earthiness of the damp soil and the sweet, sharp scent of wildflowers grounded him even as his muscles tensed with anticipation. A flicker of unease crept along his spine, chased by the cool touch of the wind, stirring a primal alertness. His heart pounded a mixture of readiness and uncertainty as his gaze locked on Verdantia's towering, luminous form.

"This will not be a mere exercise in riding," Verdantia said, her voice deep and resonant. "You have the basics, but now you must learn what it means to be a dragon rider. You must face the challenges that will forge our bond."

Thalorian straightened, his expression firm. "I'm ready."

Verdantia's lips curled into a subtle, knowing smirk, a flick of her tail adding a playful flourish—a rare glimpse of her amusement laced with a warmth that hinted at their growing bond. Her ancient eyes glinted, both challenging and reassuring. "We shall see."

She crouched low, wings folding tightly, the leathery membranes whispering as they pressed against her sides. Thalorian climbed onto her back, his palms clammy against her cool ridges.

"The first test," Verdantia said, "is trust. You must trust me entirely to be my rider, even when it defies reason."

Before he could respond, flashes of doubt and triumph flooded his mind. Would he falter or rise to the challenge? His breath hitched as Verdantia launched into the sky, the wind stealing his breath.

"Hold tight," she commanded, then folded her wings into a terrifying dive.

The world spun sky, earth, chaos. Fear gripped him, but exhilaration sparked within.

"Do not fight it!" she urged.

He forced his grip to loosen, the wind roaring past, his body weightless. Then, with a sudden snap, her wings unfurled. The glide smoothed, tension melting into exhilaration.

"Good," she praised. "You did not let fear consume you."

With a final swoop, Verdantia arced gracefully through the sky before descending, her mighty wings stirring the glen's grass as she landed. "Now, balance. Move with me, not against me."

Her steps were sharp, deliberate, uneven strides slicing through the glen. Quick bursts. Sudden pauses. She weaved between trees, each shift unpredictable. Thalorian's breath hitched, quickening. Slowing. With a sudden leap, his body jolted, struggling to synchronize with her wild rhythm.

"Do not grip so tightly," Verdantia snapped.

His fingers twitched, instinct urging him to cling for stability. Each jolt knocked his balance askew, fast corrections burning his muscles. Sweat trickled down his brow.

"A dragon is not a horse. Firm but flexible. Trust my strength to carry you."

He exhaled and loosened his grip. He let her movements guide him, the shift of her muscles, the surge of her leap, the glide of her landing. Rhythm emerged, his body answering her motion.

A log low, broad. Verdantia crouched. Thalorian felt it, sensed it. He leaned forward before she jumped. They landed as one.

"Better," she praised. "But balance is not just about your body. You must also listen."

"Listen?" he echoed.

"Not with your ears. With your intuition. Feel my rhythm. Anticipate my next move."

Her pace turned wild—sharp turns, sudden stops, erratic leaps. Thalorian's breath came in sharp bursts, his pulse hammering as he fought to keep up, muscles screaming in protest against the relentless shifts. Thalorian closed his eyes briefly. No sight, just sensation. The coil of her muscles. The angle of her turns.

Verdantia leaped, and he moved with her. He shifted with a sharp twist and was centered. They moved as one.

When they stopped, Verdantia glanced back. "Good. You are learning."

Thalorian, muscles burning and limbs heavy, felt exhaustion and satisfaction in equal measure. He had pushed himself. He had improved.

"That was more challenging than I expected," he admitted, his breath still short but his spirit alight.

Verdantia's lips curled in a faint smile, her eyes shimmering with knowing mischief. The warm scent of the wind, tinged with wild earth, brushed past as a low, approving rumble echoed in her chest. She shifted her weight slightly, the smooth stretch of muscle beneath her emerald scales radiating power and ease. Her wings flexed, their edges catching the light in shimmering arcs. The flick of her tail and the subtle flare of her nostrils hinted at a more profound satisfaction—an unspoken acknowledgment of Thalorian's progress.

"And that was only the beginning. Balance is about surviving the ride and becoming part of the dragon. We will refine this further as we progress."

With a mighty beat of her wings, they launched skyward. The sudden burst of air whipped against Thalorian's face, his silver-streaked hair tugging free as the glen shrank beneath them. His heart pounded in his chest, the sharp rush of ascent tightening every muscle.

Verdantia banked smoothly to the left, a gentle, sweeping curve. Thalorian felt the pull of gravity and fought the instinct to tense. Instead, he leaned into the motion, his body recalling the rhythms he had learned on the ground.

"Good," Verdantia praised, her voice calm against the roar of the wind. "But the sky rarely stays gentle."

Without warning, she snapped to the right. Thalorian's body jerked with the sudden motion, his stomach twisting as his grip tightened instinctively before he forced himself to relax into the movement. The sudden shift made Thalorian's stomach lurch, but he adjusted quickly. The wind howled, and then they plunged into a dive, air screaming past his ears. His pulse quickened, but his posture remained loose, his trust in her absolute.

The dive ended in a smooth glide, the air rushing quieter around them. "Adaptability is key," Verdantia said. "The sky is unpredictable. You must flow with it, not fight it."

Thalorian's resolve sharpened. He welcomed the barrage of maneuvers Verdantia threw at him: rapid ascents, jarring stops, tight spirals, each testing his instincts and balance to the limit.

Then came the next challenge. "You must stand," she declared, her voice rippling with gravity. "One day, you may need to fight while riding."

His breath hitched. Doubt clawed, whispering of falls and failure. But he crushed it. Verdantia believed in him, and he would not falter. The wind burned his skin as he crouched, his breath shuddering with the weight of the challenge. His palms pressed against the warm, living emerald beneath him, seeking stability and reassurance. Fear coiled in his gut, but he forced it down, gripping onto determination instead.

"Feel my movements," she instructed. "Let your core, not your legs, guide your balance."

He closed his eyes briefly, centering himself, then rose, his legs trembling but his core firm. The wind struck him hard, testing his resolve, but he remained rooted, his body adjusting instinctively as Verdantia rolled slightly left and right. The connection was growing, his reactions sharper, his anticipation keener.

Verdantia accelerated. The strain in his muscles turned searing as he fought to stay upright through every sudden drop and jarring twist, yet a spark of confidence ignited within him. Each movement felt more instinctive, his body learning to anticipate rather than react. The wind stung his eyes, and sweat burned his brow, but he gritted his teeth, moving in unity with her living rhythm. A sharp dive came. He crouched instinctively, brushing her ridges for stability before rising again as they leveled.

"You're learning," Verdantia said, warmth in her voice. "But remember, this is not about mastery. It is about trust. Trust in me and trust in yourself."

Thalorian nodded, his confidence growing with each passing moment. The wind carried the earthy scent of leaves and sky, its crisp touch cool against his skin, while the soft rhythm of Verdantia's breath echoed beneath him, a steady pulse of warmth and power. His pulse thrummed, but it was not from fear. It was from exhilaration, from the unbreakable bond forming between them. His mind flashed with thoughts of how far he had come—from the desperation of his first ride to this harmony, where trust replaced terror. The wind rushed past him, no longer a force to fear but an ally, guiding him alongside Verdantia. This was more than training; it was a bond forged between rider and dragon with each passing moment. The calm wind's whisper against his skin and the rhythmic thrum of Verdantia's wings surrounded him, deepening his exhilaration. Fear had once ruled him, but now, he felt attuned to her every motion. Trust in the wind, himself, and his dragon fueled him. This was more than training; it was the forging of a bond.

Without warning, Verdantia shifted sharply. Thalorian's body lurched, his grip tightening instinctively as his stomach flipped. His muscles tensed in protest, but he forced himself to adjust, fighting the urge to resist the sudden movement. Thalorian's heart leaped, instinct screaming as the angle sent him sliding. His mind flashed with panic and determination; there was no time to think, only to react.

The air roared past him, sharp and wild, slicing his breath short. His skin stung from the relentless force, and every muscle strained against the chaos of the fall. Desperation pounded through him, but Verdantia's voice cut through the confusion.

"Focus, Thalorian!" A flash of doubt pierced his thoughts: should he fear or trust? His heart pounded, but he clung to the bond they had forged. Trust. It had to be trusted. "Spread your arms and legs to slow your fall!"

His pulse hammered, but he obeyed. Arms wide, legs braced, the wind's bite softened, and he felt a fragile control. Fear still lurked, but trust rose stronger.

"Use your magic, Moon Elf! You must control your descent. NOW!" Verdantia's command rang with urgency.

Heat sparked within him, pure and primal magic. It coursed through his veins, liquid moonlight unfurling from his core. The air thickened, cushioning his descent. The world sharpened—sound, wind, and sky, his senses alive with magic's pulse.

They practiced the fall multiple times, and each plummeted, refining instinct into mastery. Shorter breaths. Faster reactions. Sweat streaked his skin, and his muscles burned, but he no longer fought the fall he commanded. By the final attempt, instinct and magic flowed as one.

When Verdantia caught him, her voice carried something new approval. "You're learning," she said, the warmth beneath her words unmistakable.

"Trust in me and yourself. The sky is not your enemy. It is your ally, as am I."

Thalorian's chest heaved, the lingering rush of adrenaline fading into steady resolve. His limbs ached, but his heart beat with clarity. He had fallen and risen. And he was ready for more.

Verdantia landed gracefully in the glen, the rush of air from her wings sending leaves swirling in chaotic eddies, scattering dust and petals in a fleeting dance. The trees trembled with the force, their branches whispering in response, while the scent of churned earth and fresh greenery filled the air. Thalorian exhaled, his chest rising with the weight of realization. Pride mingled with exhaustion—how far he had come from the uncertain rider of his first flight. Now, the sky felt like an extension of himself, limitless and alive. He braced against the gust, his cloak billowing as his boots pressed firmly into the earth. The glen welcomed them in serene contrast to their trials: leaves whispered overhead, the scent of moss and wildflowers filling the crisp air, and distant birdsong threading the stillness.

Thalorian dismounted, his limbs aching but his resolve unshaken. He felt the burn of his training, but more so, he felt the fire of purpose.

"Now," Verdantia began, her emerald gaze sharp and knowing, "we move to combat. The weapon you wield on my back will define your role in battle."

Thalorian's jade fire eyes met hers, his voice steady. "I plan to wield the Arborblade."

Verdantia's expression was unreadable, but the subtle flick of her tail and the slight narrowing of her eyes hinted at a deeper contemplation. "The blade of emerald light, tempered by the Moon Elves. It is a powerful choice but demanding. Its length and weight will test you, and its power will demand precision."

Thalorian's voice carried his certainty. "I understand."

"Then begin without it," Verdantia instructed. "First, you must feel it. Visualize its weight and know its reach. Only when your body moves as if the blade is already in your hand will we bring the weapon itself."

Thalorian climbed onto her back once more, his body sinking into a familiar rhythm as Verdantia rose into the sky, her wings cutting through the breeze.

"Imagine the Arborblade," she commanded. "Feel it."

Thalorian's eyes fluttered shut as a wave of energy coursed through him, the air around him thickening with unseen force. A tingling heat spread from his core to his fingertips, and for a moment, it felt as though the blade pulsed with his very heartbeat. He felt the cold weight of the hilt, the textured grip fitting his palm, and the soft, resonant hum of the blade's power. A thread of his Moon Elf heritage pulsed, echoing his lineage. The imagined blade felt real, a part of him.

"Strike!" Verdantia's voice was sharp and sudden.

Thalorian's body answered before his arm swung through the air, the imagined blade's arc pulling his balance. Verdantia twisted mid-air, testing his poise.

"Good. Faster."

Their tempo sharpened. Verdantia's dives and turns became erratic, and each lurch tested his instinct. The wind lashed his face, and his breath quickened. His muscles burned, his heart pounded, and he fought to keep his body fluid, his strikes swift and sure.

"Your weapon is more than a tool; it is an extension of your very essence, as vital as breath and as unyielding as the sky itself." Verdantia's voice deepened. It is like our bond, two forces moving as one. As you trust me to carry you through the sky, trust your blade to carry your will into battle." Verdantia's voice surged through the wind. It is you. If your body falters, your blade will fail."

The lesson struck deeper than her words. Thalorian's movements smoothed, his imagined strikes blending with Verdantia's rhythm. He felt the power of his body and mind aligning. The Arborblade was not something he wielded; it was an extension of his will.

A flicker of mastery kindled within him, and he felt a pure, unmistakable connection. He was no longer reacting. He was riding, striking, being.

His breath was hard, his muscles quivering, but his spirit soared with newfound certainty. He had moved beyond mere training. This was transformation. Each motion and strike had reshaped him, carving away doubt and forging something more substantial. He was not just learning; he was becoming.

And for the first time, he felt that he was not just a rider. He was one with Verdantia. One with the sky. And he was ready for what lay ahead.

Thalorian dismounted briefly, his eyes drawn to the Arborblade resting against a tree at the edge of the glen. Unlike any ordinary sword, it pulsed with a faint, living heartbeat, its emerald-hued hilt shimmering as if woven from forest light. As Thalorian's fingers wrapped around it, a gentle warmth seeped into his skin, the surface smooth yet pulsing like the rhythm of a slumbering beast waiting to awaken. He recalled simpler weapons, cold steel, lifeless and inert, but this was different. The Arborblade resonated with power, whispering echoes of the Moon Elves and the forest's ancient wisdom. As he gripped the hilt, warmth spread through his palm, a soft pulse synchronizing with his heartbeat. The blade felt alive, an extension of nature itself.

Verdantia watched, her gaze laced with pride and challenge as if measuring his resolve. "The Arborblade is no ordinary weapon," she said, her voice steady. "It is like our bond, both shield and spear, destruction and renewal. Its power flows from the natural world and with your intent. Strike precisely; it will protect you as fiercely as it attacks."

Thalorian mounted, the blade's runes faintly aglow against his shoulder. Verdantia soared, cutting through the sky. "Focus your energy," she commanded. "The blade will answer your will."

The hilt felt warm and alive as he swung. Emerald light flared, a luminous arc trailing the strike. His breath quickened as the weapon felt heavy yet fluid, powerful yet requiring balance.

Verdantia conjured shadowy figures, their forms twisting with malice, their movements eerily fluid yet jagged, like fractured reflections in rippling water. Hollow eyes gleamed with an unnatural light, and their clawed hands flickered between solid and spectral, shifting as if caught between realms. They circled, flickering between shape and smoke. The air felt charged, and the scent of cold magic hung sharp. Thalorian swung the blade and erupted in the green light, the phantom splintering into dark wisps. Another shadow lunged, and instinct guided his second strike, the blade's power shielding him with a burst of emerald energy that deflected an incoming blow.

Verdantia twisted beneath him, and he felt the dance, the blade, the bond, the battle. Shadows closed in, but his strikes were fluid, his breath in rhythm with Verdantia's wings. One shadow darted low, and his swing faltered for a heartbeat, doubt lashing through him before his blade met its mark, dispersing the final threat.

The last shadow dissolved, silence reclaiming the sky. Thalorian's grip on the Arborblade tightened as he let out a slow breath, the weight of the battle settling over him. He had not just fought. He had endured, adapted, and risen beyond his limits. A newfound certainty settled within him, his bond with Verdantia and the blade now unshakable. Thalorian's chest heaved, his arms tingling from exertion. For an instant, he felt it: mastery, not of the blade alone, but of himself.

Verdantia's voice broke the hush, layered with approval and expectation. "You've done well," she said. "But remember, the Arborblade, like me, answers trust and purpose. Wield it for more than yourself. Wield it for the world."

Thalorian dismounted, the blade's warmth fading to a steady pulse in his hand, a quiet reassurance of the bond they had forged. It no longer

blazed with newfound energy but settled into something more profound, an understanding, a promise that its strength would always
answer his call. "I understand," he said softly, his voice edged with
resolve. "And I will not falter."

As Verdantia landed gracefully in the glen, the sunlight filtering
through the canopy reflected off her emerald scales. Thalorian slid
from her back, his boots meeting the earth with an extraordinary,
grounding firmness. The faint scent of moss and wildflowers reached
him, anchoring him in the moment. The Arborblade remained in his
hand, its faint glow a subtle reminder of the power they had unleashed
together.

He stepped forward, placing the blade gently on the ground. His
jade fire eyes met Verdantia's, a question burning within as much
about himself as hers. Doubts pressed in, his mind flashing between the
crushing weight of his earliest defeats, the missed parries, the bruises
from failed landings, the moments he felt unworthy, and the rare, fleeting victories where instinct had guided him truly, where Verdantia's
approving gaze had made him believe he could be more. What had
brought him here, fate or something within him that he had yet to see
truly?

"Verdantia," he began, his fingers shifting slightly on the hilt, a brief
tremor betraying his hesitation before he steadied his grip, his voice
steady but weighted, "Why did you choose to train me yourself? Why
not another?" His hand, almost unconsciously, tightened against the
worn hilt before loosening a gesture of tension and trust.

Verdantia's eyes shimmered with ancient wisdom, and her head inclined slightly as if acknowledging a truth only she could fully grasp.
"It was not simply what you did or said," she replied, her voice resonant
with certainty, "but what I sensed, like the earth knows the roots
beneath it. Dragons see beyond the surface. In you, I felt potential and
purpose waiting to rise through fire and trial."

Thalorian's brow furrowed, his hand brushing over the Arborblade's cool, rune-etched hilt, its pulse steady like a heart beneath his fingers. "But how could you know that from a single moment?"

"It was never just a glance," Verdantia answered, her gaze softening. "It was a connection. We do not look we feel. And what I felt in you was more than strength. It was a bond waiting to be forged through trust and trial."

The word bond echoed in his mind, strengthening his understanding of leadership. It was more than command, more than power. Knowing that leadership meant making choices others could not bear, the cost so others could stand, weighed on him but sparked something sharp and bright within.

He pressed his palm against Verdantia's scales, cool, smooth, and thrumming faintly with her life's energy. "I won't let you down," he said, his voice soft but unshakable.

Verdantia's wings folded with a gentle rustle, and her voice, steady and prosperous with conviction, carried the warmth of absolute certainty. A knowing glint flickered in her emerald eyes, her gaze unwavering as if seeing who he was and who he would become. "I know you will not. That is why I chose you."

The glen settled into a sacred hush, broken only by a bird's distant call and the wind's sighing through the trees. The silence felt like a pact, a promise sealed beyond words. As Thalorian retrieved the Arborblade and began the path back to the training grounds, the earth felt firmer beneath his steps, the scent of moss and wood a companion to his resolve. Verdantia walked beside him, her towering shadow not a weight but a shield, a silent sentinel of his purpose, path, and promise.

Chapter 25

The Assassin's Shadow

The air shimmered with dark energy. A low, crackling hum threaded through the atmosphere like static before a storm. An unnatural force pulsed around him, clawing at his very essence. A cold, prickling sensation spread over his skin, like spectral fingers raking down his spine. The man resisted the call, his mind racing with excuses to ignore it, even as a creeping sense of dread coiled tightly around his thoughts. Yet, the pull grew more vigorous, twisting his gut with an unnatural dread. He staggered, clutching at the air as if to anchor himself, but it was futile. The pull overwhelmed him before he could act on his defiance, and the world around him shifted.

The oppressive heat of Fel Thalor wrapped around him like a living thing, and a thought pierced his mind. This place felt like the breath of something ancient and malevolent, watching, waiting for him to falter. It pressed against him, constricting his breath with an unbearable weight as though the very air sought to smother him. The glow of molten lava pulsed like a heartbeat, its heat searing his skin even from a distance. A low, rhythmic rumble vibrated through the ground beneath his feet, accompa-

nied by the occasional hiss and crackle as molten rock shifted and bubbled. Acrid sulfur lingered in the air, mixing with the metallic tang of
old blood, intensifying the suffocating atmosphere of this cursed place.
The glow of molten lava cast jagged, flickering shadows on the altar,
its stones etched with ancient, bloodied runes, sigils of long-forgotten
oaths, and dark pacts sealed with sacrifice. Their lines pulsed faintly
as if still thirsting for the essence they once consumed, whispering
remnants of power lost to time. A faint metallic tang clung to the air,
a cruel reminder of the sacrifices once made here.

The man swallowed hard, his gaze falling on the figure standing
before the altar, cloaked in darkness.

The mysterious stranger turned slowly, the faint whisper of their
cloak brushing against the stone floor, their fingers trailing along the
edge of the altar as if drawing power from its ancient runes, carrying a
trace of something sharp and metallic, like distant smoke or scorched
air, their silver hair catching the crimson glow of the lava. A faint smirk
crossed their face, a mix of amusement and disdain. "I thought I made
it clear," they said, their voice cold and sharp, "when I summon you,
you appear. Immediately."

The man clenched his fists, his nails biting into his palms. The
sharp sting barely registered through the heat of his anger. His breath
quickened, tension coiling through his body, every fiber screaming to
retaliate, to resist. But he could feel the weight of the stranger's power
pressing down on him like an iron vice. He bowed his head slightly, his
voice a low murmur. "What do you want now?"

The stranger's smirk widened, accompanied by the faint crackle of
molten rock and the distant hiss of escaping steam, as if the environ-
ment mirrored their hostility, their eyes gleaming with a dangerous
light. "What I want," they said, stepping closer to the altar, "is for you
to remember your place."

The man straightened, a flicker of defiance flashing as he met the stranger's piercing gaze. "How is it," he began, his voice edged with frustration, "that you came to hold this... pledge my father made centuries ago? The Shadowwalkers are gone, dead, and forgotten, their power little more than whispers of a bygone age. Whatever pact he made should have died with them."

The stranger's lips curled into a slow, predatory grin, their eyes gleaming with cruel satisfaction. "Do not concern yourself with matters beyond your understanding," they said, their voice dripping with mockery. "The pledge is mine now, passed into my hands by means you cannot comprehend. That is all you need to know."

The man's jaw tightened, and a fleeting image of his father's shadowed face flashed through his mind, a reminder of debts and betrayals long buried. His teeth pressed together, and bitterness curled through his thoughts, sharp and cold. His fists clenched as he resisted the urge to lash out. "It's a good thing they're gone," he muttered, almost to himself, his tone bitter.

The stranger tilted their head in a slow, deliberate motion, the silver strands of their hair catching the fiery glow of the altar's light. Their eyes narrowed slightly, gleaming with quiet menace as if savoring the helplessness of their opponent. Their lips curled ever so slightly, a glimmer of cruel amusement flickering in their eyes as if savoring some unspoken victory. "Perhaps," they said with a shrug, their voice calm but cold. "Or perhaps not. Either way, your father's foolishness binds you now. And you will do as I command."

The man inhaled sharply, the scent of sulfur burning his nostrils and the heat pressing against his throat like a smothering hand, forcing himself to focus. "What do you want this time?"

The stranger's gaze narrowed. A faint, almost imperceptible hum of dark energy rippled through the air, thickening the tension around them. Their tone was laced with cold, measured cunning. "Prince Gailen. Has he been trained as a dragon rider yet? His bond with Aurelia could tip the scales against me, and that must not be allowed to happen." Their voice was laced with something more than curiosity and anticipation mingled with malice.

The man hesitated. A fleeting memory of his father's warnings flashed through his mind—words about trust, loyalty, and the cost of betrayal. His pulse pounded in his ears, resentment churning in his gut as he wrestled between duty and self-preservation. Despite the heat of Fel Thalor, a chill slithered down his spine, a warning or an omen; he could not tell. If he revealed too much, he risked sealing Prince Gailen's fate. If he said too little, the stranger might suspect deception—and the consequences of that could be even worse. His thoughts churned, but in the end, he settled on caution. Finally, he shook his head. "No, not yet. But it could happen soon. The dragons are preparing for their riders, and his training is inevitable."

The stranger's expression darkened slightly, though the smirk remained. "Good. Then there is still time to act."

The man's eyes narrowed as he glanced at the stranger, unease creeping into his voice. "What does that mean?"

The stranger's smirk faded, their brow twitching as their stance shifted subtly. A predator gauging its prey, they exuded a quiet menace, their narrowed eyes gleaming with calculated malice. Their fingers twitched at their side as if resisting the urge to act, and a slow breath escaped their lips, controlled yet brimming with restrained menace. They took a measured step forward, their presence looming as though the heat bent to their will. "It means I have arranged for the Obsidian dragons to test the defenses of Crystal Vale. During the skirmish, certain... opportunities will arise."

The man stiffened, his pulse quickening and a cold sweat breaking along his neck. Every muscle coiled with tension, his unease deepening into dread. "What kind of opportunities?"

The stranger's eyes gleamed with malice, and the air thickened with oppressive heat. The firelight cracked faintly as if charged with unseen energy, hardening their expressions as they leaned forward slightly. The firelight cast sinister shadows across their faces. "To ensure Prince Gailen is eliminated before he can become a dragon rider, his connection to Aurelia must never be fully realized."

The man took a step back, his thoughts racing. Was there any escape from this trap, or was he already ensnared with no way out? Shaking his head vehemently. "No. That cannot happen. No matter what you threaten or do to me, I will not be part of that." His voice carried a finality, a spark of defiance that even the stranger's oppressive presence could not extinguish.

The stranger's gaze turned icy, and time seemed to slow, the heat of Fel Thalor pausing as if the world struggled to comprehend such defiance. A subtle shift rippled through the air, thick with disbelief, the smirk vanishing from their faces as their voice dropped to a low, menacing growl. "You dare refuse me?"

The man's jaw clenched, but he stood firm. "Yes. Killing him is a step too far. I will do many things under this cursed obligation, but I will not take the life of someone who trusts me, especially not a prince."

For a long moment, the air between them was thick with tension. The stranger's silver hair shimmered in the light of the molten lava as they considered the man's words. Their fingers tapped absently against the stone altar, a slow, deliberate rhythm betraying their inner calculation. Their expression was unreadable, but the faintest flicker of annoyance crossed their faces.

"Fine," the stranger said, their voice sharp and curt. "Then ensure he is injured badly enough not to complete his training with Aurelia. He is no threat if he cannot rise to his potential."

The man's defiance faltered, the oppressive heat pressing against his skin and the distant crackle of molten rock filling the air, heightening the tension of his wavering resolve, weighed down by the crushing reality of his servitude. The memory of his father's trembling voice as he sealed their fate echoed in his mind an oath sworn in desperation, shackling not just himself but his entire bloodline. He had been just a child then, too young to grasp the weight of those words. Now, standing in the searing heat of Fel Thalor, he felt their burden pressing down on him like an iron chain, unrelenting and absolute. Fear warred with duty, but in the end, the chains of his obligation held firm, dragging him into reluctant compliance. He wanted to argue, to refuse outright, but he knew the limits of his position. Finally, he gave a slight nod, his voice tight. "I will ... see what I can do."

The stranger's smirk returned, thin and dangerous. "Good. Do not fail me again." Without another word, the stranger turned and vanished into the oppressive shadows, leaving the man alone in the suffocating heat of Fel Thalor.

As the silence enveloped him, a faint hiss of steam escaped from a nearby fissure, and the crackling of cooling lava whispered through the oppressive stillness, mirroring his inner turmoil. The man's fists unclenched, trembling slightly. His gaze fell to the jagged altar, and a bitter thought took hold: why had his father done this to their family? The weight of his father's choices pressed heavily on his shoulders, an unbreakable chain forged from blood oaths and desperate bargains. His father had sworn fealty to the shadows, sacrificing their family's freedom for power he never truly controlled, dooming his lineage to servitude under unseen masters.

Could the bond be broken? A fleeting image of his childhood self surfaced, standing in a sunlit grove, dreaming of a life free from shadows and debts he never chose. The memory brought a pang of longing, sharpening his desire to reclaim his stolen freedom. For the first time, the thought struck him with a spark of desperate hope, igniting a whirlwind of emotions he could scarcely contain. Fear of the unknown war with a deep yearning for freedom and, beneath it all, a lingering anger at his father's long-forgotten choices. But another fear gnawed at him: if his betrayal were discovered, would his old friends, and even the new ones he had made, turn against him? Would he be left utterly alone, cast aside as a traitor with no place to belong?

The spark grew into a fragile ember, rekindling the memory of a time when he had dreamed of forging his path, free from the weight of past sins. He saw himself as a boy, running through the golden fields beyond his family's estate, arms outstretched like wings, believing momentarily that he could escape the legacy that bound him. The wind had carried his laughter then, unburdened by fear, before reality had tightened its grip and dragged him back into the shadows. That dream had never indeed died. It had only been buried beneath the weight of obligation. It illuminated the faintest glimmer of a future unbound by shadowy chains, where he could reclaim his name and choices. Was there a way to free himself from this shadowy obligation, to finally end the cycle of manipulation and control? The idea seemed distant, almost impossible, but it refused to leave him.

With a determined breath, his heart pounding and his hands trembling with the intensity of his resolve, he turned away from the altar, the acrid stench of sulfur lingering in his nostrils as he strode toward the edge of the volcanic expanse. Crystal Vale awaited him, and he knew that despite the stranger's command, he could never bring himself to harm Gailen. He remembered the first time he had seen the boy train determined, full of hope, and carrying the weight of a future he barely understood. He had seen that same light in another once, long ago, a friend who had trusted him before fate had torn them apart.

Failing Gailen now would mean repeating the past, and that was something he could never allow. The thought of carrying out such a vile act seized him, a cold, twisting weight in his chest. Could he genuinely cross that line? His breath came in uneven bursts, his fingers clenching and unclenching at his sides. A cold sweat prickled along the back of his neck, and the weight of the decision settled deep in his bones like an unshakable chill. His mind spiraled: How did it come to this? What would he become if he followed through? The conflict churned his stomach, guilt and duty clashing in a brutal, chaotic storm. His mind spun with guilt and defiance, torn between the looming threat of the stranger's wrath and the growing resolve to shield Gailen at all costs.

Each step toward Crystal Vale felt heavier, the heat shimmering off the rocks in waves that distorted the air, making the horizon waver like an unreachable mirage. The acrid scent of sulfur clung to his lungs, burning with every breath, and the crunch of ash beneath his boots was a stark reminder of the desolation surrounding him. Every movement felt sluggish, as though the ground sought to hold him back, forcing him to push forward with sheer will alone. He felt burdened by the knowledge that his choice could reshape both fates. He needed a subtle, careful plan to keep Gailen safe without revealing his defiance. The stranger would be watching, waiting for signs of treachery, but if he played this right, he might find a way to break free from the chains that bound him. The prince deserved a chance to fulfill his destiny, and the man resolved to protect him even if it meant defying the stranger's will.

Chapter 26

Whispers of a Deeper War

Verdantia and Aurelia stood on the edge of the training grounds, their gazes sweeping over the assembled riders and dragons. The scent of freshly churned earth, warm and rich from the sun's lingering heat, mingled with the faint smokiness of extinguished training fires. A light breeze carried the distant murmur of voices and the occasional scrape of boots against gravel, grounding the scene in the rhythm of the training grounds. The distant clang of metal against metal echoed from the sparring ring while the rhythmic flap of dragon wings stirred dust into the evening glow. The last remnants of the day's light bathed the scene in a warm hue, but the weight of their thoughts dimmed the moment.

"The training is complete," Verdantia said, her voice low and contemplative. "They are as ready as they can be, but no amount of practice will fully prepare them for what lies ahead."

Aurelia nodded, her crystalline eyes reflecting the fading sunlight. A gentle breeze brushed over her scales, cool and fleeting against the warmth of the evening. For a moment, it felt like a distant echo of something comforting, a reminder of peaceful skies before the storm. But the sensation was fleeting, unable to dispel the weight pressing down on her heart. A quiet storm of thoughts swirled within—a cold weight settling deep in her chest. Memories of past battles and the weight of those they had lost pressed heavily upon her. Yet, beneath the sorrow, an unshakable resolve burned a vow to protect those who remained. She knew the riders were prepared but doubt still crept at the edges of her mind. Would their training be enough? Would they have the strength to endure what was coming?

"Experience will be their true teacher now. Only in facing the dark dragons will they truly learn what it means to fight and survive."

The two ancient dragons watched as the riders laughed and talked, their camaraderie a fragile shield against the dangers that loomed ever closer. The distant cry of a hawk broke the calm, its sharp call carrying an unspoken warning. Aurelia's gaze lifted to the sky, her thoughts darkening. It was an omen, a reminder that peace was fleeting. The cry lingered in her mind, echoing a premonition she could not shake just as the warning bell would soon shatter the stillness. Aurelia's gaze lingered on Gailen, who stood with Ong and Keisha, his youthful determination tempered by a growing sense of responsibility. She saw promise and vulnerability in his stance, and her heart ached with the weight of responsibility.

"We must protect them as best we can," Aurelia said softly. "They carry the future of Vacari on their shoulders, even if they do not yet realize it."

Verdantia inclined her head. "They will learn. And when the time comes, they will rise to the challenge or fall trying." A flicker of pride and worry intertwined. Every battle had its cost.

The ancient dragons exchanged a quiet glance, Verdantia's tail flicking slightly while Aurelia's wings shifted, their silent communication speaking volumes. A moment of shared understanding passed between them, their eyes flickering with unspoken resolve. Heavy with concern, their watchful gaze returned to the riders, their thoughts weighed down by the uncertainties of the battles ahead.

The air grew heavier as they discussed the crucial decision: splitting the dragons and riders into two groups, one to protect Crystal Vale, the other to guard Emerald Woods. It was a necessary strategy, but the risks were undeniable, especially with many riders still new to their bonds. Dividing their forces meant weakening their defenses; any mistake could cost them dearly. Ensuring both regions remained defended without weakening either force was vital. The wind stilled, and an uneasy hush fell over the grounds as if the earth held its breath.

Deep and resonant, a faint rumble stirred beneath their feet like something massive was shifting far below. Verdantia and Aurelia recognized the sound instantly, not an ordinary tremor but the stirring of an ancient dragon, a presence long unseen yet impossible to forget. Verdantia's emerald gaze sharpened, her instincts warning her of imminent danger just as the sharp clanging of the warning bell shattered the air.

Heads turned sharply toward the source of the warning bell's sound. The clatter of boots on the stone broke the silence, a sound of urgency, raw and breathless, as a breathless messenger raced toward them, his face pale, and his voice trembling.

"Obsidian dragons!" he gasped, clutching his side. "They've been spotted near Crystal Vale!"

The group fell into a tense silence. Aurelia exchanged a glance with Verdantia, her crystalline eyes reflecting the moment's gravity. Verdantia nodded, her emerald gaze hardening as she turned to the assembled riders.

"To Crystal Vale," Verdantia commanded, her voice ringing with authority. "Everyone, prepare yourselves. Move now!"

The dragon riders quickly mounted their dragons, the once-calm training grounds erupting into a flurry of motion. The thunder of boots pounded against the earth, blending with the whoosh of mighty wings. Dust and the sharp scent of churned earth filled the air as shadows of massive forms swept across the ground. The powerful downdraft from dragon wings sent loose debris swirling, the rush of wind carrying their ascent's deep, rhythmic beats. Riders shouted commands, their voices rising above the growing roar as they prepared for the flight.

Gailen stepped forward, his heart pounding, his gaze fixed on Aurelia. "What about me?" he asked, his voice steady despite the tension thrumming through his chest.

Aurelia's crystalline eyes softened, a glint of something maternal beneath their icy sheen, but her voice remained steel-edged. "Not yet, Prince Gailen. You are untrained, and I will not risk your life unnecessarily. Protecting the people from the ground is where your strength is needed most."

Gailen's jaw tightened, his teeth pressing together as frustration flared in his chest. He believed he was ready and trained enough to stand beside the others. But did Aurelia see him as nothing more than an inexperienced boy? Doubt gnawed at him. Was he genuinely unready, or did Aurelia underestimate him? The sting of being sidelined burned against his pride, but a colder truth whispered: failure in battle meant death. His fists clenched, nails biting into his palms as he shoved the bitter spark of resentment down. Now was not the time for pride. He had to prove himself, even if it meant waiting a little longer.

Aurelia's crystalline form shifted, her mighty wings spreading wide as she prepared to take flight. She paused, her voice softening to a near whisper, just for him.

"But know this," she said, her wings catching the amber glow of the fading sun, "after this, your training will begin in earnest. Vacari will need you not as a prince but as a warrior."

A flicker of determination sparked in Gailen's eyes, though it was tempered by the realization that he had not yet received the training he needed for this battle. The tension in his stance eased, replaced by a quiet resolve he would learn, he would train, and when the time came, he would be ready. He stepped back, his shoulders squared, allowing Aurelia to join the others.

With a powerful beat of wings, Aurelia ascended, the sunlight catching the crystalline facets of her scales, scattering shards of rainbow light across the sky. The other dragons followed, their vibrant wings slicing through the amber twilight as they soared toward Crystal Vale. Below, the dust settled, and Gailen stood alone, his heart pounding, his resolve burning.

On the ground, Gailen turned to Ong and Keisha, who had remained at his side. "Let's get to the city walls," he said firmly. "If the dragons are spotted, there is no telling what the Obsidian dragons might do. We need to make sure the people are safe."

Ong nodded, a determined glint in his eye. "Agreed. Let us move."

The group arrived in Crystal Vale to see the unsettling sight of the Obsidian dragons circling high above. Their wings carved through the sky with a thunderous rhythm, each beat stirring hot gusts that carried the acrid scent of smoldering embers. Ash and soot drifted through the air, clinging to skin and stinging eyes. Citizens hurried through the streets, pulling scarves over their mouths and ushering children into doorways. Some stood frozen, their faces pale with fear, while others whispered prayers to the guardians of Vacari, their voices trembling as the sky darkened with looming wings. Jagged and shifting shadows stretched long over the pristine waterfalls and ancient stone streets, casting the city in an eerie half-light.

Keisha's sharp eyes swept the unfolding chaos. The air burned with the bitter tang of smoke, laced with the salt of sweat and fear. Citizens screamed, their cries raw and desperate as they clutched loved ones or scattered like startled birds. Boots pounded the stone streets. Each panicked footstep echoed the urgency of survival. Her pulse quickened. This was the kind of moment that separated leaders from survivors. Lives hung on every choice she made.

Her gaze landed on Valeon, who stood near a cluster of panicked townsfolk. His stance was tense, and his shoulders squared like bracing for impact. His jaw tightened, and his usual easy confidence was absent, replaced by a sharp focus that mirrored the urgency in Keisha's own heart.

"Valeon!" she called, her voice clear and firm over the rising panic. "Get the citizens to safety and take them to the palace. It is the strongest shelter we have." Her tone left no room for doubt, and in her eyes blazed the resolve of someone who knew that every second mattered.

Valeon's usual humor vanished, replaced by cold, focused urgency. Without hesitation, he raised his voice above the din: "Follow me!" His steady and confident call became an anchor for the frightened crowd. He guided them swiftly toward the palace gates, his sharp eyes scanning for stragglers, his heart pounding with the singular need to protect.

Inside the palace, the frightened citizens huddled close, their whispers blending into a nervous murmur. Slowly, as the walls stood firm around them and Valeon's presence remained unwavering, their fear began to lessen. Wide eyes darted to the towering windows, where the shadows of wings flashed across the glass. Valeon stood firm, his voice steady despite the tension tightening his chest: "Stay here. The palace will protect you." The crowd's fearful murmurs softened, replaced by murmurs of gratitude and a fragile, flickering hope.

With one last glance to ensure they were secure, Valeon turned and headed back out, determination etched into his face.

Meanwhile, Ong climbed the tower overlooking Crystal Vale, his movements swift and purposeful. Gailen followed closely behind, and his expression focused as he adjusted his sword at his side.

"From up here, we'll have a better view of what's happening," Ong said, his voice steady. The chill wind tugged at their clothes, carrying faint echoes of roars and cries from below.

The wind was sharp and cold atop the tower, biting through their cloaks and raising goosebumps on their skin. Ong narrowed his eyes against the chill, his body instinctively tense, while Gailen's fingers flexed around his sword hilt, the cold sharpening his senses rather than numbing them. The distant clamor of chaos screams, the clang of weapons, and the haunting, guttural roars of dragons pressed against them, an ominous reminder of what loomed ahead. The city's familiar streets, now laced with shadows and panic, sprawled beneath them like a battlefield waiting to ignite.

Gailen's eyes swept the horizon, his grip tightening around the hilt of his sword, but his gaze was clouded by the battle raging within him. The hilt of his sword felt cold and heavy in his palm, a symbol of the duty he bore and the fear he dared not show. His heart pounded, each beat a question he could not silence: Was he ready, or would his inexperience lead them all to ruin?

The Obsidian dragons' movements were methodical, their circling pattern unnervingly precise, like predators awaiting the perfect moment to strike. The dying light of the evening gleamed off their onyx scales, casting shifting, jagged reflections across the city below. They moved in calculated unison, each shift in formation deliberate, their massive wings slicing through the air with eerie synchronization, an unspoken signal that they were more than just beasts. They were hunters, waiting for the moment to descend.

"We'll focus on reinforcing the ground defenses," Ong said, his voice steady as he pointed toward the city's outer walls. "If they attack, the barriers will be their first test. Let us make sure they fail it."

Gailen's fingers flexed, tightening around his sword's hilt until his knuckles whitened. His voice, low and firm, held no hesitation: "We'll be ready."

But beneath his resolve, his pulse hammered with the weight of everything that rode on those words.

On the ground, Keisha stood at the center of a group of mages, her bow slung across her back as she raised her hands to channel her magic. Her heartbeat quickened, pounding in rhythm with the raw power gathering at her fingertips. Nearby, dragons without riders landed with earth-shaking grace, their presence towering and reassuring as they lent their magic to the effort. The air thickened, humming with power, and the scent of charged ozone stung Keisha's nose.

"Focus!" Keisha commanded, her voice cutting through the tense air like a blade. "We need a barrier in place before they test our defenses!"

The mages nodded, their faces taut with concentration, hands glowing as arcs of energy crackled between them. Keisha's magic joined theirs—threads of emerald light, vibrant and alive, weaving seamlessly into the dragons' shimmering power. A tingling warmth surged through her fingers, spreading up her arms as the magic pulsed with her heartbeat. The air sizzled, crackling with raw, untamed energy as the barrier began forming.

A translucent dome emerged, a shimmering shield of interwoven magic, its surface rippling like liquid glass. The mingled power of mages, dragons, and Keisha's will resonated in its radiant pulse.

Keisha glanced skyward, her cold, sharp gaze on the ominous forms above. Her fingers curled into fists at her sides, her stance shifting subtly as if bracing for the inevitable storm. "Let's hope it's enough," she murmured, her voice low but resolute.

Nocturna, the ancient Obsidian dragon, hovered with a presence that choked the air. A heavy weight pressed upon the defenders, their breaths growing shallow as if the atmosphere recoiled from her presence. Some staggered, gripping weapons tighter, while others instinctively braced as though expecting an unseen force to crush them beneath its might. Her wings' steady, thunderous beat cast sweeping shadows over the city below. Like liquid night, her black scales caught the dim light and flared with an ominous sheen. Her silver eyes, streaked with violet, cold, ancient, and pitiless, scoured the defenses scornfully.

Pathetic.

She had seen it all before. She had witnessed courage burn to ash and resolve to crumble to dust. She remembered Aelthmar's ruins and how the cries of the fallen had pierced the smoke-laden sky. Brave, yes. But bravery did not matter. Only inevitability did.

Victory was never a question of if. It was only a question of when. She had razed strongholds before and watched noble warriors crumble beneath the weight of inevitability. The fall of Aelthmar had been the same: a proud city reduced to ruin, its defenders valiant but ultimately powerless. This battle would be no different.

A sneer curled through her voice as she tasted the city's desperation, their barrier a fragile shell she would shatter like glass.

"Begin," she commanded, her voice a seismic tremor laced with ancient power. The air itself seemed to recoil from her decree.

The Obsidian dragons answered in chilling unison, their roars blending into a symphony of destruction. The air itself quivered with the force of their cries, a deep, resonant vibration that rattled windows and sent loose stones tumbling from rooftops. The ground beneath Crystal Vale trembled as if recoiling from the sheer magnitude of their power, dust rising in shuddering waves as the city braced for the inevitable storm. They dove, swift and merciless, releasing jagged torrents of dark energy that streaked toward the shimmering barrier. The first impact crashed against it with a deafening boom, sending ripples of luminous strain across its surface. The ground trembled beneath the force, cracks spidering through the cobblestones of Crystal Vale's streets.

Emerald and crystal dragons, their scales flashing like fractured sunlight, rose with their riders to meet the threat. The sky erupted into chaos, blinding bursts of magic, the thunder of wings, and the primal clash of claws on the scale. The cries of wounded dragons and the furious shouts of their riders wove into the cacophony of battle.

From her vantage, Nocturna watched the defenders' defiance with growing irritation. Their stubborn resistance was a small but increasingly vexing pebble in her talons. She bared her fangs, silver eyes, streaked with violet narrowing to slits.

"These riders," she bellowed, her voice crashing through the sky, "are not worth the trouble." Her wings flared wide, sending a turbulent gust downward. "Their defiance is a whisper in the wind. And I will silence it."

Her scorn twisted into something colder, and impatience edged with a flicker of contempt as the barrier held firm against the initial onslaught. The defenders did not scatter as expected; instead, they pushed back with surprising coordination. A defiant and unwavering rider led a counter-strike that disrupted the precision of her assault, gnawing at her patience like an unrelenting thorn. She considered descending to tear through their ranks and bring this nuisance to an abrupt, blood-soaked end.

But then—

The air thickened, and an invisible force pressed down, instantly halting the battle. Dragons, both obsidian and crystal, paused mid-air, their instincts whispering power beyond comprehension. The ground beneath the defenders quivered, and an ancient and commanding pulse surged through the battlefield.

A hush fell, and eyes turned skyward.

Two radiant forms descended through the fray.

Verdantia and Aurelia.

Their majestic forms gleamed with an ethereal brilliance, the colors of life and crystal, nature, and light, merging into a breathtaking force. A ripple of awe coursed through the defenders, some lowering their weapons in reverence while others straightened with renewed resolve. Even the dragons paused, their heads lifting in silent acknowledgment of the ancient power now standing among them. The air around them seemed more precise, the battle holding its breath.

Verdantia's voice, rich and sharp as the crack of thunder, sliced through the silence.

"Do you think us so foolish, Nocturna," she called, her eyes blazing with ancient fire, "as to send our charges into battle without our support? You underestimate us."

Her words were a blade, calm, cold, and undeniable.

Nocturna's wings beat heavily, her massive frame holding steady, but her eyes—those ancient, pitiless eyes—flashed with something rare and raw—recognition laced with a flicker of doubt. She had faced many foes and shattered countless defenses, but the presence of both Verdantia and Aurelia was an unforeseen challenge. The weight of their combined power pressed against her instincts, urging caution where she had once been confident of triumph. A flicker of doubt buried but present.

She snarled, the sound low and venomous, but the beat of her wings shifted—less offense, more calculation. She did not answer. But her silence was acknowledgment.

Then came Aurelia's voice, softer but unyielding crystal striking granite.

"Look closer, Nocturna," she said, the crystalline glow of her scales reflecting in the shadows of her adversary. "Among these riders stand not only the inexperienced. Among them are moon elf warriors trained in the fires of Etharyon. They do not shatter easily."

Her words carried weight as a warning, not a boast.

The battle briefly paused. Now, it sat on the edge of a blade. The players were set, and the lines were drawn.

And the storm—

It was about to break.

Nocturna's silver eyes, streaked with violet, flicked toward the riders, narrowing as she caught sight of several moon elves' silver-haired and wielding bows that pulsed with ethereal light. A flick of her tail betrayed her irritation, her claws flexing against the air as if itching to rend the arrogance from their words. Her wings gave a subtle twitch, a restless motion barely contained beneath the weight of her pride and fury. These were not mere recruits but seasoned warriors; their magic homed in the fires of Etharyon's ancient teachings. She had dismissed them too quickly, assuming this would be another effortless conquest.

A slow realization settled over her: these warriors were not ordinary. A flicker of unease stirred within her, cold and unwelcome. Could she have miscalculated? She masked the fleeting doubt with a low, guttural growl. But the truth burned in her mind: if the moon elves wielded Etharyon's forgotten magics, this battle would be anything but simple. A shadow of uncertainty flickered across her expression, starkly contrasting with the unshakable confidence she had carried moments before. She had commanded countless battles and reduced defiance to dust, but now, the presence of two Ancients and the unexpected strength of the defenders unsettled something deep within her. The doubt was brief, almost imperceptible, but it was there.

Verdantia stepped forward, her wings unfurling wide, casting an imposing silhouette against the burning sky. The air rippled with her power, shimmering like heat above sun-scorched earth. When she spoke, her voice carried with it the weight of the ancient and the immutable.

"Leave, Nocturna," she warned, her voice resonant with authority. "Emerald Woods and Crystal Vale are protected. Test us further, and it will not end well for you."

Aurelia's crystalline eyes locked onto Nocturna's, glinting with cold certainty. "This is your only warning," she said, her voice like a blade poised above a thread.

Nocturna's wings beat once, the air booming beneath their power. She had expected resistance, but not both Ancients. The weight of their combined presence pressed against her instincts, demanding caution where she had once felt assured of victory. She held her ground, her gaze burning with calculation and pride. But in the brief flicker of her pupils there was something new hesitation. She did not answer.

But then—

A sudden, sharp cry split the air. One of the smaller Obsidian dragons broke formation, its obsidian forming a jagged shadow against the storm-lit sky. Wings tucked and eyes blazing, it dove with lethal intent straight for the tower where Prince Gailen and Ong stood.

From the tower, Ong's sharp eyes caught a dark streak cutting through the sky, its form growing larger with each passing second. The wind howled in its wake, rattling the stone beneath his feet as the dragon's shadow swallowed the light. His breath hitched a heartbeat's pause before instinct took hold. Urgency ignited in his chest, and the familiar battle tension coiled through his body. The weight of his dragonlance felt natural in his grip, his muscles recalling a thousand battles.

His gaze snapped to Gailen, a flicker of worry flashing in his eyes. Too soon, his instincts screamed. The prince had fought valiantly, his spirit undeniable, but this was different. Ong's mind flashed with the memory of their first training. The prince was collapsing, exhausted but unyielding, his determination burning brighter than his fatigue. I swore I would protect him.

The promise surged through his veins, driving his arm as he raised his dragonlance. With a sharp exhale, he hurled his body one with the weapon, calculating the trajectory the instant it left his grip. The lance tore through the sky, a gleaming streak of steel and magic struck true.

The impact pierced the dragon's wing, sending it into a spiraling dive. A guttural shriek of pain tore from its throat, and its flight faltered. But not enough.

Wounded but enraged, the beast corrected its path, its eyes locking on the tower again.

"Ong!" she heard—

No—

"Keisha!"

Ong's voice. Urgent. Commanding. "Protect the Prince!"

Her body reacted before her mind. She spun, heart pounding, exhaustion like molten lead in her limbs. She felt the burn of every spell cast, every barrier raised. Her breath was shallow, her chest tight, and her legs trembled under the crushing weight of fatigue. But she would not stop.

A surge of doubt clawed at the edges of her mind. Can I hold it?

No. There was no time for doubt. Only action.

With a ragged inhale, she reached.

The emerald light roared to life from within her, surging through her veins and from her fingertips, weaving into a shield of raw, unbreakable will. It flared in a brilliant arc, green and shimmering, rippling with her resolve as it expanded around the tower in a protective dome. The force of the dragon's impact against the barrier was cataclysmic—

BOOM.

The shockwave hammered through the structure, the ground beneath them shuddering with the force of the blow. Stone cracked, dust and shards of debris cascading from above. Keisha gasped, the barrier holding but barely. Every muscle in her body burned as if she was seared by the magic she poured forth. Her vision blurred at the edges, dark spots dancing before her eyes. A sharp ache throbbed behind her temples, and her fingers trembled, raw from the force of her will. She clenched her jaw, forcing herself to remain upright, to hold on just a little longer. Her knees nearly buckled, her body screaming against the strain. She tasted copper—blood—from where she had bitten her lip. A bead of sweat traced a slow line down her temple.

The Prince staggered as the impact rattled the tower. His vision blurred, and a searing pain shot through his arm, a sharp, burning line across his flesh. The dragon's dark energy had pierced the barrier's fringe, cutting through its edge and grazing him.

His knees threatened to give, but he ground his boots into the trembling stone, forcing himself upright. His hand flew to his arm, hot, wet, and slick with blood, but the wound was shallow. I am still standing.

And then Ong was there.

A firm, a steadying hand gripped his shoulder. "You're hurt," Ong's voice was tight but measured, and his eyes scanned for worse.

"I'm fine," Gailen gritted out, his voice rough with pain but steady with resolve. "It's nothing."

Ong's eyes met his, both relieved and proud. His grip tightened briefly on Gailen's shoulder, a silent reassurance before he turned his focus back to the battlefield. "Stay close," he ordered, turning his body to shield the prince.

Above them, the emerald barrier wavered, flickering from the force of the impact. Keisha's breath came in ragged gasps, her arms trembling from the strain, but her eyes blazed with determination. She dug deeper, past the pain and the weariness, and pushed.

Her magic flared brighter, the barrier surging back to strength. It crackled with raw energy, pulsing coordinated with her hammering heartbeat. The air hummed with its power, a tangible force pushing against the darkness as if fueled by her sheer will alone.

Her voice, hoarse but unyielding, rasped through the chaos:

"I. Will. Not. Break."

The battle roared on. But at that moment, beneath the shield, she had forged with will and sacrifice.

A hush of awe rippled through the defenders, some glancing at Keisha with renewed determination. Wounded fighters found their footing again, standing taller, weapons gripped tighter. Fragile yet defiant hope rekindled in their eyes as they braced for what came next.

They stood unbroken.

High above the battlefield, Aurelia's crystalline gaze locked onto the chaos below. Her heart, a core of ancient power, burned with protective fury as her eyes fell on Gailen and Keisha within the crumbling barrier. Her wings flared wide, catching the fractured light like a thousand shattered stars.

"Nocturna!" she roared, her voice splitting the heavens, carrying the resonance of ages. The very air seemed to tremble under the force of her call.

Nocturna's head snapped toward the voice, her emerald eyes narrowing into slits. She turned to face Aurelia, and for the first time, she felt the cold brush of unease as the crystalline dragon rose, her form blazing with a searing, brilliant light.

"You were warned," Aurelia's voice rang out, cold as glacial ice, every word a promise and a verdict.

Power surged around her, blinding and pure, a corona of radiant energy. Nocturna's wings tensed instinctively, her body coiling in preparation. A flicker of instinct told her to brace, to counter—but the sheer force of the energy sent a ripple of unease through her core, momentarily halting her response. With a crackling crescendo, she unleashed it. The sky ignited as the cascade of light, molten and furious, exploded forward and struck Nocturna with staggering force. The impact sent shockwaves rippling through the clouds, tearing through the battle-churned air like a storm-given form.

Before the echoes of Aurelia's strike had faded, a second force converged—

Verdantia.

Emerald and primal, her form shimmered with the raw power of nature's heart. Magic coursed through her like the pulse of the earth itself. With a sweep of her wings, a vortex of green energy spiraled into being ancient, untamed, and unrelenting. The verdant storm struck Nocturna, a living tempest of nature's wrath.

The twin onslaughts collided with Nocturna, forcing a roar of pain from her throat with a sound both defiant and anguished. The raw force hammered against her, her body whipped backward, wings struggling against the sheer, unrelenting intensity.

Nocturna's roar tore through the sky, a sound of fury and wounded pride as she fought to regain control. Her body, bruised and scorched, trembled from the combined force of light and earth. Her breath came in ragged gasps, each inhale sharp and shallow. Her wings faltered mid-flight, the once-powerful beats now unsteady, struggling against the pain searing through her muscles. A deep, burning ache coiled in her chest, each movement sending sharp lances of agony rippling through her frame. Yet, through the torment, her defiance refused to wane. She beat her wings hard, their motions labored and searing with pain. But her silver eyes, streaked with violet, dimmed by agony, burned with venomous defiance.

Aurelia's voice rose again, unchanged, unyielding, undeniable. Nocturna's lips curled into a silent snarl, her tail flicking sharply, a restless, involuntary motion betraying her frustration. For the first time, hesitation flickered in her stance, the weight of Aurelia's command pressing against her pride. She did not answer, but her silence spoke volumes.

"Leave, Nocturna!" she commanded, her voice the song of judgment. "And hear me clearly—never again target Prince Gailen. He is protected, and I will not tolerate such insolence."

The power in her words reverberated through the sky, as immovable as the mountains and as sharp as tempered steel.

Nocturna hovered, her wings battered, her breath labored, and her pride—

Wounded.

Her gaze flicked between Aurelia and Verdantia, two ancient and united forces standing between her and the victory she had thought inevitable. Her body screamed from their assault, and the bitter taste of failure curdled in her throat.

They were stronger than she had anticipated than she had believed possible. And though her pride howled for vengeance, her instincts, honed by centuries of conquest and survival, whispered a colder truth:

To fight on would mean destruction.

Aurelia's radiant force had burned through her defenses. Verdantia's primal might have fractured her resolve. And together, they were a wall of power she could not break.

Her breath came in slow, measured bursts, each a battle to contain the tempest within. The searing ache in her wings, the memory of their combined might still be blistering her scales, gnawed at her pride. Fury roared through her blood, but with it came the sharp edge of reason.

Retreat.

Nocturna's wings gave a slow, bitter beat, the motion filled with reluctant acceptance. Her silver eyes, streaked with violet lingered on Aurelia and Verdantia, burning with defiance. But she knew this was not her moment. With one final, seething glare, she turned away, her battered form vanishing into the storm-lit sky.

The word tasted like ash and humiliation, but the alternative was annihilation.

For the first time in an age, a flicker of something cold and foreign crept into her silver eyes, streaked with violet: Fear.

Was this what the stories had spoken of? The ancient power of the twin guardians Aurelia, the light that shattered shadow, and Verdantia, the earth that bore no trespasser?

Her jaw clenched, and her eyes burned with the bitterness of knowing.

This was not her victory. Not today.

But there will be another day.

There always was.

Below, the Obsidian dragons faltered, withdrawn but shaken, their rigid formation breaking apart. For the first time in memory, they were not advancing, not striking, but retreating. Confusion rippled through their ranks, an unspoken shock settling over them. This was not how battles ended for them. This was not their way.

The rhythmic pattern of their circling wavered, their dark silhouettes shifting in uncertainty. Once thick with their predatory hunger, the air grew heavy with hesitation. Their leader, their indomitable queen, hovered, not striking but weighing. And in that hesitation, the certainty of their conquest cracked.

The defenders, bruised and weary, saw it. Felt it. And in that fragile pause, hope flared anew, raw, and bright.

The battle was not won.

But—

It was not lost.

Chapter 27
The Legacy of the Crystal Bow

O ng turned to Keisha, his brow furrowed in thought. The battlefield around them was a chaotic tapestry of scorched earth and shattered weapons, the acrid scent of burnt magic lingering in the air. Distant cries of the wounded mixed with the whisper of the wind, carrying the weight of what had just transpired.

The tension in the air crackled less the residue of battle, more the sharp edge of something unseen. Keisha exhaled slowly, her fingers tightening around her palm for a heartbeat before relaxing. A flicker of realization crossed her face, her emerald eyes narrowing as her gaze swept the battlefield. Her mind raced, piecing together the fragments, the timing, the precision, the target.

Ong's voice was low but edged with certainty. "Why do I feel like this was more than testing our defenses?" His eyes, sharp and searching, flicked to Keisha. "It seemed like an attempt to eliminate Prince Gailen or at least hurt him badly enough that he couldn't train."

Keisha's gaze sharpened, her voice measured but laced with tension. "I agree. Something feels off about the timing and precision of the attack. This was not random."

Her eyes drifted toward Gailen. He held himself upright, his breathing steady but shallow. The tension in his jaw, the rigid set of his shoulders, each detail betrayed the pain he refused to acknowledge. The wound itself was not grave, yet the weight of its intent settled deep in his bones, a stark reminder of how close he had come to something far worse. He stood firm, but his left arm, still cradling the shallow wound, betrayed his pain. His expression, taut with determination, did little to mask the strain.

"Let's head to the grove," Keisha said, her voice soft but decisive. "We can discuss this properly there."

The grove was a sanctuary, a pocket of untouched serenity amidst battle scars. The towering trees, their leaves kissed by lingering twilight, swayed gently, their soft rustling balm against the tension that clung to the air. The rich scent of damp earth and blooming flora painted the air with life, yet the echoes of the recent battle lingered like the final tremors of a fading storm.

Aurelia and Verdantia stood side by side, their majestic forms towering with an aura of ageless power. The light filtering through the canopy caught on Aurelia's crystalline scales, scattering fractals of color across the clearing, while Verdantia's emerald form pulsed faintly with the quiet rhythm of the earth itself, her very presence exuding an air of calm strength. Verdantia's emerald form, deep and vibrant, seemed almost one with the world itself, her presence both guardian and sentinel. Their gazes, sharp and knowing, swept over the group as they arrived.

King Manard, Prince Gailen, Ong, and Keisha entered the grove together, their expressions shadowed by the weight of what they had faced and now feared.

Aurelia's crystalline eyes fixed on Gailen, her voice smooth but laced with concern. "How is your wound, Prince?"

Gailen straightened under her gaze, his posture firm despite the lingering ache. "It's nothing serious," he replied, his voice steady though tight with restrained pain. "Keisha's magic absorbed most of the blow."

His eyes flicked toward Keisha, gratitude briefly softening his features.

Keisha, however, barely acknowledged it, her attention locked on him not out of indifference but because the weight of realization pressed down on her. Her fingers, where they curled around the hilt of her dagger, betrayed her unease, the tension coiling within her like a silent storm. The sight of his blood, however slight, unsettled something deep within her, a tension that knotted in her chest. She had seen battle wounds far worse than his, yet this one felt different. It was not the severity but who had been struck.

It was close. Too close.

The weight of it pressed down, a leaden whisper of responsibility, sharper than any blade. Even the most powerful mages, such as her father, could not always prevent disaster. The thought gnawed at her, a stark reminder that skill and strength did not guarantee safety. She had shielded him this time. But what about the next?

A somber silence descended over the grove, thick with unspoken thought. King Manard stood with his hands clasped behind his back, his profile carved from stone, his jaw tight with contemplation. Though fixed forward, his gaze carried the gravity of a father and a ruler. His son had survived this time.

Beside him, Ong exhaled slowly, his brow deeply furrowed, his arms crossed in a stance that spoke both protection and readiness. His instincts screamed that something was amiss: the attack's precision, the target choice. It was not conquest. The enemy sought disruption.

Aurelia and Verdantia remained still, yet their presence was an unspoken force. Their ancient eyes swept the group, weighing the echoes of battle and the tremors yet to come.

With all its natural beauty, the grove pulsed with an unspoken anticipation as if the land held its breath in waiting. The wind carried the faint
song of distant water, and the trees whispered their secrets in the breeze,
but beneath the harmony was a pulse and an unspoken warning.

Aurelia's voice broke the silence clear, crystalline, and undeniable.

"This attack was not a coincidence," she said, her tone edging with
ancient wisdom's certainty. "It was deliberate and targeted."

Her eyes, hard and knowing, settled on Prince Gailen.

"Their goal was not victory," she continued. "It was you."

The truth, spoken aloud, rippled through the clearing, shifting the air
as if the trees themselves acknowledged it. A shiver ran through Gailen's
spine, his fingers instinctively tightening at his sides. Keisha exhaled softly,
her breath barely audible, while Ong's jaw tensed, his stance subtly shifting
as if bracing for an unseen threat.

And with it, the unspoken question:

Why?

King Manard turned to his son, his expression unreadable but his voice
steady, weighted with challenge and trust. "Gailen, do you still wish to
continue your training after what happened today?"

Gailen did not hesitate. His blue eyes met his father's with unwavering
resolve, the fire of purpose burning within them. "Yes, Father," he answered firmly. "More than ever."

A flicker of approval touched King Manard's lips, a rare, fleeting smile of
pride that carried the weight of generations. His gaze lingered on Gailen,
not just as his son but as a warrior stepping into his legacy. For a brief
moment, the hardened lines of a king softened, revealing the father beneath—the one who knew the trials ahead but trusted in the strength
he saw before him. With a subtle gesture, he beckoned a nearby soldier,
who stepped forward bearing a large, ornately decorated box. The polished
wood glinted in the soft light, and the intricate carvings on its surface told
stories of battles long past.

The soldier bowed respectfully, presenting the box to Gailen.

King Manard's voice carried the weight of lineage and legacy. "This," he said, his eyes never leaving his son, "is the C Crystalbow. It was wielded centuries ago by one of our ancestors, a dragon rider who stood where you now stand, who fought to protect Crystal Vale and its people. Today, it becomes yours."

Gailen's breath caught as he carefully lifted the lid. Reverence and awe washed over him in a wave, stealing the air from his lungs. Within, nestled on velvet as dark as midnight, lay a weapon forged from the bones of legend.

The Crystalbow was pure crystal, smooth and flawless as if carved from the heart of a star. It carried a faint, tingling energy that danced along his fingertips like the magic within it stirred to life at his touch. It glowed with a soft, ethereal light, the pulse of ancient magic thrumming faintly beneath its polished surface. Along its limbs, emerald inlays formed intricate patterns like vines curling around the weapon's core, each gem flickering with a life of its own. The air around it felt charged, as though the Crystalbow knew its new bearer.

Gailen's fingers trembled slightly as he touched the cool, glass-like surface. The crystal felt impossibly smooth, yet it seemed to respond to his touch with a faint, living warmth. At that moment, the weight of history pressed down on him in his hands and heart. This was more than a weapon. It was a vow.

The soft chime of crystalline scales heralded Aurelia's approach, and her faceted and luminous eyes widened in recognition. A rare flicker of profound reverence and urgency passed through her features, and her soft voice carried enough power to still the air around them.

"That Crystalbow," she said, the words more a revelation than a statement, "is no ordinary weapon."

Her gaze met Gailen's, and he saw both knowledge and warning.

"It is an extension of its wielder's soul," she continued, her voice a chord of ancient memory and power. "It can fire radiant arrows, pure and swift, and at times, crystalline shards, each capable of piercing even the thickest dragon scales. But that..." her eyes seemed to peer into something unseen, "...is only the beginning of its power."

Aurelia's voice softened, but the weight of her words pressed deeply into him. Gailen swallowed hard, his fingers tightening instinctively around the Crystalbow as a slow breath escaped him. His pulse thrummed in his ears, the enormity of the moment settling in his chest like a stone. "Its true strength lies dormant. It will awaken only when our bond is forged and you and I, Prince Gailen, are united not just by oath but by trust, understanding, and battle. Only then will you unlock its full power."

Gailen's hand brushed over the emerald inlays, their glow reflecting in his eyes. The crystal felt cold, but the pulse beneath its surface was alive like a heart waiting to beat in time with his own. His voice, though low, rang with determination.

"Then I will make sure I'm ready," he said, his tone firm, each word a vow. "Ready to wield it properly and forge that bond with you."

Aurelia's crystalline form shifted, and rare approval was in the glint of her many facets. "Then we shall begin," she said, her towering form casting a long, protective shadow over him, a silent vow of her own.

King Manard stepped forward, his warm, strong hand resting on his son's shoulder. "You carry the legacy of those who came before you, Gailen," he said, his voice low but resonant with pride. "This Crystalbow is a symbol not just of power but of duty. Let it remind you of the strength within you and the responsibility you now bear."

Gailen lifted the Crystalbow from its velvet cradle, his grip steady despite the magnitude of the moment. Though it rested lightly in his hands, the weight of its history and expectation pressed heavily upon him, a burden far greater than its physical form. The weight felt perfectly balanced not only in his hands but also in his heart. Yet beneath the physical heft lay something more significant: the echoes of those who had wielded it before him—heroes, protectors, riders.

As he turned the Crystalbow in his hands, the emerald light danced against his skin, casting reflections that seemed to reach into his soul. He could almost hear the whispers of those who had stood where he now stood, who had faced their battles and doubts.

Aurelia's gaze was steady and knowing, holding his with quiet understanding. She saw the storm of thoughts behind his eyes, the excitement, the fear, the question every warrior asks themselves before their first test: Can I be worthy of this?

But she also saw something more beneath the uncertainty, beneath the burden.

She saw resolve.

Gailen drew in a slow breath, his grip tightening, not in fear but in acceptance. "This Crystalbow protected Crystal Vale before," he thought, his resolve crystallizing. "Now, it is my turn. My turn to protect the city, the dragons, and the legacy of those who came before me."

A presence at his side, Keisha.

Her eyes, green as forest depths, watched him with something more profound than approval and understanding. She recognized the moment for what it was: not just accepting a weapon but accepting a burden, a choice.

She, too, had stood at the precipice of duty, feeling the weight of expectation and the fire of resolve battling within. That moment had been when she regained her magic and archery skills and finally understood that she had always been a part of the Eladrin, even when she had not believed it. Seeing that same fire in Gailen now stirred something within her, a flicker of pride and hope.

"You carry more than a Crystalbow, Gailen," she said softly, her voice laced with meaning. "You carry hope. And that," she added, a small, knowing smile curving her lips, "can be the strongest weapon of all."

Aurelia inclined her head, her form shimmering, the refracted light casting faint rainbows across the grove. Her smooth and confident voice carried both promise and challenge.

"And soon," she said, "you will carry more than hope. When our training is complete, you will understand the true strength of this Crystalbow and yourself."

Gailen nodded, the weight of the Crystalbow in his hands no longer a question but a promise. The journey ahead would be extended. Grueling. Forged in battle and trial.

But he was ready to bear it.

Clear and unshaken, his eyes lifted again toward his father, Aurelia, and the path that stretched before him.

"I will not fail," he said, the words no longer a vow to others but himself. "Not Crystal Vale. Not the dragons. And not the legacy I now carry."

The echoes of the hero's past seemed to stir within the Crystalbow, a pulse like a quiet heartbeat, steady and ancient as if the weapon acknowledged his oath and awaited the moment to unleash its true power.

Keisha watched, the smile on her lips faint but discernible.

Hope, she thought, is fragile. But in the hands of the right soul tempered by resolve, strengthened by purpose.

Hope can become unbreakable.

With that, the grove seemed to breathe, accepting his vow. A gentle wind stirred the leaves, whispering through the branches like a quiet acknowledgment. The trees swayed ever so slightly, limbs creaking as if bearing witness to the unspoken promise. And in the Crystalbow's heart, a faint pulse of light flickered.

—waiting.

For the day, it would awaken.

Chapter 28

Bonds Rekindled

Aurelia observed Gailen, noting the tension in his posture and the lingering exhaustion etched into his face. Shadows lingered beneath his eyes, subtly undermining the rigid composure he struggled to uphold. His shoulders were squared, his stance firm, but there was a weight behind his gaze, an unspoken strain from all he had endured.

She turned her attention to Keisha. "Check his injury," she commanded, though the subtle softness in her voice hinted at concern. Her gaze lingered on Gailen a moment longer. "You are important to us, Gailen. I will not risk your safety for the sake of haste."

She exhaled slowly. "I want to begin his training as soon as possible, but not at the cost of his well-being. This assassination attempt was too close a reminder that the enemies of Vacari are more cunning than we anticipated."

Keisha nodded, her red hair catching the golden light, a brief shimmer dancing across the strands as she stepped forward. Her green eyes flicked to Gailen's wound, a glimmer of concern flickering beneath her usual confidence. Each step carried a quiet determination, not just to heal but to reassure him. She placed a light hand on his forearm, a steady, grounding, unspoken touch, a request rather than a command.

Thalorian stepped aside, inclining his head slightly as Keisha explained what she needed to do. Gailen tensed, his arms crossing tightly over his chest.

"This isn't necessary," he protested. "I told you I'm fine."

Thalorian raised a brow, his jade fire eyes gleaming with amusement. "Let her do her job, Prince. You will need to be in top condition for what is ahead."

He tilted his head slightly as if weighing his following words. "The training will test you in ways you have not even begun to imagine."

Ong stepped forward, his expression serious, eyes narrowing with concern and expectation. A subtle crease formed between his brows, revealing the weight of his thoughts, the unspoken resolve of someone who had seen both failure and triumph in the trials ahead. "He is right." His arms crossed over his chest, a stance not just of authority but unwavering certainty.

"Dragon-back training is not just about physical endurance," he continued, his voice dipping lower, carrying the weight of experience. "It is about mental and emotional strength. You will face challenges that test your patience, push your resolve to its limits, and demand unwavering focus even in fear."

Ong's gaze sharpened. "The bond with your dragon will amplify every emotion you feel. If you cannot master them, you risk losing that connection altogether. You will need every bit of focus and health to endure what Aurelia has planned."

Gailen sighed, tension flickering across his face. His protest faded as he rolled up his sleeve, exposing the bandaged wound. "Fine," he muttered. "But only because you won't leave me alone otherwise."

Keisha smiled faintly and began her work, her movements quick and efficient but not rushed. Her fingers brushed against his skin, and a faint warmth pulsed from her touch, a stirring of energy beneath the surface, subtle yet potent.

A tingling sensation spread through the wound, neither painful nor soothing, but an unfamiliar tug, as if unseen threads of energy were weaving bone and flesh back into place. The faintest hum of power vibrated in the air as she worked, each movement precise and controlled.

She probed the area gently, nodding to herself. "It's superficial," she confirmed to Ong. "The wound is already healing well. He should be fine to start training, though he must avoid straining it unnecessarily."

Ong nodded, his shoulders relaxing slightly. "Good. Then we can proceed."

"Not so fast," Keisha interjected, her emerald eyes narrowing slightly. She turned to Ong, her expression unreadable but firm. "You should accompany him, just in case."

Ong looked at her, surprise flickering across his face, uncertainty shadowing his features. "I was going to see which dragon I could borrow for the duration," he began, but Keisha raised a hand, stopping him with a firm look.

"You don't need to borrow any dragon," she said, her voice steady. "You have Amara. You saw her just a few months ago. Do you think she forgot you?"

Ong blinked. "Amara knows I'm here, but she's in Purplefire."

Keisha smiled knowingly, catching the slight furrow in his brow and the way his fingers flexed at his sides, subtle signs of the doubts lurking beneath his words. "You have a bond with her, Ong. That bond has not weakened with distance or time." She held his gaze. "Remember when I was a prisoner of Vuarus and Phoenix? You heard me, didn't you? Felt my call?"

Ong's expression shifted, a flicker of realization in his eyes. "I... did. I just thought."

"That bond is still stronger than you realize," Keisha said, her voice softer now. "Amara will hear you if you reach out. Trust in that connection. Reach for her. She will come."

Ong nodded slowly, Keisha's words settling deep within him, stirring a conflicted longing. He wanted to trust her and believe in the bond he once had with Amara, but doubt coiled in the back of his mind, whispering of time lost and connections frayed. Yet, something in Keisha's certainty chipped away at his hesitation, urging him to try. A part of him wanted to believe her, but another part resisted. Time and distance had a way of unraveling bonds, trust, and even certainty. What if Amara had moved on? What if she no longer felt their connection? The thought unsettled him.

But there was only one way to find out.

Keisha patted his arm, her touch light but grounding, offering a silent reassurance that steadied the doubt lingering within him. "It's time to rely on that bond again."

Ong looked at her, his brow furrowing. "How do I connect with Amara? Our bond has always been strong, but this feels... different. I do not know where to start."

Keisha's smile was gentle and reassuring. "It is different but simpler than you think. Just reach out with your feelings. Let her know you need her. Do not overthink it. Trust the connection."

Ong tilted his head, skepticism flickering in his eyes as doubts gnawed at him. What if distance had dulled their connection? What if Amara had moved on without him? The uncertainty coiled tight in his chest, but a small part of him clung to the hope Keisha offered. "And if she does not hear me? What if I cannot do it?"

"She will," Keisha said without hesitation. "It might take a few tries, but you will know when she does. It is not something I can explain. It is something you will feel."

Her confidence was unshakable, but doubt still gnawed at him. What if she was wrong? He hesitated for a moment, then exhaled, giving a reluctant nod.

"Alright. Let us try this."

Stepping away, Ong closed his eyes and inhaled deeply, centering himself. The distant rustling of leaves filled the silence, an occasional gust sending them whispering in waves. The faint chirp of night insects rose and fell in the underbrush, a rhythmic pulse against the hush of the night. A cool breeze ghosted over his skin, carrying the scent of damp earth and lingering embers from the earlier battle.

He exhaled slowly, pushing aside his doubts. Focus.

His thoughts reached for Amara, her power, her presence, and the unspoken trust between them. He remembered the times they had flown together, how her strength had steadied him, and how her eyes had held understanding without words.

Amara, I need your help.

His chest tightened, a wave of longing and desperation surging through him, wrapping around his pulse like an unspoken plea. The intensity of it wavered between weakening his resolve and pushing him forward, a battle between fear and hope waging within him.

Nothing.

Ong exhaled, frustration mounting with each silent moment. Was their bond truly broken? Had too much time passed, or was he not strong enough to reach her? The questions gnawed at him, feeding the doubt clawing at the edges of his mind. The bond felt distant, like reaching for something that no longer existed. Doubt curled around him, whispering that perhaps too much time had passed, that what they once had was beyond repair. His fingers curled into fists, breath coming in shallow bursts.

Then, just as despair threatened to take hold, Keisha's voice cut through the haze.

"Try again."

Ong looked at her, catching her encouraging smile. She believed in this. She believed in him.

He nodded. Once more.

Closing his eyes, he reached out again, more profound this time, past his doubt and fear. He called her name, not just with thought but with feeling.

Amara, I need you. Please.

Still, silence.

Ong opened his eyes, shaking his head. "I do not think this is going to work, Keisha. Maybe the bond is not as strong as you think."

Keisha did not waver. "It is." Her voice was steady, unwavering. "You just need to trust it and yourself. One more time, Ong."

He hesitated, then took a slow, deep breath.

One last time.

Closing his eyes, he pushed away his fear, doubt, and hesitation. He focused on Amara not just as a thought but as a presence and certainty. He felt the powerful beat of her wings, the warmth of her fire, and the steady, unshakable loyalty they had always shared.

Amara, I need you.

This time, he did not just call out. He opened himself completely.

The air around him shifted. A warmth coiled through his veins, slow at first, then building—not a whisper but a pulse, an echo of something vast and eternal. It seeped into his limbs, chasing away the chill of doubt like the first rays of dawn banishing the night.

His breath hitched. His heart pounded.

The warmth grew, curling around his core, steady and strong a tether reconnecting to something beyond his reach. It was more than just a feeling; it was a rekindling of trust, a bridge spanning the chasm of doubt and distance. It reminded him of who he was, who they were together, and the bond that had never truly broken. A familiar yet distant presence stirred at the edge of his consciousness.

His pulse steadied. The tension in his body melted away.

And then he felt her.

It was not words, not sound, but an acknowledgment. A presence pressing against his mind like a reassuring embrace. It surged through him, a silent recognition, a long-lost echo answering his call.

Ong's eyes shot open. The sheer certainty of her presence lifted his chest, and he rose and fell with its weight. He turned to Keisha, a mix of relief and amazement flashing across his face.

"I think... she heard me."

Keisha grinned. "I told you. You would know."

Ong exhaled, steadying himself. He turned to Gailen, newfound confidence settling into his stance.

"Amara will come. We should head to Aurelia now and begin your training."

Gailen nodded, his expression resolute. "Then let us go. I am ready."

Chapter 29
Lessons in Trust

They found Aurelia resting in the grove, her crystalline form shimmering like captured starlight in the dappled sunlight. Ong stepped forward, his expression serious.

"Aurelia, Gailen's injury is not serious. Keisha has confirmed he is well enough to begin his training." His tone held certainty but also the weight of responsibility. "Her knowledge of healing and the mystical arts ensures there's no doubt Gailen is ready."

Aurelia's piercing gaze shifted to Gailen, who straightened under her scrutiny. His muscles tensed as a mix of resolve and unease settled over him. He fought the instinct to avert his gaze, determined to meet her stare head-on despite the flicker of doubt curling in his chest. The depth of her stare was unnerving, as if she could see past his composure and the uncertainty beneath.

"Then it is time," she said, her voice resonating with ancient wisdom. "We will travel to the place I have chosen for his training."

Ong nodded, then turned to Gailen. "Don't forget the Crystalbow." His tone was firm. "You'll need it."

Gailen reached down, lifting the Crystalbow from its case. The smooth, cool surface hummed beneath his fingers, pulsing with an almost sentient energy. A reminder of the responsibility he bore.

This was no ordinary weapon.

The Crystalbow, forged by Vacari artisans of old, was said to channel the wielder's very essence, amplifying both skill and intent. Legends spoke of warriors who had wielded it in battles long past, their victories and sacrifices etched into the weapon's core. Some claimed it carried echoes of their strength, a silent testament to those who had come before, waiting for the next worthy hands to continue its legacy. As his fingers curled around its frame, a faint, rhythmic warmth pulsed through his palm as if acknowledging his grip.

It carried more than weight. It brought a legacy.

The Crystalbow had passed through generations of warriors, each leaving their mark upon its legend. Now, it was in his hands.

A knot of unease formed in Gailen's chest, tightening like a vice. His breath hitched, and his fingers clenched instinctively around the Crystalbow's grip, its warmth pulsing against his palm as if sensing his hesitation. Was he genuinely worthy of it? Could he live up to the expectations placed upon him? Doubt whispered like a gathering storm, but a spark of determination refused to be extinguished beneath it.

He remembered the first time he had faced a challenge that had seemed insurmountable—when he had stood, barely more than a boy, against seasoned warriors in combat training. He had doubted himself then, too. But he had learned. Adapted. Endured.

And he would do so again. The weight of past battles pressed against his mind, but so did the fire of resilience. He inhaled deeply, feeling the Crystalbow's pulse steady his resolve, a silent promise that he was ready for whatever lay ahead.

Gailen squared his shoulders, gripping the Crystalbow more firmly. He would prove himself not just to Ong, not just to Aurelia, but to himself.

Then, movement caught his eye.

A shadow rippled across the ground, stretching wide and imposing. A gust of wind stirred the leaves, carrying the crisp scent of rain and earth.

Gailen's breath caught as a dragon descended from the sky, her massive wings unfurling like banners of amethyst fire.

She landed with effortless grace, the ground trembling slightly beneath her massive form as a rush of displaced air sent leaves swirling in her wake. She was a shimmering force of nature. Her deep, gleaming purple scales caught the sunlight, shimmering like polished amethyst gems, casting a mesmerizing glow that danced with every movement. Each movement was fluid, controlled by a quiet display of absolute power.

Gailen barely breathed. "Who is that?" His voice was barely above a whisper.

Ong smiled, stepping toward the dragon as she landed. "This," he said, turning back to Gailen, "is Amara."

The amethyst dragon regarded Gailen, her wise, ancient eyes studying him before shifting to Ong.

"So, this is the young Prince?" Her voice was melodic, edged with amusement. "He looks far more capable than you did during your training."

Ong chuckled. "I'll take that as a compliment, Amara."

She lowered her head slightly, her gaze softening. "What do you need of me, Ong?"

Ong explained the situation, his voice measured, carrying the weight of the danger they had faced. Amara's gaze darkened as he spoke of the assassination attempt and Aurelia's decision to begin training immediately. A flicker of unease passed through her expression, subtle yet unmistakable.

Her wings shifted slightly, a silent, instinctive reaction to her growing concern.

"I need your help watching over Gailen and Aurelia during this process," Ong said. "It's vital that he completes his training."

Amara tilted her head, a teasing glint in her eye. "You're starting to rely on me more, Ong. It's almost endearing." Her voice carried the familiar playful edge she had always used with him, a mix of jest and sincerity.

Ong smirked. "It's called trust, Amara." He met her gaze steadily. "You taught me that."

Aurelia turned her attention back to Gailen. "Climb on my back." Her tone was firm, leaving no room for hesitation. "Hold on tightly. The place I have chosen for your training is not far, but the journey will test you."

Gailen nodded, his grip tightening around the Crystalbow. Its weight felt different now; it was not just heavy but expectant.

As he approached Aurelia, his fingers brushed along the Crystalbow's surface again, and the pulse of energy within it flared ever so slightly alive, waiting.

Was it sensing his resolve? Or testing it?

A swirl of emotions churned within him: excitement, doubt, the thrill of the unknown. Was he genuinely ready? Or was he still just a boy grasping at legends greater than himself? If he failed, it would not just be his burden to bear. It would be a mark upon those who believed in him. The weight of expectation loomed large, yet a spark of determination flickered within it, refusing to be extinguished.

He took a steady breath. He would find out soon enough.

He climbed onto Aurelia's back with practiced movements, settling into place. Beneath him, he felt a subtle shift, a pulse of energy thrumming in the space between them—a connection, tentative but promising, like the first step onto an uncharted path.

Gailen wondered how this newfound link might shape his training. Would he rise to meet the challenges ahead? Or would the weight of expectation crush him before he even began?

Only time will tell.

Amara watched them, her wings flexing slightly. Her gaze lingered on Gailen, not judging but assessing and measuring the potential within him, sensing the raw determination that had yet to be fully realized.

"I'll be right behind you," she said to Aurelia. "Let's see if the young Prince is truly worthy of his potential."

Aurelia's wings spread wide, their crystalline edges catching the sunlight like shards of a shattered rainbow.

With a mighty leap, she took off.

Gailen held on tightly, his excitement mingling with determination, his heart hammering as the wind roared around him.

Amara followed, her amethyst form cutting through the sky, a guardian in flight.

Together, they soared toward the training ground for the test, determining Gailen's skill and fate.

As they descended from the sky, the training ground unfolded beneath them—an untouched sanctuary hidden within the wilds. A wide, secluded clearing stretched below, encircled by towering crystalline trees that shimmered under the sun, their translucent branches refracting the light into fragmented rainbows.

A gentle breeze stirred the leaves, sending soft chimes through the air, an eerie and mesmerizing sound. The trickle of water from a nearby stream threaded through the clearing, its melody blending with the quiet rustle of leaves.

The crisp and fresh scent of damp earth and blooming flowers filled the air, stirring memories of his childhood when he would escape into the palace gardens, losing himself among the blossoms while his father's voice echoed in his mind, urging him to find strength in solitude. Gailen inhaled deeply, the fragrance stirring a strange sense of nostalgia, a whisper of home, of quiet mornings spent wandering the royal gardens.

Sunlight filtered through the crystalline canopy, casting shifting patterns of gold and silver onto the forest floor. The ground beneath them was smooth, touched by time yet untouched by war, a space that felt both ancient and sacred. Legends spoke of warriors who had trained upon this very soil for a long time, their spirits lingering like whispers in the wind. It was said that those deemed worthy could feel the echoes of their predecessors, guiding them toward their destiny. Despite its tranquility, an undercurrent of expectation lingered, a quiet promise of trials ahead.

Aurelia landed first, her crystalline wings folding against her sleek form with practiced grace. Gailen dismounted carefully, his boots sinking into the soft earth as he steadied himself.

Nearby, Amara descended in a sweeping arc, her amethyst scales glowing like polished gemstones in the sunlight. She landed fluidly, her wings folding neatly at her sides. Ong slid off her back, his gaze sweeping over the clearing, assessing and measuring.

He gave a slight nod. "This will do."

Amara's sharp gaze flicked toward Aurelia. "We'll stay close," she assured her. "If there's any threat, we'll deal with it."

Aurelia inclined her head slightly. "Your presence is reassuring, Amara. Thank you."

Then, she turned her focus to Gailen.

"Before we begin, hand Ong the Crystalbow." Her voice carried quiet authority. "It will remain with him until the time comes when you are truly ready to wield it."

Gailen hesitated, his fingers tightening around the Crystalbow's grip.

He had always been told that strength alone was never enough and that a warrior must bear the weight of responsibility, not just the weapon itself.

Memories of his father's lessons surfaced in his words of caution, wisdom hard-earned through battle.

Was he genuinely ready?

The Crystalbow felt heavier in his grasp, not just in weight but in significance.

Doubt curled at the edges of his thoughts, whispering questions he did not have the answers to. His pulse quickened, fingers tightening around the Crystalbow as a cold weight settled in his chest. The uncertainty clawed at him, but he forced himself to take a steadying breath, willing the doubt to loosen its grip. What if he failed? What if the Crystalbow's true potential remained beyond his reach?

His grip faltered for the briefest moment.

Then, a flicker of determination rose within him.

He had come too far to let uncertainty rule him now.

With a steady breath, he stepped forward, holding the Crystalbow out to Ong.

For a moment, he hesitated.

Then, with quiet resolve, he released it.

Ong carefully accepted the weapon, his fingers closing around the smooth crystal frame.

"Keep it safe," Gailen said, his voice steady though a trace of unease still lingered beneath the surface.

Ong smiled, his grip firm. "You have my word. It will be here when you are ready."

Amara watched the exchange, her sharp gaze flicking between them. A knowing glint flickered in her eyes as if she could already see the path ahead for Gailen, one filled with trials but also with potential waiting to be realized. Her tone, though firm, carried something else, a quiet assurance.

"Focus on your training, Prince." The title held neither mockery nor reverence, only expectation. "You'll need every bit of it."

Aurelia's crystalline gaze softened. "Come," she beckoned, sweeping her tail toward the center of the clearing. "We have much to do and little time to waste."

Gailen exhaled, pushing away lingering uncertainty as he followed Aurelia.

Behind him, Ong remained still, his gaze locked on Gailen's retreating form. He tightened his grip on the Crystalbow, its physical and symbolic weight.

He would ensure Gailen's training proceeded without interference.

Amara shifted beside him, her wings flexing slightly before settling. Her voice was thoughtful, edged with curiosity and amusement.

"Let's see what the young Prince is made of."

She settled into a protective watch near Ong, her gaze unwavering as Gailen took his first steps toward the unknown.

Aurelia turned to Gailen, her crystalline wings catching the dappled sunlight and scattering flecks of gold and silver across the clearing. She flicked her tail once, a measured, deliberate motion that sent a ripple through the grass beneath them. Her piercing gaze settled on him, assessing, weighing, measuring.

"Before you can even think about becoming a dragon rider, you must learn to ride a dragon properly." Her voice carried a quiet authority tempered with the slightest hint of amusement. "And that," she said, tilting her head, "is no small feat."

Gailen met her gaze, his stance firm. "I'm ready."

Aurelia's crystalline eyes narrowed slightly. "We'll see."

She lowered herself just enough for him to climb onto her back.

For a brief moment, Gailen hesitated. This was his first actual step. His pulse pounded in his ears as he stepped forward, his fingers grazing the ridges of her scales. The crystalline texture was cool and smooth, yet beneath the hard exterior, he could feel the faint pulse of warmth—a steady, living energy thrumming through her body.

He swung himself up, settling into place. A rush of exhilaration surged through him, mingled with a nervous flutter deep in his gut. The sheer magnitude of the moment tightened his grip instinctively, as if holding on harder could somehow steady his thoughts.

Then, Aurelia moved.

The abrupt shift nearly sent him tumbling sideways.

"Balance is the foundation," she said, her tone edged with warning. "Without it, you are nothing more than dead weight."

Gailen gritted his teeth. "I got it."

"Do you?" Aurelia asked sharply.

Then, without warning, she leaped into the air.

The world tilted violently.

A rush of wind roared past his ears, thrilling and intoxicating, before his stomach lurched, the exhilaration giving way to sudden panic as they shot skyward. The ground blurred beneath him, his grip faltering as the vastness of the sky threatened to consume him. The sudden motion ripped his grip free, his fingers scrambling to find purchase. Gravity yanked at him, and before he could react.

He fell.

The impact knocked the breath from his lungs as he slammed into the grass with a muffled thud.

From the sidelines, Ong winced. "That's going to hurt."

Gailen groaned, rolling onto his back and staring at the sky in disbelief. His body ached from the impact, but his pride stung sharper. Frustration burned in his chest, tangled with the sting of embarrassment. He clenched his fists, forcing himself to push past the humiliation. This was a lesson, not a defeat.

He glared at Aurelia as she landed nearby, her expression unreadable. "Was that necessary?"

"It was," she replied without hesitation. "You must learn to adapt quickly. The skies are unforgiving. In battle, hesitation is death. Again."

Grumbling under his breath, Gailen climbed back onto her back. This time, he braced himself, gripping tightly, determined not to fall again.

Aurelia took off.

The force slammed into him, knocking him back, but he held firm, adjusting to the rush of movement. He lasted a few seconds longer until she executed a sharp bank to the left, and his balance shattered.

The world flipped.

A startled yell ripped from his throat as he was wrenched off her back, tumbling downward again.

Another impact. More bruises. More frustration.

Aurelia landed, her crystalline wings folding. "You're leaning too much to one side," she observed, noting how he instinctively shifted his weight to counterbalance her movement. "You're fighting against me instead of moving with me," she said coolly. "Your body must move with mine, not against it."

Gailen pushed himself up, his muscles screaming in protest. Dirt smudged his hands, his breath coming in sharp bursts, but his eyes burned with defiance.

Again.

The third time, he focused on the rhythm of Aurelia's movements, forcing himself to match her shifts. When she launched into the air, he adjusted before she banked, anticipating the motion. His grip loosened slightly, his muscles no longer locked in rigid tension.

For a moment, he wobbled. But he did not fall.

"Better," Aurelia said. But her tone remained critical. "You are gripping too tightly. Relax, or you will burn out before we even begin."

The subsequent few attempts saw progress but also more failures. Each fall was met with growing frustration, the impact bruising his body and ego. His limbs throbbed with the growing aches, and every movement sent a dull ache through his battered muscles. Yet, each painful landing only hardened his resolve. Every mistake gnawed at him, but a realization took root, and these were not failures. They were lessons.

Each time, he learned something new.

One fall taught him that gripping too hard threw off his balance—his arms ached from the strain, his fingers numb from the pressure, and by the time he realized the mistake, he was already tumbling toward the ground. Another taught him to feel Aurelia's movements rather than react to them. Slowly, painfully, stubbornly, he began to adjust.

His balance steadied.

His grip became fluid rather than forced.

And then he was riding.

After hours of relentless effort, Aurelia finally landed smoothly, allowing Gailen to dismount.

He was drenched in sweat, his arms sore, his legs unsteady, but a small smile tugged at his lips.

He had done it.

Aurelia regarded him for a long moment, her gaze lingering as a subtle nod accompanied the barest hint of approval. Then, with a faint glimmer in her crystalline eyes, she said, "You're starting to look like a rider."

Gailen's chest swelled slightly, not with arrogance, but with relief.

The road ahead was still long, but this victory, however small, ignited something within him—a confidence he had not felt before.

"But this was just the beginning," Aurelia warned, her voice returning to its steely tone. "Now, we push further."

Ong approached, offering a canteen. "Not bad, Prince. You did not even break anything."

Gailen chuckled, taking a long drink, the cool water soothing his parched throat. "I'll take that as a victory."

Nearby, Amara watched the exchange, her amethyst eyes gleaming with amusement.

"He has a long way to go," she mused, "but there's potential."

Aurelia nodded, her crystalline gaze sharp and knowing.

"The real challenge begins now."

The weight in her voice sent a shiver down Gailen's spine. Her wings twitched, an unspoken anticipation coiling beneath her composed exterior. A faint gleam in her eyes hinted at the hardships still to come, the trials that would test him in ways he could not yet fathom.

She lowered herself again, her iridescent wings shimmering like polished ice, a faint crackling sound accompanying their movement as they shifted in the light. Her tail flicked, sending a swirl of dust spiraling into the air.

"Climb back on." The command left no room for hesitation.

"This time, we go higher."

Her voice softened, just barely.

"You must learn to trust yourself and me."

Gailen's breath hitched. Higher.

He glanced upward, the vast sky stretching endlessly above them, an unbroken canvas of blue and white.

What would it mean if he failed here if he fell from that height? Would he be able to survive the impact, or would the pain and injuries be enough to end his training before it had truly begun?

Would it prove he was not ready? That he would never be?

Doubt coiled around his thoughts, whispering of expectations too high to reach.

The memories of his earlier falls flashed in his mind, the helplessness, the impact, the bruises that had barely begun to fade.

His fingers curled into fists, tension rippling through his body.

Then, a slow, measured breath drew in steadiness and forced out doubt. The tension in his shoulders eased slightly, his heartbeat settling into a steadier rhythm as clarity took hold.

Exhale.

The pounding of his heart slowed. His grip loosened, and the trembling in his hands steadied.

He had come too far to let fear win now.

Even as the thought of falling from a greater height sent a chill through his spine, he steeled himself and climbed onto her back.

This time, his grip was firmer and more deliberate. But even so, the slight tremor in his fingers betrayed his nerves.

Aurelia felt it.

"Remember what you've learned." Her voice was firm, steady. "Stay relaxed. Move with me. And above all, do not panic."

Gailen swallowed hard. "I'll do my best." His voice was steadier than he felt.

Without further warning, Aurelia launched into the air.

The ground vanished beneath them.

The sudden force slammed against him, knocking the breath from his lungs. His chest tightened, a sharp pressure blooming beneath his ribs as his vision blurred momentarily from the impact.

The wind roared in his ears, drowning out all the other sounds. The rush of air stung his face, and as they climbed higher and higher, the world below shrunk into insignificance.

Gailen's fingers dug into the crystalline ridges, his knuckles white. The sharp pressure bit into his skin as his grip tightened against the relentless force of the wind.

The texture was smooth yet glass-like beneath his grip, a chilling contrast to the burning strain in his muscles. Every instinct screamed at him to hold tighter, as if sheer force alone could keep him from falling.

Then Aurelia's voice cut through the wind, sharp as a blade.

"Loosen your grip! Trust my movements!"

He exhaled shakily, his breath barely audible against the wind's roar.

He forced himself to ease his hold with effort, the tension in his shoulders slowly unwinding.

As they climbed higher, the temperature plummeted. The air grew thin, crisp, and sharp against his skin. The endless sky swallowed them whole, stretching in every direction, an ocean of infinite blue and weightless clouds.

For a moment, a quiet awe settled over him.

This... this was what it meant to fly.

Then, the world tilted.

Aurelia banked suddenly to the right.

Gailen's stomach dropped, his body lurching as he scrambled to counterbalance the motion.

Before he could recover, she twisted sharply left and plunged into a sudden dive.

His heart slammed into his ribs.

The force threatened to rip him away, gravity clawing at his body. His hands clenched around the ridges of her back, his breath coming in ragged bursts.

Do not panic.

Aurelia's voice rang out, barely audible over the wind.

"Keep your body aligned with mine! Let your instincts guide you!"

Instincts.

Gailen gritted his teeth.

What instincts?

Aurelia leveled out briefly, then twisted into a tight spiral.

The motion was disorienting, a blur of sky, ground, sky, ground. His vision spun, his breath caught, and for a fleeting moment, panic clawed its way back in.

Then, he forced himself to focus.

Breathe.

He stopped reacting to the motion and started feeling it.

The way she moved was fluid, controlled, and precise.

He adjusted his weight before she banked.

This time, he moved with her, not against her.

The tension in his muscles eased just slightly. The burn in his arms remained, but it no longer fought against her rhythm.

His heart was still racing.

But he was not falling.

Aurelia ascended again, the clouds parting around them as she surged higher, slicing through the sky with effortless power.

Gailen's breath hitched, his senses torn between exhilaration and unease. The vastness of the sky stretched endlessly, making him feel both insignificant and infinite on the edge of something far more significant than himself.

Aurelia's voice cut through the wind. "Hold on."

There was a challenge in her tone before Gailen could brace himself.

She rolled.

Aurelia twisted into a barrel roll, spinning through the air with a fluidity that belied her massive size.

The world became a blur of sky and earth, rotating at a dizzying speed.

Gailen's stomach lurched violently, and his body whipped sideways as the centrifugal force tore at him. He gritted his teeth, pressing his body tight against her back, his muscles straining against the relentless pull.

The sheer force of the spin made it nearly impossible to hold on, his vision tunneling as the movement threatened to overwhelm his senses.

Then, suddenly, they leveled out.

Gailen gasped for air, his pulse hammering in his ears.

He was still on.

A rush of pride surged through him, mingled with relief and exhilaration. The ache in his muscles reminded him of how far he had pushed himself, but for the first time, he felt a flicker of confidence that was real, tangible, and earned.

Aurelia glanced back at him briefly. "Not bad."

But there was no relief in her voice.

"We're not finished yet."

Before he could catch his breath, she dove into a series of tight loops and sharp turns, each movement a test, each shift in direction demanding precise adjustments.

Gailen faltered more than once, slipping precariously but managing to recover before he could fall.

His arms trembled from exertion, his muscles burning from the relentless strain.

His palms were raw, scraped, and blistered from gripping too tightly. Each movement sent a sharp sting through his hands as the cool air aggravated the tender skin.

When Aurelia brought them into a steady glide, his body ached from head to toe, and his every breath was labored.

The air stung his skin, his lungs gasping for relief as the last remnants of adrenaline coursed through his veins.

Aurelia's flight slowed, giving him a moment to compose himself.

"You're improving," she said, a rare note of approval in her voice. "But you still have much to learn."

Gailen dismounted with effort, his legs like water beneath him. He swayed slightly as his feet met the ground, the solid earth beneath him feeling foreign after so long in the sky.

He exhaled sharply, looking up at Aurelia with exhaustion and raw determination.

"That was... intense."

Aurelia folded her wings. "You'll face far worse in battle."

Her crystalline body gleamed beneath the midday sun, her gaze measuring, assessing, searching for weakness.

Then, with a flick of her tail, she said, "Today, you learned to trust me." Now, you will learn to trust yourself."

Then, her following words sent a chill through him, a shiver tracing its way down his spine as his muscles tensed involuntarily.

"You must learn to stand on my back."

Gailen blinked. "...Stand?"

"While we're flying?"

"Precisely."

She lowered herself slightly, her crystalline scales glinting like polished armor.

"Though your weapon may not require this skill often, the battlefield is unpredictable. There will come a time when standing on my back will be your only option, whether to steady a shot or launch an attack. If you cannot master your balance, you will not last."

The weight of her words settled heavily on him.

His muscles were already screaming, his legs burning with fatigue, his hands sore and raw, his entire body on the verge of collapse.

And now... she wanted him to stand?

His fingers flexed at his sides, a flicker of doubt slithering through him.

Could he do this?

Then, beneath the exhaustion, beneath the ache, something deeper stirred.

A desire. A drive. He needed to prove himself.

His jaw tightened. His stance straightened.

"Alright," he said, resolve hardening his voice. "Let's do it."

He climbed onto her back, his movements slower this time, more careful.

Settling into place, he took a measured breath.

Aurelia waited, patient yet watchful.

"Stand slowly." Her voice was even, unwavering. "Trust my movements. I will keep you stable, but you must trust yourself."

His hands pressed against her scales, cool beneath his fingertips.

Deep breath.

Gailen shifted his weight, pushing himself upward.

His legs wobbled violently as he straightened, every fiber of his body resisting the unnatural movement.

The ground was gone. The sky was endless. There was nothing but him and Aurelia.

His arms shot outward instinctively, desperate for balance, but the sudden motion only worsened his instability, sending him teetering dangerously to one side.

A gust of wind rushed past him, setting him off-kilter. He wavered dangerously, his pulse spiking.

If he fell now, it would not just be a failure; it could be the end of his training, perhaps even his life. The sky offered no second chances.

Aurelia's voice was a steady anchor. "Focus. Feel the connection between us. Trust me."

Gailen clenched his jaw. This was no longer about skill; it was about trust.

Slowly, he closed his eyes.

He let himself feel Aurelia beneath him. The subtle shifts in her flight, the steady rhythm of her breathing, the silent promise that she would not let him fall.

The tension in his legs eased.

The trembling subsided.

His balance steadied.

He opened his eyes.

For the first time, he was standing. A surge of triumph rippled through him, pushing past the exhaustion and the fear. This was more than just balance; this was trust and control, a step toward becoming the warrior he was meant to be.

Good," Aurelia said. "Now, we take it further."

Before Gailen could ask what she meant, Aurelia moved.

Her steps were slow at first, deliberate, testing. Gailen's arms shifted instinctively, counterbalancing each subtle motion.

"Not bad." There was a hint of approval in her tone.

Then, without warning, she leaped.

Gailen's stomach plummeted.

The wind slammed into him like an icy wall, tearing at his clothes and stealing the breath from his lungs. The cold bit his skin like needles, numbing his fingers even as he struggled to hold on. His vision blurred from the force of the ascent, and for a brief, terrifying moment, the sheer height sent a spike of fear down his spine.

His body reacted instinctively. Knees bent. Core tightened. Weight adjusted.

Aurelia leveled out, the world stretching infinitely in all directions.

The view was breathtaking, but there was no time to admire it.

Aurelia began a slow banking turn.

Gailen leaned with her, his mind racing to anticipate the movement.

"Trust me," Aurelia's voice carried through the wind. "Feel my movements."

He nodded, focusing on each subtle shift in her flight. Every tilt, every correction demanded precision and instinct. The more he resisted, the more unstable he felt, but the moment he moved with her, balance became second nature.

Then, her following command caught him off guard.

"Now, pretend to draw your Crystalbow."

Gailen's heart jumped. "What?"

"In battle, hesitation is death. Imagine you are aiming at a target."

This was a test.

Gritting his teeth, Gailen reached for an invisible Crystalbow, nocking an arrow that wasn't there.

His stance wavered. The wind pressed against him, a constant enemy, unrelenting.

He spread his arms wider, adjusting.

His muscles screamed in protest and balance, teetering on a razor's edge.

For a moment, his mind drifted to Vacari, to his first steps beyond its borders, to the weight of expectation that had followed him since. The uncertainty had been suffocating, the fear of failing ever-present. Yet each challenge had forged him more vigorously, and each hardship had taught him resilience. Just as he had conquered those trials, he knew he had to destroy this one.

The uncertainty, the loneliness they had tested him just as much as this moment did now.

But he had endured. And he would endure it again.

Doubt flickered in his mind. What if he lost his balance? What if he failed?

No.

He pushed his thoughts aside, focusing instead on his Crystalbow's imagined weight and Aurelia's steady rhythm beneath him.

The moment of distraction cost him.

Aurelia dove suddenly.

Gailen tilted forward too far.

His balance snapped.

He fought to regain it, crouching slightly, adjusting just in time.

His heart pounded.

Then he straightened again, raising the invisible Crystalbow with new-found confidence. His movements were steadier, his grip firmer, and a quiet certainty settled within him.

Aurelia's wings tilted slightly.

"Good."

But they were not done.

Aurelia weaved through the air, dipping into a slow roll, then shifting into a sharp, spiraling climb.

The sudden shifts in direction threatened to unseat him, forcing him to react with instinct.

His body burned from the effort, his hands aching from gripping too tightly.

Then, a moment of reprieve.

Aurelia bent her wings inward, creating a shield against the worst of the buffeting winds.

Gailen breathed. He adjusted and centered himself.

Then, just as quickly, she expanded her wings again and surged forward.

The sudden movement tested every ounce of his strength, but he held firm, his body swaying with her instead of fighting against her.

When she finally descended, landing gracefully, Gailen dismounted—shaky, exhausted, but victorious.

His breath came in sharp bursts, but a sense of accomplishment settled over him.

Aurelia lowered her head, meeting his gaze.

Then, a rare display of approval.

She extended her wings slightly, curving them over him in a protective arc. Gailen's breath hitched at the unexpected gesture, and a mix of relief and quiet pride settled in his chest. It was a rare acknowledgment, a sign that he was earning her trust, and for the first time, he truly felt like he belonged.

A faint hum of satisfaction resonated in her chest.

"You are beginning to understand."

Gailen felt the shift in her tone, the acknowledgment, the silent reassurance that he was on the right path.

But then her voice turned firm again.

"Understanding is only the first step."

She straightened, her crystalline body glowing in the midday light.

"Standing on my back is not just about skill but about trust. Trust in yourself and me. Without that, you will not succeed."

Gailen nodded, his breath still heavy, his body aching but his mind clear.

"I think I'm starting to get it."

"Good," Aurelia said. "Because the real challenges are still ahead."

She watched as Gailen approached once more, his steps slow but resolute.

She had given him a brief reprieve, but she knew that what came next would push him beyond anything he had faced so far. He had learned how to stand, but now he would have to learn how to fall and rise again.

Chapter 30
Ascension of the Dragon Rider

As Gailen approached, Aurelia lowered herself, her crystalline scales shimmering like polished glass in the light. "Are you ready for the next phase?" Her voice was calm but carried weight.

Gailen exhaled deeply. "I think so." He glanced at Ong, who stood with Amara nearby. "Anything I should know?"

Ong smirked, arms crossed. "Trust.

He had done it before when Aurelia had thrown him into the skies and forced him to find his balance when he had stood on her back despite the fear threatening to consume him. Each time, he had survived because he had trusted her, trusted himself. This was no different. Trust yourself."

Amara lowered her head slightly, amusement flickering in her amethyst eyes. "You know what's next, don't you, Ong?"

Ong's smirk widened. "I do. And let us say no one warned me about it." He glanced at Gailen, his smirk deepening. "Why should I make it easier for him?"

Amara chuckled, a low, rich sound vibrating through the air. "Cruel, but fair."

Gailen, oblivious to Ong and Amara's exchange, climbed onto Aurelia's back, adjusting his grip on her scales.

"What's next?" He tried to sound confident. He was not sure he succeeded.

Aurelia spread her wings and launched into the sky. The rush of wind stole his breath, pressing against him like an unrelenting force, making every movement feel sluggish as they climbed higher than before. Below, the lush greens of the forest blurred into a sea of shifting color, the ground growing distant, unreachable.

Once they leveled out, Aurelia glanced back at him. "Now, we teach you how to fall."

Gailen's stomach twisted. "Fall?" The word barely left his lips, his mind rejecting its absurdity. His fingers tightened instinctively on Aurelia's scales, his knuckles turning white.

This had to be a joke. His stomach clenched, and a nervous laugh almost escaped, but Aurelia's unflinching expression stole any hope of humor. She was serious.

"Yes," Aurelia's tone was unyielding. "A rider must understand how to respond when separated from their dragon. It may happen in battle. It may happen because of a mistake. You must learn to react with clarity, not panic. Trust is vital not just in me but in yourself."

He swallowed hard. "And what exactly does 'learning to fall' entail?"

Aurelia did not answer. Instead, she tilted her wings sharply. The world vanished beneath him.

For a heartbeat, he felt nothing. Then he fell. The wind roared in his ears, tearing at him, twisting him. His body flipped uncontrollably, the air stinging his skin like icy needles. His limbs flailed uselessly, the world spinning around him in a dizzying blur. A wave of vertigo crashed over him, disorienting and sickening, as time stretched into a slow-motion nightmare. Weightlessness wrapped around him like a vice. His chest tightened. His thoughts fractured. The ground was rushing toward him, fast, too fast.

"Calm your mind." Aurelia's voice cut through the chaos. "Focus."

Gailen gasped, forcing air into his lungs. He closed his eyes for a heartbeat, shutting out the terror clawing at his mind.

Trust. With a desperate breath, he stilled. He spread his arms slightly, adjusting, shifting. The descent did not stop, but it slowed. He could feel the air differently now from the shift of the wind. The fear remained, but he was no longer drowning in it.

Then, a shimmer of crystal-blue scales appeared beneath him, catching the sunlight in dazzling bursts and reflecting the sky in shifting hues of sapphire and silver. Aurelia caught him effortlessly, her movements smooth and controlled. She did not even pause. "Again."

Gailen barely had time to prepare before she tilted her wings once more. He fell. This time, he fought the instinct to flail.

He forced his breath to steady, and his body angled more deliberately. The panic was still there, clawing at the edges of his mind, but he pushed it back.

Again, Aurelia caught him. "You're improving," she said as she climbed again. "But you must trust entirely. Trust that I will come for you. Trust that you can remain composed."

By the fall of the fourth, something inside Gailen shifted. The fear was still there, but it no longer held him captive.

Each descent taught him something new. At first, he resisted and fought the air like an enemy, his muscles locking as if bracing for impact. Each gust felt like a force trying to wrench him off course, gravity becoming his opponent.

Now, he embraced it. He was not just falling anymore. He was learning how to control the descent. How to move with the wind, not against it. How to trust.

A memory flashed through his mind the day he had left Vacari. He had felt this same uncertainty, this same terror of the unknown.

But he had kept going. Step by step. Fall by fall. And now, he was doing the same here. By the final attempt, his movements were deliberate. Purposeful.

Aurelia caught him once more. But this time, she did not immediately ascend.

Instead, she landed, lowering herself so he could slide off her back. His legs nearly buckled beneath him, trembling from exhaustion, and his vision blurred briefly before he steadied himself. Every inch of him ached.

But it was a different kind of exhaustion. This was earned. He exhaled sharply, rolling his shoulders. The fatigue was profound, but it did not feel like defeat. He had fallen, but he had learned to rise.

Aurelia studied him for a long moment, her crystalline gaze unreadable. A faint flicker of something calculation and consideration passed through her expression. Then, finally, she spoke.

"Well done." Her voice held something new. Approval. "You have learned to fall without succumbing to fear." The words settled deep within him. He had not realized how much he needed to hear them. A sense of accomplishment burned in his chest, a hard-won victory after relentless trials.

Aurelia's voice turned firm again. "Remember this lesson. In the chaos of battle, it may save your life."

Gailen nodded, absorbing the weight of her words.

Ong and Amara watched from the sidelines. Ong met his gaze, nodding slightly.

Amara chuckled, her voice echoing in his mind. "I told you he'd manage."

Ong smirked, arms crossed. "Barely." Ong rolled his eyes but could not hide the slight grin tugging at his lips. Ong huffed a breathless laugh, shaking his head.

Amara's voice was teasing but warm. "Just barely," she agreed. "But he did." She turned and looked at Ong. "Though, if I recall, you also barely survived your training."

Gailen turned back to Aurelia, meeting her gaze with renewed determination. "What's next?"

Aurelia's crystalline scales shimmered, refracting the sunlight like fractured stars, casting shifting patterns of iridescent light across the sky as she hovered midair, her vast wings keeping them steady. The wind swirled around her, carrying an electrified charge that hummed the air.

Gailen adjusted his grip, his muscles still sore from the relentless training, his body aching but eager. This next phase sent him both a thrill of excitement and a coil of apprehension.

"Now, we begin combat training." Aurelia's voice was even, commanding, uncompromising.

"You will use an imaginary Crystalbow for now, mimicking the motions as if you were armed. Precision and balance are paramount. You must learn to move as one with me, to anticipate not only your actions but mine."

Gailen nodded, inhaling deeply. He closed his eyes momentarily, visualizing the Crystalbow he had glimpsed earlier.

He lifted his arms as if holding the weapon, feeling the phantom weight of the weapon settle against his palms. The imagined string was taut beneath his fingers, and a flicker of anticipation burned in his chest.

"Ready?" Aurelia asked.

"As ready as I'll ever be." Without warning, Aurelia tilted sharply.

The sudden motion yanked him sideways. His stomach plummeted. The wind snapped against him, his vision blurring as the sky twisted wildly. Gailen fought to keep his grip, his arms instinctively tightening as he tried to steady the phantom Crystalbow.

"Focus," Aurelia instructed, her voice a steady anchor. "Grip with your legs, not your hands. Your upper body must remain free to maneuver the Crystalbow."

He adjusted quickly, locking his thighs around her ridged back. His arms loosened, but his core tightened, his balance adjusting to the shift. His movements became smoother, the phantom Crystalbows steadier in his grasp.

"Now, draw." Gailen mimed pulling the invisible Crystalbowstring, his arms trembling from exertion.

The imagined Crystalbow felt heavier, as if training had given it actual weight, pressing against his fingers with a tangible resistance. The sensation grounded him, making the training feel more real. Each motion sharpened his focus, and each draw tested his endurance.

The strain of balancing made his breath come in sharp bursts, sweat trickling down his temple as Aurelia banked hard left. His stomach flipped, but he adjusted, shifting his core with her.

"Fire at the targets below," Aurelia commanded.

Gailen's gaze flicked downward. Dark silhouettes and phantom shapes of enemy dragons shifted against the treetops. His breath steadied. He aimed. He released. His body swayed with Aurelia's motion, his focus narrowing to the perfect trajectory of the shot.

"Good." Aurelia's tone held approval. "Now, let's add complexity."

Before he could respond, she dove. The wind screamed past his ears, stinging his skin like a thousand tiny blades and pressing against him like an invisible wall, threatening to throw him off balance.

His lungs tightened, the air rushing violently against him. The ground surged toward him at breakneck speed.

"Shoot."

His mind screamed that it was impossible, but instinct overrode fear. He mimed another shot, adjusting for the rapid descent. His grip wavered, but he recovered, muscles burning.

Again, Aurelia leveled out and then shot into a steep climb. Then she twisted.

The world snapped sideways. His stance faltered, but he corrected it just in time. He drew the Crystalbow string again, aiming at the newest target. This was no longer just about reacting.

This was about anticipation. The speed increased. The angles shifted. The chaos grew, and so did his clarity.

Aurelia spiraled, dove, and even flipped entirely, forcing Gailen to match her movements. At first, he struggled, his body lagging behind each shift, but gradually, instinct took over. He began to anticipate her motions, adjusting before she even moved, his body synchronizing with hers in a calculated, precise rhythm.

Then, she simulated an attack. A sharp tilt, his balance shattered. He slipped.

Gailen slid down her flank, his fingers burning as he fought to hold on. The wind howled in his ears, whipping his clothes.

His leg barely caught on a ridge, pain lancing through his thigh, momentarily clouding his focus. He gritted his teeth, forcing the agony aside, knowing that hesitation could mean another fall.

His breath came in ragged bursts. Panic flared.

Then Aurelia's voice cut through the storm. "Hold your Crystalbow."

His muscles screamed, but he tightened his grip. His chest heaved, but he forced himself to breathe.

The phantom Crystalbow remained steady. With a final burst of effort, he swung himself back onto her.

Just before she tilted again, this time, he was ready. He fired, the phantom arrow flying true.

Aurelia slowed, her approval unmistakable. "You're learning to fight and trust yourself and me."

Gailen sat back, gasping for breath, his heart hammering against his ribs. His chest ached from the exertion, his fingers trembling slightly as the adrenaline coursed through him.

His muscles burned, but the thrill of progress drowned out the fatigue.

He wiped the sweat from his brow, a determined smile creeping onto his face. "What's next?"

Aurelia turned her head slightly, her crystalline eyes glinting.

"Next, we test what you've learned in a real scenario."

As the sun dipped toward the horizon, Aurelia descended into a clearing, her crystalline wings folding with fluid grace. The light caught on her scales, casting shimmering reflections across the glade as she settled, her presence both commanding and serene.

She remained still momentarily, allowing Gailen to steady himself, then gestured subtly with a tilt of her head.

From the shadows, Ong stepped forward. In his hands, he held the ornate Crystalbow.

Its polished surface glinted with an ethereal glow, the emerald inlays catching the golden hues of the fading sun. The air around it hummed, almost imperceptibly, like a weapon that recognized its purpose.

Aurelia's voice was steady, resonant. "This is yours." She paused, letting the words sink in. "Use it wisely."

Gailen reached out. His hands trembled as his fingers curled around the Crystalbow's calm surface.

The moment his skin met the polished crystal, a pulse of energy surged through him, tingling like lightning beneath his fingertips. It was exhilarating yet almost overwhelming in its intensity.

His breath hitched. It was heavier than he expected, not just in weight but in meaning. This was no longer just training. This was real. The path of a dragon rider was no longer a distant goal but a reality unfolding in his hands. His pulse quickened, his grip tightening as the weight of destiny settled onto his shoulders.

Ong stepped closer, his expression unreadable. Alongside the Crystalbow, a quiver rested in his grasp. Gailen's breath caught as he saw what was inside. Not ordinary arrows. These were forged of pure crystal, their cores glowing faintly as though alive.

The light within them shifted, flickering like liquid fire, moving with an unseen rhythm. A faint tingling sensation ran up his arm as his fingers brushed over them. The arrows reacted. They were aware of him.

Their light pulsed soft at first, then stronger, coordinated with the rhythm of his heartbeat. A slow, creeping realization settled over him. They were not just weapons.

They were extensions of the will, purpose, and bond between rider and dragon. Holding them, Gailen felt a strange sense of unity, as though they were more than weapons; they were a promise, a bridge between his past struggles and the battles yet to come. For the first time, he understood what it meant to wield something as a tool and a reflection of himself and Aurelia.

"These are... actual arrows?" Gailen asked, his voice barely above a whisper.

Aurelia nodded, her gaze unwavering. "They are manifestations of the bond between the Crystalbow, its wielder, and the dragon who empowers it."

Her words resonated in the still air, heavy with meaning. "This connection is forged through trust, shared energy, and mutual purpose. The Crystalbow draws strength from both our spirits, creating a harmony that makes its power unique."

Gailen swallowed hard. The Crystalbow felt different now. More than a weapon, it is a conduit of something greater. "But what makes them different from ordinary arrows?" he asked, his grip tightening as he studied the flickering glow within each crystalline shaft.

Aurelia's crystalline gaze gleamed with knowing. "They do not simply pierce." She stepped closer, her wings shifting subtly as if emphasizing the weight of what she was about to say.

"Each arrow can be imbued with purpose shaped by your intent. Some will shatter on impact, releasing a storm of razor-sharp crystal shards, cutting through enemies like falling glass. Others will explode outward, unleashing bursts of concussive force that can instantly tear through armor and scatter foes. Some will radiate light brighter than the sun, capable of blinding enemies or illuminating even the deepest darkness. And then some can disrupt magic, unraveling enchantments mid-flight or breaking through barriers woven by the most potent spellcasters."

She lowered her head slightly, locking eyes with him. "The Crystalbow will respond to your will, Prince Gailen. Let your thoughts shape their energy. Let your purpose guide its aim. This weapon does not simply obey; it resonates. It is an extension of you, amplifying your intent until it becomes reality."

Gailen stepped into the clearing, the weight of the Crystalbow settling into his grip like a tangible promise.

Aurelia watched him intently, her crystalline wings tucked elegantly at her sides.

Raising the Crystalbow, he knocked one of the glowing crystal arrows onto the string. The moment he drew it back. A pulse of raw energy surged through him.

It was as though the Crystalbow and arrow were alive, their power threaded into his heartbeat, into Aurelia's presence beside him.

"Focus." Aurelia's voice was steady, a grounding force amidst the storm of power coiling within him. "Let the Crystalbow guide you."

Gailen's hands trembled slightly, the strain of his earlier training coiled in his muscles like embers waiting to ignite. Yet, it was not just fatigue.

Beneath the ache, nervous anticipation churned, pressing against his ribs. The Crystalbow hummed against his fingers, its energy pulsing with his heartbeat. It was listening. Waiting.

Some of him feared failing, fearing losing control just as he had when Aurelia first chose him, declaring that he would one day lead the crystal dragons. The weight of that responsibility had once seemed unbearable, but now, standing here with the Crystalbow in his grasp, he realized that trust was what had brought him this far.

But the energy coursing through the Crystalbow soothed that doubt, whispering of trust. This was not just a test of skill. It was a test of his bond with Aurelia.

And if he faltered, it would not only be his failure. It could sever their connection. He closed his eyes for a heartbeat, feeling the Crystalbow's resonance with his pulse, with the energy thrumming beneath Aurelia's crystalline scales.

When he exhaled, he was ready. He opened his eyes. He aimed. The distant tree stood unmoving, waiting as if daring him to strike.

He released the string. The arrow shot forward with a crystalline hum, slicing through the air like a streak of light. Then impact. The arrow struck true, and the tree shuddered upon contact. Cracks splintered outward from the point of impact, glowing with the same ethereal light that pulsed within the arrow. The energy rippled, sending jagged fractures through the bark before dissipating in a cascade of shimmering embers. Shimmering sparks erupted from the target, cascading outward in a beautiful yet deadly display.

Gailen blinked. His breath came fast, his heart hammering, his chest tightening as a tremor ran through his fingers. "It exploded?" A mix of awe and unease flickered across his face. The sheer power he had just unleashed sent a shiver down his spine.

Was this indeed something he could control? Or had the Crystalbow reacted on its own?

Aurelia nodded, the faintest trace of approval in her voice. "A burst arrow. Your intent determines the energy released."

She studied him. "Try again. But this time, focus on creating a beacon of light. Something to guide your allies in the dark."

Gailen swallowed, gripping the Crystalbow tighter. He nocked another arrow, his fingers steadying against the string. This time, he visualized the arrow illuminating the battlefield, cutting through the shadows like a guiding star. When he let go, the arrow flew true.

It struck the tree, but instead of shattering, it ignited into a blinding pulse of white light. The clearing was bathed in an ethereal glow, chasing away the creeping dusk.

Gailen turned to Aurelia, his eyes wide with astonishment. "This is incredible."

Aurelia's crystalline gaze gleamed. "You're beginning to understand." Her wings unfurled slightly, a silent command.

"Now, move with me." Her tone hardened. "In battle, you will not have the luxury of standing still. Hesitation could mean defeat and the loss of those who depend on you."

Her voice lowered, edged with something heavier. "You remember your last battle, do you not?"

Gailen stiffened. He did. The moment when he had hesitated. When it had cost nearly everything.

Aurelia's voice pierced him, striking a chord of guilt and determination. The memory of his past hesitation resurfaced, but instead of paralyzing him, it fueled his resolve. "If you falter again, the consequences will not just be yours to bear. They will be ours." She leaped into the sky, her wings slicing through the wind.

Gailen scrambled onto her back, gripping the Crystalbow tightly. They soared higher, the air turning colder. Then, a sharp bank to the right. Gailen reacted instantly, nocking an arrow mid-motion. Below, imaginary targets moved through the trees. He fired. Missed.

"Faster," Aurelia commanded over the wind. "An enemy will not wait for you to adjust."

He adjusted his stance, his muscles screaming from the effort. Another shot—this one struck. Again, a direct hit.

Aurelia twisted into a steep dive.

Gailen's breath tore from his lungs, but he did not falter. He drew, released, drew, released. The arrows responded seamlessly, mirroring his intent. With each shot, he felt a growing sense of control, the power no longer foreign but an extension of himself. Yet, a sliver of unease remained: was it his mastery guiding them, or was the Crystalbow still shaping the outcome? Some burst into blinding light, illuminating targets in the deepening twilight. Others shattered into lethal shards, scattering in precise arcs. One emitted a pulse of energy so strong the air seemed to ripple as it struck.

Aurelia leveled out. The wind rushed past them as silence settled between them—thick with unspoken understanding, a pause heavy with the weight of progress and the challenges still ahead.

"Impressive." Aurelia's voice carried something new.

Not just approval. Something deeper. Recognition. "You are adapting well. But there is more to learn." She banked gently, descending back toward the clearing. "This Crystalbow will grow with you, as will our bond."

Gailen exhaled, his muscles aching but his spirit burning with determination. Aurelia's gaze met his as they landed.

"Use it wisely, Prince Gailen. For it will be both a weapon and a symbol of the leader you are becoming."

As they descended into the clearing, Gailen dismounted, his mind racing with the possibilities before him. He held the Crystalbow with renewed reverence, no longer seeing it as a mere weapon but as a testament to the legacy he was now bound to. A feeling he had known before when he returned home, stepping back into the weight of expectation and duty, settled over him again. But this time, he did not shrink from it. He embraced it.

Aurelia folded her gleaming crystalline wings, her piercing gaze locked onto him as if weighing his readiness one last time. Gailen held his ground, resisting the urge to shift under her scrutiny. A flicker of uncertainty stirred in his chest, but he pushed it aside, meeting her gaze with quiet resolve. Amara stepped forward, her amethyst scales shimmering under the waning sunlight. She regarded him with quiet amusement, her keen eyes flicking toward the Crystalbow in his hands. "That Crystalbow now belongs to you, Prince Gailen," Amara said, her voice carrying an air of ancient wisdom laced with something almost playful.

Gailen raised an eyebrow. "You know about this Crystalbow?"

Amara's chuckle was deep and knowing. "Yes, Prince. I have been around far longer than you." Her violet gaze drifted past him as if recalling something long buried in time. "I saw it wielded in battle generations ago. One of your ancestors stood atop a ridge as enemy forces surged toward him.

The Crystalbow was raised high, its crystal arrows illuminating the battlefield like falling stars. Each shot carved light through the darkness, cutting through enemy ranks with such precision that their formations crumbled. The tide of the war shifted with every glowing arrow that fell as if the heavens themselves had intervened."

She paused, her expression unreadable. "Even now, the sight of it remains vivid." Her eyes met his again, sharper this time. "It is a weapon of great power and great responsibility."

Gailen exhaled, glancing down at the Crystalbow. Its surface was cool beneath his fingertips, yet a faint energy pulse throbbed within as if the weapon itself was alive and aware of his touch. Its surface pulsed faintly, responding to his touch as though it, too, acknowledged the weight of what it had just become. A flicker of doubt coiled in his chest. Could he indeed wield this power as his ancestors had? Or was he merely carrying the shadow of something greater than himself?

Before the thought could fully form, Aurelia stepped closer, her crystalline gaze unwavering.

"Now you understand why I chose you," she said. Her words carried the certainty of an oath. "The crystal Crystalbow obeys only the commands of one who understands its nature and has forged a bond with a crystal dragon. You have proven yourself, Gailen." The weight of her words settled deep within him, stirring a mix of emotions.

Excitement burned like embers beneath his ribs, but so did doubt. Still, when he met her gaze, it was with resolve. "What more do I have to learn?"

Aurelia tilted her head slightly, her expression unreadable. "You have mastered the basics. But there is still much to be done." Her wings shifted somewhat as if bracing for what came next. "Your bond with me will strengthen with time. And your true potential will only emerge through practice, experience, and battle. Sometimes, that may mean protecting Crystal Vale from attacks. Be ready."

Gailen nodded, absorbing the weight of her words. There would be no rest—only preparation for what was coming.

Amara and Aurelia exchanged a silent glance before lifting into the sky, wings catching the light as they turned toward Crystal Vale.

Gailen rode with Aurelia, his grip firm around the Crystalbow, while Ong soared beside them on Amara's back.

The city shimmered beneath the afternoon sun as they descended, landing near the palace gates.

Gailen dismounted, his mind still buzzing with the day's revelations, when Ong's voice cut through the air.

"Gailen."

Gailen turned as Ong strode toward his quarters.

He stopped. Ong's expression was unreadable, but his tone was serious. "Protect the Crystalbow. Keep it hidden. Be wary of who sees it."

A weight settled in Gailen's gut. "I will," he assured, gripping the Crystalbow tighter. Then, without another word, he disappeared into the palace.

Amara's large violet eyes flicked toward Ong, narrowing slightly. "What was that about?" she asked, tilting her head.

Ong's jaw tightened, and his expression darkened. "The attack." His voice was low and clipped. It was too deliberate. Someone knew exactly where and when to strike." He exhaled sharply, his gaze drifting toward the city. That level of coordination is no coincidence."

Amara's tail lashed subtly, a slow, deliberate motion of unease. "You believe someone informed them?"

Ong's lips pressed into a thin line, his gaze shifting briefly to the side as if weighing his following words. A flicker of hesitation crossed his face before he spoke. "The obsidian dragon didn't just attack. It targeted Gailen directly. Ignoring all else." He turned back to Amara, his expression unreadable. "They've never fought in Vacari before. Unless someone told them, they had no reason to know who Gailen was."

Amara let out a low growl, her muscles coiling. Her gaze flicked back toward the city walls as if she expected danger to be watching. "That is... troubling." Her voice was measured, but the sharp edge of caution was unmistakable. "None of the obsidian dragons should know him. And yet, they targeted him with precision."

Ong's fists clenched. "That is what worries me." His voice was low now, barely above a whisper. "Someone is working against us from the shadows. And I suspect they are closer than we realize."

Amara's tail swished, her agitation unmasked. Her stance stiffened, weight shifting as if preparing for an unseen threat. Her eyes narrowed a flicker of unease, sharpening her usually steady gaze. "Then we must be vigilant." She cast one last lingering glance toward the city. "Whoever orchestrated this... will not stop."

Their thoughts were heavy with implications. The attack had been a warning. An unseen force was moving against them, and the actual threat had yet to reveal itself.

Chapter 31
Bonds Beyond Boundaries

The following day dawned soft and golden, light spilling over the spires of Crystal Vale like liquid fire. The city shimmered beneath the morning sun, its crystalline towers reflecting the light in cascading prisms of amber and gold. A crisp breeze carried the scent of damp earth, dewy grass, and distant hearth fires, mingling with the faint hum of a city waking to life.

Yet, beneath the serenity, a subtle unease lingered a quiet tension that had settled over the city, unspoken yet palpable. The sunrise had not erased the tensions of the previous day; they had only momentarily softened.

Prince Gailen adjusted the clasp of his cloak, his fingers brushing against the polished metal, cool and solid beneath his touch. Its weight was a quiet reminder of duty as he strode toward the throne room. His steps echoed against the stone floors, each a reminder of the weight of his summons. Though the call pressed upon him, he reminded himself this was what he had trained for.

This was his moment to prove himself. Memories of sleepless nights in the training fields, exhaustion pressing against his limbs as Aurelia watched with sharp, unwavering eyes, surfaced in his mind.

At his side, Ong moved with the steady ease of a warrior, his expression calm but ready. Beside him, Keisha's sharp gaze scanned their surroundings, her body taut with instinct as though vigilance remained necessary even within these hallowed halls.

The throne room doors loomed ahead, their carved surfaces depicting scenes of Crystal Vale's storied past. Two guards flanked the entrance, armor gleaming beneath the fractured light from the high windows.

At a silent nod from Keisha, the guards pressed the doors open, revealing the grandeur within.

King Manard stood before his throne, his regal posture unshaken, yet faint lines of worry etched the corners of his face. The crown atop his head glinted as he watched them enter, its weight a reflection of burdens beyond what he spoke. His gaze flicked to Gailen, softening slightly, but something heavier lay beneath that moment of warmth. Expectation. Judgment.

"Father," Gailen greeted, bowing deeply. His voice carried a quiet confidence that had taken root since his return.

"Your Majesty," Ong and Keisha echoed, bowing in unison.

King Manard gestured for them to rise. His voice was steady and measured. "Prince Gailen, Ong, Keisha. I trust your time with Aurelia has been... fruitful. The safety and future of Crystal Vale rest on those who defend it. I trust you understand the weight of this duty." His gaze lingered on his son, searching as if trying to see past the surface to determine whether he had grown.

For the briefest moment, doubt stirred in Gailen's chest. His breath hitched, and his fingers curled slightly before he forced them to relax. He straightened subtly, steeling himself against the uncertainty creeping in. Had he done enough? Had he proven himself worthy? Aurelia had trained him, tested him, but was that sufficient to quell the doubts in his father's eyes? He straightened his shoulders. He would not falter now.

"I have called you here," King Manard continued, "to understand how this training has prepared you for the challenges ahead. It is your duty as my heir and protector of this land to stand ready for what may come."

Gailen glanced at Ong. They exchanged a silent understanding, and Ong gave a slight nod, conveying trust and steadfast support.

Keisha folded her arms, her quiet confidence, a steady presence beside him.

Gailen had seen firsthand why the people of Crystal Vale respected her not just for her skill or the legacy of her lineage but for something far more significant. They had seen her at her weakest. After her captivity. After her torture. They had witnessed her arriving in Crystal Vale fragile, drained, stripped of magic and even the strength to draw her bow. Yet even then, she had stood beside them, hauling stones with shaking hands. Her breath labored, but her resolve was unbroken, helping them rebuild. Even in her most broken state, she had offered them her hands, will, and heart. Not as a warrior. Not as a legend. But as someone who refused to turn away from those in need. Because of that, she gave them everything when she had nothing. They had never forgotten her.

And neither had Gailen. That respect helped shape his trust in her, reinforcing his sense of purpose. Taking a deep breath, Gailen stepped forward.

His father's scrutiny did not waver. But neither did Gailen's voice.

The training was more than I expected, Father," he said, his tone even. "It has tested my limits and shown me the strength I must still build. Aurelia's guidance was... enlightening." King Manard's brow lifted slightly, but he did not interrupt. Instead, he turned his gaze to Ong and Keisha.

"And you two? Are you confident in what has been accomplished?" Keisha's lips quirked into a faint smile.

"Your Majesty, Prince Gailen has taken his first steps well, but there is still a path ahead. No training is complete without experience. But," she glanced at Gailen, "he has proven he is ready to walk that path."

Ong's voice was steady, unwavering. "He has shown promise, and the bond with Aurelia will only strengthen with time. If he continues this course, Crystal Vale will have a dragon rider to be proud of."

King Manard studied them all for a long moment, his gaze shifting between them, thoughtful yet unreadable. A flicker of something—pride, hesitation, or perhaps a quiet acceptance—crossed his face before settling into measured contemplation. His gaze returned to his son. For a heartbeat, the weight of past kings seemed to whisper in his mind. Had Gailen genuinely become the leader Crystal Vale needed? But there was something different in his son's gaze. Something unspoken. Not just duty. Conviction. And for the first time, Manard believed that perhaps the kingdom was in capable hands after all.

"Very well." The words came not as a dismissal but as a confirmation. "We will discuss the details shortly. But first, let us ensure that all preparations are in place. For the challenges we know... and those yet unseen."

Gailen exhaled, feeling the weight of his father's expectations settle upon him. But for the first time, it did not feel suffocating. Instead, it felt like purpose.

Aurelia had forged him in discipline, shaping his focus and strength. Ong had driven him toward resilience, testing his endurance at every turn. Keisha had shown him trust, grounding him in the bonds defining his path forward. And his father, at last, was beginning to see not just a prince. But a leader. A protector of Crystal Vale. For now, the shadows outside the castle walls could wait. Inside, something far more substantial than war was being forged. A bond of trust. A bond that would decide the fate of a kingdom.

Gailen stepped forward, his movements steady, but a flicker of something new burned in his eyes. His gaze sharpened, his shoulders squaring slightly as if carrying the weight of something greater than himself. Pride. Conviction. Ong gave a slight nod of approval, and King Manard leaned forward, his fingers tightening subtly around the arms of his throne. He was listening. Gailen took a steady breath and began.

"It began with basic riding," he explained, his voice firm, carrying the weight of experience rather than mere words. "But riding Aurelia isn't like riding any other dragon. She demanded trust. Precision. Adaptability. At one point... she deliberately cast me from her back mid-air." The words hung in the air, and King Manard's fingers twitched.

Gailen continued, his tone unwavering. "She did it to teach me how to react. To trust her judgment. The world spun violently as I tumbled, the wind a deafening roar in my ears. For a moment, a single, paralyzing heartbeat of panic took hold. Then, the training kicked in. My limbs snapped into position, my body adjusting instinctively. I forced my mind to still. And when Aurelia caught me, my breath came in ragged gasps, but I understood then."

Trust is not blind faith. It is forged in moments of trial." Gailen's fingers tightened slightly at his sides. "In that moment, I wasn't just relieved. I realized trust is not something given freely. It is earned, again and again, in moments like that."

King Manard's eyes narrowed, his shoulders rigid as the weight of those words settled upon him. His jaw tightened slightly, and a flicker of unease crossed his face before he masked it carefully. Cast him off? His son, his heir, plummeting from the sky, trusting he would not die? A flicker of unease tightened his chest. Had this training indeed been necessary? Or had Aurelia risked his son's life needlessly?

His mind warred with itself, the ruler within him, knowing that great warriors were only forged through great trials, while the father within him recoiled at the thought of his son falling through the open sky with nothing but instinct to save him. His grip on the arms of his throne tightened. "Cast you off?" he repeated, his voice carrying a mix of disbelief and something dangerously close to concern.

Gailen held his ground. He did not flinch nor waver.

"It wasn't easy," Gailen admitted, his tone deliberately lighter to reassure his father. "But I understand now why it was necessary. There will be moments when I may have to act without hesitation, without fear, even in the face of death. Aurelia needed me to experience that."

Ong turned toward him, a knowing glint in his eye. "You weren't alone in that," he said. "I had to do the same with Amara. And Thalorian had to with Verdantia. None of us liked it. But it was necessary. It's a lesson we all face sooner or later." The words settled over Gailen, heavier than he expected.

His eyes widened slightly, his breath catching as the realization settled in. A sense of reassurance washed over him, threading through his thoughts like a binding thread. This was not just his trial. It was not a test meant to single him out. This was a rite of passage. One shared by every dragon rider before him. And at that moment, he no longer felt isolated in his trials. A sense of reassurance washed over him, threading through his thoughts like a binding thread. He was part of something greater. A bond of perseverance. A bond of trust. For the first time, he truly belonged. He straightened slightly, the flicker of pride warming his chest.

King Manard nodded slowly, though his brows furrowed with lingering concern. The weight of his dual roles bore down on him: father and king, protector and ruler. He wanted to trust that this trial had strengthened Gailen. But doubt gnawed at him. Had he prepared his son for the burden of leadership? Or had he merely exposed him to dangers he could never undo? The memory of his youth flickered in his mind the first time he had led soldiers into battle, and the fear masked behind a hardened exterior. He had survived, but not without cost. Not without lives lost under his command. That weight had never indeed lifted. Would Gailen one day bear the same scars? Or had he unwittingly set his son on a path where survival meant carrying burdens too significant to bear?

The thought unsettled him. He had fought wars. He had seen betrayal unfold within his court. And he knew better than anyone how power drew unwanted attention. Yet, he also recognized the fire in Gailen's eyes. The same determination that had burned within his own long ago. Still, the weight of his duty as a father clashed against his role as a king. He could not protect Gailen from the world.

But he could prepare him for it. His fingers curled slightly. "And the Crystalbow?" he prompted.

Gailen gestured toward the weapon at his side. The Crystalbow shimmered, its surface catching the light in shifting hues of blue and silver. Intricate carvings laced its limbs, ancient symbols whispering of its storied past. This was more than a weapon.

It was a legacy. Bound to him as much as Aurelia herself. "It's more than a weapon," Gailen said evenly. "It's a legacy." He ran his fingers lightly along the carvings, feeling the energy humming beneath his touch.

"Aurelia explained its significance and its power. It is tied directly to my bond with her. It has abilities I've only begun to understand."

His gaze flicked to Ong. "But Ong has advised me to keep it well-guarded."

King Manard's attention snapped to Ong. His expression darkened slightly. "Guarded? Why such secrecy?"

Ong stepped forward, his stance firm and assured. His sharp gaze swept the room, assessing unseen threats. His voice was low and deliberate when he spoke, each word carrying the weight of his concern. "Your Majesty, the attack during the obsidian dragon incursion raised concerns. The dragon did not just attack. It headed straight for Prince Gailen. Ignoring every other viable target."

King Manard's brows furrowed deeper.

Ong's expression remained unreadable, but his following words cut through the chamber like a blade. A subtle tension rippled through the room. Keisha's fingers curled slightly at her sides, her gaze sharpening. King Manard's jaw set, his grip on the throne's arms tightening almost imperceptibly. Even Gailen felt a chill settle in his chest, the weight of Ong's statement pressing down like an unspoken warning. "Obsidian dragons have no prior engagement with us in Vacari. Their precision in singling out the prince is unsettling, suggesting a foreknowledge of his location and importance." His jaw tensed slightly.

"This makes the Crystalbow and its potential a risk." King Manard's face grew stern. The weight of Ong's words settled over him, heavy and undeniable. A flicker of unease slipped through his mind. Betrayal. The word lingered like a sickness in his thoughts.

He exhaled sharply. He would convene with his council. They would strengthen their defenses. And they would uncover the truth behind this attack. "That is troubling indeed," he said, his voice low. "To target Gailen specifically implies betrayal or espionage. If that is the case, our defenses must be strengthened. And the Crystalbow's existence must be kept from untrustworthy ears."

Ong nodded, his gaze steady. "Keisha and I will assist in strategizing these defenses. But vigilance is essential. Whoever orchestrated this attack will try again."

King Manard's eyes softened slightly as he turned back to Gailen. "You've proven yourself capable, my son. But trust the wisdom of your allies. Keep your guard up. We will uncover the truth behind this treachery together."

Gailen nodded, his determination unwavering. "I understand, Father. I won't let you or Vacari down."

King Manard studied him for a long moment. Then, at last, a faint smile crept onto his lips. His shoulders eased slightly, the rigid tension in his posture softening. He gave a slow, measured nod, an unspoken acknowledgment of the growth he saw in his son. "I know you won't." Yet beneath the pride, a single, unspoken worry remained in his eyes. Would strength alone be enough for the trials yet to come?

Keisha stepped forward, her expression calm yet resolute. "Your Majesty," she began, her voice steady. "Prince Gailen has taken an important first step in bonding with Aurelia. However, that bond needs to be strengthened further." She paused, her gaze shifting. "And not just him."

She cast a pointed glance at Ong. "Ong, too, needs to deepen his bond with Amara. When he attempted before, hesitation held him back. It will always limit them if he cannot push past that."

Ong's jaw tightened slightly, but he did not argue. He knew she was right.

Keisha turned back to King Manard, her stance unshaken. "Strengthening this bond will help them overcome hesitation and fully connect with their dragons."

"It's a vital skill, and I believe I can help teach it." Her emerald eyes flickered slightly. "I also suggest we include Thalorian."

King Manard raised a brow, curiosity sparking in his expression. "Strengthen the bond, you say? And how exactly do you propose to do this?"

Keisha's lips curved into a soft, knowing smile. Her tone was patient but confident. "By teaching them to reach out to their dragons through their feelings."

A brief flicker of skepticism passed through the King's eyes.

Keisha noticed and clarified. "This is not magic, Your Majesty." She held his gaze steadily. "It is about trust—understanding their connection with their dragons. A dragon rider does not command their dragon. They feel them. Know them.

Just as Ong felt my pain when I was held captive by Phoenix and Vuarus. Just as I once sensed Kimras' distress amid battle. This bond allows communication if they believe in it and understand how to harness it."

King Manard's expression softened, shifting from skepticism to intrigue. "That sounds almost like a magical ability," he admitted. "Are you certain such a thing can be taught?"

Keisha nodded, her confidence unwavering. "It can. It is not magic but a profound connection. Dragons, especially noble ones like Aurelia and Amara, are deeply intuitive. They will respond if the bond is strong, no matter the distance. It takes practice, trust, and understanding, but I know they can learn."

A long silence stretched between them. Then, Manard turned his gaze to his son. His tone was measured but firm. "Gailen, are you willing to learn this?"

Gailen hesitated for a moment. His mind turned over everything that had happened. The weight of responsibility pressed against his chest, mingling with the thrill of the unknown.

He could still feel the rush of wind from his fall off Aurelia's back, the sharp bite of uncertainty gripping him before trust took over. If this connection were real, it could strengthen his bond with Aurelia... Then, he was ready for what lay ahead. The unknown no longer scared him.

It called to him.

His fingers tightened slightly around the Crystalbow. Then, he met his father's gaze, his voice clear, unwavering. "It seems... unconventional." His lips quirked slightly. "But if it helps me as a dragon rider, I trust Keisha's expertise."

He nodded firmly. "I am, Father. If it strengthens my bond with Aurelia and helps Vacari, I will do whatever is necessary."

King Manard studied him for a moment, then allowed a faint smile. A flicker of pride shone in his eyes. Then, he turned back to Keisha. "Then you have my blessing. I will see to it that Thalorian meets you in Emerald Woods."

Keisha bowed respectfully. "Thank you, Your Majesty. I will make the necessary preparations." She turned to Ong and Gailen, her voice steady. "I will meet you both in Emerald Woods. Gather what you need. Be ready."

With that, the group dispersed, each carrying the weight of the challenges ahead.

Keisha's mind raced, calculating the best way to guide them forward.

Ong's protective instincts flared, already strategizing how to keep them safe.

Gailen felt the enormity of his journey settled over him.

But amidst the uncertainty, a spark of determination burned.

This was more than training. It was the path to becoming the warriors and guardians Vacari needed. The trials ahead would not just test their abilities.

They would define their future.

Keisha set off toward Emerald Woods.

Ong and Gailen turned toward the city, their thoughts already on Thalorian.

Soon, the lessons would begin.

And they would learn that true strength was not just in battle.

But in the bond they shared with their dragons.

Chapter 32

A Bond Forged in Trust

The morning sun bathed Crystal Vale in a soft golden light, but Ong's thoughts were already on the journey ahead. "Emerald Woods," he murmured, adjusting his saddle. "Time to strengthen the bonds with our dragons."

Thalorian and Gailen stood nearby, finishing their preparations, when Valeon appeared. He had a curious glint in his eye and an eager smile plastered across his face. He leaned casually against a post, his presence almost too nonchalant.

"Where are you all off to?" Valeon asked, his tone light but laced with unmistakable curiosity.

Ong glanced at Gailen, who sighed, already bracing for what was coming. "Emerald Woods," Gailen replied. "We have training to do."

Valeon's grin widened, his eyes alight with mischief. This was his chance. He had spent too long on the outskirts of their group, always the outsider looking in. Maybe today, he could prove he belonged. He rocked on his heels, barely able to contain his eagerness. "Sounds exciting! Can I come?"

Thalorian arched a brow, already predicting the chaos if Valeon joined them.

Gailen suppressed a groan, recognizing the familiar look in Valeon's eyes—one he had seen too many times before, usually right before an ill-advised adventure or a half-baked scheme. He found Valeon both amusing and frustrating in equal measure. He was not just seeking excitement but acceptance and a place among them. Still, that did not make his persistence any less exhausting. He pinched the bridge of his nose. "Valeon, this isn't exactly thrilling. We are learning to communicate with our dragons, which is less entertaining than you think. You'd be bored within minutes."

"I won't be bored!" Valeon protested, stepping closer. "I swear, I'll be good. Besides, maybe I'll learn something useful."

Thalorian folded his arms, exchanging a knowing look with Ong. "Useful," he repeated, a faint smirk tugging at the corners of his lips. "You?"

"Yes, me!" Valeon shot back indignantly.

Ong let out a long sigh, rubbing the back of his neck, already weighing the potential outcomes of letting Valeon join. Would he be an asset or just another distraction? Either way, keeping an eye on him would be necessary. Torn between exasperation and reluctant amusement. "Fine," he said, pointing a finger at Valeon. "But only if you're on your best behavior and stay quiet when Keisha is teaching us. We don't need distractions."

Valeon's face lit up. "Of course! I'll be as quiet as a dragon."

Thalorian raised an eyebrow, stepping forward so his towering form cast a shadow over Valeon. The younger man stiffened slightly, his grin faltering as his eyes darted between Thalorian's imposing stance and the escape routes around him. He swallowed, forcing a chuckle, but the flicker of unease in his gaze betrayed his bravado. He glanced upward as if reconsidering his enthusiasm. "No," Thalorian said firmly, "you'll be as quiet as a fairy. And if you're not, I'll have Kaelorn and the fae in Emerald Woods put you to work."

At that, Ong and Gailen burst into laughter. Valeon's grin faltered slightly. "Work? In Emerald Woods? Surely you would not..." he began, trailing off under Thalorian's unwavering gaze. "Alright, alright, I'll be quiet!"

"See that you are," Thalorian replied, amusement flickering.

With Valeon now tagging along, the group adjusted to his presence, some with amusement, others with wary resignation, before resuming their journey. The rhythmic clatter of hooves on the dirt path blended with the crisp morning air, a quiet energy settling among them as the day's challenges loomed. Laughter and light banter eased the anticipation of the training ahead, though each carried their thoughts about what was to come.

Ong focused on the discipline and control needed to bond with Amara, determined to overcome his past hesitations. Memories of past failures haunted him, moments where doubt and fear had clouded his ability to connect. This time, he would not allow uncertainty to hold him back. Gailen, still unsure of how deep his connection with Aurelia could go, wrestled with the weight of his role as a dragon rider. Thalorian, ever the pragmatist, viewed the training as another test of endurance, while Valeon, despite his usual mischief, secretly hoped he could prove himself useful. As they rode, Ong nudged Valeon playfully with his elbow, earning an exaggerated huff from the younger man. Gailen shook his head with a smirk while Thalorian merely sighed in amusement. The camaraderie between them grew stronger with each step, each finding their resolve in the shared journey ahead.

The serene expanse of Emerald Woods greeted them with dappled sunlight filtering through towering trees, painting the forest floor in hues of gold and green. A faint magic shimmer hung, weaving around tree trunks like ethereal mist. It crackled softly in the underbrush, sending occasional sparks of light skittering across the ground. The energy tingled against their skin, leaving a faint warmth in its wake, and sent a gentle hum through their bones as if the forest itself pulsed with quiet awareness. It shifted with the breeze, occasionally sparking faint glimmers of color that danced in the periphery of vision as if the forest itself were aware of its presence. The soft rustling of leaves whispered secrets of an ancient past, and the distant call of unseen creatures hinted at the mysteries hidden within the woods. The air hummed with life, the rustle of leaves, the distant chirp of birds, and a faint, otherworldly breeze whispered of magic.

Keisha stood waiting near a clearing, her sharp eyes immediately catching sight of Valeon among the group. Amusement flickered in her gaze as she took in his eager attempt to fit in. Her brow arched slightly, and a teasing smile tugged at her lips, a flicker of amusement dancing in her gaze.

"Valeon," she greeted, hands on her hips. "Did they bring you along to help retrieve supplies from Kaelorn?"

Gailen chuckled, shaking his head. "It's possible," he replied, "though we did warn him he might be put to work if he doesn't behave."

The group shared a laugh, and Valeon's cheeks flushed faintly as he muttered under his breath, trying to appear unaffected by the teasing.

Keisha motioned for everyone to sit in a circle in the clearing. Her movements were fluid and deliberate, exuding a quiet confidence that demanded attention. The group responded immediately, their casual banter fading into focused anticipation. Thalorian, typically unreadable, inclined his head slightly in acknowledgment while Gailen straightened his posture as if steeling himself for what was to come. The unspoken respect she commanded was evident in how they followed her lead without hesitation.

"Alright," she began, her tone calm and instructive, her gaze steady as if ensuring she had their full attention. "Today's goal is connecting with your dragons through emotions and feelings. You cannot rush this, and it requires focus and trust. Valeon," she added, turning to him with a pointed look, "you'll stay back. This part isn't for you."

Valeon scratched his head, visibly confused. Was he missing something obvious? He had thought this training was for everyone, yet once again, he found himself on the outside looking in. He shifted uncomfortably, his brows knitting together as frustration flickered across his face. It felt like another moment, and he was left on the sidelines, watching the others move forward. Was he not ready, or did they not believe he could contribute? He frowned slightly, wondering why he was being excluded yet again. Was this indeed something he could not grasp, or did they not trust him to take it seriously?

"Uh... not to be dense or anything," Valeon said, glancing around as a hush settled over the group. A few exchanged uncertain looks, some shifting as if debating whether to respond. "But... I don't see any dragons here."

The air shifted.

Thalorian's gaze flicked to Valeon—sharp, assessing, but not hostile. Gailen straightened slightly, his posture alert, while Ong crossed his arms and leaned back, more thoughtful than irritated. Keisha's fingers tapped against her knee once, then stilled. She looked at Valeon for a long moment before speaking, her voice quiet but steady.

"This part isn't for everyone, Valeon," she said, gently breaking the silence. "It's for those who've already bonded."

He blinked. "Bonded?"

"With a dragon," she clarified, her tone patient. "What we're doing here relies on that connection. It's not just about being in the same space—it's about resonance. Feeling each other, trusting each other without words."

Valeon shifted, the tension in his shoulders rising. "So I'm not included because I didn't want to ride?"

"It's not a punishment," Keisha said softly. "You made it clear you weren't ready for dragonback training. That's your choice. But without a bond, this part of the training wouldn't make sense. It's not something you can fake your way through."

He looked down for a moment, letting the weight of her words settle. Then he nodded.

"Thank you," he said quietly. "I understand now. Riding a dragon still isn't for me... but I'd like to watch, if that's alright."

Keisha's gaze softened, and she gave a single nod. "Of course."

Then, without a word, Thalorian reached over and tapped Valeon firmly on the shoulder. Not a reprimand—a signal. He wasn't unwelcome. Just on a different path.

A quiet fell over the group again as they settled in, focus returning to the task at hand.

"Quiet," Thalorian said, his voice low but resolute. "This isn't the moment for commentary."

Valeon raised his hands in mock surrender. "Alright, alright. Silent as a fairy in moonlight," he muttered under his breath.

A flicker of amusement passed across Thalorian's face—a rare crack in his stern demeanor. The smirk was subtle, fleeting, but real.

And for the first time in a long while, Valeon felt like he belonged.

Keisha shook her head with a small smile, her focus returning to Ong, Thalorian, and Gailen. "Now," she said, her voice softening, "close your eyes and concentrate. Think of your bond with your dragon as a companion and an extension of your heart. Feel for them, reach out with your thoughts, and trust they will respond."

The three men nodded, their expressions growing serious as they began to focus. The clearing settled into a hush, every rustle of the leaves and distant bird call magnified by the stillness surrounding them. Gailen's heartbeat thudded in his ears, the rhythmic pulse contrasting with the quiet around them. The faintest breeze stirred the air, carrying the scent of earth and pine as if the forest held its breath alongside them. A subtle tension settled over the group, anticipating threading through the air like an unspoken current rippling beneath the quiet of the woods. Valeon, despite his earlier protests, sat back and watched quietly, his curiosity piqued as the session began.

Keisha closed her eyes, a serene expression washing over her face. She inhaled slowly, a quiet warmth spreading through her chest, grounding her in the familiar presence of Kimras. At this moment, she was glad to help others, share what she had learned, and offer them the guidance they needed. She was reaffirming her connection, allowing herself to sink into the comforting presence of her dragon, a reminder of the trust built over years of companionship. "I will join you in this," she said gently, her voice carrying a calm reassurance. "Sometimes, the best way to learn is by seeing it done."

The group fell into silence once more as Keisha began the process. Her breathing slowed, deep and even, and she lightly touched her heart. "Focus on your feelings," she instructed, her voice smooth as a flowing stream. "Think about your bond with your dragon—the times you've shared, the trust you've built. Let those emotions guide you. Feel the connection, like a thread linking you to them, no matter the distance."

Ong, Gailen, and Thalorian followed her lead. Ong's brow furrowed slightly, his body tense as frustration gnawed at him. He was always hardest on himself, replaying past failures in his mind, the uncertainty, the fear of not being worthy of Amara's trust. He recalled the moment she had hesitated in mid-flight, sensing his doubt, nearly sending them both into a dangerous spiral. That failure still lingered, a shadow he was determined to overcome. He exhaled deeply, releasing the tension, reminding himself that this was a moment to rebuild that connection, not dwell on past hesitations: the uncertainty, the fear of not being worthy of Amara's trust.

Thalorian's expression remained composed, though his lips pressed into a thin line as he concentrated. Gailen, meanwhile, sat with his hands resting on his knees, his head tilted slightly upward as though searching the skies for something unseen. He longed for reassurance, some sign that Aurelia was with him even now, that their bond was as strong as he had hoped. Doubt lingered at the edges of his thoughts, but he forced himself to breathe, to trust in the connection that had always been there, waiting to be felt.

Keisha's voice softened, becoming almost a whisper. "Let the bond guide you, not force it. It is a natural thing, like the roots of a tree stretching toward water or the sun. Trust that your dragon feels the same connection and will respond in kind."

For a long moment, there was nothing but the sounds of the forest wind through the leaves, the distant chirp of a bird, and the rustling of a squirrel in the underbrush.

Then, a subtle shift occurred. The wind hesitated, a fleeting pause as though the forest had drawn in a breath, waiting in silent anticipation. A flicker of movement played across the dappled light, casting fleeting shadows that danced along the ground. The air seemed to grow denser, infused with an unspoken energy. A faint tingling sensation danced along their skin as if the very essence of magic brushed against them. Tiny motes of light flickered in the air, pulsing softly in rhythm with their breaths, the energy wrapping around them like an unseen current drawing them closer to their dragons. A gentle warmth spread through the clearing as if the forest had paused to acknowledge the bonds forming within its embrace.

Ong inhaled sharply, a subtle shiver running down his spine as the warmth seeped into his core. Relief flooded through him, mingling with a sense of awe at the undeniable presence of Amara. The connection felt more substantial and more accurate than ever before. Thalorian's usually rigid posture softened, his shoulders relaxing like an unseen weight had lifted. Gailen let out a slow breath, his fingers twitching slightly as if drawn to something unseen. The presence of their dragons was undeniable, weaving through them like an invisible thread, tethering them in unspoken unity. The soft hum of the woods deepened, resonating with an almost imperceptible harmony, a quiet reminder of the magic linking dragons to their riders.

Ong's posture straightened, his face softening as a faint smile touched his lips. "Amara," he murmured as if the name held the power to bridge worlds. A ripple of emotion washed over him, a mixture of warmth, reassurance, and an almost playful sense of acknowledgment. His eyes fluttered open briefly, meeting Keisha's, and he nodded. "I felt her."

Keisha returned the nod, her own eyes still closed. "Good. That's the connection you'll call on when you need her, no matter the distance."

A faint shimmer seemed to cross Thalorian's features, his usually stoic expression softening as his lips parted slightly in awe. A deep sense of connection and reverence flickered in his gaze, returning him to the first time he had bonded with Verdantia. He remembered the weight of her gaze, the silent understanding between them, and the moment he realized she had chosen him just as much as he had chosen her. Now, standing in the clearing, that same certainty settled over him, grounding him in the moment. His breathing grew steady, almost rhythmic, and a faint whisper escaped him. "Verdantia." His tone was reverent as if speaking her name bridged the expanse between them. A deep sense of belonging and strength radiated, grounding him in the moment.

Lastly, Gailen sat in stillness, his brows furrowed in concentration. A sense of warmth enveloped him, but it was different from the others—it was protective, strong, like a shield wrapping around him. For a brief moment, he felt Aurelia's presence in a way he never had before, a silent vow of guardianship echoing through their bond. His breathing hitched slightly before evening out, and a soft glow lit up his features. "Aurelia," he murmured, the name spoken with a newfound understanding and respect. He felt a warmth, like sunlight breaking through clouds, and a surge of reassurance flowed through him. The bond was there, faint but steady, waiting to grow stronger.

Keisha smiled, her connection bright and palpable as her thoughts brushed against Kimras. She remembered how difficult it had been at first, how she had questioned whether she was truly worthy of such a bond. The uncertainty, the doubt those feelings had nearly kept her from reaching out. But now, she could see the same struggle reflected in them, filling her with purpose. Helping them forge these connections made all the struggles worth it. Now, standing as a guide for the others, she felt a deep sense of fulfillment, knowing that the bonds forming here would only grow stronger with time. A soft rumble of acknowledgment echoed in her mind, a reminder of the ancient dragon's steadfast presence. Opening her eyes, she glanced at each of them, her pride evident.

"You have taken the first step," she said, her voice filled with warmth. "The bond is there, waiting to be strengthened with time and trust." As her words settled over them, Ong felt a quiet pride swell within, thinking of Amara's playful yet steadfast presence. Thalorian's mind lingered on Verdantia's unwavering strength, a steady reminder of the connection he now cherished. Gailen, too, marveled at the newfound clarity in his bond with Aurelia, a beacon of light guiding him forward. Each of them felt a more profound sense of purpose, their connections solidifying not just with their dragons but with one another as companions on this journey.

Valeon, uncharacteristically quiet, watched the scene unfold with wide eyes. A strange tightness gripped his chest, his fingers curling slightly as if grasping something just out of reach. A peculiar longing coiled in his chest, a realization stirring deep within him he had always been an observer, never a participant in something so profound. For the first time, he questioned whether his path lay in more than just fleeting adventures, whether he, too, could find a connection that anchored him as profoundly as the dragons did their riders. He had always joked, always played the part of the outsider, but now, for the first time, he wondered what it would be like to share such a bond. Would he ever experience something so profound? He felt an unfamiliar tug in his heart, a mix of wonder and longing as if he were glimpsing a world he could never fully be part of. For once, he said nothing, merely absorbing the significance of what he had just witnessed.

As the connection exercise concluded, the group sat in contemplative silence. The weight of their shared experience settled over them like a gentle veil. Ong was the first to break the quiet, his voice thoughtful yet tinged with awe.

"It is...indescribable," he began, looking at Keisha. "I have fought beside Amara before, but this... this feels deeper. It is like she is a part of me, even when she's not physically there."

Keisha nodded, her gaze warm, her expression carrying the quiet confidence of someone who had walked this path before. She recalled her early days, the uncertainty that had once gripped her, the long nights spent wondering if Kimras truly trusted her as she trusted him. It had taken time, patience, and understanding to forge their bond, but now she stood as living proof of what was possible. There was an understanding in her eyes, a patient reassurance that each of them was precisely where they needed to be on their journey. "That's the essence of the bond. It is more than just fighting together; it is understanding one another on a level words cannot capture. It's about feeling their presence in your very soul, knowing their strength and trust are as much a part of you as your heartbeat."

Thalorian, ever composed, allowed a faint smile to curve his lips. The quiet camaraderie in the group, the unspoken bonds forming between riders and dragons, stirred something deep within him. He had always relied on his strength, but at this moment, he was reminded that true strength came from trust and unity. For the first time in a long while, he felt a deep sense of belonging, an unspoken understanding shared between him and Verdantia. It was a quiet reassurance, a reminder that even the strongest did not stand alone. "Verdantia's presence was... grounding," he admitted. "It's like she reassured me that no matter the odds, we are stronger together." His tone softened. "It's humbling to know such power stands beside us, not because she has to, but because she chooses to."

Gailen, still processing the connection, exhaled slowly, his fingers brushing against the ground as if grounding himself before he finally spoke.

"Aurelia... she feels like light itself. Warm, steady, guiding. I have always respected her, but now... I realize there is so much more to understand. It is not just about riding her or asking for her strength. It is about proving myself worthy of her trust every step of the way. I think... I need to approach everything with her differently from now on." He paused, searching for the right words. "Now I feel like I'm finally beginning to understand why she chose me. It's not just about riding her; it's about earning her trust and partnership."

Keisha's smile widened. "Exactly. That is what it means to be a dragon rider. It is not about dominance or command but about unity and mutual respect. You'll find that the stronger your bond, the more you'll be able to achieve together."

Valeon, who had been unusually quiet, shifted his weight, rubbing the back of his neck before finally speaking, his tone softer than usual. "I... I did not know it was like that," he admitted, his gaze shifting between the others. "I thought riding a dragon was just... You know, it is a fancy way to get around and fight. But seeing this... it is not just riding. It is a bond, a partnership. Something special."

Thalorian raised a brow, a faint trace of amusement in his voice. "Insightful, Valeon. Perhaps there's hope for you yet."

Valeon shot him with a half-hearted glare, his usual smirk faltering as his expression shifted. The amusement in his eyes faded, replaced by something more introspective. His gaze lowered slightly, and uncertainty flickered across his face briefly before he took a steady breath and straightened his shoulders. Beneath the teasing, a quiet respect lingered. He envied them sometimes, not out of jealousy but because they knew exactly where they belonged. He had always laughed and shrugged off more profound thoughts, but now, for the first time, he felt a glimmer of hope, wondering if he, too, might find a place where he truly belonged. "I mean it. Watching you all... I get it now. It is not something everyone can do. And honestly, I don't think I could handle it."

Ong chuckled. "You're more self-aware than I gave you credit for, Valeon."

Keisha leaned toward Valeon, her expression gentle, a quiet certainty in her eyes. She had always believed that everyone had a place. It was just a matter of finding it. "It's not about who can or can't handle it. Everyone has a role to play, and it is just as important. You don't have to be a dragon rider to make a difference." Valeon's gaze dropped for a moment, his brow furrowing in thought. Her words resonated with him, stirring something he could not quite name—a mix of humility and the faintest flicker of hope that he might find his place.

Valeon looked at her, his usual bravado replaced with a rare moment of sincerity. "Maybe. But after seeing this, I understand better why you all fight so hard and why the dragons fight with you. It's... inspiring, in a way."

Keisha nodded, her smile soft. "That's all that matters, Valeon. Understanding what we fight for and why we stand together."

Valeon exhaled slowly, absorbing her words. His fingers curled slightly at his sides, a quiet tension settling in his chest before easing into something softer understanding. For the first time, he felt he was looking at his life from a new perspective that he had never allowed himself to consider before. All his life, he had searched for excitement, for adventure, but now he realized that purpose was something different. It was not about proving himself. It was about finding where he truly belonged. And for the first time, he considered that his place might not be where he had always imagined. He had always sought adventure, craved excitement, chasing fleeting thrills without ever considering what lay beyond them. But this was something different rooted in connection, something greater than himself. This was what he had been searching for: a sense of belonging beyond fleeting adventure. For the first time, he wondered if his path lay not in proving himself through reckless bravado but in finding where he could truly belong.

The group fell into a reflective silence again, and each person lost in their thoughts, the bonds they had experienced still fresh and resonant. The golden light streaming through the canopy seemed to pulse gently as if the forest breathed in harmony with their newfound connections. A soft breeze carried the earthy scent of moss and blooming wildflowers, grounding them in the serenity of Emerald Woods while the distant trill of a bird echoed like a quiet song of acknowledgment.

Keisha reached into a small pouch at her belt and pulled out several smooth stones, each shimmering faintly with an inner light. These stones, crafted by the ancient dragon sages of Vacari, had been infused with the essence of dragonfire, a gift passed down to those who proved themselves worthy of an actual bond. "Take these," she said, handing one to each. "These stones are imbued with a trace of dragon energy. They will help you strengthen your connection, making it easier to reach out when distance separates you." She watched as they turned the stones over in their hands, sensing the faint warmth that pulsed from within. "Use them wisely, and trust in the bond you share."

"And now," she said, her tone lighter, "we head back to Crystal Vale. There is still much to do."

The group began their journey back, the serene beauty of Emerald Woods giving way to the familiar paths leading to Crystal Vale. As they walked, Gailen ran his fingers over the smooth surface of his stone, feeling the faint warmth pulsing from within. Ong glanced at his own, a thoughtful expression crossing his face as he considered his bond with Amara. Even Thalorian, usually unreadable, held his stone with quiet reverence. As they departed the woods, each carried a newfound strength and clarity, ready to face whatever lay ahead. Though their steps were the same, their hearts carried something different: a renewed sense of purpose and a deeper understanding of the bonds that tied them together.

Each of them, in their way, had found clarity in these woods, and as they left its embrace, they carried that strength with them, ready to face whatever lay ahead. Though their mission had been simple, their bonds felt stronger, a testament to the unity and trust that defined Vacari.

Chapter 33

A Sanctuary in the Woods

They had barely left Emerald Woods when the sky stirred above them. A shadow passed overhead, its emerald scales glinting in the sunlight as it circled lower. The dragon landed gracefully before them, its eyes locking onto Keisha with quiet urgency.

"Keisha," the dragon's voice resonated through their minds. "Kaelorn has requested your presence. He says it is of great importance."

Ong exchanged a glance with Gailen, and Keisha's expression hardened in thought. If Kaelorn was asking for her specifically, it had to be serious. "We'll return," she decided. With that, they turned their mounts, returning to Emerald Woods again.

They returned no sooner than the leaves stirred, rustling softly as Kaelorn stepped from the shadows, his confident stride faltering slightly. Beside him fluttered a glowing fairy, her tiny form casting a gentle light over his face. For someone rarely unsettled, his expression carried an unusual hint of nervous anticipation.

Keisha rose to meet him, her brows furrowing in curiosity. "Kaelorn, you look troubled. Is something on your mind?"

He hesitated, glancing at the fairy, who gave him an encouraging nod before perching delicately on a nearby branch. Kaelorn exhaled deeply, his fingers curling slightly at his sides as though steadying himself. A storm of uncertainty swirled within him, his mind torn between the weight of his request and the fear of how it might be received. He had long carried this thought, yet speaking it aloud made it feel all the more accurate as if voicing it would set a path in motion he could no longer turn away from. Doubt flickered in his mind, but he pushed it aside, straightening his shoulders and stepping closer to Keisha with a determined glint. He could not help but recall something she had said to him before words that had lingered in his mind.

"There's something I've been considering for some time now," he began, his voice steady but tinged with seriousness. "And after speaking with the fae who reside here, I believe this may be the right moment to make my request."

Keisha tilted her head, intrigued. "Go on."

Kaelorn's gaze scanned the group before settling on Keisha. He caught the quiet curiosity in Valeon's eyes, the measured wariness in Thalorian's gaze, and the unreadable expression on Gailen's face. Ong's arms were folded, his stance one of careful consideration, while Keisha's expression remained steady, though a glimmer of intrigue flickered within her gaze. Gailen shifted slightly, his expression unreadable, while Ong folded his arms, listening intently. Thalorian's sharp eyes lingered on Kaelorn, his usual stoicism masking any thoughts he might have had. Valeon, uncharacteristically quiet, watched with a hint of curiosity as if seeing Kaelorn in a new light. He had always viewed Kaelorn as distant, someone who existed on the fringes of their world, yet now he wondered if there was more to him than he had assumed. For the first time, he saw not just a warrior but someone searching for his place, something Valeon understood all too well. The air between them grew heavier, and the weight of Kaelorn's words settled over the group, each understanding the significance of what was to come.

My people, the Luminara, are unlike the other elves of Vacari. We are wanderers by nature, always moving, never settling. It has been our way for generations. But with the rise of the dark dragons and the increasing unrest, I have started to wonder if this nomadic existence is sustainable. If it is even wise."

Keisha's expression softened. "Tell me more about your people, Kaelorn. I have met many kinds of elves, but you have always seemed... different. What makes the Luminara unique?"

Kaelorn nodded, a quiet breath escaping him as relief mingled with anticipation. He had waited long for this chance to speak, to voice the thoughts that had weighed on him for so long. Hope flickered in his chest, a quiet yet persistent feeling that perhaps this moment could mark the beginning of something new for his people. He had carried this thought for so long, uncertain if it were merely a dream or something he could make a reality. "The Luminara draw strength from both the sun and the moon, balancing opposing forces within us. Our connection to the natural world is profound, but we are not tied to one place. Instead, we find power in the journey, in experiencing the world's many facets."

He paused, his voice softening. "This has always been our strength but has also made us vulnerable. Without a place to call home, we are scattered and fragmented. And as much as I have resisted the idea, I am beginning to see the need for a sanctuary as a place where the Luminara can gather, protect each other, and contribute to the greater good."

Keisha listened intently, her eyes reflecting deep understanding. She knew what it was like to search for belonging, to wonder if the path she walked would ever lead her to a place she could truly call home. Seeing that same uncertainty in Kaelorn now, she felt an undeniable connection to his struggle, a quiet resolve building within her to help him find the answers he sought. "And you believe Emerald Woods could be that sanctuary?"

Kaelorn nodded earnestly, though a flicker of uncertainty remained in his eyes. He had spent his life embracing the freedom of the Luminara way, yet now, the thought of a change of settling, even for a sanctuary, unsettled him. Would his people see this as a necessary step forward or a betrayal of their traditions? This was not an easy admission for him, nor was asking for help something that came naturally. But he had come to understand that strength was not only in solitude but also in knowing when to seek a place to stand and fight for something greater than oneself. "The fae here have welcomed me, and I have proven myself to them over time. But I have often wondered if I could truly find my place among them. Something you said to me once gave me hope that even someone like me, a wanderer, could belong. If the Luminara can make their homes in Emerald Woods, maybe there is hope for me as well."

The fairy, silently observing, fluttered closer, her voice chiming like a delicate bell. Kaelorn's breath hitched briefly, his fingers twitching slightly as if resisting the urge to reach out. Sensing the moment's weight, Keisha straightened subtly, her eyes reflecting the gravity of the fairy's silent support. She hovered near Keisha, leaning in to whisper something softly in her ear before drifting toward Kaelorn. With a graceful movement, she settled onto his shoulder, her tiny glow casting a warm light over him, a silent show of support. "Kaelorn has always been a friend to us. He has protected our grove, shared his magic when we were in need, and showed respect for the forest's ways. If his people are like him, we would welcome them."

Keisha studied Kaelorn carefully, weighing the sincerity in his eyes. She shifted slightly, her fingers brushing against the hilt of her blade, a subconscious habit when deep in thought. A slow breath steadied her, grounding her in the gravity of his request. Hope stirred within her, a quiet belief that this request could bring something meaningful to Kaelorn and the balance of the forest. A part of her wanted to accept without hesitation, as she had always believed in finding places of belonging, but she knew the gravity of his request. The balance of the forest, the fae, and the lives of his people would all be affected. Was she ready to advocate for such a change? Would the fae agree? Taking a slow breath, she steadied herself, carefully choosing her words.

"Kaelorn, this is not a small request, and it will affect not just you but the fae and the Luminara. I will need to think about this and speak with the fae and the other guardians of this forest. But I promise you, I will give your request the consideration it deserves."

Kaelorn bowed his head in gratitude, exhaling slowly as the tension in his shoulders eased. His fingers, which had been curled into fists, gradually relaxed as though he was releasing a weight he had carried for too long. The group exchanged glances, and the weight of his request settled in. Gailen gave a slow nod while Ong crossed his arms, thoughtful. Thalorian remained quiet, his sharp gaze unreadable, but there was no disapproval in his stance. Valeon, for once, said nothing, simply watching Kaelorn with something akin to newfound respect. He had always assumed Kaelorn was content in his solitary existence, but now he saw the weight the elf carried, the longing for stability, for something more. It was a feeling Valeon understood all too well, though he had never admitted it aloud. "Thank you, Keisha. That is all I could ask for."

The fairy chimed again, her wings glowing brighter. "We will speak with our kin as well. If Kaelorn's people share his heart, they will be welcome here."

As the group settled into a quiet moment, Gailen glanced at Ong, hesitation flickering in his eyes. Finally, he spoke, his voice soft but deliberate. "Ong, can I ask you something?"

Ong turned to him, his expression a mixture of curiosity and patience, his fingers idly tracing the hilt of his blade as if grounding himself in the moment. "Of course, Prince Gailen. What is on your mind?"

Gailen took a deep breath, his gaze shifting briefly to Keisha, who gave him a gentle nod of encouragement. "The alliances... they were not like this when I left Vacari. It feels like they have grown into something more than I ever imagined. How did this happen? Why has Vacari become so... united?"

Ong glanced at Keisha, seeking her silent permission to answer. He had always respected her instincts, knowing that her wisdom often saw beyond the moment. A part of him hesitated; this story belonged to both of them, but as she nodded, her steady expression reassured him. This was their shared history, and it was time to tell it. She nodded, her expression calm yet supportive. Ong exhaled and turned back to Gailen.

"It's a long story," Ong began, his voice steady but tinged with emotion. "When I first met Keisha, I thought strength and courage were enough to solve anything. But I learned quickly that Vacari's strength comes from more than just might. It comes from its people, their willingness to fight for themselves and each other."

He paused, his gaze distant. "When Phoenix seized Goldmoor, I thought I could save the King and Queen alone. I was wrong, terribly wrong. Keisha and Pumpkin saved me. They reminded me of something I had forgotten true strength comes from relying on others, from trust."

"But it was more than that," Ong continued. "During that dark time, when Keisha was captured and tortured, the people of Vacari did not turn away. They did not fall into despair, even when her suffering was shown as a warning. Instead, they came together. Her courage inspired them. It made them see that this land is not just a collection of territories. It is a home. And a home is worth protecting, no matter what the cost."

Keisha's lips curved into a faint smile as she listened, though a shadow of old uncertainty flickered beneath it. The memory of her past struggles surfaced how she had been broken, stripped of her magic and skill with the bow. She had doubted her place and questioned if she could ever stand firm again. But at that moment, the people of Vacari had shown her their unwavering belief, lending her the strength she had thought lost. She recalled the moment she first stood before the people of Vacari after her rescue. She was not strong and resolute but broken, unsure of who she was anymore. She had questioned whether she belonged and could still fight for a land that once felt like home. Yet, in that moment, she had seen the unwavering resolve in their eyes, a strength that had steadied her when she could not find her own.

Ong paused again, his voice soft yet powerful. "That is why these alliances have formed, Gailen. Not because of politics or convenience but because of love, sacrifice, and the belief that together, we are stronger than we could ever be apart. It is personal for everyone here."

The group fell silent, the weight of Ong's words settling over them. Gailen swallowed hard, his hands tightening briefly into fists before relaxing. Thalorian shifted his stance, his sharp gaze flickering between Ong and Keisha. Valeon let out a quiet breath as if absorbing the gravity of it all while Ong glanced around, reading the silent agreement in their eyes. Gailen's eyes shimmered with unshed tears as he looked at Ong, his voice trembling. "I think... I finally understand. Vacari's strength is not just its people or lands. It is the bond we share, the way we stand together, even in the face of darkness. Now, I see it."

Ong placed a firm hand on Gailen's shoulder. Its steady weight grounded Gailen, anchoring him in the moment. A wave of warmth spread through his chest from the touch and the unspoken reassurance it carried. In Ong's eyes, he saw not just a warrior but a brother-in-arms who believed in him even when he struggled to believe in himself. The burden of responsibility felt a little less heavy for the first time because he knew he was not carrying it alone. "You are a part of that, Gailen. And as long as we stand together, Vacari will endure."

Keisha stepped forward, her voice gentle but resolute. "Vacari's strength is not just in its alliances but in its heart. And that heart grows stronger whenever someone chooses to fight for it, protect it, and believe in it."

The fairy perched nearby chimed in with a melodic voice. "Even the smallest light can shine brightly when surrounded by others. Vacari has become a tapestry of lights, each unique yet part of the same whole."

Gailen smiled through his tears, his resolve hardening as the weight of responsibility settled. He inhaled deeply, squaring his shoulders as if bracing himself for the road ahead, the burden now feeling less like a weight and more like a purpose. He had always considered duty a burden, something imposed upon him by birthright. But now, he understood—it was not about obligation but choice. He saw that authentic leadership was not ruling but standing beside those who believed in something greater than themselves. For the first time, he embraced the weight, not as a burden, but as an honor. He had always carried the title of prince, but now he understood the burden entailed leadership and the duty to protect, inspire, and uphold the unity forged through sacrifice. "Then I will do my part to keep that light shining. For Vacari. For all of us."

The group nodded, the moment binding them closer as they prepared to face the challenges ahead.

Keisha turned to Kaelorn, and her expression was thoughtful yet resolute. Hope flickered in her heart, a quiet wish that Emerald Woods would always remain protected, a sanctuary for those who sought harmony within its embrace. "Kaelorn, I have your answer," she began, her voice steady. "If the fae agrees, your people can make their home here. But there is one condition—your people must build their homes with nature, not against it. The balance of this forest is delicate, and it must be respected."

Kaelorn's expression softened with gratitude, his shoulders relaxing as he exhaled a quiet breath of relief. Yet, a fleeting doubt lingered: was this the right path for his people, or was he leading them into the unknown? But as he looked at Keisha and the others, the weight of uncertainty gave way to a quiet realization. This was not about abandoning tradition but forging a future where the Luminara could belong and thrive. His fingers brushed against the hilt of his blade, a subconscious gesture as if grounding himself

in the reality of this moment. The weight of years spent wandering, the uncertainty of a proper home, seemed to lighten, replaced by the quiet hope
that this decision would finally give his people a place to belong. This was
more than just securing a home for his people; it was the first step toward
something more significant. For so long, he had lived with the belief that
his people were meant to drift, never to put down roots. But now, standing
here with Keisha and the others, he realized that belonging did not mean
losing their way. It meant choosing a place where they could finally stand
together, stronger than before. He stepped forward and bowed slightly.
"You have my word, Keisha. My people will honor the forest, not disturb
it. We seek harmony, not dominion."

The fairy flitted forward, her wings glowing brighter. "Do not worry,
Keisha. The fairies will guide the Luminara in creating homes that blend
seamlessly with the forest. You have our promise."

Keisha smiled, her heart lighter. "Thank you."

Nearby, Valeon lingered in silence, Kaelorn's words continuing to echo
in his thoughts. A swirl of emotions twisted inside him, hoping that he
might finally carve out a place for himself and fear that he never honestly
could. His fingers curled slightly at his sides, his stance shifting as he wrestled with uncertainty. The familiar urge to deflect with humor lingered
on his tongue, but for once, he stayed quiet, letting the moment's weight
settle. He had long wondered about his place in this growing alliance,
questioning whether he could ever belong. Keisha's earlier words to him.
"Belonging isn't given, Valeon; it's earned," resurfaced in his mind, stirring
a mix of longing and uncertainty. He was unsure what he was searching
for, only that he felt adrift, unsure of where he truly belonged. He had
always felt like an outsider, masking uncertainty with bravado, but now
he wondered if there was a different path for him. Could he genuinely
earn a place among them through skill, trust, and purpose? The thought
unsettled him, yet for the first time, it also gave him something to strive
for. Watching the Luminara's hope for a home rekindled a flicker of his

own. Perhaps there was still a place for him among them if he could prove himself worthy.

The fairy gave a final nod before following Kaelorn into the forest, her delicate wings leaving behind a faint shimmer like the last notes of a whispered melody. As he turned to leave, Kaelorn's gaze flickered to Gailen's hands, noticing the way he flexed his fingers as if trying to ease discomfort. He said nothing, but a thoughtful expression crossed his face. There would be time to speak of it later once his people arrived.

Keisha watched them go, a sense of peace settling over her as the golden light filtered through the canopy, casting dappled patterns on the forest floor. She drew a slow, steady breath, letting the moment's tranquility settle within her. As she exhaled, her shoulders eased, releasing a weight she had not realized she had been carrying. It was a rare feeling she had not known for a long time. So much had changed since the days when she doubted her place in Vacari and questioned if she was more than just a survivor. Standing among those she had fought beside, those who had become her family in ways she never expected, she felt something close to certainty. They had all come so far together. A gentle breeze carried the scent of moss and blooming flowers, wrapping around her like a quiet reassurance. She turned to Gailen, her eyes warm. "Thank you, Gailen. Your words today reminded me of something important. Sometimes, we need a fresh perspective to see what has been before us all along."

Gailen's cheeks flushed faintly. "I only spoke what I felt. Vacari's strength has always been in its people and their bonds."

Keisha nodded, the group exchanging knowing glances. Ong crossed his arms, a faint smile tugging at the corner of his lips, while Thalorian gave a single, approving nod. Valeon, for once, said nothing, his usual smirk replaced with quiet contemplation.

Keisha turned her gaze toward the path ahead, her thoughts shifting from the moment's peace to the challenges still looming. The alliances had strengthened, but their enemies had not disappeared. There was still much to prepare for, and she knew the road ahead would test them all in ways they had yet to realize.

Chapter 34
The Weight of Shadows

The molten glow of Fel Thalor's lava pits bathed the cavern in smoldering orange and crimson hues. Jagged and restless shadows danced across the uneven rock formations, shifting like phantom figures in the oppressive heat. Stalactites loomed like fangs from the ceiling while the floor bristled with treacherous outcroppings. The cavern pulsed with the deep, guttural rumble of shifting magma, its heat-laden breaths echoing through the stone. Cracks and hisses of cooling rock interspersed the steady churn; each sounds a reminder of the volatile force beneath. The sound resonated through the chamber, pressing against his skull like a relentless drumbeat, each bubbling surge a reminder of the raw, volatile power beneath his feet. The air shimmered with suffocating waves of blistering warmth, distorting the space like a living, breathing inferno. The magma's restless bubbling mirrored the simmering anger of the figure pacing at the abyss's edge.

The man approached cautiously, each step measured, his heart pounding beneath the weight of the summons. His throat tightened with every breath, the oppressive heat clawing at his lungs. A faint tremor ran through his fingers before he clenched them into fists, willing himself to maintain control. A thousand grim possibilities raced through his mind, each more damning than the last. He had been summoned before, but it felt different and heavier this time. The cavern seemed to close around him, the oppressive heat only amplifying the cold dread settling in his bones. This meeting was no mere formality.

The enormity of his failure gnawed at him, whispering doubts that coiled like serpents around his resolve. The molten depths below crackled mockingly, a reminder of the dangers he had unleashed and the expectations he had failed to meet. Not a trust that would trouble him, but the trust of the one who had orchestrated everything from the shadows, the one whose wrath he now feared most. The closer he drew, the heavier his limbs felt, as if his guilt itself sought to drag him into the fiery depths. The memory of his last failure haunted him the moment he had hesitated, allowing Gailen the time he needed to forge his bond with Aurelia. If he had acted sooner and had not wavered in the face of doubt, the prince would never have completed his training. That failure was his burden, which grew heavier with each step toward his master's wrath. He halted just within the cavern's shadows, watching as the figure cloaked in an aura of menace and authority continued their restless pacing.

Then, abruptly, they stopped. A sharp turn, a piercing gaze. The ambient glow from the lava carved harsh lines across their face, illuminating the fury in their eyes.

"You're late." The words were venom, spat with a force that made the man flinch.

He bowed his head slightly, his voice subdued. "My apologies. I came as soon as I felt your summons."

"Not soon enough." The figure resumed their pacing, their tone razor-sharp. "Do you understand the magnitude of your failure?" They stopped again, their voice rising with cold fury. "Gailen has been trained and is bonded with the crystal dragon! That bond amplifies his power beyond human limits, granting him access to the dragon's knowledge, strength, and legacy. His potential to disrupt our plans grows exponentially with each passing moment. He is more of a threat than ever before."

The man swallowed hard, his hands trembling at his sides. "It was not something I could prevent, not with Aurelia overseeing his training. You knew this was a possibility."

The figure turned sharply, its cloak billowing like a storm-driven wave, its fabric twisting and snapping through the heated air as if alive with their fury. The edges curled and snapped with the movement, casting shifting shadows against the molten glow as they advanced a step closer. The ambient glow of the lava illuminated the sharp ridges of their face, casting shadows over hollowed cheeks and eyes that burned with an eerie, unnatural light. A thin scar traced down one side of their jaw, a reminder of past violence that only added to their imposing presence. "Do not presume to lecture me on possibilities." Their voice dropped to a dangerous hush, a blade's edge of controlled fury. "You were tasked with ensuring he would never become a dragon rider. And yet, here we are."

The man felt the searing heat of the magma at his back, its blistering waves licking at his skin, while the icy grip of his master's fury pressed against his chest like a frozen vice. The contrast was suffocating, a cruel clash of elements that trapped him between fire and frost. A bead of sweat trickled down his temple, evaporating before it could reach his jaw. His breath hitched between the suffocating heat and the chill coiled around his ribs, a suffocating contrast that left him helpless. He forced his voice to remain steady. "It was not as simple as you think. Aurelia watches him like a hawk, closer than even I anticipated. She is a shadow that never fades, always scrutinizing my every move. And she is not alone. Others, loyal to her or simply wary of anything suspicious, linger nearby, ready to act at the slightest sign of trouble. It is not as if I have free rein. Every step I take feels like walking a blade's edge."

The figure's eyes narrowed. "Excuses. That is all you ever offer." Their voice was colder now, contemptuous. "Do you think I care about the obstacles? I care about results." Their fists clenched, and the air between them felt taut, stretched thin by the weight of expectation and failure.

The man clenched his jaw, lowering his gaze further in silent submission. Fear curled in his stomach, a gnawing ache of failure and dread. But beneath the fear, a flicker of something else stirred resentment. He had done everything within his power, yet it was never enough. His master's expectations were a noose, tightening with every misstep, suffocating any sense of control he had left.

A long silence stretched between them, broken only by the bubbling hiss of the lava below. The oppressive quiet pressed down like an unseen force, winding the tension tighter with each passing second, coiling it like a taut wire ready to snap. His breath shallowed, his chest tightening as though the very air conspired to smother him beneath the weight of unspoken words. The man dared not lift his gaze, fearing what expression he might find on his master's face. His pulse pounded in his ears, a steady, relentless drumbeat of dread. He braced for the following words. Or worse, the following command.

Then, the figure's tone softened at last, though it carried no warmth. "I have other plans in motion. But for now, you will observe. You will keep me informed of every movement, every decision, every whisper."

The man hesitated, his fingers curling into fists at his sides. A surge of defiance flickered within him, a desperate urge to push back against the command, to reclaim even the tiniest shred of his own will. But the thought was fleeting, swallowed by the cold grip of fear. He had seen the depths of his master's power and had witnessed firsthand what happened to those who defied them. Resistance was a fool's gamble he could not afford to make. "I cannot provide constant updates. It is not as easy as you make it sound."

The figure's glare darkened the silence that followed, their lips pressing into a thin line of displeasure. Their stance was rigid, a coiled force ready to strike, and their fingers twitched ever so slightly as if resisting the urge to act on their anger. The unspoken threat hung in the air, thick and suffocating. The lava crackled beneath them, amplifying the weight of the moment.

The man exhaled, finally bowing his head in reluctant surrender. "But I will do what I can. I will send reports more frequently."

"You will." The figure's voice was ice, unyielding. "And they will be thorough. If I find out, you are withholding anything..." They let the warning hang in the air, heavy with promise. Then, without another word, they turned, their silhouette vanishing into the shimmering haze of heat and shadow.

The man remained where he stood, staring into the restless magma. The weight of his situation pressed upon him, an unrelenting force that smothered every thought and breath.

As the mysterious figure disappeared into the fiery haze of Fel Thalor, the man let out a long, weary sigh. The oppressive heat of the lava pits seemed to ease slightly, yet the confrontation had left a far heavier burden on his heart.

Turning from the molten abyss, he strode toward the jagged mountain range that framed Fel Thalor. The air cooled with each step along the rocky ascent, offering a fleeting reprieve from the suffocating cavern below. At last, he reached a narrow ledge overlooking the barren valley beyond, its desolate expanse bathed in the faint glow of lava threading through the earth like veins of liquid fire.

He sank onto a weathered stone, resting his head in his hands. What have I gotten myself into? The question echoed in his mind, a relentless whisper of regret and dread that refused to be silenced.

Leaning back, he gazed at the darkening sky, where the first stars pierced through the veil of twilight. Memories surfaced unbidden, unwanted—of a choice he had never made. A pact, sealed in desperation long before his time, had bound his family to the will of Maelgrim Shadowwalker. His father had struck the bargain in the shadow of war, swearing their lineage to a master whose reach was inescapable. The terms had never been fully explained to him, only that it was a tether from which there was no release.

Why, Father? The thought was bitter, edged with resentment. Why did you bind us to Maelgrim? Why entangle our family in something that should have ended with you?

The worst thing about it was that his father had been the only one to gain anything from that cursed deal. He had wielded power and influence, secured protection that kept enemies at bay, and enjoyed the privileges of his pact until the moment he was gone. Whatever power, protection, or favor he had received had died with him, leaving nothing behind but the weight of servitude for those who remained. The rest of them had inherited nothing but chains, forced to bear the cost of a bargain they had never agreed to.

The weight of that ancient pledge bore down on him like the mountain itself, a chain forged by promises he had never made yet was condemned to carry. Beneath the suffocating burden, a spark of defiance smoldered, buried deep where no one could see. He loathed the role forced upon him and resented fate's hand, but he had learned to mask his true feelings well. Outwardly, he bowed to expectation, but the fire of resistance had not yet been extinguished inside. His chest tightened, each breath feeling shallower, as if the very air conspired to remind him of his imprisonment. The pressure coiled around his ribs, an invisible grip that refused to release, no matter how much he wished to break free. His fists clenched in frustration, his voice barely a whisper as he spoke into the empty night.

"At least Gailen is safe. For now."

But the words rang hollow. The mysterious figure's warning loomed in his mind, their next move shrouded in uncertainty. Uncertainty was what terrified him most. He had seen firsthand how ruthless they could be and how far they were willing to go to achieve their goals.

Another heavy sigh escaped him as he pushed himself to his feet. Before him, the journey back to Crystal Vale stretched long and uncertain. Each step forward was another step deeper into the treacherous web he could not untangle himself from. Every lie he told only wove the strands tighter. Every report sent another thread binding him to a fate he despised. If his deception were uncovered, the consequences would be dire, not just for him but for anyone caught in the wake of his betrayal. And yet, if he did nothing, the darkness he served would consume everything he had left to protect. His movements were slow, his thoughts a tangle of worry and regret.

As he descended the mountain, the distant lights of Crystal Vale flickered like beacons of a life he could never indeed return to. He recalled nights spent in the training grounds, sparring under torchlight with allies who had once trusted him without question. The laughter and shared victories felt like a cruel illusion now, a past he could no longer touch. The warmth of companionship had been replaced with the cold weight of deception, and no matter how much he longed for it, there was no turning back. He missed the ease of laughter shared over an evening fire, the warmth of friendship untainted by secrets. Once, he had walked those streets without the weight of betrayal pressing against his ribs. Now, that world felt like a distant memory, slipping further from his grasp with every step he took. He wished gods how he wanted things to be different. That he could break free from the shadow looming over him.

But he could only walk one weary step at a time now.

Each step reminded him that he straddled the line between loyalty and treachery. He had just promised to provide reports, to be the eyes and ears of a master he loathed. Yet, deep inside, he had hesitated, his reluctance nearly slipping past his lips before fear had silenced him. Every report he sent would keep him trapped, but every omission carried the risk of discovery. No matter what he did, the walls of his deception closed in tighter. The weight of his obligations clashed with the gnawing guilt of his deceit.

And no matter how far he walked, the battle within him would never truly end. The same struggle had plagued him since the day he learned of his family's debt, the war between duty and defiance, between self-preservation and the longing for freedom. No distance could erase the chains he bore nor silence the quiet voice within him that still dreamed of breaking them.

Chapter 35

Shadows in the Sky

The morning air of Crystal Vale lay still and crisp, an eerie hush settling over the land as if the world hesitated. The quiet felt unnatural, thick with unspoken warning, masking the storm's approach. Yet, beneath this tranquility, the land held its breath, bracing for the chaos. The first sign of trouble appeared above as shadows streaked across the sky. The silhouettes of Obsidian dragons cut through the clouds, their dark forms glinting like shards of volcanic glass against the sun's rays. Their arrival was not a full-scale assault but a calculated test, a probing of Crystal Vale's defenses.

The warning bells tolled, echoing across the crystalline spires of the city. Soldiers scrambled to their posts, and the dragon riders swiftly assembled under Aurelia's command. Among them was Prince Gailen, astride the luminous form of Aurelia, her scales gleaming with an iridescent glow that repelled the encroaching darkness. Clutching the Crystalbow, he felt its physical and symbolic weight pressing against him, a relic forged in ages past, imbued with the essence of the first Crystal Dragon. The heft of it, though not cumbersome, was a constant reminder of the responsibility it carried, its presence grounding him even as the tension of battle loomed. The Crystalbow hummed faintly beneath his grip, a steady, pulsing warmth radiating from its core as if responding to his presence. Legends spoke of its power awakening only for those deemed worthy, those who carried the fate of Crystal Vale. The enormity of his role pressed down on him, tightening his chest and making his palms slick with sweat. Yet, amidst the chaos, he drew strength from the bond he shared with Aurelia, the connection anchoring him to his purpose.

"Gailen," Aurelia's voice resonated, calm but commanding through their bond. "This is no ordinary skirmish. The Obsidian dragons are testing us. Be vigilant and use this chance to learn the Crystalbow's full potential."

He nodded, his grip tightening around the Crystalbow as Aurelia launched into the sky with a powerful thrust of her wings. The world below blurred into a patchwork of green and silver as they ascended, the wind tearing at his hair. Around him, other crystal dragons rose to join the fray, their riders armed and ready.

The Obsidian dragons struck first. One dove sharply, its wings slicing through the air as it unleashed a volley of dark flames aimed at the city's outer barriers. Crystal dragons intercepted, their luminous breath clashing with the dark flames in a dazzling explosion of light and shadow.

"Aurelia, take us closer!" Gailen commanded, his voice steady despite the chaos.

She obeyed, weaving through the aerial melee with practiced grace as the wind howled around them, carrying the distant clash of steel and the roars of battling dragons. Gailen drew the Crystalbow, its ethereal string pulling taut beneath his fingers. As he released the first arrow, it materialized mid-flight, a radiant projectile that burst into a cascade of light upon impact, scattering an attacking Obsidian dragon.

"Good," Aurelia praised. "Aim for their wings that will force them to retreat or land."

Another Obsidian dragon swooped low, aiming for a gap in the defensive lines. Gailen pulled the Crystalbow string again, focusing on his target. This time, the arrow split into three radiant shards, each finding its mark. The dragon roared in frustration, veering off as its balance wavered. Gailen's confidence wavered momentarily as he marveled at the Crystalbow's response, a mixture of exhilaration and unease coiling within him. The power was undeniable, yet the sheer intensity of its synergy with him sent a shiver down his spine. His breath hitched, and his fingers trembled slightly on the string. It almost felt alive in his hands, pulsing with its own will, sensing his intent, and adjusting to his grip. Each shot felt more fluid, the Crystalbow's energy aligning seamlessly with his own as if forging a deeper connection with every string pull.

"Impressive," Keisha's voice crackled through the riders' communication crystals. "The Crystalbow seems to be responding well to you, Prince."

"Let's hope it keeps doing so," Gailen muttered, already preparing for the next strike.

Above, the Obsidian dragons regrouped, their leader, a hulking beast with volcanic scales, her molten eyes scanning the battlefield ruthlessly. She roared orders, her voice a deep, guttural tremor that rolled through the air like thunder. The sound rattled the stones beneath them, a force that sent shivers through the battlefield. The force of it sent ripples through the clouds, vibrating in the bones of those who heard it, a primal command that compelled obedience. Her forces shifted into a more coordinated formation, each movement calculated to probe for weaknesses in the city's defenses. The skirmish was far from over, and the defenders of Crystal Vale braced themselves for the next wave.

On the ground, Keisha stood amidst a group of mages, her hands glowing with vibrant energy as she coordinated the creation of a protective barrier over the city. The crystalline spires of Crystal Vale shimmered with a faint magical glow, amplifying the power of the spellwork, but the process was too slow for her liking. The mages strained under the effort, their energy draining as they struggled to maintain control while the sheer magnitude of the barrier fought against being shaped. She clenched her fists, her mind racing as she calculated how much longer they needed.

"Focus!" Keisha called to the mages, her voice cutting through the chaos. "We need this barrier stronger and faster. If the Obsidian dragons find a weak point, they exploit it."

The mages nodded, sweat glistening on their brows as they channeled their energy. The dragons without riders circled above, their auras merging with the spell, adding layers of protective energy. Keisha extended her hands, weaving strands of light into the growing barrier. The energy refracted off the crystalline spires, scattering shimmering reflections across the battlefield, making the city seem alive with magic. A tingling warmth spread through her fingertips, the magic pulsing like a heartbeat coordinated with hers. The energy crackled against the air, shimmering like liquid sunlight as it fused with the city's crystalline structure. Each thread of magic pulsed with warmth, sending tingling sensations up her arms as the barrier thickened, resisting the relentless pressure of the assault above. A faint hum resonated in the air around her, the magic heat warming her fingertips as the light strands shimmered and pulsed with energy. The effort left her breathless, but she did not falter. This city's survival depended on her resolve.

"Keisha," Shael, a young mage, beside her stammered, "they are closing in!"

"I see them." She gestured toward a gap in the barrier, her magic surging to close it. "Hold steady. We are almost there."

Above them, the Obsidian dragons intensified their assault, testing the defenses with dark fire and physical strikes. Each blow sent ripples through the barrier, but it held—for now. Keisha spared a glance upward, her heart pounding at the sight of the ongoing battle. She felt the weight of each mage's effort, their shared desperation fueling the fragile barrier.

On one of the city's towers, Ong Swifthammer stood like a sentinel, his dragon lance gleaming in the morning sun. He watched the dragons' movements with a calculating gaze, ready to strike. When one of the smaller Obsidian dragons broke formation and dove toward the city, Ong sprang into action.

"Not today," he growled, hurling the lance with deadly precision. The weapon struck true, piercing the dragon's wing and sending it spiraling toward the ground. Ong retrieved the lance with practiced ease, yanking it from the fallen dragon's wing. The weapon vibrated in his grip, still humming with residual energy, while the dragon let out a pained, guttural growl, its claws scraping against the ground as it struggled to rise. His movements were fluid and unyielding, a testament to years of honed skill. He exhaled sharply, steadying himself. The Obsidian dragons were unlike any foe they had faced before; their tactics were unfamiliar, and their strength was overwhelming. Every battle demanded precision, but today felt different, more desperate. He could not afford a single mistake.

Another dragon attempted to flank the city, but Ong was faster. He raised the lance, its tip glowing with a faint energy, and thrust it forward. The dragon roared in pain as the lance connected, forcing it to retreat.

"Keisha!" Ong called, his voice carrying over the distance. "How is that barrier coming?"

"It is almost done!" she shouted, sweat beading her forehead. "But we need a few more minutes. Keep them off us!"

"That is the plan," Ong muttered, scanning the sky for the next threat. He braced himself, his grip on the lance tightening as he prepared to intercept another strike. The fragile balance between defense and destruction teetered on a knife's edge.

Above, Gailen and Aurelia maneuvered through the skies, intercepting dragons that strayed too close to the mages. Gailen's focus sharpened as he drew the Crystalbow again, a radiant arrow forming at his fingertips. The Crystalbow's power no longer startled him as it once had; now, it felt natural, an extension of his will. A soft hum vibrated through his hand, the arrow pulsing warmly as though responding to his determination. He loosed it in a single fluid motion. The glowing shaft streaked through the air and struck a dragon's tail, diverting its path just enough to miss the barrier.

"Aurelia, we need to buy them more time," Gailen said, his voice steady despite the chaos.

"We will," she replied, her crystal wings beating in rhythm with his. "Trust in the bond, Gailen. Together, we are stronger than they expect."

Below, the battle raged on. With Keisha's guidance, the shimmering barrier flared to completion just as the Obsidian dragons regrouped for another assault. The dome of light pulsed, a steadfast bulwark between Crystal Vale and destruction.

From above, Gailen's gaze locked onto Nocturna, the ancient Obsidian dragon. She hovered like a storm cloud on the horizon, her dark scales gleaming with an unnatural hardness. The air around her seemed to tremble, charged with an unseen force prickling against the skin. A faint wind spiraled outward from her form as if the battlefield recoiled from her presence, amplifying the eerie calm that held the combatants in suspense. For a moment, the battle seemed to pause, warriors hesitating as if caught in the grip of an unseen force, the tension stretching unbearably before the inevitable chaos resumed.

"Aurelia," Gailen called, his grip tightening on the Crystalbow. "She is the one orchestrating this. We need to stop her."

"She is formidable," Aurelia acknowledged, her tone unwavering. "But we are not without strength. Trust in yourself, Prince Gailen. Trust in us."

The Crystalbow thrummed in his hands, responding to his intent. Gailen exhaled slowly, feeling the energy pulse aligning with his heartbeat. For a fleeting moment, he wondered if he was wielding the Crystalbow or if it was guiding him. A brilliant glow pulsed from the crystal, synchronizing with the rhythm of his heartbeat. The energy coalesced into an arrow unlike any before, its radiance crackling, alive. He released the string. The arrow streaked toward Nocturna, a comet of pure light.

It struck true. Energy exploded upon impact, sending Nocturna reeling. A thunderous roar tore from her throat, not out of pain but shock. She struggled to steady herself, her wings faltering for the first time. Her molten eyes locked onto Gailen, burning with fury... and a flicker of respect.

"You dare!" Nocturna's voice rumbled across the battlefield, an echoing growl that sent shivers through the air. She flared her wings wide, but the strike had disrupted her control over the Obsidian dragons. Some hesitated, uncertain, while others grew more frenzied, lashing out with renewed aggression.

On the ground, Keisha felt the barrier thrum with stability, their collective magic fully realized. Relief coursed through her, but there was no time to falter. She poured more energy into the spell, her hands glowing as the dome shimmered defiantly against the Obsidian assault.

A deep, resonant roar split the sky, carrying with it an unmistakable echo of power, one that did not belong to the Obsidian dragons. The air quivered as an emerald glow flickered on the horizon, piercing through the smoke and shadow veiled the battlefield. The eerie contrast between the verdant light and the darkened sky cast an almost ethereal radiance, heralding the arrival of a long-awaited force.

Keisha's breath hitched as a majestic emerald dragon soared over the treetops of Emerald Forest. Its mighty wings cut through the air like blades, sending wind gusts rippling across the battlefield. The air vibrated with its wings' deep, rhythmic beat, each movement carrying the weight of untamed strength and long-awaited salvation. The battlefield stilled. Defenders, mages, and warriors alike froze, eyes lifting in stunned disbelief.

A soldier dropped to his knees, tears streaming down his face as he recognized the emerald dragons from long-told legends. Another clenched his fist and thrust it skyward in defiant triumph. Gasps of astonishment rippled through the ranks, growing into a swell of cries and thunderous cheer.

Hope surged anew, igniting a renewed fire in the defenders' hearts. Strength returned to weary limbs, and blades rose with a steadier grip. The tide had shifted, and with it came the unshakable belief that victory was within reach. Yet the battle was not over. Nocturna still loomed, and the Obsidian dragons, though shaken, were not yet defeated.

A host of emerald dragons followed, their scales gleaming like verdant jewels in the sunlight. At their head, Thalorian rode Verdantia, his silver hair streaming behind him like a banner of salvation.

Keisha exhaled, watching the impossible unfold before her. "They came," she whispered, awe threading her voice.

Beside her, a crystal dragon nudged her shoulder, its gaze alight with smug satisfaction.

Keisha huffed a quiet laugh. "Ah. So, it was you who fetched them. Well done." She reached out, wrapping her arms around the dragon's neck in a brief embrace, feeling its breath's steady rise and fall beneath her touch. The warmth of its scales was grounding, a silent acknowledgment of the trust and bond they shared.

Verdantia's roar echoed across the battlefield, a rallying cry. The emerald dragons dove into the fray, their coordinated strikes forcing the Obsidian dragons back. Emerald energy burst from Thalorian's Arborblade in sweeping arcs, each strike finding its mark."

From the tower, Ong's voice rang out. "Nocturna is losing control of her forces! Keep up the pressure!"

Above, Nocturna's snarl twisted into something dangerous as she took in the emerald dragons' arrival.

Gailen and Aurelia circled her, determination burning in their eyes.

Gailen drew his Crystalbow once more. This time, the arrow that formed pulsed with a vibrant emerald hue, its light richer and more profound than any before. Unlike the crystalline radiance of previous arrows, this one shimmered with the raw energy of the emerald dragons, a living force bound to the battlefield itself, as though drawing strength from Verdantia's presence. A surge of energy rushed through him, not overwhelming, but steady and sure, like an unbreakable thread linking him to something greater. He could feel the Crystalbow responding to the emerald dragons' presence, amplifying his resolve with their power.

"For Crystal Vale," he vowed.

The arrow streaked through the air, slamming into Nocturna's wing. She let out a furious roar, wings beating wildly as she fought for control. The tides had shifted against her.

Below, the defenders surged forward with renewed fervor. The emerald and crystal dragons worked in tandem, their magic reinforcing the barrier, their might turning the battle.

Nocturna's molten gaze swept over the battlefield, her wings twitching with barely restrained fury. How had this battle slipped from her grasp? She had been so confident of their victory, of their overwhelming power. Yet now, her forces faltered, her command crumbling like a brittle stone. She flexed her talons, her tail lashing in agitation as she adjusted her flight, her movements no longer fluid but sharp, erratic. A low growl rumbled from her throat, the sound vibrating through the air like distant thunder. She had underestimated them. The power of the Crystalbow had caught her off guard. The arrival of the emerald dragons had shattered her command.

A guttural snarl tore from her throat. Dark energy crackled around her.

"This is not over," she hissed, her voice like a whisper of impending doom.

She flared her wings, signaling her forces. The Obsidian dragons veered away one by one, their movements hesitant, reluctant to abandon the fight, yet bound by her command as they disappeared into the horizon.

Yet, even as they vanished, Nocturna's presence remained an unspoken promise that she would return more vigorously and relentlessly. The storm had only begun. Her lingering snarl echoed through the sky, a ghostly warning that refused to fade. The darkened clouds churned in her wake, a shadow stretching long over the battlefield, a reminder that this battle was only the beginning.

Chapter 36
A Golden Warning

As the first light of dawn crept over the horizon, its golden glow reflected off the crystalline spires of Crystal Vale, casting the city in an ethereal brilliance. Despite the tranquil morning, tension hung thickly in the air. Citizens still whispered about last night's battle, their eyes shadowed with fear, while the city's leaders braced for the inevitable return of their enemy. A hushed stillness clung to the streets, broken only by the distant scent of smoke lingering in the aftermath of battle. The echoes of conflict still haunted the minds of its defenders, a stark reminder of how close the city had come to falling.

The obsidian dragons had tested their strength, and while Crystal Vale still stood, the fight had laid bare its vulnerabilities. Obsidian fire had scorched the city's outskirts, its searing heat leaving blackened scars on the ground. The defenders had fought with everything they had, blades clashing against scaled hides, arrows finding their marks in the chaos. They barely repelled the assault before it reached the inner gates, their strength waning as the enemy withdrew into the night. They had won the night, but only just. Another attack, more extensive and more coordinated, would break them.

Prince Gailen strode purposefully alongside Ong and Keisha, his Crystalbow still slung across his back. The weight of responsibility pressed against his shoulders, a silent reminder that the fate of Crystal Vale rested heavily upon him. There was no room for hesitation, not now. Though his expression remained composed, uncertainty gnawed at him. Their boots echoed against the polished stone streets as they made their way toward the palace, past citizens who bowed their heads in respect. Their gratitude was evident, but so was their worry. They understood that last night had only been the beginning.

As they neared the palace gates, Keisha glanced at Gailen, her voice calm but firm. "You know he will be concerned about you fighting from Aurelia's back."

Gailen smirked. "He is always concerned, Keisha. But this time, he will have to set that aside. We have bigger issues."

Ong exhaled sharply, adjusting his dragon lance over his shoulder with a resolute nod. "Let us hope his fatherly instincts do not overshadow his duty as king. We need him focused."

The palace doors swung open as the guards recognized them, granting swift passage into the grand hall. Sunlight streamed through the arched windows, illuminating the crystalline architecture, but the beauty of the space offered little comfort against the looming threat.

In the throne room, King Manard stood with his advisors, his posture rigid, his expression grave. A flicker of relief crossed his face at the sight of his son, though it was fleeting. He dismissed his advisors with a wave and stepped down from the dais to meet them.

"Gailen." His gaze swept over his son, scanning for injuries before shifting to Keisha and Ong. "You three held the line last night. I trust this meeting is about the attack?"

Gailen nodded. "Yes, Father. The obsidian dragons were testing us. We managed to repel them but are not ready for a full-scale assault. If we do not act now, we will not survive the next battle."

Keisha stepped forward, her voice steady. "That skirmish was a prelude. They were probing our defenses, testing our response time. I saw the same tactics when Zylron tested Goldmoor's defenses. He struck at weaknesses until they crumbled, and if not for Kimras, they would have fallen completely. I fear they will do the same here. They have already found weaknesses, like the delay in activating the barrier. They will exploit them if we do not address them when they come in force."

Ong folded his arms, his jaw set, his gaze unwavering. "The barrier worked, but it was too slow. Last night, we would've lost lives without the crystal dragons and Keisha's magic. That is not a gamble we can afford."

King Manard listened in silence, his hands clasped behind his back, his brows furrowed in thought. When he finally spoke, his voice was measured. "I see. What do you propose?"

Gailen exchanged glances with Ong and Keisha before answering. "First, we strengthen the barrier. Keisha will not always be here to reinforce it. We need it faster, more dependable."

Keisha added, "I can train more mages to focus on fortifying it. And we need a warning system, a combination of magical and physical defenses to alert us before the dragons reach our gates."

Ong's voice was firm. "More watchtowers. Better coordination. Stronger weapons for the guards. If we do not prepare now, there will be no later."

The king paced, his fingers tapping lightly against his forearm as he weighed their words. His jaw tightened, a shadow flickering across his face as doubt crept into his eyes. He exhaled slowly, pressing his lips into a thin line, his usual confidence wavering under the weight of their concerns. He had trusted in Crystal Vale's defenses. He had believed they were enough, but last night had shattered that illusion. If he failed to act swiftly, his people would suffer for his misjudgment.

Finally, he stopped, his gaze lingering on the floor as doubt flickered across his face. The weight of responsibility pressed down on him, his mind racing through the possibilities. With a slow inhale, he steadied himself and turned to them.

"You have given me much to consider. You are right, and Crystal Vale cannot remain vulnerable. I will convene the council immediately to implement these changes." His gaze drifted toward the ornate windows, where fractured sunlight painted the throne room in shifting gold and white. "I had hoped our defenses would hold longer. I was wrong. We cannot afford another mistake." He inhaled sharply, squaring his shoulders. "Gailen, oversee the preparations. Keisha, assist with the magical components. Ong, ensure the warriors are ready."

The three nodded, determination hardening their expressions.

Gailen was already calculating the reinforcements. They needed more mages trained in barrier magic, additional archers positioned along the outer walls, and dragon-mounted scouts to provide early warnings. Every detail mattered; any gap in their defenses could mean devastation when the enemy returned. Keisha's mind whirred with magical schematics. Ong clenched his jaw, vowing his warriors would not be caught unprepared again.

"Thank you, Father," Gailen said. "We won't let you down."

King Manard placed a firm hand on his son's shoulder, his expression momentarily softening. "I know you will not. Be careful, all of you. The safety of Crystal Vale depends on your efforts."

A renewed sense of purpose filled them as they left the throne room.

The obsidian dragons had given them a warning.

Crystal Vale would be ready.

Stepping into the sunlit courtyard, the tension from the throne room clung to them like an unspoken weight, tightening Gailen's chest and setting Keisha's jaw. The warmth of the morning did little to ease the stiffness in their shoulders or the lingering unease in their minds. The morning warmth wrapped around them, yet it did little to dispel the chill of uncertainty lingering in their minds. Gailen exhaled slowly, his father's words still pressing against his thoughts. The truth of their vulnerability had never been more evident, and the urgency of their next steps loomed like an approaching storm.

Keisha adjusted the straps of her satchel, her gaze thoughtful as she turned to Gailen and Ong. The memory of Goldmoor's struggle surfaced in her mind, a stark reminder of how unprepared they had been. They could not afford the same mistakes here. "We should speak to Kimras," she said, her voice measured but firm. "Goldmoor had to reinforce its defenses after Zylron's attack. They might have strategies that could help us here."

Ong nodded, shifting his dragon lance against his shoulder. "That is true. Goldmoor improved their barriers and defensive coordination after Zylron's assault. What we are facing now feels too similar to ignore. Kimras has seen more battles than most of us combined. His insight could be invaluable."

Keisha looked at Gailen, waiting for his decision.

Gailen considered their words, his brow furrowing. After a moment, he nodded. "That makes sense. We would be foolish not to take advantage of Kimras's experience. If he can spare the time, it could make all the difference. Let us contact him."

A small smile touched Keisha's lips at his decisiveness, a wave of relief and admiration washing over her. Seeing Kimras again, knowing his wisdom and experience would guide them, steadied the uncertainty that had gnawed at her since the battle. Lifting her hand, she focused on the emerald amulet around her neck, its soft glow pulsing with her thoughts. A faint, melodic energy hummed as she reached across the vast distances separating them.

Moments later, her eyes fluttered open, a flicker of hesitation crossing her face before settling into quiet satisfaction. "Kimras is on his way," she announced. "He will be here within the hour. He said to be ready for a detailed discussion."

Ong grinned, pushing himself off the wall. "That's Kimras for you. It's straight to the point; no time wasted."

Gailen chuckled. "Good. We will need every moment to prepare. Let us find a solid meeting place and start planning."

With renewed urgency, they quickened their pace toward the city's southern lookout, their strides firm and purposeful. The distant hum of the marketplace still reached them, starkly contrasting with the battle-worn silence hanging over the city's defenses. The towering spires of Crystal Vale loomed ahead, their gleaming surfaces reflecting the urgency in their hearts. Gailen's jaw tightened with determination while Ong adjusted his grip on his dragon lance, ever watchful. Keisha's fingers brushed against the emerald amulet at her neck as if drawing reassurance from its glow. There was no time to waste. Gailen's mind churned with possibilities, weighing strategies, weaknesses, and the questions they needed to ask. Would Kimras's knowledge be enough to shore up their defenses? Or were they already too far behind? The weight of responsibility pressed heavier with each step, but there was no room for doubt now.

They reached the Crystal Grove, a serene sanctuary bathed in fractured sunlight filtering through crystalline trees. The air carried a crisp, almost musical hum, resonating through the grove, while the faint scent of blooming flora mingled with the cool freshness of the shaded sanctuary. A radiant statue of Aurelia stood at its heart, her elegant form immortalized in shimmering stone.

Nearby, the honest Aurelia rested, her presence commanding yet serene.

Gailen's chest tightened with familiarity and comfort. She had always been more than a guardian; she was a guiding force, a steady beacon in times of uncertainty. Memories of battle, quiet conversations, and their unspoken bond rushed through him.

Her sleek scales shimmered in the dappled light, casting fragments of rainbows across the grove. She shifted slightly, her tail flicking gently against the ground, sending a ripple of light through the clearing. As she moved, the colors danced along the ground, reflecting in the wide eyes of those who gazed upon her, a living embodiment of crystalline majesty. Her long tail curled at the monument's base, her crystalline body as still as the statuesque tribute beside her. Yet, her eyes, ancient, wise, held a knowing intensity as they met Gailen's gaze, a silent challenge wrapped in reassurance.

"Aurelia," Gailen greeted, his voice warm. "Kimras is on his way to help coordinate the defenses."

Aurelia inclined her head, her voice resonating like a distant chime. "That is good news, Prince Gailen. His wisdom will serve you well." She paused, her gaze flickering toward the distant sky. "I will remain here until his arrival."

The weight of the battle still loomed over Crystal Vale, but with each decisive step, they moved closer to securing their future.

Keisha and Ong exchanged a glance before Ong gestured toward a nearby bench beneath a crystalline tree. "Let's give them a moment," he murmured.

Keisha nodded with a quiet breath of relief and followed him to the shaded seat. From their vantage point, they watched as Gailen stood with Aurelia, allowing the prince a moment to connect with his dragon.

Gailen stepped closer, his fingers brushing instinctively against the Crystalbow slung across his back. The Crystalbow's surface was cool to the touch, yet beneath his fingertips, a faint hum of energy pulsed like a heartbeat responding to his presence. The smooth surface tingled beneath his touch, a subtle warmth radiating through his fingertips as if the bow acknowledged his presence. A memory stirred the first time he had wielded it, the way it had thrummed in his grip, almost as if it recognized him. Even now, it felt like more than just a weapon. It was a part of him, a silent promise of strength and unity.

"I've been thinking about the skirmish," he began, quiet but thoughtful. "That moment when the Crystalbow... responded to me. It felt like it was not just me using it. It was alive, an extension of both of us."

Aurelia regarded him with deep, contemplative eyes, her tail curling slightly around the statue's base as she shifted, ever watchful. "The Crystalbow is no ordinary weapon, Gailen. It was forged with the essence of the Crystal Dragons who came before me. It recognizes your bond with me, and through that bond, it reveals its true potential. The Crystalbow will respond to your will as you grow stronger, but it is also a guide, teaching you to trust in our connection."

Gailen's breath hitched slightly at the realization. "So, when that shot struck Nocturna and disrupted her balance... that was us?"

Aurelia inclined her head. "Indeed. Your will, combined with the Crystalbow's power and our bond, created that force. It is a reminder that you are never alone in battle, Gailen. We fight together as one."

Gailen absorbed her words, his mind racing with possibilities. What if he could channel the Crystalbow's energy more precisely, striking with unwavering accuracy? Could he use its power to shield allies or disrupt enemy formations? The thought of wielding such control was both exhilarating and daunting. What else was the Crystalbow capable of? Could he learn to control its power deliberately, or would it only answer in moments of dire need? The thought thrilled and unsettled him in equal measure. If he mastered it, it might turn the tide of battle. But if he failed... it could cost them everything.

"It felt incredible," he admitted, "but also daunting. What if I fail? What if I cannot control its power when it truly matters?"

Aurelia lowered her massive head, her gaze steady yet gentle. "You will not fail."

Her voice resonated through him, steady as the earth, unwavering as the stars.

"The Crystalbow chose you for a reason, Gailen. It saw your potential, your courage, your resolve. It recognized the strength within you, the unwavering determination that sets you apart." She continued, "Trust in yourself as I trust you, and let that trust guide your actions. Our bond will only grow stronger with time and experience."

Gailen let out a slow breath, her words settling deep within him. He was not alone in this. He had never been.

"Thank you, Aurelia," he said softly. "I'll do my best to honor this bond and what it represents."

Aurelia's lips curved in what might have been the faintest hint of amusement, revealing the glint of her fangs more reassurance than a threat, a silent promise unspoken yet understood.

"I have no doubt you will, Prince Gailen," she said. "Now, take a moment to rest and reflect. The road ahead will demand much from you, but you are not walking it alone."

Across the grove, Keisha glanced at Ong. They heard Gailen and Aurelia's quiet and measured voices weaving together from their bench like a melody of understanding.

"He's growing into his role," Keisha murmured, a note of pride in her voice.

Ong nodded, a small smile tugging at his lips. "He has the heart for it. That is what makes the difference."

They settled back, letting the peaceful aura of the grove surround them. Yet, in the distance, a faint rustling echoed through the trees as a reminder that peace was fleeting and the shadows of uncertainty still lingered on the horizon. Yet, beneath the stillness, an unspoken tension remained—a lingering sense of vulnerability, as if the air held the weight of the battles yet to come. The arrival of Kimras would bring new challenges and decisions that could shape the fate of Crystal Vale.

For now, they allowed themselves this brief moment of tranquility in the presence of the majestic crystal dragon and her rider, knowing it would not last.

As the peaceful stillness of Crystal Grove enveloped them, Valeon rounded the corner, his eager stride betraying his excitement. His expression mixed curiosity and admiration, and his gaze locked onto Gailen. Gailen met his gaze and smiled.

"That was incredible earlier!" Valeon exclaimed, barely containing his enthusiasm. "The way the Crystalbow worked, the dragons, the battle, everything! How did it feel up there, Gailen? Were you scared at all?"

Gailen chuckled, exchanging a glance with Ong, his stance relaxing slightly as amusement flickered in his eyes. Ong smirked knowingly, recognizing the familiar excitement in Valeon's voice. They had both faced the chaos of battle more times than they could count, and words often fell short of describing the experience.

"It was intense, Valeon," Gailen admitted. "But when you are in the air with Aurelia, there is no time for fear. It is all focus and trust."

Valeon's eyes widened with wonder. "Trust, huh? I cannot even imagine... What about you, Ong? Were you nervous up on the tower?"

Ong exhaled with a knowing look, leaning back against the bench. "Nervous? Nah. I only worried about whether the tower would hold up with everything happening around it."

Valeon grinned, his mind racing with more questions. "And the obsidian dragons—do you think they will return soon? How do you—"

His words faltered, his eyes suddenly going wide as a massive shadow swept across the grove. His body tensed, panic creeping into his voice. "What is that? Another dark dragon? Are we under attack again?"

Keisha, who had been quietly observing, glanced up and immediately caught the telltale glint of gold against the sunlight. A knowing smile tugged at her lips as she placed a reassuring hand on Valeon's shoulder.

"Relax, Valeon," she said, her voice calm. "That is not an enemy. That's Kimras."

Even as she spoke, the golden dragon descended with effortless grace, his massive wings stirring a powerful gust that sent leaves swirling through the grove. His landing was a powerful yet fluid motion, his enormous form settling with a controlled force that sent a tremor rippling through the ground. His scales shimmered like molten gold, casting warm light across the grove. The very air crackled with energy.

Valeon stumbled back, awe and a touch of fear flashing across his face. His breath hitched as the sheer magnitude of Kimras's presence settled over him. Gailen straightened instinctively, feeling the sheer power of Kimras's presence settle over them, a quiet, unspoken command woven into his very being.

Keisha stepped forward without hesitation, warmth in her smile as a surge of joy filled her at the sight of her old friend. She wrapped her arms around one of Kimras's massive forelimbs in a familiar embrace, the reassurance of his presence settling a lingering tension in her chest. He was here. He would help them, as he always had. "It's good to see you, Kimras."

The golden dragon inclined his head, his deep voice carrying a rich warmth that matched his brilliant hue. "And you, Keisha. It seems Crystal Vale has been busy since we last met."

Valeon's jaw slackened as he watched the exchange unfold. His gaze darted between Keisha and the towering dragon, his mind struggling to process the grandeur before him. Leaning closer to Gailen and Ong, he whispered in stunned disbelief, "She rides that dragon? He is enormous!"

Ong chuckled, clapping Valeon on the back. "That is right. Kimras is Keisha's bonded dragon. You will get used to it eventually."

Gailen chuckled softly, a glint of amusement in his eyes at Valeon's astonishment. "It is something to see. But you start to understand the bond once you are up close with a dragon-like Aurelia or Kimras. It is not just about size. It is about trust."

Valeon nodded absently, his eyes never leaving Kimras as the golden dragon lowered his head, speaking quietly with Keisha. He let out a slow breath, his shoulders loosening slightly as the initial shock gave way to quiet awe. "I don't think I'll ever get used to it," he murmured, more to himself than anyone else. "But it's amazing."

The group settled into the grove, the weight of Kimras's presence shifting the atmosphere. Though they allowed themselves a brief moment of awe, the quiet tension remained. His arrival marked the beginning of a meaningful conversation that would determine the fate of Crystal Vale.

For now, they let themselves marvel at the strength and majesty of one of Vacari's most legendary dragons, knowing that the stillness of the grove would soon be shattered. In the distance, a branch snapped, the sound sharp against the quiet a reminder that something unseen lurked just beyond their sight. The threat loomed ever closer, pressing against the edges of their awareness like a distant storm waiting to break.

Kimras turned his golden gaze to Gailen, his tone firm and commanding. His massive wings folded neatly at his sides, his robust frame radiating an aura of quiet authority. His voice carried the weight of experience when he spoke, his piercing eyes locking onto Gailen with unwavering intensity.

"Goldmoor had to implement additional precautions after the first attack," Kimras said. "We placed warning systems on our magical and mechanical towers to detect hostile dragons before they reached the city. Crystal Vale must do the same immediately. Without early warning, your defenses will crumble under a coordinated assault."

Gailen listened intently, nodding in agreement though unease stirred beneath his composed exterior. The weight of expectation pressed against him, and memories of past battles flashed in his mind, moments where hesitation had cost lives. He wondered if he were genuinely ready if his decisions would be enough to protect those who relied on him. The dark dragons unsettled him the most—this was not just another skirmish. When they returned, it would be with full force, and Crystal Vale might not withstand the storm. The reality of what lay ahead pressed heavily upon him. This was not just a test of Crystal Vale's defenses. It tested his ability to lead them through the coming storm.

"What else should we expect, Kimras?" he asked.

The golden dragon rumbled deeply, his voice resonating with authority. "Expect the obsidian dragons to ally with the black dragons. Together, their combined strength and tactics will be devastating. The obsidian dragons wield sheer force, while the black dragons thrive on cunning and manipulation. They will strike as one, overwhelming your defenses while sowing chaos within your ranks. Their goal is to destroy Crystal Vale and demoralize your forces. This will not be a single battle. It will be a war of attrition."

Kimras turned his gaze to Aurelia, his expression thoughtful yet profound. Aurelia inclined her head, a small smile forming as she acknowledged him with quiet respect. She flicked her tail, her crystalline scales catching the light as she lifted her head to meet his gaze with unwavering determination.

"Aurelia, I suggest you and Verdantia work together to integrate the crystal and emerald dragons here in Crystal Vale and Emerald Woods. A unified front will strengthen your defenses. Expect a dual assault one that tests both cities simultaneously. They will attempt to divide your forces."

Aurelia inclined her head, her tone resolute. "We will prepare for that, Kimras. Verdantia and I will coordinate with our dragons and allies to ensure no city stands alone."

Gailen glanced at Ong, concern flickering in his eyes. "Ong, what do you think? How do we prepare for an attack like this?"

Ong straightened, his expression serious as he addressed Gailen. "Zylron attacked Goldmoor with red and white dragons while Glaciera led another assault simultaneously. It was not just their strength but also their coordination that made them dangerous. Kimras and Amara had to split their forces of gold and amethyst dragons to defend both fronts. We will need to do the same here."

Gailen absorbed the information, nodding slowly. "Then we must strengthen our alliances immediately. Both Crystal Vale and Emerald Woods need to be ready."

Kimras let out a deep rumble of approval, his golden eyes narrowing with urgency as his tail flicked once against the ground, a subtle sign of his mounting concern. "Good. Take swift action, Prince Gailen. Every moment counts." His wings flexed slightly as if restless, needing immediate movement, his posture rigid with the weight of unspoken warnings.

He turned to Keisha. "Ensure the mages work closely with the dragons to fortify the barriers and establish the early warning systems. If those fail, the city will be left vulnerable to surprise attacks. If that happens, there will be no chance of rallying the defenses, and the destruction could spread to the inner sanctum. Countless lives will be lost."

Keisha inclined her head, her expression steady. "I will see to it immediately, Kimras. The mages and dragons will work as one."

Kimras nodded, his towering presence exuding confidence and authority. His presence calmed them, reassuring them they were not alone in this fight. He had seen countless battles and had endured trials that few could comprehend. The last battle in Goldmoor was proof of his strength. He had hurled Zylron into a mountain, forcing the dark dragon to retreat. That memory steeled their resolve, reminding them that even the most formidable enemies could be defeated. Instinctively, the group straightened as if standing before a battle-hardened general.

Gailen felt a surge of determination settles in his chest. Keisha's eyes flickered with newfound urgency. Ong gripped his dragon lance tighter, readying himself for the challenges ahead.

Kimras turned back to Gailen, his golden eyes filled with quiet expectation. "Prince Gailen, you have shown great promise, but the days ahead will test your resolve. You will face battles that demand not just strength but strategy. Moments will come when a single decision will determine the fate of Crystal Vale. Trust in your allies. Do not hesitate to call for aid when the weight of leadership becomes too heavy."

Gailen bowed slightly. "Thank you, Kimras. Your guidance means a great deal. We will see this through."

Kimras stepped back, spreading his massive golden wings in preparation for departure. He cast a final glance at Ong. "I must return to Goldmoor. If you need me, have Keisha call—I will come."

Ong nodded, his voice steady. "We will. Safe travels, Kimras."

With a powerful thrust of his wings, Kimras took to the skies, the deep, rhythmic beats echoing through the grove. Sunlight fractured across his golden scales, casting fleeting halos of light as he ascended. Leaves swirled in his wake, dust spiraling in delicate eddies before settling again as if the grove acknowledged his departure. His golden form gleamed brilliantly in the sunlight, a beacon against the sky as he soared toward Goldmoor.

For a long moment, the group remained still, their gazes following his retreating figure.

Gailen clenched his fists, feeling the weight of responsibility settles heavier upon his shoulders. Doubt whispered at the edges of his mind: was he ready for what lay ahead? But beneath the uncertainty, a spark of determination burned. He could not afford to falter now. Doubt gnawed at the edges of his resolve. Could he genuinely lead his people to victory? The battle had tested him, but the war ahead would demand far more. He had Aurelia as his ally, but was that enough? The uncertainty pressed against him, a silent whisper of fear he refused to voice.

Keisha exhaled softly, her expression firm and determined.

Ong adjusted his dragon lance, his grip tightening as his jaw set in determination. The resolve in his posture mirrored the unspoken commitment they all shared. His eyes narrowed with focus as if already preparing for the battles to come.

Gailen turned to Keisha, Ong, and Aurelia, his expression resolute. "Let us get to work. We have no time to waste."

The three exchanged determined nods.

The actual test of leadership loomed ahead, a relentless tide of darkness ready to crash against their defenses.

They would be ready.

Chapter 37

Unity in the Shadows

E merald Woods' tranquility shattered, replaced by a violent tremor that shook the earth beneath the towering trees.

A deafening roar tore through the canopy, sending flocks of birds screaming into the sky. The air vibrated with the force of the sound, a crushing wave pressing against their chests and rattling the leaves around them. Thalorian's grip tightened on the Arborblade as his ears rang, his instincts screaming that this was no ordinary threat. Xalzorath, the ancient black dragon, loomed above, his massive wings beating with such force that the ground trembled beneath him. Each beat of his wings sent shockwaves through the air, rattling the emerald leaves and sending creatures darting for shelter.

His piercing, hate-filled eyes swept across the vibrant expanse below, dark contempt radiating from his presence.

"Emerald dragons," he sneered, his voice laced with venom. "Your time has come. You will answer for the sins of your kind."

Thalorian stood at the edge of the grove, the shimmering light of the Arborblade reflecting off the lush foliage. He tightened his grip on the hilt, his expression resolute. Beside him, Verdantia unleashed a thunderous cry, her emerald scales catching the dappled sunlight as she launched into the air to meet the threat.

Deeper within the woods, Kaelorn worked alongside the fairies, his magic interwoven with theirs to strengthen the barrier encircling the forest's heart. His hands glowed with golden light as he poured power into the enchantments, guiding the fairies with firm but steady instructions.

"Stay focused together. We can hold the line!" he called, his voice cutting through the chaos.

The magical beings darted through the air, glowing like fireflies as they wove intricate spells, reinforcing the barrier that shimmered faintly around the sacred glade. But despite their efforts, the attack had come too suddenly, and gaps remained.

Kaelorn's sharp eyes tracked the weak points, his jaw tightening as urgency surged. The shimmering energy wavered and flickered under the relentless assault, and with every pulse of dark magic, the risk of failure grew more dire. Some areas thinned dangerously, the barrier barely holding as dark energy clawed at its edges. His voice commanding, he barked, "Reinforce the northern perimeter! We cannot afford a break in the defenses!"

A rush of dark energy crackled through the air as Xalzorath dove with terrifying speed, his talons slamming into the barrier. The magical shield trembled beneath the impact, its glow flickering as veins of darkness spread through it like cracks in glass.

Thalorian exchanged a look with Verdantia, his voice calm despite the storm brewing around them. "We cannot let him reach the heart of the forest. Focus on the others and leave Xalzorath to me."

Verdantia nodded sharply, her wings slicing through the air as she veered toward a cluster of smaller black dragons. With a mighty breath, she unleashed a surge of emerald fire, forcing them to scatter before they could descend upon the woods.

Kaelorn, still directing the fairies, caught sight of Xalzorath preparing another devastating blow. The dark dragon reared back, his molten gaze fixed on the flickering barrier.

Kaelorn's voice rang out. "We need more power here! Strengthen the wards before he breaks through!"

The barrier flared brighter as their magic intensified, but Xalzorath's fury only grew. His next roar shook the air like rolling thunder.

"You think your petty magic can stop me?" he bellowed, his voice echoing from the abyss. "I am vengeance incarnate!"

Thalorian took a deliberate step forward, the Arborblade pulsing with light in answer to his resolve. His gaze locked onto Xalzorath, unyielding.

"Lle'kerym naa amin," he declared. "A'ta amin Emerald Woods ar' kaima i'naur Verdantia ar' i'Arborblade! (Your battle is mine. Leave the Emerald Woods or face the fire of Verdantia and the Arborblade!)

Xalzorath's eyes narrowed, his massive form pivoting toward the Moon Elf warrior. Thalorian's grip on the Arborblade tightened, his muscles coiling with tension as he braced for the inevitable clash. His molten gaze burned with contempt as his lips curled into a sneer.

Vorthis di wer virlym jacioniv," Xalzorath hissed, his words laced with dark amusement. "Wux shilta loreat shafaer dout versvesh. (Fool of the emerald brood. You will drown in your pride.)

Thalorian's pulse quickened, but he forced himself to steady his breathing. Doubt clawed at the edges of his mind—memories of a battle lost, of comrades falling because he had hesitated. He exhaled slowly, forcing the weight of the past aside, anchoring himself in the moment. He would not falter again. There was no room for doubt. He exhaled slowly, centering himself, his grip tightening on the Arborblade. The weight of his duty pressed heavily upon him, but resolve burned in his gaze. There would be no retreat.

His response was swift. Emerald light flashed as he swung the Arborblade in a precise arc, unleashing a wave of energy toward the black dragon.

Xalzorath snarled, twisting through the air unnaturally to evade the attack. Shadows flickered in his wake, his fury intensifying.

Meanwhile, Kaelorn and the fairies wove their magic into the very heart of the forest. Emerald-hued vines and gnarled roots surged from the earth, twisting toward the smaller black dragons as they attempted to breach the barrier. They crackled with raw magic, their surfaces glowing faintly with emerald energy, emitting a sharp, earthy scent as they curled and tightened around their prey. They coiled around wings and limbs, twisting and tightening, locking the creatures in place. Furious roars filled the air as the dragons thrashed and clawed at their restraints, their movements growing more desperate with each passing second.

The Emerald Woods seemed to rise in defiance, ancient trees swaying, their leaves rustling like a whisper of resistance. This was a rallying cry to the defenders, a testament to the forest's will to endure. But to the invaders, it carried an eerie edge, a silent promise that the woods would not fall without a fight.

Xalzorath let out a guttural growl, his claws raking through the air. A pulse of dark energy followed, sending shockwaves through the grove as he lunged for Thalorian. The sheer force of his momentum shook the ground beneath them.

Thalorian sidestepped, his blade moving like a dance, a blur of radiant green as he countered with another strike of light-infused energy. The force of his attack met Xalzorath's charge head-on, sending a shockwave of emerald and obsidian energy outward. Xalzorath snarled, his wings faltering mid-flight before he corrected, his gaze burning with renewed fury. Their clash sent luminous ripples through the battlefield, casting eerie shadows that flickered in unnatural patterns.

A young emerald dragon burst through the thick canopy, its wings beating furiously as it rejoined the fray. A triumphant roar split the sky, but it was not alone.

Aurelia descended like a beacon of light, flanked by a squadron of crystal dragons.

Gailen gripped his Crystalbow atop her back, his expression carved with fierce determination. Beside them, Verdantia let out a roar of approval, rallying her emerald brethren as reinforcements surged into battle.

From the skies, Keisha, riding atop one of the crystal dragons, surveyed the battlefield below.

She instantly remembered stepping into Emerald Woods as a child, the quiet magic embracing her like a long-lost friend. Now, that same sanctuary trembled beneath the weight of war. Its whispers of peace drowned beneath the howls of battle.

She would not let it fall.

Her sharp eyes scanned the battlefield, taking in the beleaguered fairies, the wounded warriors, and the barrier, its cracks spidering outward like veins of fragility.

No. This forest was more than a battleground. It was alive, breathing with ancient magic, a sanctuary of power and memory. Its loss would be more than strategic and a wound upon the land itself. Her jaw tightened.

Leaping gracefully from her dragon's back as it descended, she landed beside Kaelorn, her hands moving in fluid patterns. Kaelorn exhaled sharply, a flicker of relief crossing his face before he refocused, his grip on the swirling golden energy tightening. The barrier flickered dangerously, its edges rippling as if on the verge of collapse. Every pulse of magic strained against the relentless assault, sweat forming at his temple as he fought to keep the defenses intact. The urgency in his movements did not wane, but the tension in his shoulders eased slightly at her arrival. Light gathered at her fingertips, intertwining seamlessly with the magic of the fairies and Kaelorn's golden energy.

"Let us strengthen this!" Keisha commanded, her voice cutting through the chaos like a blade of clarity. "We cannot let them break through!"

Kaelorn's relief was evident, though his focus never wavered. "Your timing is impeccable. They were moments away from breaching the heart of the woods."

Together, their magic surged, raw energy crackling through the air as the barrier flared brighter, solidifying into a shimmering dome of protection.

The black dragons struck talons raking, fire-spewing, yet their attacks met an impenetrable wall of power. The barrier pulsed with defiant energy, each strike sending ripples of luminous force across its surface. It shimmered and flared with each impact, absorbing the fury of the assault and pushing back with bursts of radiant resistance.

The barrier pulsed with defiant energy, absorbing each strike and retaliating with radiant bursts of power. It held—for now.

Above, Aurelia and Gailen locked onto Xalzorath, the massive black dragon's fiery gaze smoldering with cruel amusement. His lips curled into a sneer, his wings flexing as tension rippled through the air. His claws twitched restlessly, eager to rend flesh.

"You think reinforcements will save this pathetic forest?" Xalzorath drawled, his voice like rolling thunder. "It only delays the inevitable."

Gailen's grip tightened on his Crystalbow. "You'll find we're harder to destroy than you think."

He loosed an arrow in a single, fluid motion. The crystalline shaft streaked through the sky like a comet, colliding with Xalzorath's chest in a radiant light. A shockwave rippled outward, momentarily distorting the air around him as he staggered mid-flight.

A thunderous roar tore from his throat, shaking the trees and sending leaves spiraling as the air trembled with his fury. His tail lashed through the sky, dark scales glinting as he fought to regain control, his anger boiling over like molten fire.

Verdantia seized the opening. With a powerful beat of her wings, she unleashed a torrent of emerald fire, its searing heat carving a path through the sky. Xalzorath recoiled, the flames licking at his dark scales, momentarily forcing him to retreat. Below, Thalorian wasted no time. Gripping the Arborblade, he leaped onto Verdantia's back, settling into position with practiced ease.

"Keep him distracted!" he called to Gailen. "We'll strike from his blind spot."

On the ground, Ong had scaled one of the tallest trees, its ancient trunk thick with gnarled roots. From this vantage point, he surveyed the battlefield, his dragon lance poised to strike.

A swift-moving shadow flickered over Ong's perch, one of the smaller black dragons diving through the canopy, its talons gleaming as it aimed for the forest below. Instinct flared in his veins as a smaller black dragon plummeted through a weak point in the canopy, talons gleaming as they reached for the forest below. In a fluid motion, Ong launched his dragon lance, its tip glowing faintly with energy, piercing the beast's wing and sending it spiraling into the branches. Again and again, he drove back, attacking dragons, buying Keisha and the fairies precious seconds to fortify the magical barrier.

"Do not get too comfortable up there, Ong," Keisha called over the din, amusement threading her voice. "We'll need you on the ground soon."

"I'm better company up here," Ong shot back, a grin evident in his tone. "Besides, I've got the perfect view to keep these pests away!"

Aurelia soared closer to Xalzorath, swift and deliberate movements weaving through battle currents like a streak of light.

Gailen readied another arrow, a surge of power pulsing through his fingertips as he drew the bowstring. The weapon hummed in response, its energy merging with his will, guiding his aim with an almost sentient precision.

This time, the arrow glowed brighter, pulsing with raw energy. He released it.

The arrow struck Xalzorath's wing, detonating in a flash of radiant energy. The force jolted through his massive frame, sending arcs of light crackling along his scales. He snarled, a raw sound of rage and pain mingling in his throat, his flight wavering for the briefest moment.

Xalzorath let out a snarl, a guttural sound that vibrated through the air. His fury igniting the space around him in waves of heat warped the air, distorting the battlefield in a shimmering haze. His massive chest heaved with rage, plumes of smoke curling from his nostrils. His smoldering gaze locked onto Gailen with the intensity of a predator marking its prey.

"You dare to strike me, fledgling?" Xalzorath's voice rumbled, low and ominous, like the first tremors of an earthquake. Shadows flickered around him, the air thickening as if reality itself recoiled from his wrath. His claws flexed, talons gouging the earth below as his tail lashed, his rage barely contained.

Gailen met his gaze unflinchingly, his Crystalbow steady in his hands. "I dare."

Keisha, her focus unbroken, poured more energy into the barrier. The air around her shimmered, crackling with raw power as tendrils of light pulsed outward, reinforcing the magical shield. A faint hum vibrated through the ground beneath her feet, echoing the intensity of her magic. The very earth beneath her glowed softly, a testament to the sheer force she channeled. The energy coursing through her veins burned hot, making her limbs feel sluggish and her vision blur at the edges, draining her reserves faster than she liked, but she pushed on. The barrier had to hold.

"Almost there," she murmured, sweat beading on her brow, her breath ragged from exertion.

Above, the young emerald dragon that had fetched reinforcements dove into the battle again, joining Verdantia in a synchronized assault against Xalzorath. Their combined strikes forced the ancient black dragon to shift his position, exposing a weak spot.

Thalorian seized the opportunity.

With a decisive movement, he channeled the Arborblade's energy into a devastating slash. The blade sang through the air, leaving a streak of emerald light before cutting deep into Xalzorath's flank.

A roar of pure agony tore from the black dragon's throat, reverberating through the battlefield like a shockwave. The ground trembled beneath the force of his pain, sending cracks spidering through the earth. Leaves and debris swirled into the air, and the defenders flinched as the sheer force rattled their bones, their ears ringing from the deafening sound. The defenders flinched, some instinctively covering their ears as the sheer force of Xalzorath's pain rattled their bones.

Xalzorath reared back, his massive wings flaring as he retreated toward the forest's edge.

"They're falling back!" Kaelorn shouted, his voice tight with hope, though his muscles remained tense as if expecting a feint.

Yet, even in retreat, Xalzorath's fury burned. He turned, his molten gaze sweeping over the battlefield, his wounded flank pulsing with dark energy. His tail lashed, gouging deep trenches into the earth as frustration twisted his snarling features.

His voice dripped with venom.

"This is not over. Emerald Woods will burn, and the emerald whelp will fall."

Then, with a final, guttural snarl, he took to the skies, the remaining black dragons following their leader as they vanished into the growing twilight.

With the enemy retreating, the defenders began to regroup.

Thalorian and Verdantia landed together, their bond evident in their synchronized movements. Ong slid down from the tree, his lance still ready in case of a final, desperate attack.

Keisha let out a slow breath, her hands trembling slightly as she released the barrier's hold. The magical dome pulsed one last time before stabilizing, but even then, the weight of the battle pressed upon her shoulders.

"We did it," she murmured, meeting Kaelorn's gaze. "But we'll need more than luck next time."

A powerful downstroke of wings sent a swirl of dust and leaves into the air as Aurelia landed gracefully. The ground trembled slightly beneath her weight as Gailen dismounted, his Crystalbow glowing faintly. He flexed his fingers, still feeling the residual energy from the Crystalbow's power coursing through him. The realization of what he had just done, what they had all done, settled heavily on his chest. A mix of exhilaration and dread coiled within him. They had won this battle, but the weight of leadership pressed harder than ever. The enemy would return more vigorously and more prepared. Was he ready for what came next?

Ong strode forward, brushing off his tunic. Thalorian stepped down from Verdantia's back, his expression unreadable as he rested a hand on the Arborblade's hilt. Kaelorn moved toward the heart of the grove, glancing around at the defenders, his mind already turning toward the next steps.

They exchanged weary but determined looks, the echoes of battle still fresh in their minds.

Keisha brushed back her damp hair, her limbs heavy with exhaustion, the lingering hum of magic still thrumming in her fingertips as if unwilling to fade. The weight of responsibility pressed down on her shoulders, battle tension still thrumming through her veins. She exhaled sharply, then turned to the others, determination flickering in her weary gaze.

"This was too close," she said thoughtfully. "The defenses of Emerald Woods need to be strengthened immediately. The barrier must be ready at a moment's notice."

Thalorian nodded, his grip tightening on the Arborblade. "Keisha's right. We cannot afford to be caught off guard again. Xalzorath is relentless, and next time, he will strike harder."

Ong furrowed his brow, crossing his arms. His mind drifted back to another forest battle.

"In Purplefire Woods," he began, his voice thoughtful, "Amara used the forest itself against Glaciera and her dragons. She called upon the ancient trees and the land to turn the tide." He looked around at the towering trees of Emerald Woods. "Could we do something similar here?"

Verdantia tilted her great head, her emerald eyes shimmering with intrigue. "The forests of Vacari are alive, each with its spirit. Emerald Woods is no exception. It may not be exactly like Purplefire, but if we work together, we can awaken its defenses."

Kaelorn's eyes lit with understanding. He stepped forward eagerly. "The fae have long preserved the harmony of this place. If we amplify that connection with the help of the emerald dragons, we could create something even more potent."

Keisha's mind raced, the beginnings of a plan forming.

"If we merge the fae's magic with the emerald dragons' strength," she said, her voice thoughtful but urgent, "we could create an enchantment that binds the forest to the barrier. That way, any attack would meet resistance from both the magic and the land itself."

Silence fell over the group as they considered the possibility of a strategy that could not just defend Emerald Woods but empower it.

And this time, when Xalzorath returned...

They would be ready.

Ong's expression grew serious. "And if anyone knows how to make a forest fight back, it's you, Keisha."

Keisha let out a short laugh, shaking her head. "I suppose I have a habit of turning nature into a weapon."

She rolled her eyes but could not suppress the small smile tugging at her lips. "It is worth a try. What do you think, Verdantia?"

The emerald dragon lowered her head, her piercing gaze meeting Keisha's. "It is a wise plan. Emerald Woods has slumbered for centuries, its power untapped. If we awaken that power and weave it into the barrier's magic, it will become a formidable defense."

Standing beside Aurelia, Gailen spoke up. "How long will it take? We do not know how much time we have before the next attack."

Keisha exchanged a look with Kaelorn, urgency flashing in their eyes.

"If we start immediately," Kaelorn said, both urgent and determined, "we could have the initial enchantments in place within a few days. Strengthening them further would take longer, but it should be enough to hold off another skirmish."

Ong nodded, his stance firm. "Fae, mages, all hands on deck."

A sense of unity filled the air as the group moved to carry out their tasks.

The bonds between them, dragon, rider, fae, and human, seemed to solidify as if the forest acknowledged their resolve.

The leaves whispered in the breeze above, rustling like a hushed chorus of determination.

The scent of damp earth and wildflowers clung to the air, weaving with the sharp, electric tang of magic a reminder that nature and power stood side by side in defiance.

Keisha turned to Gailen and Aurelia, her tone decisive. "Gailen, can you work with Aurelia to bring more mages and crystal dragons to Emerald Woods? We need their help."

Gailen met her gaze and nodded. "We'll leave immediately."

Verdantia lifted her wings slightly, addressing the group. "I will guide the emerald dragons in awakening the forest's defenses. Kaelorn, will the fae assist?"

Kaelorn bowed slightly. "With everything we have."

Keisha's expression softened as she looked around at her allies, their faces set with determination. "We have come this far together. Emerald Woods will be lost if we fail, but we won't fail."

Kaelorn and the fae moved toward the heart of the woods, their voices murmuring spells as they attuned themselves to the land.

Ong secured his weapons, his sharp eyes scanning the treetops for the best vantage points.

Keisha and Verdantia exchanged a final glance, already mapping out the following steps to fortify their defenses.

A low, thrumming energy pulsed through the roots and branches, sending a faint vibration through the ground beneath their feet. The air crackled with latent magic, raising the hairs on their arms as if the forest was awakening, readying for war.

Aurelia turned to Verdantia, her crystalline eyes filled with urgency. "Before we go, I need to share a suggestion from Kimras." Her voice was measured but firm. "He believes we should mix our forces emerald and crystal dragons in both locations. The obsidian and black dragons will coordinate their attacks to try and destroy Crystal Vale and Emerald Woods simultaneously."

Verdantia tilted her head thoughtfully, her emerald scales gleaming as she shifted. "Kimras's wisdom is unparalleled. A united front will make us stronger. I will send word to my emerald dragons to coordinate with the crystal dragons. Together, we will ensure both territories are fortified."

Aurelia nodded. "Then we must go now. Every moment matters."

Gailen and Aurelia launched into the sky, their forms cutting through the air as they set out to gather reinforcements.

Keisha's gaze swept across the towering trees surrounding them, the weight of the recent battle still pressing on her mind. They had fought hard, but it had been too close. She exhaled, steeling herself before speaking. "We also need a better early warning system." The current setup is not fast enough, especially against dragons that move as quickly as these."

She paused, then continued, her mind already racing with possibilities. "A magical sentinel, enchanted to attune itself to the pulse of the forest, could detect disturbances long before an enemy arrives, giving us time to respond."

Kaelorn nodded, his expression serious. "That is an excellent idea. The fae can enchant the sentinel with detection magic, anchoring it to the forest's natural energy. It will work seamlessly with the barrier."

Ong crossed his arms, a grin tugging at the corner of his mouth. "Leave it to Keisha to think of something like that. A magical early warning? Brilliant."

Keisha rolled her eyes, though a faint smile crossed her lips. "It is practical, Ong, not brilliant. We cannot afford to be caught off guard again."

Verdantia turned to the assembled group, her voice steady, resonating with determination. "We have much to do, but we are not alone. With the fae, the dragons, and our allies working together, Emerald Woods will not fall."

A murmur of agreement rippled through the group, their expressions a mix of resolve and determination.

The air around them seemed to hum with purpose, as if the forest recognized their unity and lent its silent strength to their cause.

The light filtering through the canopy shone brighter, casting shifting patterns across the forest floor.

A quiet promise that Emerald Woods would not fall without a fight.

Chapter 38

Strength in Unity

In Crystal Vale's radiant morning light, the air buzzed with an urgency that had become the city's new normal. Preparations to enhance the city's defenses were in full swing. Craftsmen reinforced barricades, mages enchanted protective wards, and scouts sharpened their weapons for the battles ahead. The city's atmosphere crackled with anticipation. The recent skirmishes had left lingering tension, but they also galvanized the people into action, each resident determined to protect their home.

Prince Gailen strode purposefully through the palace corridors, but briefly, he slowed his steps, his fingers clenching at his sides. A shadow of doubt flickered across his face before he exhaled sharply, steadying himself. The weight of responsibility pressed against his chest, the echoes of past decisions lingering in his mind. Doubt threatened to creep in. Was he indeed prepared for what lay ahead? The memory of his near failure in Emerald Woods haunted him, the hesitation almost costing lives. Had he learned enough? Had he grown strong enough to ensure it would not happen again? He exhaled sharply, pushing the uncertainty aside, and resumed his determined pace, heading to speak with his father, King Manard. His mind replayed the events of the attack on Emerald Woods and the recommendations made by Kimras. While Aurelia and Verdantia were now aligned to bolster defenses, there was still much to do. He trusted his team, but a nagging unease clung to him. What if the dark dragons shifted their strategy? What if they were not prepared for the right kind of attack? Dismissing the thought, he pressed forward, his jaw set with determination.

In the palace, Gailen stood before his father, recounting the attack on Emerald Woods. King Manard listened intently, his hands clasped tightly together. His face grew stern as Gailen detailed the coordinated efforts of the Black Dragons and their leader, Xalzorath.

"We cannot ignore their tactics, Father," Gailen said firmly. "They are testing us, probing our weaknesses. We must ensure they find none."

King Manard exhaled deeply, his gaze fixed on the Vacari map on the wall. The map was a sprawling testament to the kingdom's history, with inked battle routes, defensive strongholds, and key trade paths. Faint etchings of past conflicts ran along their borders, a silent reminder of the struggles that had shaped their land. It was more than a strategy tool; it was the record of a kingdom's survival. The map, marked with faded ink and battle-worn annotations, had witnessed every significant campaign—a silent testament to the kingdom's struggles and victories. It was more than a chart of land; it was a history of survival, a reminder of the cost of complacency.

"Emerald Woods holds against the Black Dragons, and Crystal Vale must stand as its counterpart against the Obsidian. But this requires more than just defense. Our people must be prepared to fight—should the worst come."

"That is why I came to you," Gailen replied. "I have spoken with Aurelia, and we are making progress. The towers have warning systems, and the mages train with the Crystal Dragons to fortify the barrier. But we need more. Supplies, reinforcements... and your support."

King Manard rose and placed a hand on Gailen's shoulder. "You have my support, my son. I will do all I can to ensure Crystal Vale remains strong. Keep me informed of every step."

Gailen nodded, a sense of determination flooding him. The doubt that had clung to him moments ago dissipated, replaced by the steady resolve of a leader who knew the weight of his choices. This was his path, and he would walk it without hesitation. He felt the weight of responsibility settle on his shoulders, yet it no longer felt daunting. It felt like purpose. Every decision, every action from this moment on carried the fate of their kingdom. He would not falter. "I will, Father. Together, we will protect Vacari."

Ong and Valeon, meanwhile, stood at the base of one of the farthest towers. Valeon shifted nervously, the tools in his hands clinking as he adjusted his grip. "So, we are just... putting these in the towers? That is it?" Valeon asked, tilting his head at the intricate magical warning device.

Ong's expression remained focused as he began climbing the tower's stone steps, his dragon lance, his trusted weapon, strapped securely to his back. His movements were measured and confident, each step revealing the ease of someone accustomed to such tasks. Years of working with dragons and fortifications had honed his instincts, which showed calm precision in his actions. "Not 'just' putting them in, Valeon. These warning systems are enchanted to detect dark dragon movements within the region. They are sensitive, precise, and our first line of defense. So, no mistakes."

Valeon sighed, trailing Ong up the stairs. He hesitated before speaking again, gripping the railing tighter. "You make it sound so... simple. But what if the enchantment fails? Or?"

"Then we'll fix it," Ong cut him off, his voice steady. "That's why we are installing multiple layers of warnings across the Vale. Redundancy. You will learn that's key in situations like these."

As they reached the top, Ong unlatched the first device from its protective case. Valeon watched in awe as the glyphs on the crystal sphere shimmered with an ethereal glow. His breath caught slightly, and this was not just another mundane tool; it pulsed with power. "See this? It reacts to specific frequencies tied to the Obsidian and Black Dragons. If they approach Crystal Vale, even subtly, this will activate."

Valeon leaned closer, his curiosity overcoming his unease. For the first time, he saw the intricate magic behind Crystal Vale's defenses not as an abstract concept but as something tangible, something he could help protect. The weight of responsibility shifted from daunting to exhilarating. His fingers steadied against the cool stone railing, and he took a slow, deliberate breath, grounding himself in the moment. His breath hitched, and a cold bead of sweat trailed down his temple. The device's glow cast eerie reflections in his wide eyes, the weight of responsibility settling heavily on his chest like an unseen force. His breath hitched slightly, and his fingers twitched against his side as he fought the lingering tension in his chest. "And... what does it do? Just sound an alarm?"

Ong nodded, carefully placing the device in a recessed slot designed for it. "An alarm, yes, but it also sends out a signal to our forces. This is not just for the city; it ties directly to the dragons Aurelia and the others. The moment it is triggered, they will know."

Valeon's eyes widened, his fingers twitching at his side. A mix of awe and trepidation swirled within him, and this was more than just a tool; it symbolized responsibility. Doubts gnawed at the edges of his confidence. Could he genuinely rise to the challenge? He exhaled slowly, willing himself to focus. Yet, beneath his uncertainty, a flicker of determination sparked, urging him forward. "That's incredible," he murmured with a hint of wonder. For a moment, he imagined himself as more than a hesitant bystander capable of meaningfully contributing to Crystal Vale's defenses.

The faint hum of the installed device followed them like a reassuring whisper, a low vibration that resonated through the stone beneath their feet. It pulsed in a steady rhythm, neither harsh nor overpowering but present enough to be a constant reminder of the silent vigilance now guarding

Crystal Vale. Above them, the skies remained clear, but the memory of the obsidian shadow lingered in both their minds. A sudden gust of wind rustled through the trees, carrying a distant, echoing whisper, an eerie reminder of the danger that loomed just beyond their sight, urging them forward. They could still see it in their thoughts: the massive, winged silhouette blotting out the sun and the chilling roar that had sent even the bravest warriors to their knees. Its presence had been an attack, a warning, a promise of the destruction that would come if they faltered. It had first appeared during the attack on Emerald Woods, a dark omen that sent shockwaves through their defenses. The shadow's presence had sown chaos and fear, a stark reminder of the enemy's growing strength and cunning.

As the sun dipped lower in the sky, casting a warm amber glow over Crystal Vale, Ong and Valeon returned from their tower installations. Their muscles ached from the long hours of labor, and sweat clung to their brows, but there was a quiet satisfaction in their steps. Ong shot Valeon a glance, offering a brief nod of approval. Valeon hesitated momentarily before nodding back, the silent exchange carrying the weight of shared effort and growing camaraderie. The tension of the day's work still lingered in their minds, a reminder of the weight of their task. But the knowledge that they had strengthened Crystal Vale's defenses gave them a renewed sense of purpose, filling them with quiet satisfaction. Their steps were steady but purposeful, and their task was completed with a sense of accomplishment.

As they neared the central square, they spotted Keisha standing at the head of a group of mages near the training grounds. Her presence was commanding yet calm, her voice blending wisdom and determination. She folded her arms, her gaze unwavering as she studied the gathered mages, a quiet confidence radiating from her stance.

"Understanding the connection between your magic and the dragons is not just a lesson; it's a necessity," Keisha explained, her tone measured and firm, her voice carrying the weight of experience. She met each mage's gaze with steady resolve, her stance strong yet composed, exuding an authority that instilled trust and expectation. A slight tilt of her chin and the firm set of her shoulders reinforced her authority, exuding a presence that demanded attention and respect. Her words drew a mix of determined nods and hesitant glances, the gravity of her lesson settling upon them like an unspoken challenge. Some seemed inspired, their postures straightening with resolve, while others exchanged nervous looks, the weight of her statement sinking in. She gestured toward one of the Crystal Dragons that rested nearby. "When the time comes to strengthen the barriers or defend this city, the energy between your magic and theirs could mean the difference between success and failure."

Valeon slowed his pace, his attention drawn to her words about the deep connection between magic and the dragons. A strange sensation stirred within him, like a whisper in the back of his mind, urging him to listen more closely. The air around him felt charged, as if the very magic Keisha spoke of was subtly responding to his presence. For the first time, he wondered if magic was something he had never truly understood. His fingers curled slightly at his sides, and he exhaled slowly as if steadying himself against an invisible force. The idea of magic as something living, something reciprocal, sent him a ripple of unease and intrigue. A flicker of longing stirred within him. Was that the key he had been missing? He had always viewed magic as a tool, a force to be harnessed, but never as something living, something reciprocal. The way she spoke of it as if it were not just a skill but a bond forged through trust made him question everything he thought he understood. He stopped out of earshot, nudging Ong lightly and whispering, "Is she always this confident?"

Ong paused, a small smile flickering across his lips, his eyes momentarily distant as he recalled a memory long buried but never faded. He remembered how Keisha had once stood at the edge of despair, stripped of her magic and skill with the bow. He had watched her struggle and fight to reclaim what had been stolen from her. Through relentless training, sheer determination, and the unwavering support of those who believed in her, she had risen again stronger, wiser, and unbreakable. His fingers flexed slightly at his side, betraying the weight of past struggles, yet the warmth in his expression spoke of pride, not just in Keisha but in the journey that had led her to this moment. ""Now she is," Ong said, his voice quiet but steady—laced with pride and something sharper beneath. "But it wasn't always like that. After what Vuarus and Phoenix did to her... she didn't just lose her magic. She lost her confidence, her aim, the fire that made her who she was. She doubted everything—her strength, her purpose, even whether she still belonged at all."

He paused, jaw tightening slightly. "But Keisha doesn't stay down. With the help of those who stood by her, she fought her way back. Every bit of strength you see in her now—she earned it."

His gaze met Valeon's. "That confidence? It wasn't handed to her. She bled for it. Trained for it. Faced battle after battle, proving not just to others, but to herself, that she was still whole—still powerful. And no one's taking that from her again."

Valeon nodded thoughtfully, his gaze still fixed on Keisha. "She makes it look so natural."

"Because she believes in what she's doing," Ong said. "That is what makes her strong. But do not mistake that confidence for a lack of challenges. She has been through more than most, and every step she has taken has shaped the leader you see now."

Valeon gave a slight nod of understanding, his usual playfulness giving way to a rare moment of reflection. He realized that confidence was not granted but forged through trials and perseverance. Keisha had fought to reclaim her strength, and perhaps, in time, he could do the same. Together, they resumed their walk, weaving through the busy square as the preparations for Crystal Vale's defenses continued.

As they passed Keisha and her group of mages, Ong glanced over and gave her a small wave of acknowledgment. She caught his eye briefly, her lips curving into a faint smile before returning to the mages.

"Alright," she said to them, her voice clear and steady. "Let us practice. Reach out to the dragon nearest to you. Start by focusing on its presence, then extend your magic toward it like an offering. Let it guide you as much as you guide it."

Valeon turned to Ong once more as they walked away. "You think she'd teach me that someday?" he asked, half-joking.

Ong chuckled. "You? Only if you learn to sit still long enough."

Valeon grinned, rolling his eyes in mock exasperation, nudging Ong lightly in the ribs as he did. "I suppose miracles can happen," he quipped, his tone playful but tinged with curiosity.

They both laughed, their spirits lighter as they made their way toward the next task, yet beneath the humor lingered an unspoken tension. The weight of what was coming pressed at the edges of their thoughts, a silent reminder that these moments of levity were fleeting in the shadow of what lay ahead. The shadow of war loomed, but at that moment, Crystal Vale felt like a city brimming with hope and strength, the distant clang of metal on metal and the rhythmic chants of mages blending into a resolute symphony. Valeon inhaled deeply, the scent of burning incense and fresh parchment filling the air, grounding him in the moment. He closed his eyes briefly, steadying his breath, letting the familiar scents anchor him amid the uncertainty. He silently wondered if this was how warriors of old had felt before battle, poised between fear and unwavering determination, fortified by its walls and the bonds of those who defended it.

As the last rays of sunlight bathed Crystal Vale in a golden glow, Prince Gailen emerged from the palace, his expression thoughtful yet resolute. He spotted Ong and Valeon approaching from the training grounds, their strides purposeful after completing their duties.

"Ong," Gailen greeted, "how did the installations go?"

Ong gave a slight nod. "The warning systems are in place. If the obsidian dragons approach, the towers will alert us in time to prepare."

Gailen exhaled a breath of relief, his gaze sweeping across the bustling square. He took in the determined faces around him, the way people moved with urgency yet purpose. Despite the looming battle, the city stood resilient, its people unwilling to falter. He knew that every decision he made would shape their fate, and that weight pressed against his chest, a constant reminder of his responsibility. The scent of burning torches and freshly sharpened steel mingled with the crisp evening air. At the same time, the rhythmic clang of hammers and the murmur of determined voices filled the space, a testament to the city's unwavering resolve. The town was alive with preparations, every corner filled with determined figures fortifying Crystal Vale's defenses. "Good. We are as ready as we can be."

His eyes landed on Valeon, his gaze sharp yet unreadable, a quiet intensity behind it. Valeon shifted slightly under his scrutiny, feeling expectations settle over him like an unseen force. Gailen turned fully toward him. "Valeon," he began, his tone thoughtful yet firm, "I have a special task for you when the dragons attack in full force."

Valeon blinked, stumbling back as if Gailen's words had knocked the breath from his lungs. His arms folded across his chest in a defensive reflex, as though shielding himself from a blow that hadn't landed yet. His stance shifted—unsteady, uncertain as the weight of expectation bore down on him.

A tightness seized his chest. He drew in a breath, but it caught halfway, shallow and sharp. Cold sweat formed at his temples, and his fingers twitched at his sides, a silent betrayal of the rising storm within.

He was a slight-built human, young, with sharp but forgettable features that faded easily beside the bolder figures around him. His dark, unruly hair fell into anxious blue-gray eyes, which flicked about as he dragged a hand through it—a habit that surfaced whenever he felt cornered. Dressed in plain, practical clothes suited to life in Crystal Vale, he still looked like someone who didn't quite belong among warriors and mages—especially now.

"Me?" he stammered, his voice tinged with disbelief. "What can I do? I cannot fly a dragon; I am a poor fighter. I cannot do anything important."

Gailen smiled gently, shaking his head. "Every task is important, no matter what it is. Whether fighting on the front lines or aiding the wounded, every role plays a part in securing victory." During the battle, I need someone I trust to assist the wounded. Tending to them and ensuring they get to safety can save lives."

Valeon stared at him, swallowing hard as he absorbed the weight of Gailen's words. For a moment, he seemed unsure, his usual carefree demeanor replaced with a rare glimpse of vulnerability. Finally, he straightened slightly, nodding. "I... I would be honored if you could trust me with this," he said, quiet but resolute.

Ong clapped Valeon on the back, a wide grin breaking through his usual composed and serious exterior, a rare glimpse of the warmth he often kept hidden. Valeon tensed at first, his eyes widening in surprise. He had not expected to be entrusted with anything. The thought of responsibility unsettled him, but as he met Ong's encouraging gaze, a flicker of acceptance settled in. He let out a small, breathy laugh, the tension in his shoulders easing slightly. The weight of responsibility still loomed over him, but at that moment, he felt a spark of reassurance, a reminder that he was not alone in this fight. "Good. It is settled." He turned to Gailen. "Now, we should head to Emerald Woods and see if there is more we can do there. If Emerald Woods falls, Crystal Vale will become more vulnerable."

Gailen nodded, his gaze serious, though a shadow of doubt flickered in his mind. He had prepared as best he could, but the uncertainty of war weighed heavily. Every choice carried consequences, and while he believed in their strategy, he could not ignore the possibility of unforeseen challenges.

He thought of his father, the lessons of leadership instilled in him, and the countless warriors who had stood where he now stood, bearing the weight of an entire kingdom. His mind lingered on the battles that had come before, the hard-won victories etched into the history of Vacari. The responsibility was immense, but he could not afford to falter.

For a moment, he allowed himself a fleeting thought about how much rested on their shoulders, how many lives depended on their success. Shaking off the weight of doubt, he steadied himself with a resolve that burned brighter than his fears. "You are right. Let's go."

Chapter 39
The Forest Awakens

The trio arrived at Emerald Forest, where sunlight filtered through dense emerald canopies, casting an otherworldly glow over the landscape. The air hummed with latent magic, carrying the scent of damp earth and blooming flora as if the forest hesitated to awaken, still scarred by past destruction. Once vibrant and teeming with life, it had been shattered, and now it struggled to reconnect with its history, its magic hesitant, as if unsure whether to trust again. The once-vibrant energy seemed tangled as if waiting for a familiar presence or a forgotten melody to stir it from its deep repose.

Kaelorn stood in a clearing, his presence steady and assured as he directed the fairies with precise gestures and composed words. The faint rustle of their delicate wings filled the air, accompanied by a soft, melodic hum that shimmered like stardust. Their glow pulsed gently with each movement, weaving light patterns through the clearing as they responded to his commands. His eyes narrowed slightly in concentration, his fingers moving with practiced ease as he orchestrated their efforts, ensuring each note of their melody was in harmony with the forest's energy. Now and then, his fingers brushed against the rough bark of an ancient tree as if drawing strength from its deep roots. His gaze lingered on the forest, his connection to the land evident in how he moved, attuned to its rhythms and the slumbering power beneath its surface.

The fairies danced around him, iridescent wings catching the light as their songs drifted through the air like a whispering breeze, echoing the forest's slow pulse. Kaelorn paused now and then to exchange quiet nods with the young emerald dragons resting among the boughs, their golden-green scales glinting between the leaves. His calm presence grounded the gathering, a silent testament to the bond he shared with both fairies and dragons.

The dragons occasionally rumbled low, a sound more felt than heard, while the fairies flitted through the canopy, leaving faint trails of light as their music tried to coax the forest awake. Yet the magic remained dim—flickering briefly, then vanishing like breath on glass. The air hung heavy, laced with a reluctance that spoke not of resistance, but of weariness. As though the ancient enchantments slumbering in the trees needed more than song or light. They needed presence. Power. Something long lost to stir them fully again.

Kaelorn looked up as Ong, Gailen, and Valeon approached. His expression was grim but hopeful, though a flicker of unease lingered in his gaze. The weight of responsibility pressed heavily on his shoulders—so much depended on rekindling the forest's magic. He exhaled slowly, steadying himself before speaking. "You've come at the right time," he said. "We're trying to wake the forest's magic to aid in our defense, but it's proving more difficult than expected. It seems reluctant, perhaps too long dormant."

Gailen frowned, taking in the scene. "What do you need from us?"

Kaelorn hesitated for a moment before his gaze settled on Ong. "Keisha has a way with magic, especially with nature. I believe her presence might be the key. Could you contact her?"

Before Ong could answer, a young emerald dragon leaped down from its perch and stepped forward, its scales gleaming like polished jade. "I will go," the dragon offered, its voice youthful but determined. "I can reach her quickly."

Kaelorn nodded, gratitude flickering in his eyes. He understood better than most that Keisha's magic was deeply connected to the forests, her presence like a bridge between the land's dormant power and the awakening it needed. If anyone could coax the magic back to life, it was her. "Thank you. Tell her that we need her guidance desperately."

With a quick nod, the dragon spread its wings and took off, the powerful beats creating a gust that ruffled the leaves below. The group watched it disappear into the horizon, a small but vital hope carried on its wing.

Ong returned to the forest, surveying the towering trees that formed their natural defenses. Their thick, interwoven canopies created an almost impenetrable shield, while their massive roots anchored the land, forming natural barriers against intruders. The enchantments lingering within their bark pulsed faintly, remnants of ancient wards designed to repel unwelcome forces. "We can't just sit idle. The magical sentinels need to be installed while we wait." His eyes scanned the canopy, landing on several towering trees at the forest's edge. "Those are perfect. If we place sentinels on all of them, we'll cover the widest range possible."

Valeon tilted his head back, tracing the massive trunks that stretched endlessly skyward, their towering forms a testament to the forest's age and resilience. The rough texture of the bark, ancient and weathered, stood as a testament to the forest's long history. A faint rustling of leaves echoed above as if whispering secrets of the past to those who dared to listen. A deep awe settled over him, making him feel insignificant and inspired. The sheer scale of the trees reminded him of his limitations. Yet, simultaneously, something about their towering presence filled him with a quiet determination and an urge to prove himself worthy of standing among those who had already earned their place in this fight. "All of them?" he asked, a note of doubt creeping into his voice. "That is... ambitious."

Ong grinned, clapping Valeon on the back. Valeon let out a small chuckle, but the lingering doubt in his eyes betrayed his uncertainty. Still, he straightened his shoulders slightly as if trying to embrace Ong's confidence. "Ambitious, yes. Necessary. Each one increases our chances of detecting any attack before it reaches the forest's heart."

Gailen nodded in agreement, his expression resolute. "Then let's get started. The sooner we set these up, the better prepared we'll be."

As the three began their task, the fairies continued their efforts, their songs growing louder and more intricate, while Kaelorn orchestrated their coordination. The young emerald dragons observed the proceedings with keen interest, their gazes flickering toward the sky now and then, anticipating the return of their messenger with Keisha.

Ong climbed to the first tree, securing the magical sentinel with practiced ease. The magic-infused device pulsed faintly as it contacted the bark, its energy weaving into the ancient wood like a whispered incantation. The tree seemed to respond, its aura shifting slightly as the enchantment took hold, reinforcing the protective wards that had lain dormant for so long. The thick bark was rough beneath his fingers, and as he reached for a secure hold, a brittle branch snapped unexpectedly, nearly causing him to lose his balance. He exhaled sharply, adjusting his grip before pressing forward, the minor setback only adding to his determination to complete the task. Below, Valeon worked diligently on another tree, his usual air of uncertainty replaced with quiet focus. Gailen, ever the leader, moved swiftly between them, ensuring the sentinels were correctly aligned to create an effective network.

As the final sentinel was secured, Ong descended from his tree, wiping sweat from his brow. "That should do it," he said, satisfaction evident in his tone. "Now we wait for Keisha and see if she can work her magic."

Moments later, the sound of rustling leaves and faint footsteps signaled Keisha's arrival, her presence immediately bringing a calming focus to the chaotic efforts in Emerald Woods. The fairies and dragons turned toward her, some smiling knowingly, and all had heard of her unique connection to the forests. Her emerald eyes swept over the scene, taking in the young jade-scaled dragons, the struggling fairies, and the subdued magic of the forest. The air carried the scent of damp earth and blooming flora, mingling with the faint, whispering hum of lingering enchantments. She approached Kaelorn with a steady purpose.

Kaelorn stepped forward, inclining his head respectfully. "Keisha, we're doing everything possible to wake the forest, but it's resisting. We need your guidance. Your magic might be what's missing."

Keisha gave a soft chuckle, shaking her head at his earnestness. He meant well, but there were still pieces he hadn't seen. "My magic can help," she said gently, "but it's not the kind of help you need." She looked upward toward the thick canopy. "This is Amara's domain as much as the emerald dragons'. You need her wisdom to awaken the forest's true power."

Kaelorn blinked. "Amara?" he asked, the name unfamiliar.

Keisha turned back to him, her expression softening. "You'll understand when she arrives. Trust me—if anyone can stir the heart of this forest, it's her."

Ong let out a quiet sigh, running a hand through his hair as realization struck. "Of course! I should have thought of that." Without hesitation, he pulled out a small enchanted stone used for communication. He activated it and called out to Amara. Within moments, her melodic yet commanding voice resonated through the stone.

"I hear you, Ong," Amara's voice came through, warm yet resolute. "I am on my way. Tell them to hold fast until I arrive."

Ong looked up, a relieved grin spreading across his face. "She is coming."

Keisha gave a slight nod of approval before turning her attention to the fairies, who had gathered nearby, their glowing forms flickering with anticipation. "Even with Amara's help and the dragons working to-gether, you'll need more strength to maintain a barrier. The forest is vast, and the enemy will exploit every weakness."

One of the fairies, a delicate figure with shimmering wings and a voice like tinkling bells, fluttered closer. "We know," she said, her tone tinged with concern. "If we wake the forest, the barrier will draw from its magic, weakening us. We will need more help to sustain it."

Keisha frowned thoughtfully, her gaze drifting toward a nearby glade. She considered the allies who might be able to aid them—per-haps the elder dryads who once tended to these woods or the guardian spirits rumored to slumber beneath the roots. If the forest had yet to awaken fully, they perhaps needed to call upon those who had once nurtured it, those whose presence could rekindle its ancient power. Sunlight filtered through the canopy, illuminating the clearing with an almost ethereal glow, shifting as the leaves swayed gently in the breeze, casting ever-changing patterns across the forest floor. The air carried the faint scent of moss and wildflowers, and a quiet energy pulsed beneath the surface as if the land held an unspoken memory waiting to be unlocked. She took a slow breath, letting her thoughts settle before addressing the group. "Then we'll find the help you need." She turned and began walking toward the glade, her movements purposefully yet measured.

The glade, bathed in dappled sunlight and alive with the whispers of unseen creatures, seemed to embrace her presence. A soft hum of magic stirred in the air, the leaves quivering as if responding to her arrival. Tiny motes of golden light drifted from the branches, lingering briefly before vanishing into the air as if the forest were stirring awake. Keisha stood in the center, a flicker of hope igniting in her chest, her hands resting lightly on her hips as her mind raced through possibilities. The answer was in the intricate tapestry of allies and magic woven across Vacari. She just needed to find the right thread to pull.

She inhaled deeply, reaching out with her senses, feeling the pulse of the forest beneath her fingertips. Something stirred, faint but undeniable, as if the land had begun to listen. A shift in the air sent a ripple through the clearing, a gentle current of awakening magic.

"Can you sense it?" Ong asked, his voice quiet but firm. Gailen nodded, his expression a mix of awe and curiosity. "It's... alive. It feels like something has awakened like the forest is breathing."

As Amara arrived, her radiant form descended into the clearing, and a shimmering wave of energy rippled outward from her. She spread her wings wide, releasing an amethyst fire cascading through the canopy, igniting dormant runes hidden within the trees. Ancient symbols flickered to life, pulsing in rhythm with the dragon's presence as the energy flowed through the trees like a forgotten melody, awakening an ancient spirit. The air seemed to vibrate with newfound life as vines straightened, flowers unfurled, and the emerald glow of the leaves deepened.

She turned her keen gaze toward Gailen. Her amethyst eyes sparkled with an ancient wisdom as she addressed him. "You are perceptive, young prince," she said, her voice a melodic blend of strength and warmth. "The forest has always been alive, but like all living things, it needed a purpose, a purpose to rise and defend itself. Now it knows. It understands the threat and its role to protect not just its existence but also the inhabitants of Emerald Woods and beyond, including Crystal Vale."

Her words lingered, and the air seemed to shift as they did. The glow of the leaves intensified, their edges shimmering with a renewed vibrance, while the ground pulsed faintly beneath their feet, attuned to her magic. Gailen exhaled slowly, his fingers flexing at his sides as if grasping the enormity of what had just been spoken. Keisha held her breath, the weight of responsibility settling over them. The fairies hovered closer, their wings vibrating in hushed reverence, while the young dragons shifted their stances, their tails flicking with newfound determination. A hush fell over the clearing. Warriors squared their shoulders, fairies drifted in silent reverence, and young dragons rumbled in quiet acknowledgment.

Valeon stared in awe, his breath catching as he took in Amara's regal presence. He had heard of her power and wisdom but seeing her now—radiant and commanding—was something else entirely. She didn't just arrive; she *resonated*. A quiet reverence stirred within him, mingling with the thrill of witnessing history unfold before his eyes.

In that moment, he understood true leadership wasn't about dominance, but guidance, presence, and unwavering purpose. Magic wasn't merely an external force—it was a bond, a responsibility. To those who wielded it, and to those who depended on it. The realization left him both awed and humbled.

"She's magnificent," he murmured, barely above a whisper.

"She truly is," Kaelorn agreed softly, standing beside him. His eyes were wide with wonder, reflecting the glow of Amara's scales as they caught the filtered light. It was his first glimpse of her, and already he felt the weight of her presence stir something ancient in the forest—and in himself.

Ong nudged Valeon with a teasing grin. "Careful, you two. You'll have her thinking she's royalty."

Amara turned her attention to Ong, her eyes twinkling with mischief. "As for you, Ong Swifthammer," she said with a playful lilt, "I couldn't help but overhear your earlier... assessment of me."

Ong's eyes widened slightly, a sheepish grin forming as he cleared his throat. "I stand by it," he said, trying to maintain composure.

"Good," she replied, her tone affectionate beneath the tease. Her gaze slid to Keisha, who stood nearby with a knowing smile. "I'm pleased to make an impression. I'd expect nothing less. But remember, Ong—flattery only gets you so far."

Then came a deep, melodic rumble—Amara's laughter, warm and unmistakably draconic.

She stepped forward, lowering her head to the earth, and exhaled a slow, deliberate breath. A soft mist of energy spread outward, weaving into the roots of the trees. Their trunks shivered in response, resonating with a deep, awakening hum. As if answering her call, the forest shed its lingering weariness. Magic surged to the surface.

Satisfied, Amara spread her wings. The amethyst glow of her scales shimmered in the dappled sunlight as she prepared for flight. Her presence pulsed through the woods, stirring the very earth. Leaves glistened with renewed luminescence, and the air thrummed with magic—alive, alert, and ready.

"I must return to Purplefire Woods," she announced. "There are preparations to be made there as well. But know this—Emerald Woods is awake, and it will not fall easily."

With that, she launched into the sky, her mighty wings churning the air as she ascended. The group watched her go, her radiant form vanishing into the distance.

Valeon exhaled slowly, his mind still turning over the weight of her words. Keisha folded her arms, a determined smile playing at her lips as the renewed energy of the forest surged around them. Gailen, ever the strategist, turned his gaze to the horizon, already calculating what needed to be done next.

Though Amara had gone, her presence lingered, woven into the very air—a quiet promise. The forest hummed with her parting breath, alive with purpose, prepared to stand against the coming dark.

Yet even as the trees embraced their awakening, an unfamiliar presence approached—bearing an offering for the dragon riders.

Chapter 40
Warriors of Emerald Woods

The air was thick with anticipation as an unfamiliar noise stirred through the trees. The warriors stiffened, hands instinctively moving toward their weapons. The dragons lifted their heads, their sharp eyes scanning the surroundings, while the fairies fluttered closer together, sensing the energy shift.

Kaelorn stepped forward, his gaze narrowing as he signaled the fairies to stay behind him. His heart pounded with the weight of responsibility, a silent vow to shield them from whatever threat approached. The flicker of unease in his eyes was fleeting, quickly replaced by the hardened resolve of a warrior who had seen too many battles to take chances. They hesitated briefly, their wings fluttering in rapid bursts, before obeying his command, drawing closer together in a tight formation, their luminous forms flickering with unease. His stance was protective, his presence a shield between them and the unknown. "Stay close," he murmured, his voice calm but firm. "We don't know who or what is coming."

Gailen and Ong exchanged wary glances, their hands tightening around their weapons. Valeon, despite the flicker of unease in his eyes, mirrored their stance, ready to defend if necessary. The clearing, moments before filled with the lingering hum of awakened magic, now bristled with tension.

The rustling in the distance grew louder, a rhythmic shuffle interwoven with the occasional snap of twigs, approaching steadily. Though alive with magic, the forest now held its breath, waiting. The fairies fluttered anxiously, their shimmering wings quivering with nervous energy. Kaelorn tensed, preparing to take a cautious step forward, but figures emerged from the trees as he moved.

Recognition flickered in his eyes as he spotted an elder among the group, their presence a reassuring beacon amidst the tension. His shoulders relaxed. He let out a slow breath before turning to the others. "Stand down," he said, his voice steady yet filled with relief. "It is my people."

The warriors eased their grips on their weapons, and the dragons lowered their heads slightly, their keen eyes studying the newcomers. It was not just the warriors' shift in stance that reassured them but a more profound recognition of an instinctive understanding that these figures were not foes. Still hovering warily, the fairies gradually settled as Kaelorn returned to address them. "They bring no threat. We are among allies."

The Luminara stepped into the clearing, their presence a quiet yet undeniable force. Their footsteps were soft against the forest floor, barely disturbing the carpet of moss beneath them. A subtle shift in the air accompanied their arrival as if the atmosphere acknowledged their presence. As they moved, the fairies fluttered forward to greet them whimsically, dancing in midair, weaving delicate trails of glowing dust, and circling the newcomers with twinkling laughter.

The Luminara smiled, their gazes sweeping over the tiny, luminous beings with admiration and amusement. They took in the fairies' curious energy, their graceful movements adding to the ethereal beauty of the moment.

Gailen stepped forward and bowed respectfully. "Welcome," he said, his voice warm and steady. "We are honored by your presence."

The Luminara returned the gesture with nods of acknowledgment before their gazes drifted toward the dragons. They halted, eyes widening as they took in the majestic creatures before them, their awe evident in their expressions. Yet, as they observed the emerald dragons, a realization settled over them this place was more than they had ever expected. With such noble guardians present, this was not just a place of refuge but a home far more significant than they had anticipated. Their attention flickered toward Kaelorn, seeking silent confirmation of what they saw.

Kaelorn let out a hearty laugh, his eyes twinkling with amusement at the realization dawning on the Luminara. He had purposefully withheld mention of the dragons, relishing the moment of their astonishment. The Luminara exchanged glances among themselves, momentarily processing his words before soft chuckles escaped them. A shared understanding passed between them, and soon, they joined in the laughter, their initial surprise giving way to warmth. "Ah, did I forget to mention the dragons of Emerald Woods?" he asked, his tone light and teasing.

A ripple of laughter spread through the gathered warriors, fairies, and dragons alike. The tension from their arrival dissolved into shared mirth. As they did, Verdantia, the emerald dragon, lifted her head and regarded them with knowing eyes. Her presence alone commanded respect, but as she spoke, her voice carried a deep resonance filled with wisdom and authority, sending a shiver through the Luminara. It was both a welcome and a promise of reassurance that they were safe, yet a reminder of the power that protected this land. Her voice, rich and resonant, filled the space. "Welcome to your new home," she said. "May your purpose here strengthen the bonds between us all."

One of the elders turned to the others and motioned for them to bring forward the bundles they had carried, as Kaelorn requested. With careful hands, the Luminara began laying the packages on the ground, arranging them in neat rows with a sense of reverence.

Keisha glanced at Ong, her brow slightly furrowed in curiosity. Sensing her unspoken question, Ong turned toward Kaelorn. "What is going on?" he asked, his voice laced with intrigue.

Kaelorn gave a small, knowing smile but did not answer immediately. He folded his arms, glancing at the artfully arranged packages before looking back at the group, letting the anticipation build.

Gailen turned to Thalorian, his brow raised in curiosity. He hesitated momentarily before speaking, his voice carrying a note of uncertainty. "Do you know what this is about?" he asked.

Thalorian shook his head, crossing his arms. "I'm in the dark just like everyone else," he admitted, his gaze fixed on the bundles with quiet intrigue.

I noticed something after Gailen's training," Kaelorn began, his gaze shifting toward the young prince. "Your hands bore the marks of your efforts, the strain of guiding your dragon, of wielding a weapon while riding. It gave me an idea that might aid you and all dragon riders. However, the idea grew even more as I considered it further."

The Luminara finished bringing in all the packages and stepped back as they completed their task. Kaelorn stood there for a few moments, his smile lingering as the anticipation grew. He let curiosity settle over the group before the final package was placed on the ground. He motioned toward Gailen and Ong, "Go on, open one."

Gailen and Ong exchanged glances before stepping forward. With careful hands, they untied the bindings and peeled back the covering. As the fabric fell away, their breath caught in their throats. Inside lay beautifully crafted dragon rider armor and gloves, each piece intricately designed, etched with ancient symbols, and infused with a subtle, shifting glow that hinted at deep enchantments. The armor was form-fitting, adapting seamlessly to the wearer's body type, ensuring comfort and mobility without sacrificing protection. A lump formed in Gailen's throat, and Ong exhaled sharply, his fingers tightening briefly around the edge of the armor. He blinked rapidly, his usual composure wavering as the moment's weight settled over him, their emotions threatening to overwhelm them.

Kaelorn's voice was warm, carrying a note of pride as he continued.

He turned to the assembled dragon riders, and his expression filled with anticipation. "Each of you, open a package," he instructed. "The fairies must enhance the armor before it is fully ready. The enchantments they weave will ensure the armor reacts to each dragon's color, binding it further to its rider. This is a gift for you and from the fairies, meant to strengthen the connection between you and your dragons."

As the riders stepped forward, the fairies gathered around them, their delicate hands weaving intricate patterns in the air. Soft golden light shimmered from their fingertips, trailing like strands of stardust as they infused the armor with enchantments. The metal gleamed under their touch, flaring to life before settling into a soft glow. As the magic took hold, a faint hum resonated through the air, merging the armor's essence with the dragons who would soon claim it.

At Kaelorn's words, the dragon riders eagerly moved forward, each untying the bindings of their package. Gasps of wonder spread through the group as the coverings were pulled away. Keisha's eyes shimmered with unshed tears as she traced the intricate craftsmanship, her fingers brushing over the delicate engraving patterns that seemed to tell a story of past warriors and their dragons woven into the very essence of the armor. The sheer beauty of the work left her momentarily speechless.

Gailen, his hands steady, picked up the gloves and ran his fingers over the material, feeling the fine, enchanted weave beneath his touch. A slow, heartfelt smile spread across his face as he took in the thoughtfulness of the gift.

One by one, the riders turned toward Kaelorn, their gratitude shining through their expressions. One murmured in disbelief, running a hand

over the gleaming armor as if ensuring it was real. Another let out a breathless chuckle, eyes still wide with amazement. A few reverently touched their
armor, feeling the energy pulsing beneath their fingertips, while others
exchanged stunned glances, overwhelmed by the sheer thoughtfulness of
the gift.

"Thank you," Gailen spoke first, his voice filled with sincerity. The others
echoed his words, their appreciation carrying through the air, their voices a
mix of awe and heartfelt respect. Kaelorn nodded and explained the armor:
"This armor is unique. It is not just protection. It is bonded to your dragon.
When you ride, it will adjust to reflect the dragon with which you are
bonded. If you ride an emerald dragon, the armor will take on emerald
hues; if you ride another, it will match accordingly."

Kaelorn observed the warriors and dragon riders as they admired their
newly gifted armor, the hum of quiet appreciation filling the air. The
moment felt significant, yet his thoughts drifted beyond the present. He
turned to Keisha, his expression thoughtful. "Do you believe my people
can help in the coming battle?

Keisha met his gaze, considering his words carefully. The weight of his
question pressed against her thoughts. She knew the Luminara had the
heart to fight, but were they prepared for the brutal reality of war? No
amount of training could truly prepare them for the chaos of battle, the
unrelenting force of their enemies, and the weight of loss. Would their
resolve hold firm when faced with bloodshed and fear? Asking them to
stand against such darkness was not a decision she could take lightly. Responsibility settled on her shoulders, and for a moment, she hesitated, torn
between protecting them and honoring their right to choose their path.
"Their abilities could be invaluable," she admitted. "But I do not want to
push them into a battle they are not ready for."

One of the elders stepped forward, his voice steady and resolute. "We
appreciate your concern, Lady Keisha, but if Emerald Woods is to be our
home, we will stand and fight to protect it."

Keisha's eyes shimmered with admiration as she nodded, a tear slipping down her cheek. Their unwavering stance and willingness to fight for their newfound home filled her with deep respect. It was their courage and a commitment to something greater than themselves. "Then I thank you, all of you," she said, her voice full of gratitude.

She turned to the others. "Let's leave the Luminara to get acquainted with the fairies and dragons," she suggested. The riders nodded in agreement, each picking up their armor before preparing to depart.

As they turned to leave, Gailen took a deep breath. The weight of the moment settled over him. He realized how valuable his friends were and how much they had all sacrificed for this fight. Hesitating momentarily, he let the gravity of their journey sink in the battles ahead, the sacrifices already made, and the trust they had built. Then, with quiet determination, he stepped toward Kaelorn. He embraced his friend without a word, silently acknowledging their bond and the journey ahead. Then, with a final nod, he turned and followed the others, heading back toward Crystal Vale.

Chapter 41
Shadows of Defiance

The searing heat of Fel Thalor's volcanic heart pressed against Valeon as he stepped into the vast cavern. The ominous glow of molten lava sent flickering shadows dancing across the jagged walls while waves of stifling heat rolled through the cavern, pressing against him with each step. The acrid stench of sulfur clawed at his throat. Beads of sweat trickled down his temples, only to vanish before reaching his jaw, swallowed by the searing heat. Each breath carried the faint taste of ash, burning in his lungs as he forced himself to press forward. His breath came in shallow gasps. The oppressive heat wrapped around him, relentless and suffocating, prickling his skin as if the fire sought to consume him. The rhythmic crackle of the fire and the occasional rumble deep below created a grim symphony that mirrored the turmoil within his heart.

The mysterious person stood near the edge of a bubbling lava pool, pacing impatiently, their cloak billowing slightly in the oppressive heat. Their face remained obscured by shadows despite the glowing surroundings, their cloak shifting subtly in the stifling heat. As Valeon approached, he hesitated, sensing the volatile mood emanating from the figure.

"You're late," the mysterious person hissed, their voice cutting through the cavern's oppressive silence like a blade. "What news from Crystal Vale and Emerald Woods?"

Valeon bowed his head, his voice steady despite the tension from the mysterious person. "Nothing significant. They keep me occupied with trivial errands."

The air grew heavy with silence, save for the bubbling of molten rock. Valeon clenched his fists, his nails biting into his palms as he forced himself to remain still. Sweat trickled down his back, but he ignored it, his mind racing through possible responses. Every second of quiet stretched the tension further like a blade poised to strike. Then, a cruel laugh shattered the stillness, echoing off the jagged walls like a dagger striking Valeon's composure. The sound cut deep, not just because of its sharp mockery but because it was another reminder of the mysterious person's little regard for him. The laughter carried no warmth, only contempt, and Valeon felt the sting of it settle in his chest like a wound left to fester.

"Trivial errands?" the mysterious person sneered, their tone dripping with derision. "Even those are beyond your reach. It is almost amusing they trust you at all."

Valeon's jaw tightened, but he remained silent, his hands clenched at his sides. A storm of frustration churned within him, a quiet war between defiance and survival. Every word from the mysterious person grated against his resolve, but he swallowed the bitter taste of anger, knowing that one wrong move could cost him everything. He felt no guilt about deceiving the mysterious person, so why should he? He had never wanted to be in this position, never asked for it. Every word he spoke to them was a means of survival, a careful game he had no choice but to play; a flicker of frustration burned beneath his carefully composed exterior. Every insult and veiled threat lodged in his mind like a splinter, but he knew he could not afford to break. Not yet. He knew better than to respond.

The mysterious person stopped pacing and turned to face him fully, their piercing gaze burning through the shadows. "Listen closely," they said, their voice low and menacing. "When they make any changes or adjustments, no matter how insignificant you are, inform me as soon as you know the plans. Do I make myself clear?"

Valeon nodded stiffly, keeping his gaze fixed on the ground. "Yes, I understand."

The mysterious person lingered for a moment longer, their gaze an invisible weight pressing down on him. Valeon fought to keep his breath steady, resisting the urge to flinch under their scrutiny. A cold weight settled in his stomach, tightening like an unseen chain around his resolve. It was not just fear for himself. It was the fear that those he had come to care about would be hurt or worse because of his involvement. The thought gnawed at him, twisting through his mind like a shadow he could not shake. Doubt gnawed at the edges of his resolve, whispering that he would never be more than a pawn in this deadly game. His hands curled into fists at his sides, not just in defiance but to suppress the trembling that threatened to betray him. Every instinct screamed at him to leave, but he remained rooted, his breaths shallow and deliberate to keep his composure intact.

"Do not disappoint me again, Valeon. You will not like the consequences." Then, without another word, they turned and vanished into the shadows, leaving Valeon alone in the stifling heat of the volcanic chamber.

As the oppressive atmosphere began to ease, Valeon exhaled slowly, his shoulders sagging under the weight of the encounter. His mind churned with doubts, each laced with the bitter realization that he had stepped too deep into a game he barely understood. The consequences loomed over him if he failed; the mysterious person would not hesitate to punish him, but worse still was the thought of those in Crystal Vale. What if his deception brought danger upon them? What if his failure meant watching them suffer? The thought coiled around his mind like a serpent, suffocating any lingering hope that he could walk away unscathed. Was there still a way out, or had he already sealed his fate? He glared at the bubbling lava as if its restless surface mirrored the chaos within him. Shaking his head, he muttered, "What have I gotten myself into?"

He turned with measured steps and began the arduous journey back. The suffocating heat of the volcanic lair gave way to the cooler, earthy air of the forest as he trudged along the rugged path leading out of Fel Thalor. The cooler air brushed against his overheated skin, sending a shiver down his spine as it soothed the relentless heat clinging to him. It carried the earthy scent of damp leaves and moss, a relief after the suffocating stench of sulfur.

For months, the weight of the mysterious person's demands had crushed his spirit, leaving little room for hope. Every task forced upon him reminded him of his precarious position, relaying information, manipulating trust, and walking the fine line between survival and betrayal. The constant fear of exposure gnawed at him, turning even moments of solace into shadows of paranoia. Restless nights plagued him, each filled with the lingering fear of failure, while his days became a careful performance, each word measured, every glance calculated to avoid suspicion. Conversations felt hollow, and the warmth of Crystal Vale's trust was a painful contrast to the cold deception he was forced to maintain. The burden had hollowed him out, making even simple moments of camaraderie feel like distant echoes of life slipping further from his grasp. He thought of all the times they had teased him, the playful jabs and lighthearted moments that once felt insignificant. Yet, beneath it all, he knew they cared. That realization cut more profound than any reprimand from the mysterious person because, despite his deception, they had accepted him as one of their own. Each day, there had been a careful balancing act, and his every move was dictated by the need to avoid suspicion. The slightest misstep invited sharp reprimands or worse, while the unwavering trust and camaraderie in Crystal Vale stood in stark contrast, a painful reminder of all he stood to lose if he failed.

But as he replayed their conversation in his mind, a flicker of something unfamiliar, a sly grin crept onto his face.

"The only change," he muttered, recalling the mysterious person's mocking laughter. "What a fool. They practically handed me a lifeline when they said, 'when I find out."

The thought uncoiled like a serpent, bringing a sliver of defiance. His shoulders straightened slightly, his fingers uncurling from their tense grip as if shaking off invisible chains. A slow, measured breath steadied him, solidifying the resolve now taking root in his chest. For the first time in months, he allowed himself to consider the possibility of manipulating the timeline, stretching out the mysterious person's patience until it snapped or until it was too late for their plans to succeed. But the risk was undeniable. If they saw through his deception, the consequences would be swift and merciless. The mysterious person was not one to suffer disobedience, and the price of failure could be far worse than he dared imagine. If he delayed relaying critical information, claimed ignorance, or feigned incompetence, it could buy Crystal Vale and Emerald Woods precious time.

He considered the words and actions of those in Crystal Vale, their trust in him, and their belief that he could be counted on to protect their interests. The way they spoke to him with quiet confidence, the tasks they entrusted him with, and the subtle nods of approval during council meetings painted a picture of genuine faith. Their trust in him felt almost surreal, a stark contrast to the secret he carried. But he was not ready to act, not yet. Fear still gripped him too tightly. If he could stall the mysterious person long enough, he could find a way to truly protect them all without revealing his role in this dangerous game.

It was not much of a plan, and it carried significant risks. The mysterious person was not one to tolerate disobedience or failure lightly. But Valeon's options were limited; for once, he felt the faint stirrings of control in a situation where he had been little more than a pawn.

The smile lingered as he walked. "If I have to play the fool to keep them safe," he murmured, "then so be it. They will be angry, but maybe it will already be too late by the time they figure it out."

His steps grew lighter as he neared the forest's edge, the towering spires of Crystal Vale now visible on the horizon. A strange mix of relief and apprehension tightened in his chest, relief at returning to familiar ground, yet uneasy at the deception he carried within him. The sight of the city, once a beacon of safety, now felt like a sanctuary and a battlefield where every word and action would determine his fate. He longed for the comfort of its walls, the familiar voices that had come to trust him, yet the weight of deception turned that longing into unease. Each step closer brought the gnawing fear of exposure, the possibility that his carefully woven lies would unravel. Yet, beneath that fear, a spark of resolve burned. He had a part to play, and he would see it through. Though the weight of his predicament still pressed on his shoulders, the faint hope that he could disrupt the mysterious person's plans even a little offered him a renewed sense of purpose.

Straightening his posture, he pressed forward, his mind now set on what he could do from within Crystal Vale to tip the scales subtly. He would watch the council's decisions with sharper scrutiny, identify allies who might share his doubts, and plant seeds of uncertainty where needed. If he played his part carefully, he might shift the balance without revealing his true intentions. Yet doubt lingered at the edges of his mind—what if they saw through his deception? What if his carefully laid plans unraveled before he could act? The risk was significant, but so was the chance to finally take control of his fate. He could start by quietly observing the council meetings more closely, noting even the slightest shifts in tone or decisions that might matter later. Small steps, but each one could weave a subtle web of resistance against the mysterious person's plans. He would need to tread carefully but allowed himself a small victory.

The shadow of the mysterious person's control loomed over him, but for the first time in months, it did not seem quite so overwhelming. He recalled the early days of his entrapment when fear dictated his every move when even the thought of defying them felt impossible. He had spent countless nights wrestling with hopelessness, believing he was a pawn, doomed to follow orders. But now, that helplessness had begun to crack, and something else had taken root, determination in its place. A plan was formed, fragile, dangerous, but possible. It relied on deception, careful manipulation of information, and an unwavering ability to remain unnoticed. One misstep, one slip of the tongue, and the entire scheme could crumble, exposing him to the wrath of the mysterious person. The stakes were higher than ever, but it might give him the edge he desperately needed if executed correctly. He would play the expected part but carve his path in the shadows. He was done being just a pawn.

Chapter 42
The Final Command

The oppressive heat of Flameford was suffocating, pressing down like an unrelenting force. It was matched only by the boiling fury of the mysterious figure pacing back and forth in the cavernous chamber. Their steps were quick and erratic, each one echoing like a war drum against the jagged stone walls. Their clenched fists trembled with barely restrained anger, each step echoing like a war drum against the jagged stone walls. Their breath came in sharp, uneven bursts, each a measured attempt to contain the mounting frustration. Each heavy step echoed ominously, filling the chamber with an unrelenting rhythm. The flickering shadows the glowing lava pools cast twisted and stretched across the jagged walls as if the cavern recoiled from their seething presence. The dim light from the lava cast jagged silhouettes against the walls, amplifying the ominous atmosphere.

Lyra Dreadcrusher stood silently near the edge, her crimson robes gleaming faintly in the fiery glow, her expression stoic and unreadable.

"You're useless!" the figure snarled, their voice a harsh whip cracking through the molten air. "Weeks, months, and yet you have unearthed nothing from those texts about how to defeat the noble dragons! How is it that you, who claim to be an expert in the arcane, cannot decipher a single useful phrase?"

Lyra's gaze remained fixed on the floor, her hands folded neatly in front of her. Though outwardly submissive, her thoughts burned with defiance. She knew her skills were far from useless; she was one of the most potent sorceresses among the Druchii, her mastery of the arcane unmatched. But she also knew the futility of arguing with the figure during their rage. Survival demanded patience, and she would choose her moment carefully, waiting until the tides of favor shifted or a weakness in their resolve presented itself. Qellaun Deadcrusher, standing to her right, exchanged a cautious glance with her but said nothing, his body stiff with tension.

The figure continued, their voice rising with each word. "Do you think this is a game? Do you understand the importance of what we are doing here? The noble dragons are a threat to everything we have built! Every moment you waste brings us closer to failure!"

A tremor rippled through their voice—barely restrained. "If the text isn't found before Radiantus returns to Vacari—before that cursed Platinum Dragon sets foot in this realm again—then any advantage we might have had will be gone."

As the rant escalated, the figure's erratic movements caused their heavy cloak to sway. For a heartbeat, a cascade of silver hair spilled from beneath the hood, catching the lava's glow—brilliant against the oppressive dark. It vanished just as quickly, but the damage was done. This person had gone to great lengths to conceal their identity, and that brief flash of silver felt deliberate, dangerous. Why hide something so seemingly trivial? Unless it was not so trivial after all.

Lyra's breath hitched, her mind already spinning with possibilities. Beside her, Qellaun stiffened, his hand twitching toward his blade. Silver hair was common enough, but something about this felt wrong—as if the hair itself carried weight, a clue whispered in plain sight, hinting at truths far more dangerous than either of them had expected.

The figure froze mid-step, a low growl escaping their lips. They turned sharply away, lifting a gloved hand to shove their hair beneath the hood. Their voice dropped to a dangerous murmur, but the words were clear enough for those in the room. "Careless... I was careless."

Lyra's lips pressed into a thin line as she glanced at Qellaun, whose eyes narrowed but stayed fixed on the mysterious figure. The tension in the room thickened as the figure turned back toward Lyra, their temper reigniting.

"You think silence will save you, Lyra?" they spat, their voice dripping with venom. "You will return to those texts and find what I need. If you fail again, I will ensure you understand the cost of disappointing me."

Lyra inclined her head slightly, her voice calm but firm, though her fingers curled subtly against the fabric of her robe, betraying the tension she refused to show on her face. She had endured far worse than this figure's wrath before. If they thought fear alone would bend her to their will, they underestimated her resolve. Every demand, every impossible order only strengthened her determination to find a way out of this deadly game on her terms. "I understand, my lord. I will not fail." Inside, however, her mind churned with resentment and determination. She could feel the weight of the figure's expectations pressing down on her like the suffocating heat of the chamber. Yet, a flicker of defiance sparked within her a quiet resolve to prove her worth, not for their approval, but to secure her survival in the storm, she could feel brewing. She would have loved to remind them that the noble dragons had some of the scrolls they desperately sought, but she knew better. The figure's fury was already boiling over; challenging them now would be foolish. Instead, she remained silent, letting them believe she was obedient while she considered her path forward.

The figure scoffed, pacing again, the silver hair now concealed, but the memory of it lingers like a phantom in the air. "You had better not. The noble dragons grow stronger with every passing day, and we cannot afford to fall behind. If you cannot find the answer, I will find someone who can."

With one final glare at Lyra and Qellaun, the figure stormed out of the chamber, their cloak billowing behind them like a storm cloud. Their footsteps faded into the distance, leaving the room heavy with silence.

Qellaun turned to Lyra, his voice a low whisper. "Silver hair... Did you see it?"

Lyra nodded slowly, her expression contemplative. "I did."

"And yet they hide it," Qellaun mused, his gaze fixed on the figure's path. "Why?"

Lyra shook her head, her thoughts swirling with unanswered questions. "I do not know. But it is clear they do not want anyone to see."

The two exchanged a wary glance, the air around them still charged with the remnants of the figure's wrath. Without another word, Lyra turned and strode back toward her quarters, her mind racing through the ancient texts she had been pouring over for months. Whatever the answer, she knew she had to find it or risk facing the figure's wrath again.

Qellaun lingered for a moment longer, his hand resting on the hilt of his blade as he stared at the empty corridor. He had no immediate concerns, but the lengths the figure had gone to conceal their hair intrigued him. Why such secrecy? Why such an effort to hide something as simple as hair? His curiosity stirred, knowing that answers would not come quickly if they came. The silver hair was more than just a curiosity; it was a clue, a thread tied into secrets he had long suspected but never confirmed.

Qellaun had always questioned the true nature of their leader, how they seemed to know more than they should, how their presence carried an unnatural authority, and how their demands were driven by something beyond mere conquest. But this? This was proof that there was more to their identity, something deliberately concealed. And that made it all the more dangerous. His grip tightened briefly, then relaxed as a knowing smirk flickered across his lips. "Silver hair," he murmured again, a faint smirk tugging at his lips. "A secret worth keeping, indeed." With that, he turned and disappeared into the shadows.

The mysterious person emerged from the oppressive heat of Flameford's caverns into the equally stifling air outside. The jagged landscape stretched before them, barren and lifeless, save for the swirling clouds of ash and the faint glow of molten rivers in the distance. With a swift motion, they raised their hooded head, and a sharp, commanding whistle split the air. The sound sliced through the thick, stifling atmosphere, sending ripples through the swirling ash. A tense stillness followed as if the land had been put on notice. Then, a low, resonant growl answered from a distance, followed by the heavy beat of massive wings cutting through the sky. The sound echoed through the barren landscape, momentarily stilling the swirling ash. A distant rumble followed as if the land held its breath in anticipation.

From the darkened horizon, the shadows of two massive dragons loomed, their forms growing more prominent as they soared closer. Xalzorath, the black dragon, descended first, his charcoal scales gleaming faintly in the molten light. Like twin voids, his eyes were fixed on the mysterious person with a predatory gaze.

Moments later, Nocturna, the obsidian dragon, landed with quiet but menacing grace, her shimmering scales reflecting the dim light like polished glass. Her glowing silver eyes streaked with violet narrowed as she regarded the figure before her, a flicker of uncertainty buried beneath her usual stoic demeanor. Their power was undeniable, a force unlike anything she had encountered before, but the secrecy unsettled her. Why go to such lengths to hide their identity? Power and dominance were often displayed, not concealed. The contradiction gnawed at her instincts, leaving her with an unease she could not ignore. The plan was sound, but something gnawed at her thoughts, an unease she could not shake. Was it the ferocity of the coming battle or a deeper instinct warning her of unseen dangers? She had fought many battles, yet this time, a shadow of doubt clung to the edges of her resolve.

"It is time," the mysterious person began, their voice cold and resolute. "The skirmishes are over. We will no longer test their defenses. Now, we will destroy them."

Xalzorath lowered his head, his deep, guttural voice resonating like a distant thunderstorm. His massive claws dug into the ashen ground, sending faint tremors through the earth. Like a predator preparing to pounce, a subtle ripple passed through his charcoal scales as he fixed his piercing gaze on the hooded figure. "What is your will, master?"

The mysterious person turned their piercing gaze to Xalzorath first. The black dragon let out a slow, guttural growl, his claws raking against the hardened ground in anticipation. His wings twitched slightly as if resisting the urge to take flight and unleash the fury that had been building within him. His entire form tensed, ready and eager for the command to strike. The black dragon let out a slow, guttural growl, his claws raking against the hardened ground in anticipation. His wings twitched slightly as if resisting the urge to take flight and unleash the fury that had been building within him. His entire form tensed, ready and eager for the command to strike. "You will lead the assault on Emerald Woods. Your objective is simple: destroy Verdantia and the Moon Elf who rides her. Thalorian must fall. And if the Eladrin elf, Keisha, is there, eliminate her as well. Rid the forest of anyone aiding them."

Xalzorath's black eyes gleamed like polished onyx, his wings shifting with a restless energy. "As you command. The forest will be cleansed."

The mysterious person then turned to Nocturna, their tone no less commanding. "You will head to Crystal Vale. Aurelia and her rider, Prince Gailen, are your targets. Ensure their destruction. Do not fail me."

The mysterious person nodded curtly. "Good. Now prepare."

As the dragons spread their wings, ready to take flight, a rustling sound emerged from the cavern behind them. Zylron and Glaciera appeared, their red and white scales glowing faintly in the volcanic light. The two dragons exchanged glances before addressing Xalzorath and Nocturna.

"Before you go," Zylron rumbled, his fiery breath illuminating his massive fangs, "we have a suggestion."

Glaciera's icy voice followed, as sharp as a blade slicing through frost. A hush fell over the gathering, the tension thickening as her words sank in. Nocturna's wings twitched slightly, and Xalzorath's tail flicked in contemplation. The gravity of the strategy settled over them like a frost-laced wind. Even Zylron's fiery breath dimmed momentarily as if the weight of her calculations demanded a moment of silent consideration.

She had weighed every possible outcome, calculating the risks and rewards precisely. This plan, while dangerous, offered the most excellent chance of success if executed flawlessly. "Mix your dragons. Divide the obsidian and black among both groups. By splitting their forces, we can create chaos and confusion among their defenses. The simultaneous assaults will force them to thin their resources, making it impossible to mount an effective counterattack. However," she paused, her piercing gaze shifting between the dragons, "if communication falters between the groups, we risk disorganization on our side as well. Precision will be critical. A coordinated assault from both will overwhelm their defenses and leave them no room for retreat. However, if our forces lose synchronization, chaos may weaken our offensive. The benefits outweigh the risks but only if executed with flawless coordination."

Nocturna turned her head slightly, her violet eyes narrowing in thought. She fully supported the strategy, recognizing its tactical advantage. Dark dragons were not known for working well together; their nature was dominance and instinct rather than coordination. The plan was sound in theory, but would the others follow orders when the heat of battle ignited their bloodlust? A flicker of doubt stirred within her. The risk of discord was high, yet disobedience would not be tolerated. She would have to ensure their unity by force, if necessary. "An interesting strategy."

Xalzorath snorted, his dark voice tinged with approval. "It will ensure we cover both locations thoroughly. I agree."

The mysterious person listened, their hooded head tilting slightly. After a pause, they nodded. "Do it. Split your forces. Work together to destroy Crystal Vale and Emerald Woods. Let no one survive."

The dragons bowed their massive heads in unison, their wings spreading wide. With a thunderous roar, Xalzorath and Nocturna launched into the sky, their powerful forms disappearing into the swirling ash above. Zylron and Glaciera watched for a moment before retreating into the cavern, their voices echoing in quiet conversation.

"This will work," Glaciera murmured. "Their defenses will shatter."

Zylron rumbled in agreement, though a faint hesitation flickered in his molten eyes. His fiery breath cast flickering light against the cavern walls, but his claws scraped subtly against the stone, betraying a moment of doubt. The strategy was sound, yet something about the looming battle gnawed at the edges of his mind, a whisper of unease that he quickly buried beneath his hardened resolve. "It must. Failure is not an option."

In the stillness that followed, the mysterious person stood alone, their silhouette framed by the fiery glow of Flameford, the molten rivers casting twisted reflections against the barren ground. They inhaled deeply, savoring the moment, the anticipation of destruction, the inevitability of chaos. Everything had been set in motion, and soon, the world would kneel before their power. A slow, satisfied smirk ghosted across their lips as they envisioned the flames consuming the proud cities, the agonized cries of their enemies swallowed by the roar of dragonfire. The chaos and the devastation would be a fitting end to those who had defied them for too long. Every act of destruction would serve as retribution, a long-awaited reckoning for the pain and loss they had endured. Let them struggle. Let them fight; it would only make their downfall even more satisfying. Their fingers curled into a tight fist as the distant roars of dragons echoed across the landscape, a harbinger of the destruction soon to come. Their voice, a whisper laced with malice, carried on the ashen winds. "Crystal Vale and Emerald Woods will fall. And with them, the noble dragons' legacy will crumble. Vuarus will be avenged."

Chapter 43

Shattered Shadows: Aurelia's Triumph

The skies above Crystal Vale boiled with unnatural darkness. Malignant energy churned within thick clouds, their swirling depths alive with flickers of violet lightning. The storm's weight pressed down on the city like an unspoken omen. It was a force that did not belong to the natural world but had been summoned, shaped, and twisted into something primordial and wrong.

Below, the towering crystalline spires of the city gleamed faintly beneath the haze, their fractured reflections casting broken rainbows across the ground. Their fragile beauty stood in defiance of the coming storm, shimmering even as the shadows lengthened over them.

Prince Gailen stood firm from the highest tower, his silhouette framed against the turbulent sky. Beside him, Aurelia, her opalescent scales gleaming like a beacon, gazed toward the horizon. Around them, the Crystal and Emerald dragons gathered, wings rustling with restless anticipation, talons digging into stone as they prepared for the battle that would decide the fate of their home.

Then, the darkness moved.

The horizon rippled not like wind through the clouds but like something unnatural, something alive. A pulse of shifting, writhing blackness surged forward, consuming the light in its path. A wall of Obsidian and Black dragons swept down in perfect, merciless formation, their wings a seamless tide of encroaching doom.

And at their head, emerging from the heart of the abyss itself, Nocturna.

The Shadow Sovereign materialized from the living darkness, her form more like an entity than a beast, a figure that seemed to drink the light around her. Her wings stretched wide, their massive span blotting out the sky, each beat sending unnatural ripples. The shadows beneath her crawled and shifted as though the ground feared her touch.

Her obsidian scales shimmered with a fluid, spectral glow, absorbing the light rather than casting it back. They cast eerie shadows that twisted and writhed as if alive, making the air around her darker and heavier. She did not simply fly. She moved like the darkness itself, her presence a gravity that pulled everything toward oblivion. Her silver eyes streaked with violet burned like twin stars caught in a cold, calculating, infinite, dying universe.

Then, she smiled. Not a grin of arrogance nor amusement but one of certainty. "It begins."

Nocturna's roar shattered the moment.

The sound was not a mere cry. It was a force, an ancient, suffocating wave of dread that swallowed the sky. Gailen staggered, his breath catching as icy fear coiled around his spine. The dragons flinched, their wings twitching, eyes wide with primal terror. Even the air seemed to shudder beneath the weight of the sound, a pressure that pressed into their bones and threatened to crush resolve before the battle had even begun. It resonated through the air, slamming into the crystal spires and sending visible tremors through the earth beneath them. The light dimmed further as though recoiling from the force of her presence.

And then the battle erupted.

Aurelia launched herself into the storm, her wings unfurling with a brilliance that split the darkness like a blade of light. For a fleeting moment, doubt clawed at the edges of her mind—was she strong enough to face this? The weight of expectation pressed against her like an invisible force, reminding her of every battle and every hardship that had led her to this moment. She had overcome it before, but this felt different, darker, and more final. The shadows whispered her failure before she struck, but she forced them away. She could not would not yield to fear. She recalled the battle of the Emerald Cliffs when she had stood alone against impossible odds. Then, she had felt the same uncertainty, the same fear. But she had triumphed. And she would again. She shook the thought away, her resolve hardening like the crystal she commanded. There was no room for hesitation now. The crystalline barriers around her flared as she rose, their surfaces shimmering as they absorbed and deflected the onslaught of dark energy blasts and razor-sharp shadow projectiles already filling the air.

With a swift motion, she unleashed her first strike. A barrage of razor-sharp crystal shards erupted from her wings, each catching what small light remained, turning into a cascade of falling stars as they surged toward Nocturna.

Gailen held his ground atop her back, his Crystalbow pulsing with building energy. He could feel the connection between them, the magic humming between dragon and rider, each feeding into the other, their power merging into something greater than themselves.

Nocturna moved with unnatural fluidity, her obsidian form twisting effortlessly through the oncoming assault. Crystal shards missed her by mere inches, their jagged edges whistling through the air with a sharp, keening sound, slicing through the space where she had been a heartbeat before. The battlefield rippled in her wake, the force of her movement stirring unnatural winds that sent defenders reeling. She did not merely dodge. She dissolved—her body momentarily blurring into darkness, reforming an instant later. When she reappeared, she did not come alone—phantom echoes trailed her, shadow-forged replicas that mimicked her every motion with spectral precision, weaving confusion into the chaos of battle. The battlefield rippled in her wake, the force of her movement stirring unnatural winds that sent defenders reeling.

Then, she retaliated.

Her talons slashed through the air, carving through the darkness like rifts in reality itself. But she was not attacking, and yet she was shaping the battlefield. The shadows around her twisted, forming ghostly replicas of herself, flickering in and out of existence, their silver eyes streaked with violet gleaming in the chaos. They moved in tandem with her, weaving through the sky, each one a perfect echo of the original.

The Aura of Dread unfurled from her like an unseen mist, a natural force that instilled fear, making even the most courageous hesitate in her presence. Its cold fingers slithered into the minds of her enemies. Some dragons shuddered violently, their eyes flickering with primal fear as memories of past battles surfaced unbidden. Others fought against it, their claws tightening, jaws clenching as they struggled to resist the oppressive weight of despair. A few, unable to withstand the suffocating terror, let out piercing cries and veered off course, their wings trembling as they tried to escape the invisible grasp of dread. Dragons recoiled mid-flight, their wings faltering as panic clawed at their instincts. Some uttered involuntary cries, their resolve momentarily cracking, while others shuddered, eyes wide with an unshakable sense of doom. Even the seasoned warriors felt a primal fear sinking deep into their bones, whispering that resistance was futile. It was not a spell. It was a presence, a raw force of terror that dug into the bones and instincts, whispering of inevitable doom.

And for a heartbeat, just a heartbeat, even the bravest faltered.

The first clash came in a collision of raw power, a thunderous impact that sent shockwaves rippling through the battlefield. The air vibrated with the force, a deafening crack that momentarily drowned out the howling winds and the clash of wings. Sparks of energy erupted where their attacks met, scattering like stars falling against the darkened sky. The pressure of the impact sent ripples through the ground below, fracturing stone and sending shards flying like deadly shrapnel. The moment hung suspended pure, unfiltered destruction before the battle resumed in full fury. Aurelia's crystal shards expanded, growing mid-flight into jagged, cage-like formations, each shifting unpredictably, forcing Nocturna to weave through the deadly labyrinth.

But the Shadow Sovereign did not flinch. She twisted through the crystal storm, her movements almost serpentine, her wings snapping inward as she spiraled through the narrowest gaps. Then, with a growl of ancient fury, she exhaled.

A storm of obsidian shards erupted from her maw, her breath weapon razing through the battlefield like a hurricane of razors. The ground beneath splintered upon impact, deep fissures tearing through the earth as the force sent defenders tumbling, their roars of pain lost amidst the chaos. Some dragons, caught mid-flight, recoiled as the shards tore through their wings, leaving trails of darkness in their wake. Aurelia's crystalline barriers flared, absorbing the attack, but the ground below was not so lucky.

The city screamed beneath the impact of colliding titans. Buildings shuddered as the impact reverberated through their crystalline structures, fractures splintering across their surfaces. Shards rained like a fractured prism, scattering across the city in a shimmering cascade. The streets filled with terrified cries as citizens fled, shielding themselves from falling debris. Buildings trembled, their crystalline structures fracturing under the force, sending shards cascading like rain. The streets filled with terrified cries as citizens fled, shielding themselves from falling debris. Fires erupted where energy clashed against stone, painting the sky with flickering embers. The scent of burning crystal and scorched earth thickened the air, a haunting prelude to the devastation yet to come.

The obsidian storm tore through the earth, shattering stones, ripping through buildings, leaving behind nothing but blackened scars where it touched.

The heavens became a battlefield of fire and shadow. The air crackled with raw energy, thick with the acrid scent of smoke and the metallic tang of blood. The deafening roars of dragons clashed with the chaotic symphony of steel striking scale, magic crackling like thunder. The sky trembled under the weight of battle, each collision sending shockwaves through the storm-laden winds, buffeting wings and rattling bones. Dragons clashed mid-air, their roars of fury lost amid the storm of magic and steel. Fire rained from above, streaking across the darkness like falling stars, while shadowy tendrils twisted through the chaos, seeking to ensnare their foes. Below, warriors fought with desperate intensity, their eyes reflecting the flames of war, their bodies moving in a relentless dance between survival and annihilation.

As Aurelia and Nocturna tore through the sky in their vicious aerial duel, their armies collided in brutal combat below.

The Crystal and Emerald dragons fought as one, their magic weaving together in seamless harmony, offense and defense entwined in a war dance.

The Emerald dragons took to the skies first, their hypnotic scales granting them a unique advantage. The movement of their scales created an entrancing effect, drawing the eyes of enemies who gazed too long. This mesmerizing shift in color disarmed attackers, causing hesitation and confusion in the heart of battle. Their hypnotic scales shifted in mesmerizing waves, a symphony of light rippling like liquid gold. The air shimmered around them, distorting reality itself as they climbed higher. The air around them warped, shimmering as their enemies' eyes glazed over, movements slowing as though caught in an unseen current. A heartbeat of hesitation. A moment of confusion.

And in battle, a moment was all that was needed. The Crystal dragons struck with ruthless precision.

They moved like shards of light cutting through the storm, their
talons gleaming as they sliced through the disoriented enemy lines.
Some of the dark dragons panicked, their formations breaking as
they attempted to evade the deadly precision of their attackers. Others fought back with desperate ferocity, lashing out with claws and
dark magic, their roars echoing with defiance even as they fell one by
one. The air became a kaleidoscope of motion, light flashing off their
crystalline bodies as they darted between stunned foes. They ripped
through armor mercilessly, their talons slicing through wings and sending enemies spiraling toward the earth below.

One by one, the dark dragons crashed from the sky. Their shrieks
drowned beneath the roar of battle. Defenders felt the weight of each
fallen foe on the ground, some with grim satisfaction and others with
sorrow, knowing the cost of this war. Yet no one hesitated. They pressed
forward, fueled by duty, vengeance, and the unyielding need to protect
what remained. Their bodies struck the earth with bone-jarring force,
sending up clouds of dust and debris. Some writhed upon impact,
wings shattered, limbs flailing in desperate final movements before stillness claimed them. Others left deep craters in the city's broken streets,
the force of their downfall sending tremors through the ground.

Below, the war raged just as fiercely.

Shael, a Moon Elf mage at the city's heart, stood amid the swirling
chaos. Her silver hair whipped wildly in the stormwinds as she
stretched her hands forward, weaving magic into the city's protective
barriers. A deep ache pulsed in her limbs, the strain sustaining the
barrier like molten chains wrapping around her bones, but she gritted
her teeth and pressed on, drawing on reserves of strength she did not
know she had. "Hold steady!" she commanded her voice a pillar of
clarity amid the turmoil.

The barrier flickered, buckled, then flared with renewed strength, a shimmering dome of power holding back the encroaching darkness. But it would not last forever, not against an enemy this relentless.

On one of the battered watchtowers, Ong stood defiant, his dragon lance crackling with volatile arcane fire, illuminating the broken stones around him with a flickering, ghostly glow. Sparks leaped from its surface, searing the air with the scent of burning ozone. His grip tightened, and as he swung, tendrils of blue fire arced outward, scorching the air and leaving molten streaks upon the tower's weathered stones. The heat distorted the air around him, a shimmering haze that rippled like a mirage, marking him as a beacon of fury and defiance. His heart pounded, not with fear, but with the exhilaration of battle, the relentless drive to protect, destroy, and endure. He moved like a storm, the weapon a blur of searing blue light, each strike sending shockwaves of force rippling through the enemy ranks. Where his lance met flesh, scales blackened, armor melted, and enemy warriors were thrown backward, tumbling lifelessly through the air.

One dragon surged toward him, claws bared. Ong twisted. His movements were swift and precise. His lance arced upward in a sweeping strike, crackling with volatile energy. A burst of power erupted as he impaled his foe through the chest. The dragon convulsed, its body jerking violently. Then, with a final surge, the energy lanced through its form before exploding into a brilliant eruption of an enchanted fire.

Beside him, Valeon worked tirelessly, his hands steady as he moved through the chaos of wounded defenders, guiding them to safety. His heart clenched with each agonized groan, each whispered plea for help. The metallic scent of blood filled the air, mingling with the acrid tang of smoke. He focused on their faces, pain, and hope, forcing away his exhaustion. This was his purpose. He was not a warrior like Ong nor a mage like Shael, but he found his strength here amid the fallen and suffering. Every life he saved was a defiance against the destruction that threatened to consume them all. Some clung to him, their faces twisted in pain and fear, whispering words of gratitude between gasps. Others met his gaze with silent determination, their eyes hardened by battle but filled with trust. Each step he took carried the weight of their survival, and he refused to let them fall.

He did not hesitate. He did not falter. The fear that once plagued him was gone.

The boy who had once questioned his place in this war now moved with unwavering resolve. In the chaos, he had found where he belonged, not as a warrior or a sorcerer but as a force of compassion and resilience. Among those who needed him most, he had found acceptance from others and within himself.

The battle between Aurelia and Nocturna reached a fever pitch in the skies, the fate of Crystal Vale hanging in the balance. Every strike and every movement carried the weight of destiny, as two formidable forces clashed in a struggle that would determine the course of the war.

Aurelia looped beneath her adversary, banking sharply, her crystalline wings scattering bursts of refracted light through the storm. The sky shimmered, momentarily disorienting Nocturna's shadow-forged replicas, distorting their forms like vanishing specters. For an instant, Nocturna's wings faltered—her movements hesitated as the unexpected radiance fractured her vision. The blinding light jolted her senses. Not pain, but disruption. A flaw she could not afford.

With a snarl, she forced through the haze, her form snapping back into focus, fury mounting.

Gailen nocked another arrow. He had only seconds to act. He didn't aim for Nocturna's core—but her wings, the source of her terrifying maneuverability.

"Focus on her wings!" he shouted, letting the arrow fly.

The projectile streaked through the darkness, its crystalline glow illuminating the sky before it struck Nocturna's left wing. A tremor rippled through her form. Cracks spiraled across the obsidian scales, a fracture branching outward in a spiderweb of glowing light.

For the first time, Nocturna's flight wavered.

And Aurelia seized the moment.

She tucked her wings and dove like a falling star, talons gleaming with raw energy. In one fluid strike, she raked beneath Nocturna's exposed underbelly.

Contact.

A resounding crack split the sky. The impact sent shockwaves shuddering through the battlefield.

Nocturna shrieked in agony, her massive form lurching, dark blood splattering as her scales shattered like glass.

The heavens trembled beneath the force of their clash.

And yet, the war was far from over.

Nocturna's silver eyes streaked with violet flared, burning with ancient rage. She registered the pain as sharp and unwelcome, but it only fueled her wrath. There was no pain. She had endured worse, and she would tolerate this. What mattered now was retribution. Pain coursed through her body, a sensation she had not felt in centuries. Her breath came in sharp, controlled bursts as she steadied herself, refusing to yield. The wound throbbed, but the fury drowned out the pain. She was wounded but not broken. Not yet.

With a snarl, the shadows surged around her, the darkness thickening, twisting, writhing, growing stronger.

The actual test had only just begun. But Nocturna was not so easily undone.

The fractures in her obsidian scales seethed with a writhing shadow, the darkness coiling like a living thing, knitting itself back together even as the wounds throbbed with pain. Aurelia's strike had landed, but it was not enough.

Then, in the space of a single breath, Nocturna vanished. The air shuddered in her wake as if recoiling from the unnatural void left behind. A cold pulse rippled outward, distorting the very fabric of the sky. Silence rushed in like a deafening void, as if existence had hesitated in her form's absence. It was not a retreat. No hesitation. She ceased to exist, slipping beyond sight like a whisper swallowed by the void.

The air around Aurelia grew cold, the essence of the sky shuddering with unnatural energy: a flicker, a ripple in the darkness.

And then—

She was behind her. Aurelia barely had time to react before obsidian talons tore through the air, raking across her side. Pain exploded through her body.

The impact drove her off balance, her wing jerking violently under the sudden force. Her breath hitched, sharp and uneven, as a wave of dizziness threatened to pull her under. Vision blurred at the edges, the pain clawing at her focus like a relentless predator, demanding attention she could not afford to give. The wind tore past her, a sharp, whistling agony against her wounded side. The shock rippled through her body, muscles tensing in protest as pain flared along the torn membranes of her wing. Deep, jagged gashes carved through the thin protective scales near its base, sending rivulets of shimmering crimson spilling through the sky like scattered rubies.

Nocturna's silver eyes streaked with violet gleamed, the corner of her fanged maw curling into something almost smug. She had found the weakness. She had wounded Aurelia not just injured her but hindered her flight.

Aurelia forced herself to level out, suppressing the searing pain, but she felt stiffness and heaviness in her movements. It was subtle, but even the most minor disadvantage could mean the difference between survival and oblivion in a fierce battle.

Gailen felt the pain through their bond, a sharp, searing sensation that lanced through his chest as if the wound were his own. It was not just an echo but raw and visceral, a connection that blurred the line between his suffering and Aurelia's. Their shared essence pulsed with agony, yet a fierce determination burned beneath it. Aurelia did not cry out. She did not need to. He knew.

He gritted his teeth, his fingers tightening around the Crystalbow, the magic thrumming against his palm. This had to end.

His thoughts burned with a singular purpose. One final shot. One moment. One chance.

The Crystalbow hummed, resonating with Aurelia's magic, the gathered energy thrumming through the air like a heartbeat. Then, her voice whispered in his mind.

'Steady, Gailen. This is our light.'

He exhaled slowly, blocking out the battlefield, the pain, the chaos. His vision narrowed, his focus absolute. Aurelia soared higher, higher still, breaking through the lower clouds, framing herself against the darkest stretch of sky.

And then—

She unleashed it. A radiant beam of concentrated crystal light erupted from her core, splitting the storm, a celestial force that tore through the darkness like a divine spear.

At the same time, Gailen let his arrow fly. The battlefield seemed still at that moment, warriors and dragons turning toward the sky, their gazes locked on the streak of pure radiance hurtling toward its target. A hush, a heartbeat of silence, as hope and dread collided in the air before the explosion of light consumed the darkness. The two forces met mid-flight, merging in a spiraling lance of pure radiance, its glow brighter than the dying sun.

The battlefield below was bathed in light, and for a moment, everything paused. Warriors lifted their gazes, awe-struck as the brilliance washed over them, banishing the suffocating dark. The golden radiance cascaded over the battlefield like a cleansing tide, illuminating every crack and shadow with its searing glow. The once-oppressive air lightened as if the weight of fear had been stripped away, leaving behind a charged silence filled with wonder and renewed determination. Some fell to their knees, over-whelmed by the sight of hope carved into the heavens, while others let out fierce cries, their spirits reignited with the promise of victory. Fear, despair, everything Nocturna had instilled was momentarily forgotten in the wake of the radiant force above. The spiraling energy spear slammed into Noc-turna's chest, driving her backward with a force unlike anything she had endured before. Shadows rippled violently around her, writhing in agony as the light seared through her form. A guttural choked snarl escaped her, fury and disbelief mingling with the raw pain that tore through her essence. She lashed out instinctively, claws swiping at the radiance consuming her, but it was useless. The light was relentless, merciless, and for the first time, true desperation flickered in her silver eyes streaked with violet.

The impact detonated on contact, sending a concussive shockwave through the sky, its ripples cracking through the darkness like a fractured mirror.

Nocturna's form flickered violently, her shadows writhing and convuls-ing, twisting like living tendrils as they cracked apart under the searing radiance. They shrank and dissolved, peeling away in ragged, smoke-like wisps that curled and burned, unable to withstand the relentless purity of the light. But it was too much. The light burned through her essence like fire through parchment, unrelenting, unstoppable.

She let out a furious, ear-splitting shriek, her body twisting against the onslaught.

For the first time, the darkness faltered. The battlefield seemed still, warriors pausing mid-strike as they sensed the shift. The eerie, suffocating weight of Nocturna's power wavered, a crack forming in the unyielding night. She was losing for the first time, and the air trembled with the realization. Nocturna snarled, silver eyes streaked with violet blazing with rage and defiance.

She was not broken, but the fury burned her as she was forced to retreat. The humiliation of defeat seared her mind, her rage simmering beneath the surface, promising vengeance. A final echoing cry tore through the valley as she dissolved into the void, vanishing into the shadows from which she came.

With her retreat, the enemy army wavered. A ripple of confusion spread through the Obsidian and Black dragons, their once-coordinated assault now a fractured force without its leader.

Then, her command whispered through the battlefield like a dying breath, a spectral whisper that slithered into the minds of her forces. Fall back. The dark dragons broke formation, turning away, streaking toward the storm-laden horizon like fading shadows. The battle was over for now.

Nocturna's retreat was a fleeting relief, but unease lingered. They knew she would return more vigorously, more relentless. Would she come with new allies? A darker power? For now, they could only prepare, their victory shadowed by the certainty that this was merely the beginning. They knew the dark dragons would return, stronger and more determined, bringing an even more significant threat. The respite was temporary, a brief moment to gather their strength before the storm came again. Her army vanished into the storm, and a tide of darkness dissolved into the horizon like ink washing away at dawn. Yet, the battlefield still whispered of her presence, scorched earth, broken bodies, and the lingering dread in the eyes of those who had faced her. Even in retreat, she was not truly gone. Yet, they could breathe a little easier, for now, knowing they had won this battle. Plans would be made, defenses strengthened, and preparations set in motion for the war was far from over.

The land bore the scars of battle.

The crystal spires lay in jagged ruins, remnants of a proud city that had once stood as a beacon of beauty and resilience. Now, their fractured forms told a story of loss, sacrifice, and the enduring scars of battle. Once a beacon of beauty and resilience, the shattered city now bore the weight of its suffering, its broken remains whispering of a fight that had left its mark on the soul of Vacari. Their once-glorious forms had been reduced to fractured remnants, reflecting broken light across the devastated earth. Shattered crystals littered the ground, glinting weakly beneath the haze of destruction. The scorched ground smoked, plumes of vapor rising from where dragonfire had torn through the stone, leaving behind ashen scars and the acrid stench of burnt scales.

The metallic tang of spilled blood lingered, thick in the air, mingling with the distant groans of the wounded. The sky, once a maelstrom of war, lightning, and roaring fury, was eerily silent.

The war had paused, but it had not ended. The defenders stood among the ruins, wings sagging, weapons lowered, their bodies trembling from exhaustion but still standing.

They had won. But at what cost?

A hush fell over the battlefield as Aurelia descended. It was not the effortless, regal descent of a victorious dragon. It was heavy and painful, her wings faltering slightly as she remained steady.

Her right wing dipped, struggling beneath its weight, deep gashes leaking shimmering crimson down her opalescent scales. Each movement sent sharp jolts of pain lancing through her muscles, the torn membranes dragging heavily, resisting every attempt to stay aloft. Her breaths came shallow and uneven, and each inhale strained as the air had turned against her. A sharp, searing pain lanced through her muscles, each movement sending a fresh wave of agony coursing through her body. She pressed her lips together, forcing herself to breathe evenly to mask the trembling that threatened to overtake her limbs. Each slow, deliberate movement sent sharp pangs of agony through her body, but she clenched her jaw, refusing to show weakness.

The moment her talons touched the ground, she nearly collapsed beneath the sheer weight of her exhaustion. Her chest rose and fell in deep, unsteady breaths, and every inhale was laced with the bitter taste of blood. Her muscles ached like a fire had burned through them, and her wings felt like lead, each beating a silent war against the pain.

But she stood. She did not let Gailen see her falter. 'Focus on the others. I am fine.'

The telepathic words were calm, unwavering, though they carried the weight of a thousand wounds.

Gailen slid from her back, but the moment his boots hit the ground, his knees buckled beneath him. He barely caught himself, his muscles weak, trembling from the intensity of battle.

He stood still momentarily, his fingers resting against Aurelia's warm scales.

It was over. They had done it.

The words left his lips in a whisper, barely audible, more to convince himself than to declare it.

"We did it." But his voice lacked triumph.

It was exhaustion, disbelief, and the heavy weight of a battle that had claimed too many lives, reduced homes to rubble, and pushed spirits to the breaking point. A battle that should have felt like victory, but instead, felt like survival.

Shael rushed toward them, her hands aglow with golden magic, her silver hair whipping wildly in the lingering wind. She knelt beside Aurelia, pressing her palms against the wounded dragon's side.

A soft pulse of warmth radiated from her fingertips, flowing into Aurelia's wounds like a gentle light current.

"Hold on," she murmured, her voice firm yet soft, urgent but careful.

The magic stitched the torn scales together, the wounds closing beneath the golden glow. But though the bleeding slowed, though the pain eased, the exhaustion remained.

Magic could heal wounds but not erase the toll of battle. The aches remained, buried deep within muscle and bone, a constant reminder of the struggle endured. The weight of loss lingered in their minds, an exhaustion that no spell could dispel. Both seen and unseen, scars would remain long after the battle's end, etching their place in memory and spirit alike.

Valeon approached, arms burdened with bandages and supplies. He hesitated as he took in the scene of Aurelia's labored breathing, Gailen's near collapse, and the devastation that surrounded them.

He finally spoke, his voice quieter than usual. "She's... incredible."

Gailen exhaled a breath that sounded like laughter, but it was tired, worn, and drained of anything but truth. His hand still lingered on Aurelia's scales, his fingers brushing across the cooling surface of her wounds, feeling the faint pulse of her life beneath them.

"She is," he said, and there was no hesitation this time.

Then he turned to Valeon, his body heavy with exhaustion but his voice steady. "Thank you."

Valeon nodded. Some words did not need to be spoken.

A few steps away, Ong stood silent, taking in the battlefield.

His gaze swept across the smoldering remains, the figures standing among the ruins, the undeniable proof of all they had endured.

His body ached. His breath was slow. His weapon was heavy in his grasp.

And yet he smiled. It was not a smile of joy or celebration but one of quiet recognition—an acknowledgment of the struggle, the pain, and the resilience that had carried them through.

It was the smile of one who had fought and survived, who had stared into the abyss of darkness and refused to falter. "We're all incredible," he said.

It was not arrogance. Not pride. It was an unshakable, solemn realization settling over them like the weight of the battle itself. It was the certainty of what they had endured, of what they had become. And at that moment, it was all that mattered.

They all knew it. They all felt it.

But they also knew the truth that simmered beneath the silence.

The Battle for Vacari was far from over.

More shadows would rise, lurking just beyond the horizon. They knew that until they found and stopped the mysterious figure orchestrating these attacks, the dark dragons would keep coming, threatening the noble dragons and the people of Vacari. But the people would not abandon the noble dragons. They would stand, fight, and endure together. More blood would be spilled, staining the earth in battles yet to come. More sacrifices would have to be made, each a solemn price for the war far from over.

But for tonight, they had held the line.

For tonight, they had survived. And for tonight, that was enough.

Chapter 44

Verdantia vs. Xazorath

The Emerald Woods quivered under the weight of an impending storm, not of wind or rain but of fire, shadows, and vengeance. Xalzorath descended from the heavens like a living nightmare, his approach slow and deliberate, each beat of his massive wings carrying an ominous promise of destruction. The air grew thick with his presence, a suffocating weight that pressed down onto the forest. The trees seemed to shrink away from him, their leaves curling inward as though recoiling from the sheer malevolence he exuded. A creeping dread slithered through the woodland, an unnatural stillness settling over the land as if nature itself dared not breathe in his wake. His pure black scales swallowed the light, bending the air around him into an unnatural haze. It was as if reality itself recoiled, resisting his very presence. Shadows coiled and writhed at his approach, creeping unnaturally through the trees, and with them came a bone-deep chill, a warning unspoken yet unmistakable.

The massive dragon's wings sent shockwaves rippling through the air, each downstroke pressing against the trees with oppressive force. The light dimmed wherever he passed as if the forest itself recoiled from his presence. The earth trembled. The sky darkened.

Then he roared—a sound that shattered the fragile calm, shaking the very roots of the forest.

"Verdantia!"

The name was not called. It was hurled like a war cry, a sound of fury so raw it sent flocks of birds screaming from the canopy, their wings beating frantically in terror.

"I come for you! For all your kind who dared align themselves with Hespherus! This forest will burn, and you will fall!"

From the heart of the Emerald Woods, Verdantia emerged.

Her emerald scales shimmered like a beacon, reflecting the woven strands of ley-line energy that encased her form. The air around her shimmered and pulsed in rhythm with the magic, leaves trembling as an unseen force rippled through the forest. The ground beneath her seemed to thrum with life, the roots deep below responding to her presence as if the entire woodland acknowledged its guardian. The light pulsed harmoniously with the land, flowing through her like veins of living magic. The forest seemed to breathe with her, its ancient power lacing itself through her form.

She rose above the trees, her wings outstretched, the embodiment of an unstoppable, unyielding force. Perched upon her back, Thalorian tightened his grip on the Arborblade, the emerald hilt glowing faintly in response to Verdantia's power.

Her voice was measured, calm yet resolute, a voice of ages, of wisdom, of unwavering defiance. "Your quarrel is misplaced, Xalzorath," Verdantia's voice rang through the battlefield like a song carried by the wind. "Hespherus did what he needed to do to save Vacari, and in doing so, he saved me. Hespherus did nothing wrong. Do not let blind vengeance destroy what remains of this world."

Xalzorath's eyes blazed with fury. "Spare me your noble platitudes!"

His wings unfurled fully, blotting out the remaining light and casting a crushing shadow over the trees. The air around him tightened, charged with his growing rage. "You will answer for his crimes."

And then he struck. With a thunderous roar, Xalzorath surged forward, his claws cleaving through the air like scythes.

Verdantia met him mid-charge, their talons colliding in an explosion of raw power. A deafening boom tore through the forest as trees bent and cracked under the force. Leaves and debris blasted outward in a violent storm, and the air vibrated with the sheer magnitude of their clash. The ground shuddered beneath the force, cracks spiderwebbing through the earth as the impact resonated like thunderclaps. Defenders below felt it in their bones, the sheer force pressing against their chests like an unrelenting wave, leaving them gasping in the charged air. A violent gust of wind followed, flattening grass and snapping smaller branches as it tore outward. The defenders below staggered against the sudden force, their lungs filled with the raw, charged air left after the collision.

The ancient dragons spiraled upward, twisting and colliding in a relentless aerial duel. Their talons clashed, sending bursts of energy crackling through the air. They separated, then lunged again, a blur of emerald and shadow streaking across the sky. Each impact was thunderous, rattling the heavens and sending tremors cascading through the battlefield below. Every impact sent tremors through the battlefield, shaking the trees, ripping leaves from their branches, and tearing through the once-pristine canopy.

The defenders below braced themselves, their stances widening, arms shielding their faces as debris rained. The sharp sting of splintered bark and dust filled the air, the acrid scent of scorched earth mingling with the raw tang of magic. Each breath was thick with the taste of char and dirt, a grim reminder of the destruction unfolding above. "Gods above... how do you even fight something like that?" one of them muttered, her grip tightening around her sword. Another, steadier in voice but no less awed, responded,

"You don't. You survive it. And hope Verdantia wins." Some trembled, eyes wide with fear at the raw power above. Others stood resolute, gripping their weapons tightly, determination etched into their expressions. A few stared in awe, caught between terror and reverence, knowing they were witnessing legends clash.

The forest itself groaned beneath the battle. Xalzorath unleashed his Shadow Breath, a swirling maelstrom of darkness, tendrils of pure void twisting and writhing like living serpents. The temperature plummeted, an unnatural chill spreading with alarming speed, frosting over leaves, and creeping across the ground in a thin layer of ice. A biting cold seeped into the bones of those who stood too close, their breath turning to mist as they struggled against the numbing grip of the encroaching darkness. Breath came in ragged gasps, their lungs burning with the sudden cold, limbs stiffening as if frost had crept beneath their skin. Even movement became a struggle, their bodies sluggish, weighed down by the oppressive chill that leeched warmth and life from the air. The air grew thick, suffocating, as if reality itself recoiled from the presence of such void-born corruption. A crushing weight settled over the battlefield, the air shimmering unnaturally as shadows pulsed and writhed at the edges of perception. The air warped around it, its touch withering leaves to ash, reducing bark to blackened husks.

A corrosive hiss filled the air, the mist crawling forward, consuming everything in its path.

But Verdantia was ready. She summoned the winds, a roaring gale from her maw colliding with the venomous darkness mid-air. The two forces clashed, battling for dominance, and the sky was caught between pure, suffocating corruption and an unyielding breath of renewal.

The wind howled, carrying within it the hum of the ley lines, a pulse of ancient power. It was rhythmic and steady, the heartbeat of the land itself.

And the darkness began to falter. Thalorian tightened his grip.

"His attacks are relentless," he muttered, his voice nearly lost in the storm of power.

Verdantia's voice rang through their shared bond, calm but focused. Her wings flickered, adjusting subtly as if reinforcing her resolve, her breath steady despite the storm raging around her. Beneath her measured tone, a storm of thoughts swirled calculations of wind currents, the pulse of the ley lines beneath her claws, and the ebb and flow of magic coursing through the forest. She could feel the land responding to her presence, ancient power waiting to be wielded. This was not just a battle of strength but of will, of harmony against chaos. And she would not let the forest fall. "I know," she answered. "But he underestimates the forest."

Xalzorath dove sharply, his massive wings carving through the air like blades, the force of his descent sending leaves and debris swirling in his wake. Below, defenders braced instinctively, their hands tightening on their weapons, eyes widening with terror and awe. Some staggered as the gust of displaced air nearly knocked them off their feet, while others exchanged silent, grim glances, knowing the actual battle was only beginning. The air howled around him, his sheer speed a terrifying display of power.

He twisted midair with deadly precision, his charcoal claws gleaming like razor-edged scythes as they slashed toward Verdantia's flank.

But the emerald dragon rolled gracefully, evading the attack fluidly. With unshaken poise, she retaliated, unleashing a concentrated burst of ley-infused energy from her maw.

The impact struck Xalzorath's wing, sending him into a violent spiral. His massive form barreled toward the ground, twisting uncontrollably before he caught himself with a furious beat of his wings.

Below, the Emerald Woods came alive. The ancient magic, long woven into the very roots of the land, responded to the threat. A soft hum vibrated through the trees, growing into a resonant pulse, sending waves of ethereal green light shimmering through the branches. The defenders shivered as the magic surged around them, their skin tingling with the raw energy. Some gasped at the sudden rush of power, their hearts pounding as if in rhythm with the awakening forest, while others clenched their fists, steadied by the ancient force that now coursed through them. The energy crackled like distant thunder, rolling through the forest floor, awakening something ancient, powerful, and unyielding. The defenders felt it surge beneath their feet, a protective and commanding force. The air vibrated with unseen power, filling their lungs with raw magic, their bodies bracing as the earth responded to the call. Leaves shimmered, glowing faintly as the pulse of the ley lines grew stronger, binding them to the will of the land. The ancient magic, long woven into the very roots of the land, responded to the threat.

Vines, their edges glowing with the essence of the ley lines, surged upward, lashing toward Xalzorath like living tendrils.

The fairies and Luminara raised their voices in a melodic chant, a song of nature's defiance. The air trembled as their voices merged with the pulsing magic, strengthening the forest's hold on the invading dragon.

The very roots of the Emerald Woods twisted upward, seeking Xalzorath's limbs, wings, and throat. But the black dragon was not so quickly bound.

He snarled, ripping through the enchanted foliage with his talons and whipping tail. Yet for every vine he severed, more sprang forth, guided by the will of the forest's defenders.

Kaelorn stood at the forefront, his stance unwavering, shoulders squared as if bracing against the storm of battle. His presence was a beacon of resolve, a steady force amid the chaos. Those around him stole glances his way, drawing strength from his determination, their wavering courage bolstered by the certainty in his gaze. When it rang out, his voice carried authority and an unshakable belief that they could endure. His presence was a beacon of resolve, a steady force amid the chaos. Those around him stole glances his way, drawing strength from his determination, their wavering courage bolstered by the certainty in his gaze. When it rang out, his voice carried authority and an unshakable belief that they could endure. His eyes burned with determination, his jaw set with the weight of responsibility. His command rang out over the chaos, a steady anchor amid the swirling tide of magic and fury. "Pour your magic into the forest! It must hold him!"

Keisha stood among the defenders, her hands glowing with raw energy, the barrier pulsing beneath her touch. The magic tingled against her skin, crackling like static before sinking into her veins, filling her with strength and an unbearable weight. Each pulse of magic sent ripples through the air, the shield crackling like a storm barely held at bay. It shimmered with resistance, its golden runes flickering as dark energy battered against it, struggling to break through. The protective dome expanded and contracted as though alive, pushing back against the shadows with unrelenting force. It was a colossal force, a shimmering dome of protective magic, its surface rippled with golden runes that burned bright against the darkened battlefield.

She poured everything she had into it, her magic weaving through the air like threads of light, reinforcing the fragile shield against the relentless waves of destruction. Her muscles burned, her breath coming in ragged gasps as her knees threatened to buckle beneath her. A creeping numbness spread through her fingers, her grip faltering as spots danced at the edges of her vision. Every heartbeat felt like a hammer against her ribs, the strain pushing her perilously close to the brink of collapse. Each surge of energy felt like fire coursing through her veins, her vision blurring at the edges, but still, she held firm, refusing to yield. Her jaw clenched, exhaustion clawing at her, but she did not waver. This was her home. These were her people. She would not let Xalzorath take them.

The weight of the barrier pressed on her, her body trembling under the strain. Sweat rolled down her temples, her arms shaking, but her resolve burned brighter than the fire in her veins.

"We can't let him breakthrough!" she cried, her voice cutting through the chaos.

Xalzorath roared in fury, his struggle against the forest's grasp growing more violent. His breath came in ragged bursts, each exhalation laced with seething rage. Muscles quivered beneath his charcoal scales, straining against the enchanted bindings as if sheer will alone could break them. Shadows coiled tighter around his limbs, pulsing with frustration, their tendrils writhing in sync with his escalating desperation. This was not how it was supposed to be. He was power incarnate, a force of destruction, not something to be shackled like a caged beast. The indignity of it burned hotter than the pain, fueling his wrath as he lashed out, determined to tear the forest apart piece by piece. The ground trembled beneath his thrashing, cracks forming in the earth as his massive form twisted against the bindings. The defenders staggered, some falling to their knees as the vibrations rattled through their bones. Trees groaned under the strain, leaves whipping through the air like panicked birds, while the air seemed to pulse with the raw force of his defiance. His massive tail smashed against the enchanted roots, snapping some while others only tightened in response. Shadow tendrils slithered from his form, slicing through the bindings and violently tearing them apart.

Then his acidic breath spewed forth, devouring the enchanted foliage, corrupting the land beneath him with each seething drop.

Verdantia seized the moment. She dove with the force of a falling star, her claws striking true, raking across Xalzorath's exposed flank.

Thalorian raised the Arborblade, intensifying the emerald glow, and drove the weapon into Xalzorath's wing joint. The blade struck true, searing through scale and sinew with a crackling hiss. A burst of emerald energy pulsed from the wound, sending arcs of green light dancing across Xalzorath's body as the weapon dug deeper. The dragon's flesh resisted for only a moment before splitting apart beneath the raw magical force, a jagged wound glowing with residual ley power. The blade bit deep, searing through scale and sinew, sending a pain ripping through the dragon's form. Xalzorath's entire body convulsed, his wings jerking erratically as he let out a raw, guttural snarl. His talons scraped against the earth, desperately trying to brace himself, his breath coming in ragged, furious bursts. But even in agony, his rage did not diminish. It burned brighter, igniting a storm within him that was about to be unleashed.

The black dragon's roar split the sky, a cry of agony that echoed across the battlefield. But Xalzorath was not finished.

Bloodied but unbowed, he tore free from the forest's grasp with a mighty lurch. His scales were fractured, marred with deep gashes, a crimson trail dripping from his wounded wing.

Yet his eyes still burned with relentless fury. And then, he unleashed his Sonic Keening Wail.

The air vibrated as the sound wave ripped through the battlefield, a force so devastating that branches shattered, defenders were hurled backward, and the barrier wavered violently, its surface rippling like disturbed water before cracking in luminous fractures. Verdantia reeled as the sonic blast tore through the air, her wings straining against the force. A sharp pain lanced through her skull, the unnatural frequency rattling through her bones. She clenched her jaw, willing herself to focus, forcing the ley energy within her to stabilize. With a powerful beat of her wings, she pushed forward, channeling the resonance of the ley lines to shield herself, her emerald glow flaring against the onslaught. A piercing agony erupted in the ears of those caught in its wake, the sheer volume sending waves of nausea through their bodies. Their vision blurred, dark spots dancing at the edges of their sight as disorientation took hold. Limbs went weak, trembling under the relentless force, some collapsing as the unrelenting sound scrambled their senses, leaving them gasping for breath. Some clutched their heads, eyes squeezed shut, as their equilibrium faltered. Others staggered, their screams drowned beneath the overwhelming sonic assault, their chests tightening as if the air itself had turned against them.

Keisha's knees buckled, her vision swam, and a crushing weight settled over her chest like an iron vice, squeezing the breath from her lungs. It was suffocating, an unbearable force pressing down, threatening to drag her into oblivion. She could not fail. Not now. Not when so many depended on her. The pain clawed at her resolve, but she pushed it aside. There was no space for weakness, only the will to endure. Every breath felt like dragging air through the fire, her limbs trembling under the unrelenting pressure of the magic she channeled. Pain lanced through her skull, but she clenched her teeth, willing herself to endure. The barrier had to hold. She had to keep it.

She would not let it fail. But then she heard a tiny cry.

From the shield's edge, a delicate winged figure stumbled, dazed, a fairy caught in the wrong place at the worst possible moment.

Keisha's heart clenched. Cracks splintered across the barrier's shimmering surface, flickering erratically as the magic strained under the assault. The fairy was too close to the edge. There was no time to think. Keisha moved without hesitation.

She lunged forward, grabbing the fairy in both hands and tossing her back into the barrier's safety. The tiny creature clung to her fingers briefly, eyes wide with gratitude, before fluttering to safety. In that single breath of distraction, she felt the searing impact.

A massive force slammed into her, hurling her backward. Pain exploded through her ribs and shoulder, a white-hot agony that stole her breath as she crashed against the barrier's edge. Her vision blurred with white-hot agony, her ears ringing, the world spinning. A chilling numbness crept through her limbs, distant and unreal, as if her body no longer belonged to her. The weight of consciousness slipped, her thoughts scattering like leaves in a storm.

The tiny fairy fluttering inside the shield was the last thing she saw before darkness edged her vision. She was safe.

Verdantia weathered the soundwave, her emerald aura flaring brighter in defiance, crackling with raw energy as it pulsed in rhythmic waves. The magic coiled around her, rippling like liquid light, each surge reinforcing the power she wielded against the darkness. The force rattled through her bones, a deep, thrumming vibration that clawed at her senses. The frequency sent sharp pain lancing through her skull, but she steadied herself, grounding into the ancient magic that flowed through her veins. She did not falter. Her focus remained unshaken, and she will be a fortress against the storm. The air shuddered under the force of Xalzorath's wail, trees bending like reeds, leaves ripped from branches, swirling in the violent wake of his fury.

But the forest refused to fall. The dragon's breath faded into the sky, dissipating in the face of the ancient power pulsing through the woods.

Verdantia's eyes blazed, her presence unshaken. "Enough, Xalzorath," she said, her voice cutting through the din, ringing through the battlefield like a final decree.

"This ends now." The forest answered her call. The ground trembled in response, roots twisting and rising as if the land awakened to her command. The trees groaned, their branches crackling with latent energy, leaves shimmering with an ethereal glow as the ancient magic surged to life.

The air vibrated with the raw hum of ley-line energy, the very earth beneath them awakening, its pulse growing more assertive, deeper, more commanding. A tingling sensation crawled over the defenders' skin, the hairs on their arms standing on end as if charged by an unseen force. Some staggered, their breaths hitching as the power coiled through their veins, their fingers twitching with the electric thrill of magic woven into their essence. Defenders gasped as the surge of power coursed through them, invigorating their weary bodies with renewed strength. The ground trembled, not with fear, but with purpose, as if the land had joined the fight. Eyes widened in awe and determination as the ancient force wove through their veins, binding them to the forest's will.

The fairies and Luminara raised their voices once more, their chant swelling to a crescendo, weaving into the fabric of the land's magic.

From the ground, roots surged upward, thick as tree trunks, coiling around Xalzorath's limbs, dragging him toward the earth like a beast claimed by the land.

He thrashed violently, his scorched charcoal scales splitting further, but three more took their place for every vine he severed.

Above him, Verdantia circled, her wings outstretched, her form radiant with the collective strength of the Emerald Woods.

The ley lines pulsed, their emerald glow merging with her, converging on her form like an unbreakable shield.

Xalzorath snarled, his shadows twisting and lashing out violently, their jagged tendrils clawing at the encroaching light. They writhed in desperation, fraying at the edges under the relentless force, flickering like dying embers as the radiant magic constricted around him. The magic constricted around his limbs like living chains, burning against his scales with an unrelenting intensity. Every pulse of energy sent a searing pain through his body, his muscles tensing as if caught in an inescapable vise. The weight of the forest's will bore down on him, pressing into his very essence, suffocating the darkness he wielded like a blade. Desperation flickered beneath his fury, and he could feel the ley lines constricting and tightening with an unrelenting grip. His mind raced for an escape, his claws raking against the roots with frantic determination. He had underestimated the forest's will but would not be buried without a fight.

But resistance was futile. The earth itself was rising to claim him.

Verdantia drew a deep breath, the glow of the ley lines reflecting in her emerald eyes. The air seemed to hold its breath, the battlefield caught in the stillness before the storm.

For a moment, time seemed to freeze. The defenders held their breath, eyes wide with awe and trepidation. Some clutched their weapons tighter, their knuckles white, while others glanced toward Verdantia, their expressions filled with silent hope. The trees stood motionless, their leaves no longer swaying, as if the forest awaited the final blow. Even the earth, moments ago trembling with battle, grew eerily still, listening, watching, waiting. The air thickened with tension, charged with raw energy as if the land held its breath in anticipation of the final strike. The wind stilled, the echoes of battle fading into a charged silence. Energy coiled around Verdantia, luminous veins of emerald light crackling along her scales, feeding into the storm gathering in her chest. The air quivered with anticipation, the weight of an unstoppable force pressing down upon the battlefield. Then, with a roar that resonated through the very bones of the land, she unleashed her full power.

A torrent of pure emerald energy erupted from her maw, a force so blindingly brilliant that even the shadows recoiled, devoured by the radiance.

The ground shook beneath its intensity, arcs of emerald lightning crackling through the air, striking like divine judgment.

Xalzorath's form convulsed within the storm of light, his shadows torn apart at the seams, unraveling under the relentless onslaught. Rage burned hotter than the pain, a fury that refused to accept the impossible. He thrashed against the force consuming him, his mind a storm of denial. This could not be happening. He would not fall here. His muscles spasmed, his vision blurred at the edges, and a cold tendril of fear slithered through his mind for the first time. His strength drained like sand slipping through his claws, the crushing weight of the radiant energy pressing into every fiber of his being. His mind reeled, disbelief tightening like a vice around his thoughts. This was not how it was meant to end. He was darkness incarnate, the harbinger of ruin, yet he was broken, powerless against the forest's wrath. A flicker of something foreign doubt gnawed at the edges of his fury. Could he truly be defeated? His roar was not just one of pain. It was one of disbelief.

The Emerald Woods would not fall today. A collective breath of relief swept through the defenders, their exhaustion momentarily forgotten as they beheld the fading remnants of the battle. Some dropped to their knees, gripping the earth as if grounding themselves in the reality of their survival. Others raised their weapons skyward, shouting cries of triumph that echoed through the trees. The forest seemed to exhale, the tension that had gripped the land releasing in a soft rustling of leaves as if the ancient woods acknowledged its victory.

When the light finally faded, silence fell upon the battlefield.

Xalzorath lay broken on the forest floor, his body heaving with ragged, labored breaths. The forest stood victorious.

For a brief moment, the battlefield held its breath. The defenders stood frozen, their bodies trembling from exhaustion, eyes darting between the fallen dragon and the radiant Verdantia. Some pressed hands to their chests, their hearts hammering, while others exchanged silent glances of disbelief and cautious hope. A few clutched their weapons with trembling fingers, their breaths catching in their throats as they struggled to grasp the reality of their survival. Verdantia's wings trembled slightly, the immense energy she had unleashed leaving traces of fatigue in her stance, yet her gaze remained unwavering. The trees seemed to pause, their branches still honoring the victory or bracing for what was to come. The air was thick with lingering energy, the weight of what had transpired pressing down on every soul present. Then, cutting through the fragile silence, a new sound shattered the stillness.

A sharp cry. A body hitting the ground. Keisha lay crumpled near the flickering barrier, her breath shallow, her skin pale.

The moment of self-sacrifice had cost her dearly. The tiny fairy she had saved fluttered anxiously above her, its wings quivering, tiny hands pressed together in distress.

Kaelorn was the first to reach her, dropping to one knee beside her. The ground beneath him was damp and unsteady, the earth still quivering from the battle's aftermath, yet he barely noticed as his focus locked onto Keisha's still form. His breath came in short, uneven bursts, his brows drawn in tight focus. Concern flickered across his face, his ordinarily steady hands trembling as he reached out, glowing with soft light, to assess the damage.

"Keisha?" His voice was calm, but his fingers trembled as he pressed them against her injured shoulder and ribs.

Her eyes fluttered open briefly, unfocused and glassy as if struggling to anchor themselves to reality. Pain carved deep lines into her expression, her breath hitching as the raw agony flickered through her like a dying ember. "I'm—" Her breath hitched, her words lost as another wave of agony wracked her body.

Kaelorn's jaw tightened. "She took the full force of an impact meant to kill," he muttered, his magic already weaving into her wounds. "We need to get her stabilized."

Oryn rushed forward, his usually collected expression fractured with worry. "She saved one of ours," his voice was hushed, filled with quiet awe.

But not everyone saw it that way.

A nearby warrior, a Luminara fighter, his armor scratched and his face lined with exhaustion—shook his head, exhaling sharply as he ran a weary hand through his hair. His stance shifted, weight rolling from one foot to the other, his tone bordering frustration and admiration. "Damn reckless," he muttered, exhaling sharply. "We could've lost her."

Kaelorn shot him a sharp glance. "She saved a life." The warrior rubbed his jaw, grudging but unwilling to argue further.

Keisha stirred slightly, her voice a faint whisper. She struggled to keep her eyes open, her breath coming in short, uneven gasps as if every inhale were a battle of its own. Her fingers twitched against the dirt as if trying to grasp something unseen, but they lacked the strength. "Was not... thinking. Just... moved." Kaelorn let out a slow breath, pressing a gentle pulse of magic into her wounds. "That's what makes it matter."

The tiny fairy hovered close, landing near Keisha's shoulder, its small hands pressing against her cheek in gratitude. Keisha's eyelids fluttered at the touch, a faint, weary smile ghosting across her lips as she exhaled softly, reassured by the presence beside her.

And in the distance, Xalzorath stirred. The Emerald Woods fell silent.

The defenders watched as Xalzorath struggled to rise. Some instinctively tightened their grips on their weapons, bracing for another strike, while others exchanged uncertain glances, caught between disbelief and weary vigilance. The air hung thick with tension, every breath measured, every movement cautious, as if one wrong step could shatter the fragile moment between battle and retreat. His black eyes burned, a mixture of hatred, grudging respect... and something else—something unreadable, teetering between hesitation and a recognition he refused to acknowledge.

For the first time, his gaze flickered with doubt. His breath came in ragged bursts, his massive body trembling as though caught between the instinct to fight and the realization that he had lost.

Yet even in defeat, his voice was a growl of defiance. "You... think you've won."

The words were not a question but a warning. His massive wings trembled, the damage evident, but he still forced himself onto unsteady legs.

Verdantia landed gracefully before him, her eyes calm, unwavering. "It is over for now," she replied. "The forest stands, and so do its people."

Thalorian stepped forward, his arborblade glowing faintly. "And we'll be ready when you return."

Xalzorath snarled, his form flickering between corporeal and spectral, a dragon caught between the realm of flesh and the veil of shadows. His edges wavered, shifting erratically as if he were torn between two existences. Shadows coiled around him, struggling to hold him together, while faint wisps of his spectral form bled into the air, dissipating like smoke on the wind. Each flicker seemed both painful and unstable, his form convulsing in defiance of the forces trying to drag him away.

With a final, lingering glare, he turned. His form dragged itself into the darkness, each step leaving blackened scars upon the land.

The defenders watched, silent, as his wounded, towering form disappeared beyond the tree line.

His retreat was slow but deliberate, each step heavy with wounded pride and simmering rage. His posture remained rigid, his wings dragging slightly, but there was no mistaking the fury in his gaze. This was not defeat but a bitter withdrawal, a promise of reckoning yet to come. The shadows clung to him like a living shroud, trailing in his wake, staining the earth with their lingering corruption. The trees nearest his path withered slightly, their leaves curling inward as if recoiling from his presence. Even the air seemed colder where he had passed, the unnatural chill refusing to dissipate. His departure was not an absence but a mark, a scar upon the land that whispered of his inevitable return. This was not surrender. A lingering shadow stretched behind him, a dark reminder that his presence had not been erased, only momentarily subdued. As he disappeared into the forest's depths, his gaze flickered back just once, a silent promise that this battle was far from finished.

This was a promise.

The moment Xalzorath vanished, the collective exhaustion hit.

A slow, unsteady exhale swept through the ranks. Kaelorn remained kneeling beside Keisha, his hands glowing as he murmured a steady incantation, weaving magic into her wounds. The warmth of his healing spell pulsed through her, a gentle yet potent energy that seeped into torn flesh and aching bones, knitting them back together with a soothing hum.

"She'll live," he finally said. "But she won't fight again for a while." Silence.

"Good," Oryn muttered, rubbing the back of his neck. "She's done enough for now."

And with that, the defenders let out a collective sigh. Some sank to their knees, their limbs trembling from exhaustion, while others leaned on their weapons for support, their breaths coming in ragged gasps. A few clasped each other's shoulders, grounding themselves in the shared relief of survival. The weight of the battle still clung to them, but they allowed themselves a fleeting moment of rest. For now, they had won. But even as the battlefield quieted, the weight of what was to come pressed upon them. A cold breeze swept through the clearing, carrying a distant, echoing whisper as if the forest murmured a warning. The shadows stretched unnaturally long in the fading light, clinging to the edges of the land, refusing to be banished. The war had not ended; it only paused, a brief respite before the next inevitable clash. In the distance, the forest still whispered of danger, the shadows lingering where the light had not yet reached.

Chapter 45
Shadows Gather in Flameford

The fiery caverns of Flameford pulsed with heat as molten lava illuminated the jagged stone walls. Nocturna entered first, her obsidian scales gleaming faintly despite her wounds. Every step sent sharp pain lancing through her muscles, her wings aching with every shift. The deep scratches along her side burned like molten embers against her flesh, each movement a cruel reminder of the battle she had barely escaped. Yet, she forced herself to walk tall, unwilling to let the pain betray her weakness. The clash with Aurelia had been brutal, claws raking and fire searing, and neither was willing to yield. Even now, the pain gnawed at her, a bitter reminder of the battle's cost. She moved with deliberate caution, her Silver eyes streaked with violet darting around the cavern, scanning for any sign of betrayal, weakness, or unseen threats lurking in the shadows. Glaciera and Zylron, lounging near a pool of lava, rose on her arrival, their curiosity evident.

Glaciera, her icy scales shimmering like frost against the fiery backdrop, tilted her head. "Nocturna, you're injured," she observed, her voice carrying an edge of concern rare among the dark dragons.

Nocturna growled low, her pride stung like a fresh wound, an unwelcome reminder that Aurelia had bested her in battle, her strength and skill insufficient to claim victory. The fire of battle still burned within her, but the sting of her injuries gnawed at her confidence. She clenched her claws against the cavern floor, forcing herself to mask the frustration beneath her hardened exterior. "I am fine," she snapped, though her posture betrayed her fatigue. "I did my part. Aurelia suffered under my claws, her pride, and scales bearing the marks of our clash. Crystal Vale will remember the ferocity of this day."

Zylron stepped forward, his crimson-red eyes scanning her carefully. Nocturna stiffened, her wings shifting slightly, instinctually widening as if to assert dominance. Her claws flexed against the stone but met his gaze without flinching, refusing to show weakness. "Your injuries tell another story," He said, his tone almost mocking though laced with caution. "Did you weaken them enough?"

Before Nocturna could answer, a thunderous roar echoed through the cavern, drawing their attention to the entrance. Xalzorath stumbled in, one of his wings dragging limply behind him, its membrane torn and trailing ash. His movements were labored, each step dragging as if the weight of defeat clung to his very bones. Deep gouges oozed a faint, dark ichor, the slow seep of his lifeblood starkly contrasted with the fury that still burned in his eyes. Every breath came ragged, a harsh rasp against the heavy silence, but the pain did not dim his rage. It only sharpened it, feeding the smoldering ember of vengeance that refused to die. Scorch marks marred his once-flawless charcoal scales as if seared by an unrelenting inferno. His eyes burned with rage, and his presence darkened the cavern further.

Zylron moved quickly toward him. "Xalzorath, what happened?" he demanded, his voice tinged with genuine concern for the first time.

Xalzorath growled, his teeth bared, his wings trembling with barely contained fury. Vengeance burned in his chest, eclipsing even the pain that wracked his body. The humiliation of defeat gnawed at him, fueling a hunger for retribution that refused to be ignored. His entire body ached from the battle, but his rage burned hotter than his wounds. The searing pain of Verdantia's fangs piercing his wing, the humiliation of being forced back as the emerald dragon outmaneuvered him—these memories festered like an open wound, fueling the fire of his wrath.

What happened is not your concern, Zylron," he spat. "This is far from over. Verdantia will pay for the humiliation they dealt us in battle, their emerald champion mocking our strength at every turn — and so will every other noble dragon that dares to stand against us." His voice, laced with venom, reverberated through the cavern as he limped past them.

"Let the defenders revel in their so-called victory. They have paid a price," he sneered, his gaze narrowing. "Even their precious Keisha did not escape unscathed."

Nocturna, leaning against the cavern wall, let out a low, derisive snort. "Empty words," she muttered, not loud enough for Xalzorath to hear but sharp enough to cut through the silence.

Zylron's ear twitched at her remark, his gaze flickering toward her in silent reproach. Glaciera's tail curled, her muscles taut beneath scaled flesh, though she withheld any response.

The two exchanged uneasy glances. They had witnessed Xalzorath's fury before, but this time, it ran deeper — a simmering, dangerous rage that unsettled even them. Nocturna smirked, her satisfaction lingering as the others let her challenge hang unanswered in the thickening air.

Tension coiled around them like storm clouds pressing upon the cavern. Zylron's claws flexed against the stone, while Glaciera's tail coiled tighter, her wary eyes shifting between her companions. The oppressive heat did little to chase away the cold weight of distrust settling over them.

Before any further words could be exchanged, the temperature in the cavern seemed to shift. A sudden hush fell over the space, the distant bubbling of lava momentarily ceasing as if the molten river held its breath. Like the faint splintering of stone under unseen pressure, a crackling sound echoed through the cavern, sending a ripple of unease through those gathered. A thick, stifling weight pressed against their scales, and an unnatural stillness settled over the space. Nocturna's wings tensed involuntarily, Zylron's tail flicked in irritation, and Glaciera exhaled slowly as if steadying herself. Once pulsing with restless energy, even the lava appeared subdued, its glow dimming as though recoiling from an unseen force. A heavy, oppressive energy filled the space, carrying a low, resonant hum that seemed to vibrate through the very stone. Even the lava appeared to dim as if cowering in the presence of an approaching storm.

"The mysterious person," Glaciera hissed under her breath, her icy scales shimmering nervously. Zylron's molten eyes narrowed, and he straightened, bracing himself. Both knew what was coming. The memories of the last encounter with their volatile leader were still fresh, and they prepared for the inevitable storm.

The sound of deliberate, measured steps echoed through the cavern as the mysterious person entered, their dark cloak billowing slightly in the oppressive heat. Yet, with each step, the very warmth of the cavern seemed to recoil, as if the fire itself feared their presence. A ghostly chill slithered through the air, an unnatural contrast against the molten landscape, sending an involuntary shudder through even the most hardened dragons. Steam hissed where the cold met the searing heat, curling in ghostly tendrils that twisted upward as if recoiling from the unnatural presence that had entered the cavern. A faint metallic tang mixed with the sulfurous air and the subtle scrape of boots on stone heightened the tension with each step. The molten glow of the lava cast fleeting glimpses of the person's silhouette, its flickering light accentuating the tension that rippled through the gathered dragons. Their sharp intakes of breath and the subtle shifting of claws against the stone betrayed their unease as if the mere presence of the cloaked figure demanded submission. Their presence alone drained the air of warmth, leaving even the dark dragons uneasy.

The mysterious person stopped at the cavern's center, their gaze sweeping over the gathered dragons. A tense stillness gripped the chamber as the dragons instinctively stiffened under the scrutiny. Zylron's wings shifted slightly, an unconscious response to the oppressive presence, while Glaciera's tail curled tighter around her claws. Even defiant Nocturna exhaled slowly, masking any sign of unease the weight of expectation pressed upon them all, heavy and unspoken. A long silence stretched the kind that felt like the calm before an explosion, thick with tension and unstated expectations.

"Explain," the mysterious person said, their voice cold and sharp as a blade.

Nocturna stepped forward, her movements stiff, her tail flicking once in irritation before she stilled it. Her jaw tightened, but she held her head high, unwilling to show weakness. "I struck Aurelia," she said, her tone defensive. "Crystal Vale's defenses were tested, and I left her injured. It was a success."

The mysterious person turned their head slightly, their shoulders tensing ever so subtly beneath the cloak, the shadow of their hood obscuring any visible reaction. A faint shift in posture hinted at restrained displeasure, which promised consequences yet to unfold. "And yet you are injured," they said slowly, their voice cutting through Nocturna's confidence like a knife. "How, exactly, does this constitute success?"

Before Nocturna could respond, Xalzorath growled, his voice a deep rumble of anger. "Do not waste your breath on her," he snarled. "The noble dragons are resilient. They are too coordinated; Verdantia and her rider nearly crippled me." He flexed his good wing for emphasis, wincing in pain. "But this is not over. I will see them all destroyed."

The mysterious person's head turned sharply toward Xalzorath, and the cavern grew deathly quiet. Even Zylron and Glaciera, usually fearless, took a step back. The silence stretched until it became unbearable, and then the mysterious person spoke, their voice low and venomous. "Not over?" they echoed. "Do you think failure is a luxury you can afford?"

Xalzorath lowered his head, his growl rumbling low in his throat, seething rather than submitting. Anger flared in his chest. Why was he being reprimanded when he had at least dealt a blow? Keisha had been injured. That was a victory in itself. They should recognize his efforts and commend him for striking at one of their key defenders. Yet here he was, treated as though he had failed. His pride burned almost as much as his wounds, but he knew better than to challenge the mysterious person outright. "The elf Keisha was injured in the battle," he added, his voice laced with bitter satisfaction.

The mysterious person remained silent for a beat, then gave a slight nod, a shadow of a smile barely visible beneath the hood, an expression both approving and ominous, laced with a promise of consequences yet to come. Perhaps, for once, they would acknowledge the effort made—the injuries inflicted. The pain was a lesson if nothing else; maybe these wounds would forge something more substantial. It was unclear whether it was approval or something more unsettling, but the slight nod did not go unnoticed.

Zylron's tail flicked once, an instinctive reaction to the unspoken weight behind the gesture, while Glaciera's gaze lingered on the mysterious figure, her unease deepening. Nocturna, ever observant, narrowed her eyes, sensing that whatever the reaction meant, it carried implications beyond what was spoken.

The mysterious person continued, their tone rising with fury. The weight of their words pressed down like a vice, and the gathered dragons instinctively tensed. Zylron's wings twitched, his tail curling tighter, while Glaciera shifted uneasily, her claws scraping the stone. Even Nocturna, determined to hold her ground, felt the oppressive air settle around her, her muscles coiling in defiance of the unspoken threat. "Two battles." There was a pause, the weight of disappointment pressing into the silence. "Two failures." The words hung in the air, each syllable laced with scorn.

"You have tested their defenses, yes, but at what cost? Each skirmish has weakened us, with allies lost and the noble dragons emboldened. Do you not see the price we pay for these repeated humiliations? Your pride? Your strength? I see injuries, exhaustion, and excuses. Do you think this is acceptable?"

Glaciera shifted uneasily, her icy breath misting in the thick, stifling heat. The oppressive warmth clung to her like a suffocating shroud, sapping her strength with each passing moment. Her usually fluid movements felt sluggish, her frost-kissed scales radiating a faint chill in protest against the overwhelming heat. Every breath felt heavier, as though the molten air sought to smother the cold that defined her. The air pressed down like a smothering weight, charged with tension, making each inhale feel like breathing embers. The weight of the mysterious person's fury pressed down on her, a stark reminder of the thinning patience that had already claimed too many lives. She had seen their wrath before unforgiving, absolute. And now, with tensions mounting, she wondered who among them would be next to fall under their crushing expectations.

Zylron, ever the opportunist, broke the silence. "Perhaps mixing our forces was not the wisest strategy. The noble dragons have fought side by side for eons. We, however, are not known for our unity. Our kind has always thrived in chaos, not cohesion."

"Silence!" The mysterious person's voice lashed out like a whip, and Zylron fell silent, his molten eyes narrowing.

The mysterious person turned, their dark cloak swirling around them. "You will recover," they said, their voice dangerously calm now. "You will regroup. And you will not fail me again. Do you understand?"

A chorus of reluctant growls and nods followed. The mysterious person lingered for a moment, their gaze heavy on each dragon, before disappearing into the shadows. A few dragons instinctively bristled, their tails lashing in barely restrained tension. Zylron exhaled slowly through his nostrils, his molten eyes flickering with unease, while Glaciera's claws flexed against the stone, the chill of her breath growing sharper. Even Nocturna's wings tensed slightly before she forced herself to relax, masking her reaction behind a carefully measured glare. A collective exhale followed, the tension momentarily easing, though no one dared to speak first.

The cavern was silent for a long time after their departure, the only sound of the distant bubbling of lava and the soft rasp of uneasy breaths. Shadows flickered across the jagged walls, shifting like restless specters as the dragons exchanged wary glances. A faint tremor ran through the stone as if the cavern itself recoiled from the tension left in the wake of the mysterious person's fury. The walls seemed to shudder as though absorbing the weight of their wrath while an eerie silence lingered, stretching the unease between the gathered dragons. No one spoke, but the flick of tails and the subtle grinding of claws against rock betrayed the fear they refused to voice. The dragons exchanged wary glances, their tails twitching and claws scraping lightly against the stone floor as the weight of the mysterious person's words settled over them like a suffocating shroud.

Finally, Glaciera spoke, her voice a cold whisper. "We must be careful," she said. "Their patience grows thinner by the day."

Xalzorath let out a low snarl, his eyes burning with rage. "Careful or not, this is not over. They will pay. All of them." His tail lashed against the stone, sending tiny embers across the cavern floor. A tense stillness followed his words, the air thick with unspoken anticipation. Even defiant Nocturna flicked her wings in slight agitation while Glaciera's claws flexed against the stone, the only sign of unease. He turned and stalked more profoundly into the cavern, his limp barely visible in the dim light.

Nocturna glanced at Zylron and Glaciera, her silver eyes streaked with violet gleaming. "We have to strike smarter," she said. "Next time, there can be no mistakes."

Zylron nodded slowly, his molten gaze fixed in the direction where the mysterious person had vanished. "Agreed," he said, his voice low but edged with a quiet intensity. His tail flicked once, a slow, deliberate movement, as his narrowed eyes burned with something colder than fire. "Or there will be no next time."

The cavern's molten glow flickered, casting ominous shadows that twisted and stretched across the walls, distorting the dragons' forms into something darker, more menacing. Nocturna, still nursing her injuries, turned her gaze toward the others, the shifting light making her violet eyes streaked with violet gleam with an unsettling intensity. Her voice, low and quiet, broke the uneasy silence.

"The defenses were increased," she admitted, her tone betraying a grudging respect. "They were ready before we struck. Barriers, warnings, everything was in place."

Zylron tilted his head, his molten eyes narrowing thoughtfully. "They did the same in Goldmoor and Purplefire," he mused, his deep voice resonating through the cavern. "We had to fight through layers of barriers and prepared defenses. But..." He paused, his tone growing sharp. "Surely the mysterious person knew this. They are never caught off guard."

Glaciera let out a low, icy hum, her frosty breath misting in the heat, curling into thin tendrils that evaporated before they could touch the cavern floor. The sharp contrast of cold against molten air sent a ripple through the space, a silent reminder of the unnatural balance between fire and ice within their ranks. Her claws flexed slightly against the stone, a subtle sign of unease, while her gaze flicked toward the cavern's entrance as if expecting the mysterious person to return at any moment. Her eyes, sharp and calculating, flicked between the other dragons. "The question isn't if they knew," she said, her voice a whisper. "The question is... who's going to ask them?" Her words lingered in the suffocating air, drawing tense, uncertain glances from the other dragons. Even Zylron's usual bravado faltered as his molten gaze shifted away while Glaciera's icy breath misted in an anxious rhythm.

The weight of her words settled heavily over the group, stretching the silence into something thick and unspoken. Zylron's tail twitched, his usual arrogance replaced by wary contemplation. Nocturna exhaled slowly, her gaze flickering toward the cavern's entrance as if expecting the mysterious person to return. Even Xalzorath, ever defiant, remained still, his claws flexing against the stone in silent frustration.

Unbeknownst to them, the mysterious figure lingered in the shadows just beyond the cavern. Rigid with barely contained fury, their breath came slow and measured, each inhalation a battle against eruption. The air thickened beneath the weight of their wrath, the oppressive heat of the cavern folding in upon itself, stifling and unnatural. For a heartbeat, the molten glow of the lava seemed to dim, as though recoiling from the force of their restrained fury.

Their cloak trembled at the edges, the tension in their muscles betraying their composure. A faint twitch rippled through their gloved fingers before they flexed, then slowly curled into fists, knuckles paling beneath the leather.

As Nocturna's admission reached their ears, the atmosphere itself seemed to ripple, the hiss of molten lava mingling with the crunch of boots upon scorched stone — a quiet herald of the storm coiling beneath their still exterior.

"Valeon," the mysterious person muttered under their breath, their voice a venomous whisper barely escaping their hood. "That worthless fool..."

Without waiting to hear more, the mysterious person turned sharply, their cloak billowing around them as they stormed toward the towering spire where Lyra and Qellaun awaited. Each step struck the stone with a deliberate cadence, a grim rhythm that heralded the inevitable reckoning approaching them.

The tower loomed in the distance, its jagged silhouette cutting through the fiery glow of the horizon. As the mysterious person approached, their pace quickened, their frustration mounting with every step. By the time they reached the entrance, their fury was palpable, a seething energy that darkened the air around them.

The mysterious person shoved open the heavy stone door, the impact sending a resounding, resonant thud echoing through the chamber. Dust shook loose from the ceiling, drifting in lazy spirals through the dim torchlight. The hinges groaned under the force, and the door scraped harshly against the floor before slamming into the wall. Lyra and Qellaun, poring over ancient texts and strategizing in hushed tones, immediately looked up. Their expressions were unreadable, but their postures stiffened slightly, betraying their unease.

The mysterious person stopped in the center of the room, their presence filling the space like an oppressive storm cloud. Lyra instinctively took a half-step back, her breath shallow, while Qellaun squared his shoulders, though his fingers twitched at his sides. Neither dared to break the silence, their unease evident in the rigid lines of their postures. The air thickened, charged with an unseen force that sent a prickling sensation along the skin.

A subtle static filled the atmosphere, making the hairs on the back of their necks rise while the pressure seemed to press against their lungs, making each breath feel labored and shallow. A sudden shift in air pressure made the torches sputter, their flames flickering wildly as if recoiling from the force that had just entered. The temperature seemed to plummet for a brief moment, sending an unnatural chill skittering along their spines.

Lyra's breath hitched, and she tightened her stance while Qellaun's fingers twitched at his side, the tension coiling through his body like a tightly wound spring. The walls seemed to tremble under the weight of the mysterious person's presence, the flickering light casting restless, distorted shadows across the chamber. For a long moment, they said nothing. The silence hung heavy in the air, thicker than the heat that permeated the tower. The stillness clawed at their composure, demanding their attention and submission. The flickering torchlight cast eerie shadows across their cloaked figure, making them seem more extensive, more menacing.

Lyra and Qellaun exchanged a glance but wisely held their tongues. They knew better than to speak first when the mysterious person was in such a state. The silence grew heavier, pressing down on them like an invisible weight until the very walls were holding their breath. Lyra shifted slightly, her fingers twitching at her sides as if resisting the urge to move, while Qellaun's jaw tightened, his throat bobbing with a slow, measured swallow. The flickering torchlight cast restless shadows across their faces, accentuating the unease neither dared to voice.

The silence stretched, dense and unyielding, pressing into every corner of the room. The torches flickered erratically, their light casting long, wavering shadows as if the walls themselves hesitated to bear witness. Finally, the mysterious person spoke, their voice low and icy, slicing through the oppressive stillness. "Do you know why I am here?" The question, though simple, carried a dangerous edge that sent a shiver down Lyra's spine.

Lyra hesitated, her mind racing through possible responses. If she chose her words poorly, the consequences could be severe. Was this an interrogation or merely a warning? Did the mysterious person already know the answer, waiting for a confession, or was this a test of loyalty? The wrong response could shift their wrath onto her. She could feel the weight of the mysterious person's fury pressing down on her, tightening her throat like an unseen hand. Still, she forced herself to remain composed, her voice steady despite the unease in her chest. "We can only assume it pertains to the battles," she said carefully, her tone measured.

The mysterious person turned their head slightly, the shadow of their hood obscuring their expression. "Assumptions," they said, their voice dripping with disdain. "Do you think assumptions will win this war?"

Qellaun, ever the stoic, remained silent, his piercing gaze fixed on the mysterious person. He knew better than to interject when their temper was running high.

The mysterious person stepped closer, their movements deliberate and controlled. The air around them seemed to contract, thick with unseen pressure, making each breath feel heavier. Their boots struck the stone floor with an ominous rhythm, the sound sharp and measured, like the ticking of an unseen countdown. "Valeon was instructed no, commanded to inform me of any changes immediately," they hissed, their voice sharper with each word. "And yet, here I stand, blindsided by increased defenses in not one but two of our targets!"

Lyra and Qellaun exchanged another glance, this one filled with silent understanding. They both recognized the storm brewing before them. Valeon was about to suffer the consequences of his misstep, and neither wished to be caught in the aftermath. Valeon's failure or perceived failure had once again ignited the mysterious person's wrath.

The mysterious person's voice dropped to a dangerous whisper. "He defied me. And now, he will understand the cost of disobedience." Lyra stiffened, her breath catching for just a moment before she forced her posture to remain neutral. Qellaun's gaze flickered toward her, his jaw tightening as if weighing whether to speak. Neither dared to move, but their tension crackled like an impending storm."

Lyra shifted slightly, tilting her head just enough to mask the flicker of intrigue in her eyes, though the slight tightening of her grip betrayed the tension coiling beneath her composure. Her pulse quickened, a faint tremor running through her fingers as she clenched them at her sides. Each breath felt measured and controlled, an effort to mask the unease swirling beneath her composure. She knew the mysterious person never issued empty threats, and whatever punishment they had in mind for Valeon would serve as a brutal lesson. Was this merely rage, or was there a deeper strategy behind their fury? "What do you intend to do?" she asked, calm but tinged with intrigue.

The mysterious person turned sharply, their hooded gaze landing on her. Lyra drew a quick breath, their stare settling over her like a leaden shroud. A flicker of unease crossed her face before she forced it away, steeling herself against the unspoken challenge in their presence. "What I intend," they said coldly, "is none of your concern. Just know this: Valeon will have no room for error when I finish. None."

The mysterious person paused, their gaze sweeping over Lyra and Qellaun again. Qellaun's jaw tightened almost imperceptibly, his fingers curling into fists at his sides. He held their gaze without flinching, yet a subtle tension settled in his stance, like a soldier bracing for impact. Standing beside him, Lyra felt the moment's weight pressing down on them, an unspoken warning lingering in the air. "The dragons may not have achieved what was expected," they said, their voice edged with dark satisfaction, "but Keisha was injured." A brief silence followed, their words sinking in like a well-placed dagger. Lyra stiffened, her fingers twitching slightly at her sides, while Qellaun cast a sharp glance in her direction, his expression unreadable. Then, without another word, they turned on their heels and stormed out of the tower, their cloak snapping like a whip, trailing their fury in its wake. The door slammed shut with a resounding finality, sending a tremor through the floor beneath them. Lyra exhaled slowly, rolling her shoulders as if shaking off an unseen weight, while Qellaun remained rigid, his fingers still curled into fists. The charged air left in their wake was thick with unspoken tension, a lingering presence neither could ignore. The door slammed shut, leaving Lyra and Qellaun in the suffocating silence again.

Qellaun finally broke the stillness, his voice low and dry. "It seems Valeon's days of teetering on the edge are numbered."

Lyra smirked, her eyes gleaming with a dangerous curiosity. "Keisha injured... that changes things," she mused, tapping a finger against her arm. "A failure in one regard, but perhaps an advantage in another."

Qellaun nodded, his expression contemplative, his brow furrowing slightly as he exhaled a slow, measured breath. "And Valeon's failure only makes things worse. The question is, how much longer will the mysterious person tolerate it?" Lyra's smirk deepened, her tone almost amused. "Perhaps," she said softly, "but watching this unfold might be worth the chaos."

The cavern was alive with the fiery glow of molten lava, its searing heat pressing against every surface as the mysterious person stood at the threshold, contemplating the fate of their so-called agent. Valeon's repeated failures gnawed at their patience, each misstep fueling a storm of conflicting impulses within them, an urge to dispose of him swiftly, to rid themselves of his incompetence once and for all, warring against the cold logic that he could still serve a purpose if adequately disciplined. For a fleeting moment, they considered ending his life in the heart of Fel Thalor's infernal depths, where rivers of molten rock carved treacherous paths through the cavernous abyss. Their fingers twitched at their side, the temptation gnawing at them, a sharp, visceral need for immediate retribution. The thought lingered, a seductive whisper in the back of their mind, but logic intervened, a cold reminder that a swift death would be too merciful. A slow exhale, a calculated pause, and patience would yield a more satisfying punishment. The air there was thick with the acrid scent of burning stone, and the echoes of past agonies still clung to its walls. A single misstep would send him plunging into the seething void, his screams swallowed by the relentless, churning fire. A swift punishment that would bring temporary satisfaction, a fleeting moment of relief to their frustration.

Yet another thought lingered: a more calculated approach that would make him suffer the consequences of his defiance while ensuring his usefulness remained intact. The flicker of a smirk crossed their concealed faces as they relished the control they still wielded over his fate. There were more satisfying ways to deal with incompetence.

With a sharp gesture, they summoned Lyra and Qellaun to join them. The two figures appeared promptly, their expressions cautious but unreadable as they stepped behind the mysterious person. Together, they made their way deeper into the caverns where the dragons awaited.

The oppressive heat intensified as they entered the chamber, pressing against their skin like a living force. Beads of sweat formed on their brows, clinging to their skin as the thick, sulfur-laden air pressed against them like a suffocating shroud. . The molten pools cast eerie reflections onto the jagged walls, their glow shifting like restless spirits in the sweltering haze. The heat radiating from them was relentless, making the air ripple and distorting vision like a mirage. Every breath came thick and heavy, the scent of scorched stone clinging to their lungs while the humidity wrapped around them like a suffocating veil. Nocturna and Xalzorath loomed near the edge of the largest pool, their massive forms silhouetted against the fiery glow. Glaciera and Zylron stood to the side, gazes fixed on the newcomers.

The mysterious person did not wait for pleasantries. Their voice cut through the thick air like a blade. "Tell me," They demanded, "were you able to rid us of Prince Gailen?"

Nocturna shifted uneasily, her dark scales gleaming in the firelight. "No," she growled, her tone laced with frustration. "The defenses were stronger than anticipated, and the Crystal Dragon fought fiercely. Prince Gailen was no easy opponent with that enchanted Crystalbow, an ancient relic imbued with Aurelia's essence. The weapon did more than fire arrows; it channeled the dragon's power, making each shot a devastating force on the battlefield. The weapon did not merely fire arrows—it unleashed streaks of crystalline energy, each shot guided by the will of its wielder and amplified by the dragon's magic. With every release, the air vibrated with latent power, and the force of impact sent shockwaves rippling through the battlefield, making him a formidable adversary. Each arrow he loosed carried the dragon's might, striking with uncanny precision and devastating force. It is as if the connection between him and Aurelia is stronger because of it."

Xalzorath, nursing his injured wing, remained silent, his smoldering eyes betraying his fury. His claws flexed against the stone, and his tail flicked in irritation, the tension in his posture barely restrained. Lyra and Qellaun exchanged a glance but wisely held their tongues. "The emerald dragons are more powerful than we were led to believe, and the magic that pesky elf Keisha wields is strong, but thankfully, she was injured. Though I am not sure how badly, hopefully enough to keep her out of the battles for a while."

The mysterious person's gaze swept over the group, their displeasure evident despite their face remaining shrouded. The dragons instinctively braced themselves, their bodies tensing under the weight of the scrutiny. Nocturna's tail twitched, barely perceptible, while Zylron averted his gaze, his molten eyes narrowing. Even Glaciera, ever composed, exhaled a slow, frosty breath. A tense stillness settled over the chamber, unease rippling through the gathered dragons. "Pathetic," they spat. "Rest and recover, both of you. Your failures will not be tolerated again."

Without waiting for a response, the mysterious person turned to Zylron. "Prepare accommodations for the Abyssal Dragons and the Shadow Dragons," they ordered. "I have summoned them. They will arrive shortly."

Glaciera's head snapped toward Zylron, her icy gaze narrowing. Zylron's tail flicked sharply, a brief but telling gesture of irritation, though his expression remained carefully guarded. "The Shadow Dragons?" she murmured, more to herself than anyone else. "Do you think that's what we've been sensing?"

Zylron rumbled low in his throat, his molten eyes flicking to her, his expression unreadable but tense. A faint furrow creased his brow, betraying a flicker of reluctance. "It's possible," he admitted, his voice measured as if carefully weighing his words. "I've heard whispers of their return, but only in hushed tones. They are... not like us."

The other dragons nodded solemnly, their unease palpable. Tails flicked in agitation, wings shifted restlessly, and claws scraped lightly against the stone as if instinctively preparing for an unseen danger. The air seemed to grow heavier, thick with an unnatural stillness, as if even the caverns themselves recoiled from the approaching presence. The molten glow flickered erratically, casting jagged shadows that danced along the stone walls, twisting the silhouettes of the dragons into monstrous forms. A chilling undercurrent slithered through the oppressive heat, pressing against them like an unseen force. Nocturna's wings tensed involuntarily while Glaciera exhaled another slow, misting breath as if bracing herself against an unknown threat. Even the cavern seemed to react, the very stone pulsing faintly as if it feared what was coming.

In the silence that followed, Glaciera watched them leave, her icy breath misting the air. She turned to Zylron. "Do you think this is wise? Bringing them here?"

Zylron's molten gaze lingered on the doorway momentarily, his expression unreadable. His tail gave a slow, deliberate flick, and a brief hesitation passed before he answered as if weighing his words carefully. "Wise or not, it is happening. But I have heard rumors about the Shadow Dragons... ancient beings of unmatched cunning and malevolence. They thrive in the darkness between realms, their allegiance shifting like smoke in the wind. Legends tell of the night they turned against their own, abandoning an alliance mid-battle and leaving their supposed kin to be slaughtered. Even now, no one truly knows where their loyalties lie or if they have any. And I'm not sure even the mysterious person can control them."

The dragons fell silent, the weight of Zylron's words hanging heavy in the air. Glaciera shifted, her tail curling slightly in unease, while Nocturna's wings tensed, a nearly imperceptible twitch betraying her thoughts. Even the ever-composed Zylron exhaled slowly as if steadying himself against the implications of his own words. Once alive with the flickering glow of molten pools, the cavern felt colder, as if the heat recoiled from the foreboding presence of what was coming. Nocturna exhaled sharply, a thin mist escaping her maw where the fire should have been. Glaciera shifted, her frost-tipped claws scraping against the stone as unease coiled through her body. Even Zylron flicked his wings subtly as though attempting to shake off the unnatural chill settling over them. The silence stretched unbearably, and each breath was drawn with wary hesitation, the oppressive tension making even the embers seem dimmer in the suffocating stillness.

Emboldened by her position, Lyra squared her shoulders before daring to speak. "You summoned the Shadow Dragons?" she asked, her voice edged with disbelief. "Are you sure about this? Their allegiance is... fickle, at best."

The mysterious person turned sharply, their cloak snapping through the air with a rustle like a drawn blade. The heavy fabric dragged against the stone, echoing their barely contained fury. Their voice remained calm, but menace threaded every syllable. "Do not question me," they warned.

Lyra stiffened, her confidence momentarily faltering. A sharp inhale betrayed her lapse, her fingers twitching before she forced them into fists. The heat of the cavern seemed to press harder against her skin, oppressive and smothering. A spark of defiance flared within, but she buried it beneath hard-won restraint. The warning lingered like a poised blade, and she was not so foolish as to test its fall. She dipped her head in a curt nod, lips pressed to a thin line, her gaze averted.

Beside her, Qellaun shifted subtly, his presence steady but unmistakable. Though he said nothing, his posture tightened in quiet solidarity, a silent show of support for his sister. His watchful gaze never left the mysterious figure, guarded but unflinching.

Satisfied, the mysterious person turned and strode toward the tower, Lyra and Qellaun falling into step behind them.

As they reached the tower, the mysterious person slowed, their steps measured upon the ascent to the throne room. The silence stretched, weighted and uneasy, until Lyra finally broke it. "I don't understand," she said, her voice lower now, careful. "You summoned them, but... do you truly believe they will follow you?"

"You disappoint me, Lyra," came the soft reply, mockery curling beneath their words. "They will do as I command. They answer to me. And do not question me again... or else."

Lyra swallowed hard, her usual bravado caged by wary compliance. Her shoulders tensed beneath the weight of unspoken threat, uncertainty flickering in her gaze before she smothered it. Without another word, she followed them into the throne room, Qellaun close at her side, his silent vigilance unbroken as the shadows swallowed them.

Once inside, the mysterious person waved them away with a dismissive gesture. Lyra and Qellaun exchanged glances before retreating, leaving the mysterious person alone.

The room was silent save for the crackling of torches, their flames flickering uncertainly, casting elongated shadows that slithered across the stone walls. The shifting light danced over the mysterious person's face, momentarily sharpening the angles of their features before plunging them into darkness once more. A ghostly shimmer in the air hinted at something unseen stirring just beyond the reach of the fire's glow, an unsettling presence lurking at the edges of perception. A faint, almost imperceptible hum resonated through the air, like the distant echo of something unseen shifting within the darkness. For a brief moment, the shadows seemed to coil and pulse, stretching unnaturally before dissolving back into the gloom. The mysterious person's gaze flicked toward the movement, their eyes narrowing slightly, though they made no immediate reaction. A slow smirk curled at the edges of their lips as if acknowledging an unseen presence. A faint whisper of air stirred the chamber, carrying with it the lingering scent of smoldering embers and something darker, something unspoken.

The mysterious person walked to the throne and sank into it. Their fingers steepled as they leaned back, their smirk returning. Their gaze flickered toward the shifting shadows, and in a voice barely above a whisper, they murmured, "At least Keisha is out of the battle for now, Vuarus."

"Two problems, one solution," they murmured to themselves, their tone dripping with satisfaction. "Maybe it is time to push Valeon further."

They chuckled softly, the sound echoing in the empty chamber like the promise of impending chaos. The temperature seemed to drop, the air thickening as if the very walls held their breath. The shadows near the edges of the chamber wavered, stretching unnaturally as if responding to the sound, their movements eerily synchronized with the lingering echo of the laugh.

The thought of Keisha being injured, possibly out of the battles for a time, gave them a twisted sense of satisfaction. It was an opportunity, one that could be extended if necessary. Perhaps there were ways to ensure her absence lingered, to keep her from interfering at a crucial moment. It was a temporary advantage but could be exploited if correctly played one less obstacle to contend with now.

Chapter 46

Roots of Resilience

A gentle hum of magic vibrated through the air, threading through the towering trees like an old melody. It resonated through the ground and whispered through the leaves, a constant, living presence that pulsed harmoniously with the forest's heartbeat. A tingling warmth spread through the air, brushing against the skin like a comforting embrace, while the faintest echo of its song stirred at the edges of the mind. It pulsed harmoniously with the forest's heartbeat, resonating through the ground and whispering through the leaves, a constant, living presence. Verdantia stood at the edge of the clearing, her emerald scales shimmering faintly under the dappled sunlight filtering through the trees as though drawing strength from the ancient magic suffusing the air. Thalorian, his silver hair catching the same light, crept beside her, his keen eyes scanning the forest for any signs of lingering damage from the recent upheaval, the scorched bark, the shattered branches, and the disrupted earth left in the wake of the battle. Beside them, Kaelorn coordinated with the fairies, their iridescent wings fluttering as they wove together homes for the Luminara among the highest trees.

The fairies worked in mesmerizing unison, their faces aglow with joy as they wove spiraling walkways of luminescent vines linking the treetop dwellings. Suspended high among the ancient boughs, the paths glowed with gentle radiance, casting hues of silver and green, their surfaces shifting beneath each step as though responding to the movement of those who walked them. They pulsed in quiet harmony with the ancient magic woven into the land, a living testament to the resilience of Emerald Woods.

The walkways were sturdy yet fluid, adapting to the weight of those who traversed them as if guiding each step with an unseen hand. A faint hum of enchantment lingered in the air, mingling with the soft rustle of leaves and the distant trickle of hidden streams below. The atmosphere was warm but gentle, carrying the subtle fragrance of blooming flora, as clusters of bioluminescent flowers sprouted along the edges, their vibrant colors brightening the canopy with bursts of life.

Above, veils of emerald leaves filtered shafts of sunlight, dappling the scene in shifting patterns that danced across the living architecture. In that moment, Emerald Woods felt not only alive but reborn — a sanctuary carved from survival, woven with the fairies' hope and magic into something that would endure long after the echoes of battle had faded.

The Luminara stood nearby, their tall and elegant forms moving gracefully as they assisted in integrating into the forest. Their green and violet robes flowed like water, reflecting their deep connection to Etharyon. The eldest among them, Lady Sylmara, her hair like liquid silver and an air of quiet authority, guided the younger ones with calm precision.

A few steps away, Keisha lay on a bed of thick moss and woven leaves, her form still and wrapped in soft blankets. Though her breathing was steady, the strain of her injuries had left her weakened. A nearby fairy hovered close, adjusting a damp cloth against her forehead with delicate precision. They had done all they could for her here, but the decision had already been made—soon, she would be taken to Crystal Vale, where more potent magic and experienced healers could ensure her full recovery.

Kaelorn turned his gaze away from Keisha, his chest tightening at the sight of her still form. A flicker of guilt passed through him—not because he could have done more, but because he knew Ong too well. Seeing his wife like this, weakened and vulnerable, would be a bitter sight for him. Ong would not take this well. Seeing his wife like this, weakened and vulnerable, would be a bitter sight for him. He wished he could do more, but the decision had been made—she would get the care she needed in Crystal Vale. Exhaling softly, he refocused on the work at hand. The forest was healing, but there was still much to be done.

Kaelorn watched the work with satisfaction before turning to Thalorian. "The forest feels alive again," he remarked. "It's as though it's welcoming its new guardians."

Thalorian nodded, his hand resting lightly on the hilt of the Arborblade. "And the Luminara are proving themselves worthy of that trust. Their magic complements the fairies' work together, and they're forging a bond that will strengthen Emerald Woods against any future threats."

As they continued to observe, a younger Luminara approached Kaelorn, her expression a mixture of curiosity and hesitation. Her fingers tightened slightly around the scroll, the subtle shift betraying her uncertainty, while her gaze flickered between Kaelorn and the seal as if gauging the weight of the message she carried. In her hand was a sealed scroll, its wax bearing a crest unfamiliar to most but immediately recognized by Kaelorn.

"Do you know someone named Manard?" she asked softly, extending the scroll.

Kaelorn's brows furrowed as he took the scroll, carefully examining the seal. The wax felt cool beneath his fingertips, smooth yet firm, infused with a faint pulse of magic that tingled against his skin. A subtle energy thrummed within it, a quiet reminder that whatever lay within was bound by more than just tradition. It carried an enchantment that had endured the test of time. Memories of whispered negotiations and long-forgotten oaths stirred in his mind, bringing with them the weight of promises made under dire circumstances.

He had once stood at the crossroads of such alliances, knowing that the slightest misstep could fracture fragile bonds. As he held the scroll, the past pressed against the present, demanding acknowledgment. The past was never truly gone. It lingered, waiting for moments like this to resurface. He traced the edges of the wax, feeling the weight of history pressing against his fingertips. A flicker of recognition passed through his eyes, followed by a shadow of hesitation. His fingers traced the edges of the wax, feeling the weight of the years it had been in his possession.

The scroll carried more than just a message; it bore the weight of promises made and alliances tested. Kaelorn exhaled slowly, steadying himself before speaking as if bracing for the history embedded within its seal. The intricate design depicted a dragon and a tree intertwining, their forms etched with artistry that spoke of ancient ties and unbroken oaths. A faint shimmer of enchantment glinted off the wax, hinting at the scroll's importance and the magic that bound it closed. He nodded slowly. "King Manard. He is the ruler of Crystal Vale." Her expression shifted to one of quiet reverence. "This... is unexpected. I have carried this scroll for many years. It was entrusted to me by the King of Etharyon himself to be delivered only if the bonds between Etharyon and Vacari became true once more."

The weight of her words hung in the air, and even Verdantia let out a low rumble of interest. Thalorian's sharp gaze locked onto the scroll, and he stepped closer.

"What does it say?" Thalorian asked, his tone measured.

Kaelorn shook his head. "It is not mine to open. It was meant for King Manard's eyes only." He turned to Thalorian and handed him the scroll. "You should be the one to deliver this to him. But know this: if it carries the Etharyon King's seal, it may hold something deeply personal, perhaps even pivotal for both our people."

Thalorian accepted the scroll, his expression thoughtful. "I will ensure it reaches King Manard directly. But first, we must finish ensuring the forest is secure. No message, no matter how important, can take precedence over our duty here."

Verdantia growled softly with approval, her gaze lingering on the flourishing treetop dwellings where fairies and Luminara worked seamlessly. Some hovered in the air, weaving protective enchantments into the branches, while others moved gracefully along the winding walkways, exchanging knowledge and resources. The sight stirred something deep within her, a reminder of the old ways when such harmony had been taken for granted. She rumbled with quiet satisfaction, knowing they would not let it slip away this time. Their cooperation was a testament to the strength in harmony, a reassurance that Emerald Woods would not stand alone against the darkness. "The forest is resilient, but vigilance will ensure its survival. Let us finish our work here swiftly so the message reaches Crystal Vale."

Kaelorn turned back to the fairies and Luminara, his heart swelling with pride at their determination. The air around them pulsed gently with magic, a subtle thrum that resonated through the trees and carried the scent of fresh earth and blooming flora as if the very forest acknowledged their efforts. Kaelorn felt its warmth seep into his skin, a gentle yet undeniable force threading through his veins. The energy crackled faintly at his fingertips, sending a shiver up his spine, a quiet reminder that the land itself was alive, responding to their presence and purpose. He recalled the long years of division, the bitter losses that had once seemed insurmountable. Yet now, in the face of renewal, he saw something greater hope woven into the unity before him, a testament to the resilience of their people. The unity he saw before him, blending magic, will, and purpose, filled him with hope. For the first time in many years, he believed the ties between Etharyon and Vacari could heal.

As Thalorian tucked the scroll safely into his cloak, his silver eyes glinted with resolve. Whatever the scroll contained, it was clear that the future of both realms was growing ever more intertwined.

Kaelorn's attention shifted as he noticed one of the fairies hovering nearby, her tiny face etched with worry. Her delicate wings fluttered unevenly, betraying her nervous energy, and a faint tremor ran through her hands as she clutched the edges of her tunic. Her wings shimmered faintly, a telltale sign of exhaustion. He stepped forward, his voice gentle but firm. "What troubles you?"

The fairy hesitated, wringing her hands before speaking. "One of the young emerald dragons... he's injured. I tried my magic, but it did not heal him. It only made him feel better, but..." Her voice faltered, and she looked down, her wings drooping.

Kaelorn frowned, concern flashing across his face. Before he could respond, one of the Luminara stepped forward. She was a tall, graceful figure with a soothing presence and a healer's calm. "I will go with her," the Luminara said, her voice steady. "I am a healer. Let us see what can be done."

The fairy and the Luminara healer slipped into the dense foliage, their figures vanishing amid the vibrant green canopy. Shadows pooled beneath the towering trees, shifting as if alive while the hush of the forest embraced them. Leaves rustled softly in their wake, carrying the faint charge of lingering magic. The air grew cooler as they pressed deeper, tinged with the quiet whisper of unseen creatures stirring in the gloom.

Though the forest stood as a sanctuary, it still held its mysteries — some ancient, others waiting to be uncovered. Dappled light flickered through the shifting branches, casting patterns that danced across the forest floor. The earthy scent of moss and damp wood mingled with the faint trace of magic lingering in their passing, as if the forest itself watched their progress in silence.

Behind them, the group waited wordlessly, a shared tension hanging in the air as they turned to other tasks. Yet Kaelorn's gaze lingered on the place where they had vanished, his chest tightening with a familiar coil of protectiveness.

She did not look back, her steps steady and sure, and that quiet confidence sent a sharper pang through him than he expected...

Kaelorn instinctively stepped forward, his heart pulled by the deep weight of responsibility. He had promised to watch over the fairies, to ensure their safety, and the thought of stepping aside felt like a betrayal of that vow. For so long, he had convinced himself their survival depended solely on his vigilance — that without his constant watch, they would falter. But was that truly leadership, or fear disguised as duty? If he could not trust them now, how could he expect them to stand firm when the time came?

As these doubts twisted within him, Thalorian's hand settled gently on his shoulder, grounding him. The weight of that quiet gesture held understanding, as though Thalorian, too, wrestled with the same balance between duty and trust.

"Let her go without you," Thalorian said, his voice low and weighted by the moment. "If the Luminara are truly to call Emerald Woods home, they must build their own bonds with the fairies and emerald dragons. Trust them to do this."

Kaelorn hesitated, the conflict within him sharp and aching. His every instinct cried out to intervene, to stand as the guardian he had always been. Yet deep beneath that urge, he knew Thalorian's words rang true. Growth required trust — not endless guardianship. The weight of past failures lingered in the corners of his mind, whispering doubts, but he forced himself to see beyond them. This was not his path alone to walk — it belonged to them as well.

Before he could speak, Verdantia stepped forward, her luminous gaze meeting his with calm understanding. She rumbled softly, a sound rich with the wisdom of countless ages. Her expression, poised and steady, seemed to reach directly into the heart of his struggle.

"Thalorian speaks the truth," Verdantia said, her voice like the deep resonance of the earth. "The bond between the Luminara and Emerald Woods must be forged by their efforts. They cannot always rely on you to guide them."

Kaelorn exhaled slowly, the tightness in his chest easing, if only slightly. His shoulders softened beneath the weight of their counsel, his fingers flexing before settling at his sides. He managed a faint, wry smile, an acknowledgment of their wisdom and of the path he now saw more clearly.

'I suppose you're both right," he admitted, his voice touched with reluctant acceptance. "Still... it's not easy to stand back."

Minutes passed before the sound of soft footsteps heralded their return. The fairy fluttered ahead, her wings glowing with renewed energy, while the Luminara walked beside her serenely. Between them, the young emerald dragon stood, his movements steadier, the pain in his eyes replaced by quiet relief.

"He will recover," the healer assured them. "His wounds were resistant to magic, but he will be whole again with time and care."

The fairy beamed, clasping her hands together. "Thank you. I was so afraid he wouldn't make it."

Kaelorn nodded in gratitude. "You both did well. This is only the beginning of what you can accomplish together." A warm sense of hope settled within him, a rare and welcome feeling. For so long, his people had wandered, searching for a place to belong. As he watched them work side by side, he realized they had finally found a home where they could thrive, not merely survive. As he watched them, a quiet realization settled within him. He had spent so long believing that strength meant carrying every burden alone, but perhaps authentic leadership lay in empowering others to stand alongside him.

Thalorian placed a hand on Kaelorn's shoulder. "Now, we must move forward. Crystal Vale awaits, and the message we carry may shape the future of both our realms."

With a final glance at the thriving forest, Kaelorn and Thalorian turned toward the path leading beyond Emerald Woods, their journey far from over but now carrying a deeper understanding. As they walked, Kaelorn reflected on the weight he had taken when he first arrived in Vacari. He had believed then that every burden rested on his shoulders alone, that leadership meant shouldering every hardship without faltering. But now, seeing the unity between the fairies and the Luminara, he understood he was not alone. Others had stepped forward, proving that strength was not in solitude but in trust, in the bonds that made them stronger together. As they walked, Kaelorn exhaled slowly, the weight of responsibility still heavy. "Strange how much change can happen in such a short time," he murmured.

Thalorian nodded, his jade fire eyes reflecting the light ahead. "And yet, it is only the beginning."

Chapter 47

Echoes of the Past, Bonds of the Future

A tense stillness gripped Crystal Vale, the ordinarily vibrant grove subdued by a heavy air of worry. The usual chorus of birds had fallen silent, and the scent of damp earth lingered in the air as if the land held its breath. The magnificent crystal dragon Aurelia lay in the expansive healing grove, her iridescent scales dimmed by the injuries sustained in the fierce battle against Nocturna. Her breaths were slow and steady, but the occasional flicker of pain in her eyes did not escape those watching over her.

Prince Gailen paced nearby, his boots scuffing against the grass with each restless step, the soft rustle of blades barely masking his quiet sighs. His hands clenched and unclenched at his sides, his face etched with concern as his gaze flickered between Aurelia and Shael's healing hands. Shael knelt beside Aurelia, her hands glowing softly as she focused her healing magic on the dragon's wounds. Ong and Valeon were busy nearby, fetching sup-

plies and preparing the herbal salves and antiseptic potions Shael needed
to cleanse and dress the injuries.

Shael glanced briefly at Gailen as she worked, her voice calm but firm.
"You are not helping by wearing down the grass, Gailen. She is strong, and
she will pull through this."

Gailen nodded but could not stop his pacing. "I know," he said softly,
"but seeing her like this... It is hard. She is more than a dragon to me."

Ong returned with a basin of fresh water and a cloth, setting it down
beside Shael. "We've all been there, Gailen," Ong said, his voice steady.
"Watching someone you are bonded to suffer is difficult, but Aurelia is a
fighter. You must trust her strength."

A small voice broke through the tension. "Is Aurelia going to be okay?"

Everyone turned to see a child clutching a small bundle of flowers. The
little one's wide eyes were filled with tears as she approached the injured
dragon. Shael smiled warmly at the child, nodding reassuringly. "She'll be
okay," Shael said softly, her tone filled with conviction. "She just needs time
and care."

The child moved closer, her heart pounding with fear and awe. Her tiny
fingers trembled as she reached out hesitantly to touch Aurelia's massive
foreleg, uncertainty flickering in her wide eyes. Would the mighty dragon
even feel her touch? Would she know how much she cared? She swallowed
hard, determination settled in her chest as she pressed her palm against her
cool, scaled skin, silently willing her love and hope to reach her. "You have
to get better," the child whispered, her voice trembling with emotion. "We
all love you."

Aurelia slowly turned her head, her silver-blue eyes locking onto the
child with a quiet intensity. A flicker of warmth softened the pain in her
gaze, acknowledging the child's words. Her breath hitched, small hands
trembling slightly before she pressed the flowers closer to her chest, a mixture of awe and relief washing over their tear-streaked face. A flicker of
warmth softened the pain in her gaze, acknowledging the child's words.

The little one gasped softly, their grip on the flowers tightening as if willing her hope to reach her. Despite her pain, she managed a soft, reassuring rumble, and her lips curled into what could only be described as a dragon's smile. Tears glistened in her eyes as she gently lowered her head closer to the child as if to comfort them.

The child hugged her scaled foreleg tightly, and Shael wiped her eyes, moved by the tender moment. "She hears you," Shael said, her voice thick with emotion. "She knows."

Valeon, standing nearby with a tray of bandages, whispered to Ong, "Even in pain, she's thinking about others."

Ong nodded, his voice quiet but filled with pride. "That's what makes her a noble dragon."

The child released Aurelia and turned to Shael. "Please help her get better," she said, pleading.

Shael smiled gently and nodded. "I will," she promised. "And she'll be soaring through the skies again before you know it."

As her parents led the child away, Gailen approached Aurelia, kneeling beside her massive head. "You've always been there for me," he said softly. "Now it's my turn to be here for you."

Aurelia's gaze softened, and she let out a low, comforting sound as if to tell him she understood. Shael resumed her work, her magic flowing steadily, and the healing process continued, filled with the quiet determination of everyone involved.

The bond between dragon and rider, and between Aurelia and the people of Crystal Vale, had never been more evident, a connection forged in the fires of battle and strengthened in such moments. They had fought together, suffered together, and now, they would heal together. It was a testament to the resilience that bound them, the love and trust that endured, even through the darkest times.

The serene quiet of the grove was momentarily interrupted as King Manard approached, his polished boots crunching against the gravel path.

. A faint breeze stirred the leaves as if the air held its breath in anticipation. The once-muted tension seemed to shift, replaced by the quiet gravity of his presence. The faint clink of his ceremonial armor echoed through the air, each step deliberate and commanding. His every movement carried a quiet authority, intentional and assured. Yet, the worry lines on his face betrayed his fears for his son and the injured crystal dragon. His gaze swept over the scene, the glowing magic from Shael's hands, Ong and Valeon bustling to assist, and Gailen sitting protectively beside Aurelia.

King Manard approached his son, his voice warm yet carrying the weight of concern and authority, a steady presence that spoke of experience and unshaken resolve. "Gailen," he said, touching his shoulder, "I see how much you care for her. It is... reassuring."

Gailen looked up, his expression a mix of determination and vulnerability. His fingers curled against the fabric of his tunic as if steadying himself. A slow exhale escaped him, shoulders tensing before he met his father's gaze, resolve flickering in his eyes despite the weight of emotion pressing against him. "I understand why you might have doubted me," he admitted. "When I returned to Vacari, I was unsure how to let myself care again. But Aurelia... she is more than a dragon to me. She is... family."

Manard's lips curved into a rare smile. "At first, I feared you would remain guarded, always keeping the world at arm's length. I am glad I was wrong."

The quiet moment between father and son was abruptly shattered as hurried footsteps echoed through the grove, accompanied by the rustling of leaves and the sharp urgency in the scouts' voices. Ong's head snapped up, his stance shifting instinctively as his hand hovered near his weapon. Valeon exchanged a wary glance with Shael, his brows furrowing. Even King Manard stiffened, his gaze sharpening as he turned toward the approaching figures. The weight of an unspoken warning settled over them all before the first urgent words were even spoken. Two scouts rushed forward, carrying a makeshift stretcher between them.

On it lay Keisha.

Her red hair clung to her sweat-dampened forehead, her face pale, and her breathing came in shallow, ragged gasps. A crude bandage wrapped around her ribs, already stained with blood. A nasty bruise darkened one side of her face, and her shoulder sat at an unnatural angle.

Ong, who had been handing Shael another set of bandages, froze mid-motion, his fingers tightening hard around the fabric. A cold knot of dread coiled in his stomach, and for a heartbeat, everything else faded — the sounds of the grove, the murmurs of the others — until only the sight of Keisha's motionless form filled his vision. His breath caught, his grip clenching almost painfully tight before instinct forced him to move. His jaw set, chest tightening as he turned sharply toward the commotion, the steadiness he was known for buckling under rising fear. The moment his gaze locked on Keisha, something inside him snapped. His hands clenched into fists, and he surged forward, urgency burning away hesitation.

"What happened?" His voice came out sharp, edged with something raw.

One of the scouts, still catching his breath, answered quickly. "She saved a fairy. The shield was breaking, and a fairy got caught at the edge. Keisha went after her and pulled her back to safety." He hesitated, looking between King Manard and Shael before continuing. "That is when she got hit. A massive strike threw her straight into the barrier's edge. We barely got her stabilized."

Shael had already motioned them to bring Keisha closer with practiced efficiency, clearing space beside Aurelia. The great dragon shifted slightly, her silver-blue eyes narrowing as she let out a low rumble, the sound vibrating through the ground, a mix of worry and protectiveness. Her wings twitched, her gaze never leaving Keisha as if silently urging Shael to work faster. "Lay her down here," she instructed, her glowing hands reaching for Keisha's injuries. "Ong, I need more water and clean linens. Now."

But Ong did not move. His fists remained clenched, his chest rising and falling unevenly as he stared at Keisha's broken form.

Valeon nudged him. "Ong. Now."

The command snapped him out of it. Ong turned on his heel, storming toward the supply station with rigid movements, every fiber of his being coiled tight. His hands shook slightly as he grabbed what Shael needed, his breath coming too fast. He exhaled, steadying his grip before returning to Keisha's side.

Keisha stirred slightly, her eyelashes fluttering as a faint groan escaped her lips. A dull ache pulsed through her body, and she struggled to lift her heavy eyelids, the effort leaving her breath shallow and weak. "Ong..." she murmured, her voice barely above a whisper.

Ong was already kneeling beside her before he realized he had moved. His hands hovered over hers for a moment before he carefully grasped them, his grip firm but careful. "I'm here," he said, his voice low, rougher than usual. "You reckless idiot. You were not supposed to."

Keisha let out a weak chuckle, though the sound was cut short as pain lanced through her, forcing her to suck in a sharp breath. Her body tensed involuntarily, fingers curling slightly as a shudder ran through her. She squeezed her eyes shut, her jaw tightening as she tried to ride out the pain before exhaling slowly, her breath still unsteady. "And leave you... to have all the fun?"

Shael exhaled sharply but did not pause in her work. "Save your breath," she muttered, magic pulsing under her fingertips. "You'll need it for when I yell at you later."

Keisha's lips twitched into a faint smile. Ong, however, did not. His grip tightened ever so slightly around her fingers, his knuckles white.

Valeon spoke next, his voice softer now. "She is strong. She will pull through."

Ong did not answer immediately. His gaze remained locked on Keisha's face, his expression unreadable except for the tension in his jaw and the slight tremor in his grip.

A shadow passed overhead, the rhythmic beat of mighty wings cutting through the tense silence. A sudden gust followed, rustling the leaves and sending a ripple through the grass as Kimras descended, the air vibrating with the sheer power of his arrival. A golden shimmer reflected against the trees as Kimras, the golden dragon, descended into the grove. His eyes, molten gold darkened by concern, locked onto Keisha's still form. He landed with careful precision, standing protectively near her, his presence radiating silent vigilance.

Kimras's gaze flicked briefly to Ong, silently reassuring him as if to say he would ensure Keisha's safety. Ong met his eyes and gave a slight nod after a tense beat. No words were needed. The understanding between them was clear: Kimras would stand watch, ensuring she was safe.

Finally, his voice came, low and rough.

"She better."

Verdantia descended gracefully into the grove, the rhythmic beat of her wings stirring the leaves below and sending a faint swirl of dust into the air. A ripple of movement passed through those gathered, some instinctively stepping back while others straightened, gazes drawn to her emerald form. The air shifted with the weight of her presence, a silent acknowledgment of the power she carried. Her emerald scales gleamed in the sunlight, casting shimmering reflections across the clearing as she landed with a soft, controlled impact. Thalorian dismounted and approached, his expression concerned. Verdantia's gaze immediately fell on Aurelia, and she let out a low, worried hum.

"She's hurt," Verdantia said softly, her voice tinged with concern. She turned to Shael. "Is there anything I can do to help?"

Shael looked up from her work, her face tired but grateful. "Just let her know you are here. Sometimes, that is all it takes."

Verdantia nodded and stepped closer to Aurelia, her movements careful and deliberate. Aurelia's eyes softened as she let out a slow exhale, her body relaxing slightly at the familiar presence of her fellow dragon. A faint flicker of gratitude shone in her gaze, a silent acknowledgment of Verdantia's comforting presence. Lowering her head to meet Aurelia's gaze, she spoke gently. "You're lucky Amara isn't here," she teased lightly, "or she'd never let you live this down."

Even in her pain, Aurelia rumbled a soft laugh, a sound that brought a small smile to everyone in the grove.

Thalorian, meanwhile, approached King Manard and handed him a sealed scroll. "This is from the King of Etharyon," he explained, his tone formal but kind. "It was entrusted to the Luminara and brought here to you."

King Manard's expression shifted to one of intrigue as he carefully broke the seal, his fingers hesitating for the briefest moment before he pressed forward. His grip tightened slightly, the cool wax crumbling beneath his touch, as his mind raced with possibilities. Was this a call for aid, a rekindling of old alliances, or something far more personal? A whisper of unease flickered through him as he prepared to uncover whatever message lay within. The main scroll unfurled in his hands, and his eyes scanned its contents. His brows furrowed slightly, his lips pressing into a thin line as he absorbed the message. A flicker of recognition crossed his face, followed by a thoughtful pause as if the words carried a weight he had not anticipated. His expression softened, and he gave a small smile at the message. But then he noticed a more miniature scroll attached to the larger one. Gently detaching it, he held it momentarily, his fingers trembling slightly.

As he read the more miniature scroll, his face paled, his jaw tightening as his fingers clenched around the parchment. A name he had not spoken in years stared back at him, stirring a tide of emotions he had long buried. Memories of hushed conversations in candlelit halls and the final, fateful night before the war flooded his mind. He had believed this chapter of his life closed, sealed by time and loss, but now, the words before him threatened to unravel everything he thought he knew. A sharp breath escaped him, and he took a half-step back as if the weight of the words physically struck him. A flicker of disbelief crossed his eyes before the weight of realization settled in, deepening the creases on his forehead. Tears welled in his eyes briefly, and he quickly blinked them away.

Gailen, noticing his father's sudden change in demeanor, stepped closer. He asked gently, "What's wrong?"

King Manard took a deep breath, his voice steady but tinged with emotion. "This smaller scroll... it's from someone I thought was killed years ago." He paused, clutching the scroll as though it were a lifeline. "I need to read this in privacy," he added, his tone final but kind.

With that, King Manard turned and began the walk back to the palace, his shoulders slightly hunched as if burdened by the weight of the past. His grip on the scroll tightened, knuckles whitened, and his breaths came slow and deliberate, each measured as he wrestled with his emotions. His thoughts churned with emotions he had long buried: grief for the choices that had led to so much loss, regret for the unspoken words, and now, a flicker of hope that perhaps all was not lost. He could still hear the echoes of that final conversation, the promise made in desperation and shattered by war. The weight of the past pressed against him, but within it, a possibility stirred one he never dared to believe could return. Each step felt heavier, laden with the weight of the past and the uncertainty of what this revelation might mean for the future. Could long-lost ties truly be mended? Or was this merely another wound waiting to reopen?

Gailen watched him go, his own heart heavy with curiosity and concern. Meanwhile, the grove settled into a thoughtful quiet, the bonds between its occupants growing stronger despite the uncertainty of what lay ahead.

The air in the palace was thick with anticipation as King Manard strode through its grand halls, the scroll from Etharyon still clutched tightly in his hand. The towering marble columns cast long shadows under the flickering torchlight, their intricate carvings whispering echoes of Vacari's past. Chandeliers of glistening crystal refracted light into shimmering patterns on the polished floors, starkly contrasting the weight of tension pressing down on the chamber. The nobles gathered in the central chamber took notice of his grave expression and exchanged concerned glances. One of them, Lord Belathar, stepped forward, bowing slightly before addressing the King.

"Your Majesty, is something troubling you?" he asked cautiously.

King Manard shook his head, though his expression remained serious. A flicker of hesitation crossed his features, his grip tightening on the scroll as if steadying himself before he spoke. "No, nothing troubling," he said slowly. "I've received some news from Etharyon that may shape the future of Vacari."

The nobles leaned in, their curiosity piqued. Another noble, Lady Althea, spoke up. "Etharyon? What news, Your Majesty?"

King Manard held up the larger scroll. "The King of Etharyon has formally requested that trade be reestablished between our realms. This is excellent news for both Vacari and Etharyon."

A murmur of approval rippled through the room. Lady Althea smiled, but King Manard remained still, his fingers momentarily tightening around the scroll before he exhaled softly, maintaining his composed demeanor. "That doesn't sound like a problem, Your Majesty."

No, it is not," Manard agreed. "It is a step forward, a bridge that can strengthen our realms. But there is more." His voice grew quieter, tinged with emotion. "Along with this scroll, there was another. A smaller scroll from... Seraphina Frostwood."

The room fell silent, the name hanging in the air like a ghost. Some nobles shifted uncomfortably in their seats, their expressions ranging from confusion to shock. A few exchanged uncertain glances while others sat frozen, their hands tightening over the arms of their chairs. The silence stretched, heavy and oppressive, as if the air had thickened with the weight of the revelation. Lord Belathar frowned, his brow furrowing. "Seraphina Frostwood? Was she not your fiancée years ago? The one who was believed to have been killed during an attack in Etharyon?"

King Manard nodded, his jaw tightening. "That is what we believed. But according to this scroll, she was not killed. The King of Etharyon took her in after the attack."

The nobles exchanged stunned glances. Lady Althea pressed further. "But why... why would she not return to Vacari? Why now?"

King Manard's gaze dropped briefly before meeting theirs again. "Because she remarried," he said quietly. "And because she was carrying my child, a son."

A collective gasp rippled through the chamber, followed by several nobles' sharp breath intake. Some recoiled slightly, their eyes widening in disbelief, while others leaned forward, their faces tight with unease. A few clutched the arms of their chairs, their knuckles whitening, while whispered exchanges flitted through the room like the rustle of dry leaves. Some nobles remained motionless, their faces pale with shock, while others shifted uneasily in their seats, fingers drumming against polished wood or gripping the folds of their robes. A few turned to one another, whispering in hushed, urgent tones, while others sat frozen, struggling to process the revelation before them. The weight of the revelation pressed upon them all, reshaping the very foundation of what they believed about their king's past. Lord Belathar's expression hardened, his fingers drumming on the table's edge as if processing the gravity of the situation. Lady Althea's mouth fell open in shock before she quickly composed herself, her eyes darting to King Manard with curiosity and concern. "This changes everything," she murmured, breaking the heavy silence.

Lord Belathar took a step closer, his voice low but urgent. "Your Majesty, did she... did she name this son?"

King Manard nodded solemnly. "She did," he replied. "But I will not reveal his name here. This is a matter that requires the counsel of all our allies."

Lady Althea's expression softened. "What will you do, Your Majesty?"

"We will call for an immediate meeting," King Manard said, his voice firm. "Send out messenger birds to all our allies. They must know of Etharyon's request for trade and this... personal revelation. The dark dragons are still plotting, and unity will be more important than ever."

The nobles nodded in agreement, their earlier shock replaced with purpose. Some straightened in their seats, exchanging determined glances, while others clasped their hands as if solidifying their resolve. A sense of urgency settled over them, their initial disbelief giving way to decisive action.

Orders were given, and couriers and messengers began their swift preparations within moments. The hurried rustle of parchment, the clatter of boots against the stone floors, and the sharp calls of scribes dictating last-minute details filled the air, blending into a chaotic symphony of urgency. The palace bustled with renewed urgency as birds were sent soaring into the sky, their wings slicing through the crisp air. The wind carried their messages swiftly beyond the palace walls, rustling through the courtyard's banners.

Messengers hurried through the halls, their footsteps ringing across the marble floors as they clutched sealed letters destined for Vacari's allies. The weight of the moment pressed heavily upon them, urgency propelling every stride. Some courtiers paused, their gazes shadowed with both apprehension and resolve, as they watched the birds vanish into the horizon, knowing the fate of Vacari now rested on the answers those messages would bring.

As King Manard watched the flurry of activity, his thoughts lingered on the more miniature scroll and the name it contained. The shadow of the past loomed large, but the future now held a glimmer of hope and a chance to forge new bonds that might strengthen their fight against the darkness.

Chapter 48

Revelations of Blood and Bond

King Manard sat in his study, his gaze fixed on the spread of scrolls before him. Candlelight flickered softly, casting restless shadows over the parchment, while the air carried the faint scent of aged ink and melting wax. The weight of history and consequence settled heavily on his shoulders, each sealed missive a choice poised to shape Vacari's fate. The wax emblems gleamed in the dim light, silent heralds of promises and risks intertwined. His expression tightened, caught between anticipation and unease, as his thoughts circled the monumental decision ahead. The moment hung in quiet tension — hope and fear balanced on a blade's edge — as Prince Gailen entered, his steps measured yet purposeful.

"Father," Gailen began, his voice steady but curious. I have heard whispers among the nobles. What announcement do you plan to make? Is it about the alliance with Etharyon?"

King Manard looked up, his gaze softening as he regarded his son, thoughts of pride and the weight of unspoken truths flickering across his features. He felt hope for Gailen's strength and a pang of regret for the burden this revelation might impose upon him. "Partly, yes. The alliance with Etharyon is a significant development for Vacari, but a personal matter concerns our family."

Gailen tilted his head, his curiosity deepening. "Then why not tell me now, in private?"

Manard rose deliberately slowly from his chair, his robes rustling like dry leaves in the quiet chamber. The heavy fabric whispered against the polished floor, each step deliberate as he gathered his thoughts. A deep breath steadied him, though his fingers briefly tightened against the armrest before releasing. The weight of years of silence pressed upon him, and doubt whispered at the edge of his mind for a fleeting moment. Was it indeed the right time to reveal what had long been buried? His expression was grave, and his gaze fixed firmly on Gailen. Crossing the room, he placed a steady hand on his son's shoulder, his grip firm yet gentle, as if to impart reassurance and the weight of his resolve. "Because it is not just about you or me. This revelation affects us all and is best shared openly with our allies and friends present. However, if you truly wish to know beforehand."

Gailen shook his head, interrupting gently. "No, Father. If it is as important as you say, then it is only fair that I hear it alongside everyone else. You have my trust."

Manard's face softened into a rare smile, and he gave his son a slight nod of approval. "Thank you, my son. That trust means more to me than you know. For now, I ask you to consider our guests' comfort and ensure the preparations in the glade are proceeding smoothly. The announcement will take place there, with the dragons present, as their wisdom and presence lend legitimacy and gravitas to the occasion."

Gailen straightened, squaring his shoulders as determination gleamed in his eyes. He nodded, his resolve settling like an unshakable stone within him. "I will see to it. The glade will be ready, and everyone will be attended to.

As Gailen turned to leave, Manard called after him, his tone warm yet firm. "Gailen, thank you. You have shown great maturity, and I am proud of the man you have become."

Gailen paused, a faint smile playing on his lips. "Thank you, Father. I will make sure everything is perfect for the announcement."

With that, Gailen departed, his thoughts swirling with anticipation. Excitement thrummed beneath his skin, restless energy driving his steps — yet beneath that exhilaration, doubt coiled in his chest, a quiet whisper of uncertainty he could not ignore. What truth could be so great that his father hesitated to share it privately? Was it a cause for celebration, or another burden he would be forced to carry?

He clenched his fists, then slowly exhaled, forcing the doubt aside. Whatever awaited him, he would meet it with the same resolve that had carried him this far. The revelation his father withheld felt momentous, charged with the power to reshape alliances and shift the balance within Vacari. Gailen's mind raced with possibilities, each more profound than the last, leaving him poised between eagerness and apprehension. He would see the glade prepared for a day that could alter not only their lives but the fate of Vacari itself.

The glade shimmered with ethereal beauty, bathed in the bioluminescent glow of enchanted flowers that cast living patterns across the ground. Their radiance glowed in the eyes of those gathered, illuminating faces poised between hope and tension. Light danced over the polished scales of the dragons, each gleam accentuating their power and majesty as they stood in solemn vigil. A breeze stirred the ancient canopy, carrying whispers of the moment's gravity, as if the glade itself held its breath in silent witness.

Dragons of countless shades encircled the clearing, their watchful eyes catching the shifting glow. Some shifted their great forms, wings unfurling ever so slightly, tails sweeping arcs through the air in quiet readiness. A deep, resonant hum rippled through their ranks, punctuated by subtle nods and slow, deliberate movements — silent gestures that bore the weight of ages. Their presence filled the space with a timeless gravity, their wisdom woven into the very air.

Around the raised stone platform where King Manard stood, the allies of Vacari — human warriors, silver-clad Eladrin, the emerald-robed Luminara, and others still — formed a broad semicircle. United by fragile hope and hard-earned resolve, they waited beneath the watchful gaze of dragons and stars alike, poised upon the edge of destiny.

Manard surveyed the assembly, his presence commanding. Yet beneath that authority, a rare vulnerability flickered, betraying the internal conflict he carried. The burden of leadership had long weighed upon him, but this choice was no mere matter of strategy or alliance — it was about legacy, the echoes of past mistakes, and the fragile hope of a future he dared to believe in. For years, he had made decisions for the good of his people, steadfast and unyielding, but now the stakes felt deeply personal.

Though a pillar of strength to his kingdom, this moment revealed the father beneath the crown — a man keenly aware of the risks before him, balancing hope against uncertainty. He drew a steadying breath, his gaze sweeping over the expectant faces gathered before him. With measured resolve, he straightened his shoulders and began.

"Friends, allies, and guardians of Vacari," Manard's voice rang out, steady and clear, "today, we stand on the cusp of a new chapter in our shared history. As you know, the bonds between Vacari and Etharyon have been frayed for many years. Distrust, misunderstandings, and old wounds have kept us apart. But recently, new opportunities have arisen that could reshape our future."

He held up the scroll bearing the royal seal of Etharyon. "I have received a formal request from the King of Etharyon himself. He proposes that trade be reestablished between our realms and that we rebuild the bridges once burned. Such an alliance would bring strength, resources, and solidarity to our lands in the face of the threats we now face."

The crowd murmured, their whispers blending with the soft rustle of leaves. Manard raised his hand, silencing them. "But I am not a king who makes such decisions alone. Vacari has always thrived because of the wisdom and unity of its people and allies. And so, I open the floor to you, our trusted council and guardians. Let your voice be heard."

King Alex of Goldmoor stepped forward, his regal bearing unshaken, his sharp gaze sweeping across the assembly. His voice, steady and authoritative, carried the weight of experience, leaving no doubt about the firmness of his stance. "I have seen firsthand the devastation wrought by division. Etharyon's proposal is a gesture of reconciliation, one we would be wise to embrace. If this alliance strengthens our realm and safeguards our people, I see no reason to oppose it."

Lord Karrenen, standing tall and stately, followed, though a shadow of concern flickered in his eyes. His usual composed demeanor was strained by the weight of his daughter's injuries pressing upon him. He inhaled slowly, steadying himself before speaking. "I have lived long enough to know that trust is fragile, easily shattered, but vital for survival. Etharyon extends a hand of friendship. We must meet it with strength and honor. I support this alliance."

A murmur rippled through the crowd as Lysander, God of the Sea, stepped forward, a living embodiment of the tides of fate he had long guided. His wisdom had carried many through storms of turmoil, his voice shaping the currents of alliances and conflict alike. A faint mist clung to him, as if the sea itself had followed him ashore, curling around his form in silent reverence. The gleam of his shimmering trident caught the ethereal light of the glade, drawing awe-struck glances from those gathered. Rarely did he grace such assemblies, but the gravity of the moment — and its far-reaching consequences for the realm — had summoned him to stand among them. . He cleared his throat, his voice deep and steady. "The battles we face are not ours alone. Allies strengthen us, and I believe this partnership will serve us well. My vote is for acceptance."

Kimras, the gold dragon, shifted his massive form and let out a low rumble, his golden eyes narrowing in thoughtful appraisal as he entered the gathered assembly. His gaze flicked briefly toward Keisha, as if quietly measuring her condition, before settling on the crowd before him. A hush settled over the assembly, the weight of his decision rippling through those assembled. Some nodded in solemn agreement, while others exchanged glances marked by a newfound sense of reassurance. His endorsement alone began to shift the mood, steadying the assembly toward unity. When he spoke, his voice carried a deep, resonant authority, underscored by an unwavering confidence that left no doubt as to his resolve.

"Vacari thrives when united with others who respect life and light. I know of Etharyon's king; his wisdom is true. Let us accept this alliance and move forward with vigilance and hope."

The murmurs grew more optimistic as, one by one, those who gathered voiced their agreement. Heads nodded, quiet words of affirmation passed between allies, and even the dragons shifted slightly, their approving rumbles adding to the growing sense of unity. Manard's steady gaze traveled across the assembly as he spoke again. "It seems the will of our allies is clear. Shall we then put this to a vote?"

A ripple of nods spread across the assembly, and Manard called out, "All in favor of accepting Etharyon's proposal?"

A resounding chorus of "Aye" echoed through the glade, unanimous and resolute. Kaelorn, standing near the Luminara, allowed himself a rare smile.

Manard gave a slight bow of gratitude, his voice softening as a flicker of relief crossed his features. His shoulders, which had carried the weight of uncertainty, eased slightly, and his hands unclenched at his sides, betraying the depth of his emotions. This decision was more than just an alliance. It was a chance to mend old wounds to forge a future not dictated by past divisions but by shared strength and renewed hope. "Thank you, all of you.

This momentous step for our people, leading to greater unity and strength in future battles."

He paused, his expression shifting to one of hesitation. His fingers curled slightly at his sides as if bracing himself for the weight of his own words. The gravity of what he was about to reveal settled heavily on his shoulders, momentarily stealing his breath. "But before we conclude, there is... another matter I must address," he began, his voice faltering slightly as his gaze swept over the expectant crowd. "A personal revelation, one that I have kept silent about until now."

The glade grew still, anticipation heavy in the air as the allies and friends of Vacari waited for the king's following words.

The glade was silent save for the gentle rustle of leaves in the evening breeze, carrying the crisp scent of earth and faint traces of blooming flora. The air had cooled with the setting sun, casting elongated shadows across the gathered assembly as if the forest held its breath in anticipation. All eyes turned to King Manard as he straightened, his expression shifting from regal composure to a deep vulnerability rarely seen by his subjects. His gaze swept the assembly, lingering on his son, Prince Gailen, who stood to the side, curiosity and concern etched across his face.

"Prince Gailen," Manard said, his voice steady but heavy with emotion, "please stand beside me. This next announcement concerns not only me but you as well."

Gailen stepped forward, his boots crunching softly on the glade's earthen floor. He stood tall beside his father, his expression solemn, awaiting the revelation.

King Manard took a deep breath, gathering his thoughts. "Years ago," he began, his voice resonating through the glade, "I traveled to Etharyon with a woman named Seraphina Frostwood, my fiancée. She was my heart and the woman I intended to marry. But tragedy struck. As we journeyed through the forests of Etharyon, our carriage was ambushed, and I believed..." He paused, his voice faltering slightly. "... I believed she had been killed in the attack."

A stunned silence fell over the crowd before ripples of disbelief spread among them. Some nobles exchanged wide-eyed glances, their shock unmistakable, while others murmured in hushed tones, their voices scarcely rising above the charged stillness. A few leaned toward their neighbors, their words barely concealed beneath the weight of the revelation. The faint rustle of robes and the shifting of feet punctuated the silence, as though the assembly itself held its breath.

Uncertainty flickered across faces as the king raised a hand, silencing them with a quiet command. His gaze dropped to the scroll in his grasp, his fingers tightening around the parchment as if to steady himself against the storm within. A flicker of hesitation crossed his face, the magnitude of what he was about to reveal pressing upon him like an invisible force, heavy and inescapable. "Only recently have I learned that I was wrong. With the scroll the King of Etharyon sent, there was a second message from Seraphina herself."

The crowd leaned in, the weight of King Manard's words thick in the air. Ong's breath caught in his throat, disbelief and confusion crashing over him in relentless waves. His fingers clenched at his sides, as though grasping for something solid to anchor himself. His heart pounded against his ribs, a storm of emotions swirling within him—shock, anger at the years lost, and a fragile hope he scarcely dared acknowledge.

His hand found Keisha's arm, his voice barely more than a breath. "That... was my mother."

Keisha turned toward him, slower than usual, a faint wince flickering across her face as she shifted her stance. Ong steadied her instinctively, his grip gentle yet sure. She exhaled, frustration and gratitude mingling in her gaze, but she did not pull away.

Her eyes widened as realization settled, heavy and unmistakable. Whatever the revelation meant to the world, Ong remained unchanged in her eyes—fierce, loyal, burdened yet unbroken. Yet beneath that certainty, a quiet fear coiled within her: not for herself, but for him. She knew well the weight of expectation, how it could grind down even the strongest. Would he rise beneath it, or would it become another chain, tightening with each step?

Whatever the answer, she knew one truth: she would stand by him. Always.

Her fingers, stiff with lingering pain, brushed against his in silent support. Ong's grip closed over hers, firm yet careful, his warmth steadying her even as she felt the tremor in his touch. The storm within him was not his alone—it pressed against them both. Despite the ache in her ribs and the uncertainty coiling in her chest, she tightened her hold. She would be his anchor through this unexpected gale.

King Manard's voice drew them back to the moment.

"The scroll revealed that Seraphina had not been killed but taken in by the King of Etharyon. To protect her, she was given refuge. Over time, she built a new life, marrying a noble who offered her stability and support. Within Etharyon's court, she became a respected figure admired for her strength and grace despite her past."

His voice broke, but he pressed on. "She married because... because she was expecting my child. A son."

The murmurs in the crowd swelled, disbelief and curiosity rippling through the assembly.

A noble near the front cleared his throat. "A son? After all these years?"

A woman in Eladrin robes whispered fiercely to her companion. "This changes everything."

Gailen turned to his father, brow furrowed. "Do we know who the child is? And... does Seraphina still live?"

King Manard's expression softened, grief flickering across his face. "We do know the child's name," he said, quiet yet resolute. "But Seraphina passed years ago. In her final words, she explained that she sent her child to train as a warrior so he would grow in strength and purpose."

Silence settled over the glade, thick with anticipation.

Ong shook his head, whispering to Keisha, "I did not know. I did not know my mother had another child."

Keisha's fingers pressed against his arm. "Let's wait and hear who it was."

King Manard gripped the scroll as though drawing strength from the parchment itself. He exhaled, his gaze flickering to Gailen before sweeping over the expectant faces before him. He had prepared for this moment, but now that it was here, its weight pressed deeper than he had imagined.

This was not just a revelation. The unearthing of a long-buried truth would change their family's fate forever.

The wind stirred the parchment in his hands, yet he did not move. He let the silence speak first.

Finally, he said, "The Lady Seraphina has passed. But before her death, she instructed the King of Etharyon to send me this scroll... if the realms of Etharyon and Vacari ever stood as allies again."

All eyes were locked on him now. The crowd's collective breath held as if the world had stilled, waiting for his following words.

"Yes," King Manard said, his voice steady. "We have the child's name."

A ripple of murmurs spread through the assembly. Expectant gazes turned toward him, anticipation thick in the air.

"The name of the child..." Manard's gaze swept the crowd, lingering on one individual before he spoke again. "...is Ong Swifthammer, the warrior who has protected Crystal Vale all these years and made a life for himself with Lady Keisha."

Ong's head snapped up, disbelief crashing into him like a thunderclap. His breath stalled in his chest, a sudden chill racing down his spine. The ground beneath him felt unsteady, as though reality itself had shifted. His fingers curled reflexively at his sides, his pulse hammering in his ears—a relentless drumbeat of denial. The weight of the revelation bore down on him, suffocating. And yet, beneath the shock, something flickered in the depths of his soul, something fragile, something he dared not name.

His breath hitched. His fingers clenched into fists as if trying to grasp onto something solid amid the unraveling of everything he thought he knew. A torrent of emotions surged through him: shock, disbelief, a gnawing fear... and somewhere, buried beneath it all, a faint glimmer of hope he could not yet accept.

"No," he whispered hoarsely, shaking his head, his voice raw with refusal. "That cannot be me."

His gaze snapped to Keisha, the one constant in his life, the only thing that felt real in this unraveling truth.

Keisha met his eyes, her expression warm and steady, a tether in the storm raging inside him. She touched his arm, her voice soft yet firm as she whispered, "Listen to him, Ong."

Oh boy, she thought, already bracing herself. This is going to be fun. He hates council meetings.

King Manard stepped forward, his face softening, his eyes shimmering with unshed tears. A hushed wave spread through the crowd, whispers rising and falling like ripples on a pond. Nobles exchanged glances, some astonished, others unreadable. Even the dragons shifted slightly, their gleaming eyes locked onto Ong, sensing the moment's significance.

The weight of years pressed into Manard's voice as he spoke again, rich with sorrow and pride. "Yes, Lord Ong," he said, his voice thick with emotion. "You are my son. You are Gailen's brother."

Silence fell over the glade. Not the peace of calm, but a charged, breathless stillness — as though the very world was holding its breath. A noble gripped the edge of his cloak, knuckles white. Another gasped softly, pressing her hands to her lips. The weight of the truth settled over them all like a heavy veil.

Then, breaking the stillness like sunlight through storm clouds, Gailen's laugh burst into the air—warm, unrestrained, and full of life. A wide grin spread across his face as he strode forward and, without hesitation, pulled Ong into a brotherly embrace.

"If I had to have a brother," Gailen said, his voice alight with genuine joy, "I'm glad it's you."

Ong stiffened for half a heartbeat before exhaling, the rigid tension in his shoulders easing just enough to accept the moment.

Gailen turned next to Keisha, his smile no less bright. "And I have a sister as well now," he added, his voice warm with welcome.

His gaze softened as it passed over her, lingering on the bandages encircling her ribs, the exhaustion she tried so hard to mask behind unwavering eyes.

"You saved a life, Keisha," he said, quieter now but rich with heartfelt sincerity. "Even injured, you stand here with us."

Reaching out, he laid a hand gently on her uninjured shoulder.

A flicker of surprise stirred in Keisha's chest, chased swiftly by a quiet steadiness. She had expected recognition, perhaps respect — but not this warmth, this effortless inclusion. Something tightened in her chest, not pain, but a subtle weight of responsibility that had always been there, now simply named.

"Vacari is lucky to have you," Gailen murmured. "We are lucky to have you."

Ong stood frozen, the revelation settling over him like a heavy cloak, pressing against the very core of his identity. His thoughts raced, struggling to reconcile the life he had forged with the truth unraveling before him. He had spent years carving his own path, believing himself unmoored — a lone warrior, bound only by duty and the love he had chosen to give.

And yet, here he was. Not alone. Not unmoored. But tethered to a legacy he had never sought, never even imagined.

The realization staggered him. Could he accept this?

Did he even want to?

His gaze flicked to Keisha, and a deeper fear took hold in his chest. What would this mean for them?

But then, Gailen's words sank in — simple, sincere — and something inside him shifted. A faint smile tugged at the corners of his lips, hesitant at first but undeniably real. Slowly, as though learning the motion anew, his arms rose to return the embrace.

The crowd remained hushed, caught in the weight of the moment. Some exchanged stunned glances; others watched, spellbound by the unexpected joy unfolding before them. A few gasped softly, realization sweeping through them like a tide redrawing the shore.

"By the stars," an elder breathed, awe thick in their voice. "This is truly fate."

Another noble, hands clasped tightly, shook their head. "Who could have foreseen this?"

Above them, the dragons perched along the glade, their massive forms still as stone, watchful eyes fixed on the scene below as if sensing the shift in destiny.

A thought stirred beneath Ong's rising breath, quiet yet undeniable. Had his life always led to this moment, and he had simply never seen it?

He exhaled slowly, steadying himself. The embrace had settled something within him — not everything, but enough for now.

A breeze slipped through the glade, as though the land itself exhaled with him, carrying away the remnants of uncertainty as he prepared to speak.

There was still more to say.

"In the event of our father's..." He hesitated, the word father unfamiliar on his tongue, an identity thrust upon him rather than chosen. His jaw tightened before he forced himself to continue. "In the event of King Manard's passing, I want you to know I have no intention, nor will I ever desire, to be king."

A flicker of surprise crossed Gailen's face. "Are you sure? This is a lot to take in."

Ong met his brother's gaze and nodded, firm in his resolve. Then, he glanced at Keisha, and his lips curved into a rare, genuine smile.

"I have other responsibilities now," he said, his voice steady. "Looking after Keisha. Protecting E'vahona. That is where I belong."

Ong's gaze lingered on Keisha, tracing the fading bruises and the careful way she held herself—too many close calls. Twice now, he had nearly lost her, once at the hands of their enemies and now in an act of selfless sacrifice. The thought tightened his throat, igniting something fierce within him.

He could not, would not, let that happen again.

Even standing beside him, strong as ever, she was still healing. That knowledge sent a flicker of frustration through his chest, not at her, never at her, but at himself that he had not been there, that she had fought through it alone. A silent vow burned in his heart: he would be by her side from now on.

Gailen studied him, an amused glint in his eyes. "You're certain?"

"Very sure," Ong said, arms crossing. "Besides, I could never deal with the council members. Too much talking, not enough doing. I'd probably end up challenging half of them to a duel to get something done, though I doubt that's a great leadership strategy."

Gailen laughed, clapping Ong on the shoulder. "I can't say I blame you. But it's good to hear it from you directly."

Silence followed; it was not an awkward silence but one filled with weight. No one dared to speak, allowing the moment to settle and carve itself into the hearts of everyone present.

Then, Amara's voice rang out, shattering the silence with familiar mischief.

"Just because you're a prince now, Ong, doesn't mean you're getting any special treatment from me."

Laughter rippled through the gathering, breaking the last remnants of tension. Smiles spread, the weight of revelation giving way to something lighter, something real.

Thalorian, Kaelorn, and Valen stepped forward, embracing Ong in a silent show of support. When Thalorian pulled back, he smirked, giving him a knowing look.

"Well, at least now you can help me keep the others out of trouble."

Amara huffed, the glow of her amethyst scales catching the light as she flicked her tail in mock exasperation. "Good luck with that."

Another wave of laughter followed, and the moment's heaviness softened into something almost absurd. Ong chuckled, shaking his head at it all for the first time. He had spent years believing himself as an outsider warrior bound only by his choices, with no ties beyond those he forged.

Yet, here he stood, no longer just a lone blade in the world but part of something greater. Something that had been his all along.

His gaze drifted to Keisha, and he pulled her close with quiet certainty, wrapping his arm protectively around her.

"No matter what titles or bloodlines say, this matters most," he murmured. "You, E'vahona, and the life we've built that is where I belong."

Keisha leaned into him, a soft smile touching her lips. She rested against his chest, feeling the steady rhythm of his heartbeat beneath her cheek, anchoring her in the quiet certainty of this moment.

"And you will always belong here," she whispered, her fingers brushing against his hand.

The moment held quiet yet profound as if the stars themselves bore witness to the bond they had chosen over fate's decree. Ong exhaled slowly, his grip on Keisha tightening just slightly, grounding himself in the reality of now. He met her gaze, a silent promise passing between them.

No matter what comes next, we face it together.

Though the night was filled with laughter and warmth, an unspoken understanding lingered beneath it. The battle against the rising darkness was far from over. Shadows still loomed beyond the glade, waiting for their chance to strike. But for now, they stood united, drawing strength from each other before the next storm arrived.

Epilogue
The Cost of Defiance

T he chamber of Fel Thalor pulsed with a simmering tension, the walls seeming to hold their breath in anticipation of what was to come. Shadows stretched unnaturally in the dim torchlight, flickering erratically as if stirred by the sheer malice radiating from the figure pacing the chamber. The mysterious figure moved with measured steps, their boots echoing against the cold stone floor, each step a calculated pause in the storm of their thoughts.

Valeon had been summoned.

And he would answer.

The figure's gloved hands clenched and unclenched at their sides, barely containing the fury boiling beneath their composed exterior. Their minds raced, weighing punishments, and considering retribution. Betrayal—whether intentional or the result of mere incompetence—was not something they tolerated. Valeon had tested the boundaries of their patience, and that patience had worn dangerously thin.

A slow exhale. It was a deliberate turn.

They halted before the great iron doors, their gaze fixed on the entrance as if willing it to part and drag Valeon inside. Would he arrive with feigned ignorance, offering weak excuses? Or would he have the audacity to meet their wrath with defiance? The figure's lips curled slightly—a mirthless, chilling smile. It mattered little.

When Valeon arrived, he would learn the full cost of failure.

The iron doors groaned open, revealing Valeon as he stepped inside with the ease of a man who had walked into this chamber countless times before. His gaze swept the room, noting the stiff posture of the figure before him, the way their fists curled at their sides. Their anger was palpable, thick like a storm about to break. And yet, he did not seem particularly concerned.

He exhaled slowly, tilting his head slightly, a smirk playing at the corner of his lips. "You summoned me. I assume it was not just to glare at me from across the room?" His voice carried an air of careless amusement, though his sharp eyes missed nothing.

The tension in the chamber deepened. The figure took a measured step forward, the flickering torchlight barely illuminating the shadowed edges of their face. "You presume to be amused, Valeon? You were given an order, and yet I hear whispers of actions that were... less than satisfactory."

Valeon shrugged, his expression unreadable. "Oh, you know how whispers are. They tend to be exaggerated." He took another step forward, deliberately casual as if he had not just walked into the lion's den. "But please, enlighten me—what have I done to warrant such a summons?"

The figure's fists clenched tighter, their barely contained rage boiling over. "You failed to inform me of the extra precautions taken in Crystal Vale and the Emeraldwoods before the battle. Because of your negligence, the battle was lost. Do you have any explanation for this?"

Valeon exhaled sharply through his nose, his smirk widening ever so slightly. He lifted his hands in an exaggerated shrug, his tone entirely unconcerned. "I didn't have time."

The figure's fury ignited like a spark meeting oil, their presence seeming to darken the very air around them. "You didn't have time?" The words dripped with venom, each syllable sharpened with barely restrained rage. "And because of your... carelessness, everything we worked toward has crumbled to dust."

Valeon rolled his shoulders, feigning indifference as tension coiled in his gut. He masked the unease, clawing at the edges of his mind and unwilling to give the figure the satisfaction of seeing him falter. "Yes, well, that does tend to happen in war. You win some, you lose some."

The figure took a slow, measured breath as if reigning in the urge to strike him down where he stood. "And tell me, Valeon—do you intend to lose again?"

Something in Valeon's expression shifted, the careless smirk fading slightly. He lifted his chin, his gaze steady and unwavering. "You know," he said, his voice softer now, almost contemplative, "I grow tired of doing your bidding."

A heavy silence followed, thick and suffocating. The figure stilled, their head tilting slightly as if measuring the weight of his words. Then, without warning, darkness surged from their outstretched hand, a tendril of pure malice lashing out like a whip.

Valeon barely had time to react before the force struck him square in the chest, sending him stumbling backward. His balance wavered, and he crashed to the cold stone floor, a sharp gasp escaping as the pain seared through him. The tendrils of dark magic tightened, pressing down like invisible chains.

The figure stepped closer, their voice a low, dangerous whisper. "You forget your place, Valeon. And for that, you will suffer."

A cruel smile ghosted their lips before they leaned slightly, their voice laced with malice. "And I know about Keisha's injuries. You will ensure she never recovers."

Valeon's body tensed, his fingers digging into the stone as he fought against the pain. He shook his head, a defiant glint flickering in his eyes despite his predicament. "I can't do that."

The figure let out a slow, mocking chuckle. "And why is that?"

Valeon exhaled heavily, shifting slightly, ignoring the ache spreading through his limbs. "Because," he said, his voice measured despite the pain, "you're not stupid enough to cross that line. Keisha is Ong Swifthammer's wife. And Ong, in case you have forgotten, is Gailen's stepbrother. That makes Keisha a protected member of the royal family." He smirked, though it was strained. "And you won't even risk making an enemy of the crown."

The figure's eyes narrowed, their amusement fading into cold calculation. Then, their expression darkened further as they turned a piercing glare on Valeon. "What are you talking about? Ong Swifthammer is not Gailen's stepbrother."

Valeon laughed sharply, shaking his head despite the pain still lancing through his body. "Oh, that's right," he said with an air of exaggerated realization. "This is new information. Just discovered." His smirk widened as he watched the brief flicker of uncertainty cross the figure's features. "I guess you're not as all-knowing as you thought."

The figure's glare hardened, and they struck out again without hesitation. Dark energy lashed toward Valeon, slamming into him with brutal force. He gasped, the impact sending another wave of pain searing through his body. The world blurred around him, his vision dimming at the edges as he struggled to breathe.

With a sharp turn, the figure strode toward the exit, their cloak billowing behind them. Their anger had not diminished; it had merely shifted. Valeon was an unreliable tool, but others could serve its purpose.

Stepping beyond the gates of Fel Thalor, the figure's expression settled into a cold mask of determination. If Valeon did not ensure Keisha never recovered, they would find someone who would.

A slow, chilling laugh echoed through the night as the figure disappeared into the shadows, a cruel smile curling at their lips. Valeon thought he had escaped their wrath, but he would soon understand the full cost of failure. The figure could already envision the moment of Valeon's death—and the thought pleased them.

Battlecraft of Vacari

Battlecraft of Vacari

A record of the legendary weapons, gear, and craftsmanship that shaped the Dragon Wars and the rise of the alliance.

Note: A full expanded archive with detailed histories and craftsmanship notes is available on the author's official website.

Legendary Weapons

A catalogue of the renowned weapons forged and wielded across Vacari, each carrying its own legacy and power.

• Crystalbow (Gailen) — A relic forged in ages past, imbued with the essence of the first Crystal Dragon. It channels the bond between rider and dragon, manifesting in arrows of living crystal that respond to Gailen's will and Aurelia's presence. In battle, it can momentarily draw upon the power of nearby allied dragons, amplifying its might.

• Arborblade (Thalorian) — A blade of emerald light, forged by the Moon Elves and pulsing with a living heartbeat. The Arborblade is both spear and shield, a weapon of balance, drawing upon the natural world and Thalorian's intent to defend life and land alike.

• Dragonlance (Ong) — Crafted by Lord Karrenen, the strongest mage of the Eladrin, and blessed by Kadona herself. Ong's personal lance carries enchantments tied to Amara's amethyst energy, creating a powerful link between rider and dragon, and carrying the legacy of unity between Eladrin and Goldmoor.

• Eladrin Longbow of Serena (Now Keisha's) — Gifted by Lord Karrenen to Serena, a master archer of the Eladrin. Passed to Keisha, whose rare nature magic awakens the longbow's latent potential, turning it into a living extension of her will and elemental power.

Forged Gear & Equipment

A chronicle of exceptional craftsmanship, forged to endure the trials of war and the bond between rider and dragon.

• Bonded Dragon Rider Armor — Crafted of reinforced, enchanted leather and woven with stardust enchantments by the fairies of Vacari. This armor not only protects but deepens the bond between rider and dragon, shifting its hue to reflect the dragon's colors. It is form-fitting, seamlessly adapting to the rider's body for agility in battle. Each piece bears ancient engravings telling the tales of past warriors, etched with reverence. Gloves crafted to match, finely enchanted for both protection and flexibility. Note: This armor is not a skirt. It is built for real combat.

• Eladrin Dragon Saddles — Masterworks of Eladrin artistry, these saddles are forged from high-quality, supple materials and woven with magical runes to secure the rider through even the most evasive aerial maneuvers. They enhance the bond between rider and dragon, infusing comfort and control into long flights and battles alike.

Eyes of Vacari: Unique Colors & Meanings

A record of the distinctive eye colors among the people and dragons of Vacari, acknowledging their heritage, magic, or other unique traits.

• Thalorian — Jade-Fire eyes; a rare emerald brilliance with inner flame, reflecting his fierce connection to nature and the living energy of the forest.

• Kaelorn — Glade-Fire eyes; a vibrant hue of green kindled with golden sparks, echoing the life and light of Vacari's sacred glades.

• Nocturna (Dragon) — Silver eyes streaked with violet; an uncommon fusion of wisdom and shadow magic, hinting at deep, ancient powers and a storm of internal conflict.

Teaser

Celestial Convergence

T he wind carried a whisper of change.

Radiantus soared above the vast expanse of Vacari, his platinum scales reflecting the light of the fading sun. He had been gone for what felt like an eternity, yet as he descended toward familiar lands, an unease settled over him. Something was different.

The magic of the realm pulsed beneath him, shifting like the undercurrents of a restless sea. It was subtle—too subtle for most to notice—but Radiantus had walked the ages, and he could feel the disturbance threading through the land like an unseen storm on the horizon.

His wings beat steadily as he circled lower, diamond-silver eyes scanning the forests, mountains, and rivers that had long been his home. Vacari remained as breathtaking as ever, but its heart no longer beat with the same rhythm. A discord had taken root, elusive yet undeniable.

A deep rumble echoed from his chest, not of anger, but of contemplation. The balance had shifted. Forces long dormant were stirring. Whether this change would bring salvation or ruin remained unknown. He had seen the rise and fall of empires, the ebb and flow of magic, but this disturbance was unlike any before. It was neither the clash of kingdoms nor the stirrings of mortals. This was older, deeper—woven into the very fabric of the world itself.

He descended further, his shadow stretching over the land below. Somewhere in the distance, the sky trembled as unseen forces clashed beyond mortal perception. A single truth settled in his mind, heavy with the weight of an unspoken prophecy.

The war had already begun.

And the true battle had yet to reveal itself.

DRAGONS OF ACARI

Acknowledgements

Jean McEvoy

To my wonderful mother—your red pen and unwavering belief in me will never be forgotten. Thank you for always standing by me.

Caroline Otto

To my best friend from high school, Caroline, thank you for taking the time to read the rough drafts. Thank you for also being there for me during high school and believing in me now. Her friendship has meant a lot to me. She is more of like a sister.

Steven Thomas

To my dear friend, Steven, who took the time to read early drafts of the chapters. Your friendship and feedback mean the world to me.

Special Acknowledgment

This book is dedicated in part to **James Augustiniak**, whose strength and resilience inspired the soul of a prince.

Though fiction cannot bear the full weight of reality, the character of Gailen was born from the quiet courage and steady heart James has shown in the face of unimaginable challenges. His journey—marked by determination, grace, and hope—echoes through the pages, a testament to the impact one life can have on a story, and on those who carry it forward. To James: May you always know that your fight, your presence, and your light reach farther than you realize. This world I built is stronger because a part of you lives in it.

Special Acknowledgements to the Fur Babies (whose names are used in the book

Pumpkin

I rescued my little black panther over five years ago, and her playful spirit became the inspiration for Pumpkin in this book.

Casper

To Casper, Caroline Otto's spoiled fur baby, who brings joy to every moment.

www.ingramcontent.com/pod-product-compliance
Lightning Source LLC
Chambersburg PA
CBHW031043110726
47900CB00003B/791